The Norsunder War, Book II

Seek to Hold the Wind

SARTORIAS-DELES BOOKS

HISTORICAL ARC

"Lily and Crown"
Inda
The Fox
King's Shield
Treason's Shore
Time of Daughters (two volumes)
Banner of the Damned

The Young Allies as Kids Series

The CJ Notebooks
Senrid
Spy Princess
Sartor
Fleeing Peace

A Stranger to Command
Crown Duel
The Trouble with Kings

The Rise of the Alliance Series

A Sword Named Truth
The Blood Mage Texts
The Hunters and the Hunted
Nightside of the Sun
Sasharia En Garde
The Wicked Skill
Ship Without Sails
Marend of Marloven Hess

The Norsunder War II

Seek to Hold
the Wind

SHERWOOD SMITH

BOOK VIEW CAFE

BOOK VIEW CAFE

Published by Book View Café
304 S. Jones Blvd., Suite #2906
Las Vegas, NV 89107
www.bookviewcafe.com

ISBN: 978-1-63632-092-2

This book is a work of fiction. All characters, locations, and events portrayed in this book are fictional or used in an imaginary manner to entertain, and any resemblance to any real people, situations, or incidents is purely coincidental.

AUTHOR'S NOTE

This second book in the Norsunder War story runs concurrently with *Marend of Marloven Hess*, which is short and located specifically in Marloven Hess, which is why it's listed as "1.5" instead of "volume 2". There will be some overlap, but I tried to reintroduce everyone here.

The title is taken from a poem by Sir Thomas Wyatt

Whoso List to Hunt, I Know where is an Hind

Whoso list to hunt, I know where is an hind,
But as for me, hélas, I may no more.
The vain travail hath wearied me so sore,
I am of them that farthest cometh behind.
Yet may I by no means my wearied mind
Draw from the deer, but as she fleeth afore
Fainting I follow. I leave off therefore,
Sithens in a net I seek to hold the wind.
Who list her hunt, I put him out of doubt,
As well as I may spend his time in vain.
And graven with diamonds in letters plain
There is written, her fair neck round about:
Noli me tangere, for Caesar's I am,
And wild for to hold, though I seem tame.

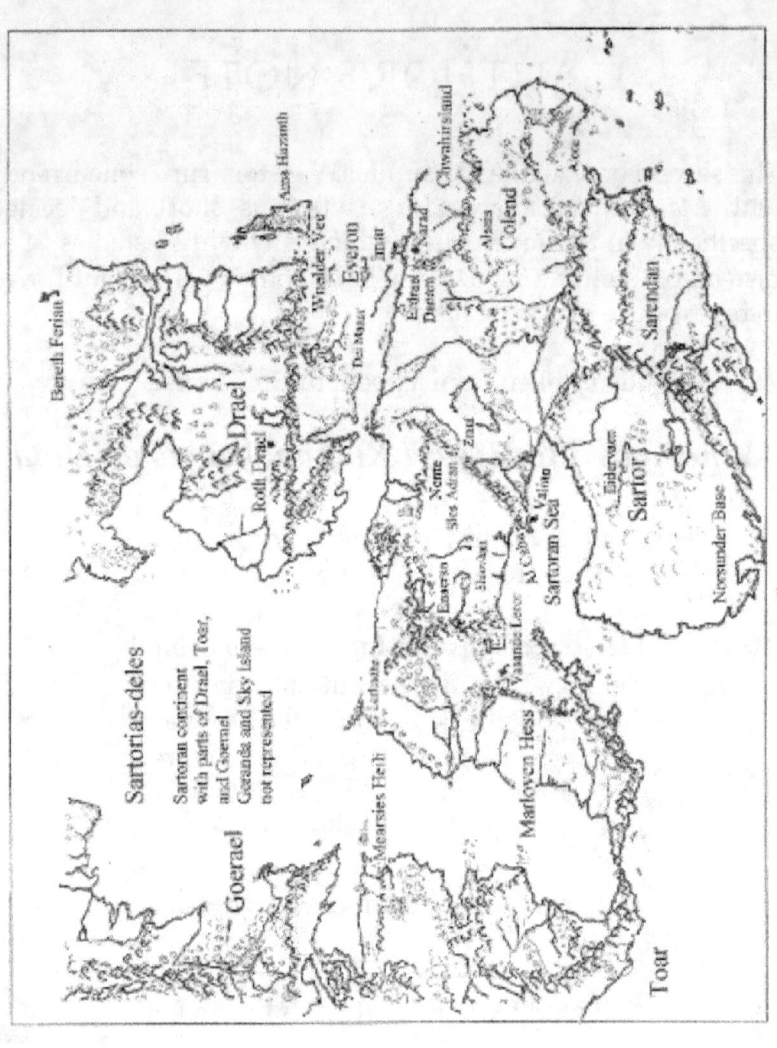

Sartorias-deles

Sartoran continent
with parts of Drael, Toar,
and Goerael
Geeradn and Sky Island
not represented

Goerael

Tour

Bereth Ferian

Drael

Rodi Drael

Anna Hazzmith

Wnalder Vee

Dei Matar

Everon

Inn

Edrael
Durian

Olwahir island

Alsais

Colend

Sarendan

Nente

Siles Adran

Znid

Eidervaen

Sartor

Neesunder Base

Esarem

Horvath

Valtia

At Cabora

Sartoran Sea

Anaeran Leror

Marloven Hess

Mearsies Heili

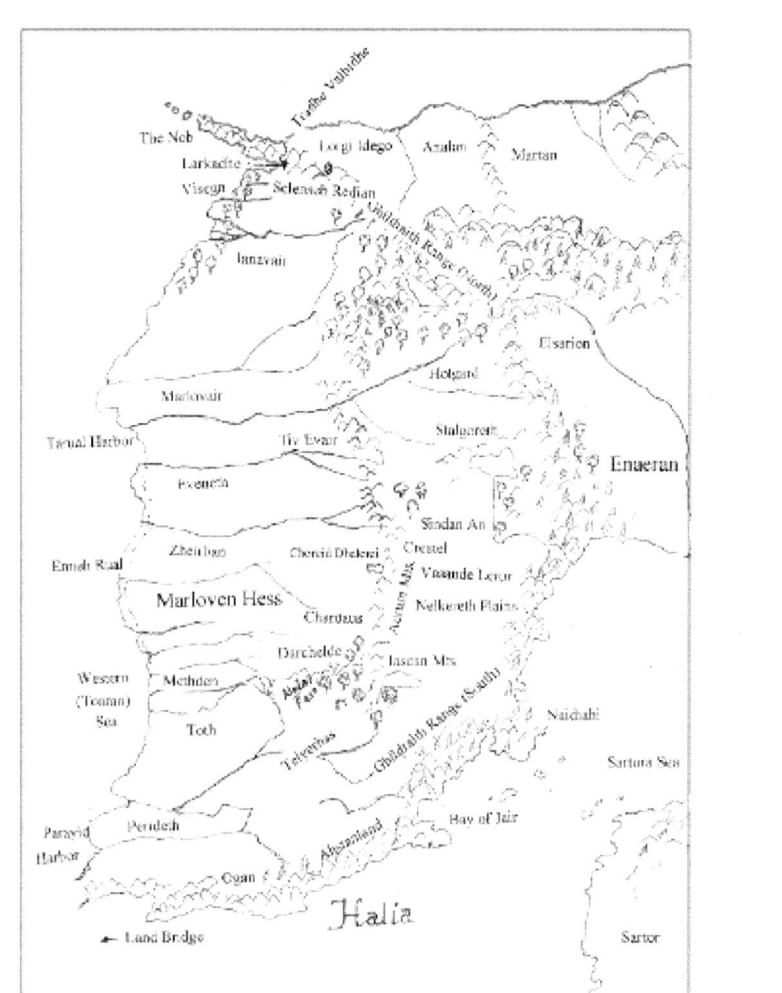

DRAMATIS PERSONAE

NOTE: This list is building off the *Ship Without Sails* List. Norsundrians, Ex-Norsundrians, and Detlev's boys at the end.

Name most frequently used comes first, so sometimes first name, sometimes last, sometimes nickname.

LIGHT MAGIC MAGES AIDING THE ALLIANCE

Erai-Yanya Vithyavadnais*: One of a long line of mages dwelling in the ruined city of Roth Drael. Trained partly by the northern Mage School at Bereth Ferian, and partly by Tsauderei, she works independently, her specialty magical wards. She has one son, ARTHUR (see BERETH FERIAN). Erai-Yanya's student mage is the Marloven exile Hibern Askan.

Evend: [deceased] One-time colleague of Tsauderei, King of Bereth Ferian (a courtesy title only) and head of the mage school there, he surrendered his life to bind rift magic from being used in Sartorias-deles by Norsunder. His place as titular king was taken by ARTHUR.

Igkai: Hermit mage living on the peninsula on the Sartoran Sea. An oddball all his life, he is a friend to birds and animals — and tolerates humans who do well by animals.

Lilith the Guardian*: A lower ranking mage and what might be called an officer of rites and rituals in Ancient Sartor, which was as close to a government as they got. She had one daughter, Erdrael, who was killed along with most of the rest of the population when Norsunder tried to wrest control of the world, for reasons explored in a volume to come. Her name is a modern adaptation, and she found herself trying to combat Norsunder on this and other worlds around the sun Erhal; she comes out of hiding beyond time whenever she finds evidence that Detlev has been in the world, acting for Norsunder's Host of Lords.

Mondros "Rosey": Big, bluff, and bearded, he began life as an exiled son of the disgraced Glenereth family, warlords of Ralanor Veleth. He studied magic, aided by Gwasan Sonscarna, Princess of the Chwahir, whom he married and had a son, REL (see SARTOR). When Mondros made it his life's goal to defeat Wan-Edhe of Chwahirsland, he stashed Rel with a trusted friend, where Rel grew up a part of the family, until the urge to travel caused him to take to the road. Father and son found one another relatively recently.

Murial of Mearsies Heili: Recluse mage, living hidden in the western wilds of Mearsies Heili. Born a princess, she supported the transfer of the throne to her niece CLAIR (see MEARSIES HEILI) on the death of her sister. Protecting the kingdom from a distance, she has seen to it that Clair got magical training.

Oalthoreh: [deceased] Head of the northern mage school in Bereth Ferian

Randon Amdrelya: Originally from Vandary, Randon is an accomplished mage who did the Child Spell when around thirteen, to avoid limiting expectations of his culture. Travels around looking for kids to rescue.

Tarael of Drael: A morvende mage of a Drael geliath, captured by the Host.

Tsauderei: Oldest of the senior mages, independent of the two leading mage schools, living in a historic mage retreat located in the mountains bordering Sarendan and Sartor in the Valley of Delfina.

FROM OFF-WORLD

Caris-Merian Rhoderan of Geth-deles: "Rhoderan" is a name adopted by her father, the disinherited and disgraced Harold Dei, who tried to take the throne of Everon a couple of times before he was booted off-world. He had three children, the middle one being Caris-Merian. She came to Sartorias-deles's northern mage school to study magic right before the invasion. An accomplished singer and a scholar, when she is not seeking revenge for her brother's death.

Les (Leskander) Rhoderan of Geth-deles: [deceased] elder brother to Caris-Merian, and a problematical figure in his home archipelago. He discovered vagabond magic, and tried to weaponize it, (he said) in order to win freedom for the underaged and poor. Very charismatic.

Mildred of Geth-deles: a martial artist.

Zairna Raadi from Sri Fortnu: A worldgate traveler and beginning mage, born a prince in a very problematic kingdom; a dragonflower inked into his neck and curling up over one ear testifies to serious rituals. Ditto the diamond earrings he never removes. Ended up at the Northern School of Magic.

June from Earth: From a parallel of Earth in even worse shape, who got caught in someone else's conflict. Has been traveling through Worldgates since, and become a sort of magical lightning rod without knowing. No matter how far or fast she goes, she cannot outrun her own shadow.

THE YOUNG ALLIES AND OTHERS,
LISTED BY KINGDOM

ALCANDAAMERA

Charlana, Queen of Alcandamer: A mage of sorts, possessor of the double crown, which distinguishes between lies and truth.

AMA HAZANTH

Crow (Prince Marseth Ghandorjien): Crown prince, keeper of the Fire Ruby (which wards storms from the island)

Barban

Dara, Leela, Yovres, Honey-blossom: vagabonds, present day

Ancient Tower that once had a window to the past, and to residents from the world Elesh Orom-alsh, guardians of the Fifth Protection of Alsheya (the cup Ethe)

Bereth Ferian

Arthur (Yrtur) Vithyavadnais: He adopted the nickname Arthur after his rescue by young world-gate crossing friends. Son of mage Erai-Yanya, he early showed great ability in learning and magic, but he was unhappy living in isolation. He was adopted as heir by Evend, the former head mage of the Bereth Ferian Mage School, and presiding King of the loose federation headquartered at Bereth Ferian. After Evend's death, Arthur shared this courtesy title with Liere Fer Eider in her persona as Sartora, the Girl Who Saved the World.

Evend: (see Light Mages)

Liere Fer Eider: Also known as the Girl Who Saved the World, she was the first of her generation to be born with *Dena Yeresbeth*. At ten years old she left her small town to escape being captured by Siamis, who had extended an enchantment over the world, which Liere later broke. The enchantment is generally known as The Lost Year, as most lived in a dream world while it lasted. She was lauded by all, and given the courtesy title of Queen in Bereth Ferian, a title with no powers or responsibilities whatsoever — but which still chafed her unbearably. Liere was the poster child for Imposter Syndrome until she went to Geth-deles for five years to study magic, and returned recently.

Chwahirsland (aka Land of the Chwahir)

Dirk Sonscarna: Son of the problematical Kessler (see below), on the verge of teenhood. Has Dena Yeresbeth and considerable martial arts as well as magical knowledge.

Jilo: Son of a lowly one-syllable sergeant, heir to elderly *Prince Kwenz Sonscarna,* he finds himself acting king of Chwahirsland, after Norsunder's removal of the previous king, who had ruled for more than a century. What that means is, he is slowly poisoning himself trying to remove the toxic accretion of dark magic enchantments over Chwahirsland, and especially its capital.

Gwasan Sonscarna: [deceased] Princess and mage, married a disinherited swordsman from Ralanor Veleth who later became the mage Mondros (SEE Mages). Their son is Rel the Traveler (SEE Sartor)

Prince Kessler Sonscarna: (SEE also Ex-Norsundrians) The single living descendant of the ruling Sonscarnas, who were systematically killed off by Wan-Edhe, blood relations notwithstanding. Prince Kessler escaped at a young age, made his way to a martial arts group where he mastered military arts. He allied with a Norsundrian mage, Dejain, and began to assemble followers for his plan to remove all hereditary rulers of the world and replace them with his followers, chosen solely on merit. When defeated, he was forced into Norsunder by Dejain, who betrayed him.

Wan-Edhe (born Shnit Sonscarna), King of the Chwahir: Descendant of the ruling Sonscarna family, has ruled for close to a century. A powerful dark magic mage, he has managed to create a powerful citadel in the heart of his kingdom where time itself is distorted in his effort to ensure that he will live and rule forever. He killed off his family and descendants, including his brilliant heir, Princess Gwasan; only his grandson Kessler escaped, but years of abuse told on Kessler's emotional landscape.

COLEND

"Bee" (Aural) Keperi: Chief scribe to Shontande Lirendi. Being blind, he does all his work by memorization.

King Carlael Lirendi: [deceased] Regarded generally as Mad King Carlael before he was assassinated by Efael of Norsunder. He was as beautiful as he was strange. He mostly existed in a world of dreams imposed by magic, from which he emerged now and then, very alert and very aware. There was a regency council made up of the chief nobles who oversaw the kingdom when he was unable to respond to the world around him, and they ruled until very recently, refusing to relinquish power, though Carlael's son Shontande had come of age.

Prince Shontande Lirendi: Son of Carlael, King of Colend, and new king.

Karhin Keperi: [deceased] She was a teenage scribe student in a small town in the west of Colend, who volunteered to function as the center of the young allies' communication network. An indefatigable letter writer, she first met Puddlenose of the Mearsieans, and gradually got drawn into the Alliance; she was murdered by one of Detlev's boys, and she is still missed.

Lisbet Keperi: Younger sister of Thad and Karhin.

Thad Keperi: Red-haired brother of Karhin, also a scribe student, but much less passionate about the scribe life. Very social, and friend to all the Alliance; he and his brother Bee are very close to Shontande Lirendi.

ENAERAN

Adon Marsael: Distantly related to the royal Elsarion family, tried to take throne. Allied with Norsunder in order to keep the throne.

Andri Malcolin Elsarion: Inherited his throne very recently, after years of civil war.

Gared Inmael: Close friend and adoptive brother of Andri Elsarion. Gared's father, the Elsarion Master of Horse, took in Andri when he was disinherited. The boys grew up together.

Marten (Martande) Eldias: Lifelong friend to Andri Elsarion.

Baras Parael Otobris: [deceased] The new king's Commander of the King's Guard.

Thadara Otobris, Duchas of Merith: The new king's Chief Minister and treasurer, who has her eye on marrying Andri and sharing his throne.

EVERON

King Berthold and Queen Mersedes Carinna Delieth: [deceased] Former king and queen, survivors of rough earlier years. Mersedes, daughter of a con man, became one of the Knights of Dei, dedicated to protecting the kingdom. They were both killed (at different times) by Henerek of Norsunder, who had come from Everon, and had been booted out of the elite Knights of Dei for countless crimes.

Prince Glenn Delieth: [deceased] Heir to the throne of Everon, and convinced that a strong army solves all questions, especially the threat of Norsunder attacking; he died in a duel with David, one of Detlev's boys, after forcing the fight on him.

Hatahra Delieth (Tahra), Queen of Everon: Younger sister of Glenn, passionate about numbers, and in her unrelenting hatred of Detlev and his boys. When the war begins, has two children, Jessan and "Carl".

Roderic Dei: Commander of the Knights of Dei, once defenders and protectors of the realm. The Knights were decimated in the war Henerek brought, and Kessler Sonscarna finished. Roderic Dei survived to serve as regent for Tahra Delieth until she reached the age of majority.

MARLOVEN HESS

Crystal Ingrid Montredaun-An: [deceased] Daughter and heir to Senrid, the king. Five years old. Her chief passion is dogs.

Daltan: Cobbler, middle aged. She is a resistance leader.

Forthan, Retren: [deceased] A young man from a farm background, Forthan is the best of the leaders to come out of the military academy. He became Harskiald, a resurrected title that means trusted commander in chief of Marloven Hess's standing army; before then, commanders in chief were appointed per mission. Struck his banner at Aladas Pass before the defeat of Marloven Hess.

Hibern Askan: Light magic student, tutored by Erai-Yanya of Roth Drael, who learned in the northern mage school. Hibern was disinherited by her family.

Indevan-Harvaldar Montredaun-An, previous king of Marloven Hess: [deceased] Second son of Kethadrend, and raised to be a scholar. Indevan was, like his elder brother, skilled in martial arts, but he was never competitive. His leadership was entirely through a likable, easy-going nature and intelligence. He traveled to the neighboring lands, where he conducted himself so well and so knowledgeably that he did a great deal to lessen the negative Marloven reputation. Married the King of Telyerhas's daughter, Lesra. Had one son, SENRID, [see below] before he was killed by his younger brother Tdanerend, who was appalled at his ideas about limiting royal power and disbanding the army in favor of a militia defense.

Kendred Montredaun-An, Prince of Marloven Hess: [deceased] Eldest son of Kethadrend, son of the grim Senrid who caused the various treaties to be made limiting Marloven Hess. Trained in martial arts at a very young age, sent to the academy too young. He had too much of his grandfather's angry drive, and when his father failed in various forays against those treaties, Kendred tried to rally the young Marloven heirs around him to take the throne. He ended up escaping over the border at a gallop with a company hot on his heels. Had two sons, both of whom he sold after unsuccessful plots. Changed his name, became a pirate before joining Norsunder, dead by age thirty.

Keriam, Janec: Career military man, Commander of the Marloven military academy, also titular head of the Palace Guard. Acted as guardian and foster-father to Senrid, protecting him from the regent as much as possible.

Senelac, Fenis: Wife to Retren Forthan, and head of horse training for the military academy, equal rank to the Master of Horse in the city guard.

Senelac, Jan: Cavalry Captain in the army, now chief of Senrid's coverts.

Senrid Montredaun-An: Young king of Marloven Hess, a mage studying both dark and light magic. First friend to Liere Fer Eider, and second to make his unity in *Dena Yeresbeth*. The Marloven army is one of the most formidable in the world.

Stad, Indevan (Van): Second in command, Marloven army

Tdanerend Montredaun-An, Prince of Marloven Hess: [deceased] Third son of Kethadrend, raised to be "shield arm" to his brother Indevan. Tdanerend was short-tempered as well as short-sighted, and uncoordinated. He tried to learn magic, but where that came easy to Indevan, as well as everything else, he had trouble learning, and eventually surrounded himself by toadies and the traditionalists who were uneasy at the changes Indevan contemplated. He married Caras, the second princess of Telyerhas, and there, too, he was unfortunate: she was ambitious, despised him as much as he came to despise her after she tried to scorn the Marlovens into setting up a court. He killed her first, before he took out Indevan and Lesra. His daughter, Ndand, was Senrid's chief companion. Tdanerend tried control spells on her, meant for Senrid, which motivated Senrid to master magic at a young age so he could fix his cousin. Tdanerend went over to Norsunder before losing the kingdom, and then his life. NDAND left the kingdom to become a musician.

MEARSIES HEILI

Aurora of Mearsies Heili: Clair's small daughter, already showing signs of being a wanderer, like her Uncle Puddlenose.

Clair of Mearsies Heili: Young queen of Mearsies Heili, a small agrarian polity on the northeast corner of the continent Toar. Niece of the hermit-mage *Murial*, and cousin to the wandering boy known only as *Puddlenose*, she has adopted a group of girls, most of them runaways. Her right-hand and designated 'heir' is *C.J.*

C.J. (Cherenneh Jenet): Found by Clair, who traveled through the World-gate, C.J. is from Earth, adopted into Clair's gang of runaways and rejects. She learns magic fitfully, and is generally regarded as the leader of Clair's gang of girls.

CJ's Gang of Girls: Falinneh and Dhana currently wear human form but are not actually human; Seshe has a mysterious past, suspected of being a runaway princess (which is actually correct); Irenne thought the world was a stage and she was the heroine of the play, which got her killed by accident by one of Detlev's boys, but she is still very much a presence among the girls; Diana is a martial artist and forester; Sherry and Gwen are followers. They are a very tight found family.

Mearsieanne: [deceased] Once Queen of Mearsies Heili, on her return to the present time, she stepped in and in the nicest way possible, shouldered aside Clair, her great-granddaughter, in order to show her how ruling ought to be done. After the invasion, she bound Mearsies Heili in a protective lattice-ward that was tied to herself, then she walked into a Selenseh Redian and surrendered her life, binding the enchantment onto her. The key is Clair.

Murial: *(see Light Mages)*

Puddlenose of Mearsies Heili: Bereft of family at a very young age, thus no one knows what his actual name was. He was abducted and used by The King of the Chwahir in his complicated plots, he was rescued several times by Rosey (Mondros, see LIGHT MAGES). He wanders the world, determined to have fun. His chief companion is a world-gate wanderer from Earth named Christoph, but sometimes he's joined by Rel (see SARTOR). Gradually he traveled on land less and on the sea more, until he was made second in command by Captain Heraford of the *Tzasilia*, former privateer.

REMALNA

Bran (Branaric) Astiar, Count of Tlanth: brother to Meliara, wife NEE

Meliara Astiar, Queen of Remalna: children Alaraec and Elestra

Nadav Savona: Vidanric's oldest friend and chief aid, son Nadav

Vidanric Renselaeus, King of Remalna: children Alaraec and Elestra

RALANOR VELETH

Flian Elandersi, Queen of Ralanor Veleth: was a princess from Lygiera, distant cousin to Garian Herlester of Drath.

Jaim Szinzar: Brother to the king, and nominal leader of the army, though Jason commands in action.

Jaimas Szinzar: Younger child of king and queen

Jason Szinzar, King of Ralanor Veleth: [deceased] military background, inherited the throne, and the care of his siblings, at a young age. His chief rival is PRINCE GARIAN HERLESTER OF DRATH

Jewel Szinzar: married to the King of Lygiera, MAXL ELANDERSI, has several children

Liara Viana Szinzar: Eldest child of king and queen

Markham Glenereth: disinherited, technically denied the Glenereth name, though the king intended that to be temporary. Liege to the king, a martial artist of superlative skill.

Lexan Glenereth: son of Markham Glenereth

SARENDAN

Darian Irad: [deceased] After his defeat in a vicious civil war, Darian Irad stepped down from the throne and ended up as a military consultant on the sister-world Geth-deles. On his nephew Peitar's assassination, Darian Irad insisted that he was a regent for Peitar's son Darian, and not a king: he had gone to Geth, where he married and had a family.

Darian Selenna: son of Peitar Selenna, and heir to the throne. Has Dena Yeresbeth.

Derek Diamagan: [deceased] Charismatic leader of the revolution, a commoner who wished to overthrow all the nobles, and institute common rule. He was a far better speech maker than he was an organizer; his revolution was a disaster. Close friend of Peitar Selenna until his assassination by Siamis, at that time nominally of Norsunder.

Lilah Selenna, Princess of Sarendan: [deceased] Younger Sister to Peitar. She, with friends *Bren* (artist), *Innon* (a noble-born accountant at heart) and *Deon* were deeply involved in the revolution.

Peitar Selenna, King of Sarendan: [deceased] Reluctant king who would rather study magic, he came to the throne after an especially vicious civil war. He, nephew to the former king, Darian Irad, was one of the leaders of the revolution, but advocated non-violent means. His accession was a compromise between the commoners, who adore him, and the nobles, who recognized that at least he is nominally one of their own; on his assassination, he was, at his own order, replaced by his uncle.

SARTOR

Atan, (Queen Yustnesveas Landis V): New young queen of Sartor, after the oldest kingdom in the world was removed from time by nearly a century. She was found as an infant on the border by Tsauderei the mage, and raised by him before the enchantment was broken. She began her queenship as a mage student with little training in statecraft, but well-read in history.

Gehlei: Former guard in the days before Sartor was enchanted for a century, escaped with the infant Atan. Raised Atan to age fifteen along with Tsauderei the mage.

Hinder and Sinder: Morvende (cave dwellers), friends of Atan.

Julian Landis: born Julian Dei, she is Atan's cousin who wore the Child Spell for a considerable time. She relinquished it on Atan's promise that she would not be considered an heir, nor a princess. She is a wanderer by nature, and was happiest when staying with Dtheldevor of Wnelder Vee's gang.

Mistress Veltos Jhaer: [deceased] Former chief of the prestige-ous Sartoran mage guild, until the enchantment the foremost mage school in the world. Now a century behind. She was fur-ther burdened by guilt for having lost the kingdom to enchant-ment, she left the guild woefully behind as they struggled to re-cover their old prestige. Assassinated by Efael of Norsunder, she was replaced for a time by Tsauderei the mage.

Old Helas: One of Rel's city guards, left from before Sartor's 100 year enchantment. Along with BEAK, a young guard.

Rel: Known as Rel the shepherd's son, and more widely as Rel the Traveler, he was happily raised by a guardian in Tser Mearsies until wanderlust caused him to leave home. Met Puddle-nose of the Mearsieans, and consequently became tangled in some of the Mearsieans' adventures. Friends with Atan, and one of the Rescuers. He was the only outsider ever invited to join the Knights of Dei in Everon; in the previous volume he discovered his parentage (SEE Mondros the mage), which he is still trying to process.

Rescuers: The name given to a band of children who had lived in a magic-protected forest during the enchantment. They sheltered Atan before the enchantment was broken. Ostensibly highly regarded as heroes by the Sartorans, there are the aristocratic Rescuers, and the non-aristocratic, Rel among them.

SLES ADRAN

Bartal na Shagal, King of Sles Adran: Allied with Adon Marsael of Enaeran, and Norsunder.

Chantala Shagal: Niece and heir to Bartal, daughter of Chantal, Bartal's sister. Cared for by her elderly nanny MARIANA, who was Chantal's devoted nanny.

Haries: Last name of the pair of artists who shelter Chantala na Shagal during the war.

Kinarde, Arandos: Sarendan-born Norsundrian placed as watch-dog and then commander over Bartal by Norsunder

Navor Mandracar: army commander and close friend of the king.

Master Orthal: runs an art school along the river. Other artists in training: LEMETH, LISI.

TELYERHAS

Havlan Casarod, King: Family the most direct descendant of the Cassadas, who were regarded as visionaries (or mad). Son of a queen known for her lack of skill at ruling but her genius for music, he had two sisters, LESRA and CARAS, who married Marloven princes and ended up dead. A scholar, he has a consort, who is also a scholar but he handles a lot of minor ruling issues. Has a son and a daughter.

Vasande Leror

Kyale Marlonen: Adoptive sister to Leander, relishes being a princess, and is jealous of Leander's attention.

Leander Tlennen-Hess: Like Senrid, a young king, though of a tiny polity that historically belonged to the Marlovens, then broke away four centuries previous. Leander and Senrid have a lot in common, and would be friends, except for Leander's jealous stepsister:

Llhei: [deceased] Sarendan-trained nanny (sister to Lizana, nurse to the royal children of *Sarendan*), governess to Kyale, remained after evil Queen Mara Jinia defeated.

Alaxandar: Captain of royal guard, quit under evil queen Mara Jinia, protected Leander.

Land of the Venn

Erenlara Sofar: Barely into her teens, princess of the Venn until her brother's death in the invasion. Has Dena Yeresbeth.

Kerendal Sofar: [deceased] Was king of the Venn, until the invasion. He committed suicide rather than submit to a blood-binding forcing him to act according to Norsunder's will. Met Rel the Traveler [see SARTOR] the one time he was able to escape Venn and his duties, as a young boy.

Wnelder Vee

Dtheldevor: Daughter of a privateer (some say pirate) who was killed when Dtheldevor was small, but not before she was taught martial arts. She became the champion for the young prince Murgeh Troiad, sailing against pirates infesting the shores, and helping to fight off an enterprising Norsundrian.

She has a hideout called Dthel Rendm, on one of the hundreds of islands off Wnelder Vee's coast. She did the Child Spell decades ago; in lived time she is in her late seventies. She accepts kids on the Wander on her ship and her island, but her most loyal shipmates are: Sarmonwilda, born a dawnsinger; Sharly, a centaur from the northern reaches, and Sidres, another centaur; Gloriel and Peridot Warren (twins, from Earth, born with mundane names) and Joey and Ellen Warren.

Her most frequent visitor who doesn't live with the privateers is Julian Dei Landis of Sartor.

Troy, King Murgeh Troiad: erstwhile king in Wnelder Vee. Though kingship is little more than a title — the guilds do what little governing is required in small, very rural Wnelder Vee — he resisted even that much, preferring to wander the world and master music, and kept the Child Spell in order to avoid royal duties. Actually considerably skilled as a bard.

NORSUNDER

Aldon: Military leader with a thirst for warfare, the bloodier the better. Wants to command the invasion in order to foster eternal war.

Alsaes: First came to notice as Kessler Sonscarna's companion in Kessler's plan to take over the world. Given a mortal wound, surrendered self in exchange for bloodknife spell to preserve his life. Extremely vain. Dyes hair blond to hide Chwahir origins.

Benin: [deceased] Ambitious mage, his specialty the soulbound (people caught at the point of death, their wills bound to the command of whoever holds the soul-bound magic). Benin tends to not wait until potential soul-bound are dead in order to experiment.

Bergan: one of Imry Llyenthur's staff, along with COLLERON, and Duin [see below] These are all typical flunkies, though Bergan sells info to whoever will buy it, most of all to Aldon.

Bostian: Ambitious Norsundrian military captain, obsessed with making himself king of Sartor.

Connanre of the Host of Lords: A charismatic musician. It's still unknown if he was turned or born without a vestige of conscience. He was the one who precipitated the Fall of Old Sartor by turning one of the rituals into a bloodbath, it is said to win the attention of Yeres. He is the Host's master spy.

Dejain: [deceased] Mage specializing in dark magic, one of a succession of Norsunder Base commanders, who tended to be summarily replaced by violence. Now deceased

Duin, Fassler: Imry Llyenthur's chief aide-de-camp. Born in Chwahirsland.

Efael: Considers himself one of the Host of Lords, the authors of Norsunder. Has a penchant for cruelty. He is the Host of Lords' chief assassin, bloodhound, interrogator, and errand boy; he and his sister Yeres consider Detlev their rival for a seat among the Host of Lords.

Elzhier: One of Connanre of the Host's best spies. She joined Norsunder as a young, angry teen.

Henerek: [deceased] Ambitious low-ranking young Norsunder military captain, originated in Everon. Wanted to be one of the Knights of Dei, but was cashiered due to excess cruelty, drunkenness, and inability to follow orders. Led a brutal war in Everon, now deceased.

Host of Lords: Authors of Norsunder, existing beyond time, readying for a second try at taking the world. Or worlds. Why, and who, they are will become clearer in succeeding volumes.

Hyath: Very young, ambitious, and cruel mage studying under Yeres.

Ilerian of the Host of Lords: Currently wears the shape of a beautiful and promising morvende, though morvende did not come out of their caves until a couple thousand years after the Fall of Old Sartor. The story put around is that his turning was Detlev's first act on emerging from Norsunder-Beyond. Ilerian is the architect of Norsunder.

Imry Llyenthur: Shares field command of invasion with Efael of the Host. A mage and a martial artist, he has Dena Yeresbeth. He's essentially a strategist.

Lesca: Apparently lazy steward in charge of Norsunder Base. Overlook her at your peril.

Svirle Treloar of the Host of Lords: He was heir to Yssel and still uses that title though Yssel is long gone. His underlings address him as "Lord Svir", the word 'lord' being an ancient title. He was the organizer of the Fall of Old Sartor, recruiting and forming plans. He is the ultimate in assumed privilege: nothing he does could be wrong because he deserves the world. It was he who lured Ilerian to the world, then discovered that he could not control this fascinating entity, so he exerts himself to function as go-between between Ilerian and everyone else.

Theronezhe of the Host of Lords: Their military chief.

Yeres: She and Efael, her brother, were born off-world and so thoroughly and spectacularly corrupted that they caught the attention of Svirle of Yssel, one of the authors of Norsunder. Yeres is a powerful mage. She and Efael gladly execute the errands that the Host of Lords, steeped in evil, consider too distasteful.

Ex-Norsundrians

Detlev Reverael ne Hindraeldrei: Chief visible mage and

sometime military leader, answerable to Norsunder's Host of Lords. Born four thousand years ago, has lived in and outside time ever since. Like his nephew Siamis, has Dena Yeresbeth. Left Norsunder in 4753: much speculation on both sides as to why.

Kessler Sonscarna: Renegade Chwahir prince with considerable military abilities, forced into Norsunder as a result of treachery by the mage Dejain. Hates Norsunder. (See *Chwahirsland* below)

Siamis Reverael: Nephew to Detlev. Formidable mage, and like Detlev, has Dena Yeresbeth. Left Norsunder previous to Detlev, after furnishing the means to free the Venn from an eight-century-year-old binding of their magic. Adopted Yanli, the last descendant of someone Siamis was close to on his first visit to Sartorias-deles. He has reason to believe that the woman, Isa Cassadas, was pregnant with his child before he was forced to return to Norsunder. They were both teenagers.

Sveneric Reverael Hindraeldrei: Detlev's son, trained with the boys.

DETLEV'S BOYS

Adam: Artist, formidable talents in Dena Yeresbeth, artist until his hands were ruined by Efael

Alaki (Ferret): Acutely observant, aware of overlapping worlds, spy

Curtas: [deceased] Strongly responsive to line and harmony, especially in building

David: Captain of the group, best in most areas

Erol: Chwahir born, plucked off a battlefield. Excellent at stealth

Edde (Noser): [deceased] Taken from another world, at best a mascot

Laban: Volatile and longing for what he cannot have, a Dei descendant

Leefan: Quiet, strong martial artist, cousin to Rolfin

Mal Venn (MV): Martial artist, studying magic, excellent sailor

Rolfin: Cousin to Leefan, superlative martial artist

Roy: Strong Dena Yeresbeth, mage and scholar

Silvanas: Martial artist and horse master

FOR MORE INFORMATION . . .

Visit the Sartorias-deles wiki at http://reqfd.net/s-d/

Part One

One

EVERYONE KNOWS THAT THE course of history is twisted by the tectonic energies of wars caused by the clashes of kings and mages; the great hold back chaos like the boulders that stand against the rushing water, and evil is the flood that changes the landscape entirely, until it is vanquished.

What we sometimes forget is that small, almost unnoticed actions — the lighting of a leaf on the water's surface, the meeting between bird and bug, and the dance of the turtle — also create widening ripples, until their consequences intersect with those of the plunging rock.

Or, the matters of kings.

This part of my story involves three quests; some sought a magical object that would aid their efforts to free the world, and some did not know until it was over that there had been a quest at all.

I must begin with an innocent who never quested, consciously or unconsciously. She would in the fullness of time serve as catalyst to great change, just as the cataract and the storm are influenced by the frog and the turtle, the wind and the air.

Chantala Shagal, Crown Princess of Sles Adran, sat in a window seat looking out over the snow-covered rooftops of Nente in tiers below her. The window seat was in a hidden alcove carved from stone, in the older part of the royal palace. She liked the feeling of complete privacy it gave, although she was aware that the entire household knew she could be found there.

Her gaze drifted over the city. The smooth white mantles of snow on the roofs and the gleaming gold and yellow and white of the stone below them gave her quiet pleasure. She could pretend it was home. The sky was blue, the clearest it'd been for at least a month. It was a beautiful day for —

The familiar anxiety churned her insides. She leaned her forehead against the diamond-paned glass of the window and shut her eyes.

Today Chantala turned eighteen, and Royal Uncle Bartal was giving a ball in her honor. Chantala shivered inwardly at the thought. She wished she were back home in Denwy. She wished her mother was alive. Mother would tell Royal Uncle Bartal to leave her be.

Her old nurse Mariana approached with quiet step. "Come, Chantala," she coaxed. "Time to get ready."

Mariana watched her uneasily as Chantala slowly left the window seat, her narrow hands clutching her elbows. Chantala's wraith-like form was shrouded in a close gown of heavy silk; no matter how rich the fabric, how clever the design, nothing could hide how thin she was. The finest gown (so the courtiers said, tittering) looked like a bag on a stork.

The walls had little nooks and shelves with lamps, books, a couple carved statues and a cloth doll — obviously rather old — with long silk-strand hair and a dress that would have graced any Royal Court.

Chantala was also far too pale; even in this dark hall one could see the blue tracery of veins beneath her thin skin, which was considered vulgar. Though no one would dare to point that out in public, not about the Royal Princess.

Sadly, Mariana reflected as she gently combed out Chantala's light brown locks, Chantala wouldn't care if they did. If she even heard it. She usually wandered about in a world of her own, one mired in her childhood. They stood directly before the huge fireplace in the bedroom. Bartal's palace was well-insulated, for a palace, and he made sure Chantala's rooms always had plenty of firesticks, but she was always cold anyway.

Mariana brushed Chantala's hair, trying to induce a shine in it. She parted it in the middle, drew it smoothly back over her ears and fitted the pearl-edged cap on her head, leaving the hair to hang free down her back.

Mariana stepped away to survey the effect, knowing

Chantala wouldn't show any interest in looking in a mirror. "Let's rub some color into your cheeks and your lips, child." Mariana held out the crushed rose petal salve. "You're so pale you'll stand out."

This was exactly the right approach: Chantala's single interest in her appearance was not to be noticed.

Someone knocked. Mariana recognized that imperative rap, and waved away the waiting maidservants, moving to the door to open it herself.

As the footman who had done the rapping bowed himself out of the way, Mariana dropped into a deep curtsey. Bartal stepped in and smiled at Chantala, who bowed her head, palms together as she made the proper dip, heir to king. "Good evening, Royal Uncle," she said in her soft, almost toneless voice.

"You are lovely tonight, dear niece," Bartal said, smiling widely and a little ironically.

Chantala thanked him gravely; in the background, Mariana's lips tightened, then she schooled her face. She remained in her low curtsey, head bowed, while Bartal extended his arm to Chantala. As soon as the door was shut on them, Mariana creaked upright again, hating Bartal anew as she set about ordering things to be comfortable and warm as soon as Chantala returned.

Bartal noticed the slight nervous tremor of Chantala's hand. He made a strong effort to smooth his voice to gentleness, though he didn't worry about her seeing his face. She never met anyone's eyes if she could help it, and even when she did, he'd discovered that she seldom recognized his expression for what it was. Things like hate, contempt, and malice passed right by. But she did feel dread—especially if she had to be an object of any sort of attention. Then there was no getting anything out of her.

If she hadn't been indisputably his heir, and the Duchas of Denwy, and surprisingly and overwhelmingly popular with the populace of that large and influential province, he would have seen to it that she suffered a tragic accident shortly after her mother's. But his two marriages had not produced an heir, and as for that supposed Birth Spell, no amount of courting mages in either light magic or dark could force it to work. Though Bartal was cynical about most things, he was very proud of the long reign of the Shagals. He had only Chantala to continue his bloodline—so he must simply pair her with some-one he had chosen, then he would have the raising of a grand-child as suitable heir.

In the meantime, cloud-minded Chantala was, but not stupid. She had proved unexpectedly adamant. She wouldn't come to court without that sour-faced Mariana, who Bartal remembered from his own childhood.

He knew well his sister had spent her time poisoning their minds against him, and though he knew his forces could reduce mighty Denwy to rubble, he did not want to sap the strength of Sles Adran, so that it became a beggarly travesty like Adon-Marsael's Enaeran. Though it suited his plans to have Enaeran weak. The time would come when he would rule the whole Arcardan Plains from Nente, and he would need strength to achieve it. Denwy was to be his backbone.

First he had to secure it by coaxing Chantala into marriage with the man he'd chosen.

He'd taken great care to praise his army commander-in-chief Navor Mandracar before Chantala and that old woman. The rest should follow, shouldn't it? A girl steeped in poetry, romanced by a handsome and dashing courtier—of course she's going to fall for him. But the romance was proceeding at the pace of ice melting.

So he worked on her as he walked her down to the ballroom. He even got her to flush with pleasure before they entered when he gallantly broke a spray of blossoms from the potted bush beside the grand doors and handed it to her with a flourish and a bow. She tucked it into her embroidered sash and was still smiling when he took her arm and they entered the ballroom.

He signaled the waiting musicians with a glance. The musicians struck up the fanfare to the promenade, and Bartal and Chantala fell into step. Everyone took their places behind them. When the two had made their circuit and reached the throne with its more modest padded heir's chair, the ball began.

Bartal was pleased to see that his courtiers were not napping. Chantala was surrounded by the most prominent peers, but Mandracar attached himself to her side until she promised him the first taltan.

It was especially galling to the ambitious that Chantala, Duchas of Denwy, had so easily attached the handsome Mandracar, but she scarcely looked at him. She was so clearly minding her steps that she could as easily have been partnered with a broomstick.

Under the expectant and watchful gaze of the king, Mandracar got her to stay next to him. But she did not know what to say to him. He was tall, well built, with glossy long black hair and a thin black mustache—Bartal had brought mustaches back in fashion, having gained a taste for them when traveling in the north. Mandracar's bronze skin made his pale hazel eyes stand out by contrast, as the glossy black mustache seemed to emphasize his strong white teeth.

Chantala found him vaguely frightening; to the court, the couple looked like a panther and a stork.

"Are you enjoying yourself, Princess Chantala?" he asked once they sat down.

"Oh, yes, thank you, Honor," she answered gravely.

"You look tired. May I fetch you anything?"

"No, thank you, Honor." She turned to watch the dancers.

Catching a glare and an impatient shooing gesture from Bartal, Mandracar cudgeled his mind for another topic of conversation. "Beautiful day, today, was it not?"

"Yes. I didn't get to watch the sunset today," she said regretfully. "It was time to get ready. Did you see it?"

At this rare return he had to answer positively. "Why yes, I did. Most beautiful. Clear sky, you know."

"I hope it is tomorrow." She smiled wistfully. "It is almost as pretty as sunset at home."

Mandracar sidled a glance. The king had better be watching. This was one of their longest conversations. "I would dearly love to see the sunsets in Denwy," he added slyly.

She smiled, her face almost becoming animated. "I have a poet in Denwy. He used to tell me such stories, in addition to writing poems. He would have come to Nente, I'm sure, but wasn't around when his majesty invited me to come. I wish I could hear from him—"

Mandracar remembered Bartal's description of the sharp-eyed old fellow in loud, ragged clothes whose figurative language made far too many references to ambition, and Norsunder, betrayal and greed. Once Chantala had been extricated from Denwy, Bartal had made certain the old nuisance vanished.

Her face was closing over again, and Mandracar said swiftly, "Do you know any of his poems?" and was able to congratulate himself once again on his success: she embarked on a long recitation.

This recitation was excruciatingly stultifying, but he was rewarded by the grim smile Bartal gave him as he strolled by with a couple friends.

Bartal had been clear. The courtship was to be as real as he could make it — that is, Chantala kept happy — or Denwy would rise in revolt. And Bartal knew that there were many among his nobles who hated his "treaty" with Norsunder, and would take any excuse to rise against him if rich, powerful Denwy led the way. But the reward, if Mandracar succeeded, would be worth the effort: his child would be the future king or queen. But he had to marry her first. Oh well. He'd done a lot worse things in his rise to power.

They danced again before passing to the next room for the midnight supper. But with this penetrating and constant cold, and the castle rooms being large and drafty no matter how sedulous the servants were about keeping fires going, dancing was becoming a way to keep warm. New ones were being introduced all the time, and people danced until they were exhausted, then sat till the cold forced them up again.

Supper consisted of hot, spicy food, and everyone ate well. Everyone except Chantala, that is. She'd been hungry when she went down but lost her appetite after being seated between the king and her swain and across from an older man whose face radiated this strange expression Chantala sometimes saw in Bartal's eyes, and who said very obscure things. Gradually she sustained the old unnamed dread feelings, and laid her fork neatly beside her plate, the delicacies so thoughtfully served her untouched.

Afterwards there was more dancing. Chantala wished she weren't guest of honor so she could have slipped off after supper as she usually did.

Mandracar, recognizing both the tiredness and the longing, steered her toward a chair. As soon as they were seated Mandracar said, watching her carefully, "I can wait no longer, Chantala. I must ask you now. Will you marry me?" First try!

She didn't look afraid, mad or coy, just blank. "Marry? You?" she repeated.

He was afraid this was another of those things her mother had deemed unworthy of explaining to her daughter, but then she said, "Why?"

He was so sick of smiling that his teeth ached. "People in our high positions have a duty..." He searched wildly for reasons she would understand, and recalled their earlier conversation, and his incremental success. "Because we can be alone together all the time and read poetry. We can leave court—" Her gaze lifted, and she actually smiled. "And go to Denwy, and I can take care of your burdens while you're free to do what you like."

Her smile broadened. For the very first time, she was almost human, even kind of pretty, in a faded late-summer wildflower sort of way. "That would be so wonderful. And would you—ride out with me?"

"Of course, of course!"

"Then I'll be glad to."

"You must call me Navor. You see I use your name." He took her hand and gravely kissed the top of it.

She jumped, startled by the contact. Obviously she would not be expecting him to fake interest in her person, for which he was grateful—he couldn't bear skinny women, and this was the thinnest one he'd ever seen. Even the touch of her hand was repellent, in that he was afraid her fingers would break if he held them in too strong a grip. (As for that future child on the throne, it would definitely be a Mandracar, and with a little conniving, Bartal would think it was a Shagal...)

A few questions about her preference revealed that she knew as little about weddings as she did about romance. She appeared to be content to leave the details up to him; the only animation she expressed was at the idea of marrying soon, that she might leave court and return to Denwy.

That was exactly what the king wanted.

Exulting with triumph, Mandracar carefully took her hand, threaded it through his arm, and escorted her as fast as she would move to Bartal, who, upon hearing the news beamed upon them and said he would let them have a court wedding two weeks hence.

The king then lifted his wine cup, and the lead musician motioned for the players to cease. The remaining guests, sensing a proclamation (and perhaps an expensive party that they would not be required to pay for) raced to get cups. Then the king offered a toast to the newly plighted couple.

As people drank to the happiness of the couple, those who knew about politics wondered if even mastery of powerful

Denwy would be worth being tied to such a rabbit, and those who didn't know about politics gave Chantala considering looks, wondering how so quiet and pale a person could have landed the lusty Mandracar, and she might be worth cultivating in the future, especially if the new duchas took to entertaining on a lavish scale.

The only sour note was the old Honor Nor, who was crying, and wouldn't say why.

Two

FOR TWO WEEKS, CHANTALA was happy enough to break the shell of numbing ice that had closed around her since her mother's death. Royal Uncle Bartal was extra kind, and did not insist she attend court functions.

When the two weeks ended, Chantala wanted to postpone the wedding because the Count of Nor, who'd departed suddenly after the ball, hadn't returned yet, but she was easily overruled by Mandracar and Bartal.

She signed the papers put in front of her that would grant her new consort equal power, and she was given a fantastically beautiful gown of pale blue velvet with golden queensblossom elaborately embroidered on it. She permitted tight-lipped, frowning Mariana to rub some rouge into her cheeks and lips, and her hair was bound in rags the night before in order to induce a wave in it.

The king hosted the wedding in the main ballroom, all court in attendance. The floor was strewn with flowers, procured from somewhere. Chantala wore a garland of white hothouse roses in her hair. Bartal had done them the highest honor by, instead of designating a married couple to perform the old ceremony, declaring he would do it himself.

And so they were married, and departed immediately for Denwy.

After two and a half weeks in his new duchy, the new Duchas of Denwy packed up his consort and his enormous entourage and started back to Nente.

Mandracar was furious.

He'd started out with what he believed to be the best of intentions. When they arrived in Denwy, Chantala led him all around the palace as she described in excruciating detail the improvements her mother had made, while carefully explaining how nothing could be changed.

The second day, when she asked him to ride out with her, this ride turned out not to be a sedate tour of the extensive outer gardens, or a gallop along an elegant avenue, but a house-to-house visit to what appeared to be every aged, poor, and disabled hanger-on who could claim blood relation, and other indigents on what was apparently a staggering charity list.

At these houses, frail and listless Chantala, who at court seemed barely able to totter across a ballroom, dispensed herbal medicines to those who needed them, inspected, discussed, and then dispatched workers to repair houses and wells and canals and roads, and a host of other tasks as boring as they were exhausting.

And Denwy paid for it all.

Everywhere they went, she introduced him, and people bowed, and simpered, and though he exerted himself to be charming, they all addressed her. He could have been speaking Venn, for all they heeded him, whereas they hung on her every word.

He stuck to it for a solid week, figuring that had to be long enough to establish his name and rank, after which he'd be able to start issuing orders of his own. But by the end of the week, after seeing in one face after another adoration for her, and for him stony distrust, dislike, and just enough politeness that Chantala didn't notice anything amiss, he realized that it wouldn't be five days or five weeks, but more like five years before he would see the slightest lessening of that distrust: Bartal's sister Chantal had done her work thoroughly and well. Every order he gave, no matter how inconsequential, if they didn't like it, they carried it to Chantala, and if it didn't match what that damned dead duchas had decreed, Chantala would painstakingly explain to him why it was impossible.

Mandracar commanded the elite King's Guard, but he could not send a battalion of heavies in to thrash some sense into these idiots, as Bartal had been firm: Denwy was not to be knocked about. He needed it too badly.

In short, in spite of those fine papers she'd willingly signed, Navor Mandracar, Duchas of Denwy and Commander of the King's Guard, came to understand viscerally why Bartal insisted Chantala be kept content: Mandracar, though a duchas now in name, was effectively powerless.

After every one of these day-long journeys to the needy, she'd preside over a vast dinner in the company of a mighty throng of distantly-related hangers-on and indigents, after which those with the vaguest literary pretensions would bore on with their latest creations, or "converse" till it was time to separate to their respective wings and retire for the night. He would drop gratefully, but he could see the lights burning in her apartments across the courtyard long after he'd gone to bed, as she went over duchy accounts.

When he (holding himself back heroically) made tentative suggestions on how they wouldn't have to be so careful with money if they raised taxes, she explained that her mother had made a law that no one below the rank of merchants or gentry could be taxed—if the king's tax was extra that year, her estates could well afford the extra (she paid a third of the required sum anyway, since by some oversight the highest peers elsewhere in the kingdom didn't seem to have to pay), and no, she needed no honor guard or border patrol of her own—whatever for?—and anyway there were very few idle young men or women in Denwy.

That night, Mandracar went to his lonely bed—though he had lovers aplenty in Nente, no Denwy woman gave him a second look—in bitterness and enraged disappointment.

The next morning he rose before she did, and rode off on his own to see what he could do. He was thoroughly brick-walled in every endeavor, and he began to see that even Bartal had underrated his sister's work. It became clear that the slightest hint of change would cause the people to rise up. And that would get him in trouble with Bartal, whose resources were extended to the maximum by the Norsundrian commander Imry Llyenthur's high-handed demands.

The people gave Bartal's local garrison the prescribed money and goods, and then lived completely around them as though they didn't exist. The border garrison commander confessed to Mandracar over beer, behind locked doors, that he'd been stuck there for fifteen years, and he'd never had a conversation outside of business necessity with even the smallest child.

To the people of Denwy, in short, the duchas's marriage only existed on paper.

Mandracar had had enough. The next night, he cornered Chantala between the evening's indigent-poetry boredom and her going off to her rooms.

"Chantala, we're going back to court tomorrow," he said, shutting the door firmly on the army of listening ears.

Her face had begun to fill out a little. Now it closed over in the old way. "Why? I thought my getting married meant I shouldn't have to go to court anymore. His majesty said he'd brought me to keep us safe, but now you're keeping me safe, just as you said."

"Because I have to talk to Bartal, and you need to — because we're going, that's why."

"But I don't wish to —"

"Too bad. Keeping you safe means we must travel together. It is the king's command," he added. Not true, but even she couldn't gainsay it. The king was the king.

So now they were on their way back.

It was an ugly Fourthday morning, bitterly cold, when they rolled into Nente. Mandracar's mood was vile because on starting out he'd decided that rather than have to ride with Chantala in the coach, he'd ride outside of it. The freeze had hit the night before while they slept at an inn. He still had no wish for Chantala's company, but he hadn't taken two coaches, and he certainly couldn't force her to ride, so here he was.

The innermost courtyard of the palace was strangely silent when they got there. One stable-boy, obviously impatient at having to remain at his post, came out to open the door for Chantala and take the bridle of Mandracar's horse after he'd dismounted.

Mandracar flung a look around the place, and said, "What's going on here? Where's everyone?"

"Brought in a pris'ner. 'Portant one. All gone on bizness inside hoping to see." The boy grinned, showing a mouthful of crooked teeth.

"Prisoner?" Mandracar repeated.

"From Enaeran, they say."

Mandracar strode inside and up the stairs two at a time,

his ironic gaze taking in a surprising number of servants who were busy polishing doorknobs and hall furniture.

The slab-faced guard before Bartal's huge study recognized Mandracar, and opened the door. The guard's eyes flicked to Chantala, who was following along behind. Mandracar had forgotten about her or he would have told her to take herself off, but the guard didn't know that, and held the door open for her, too.

Inside the warm, elaborately furnished study a disparate group stood around the king, who held out his hands to an enormous fire. The king, a courtier both Chantala and Mandracar recognized as one of Bartal's right-hand men, and two guards in mud-splashed purple, were focused on a tall, rangy young man whose yellow head was bound with a rag even dirtier than his clothes. His hands, tied tightly behind him, were a strange reddish blue, and his bony triangular face was disfigured by cuts and bruises. His large, hazel eyes crinkled in amusement.

"You will be well rewarded. Very well rewarded..." Bartal was saying to the two guards. Then his voice changed. "But where are my manners? Sit down, dear Andri, sit down. I'd never thought to have an opportunity to meet you." His thin lips curled.

"*That's* Andri Elsarion?" Mandracar asked in disbelief.

"Yes, M—" Bartal's face changed when he glimpsed Chantala still standing uncertainly at Mandracar's shoulder.

Mandracar swung around, and glared.

Bartal's smooth voice cut across Mandracar's started oath. "Good day, dear niece. How pleasant to see you back." He strolled over, took her arm, and gently but firmly escorted her to the door. "How unfortunate—your arrival coincided with that of one of our worst criminals. But you are safe, don't worry. Why don't you go to the royal suite, and have the servants prepare hot spice-milk for you. His grace will be along directly."

He flicked a look at one of the stationed liveried men out in the hall, who sprang to Chantala's other side, and escorted her to the royal wing.

There she found Mariana supervising the unpacking. A new fire was crackling brightly in the fireplace, though as yet it had little effect on the icy air of the room. Chantala sank down into a chair without removing her cloak.

"It will warm up soon," Mariana said brightly. "Where is his grace?"

"With the king. They have a prisoner," Chantala murmured, curling her legs under her and wishing she were warm. This palace was always so cold. "One of the worst criminals. But Royal Uncle invited him to sit down."

"That sounds odd," Marana said encouragingly. Instinct insisted that it was very odd.

"Is crime common?" Chantala asked, hugging her elbows close. "Remember when mother held that debate, and we were agreed that those who stole food out of desperation were not criminals, but those who did out of laziness committed crimes against the community?"

Mariana kept working.

Chantala watched idly, murmuring, "Uncle Bartal said he'd never thought to meet him."

"Who, dear?"

"The prisoner. They called him Andri Elsarion. I know that name, don't I? Elsarion…" Her voice drifted, as her gaze turned toward the fire. "I wanted to ask why he wished to meet him, but Royal Uncle said he was dangerous, but I am safe. He told me to come here and drink spice-milk."

Mariana's lips tightened over the words *He is the true king of Enaeran.* Instead, she arranged for the spice-milk, and once that was drunk and Chantala was tucked up into bed, Mariana whisked herself into the dressing room, which had once belonged to the duchas. A secret panel in one wall opened onto a passage, which she entered swiftly. A couple passages later she crouched on the floor, peering through a slit in the ceiling of Bartal's study. The slit was hidden in a lot of arabesque-work, which obscured some of her view of the study. She could see Bartal seated at his desk, but not who he was talking to. But she recognized Mandracar's voice.

"…foolishness to play your hand too soon, I agree, but don't you think if you wait too long Llyenthur might find out? And he will wish to know why you didn't even report the capture, much less turn Andri Elsarion over to him."

Bartal sat back and placed his fingertips together. "Possibly… Possibly… but I find I'd like to risk it. Andri is a very minor pawn in Llyenthur's game. But he's a major piece in mine." His smile slowly increased as he became lost in thought. After a long pause, he said, "Eh. I shall take some precautions while I plan. The two who brought him apparently killed off their compatriots, and they should be dead by now. No one else but Ganal, who I've trusted since I came to the throne, and now you, know. There will be no hindrance when I have everyone in place around Enaeran." He turned an inquiring gaze on Mandracar. "But I'm forgetting—what brings you back, my dear Mandracar? Don't tell me you find your wife too wild for you."

"That rabbit," Mandracar said with such contempt Mariana gritted her teeth and longed to drop a potted plant on his head. "You've been misled in your niece, Bartal. Your sister was even cleverer than you'd supposed." He embarked on a long and embittered description of his miserable stay in Denwy, which made Mariana grin and seethe by turns. Finally he wound up: "So I brought her back here. The only solution I can see is either to subjugate them by force or by threat."

"No. I do not wish to see force used. You know my reasons. But I do see a definite possibility in keeping her here and—regretting the onslaught of a decline in her health, shall we say, if Denwy responds insufficiently to your rule, now that the two of you are married. It will suffice to drop a hint in the ear of that dough-faced nanny. She used to champion my sister before her essay into poetic justice."

"Chantala is poetic justice?" Mandracar said blankly.

"I will explain one day. For the present, you must strive to win her favor. Make more of an effort to charm her woman, too. I believe she has a great deal to say (if not all) about what forms Chantala's likes and dislikes will take." Bartal rose. "I have several problems to ponder, such as whether it will be more effective to brandish Andri Elsarion before Adon Marsael in Enaeran, or merely his head. We will discuss this further once I make certain there are no dangling threads—but before that, you must return to Denwy without Chantala, and see what you can contrive."

Mariana heaved herself up and sped down the passageways to Chantala's suite, making and discarding plans as she did so. When Mandracar arrived to see how things were going she had almost finished unpacking, doing what remained in a ponderously slow way that precluded any suspicion of her having had time to be occupied in any other way.

Finding Mariana in the middle of unpacking, and Chantala asleep, Mandracar felt his duty had been done, and he retreated down the hall to see to his own suite's preparation.

———————⚬⚬⚬⚬———————

For Chantala, at least, things settled down to normal. She was resigned to the old patterns, even forgetting her marriage to the extent of being startled whenever anyone addressed Mandracar as the Duchas of Denwy. She became aware of his plan to go back to Denwy without her. She knew this was wrong. He did not know how the duchy was to be governed. She ought to be there long enough to make sure he did it right.

One evening, when he was paying her a duty visit, she made the tentative and timid suggestion that perhaps it would be wisest if she accompanied him to Denwy, at least for a while. Besides, she missed her home so much.

He looked at her, brows raised. "My dear Chantala. If I want suggestions from you I will ask for them. It is the king's wish that I go to Denwy." He paused, then added slyly, "He's not satisfied with its running. He thinks I will fulfill your mother's wishes best."

Of course Chantala acquiesced immediately.

Mandracar forgot the incident as soon as he left. But Mariana, who'd been arranging things in the room adjacent, recognized the timid attempt for what it was. She smiled to herself: her plans were going to be easier to accomplish than she'd thought.

Another day passed before Mandracar departed, enabling Mariana and her compatriots to act.

Late that night, Mariana touched Chantala on the cheek, waking her. Chantala sat up with a gasp, awake in an instant, and afraid. "Mariana?" She recognized her maid's face by the glow of the candle in her hand.

"Yes, dear. Up and get dressed. See, I've laid these clothes out for you."

Chantala stared at the unfamiliar thick riding trousers and the worn-looking, quilted robe, but offered no question as she slipped hurriedly out of her nightgown, so that Mariana could just as hurriedly pull the hearth-warmed dress over her. As the robe was fastened round her waist she looked over her shoulder at Mariana. "Why are we doing this?"

"Because we're going to save Denwy."

"From Navor Mandracar?"

Mariana was surprised at so much understanding. "You've seen it, too?"

Chantala studied the patched, uneven sleeves of the robe she now wore. Mariana had spent a deal of time trying to find one sold enough yet still warm. "His grace said it was the king's order to go to Denwy without me. There is no way to stop him from it. Otherwise I would."

"I believe we will be able to fix that," Mariana gloated. "Once words spreads to Denwy that the heir to the kingdom is going to safety, escorted by the king of Enaeran."

Chantala blinked in surprise. "He is?"

"Ah, we're contriving it now. Here, sit down, child. I'm going to rub this oil in your skin and hair. It isn't permanent, but it won't wear out for a couple weeks or so." She brandished a jar of greasy dark brown oil.

Chantala sat unresisting while the strange, sharp-smelling stuff was rubbed vigorously on her face, neck and arms, then into her hair, making it stiff and brown. At length, Mariana sat back on her heels and sighed. "You're going to smell like you've been eating garlic in every meal, but that's as well. Because the Duchas of Denwy is going to vanish, and a skinny whitework seamstress named Orfia has taken her place. That traitor Bartal is never going to see you again—unless he's defeated and you return in triumph. And he's not going to have Denwy without a revolution on his hands, and he's not going to have Enaeran, either." Mariana sniffed, lips poonched. "How I wish I could see his face when he finds himself doubly defeated."

Chantala looked up questioningly at Mariana. "Defeated?"

"Yes! You'll see presently. Here, put this on, and this, while I lace up your leggings." Chantala struggled into a coat, which was shaggy with hanging threads and patches, then pulled the rough, heavy cloak Mariana handed her over her shoulders. She sat still while Mariana wrapped long sewn-together rags round her legs and over and under her feet, then laced the leggings into place with string. Then she stood up. "I have some fine hemp-shoes for you, but I'll give them to you when we're outside. They'll hamper you inside, and you must be swift and silent. Come, give me your hand. We're going to use some passageways that can't be lit by a candle. I know my way, so I will lead you. Your mother learnt these passages as a child. Would you like to learn them, too?" She talked calmly, sensibly, and Chantala remained calm, merely curious.

Taking the oil with her, Mariana led Chantala by a hidden route down to a very cold, strangely echoey room. It was too dark to see much beyond an occasional dim light. It only created confusing shapes and shadows for Chantala, but Mariana never faltered in her steps, her large warm hand giving Chantala's thin, cold one reassuring squeezes every so often. At last they stopped. Chantala heard the sound of heavy breathing, coming from somewhere to her left. She pressed unconsciously against Mariana's side.

"Andri?" Mariana whispered.

"Here," came a low whisper. It was the breather. He had a juicy cold.

"Need a hand?"

"No. Thanks."

Andri's steps joined them; Chantala recognized the prisoner from Royal Uncle's study. "Mariana?" she breathed.

"Shh." Mariana squeezed her hand warningly as they stopped again, to open another mysterious door. As they went through, the cold air from outside hit them with an unpleasant shock. Snow was falling softly, and there was no sound beyond the squeaking of the snow under their feet. They crossed the stable courtyard without being heard. Mariana led the way, clutching a black shawl over her head with one hand, leading Chantala by her other, and looking neither right nor left.

There was one last passage in the palace walls, then they were in the city.

Mariana stopped, the young man as well. Two big guards also stopped. "You will have to desert now," Mariana said. "There will be no hiding this escape."

"We know," said one of the guards. "We've an escape route ready and waiting; we saw what happened to those guards who brought him. There's no serving such a king." He spat into the snow as the other guard bobbed her head in agreement.

The guards took off in one direction, and Mariana, Andri, and Chantala set out in another.

Three

THEN BEGAN THE HARDEST part of their escape so far: walking quickly, being jerked suddenly into doorways or behind walls, waiting in the freezing snow, then starting off at a swift pace again.

Chantala's feet were starting to get numb with the cold when they ducked down an alley. Mariana knocked a pattern on a window. The wooden door next to the window unbolted. A woman with carrot-colored hair opened the door a crack, then wide, and hurried them into the house. As soon as the door was shut she bowed.

Chantala was going to acknowledge it when she realized the woman wasn't even looking at her, but up at Andri.

Chantala turned his way to find the same tall, skinny young man she'd glimpsed in Royal Uncle's study. His hands looked more normal now. His mouth and eyes were smiling, but there was a look of tension in his forehead, and his eyes were ringed darkly. He was holding himself erect in a stiff sort of way that didn't look very natural.

Mariana waved a hand impatiently at the younger woman. "Get some hot water and a towel along with some warm food. He's hurt, you know."

"I'm afraid I'm beyond your aid," Andri said in a low voice, gravelly with leftover cold.

His tone made it a trivial matter, but Mariana's brows snapped together, and she said, "I'll have a look at it just the same."

Andri shrugged as he dropped gratefully into a chair.

The redhead said, "Come down into the basement. I've warmed it up, and we'll be safer there. My son will bring some food down presently..."

Soon they sat on a rug-covered floor, surrounded by boxes of preserves and old furnishings. Mariana emptied her huge apron pockets of all sorts of oddments, including the skin dye and two long and wicked-looking knives. They were heavily ornamented. Chantala recognized them as Mandracar's.

"Here." Mariana pushed the knives at Andri, who picked them up, hefted them, then smothered a grimace. These were decorative knives, probably pulled off a wall; the ornamentation was all for show, but the rest was badly made.

Still, even a bad weapon was better than nothing. He yanked one of his pants legs up and put one knife down the inside of his riding boot. He laid the other beside him.

Mariana nodded, said, "Off with your shirt, boy."

Andri shrugged, pulled off his jacket and unbuttoned his shirt, using his left hand as little as possible. Chantala blushed, wondering if she should retreat to one of the dark corners of the basement—but when she looked at his face she decided she didn't have to. Such a complete lack of embarrassment meant he didn't care at all. So she stayed put, where it was warm. Meanwhile Mariana frowned heavily at the strange cut making a jagged line down his left shoulder blade. When the red-haired woman brought hot water and a towel, she sponged at the dried blood on the cut till it was clean. The cut was completely healed over, the skin around it white, and the line where the slice had been, gray.

"How could that heal so fast?" Mariana said.

"Dark magic."

"Does it hurt?"

"Only at night. It's numb most of the time. I was cut by what's called a bloodknife. Bartal supervised himself; he's not a mage is he?"

"No," Mariana said, shaking her head. "He always hired mages. Her grace often regretted where some of these came from."

Andri pursed his lips. "I hope that means he'll do the honors at night. I suspect his efforts won't even come near Yeres at her laziest."

"What? Who?"

"Ah, nothing, nothing," he added, smiling as he pulled on his shirt.

"It's numb? Then why are you moving like that?" Then Mariana eyed the rest of him, taking in the visible bruises, and answered her own question.

Andri said carelessly, "Oh, that's from a good old-fashioned beating. I couldn't just sit there and let that horse apple prick me with that knife, could I? My hands were still useless so I kicked him." He grinned at his boots. "Must have loosened every tooth in his head," he said reminiscently. "They objected. Sprained my arm while they were at it."

"Can you defend yourself?" Marianna asked doubtfully, shifting her gaze to Chantala.

"Can use either hand."

Mariana shook her head and creaked to her feet. "Well. You'll eat before we go."

"Was hoping to hear that!" He smiled at her with real gratitude.

The red-haired woman went upstairs to fetch some food, and Mariana checked to see how Chantala took this talk of knifing and fighting. She was staring at the fire with her withdrawn look on her face.

Their hostess and a stringy girl with carrot-hair came down, the girl carrying a full tray with totally absorbed caution.

Mariana shot a glance at his mother and raised her brows.

"'S all right," the woman said. "I'd trust her further than most adults."

The girl had a comical look on her face — like she was valiantly trying to suppress a pleased grin, and appear grown-up. She sat down near the fireplace and, hugging bird-thin legs to her chest, fixed Andri with a bright, unmoving gaze that was the total opposite of Lyren-Sartora's ready scorn.

The girl seemed to be Lyren-Sartora's age. What bothered him was that this little Sles Adrani urchin shouldn't even know who he was, much less regard him as a hero. It meant that the desperate Adranis really did look to him to rescue them as well as Enaeran.

The food was a strange, pasty sort of stew, but it was hot, and he hadn't eaten any hot food since he got nailed. Before, even. When he was nearly done, he turned Mariana's way. He wanted to get going, but he owed her for the escape. If she wanted his help he'd give it. She must've freed him for a reason.

Mariana was watching her charge, who merely sat, hands in her lap, shoulders hunched, eyes on the fire. Her plate sat before her, untouched.

Andri looked at her more closely. Stick thin, squarish hands that were so thin of flesh the knuckles and bones were prominent. They were a strange brown color, as was her face. Her gray eyes reminded him somehow of Detlev's son Sveneric, the same clear, steady gaze. Her hair was badly dyed brown and stringy.

"Eat something, Chantala," Mariana said gently, touching the girl's bony wrist. Andri wondered how old she was, and decided she could be no older than fifteen or sixteen.

Chantala said apologetically, "I'm not really hungry."

Mariana's face took on the resigned look of someone fighting an old battle. "Please try. We have a long trip ahead. You will need your strength."

Chantala reached obediently for her fork with no ill will but with an utter lack of enthusiasm.

"What's the matter, want to make me look like a pig?" Andri asked her, patting his stomach deprecatingly.

Chantala looked at him questioningly, at his flat stomach, skinny hands and face, then suddenly smiled. "You are as thin as I am," she said, almost reproachfully.

She picked up her fork with no more enthusiasm than before, but at least her face didn't look so withdrawn.

Mariana shot him a look of real gratitude, so warm he sat back in surprise. He then restacked his plate, helping himself from the bowl the woman had brought down. When he was completely stuffed, he grinned up at his hostess. "Thank you," he said. "Best food I've tasted in over a week."

She smiled. "You're welcome, Enaeraneth king. Is there anything else I can get you?"

"I suppose there's no chance of having a bath?"

Mariana spoke up, though she never took her eyes off Chantala's hand in its journey from plate to mouth and back again, "I'd rather you didn't, your majesty. We must be beggars this trip. Filthy ones," she added, eyeing Chantala. "This, by the way, is *Orfia*. May's well begin by calling her that. What shall we call you?"

Andri was somewhat surprised by Mariana's apparently unquestioning assumption that he would remain with her and Chantala/Orfia. He wanted badly to find Liere, who he feared might be loitering about waiting for him, though she had promised not to. But he owed Mariana his life. It wouldn't be fair to run off and leave her when she seemed to need his help.

He smiled, every evidence of reluctance gone from face and voice. "Malcolin will do. It's my middle name, and common enough both sides of the border." He leaned back on his elbows. "So what's the plan?"

"We will leave as soon as she has eaten. We want to go under cover of this snow, which will obliterate our tracks."

The girl exclaimed, "Mama! The milk—"

"Oh! Run and fetch it. I've some spiced-milk. You must each have a glass before you start out into the cold again."

The suggestion was accepted with goodwill. Soon, with the warm taste of cinnamon and honey in their mouths, the three visitors took their leave.

The air was bitterly cold, the city dark and closed up. Houses and walls jutted black shapes against a blacker sky. Sharp and distinct rang the slightest sound. They took care not to add to them.

As great flakes drifted softly down, they made their way safely beyond the boundaries of Nente.

No one spoke until Chantala said softly, "Mariana, I'm very tired."

"We'll soon be there, little one."

As dawn blued the east, the snowfall steadily increased till, when they turned off onto a wagon track, they could barely see. But at the end of the trail was a low weather-battered farmhouse, with windows glowing a welcome gold. The front door opened almost as soon as Mariana knocked, and a tall man with a red nose pulled them inside. As soon as they were inside and the door was shut, the man embraced Mariana, wet coat and all. "I had given up all hope!"

"Bad weather indeed," she returned, smiling at the other three occupants of the room: a woman her age, and two young men around Andri's age. These were looking at Andri with ill-concealed curiosity. One of them, the younger-looking, was more of a boy, on the verge of manhood—which in some circles was defined simply by having to go to the Healer for the beard spell. He had a hungry, burning-eyed look of painful hope. He started up, opened his mouth and Mariana said as the red-nosed man helped her out of her coat, "We'll be glad enough of your fire. These, by the way, are my children, Orfia and Colin."

The boy stopped as if he'd run into a wall, then whirled around and flung himself down by the fire. He yanked a knife from its sheath by his side and began to play with it, glowering at the fire as if he were alone in the room.

The tension in the room focused on Andri. He sighed inwardly, wishing he was on horseback, alone, crossing the border out of Sles Adran.

Red Nose took them upstairs and revealed a narrow, long room secreted behind a heavy cupboard. The woman handed them an armload of heavy quilts and pillows, and left them in the dark. As they groped about to settle, they heard the cupboard being dragged back into place.

Andri cursed under his breath as he arranged himself in a cocoon of mildew-smelling quilt. He'd been a fugitive for too many years—didn't like having to trust his life to people he didn't know. But that did not stop him from catching sleep when he could.

When he woke, he sat up and pulled the blankets around his shoulders against the cold, stuffy air.

"Andri?" Mariana whispered.

"Mmhmm. How about having a talk? I've some questions for you."

Her voice was slightly guarded. "All right."

"What have you and Orfia to do with Bartal na Shagal, and how do I fit into your plans? I confess I'd be glad to be away on my own business, but I owe you, so if I can help, here I stay."

"I do need your help—desperately," Mariana's reply was prompt. "I've no illusions about my ability to get out of a bad situation, should Bartal catch up with us. Your success in that way is well known in Sles Adran."

He got the feeling she was hesitating. He said, "And?"

"Well—once the resistance heard you were with me, they'd be more likely to shelter us."

"I'm not so sure it's a good idea to let that get around."

"It must. Denwy's well-being depends upon it. She's Duchas of Denwy, a considerable principality."

Andri shifted to the other elbow. Queer how numb his arm was. Well, at least he knew it was still day. It only ached at night. "Another thing."

"Yes?" She wished she could see his face.

"Am I going to meet with the hero-treatment everywhere I go? Someone's been awfully busy on my behalf, I think."

"Stories about your defeat of Adon-Marsael hearten folks."

"As you see, I didn't win for long."

"Nevertheless. The people want you."

"Would it be graceless to say I don't want them? I'm not Bartal. One kingdom is enough for me. Besides, there's still something about this business that disturbs me. Sles Adran, from what I've heard, is very proud of the fact that the kings and queens for pretty near a thousand years have been Shagals. An unbroken line. That makes me — besides being a foreigner — practically a parvenu. We Elsarions have only worn the crown for a mere four hundred years, ever since we broke away from Sles Adran. Why not choose as hero one of the local nobles? Surely not all Bartal's relations are Norsundrian allies. And I know there are good people, suitable candidates for king, I mean, in the underground because I met one or two of them, a few weeks back."

"I can't really say," Mariana stated a little too firmly. "Bartal's supposedly secret plans for conquering all the neighboring countries aren't too popular. Well. Why worry about it now. We must escape first." Her tone was firm, hiding her determination. Desperation.

Andri had dozed again when he woke to the welcome scraping, creaking, and soon they stood around blinking in the lamplight outside. The hall was warm and unstuffy, which was a pleasant change.

"Come this way; we have some food prepared." It was the tall man with the red nose. "The sun went down an hour or so ago, but until just a while ago it was snowing fairly steadily. Has been all day." He led them into a tiny bedroom at the end of the hall. There two boys were waiting with a couple trays of food. One of them was the wild-eyed young man/boy. He sat cross-legged on one of the narrow beds, still playing with that knife. It was a really fine knife: carved handle, silver guard and long, slender two-edged blade. Andri looked at it and sighed inwardly, thinking of Mandracar's decorative but clumsy knives; Mariana had meant well, but these two blades were badly made.

There was only one chair and no table, so once again they sat on the floor to eat. Andri and Mariana ate quickly, finishing long before Chantala was half done. No one said anything, though Andri (who was covertly watching Knife Boy) was expecting him to pounce any time.

As soon as the man was out of earshot a hand grabbed at Andri's. "Are you—"

"Rothor!"

"Oh, shut up, Gerol!" the teen said violently, and turned back to Andri. "You're Andri Elsarion, aren't you!" he demanded, his eyes wide. "But you are!"

Mariana sighed in exasperation. "You know that very well. As well as the fact you shouldn't—"

Rothor cut across that with an exclamation of impatience and a jerk of his head. "Is it true, the—oh, never mind. Comes my father. Do you need me? I'll come—can fight—I don't eat much, all I ask is to help in your plans—"

"I'm afraid all my plans these days amount to helping these two to safety. After which I'm going to disappear myself."

"But you will return—To fight the Norsundrians. With help—won't you!"

Marianna watched with hidden hunger as Andri looked down at the pleading face. "Yes. But to Enaeran."

"But you'll help us!"

"If I can."

Mariana clasped her hands so tightly her knuckles cracked.

"Oh, you can," Rothor exclaimed. "I'm—take me with you!"

Andri shook his head. "Hard enough, with three. There is one thing, though—" he said consideringly.

"Name it!"

"Trade me that knife. I've two. Belong to one of Bartal's toadies. You'll get the worst of the bargain—"

"It's yours!" The teen yanked the knife from the sheath at his side, and held it out. Andri weighed it in his hand, then smiled his approval. "Here. These are badly balanced, loose in the haft. Maybe you can sell some of those idiot jewels in the hilts." He put the knives into the teen's hands, and smiled at his grinning face.

Mariana watched with that same smile she'd shown the night before, after Chantala had finished her plate. Andri wondered if he'd unwittingly made some sort of Gesture according to Sles Adrani custom, and who had been spreading these tales about him?

And why?

Four

ANDRI AND MARIANA BOTH smelled snow on the way. Their trail hugged the edge of a hill outlined in the moonlight shining down between clouds.

Mariana walked next to Chantala, annoyed with herself for forgetting snowshoes in her haste. Her feet were wet and numb so she knew Chantala's must be.

Big soft flakes fell, turning to wet on contact. Mariana gulped in air, swaying on watery legs. She was not certain how much longer she could endure—but she had to. The time couldn't be much before midnight, and already she craved rest. Chantala's head drooped. "Come, Chantala, we are going to stop." She laid a hand on Chantala's arm. "I saw a cave a little ways back."

They made their way there. Andri sank down with a grunt of pain.

Mariana settled Chantala, then rummaged in the bag. "Candles! And a firestick! Here—off with those shoes and stockings. We'll dry them out and warm them up with these." She lit the candles, then ripped off Chantala's wet shoes and socks.

It was a long process, and the cave smelled thickly of wet and singed wool long before she was done. When Chantala was warm and dry she dealt with her own sodden, icy feet, then pulled out several carefully wrapped packets of food, and a flask.

She unstoppered it, took a whiff, coughed, and said

triumphantly: "Brandy! The local pears are famous. Exactly what we need!" And she took a hearty swig, gasped, and dashed a hand across her watering eyes. "Here!" She held it out to Chantala, saw that she took some, then said, "Andri?"

There was no answer. She held a candle up. He sat near the mouth of the cave, his knees drawn up and his arms crossed and pressed between his legs and chest. "Andri!" she said more loudly.

His head turned; his face was a mask. Only his eyes glittering and reflecting the candlelight made him seem alive.

"Brandy! Want some? Warm up your innards."

"In a while," he said.

"It'll do you good now."

"I'm too lazy to get up." His smile in the candlelight was mask-like, too.

The tightness in her chest gave way to the brandy's glow. "Here." She tossed the flask to him.

He reached slowly with his good hand, picked it up, uncorked it, and took a sip. Then he took a huge gulp, gasped, and laughed breathlessly. "You're right. Just what I need. Mind if I keep it beside me?" His left arm was tucked inside his coat and his right lay beside him, fingers curled into a lifeless fist.

Mariana remembered his strange wound. "Not a bit." She blew out the candles. Chantala's weight increased slowly against her shoulder. Mariana drowsed off gratefully, as Andri silently endured Bartal's torments.

Bartal was not experienced in mental torture the way Yeres was. But from somewhere he had learned how to amplify physical sensations, especially pain. Andri had to concentrated on holding his mind-shield in spite of cold, exhaustion, and the magic that throbbed in the bloodknife wound.

Finally Bartal gave up, and Andri dropped into sleep before he'd drawn two breaths.

It was nearly dawn when Mariana turned Andri's way. He was still asleep, head thrown back against a rock. Drunk? No. She picked up the flask, to find it nearly as full as it had been when she gave it to him.

"Andri," she said insistently, her voice low and breathless. "We must get on the road."

Chantal rose obediently. Their feet crunched in the barely-formed icy crust over the snow, and Mariana's harsh breathing clouded and fell in the frigid air. The heavy snowfall stopped. They blundered onto a road, a mud-brown, narrow track down the middle created by horses passing to and fro.

That made walking easier, but both Andri and Mariana eyed the road ahead anxiously, he for a possible patrol, and she wondering how long she could endure this trek. If only she could get a deep breath!

Both were startled when Chantala's soft voice broke the stillness, "Look."

Mariana's gaze snapped behind as she braced to see Bartal at the head of a grinning band. Andri braced, turning to see what had caught Chantala's attention. She stood at the cliff edge, gazing out over the valley.

"It's so beautiful," Chantala sighed.

She wasn't spotting threat. Andri looked again, and sustained a paradigm shift. The valley stretched out below them, an expanse of white and silver and gray in scalloped layers as the rolling hills gave way to mountain peaks. Bare trees framed the whole, branches silvery-brown with frost. The stippling of snowflakes rendered this quiet world into an etching done by a master hand.

Chantala clasped her hands and began to recite a poem about two travelers coming across a scene of similar winter beauty, and the completely different ways they saw it.

Chantala finished, then turned to Mariana. "Do you remember? That's the one I wrote for Mama when we returned from visiting Cabriol." She turned back to the view.

Andri shot a surprised look at her, and then at Mariana — to find her watching him consideringly, eyes narrowed. This surprised him even more. But she said only, "Come, we're late as it is, and every moment we tarry on the road brings us closer to danger."

Chantala turned obediently, but her gaze lingered as they once more started tramping on. Presently she said with a hopeful air, "Are we going home?"

"No, dear. It'll be better if we disappear altogether, for a while." Mariana said no more; she was distressingly short of breath, the tightness in her chest like an invisible band.

Mariana clawed her tired body from landmark to landmark until they reached a one-room cottage completely hidden from the road, unless you know the notch between two ancient pines. There lived an old widow of fierce loyalty to Sles Adran.

She took one look at Mariana and insisted she take the chair by the fire, then cooked them a hot, plentiful meal. Every bit of color that reentered the drawn, tense faces of her guests gratified her, and the triumph of her night was drawing out some exhausted laughter when she expressed herself fluently and lengthily on the perfidy of Bartal.

Mariana woke aching in every joint, and for the first time on this desperate journey, short of breath before she even moved. Fear chilled her nerves, making her arms tremble as she drew in each sweet lungful of air. She *had* to survive until Chantala was safely bestowed according to the duchas's wishes.

A huge meal and three pairs of snowshoes awaited for them. Their hostess cackled, then pointed out the window. "You're going to need 'em, and no mistake! Been snowing all day! Make it that much harder for Bartal's stinking road apples." She snorted, bending to snap up the fire a little. As she did her glance fell on the three coats, and the food sack. "Also replaced that," she added. "More candles, some salt-fermented cabbage, crackleberry compote, and good cheese. And some brandy. Better for the cold than that soft stuff any day. Grandson makes it, from my prize pears." She cackled again and then drew Mariana aside to explain the route to the last safehouse.

They left after sundown, their hostess calling out admonitions and advice to them as they disappeared down the road.

The wind scoured them with icy strength. Their pace was quickened by the snowshoes, once everyone adapted to the shuffling walk necessary. They left the road entirely, which pleased Andri, and embarked on a long downhill descent, which was a relief to Mariana. Light from the full moon outlined the mountains, and transformed the world to blue-white dotted by dark forest. Shortly before midnight, Bartal attacked Andri, with vicious desperation. Mariana's breath was coming fast. Gratefully she suggested a halt.

As they sipped double-distilled pear-brandy, their tongues loosened. At Mariana's prompting, Andri regaled them with tales of his childhood, made palatable for Chantala: no danger, only stories of friends, of meals shared, of learning the language of horses.

Chantala liked these so much she began to talk in a soft voice that warmed considerably when she mentioned her mother, who had clearly been the center of her life; after a time the constant repetition of "Mother said," made Andri queasy, underscored by Mariana's flushed, avid gaze. It was as if Chantala not only never had a thought she did not share with her mother, she hadn't ever wanted one. Not just thoughts. They apparently shared their meals—eating off the same plate—as well as their days. And Mariana clearly treasured those memories, old grief creasing her face.

At dawn they set out, rounding the last tight curve of mountain road before setting out to cross the Northern plains. Despite the relatively easier trail, Mariana's strength flagged as they sought her last safe house. The tightness in her chest had become a constant pain. Maybe it was time to confide the Duchas Chantal Shagal's great plan to Andri. Surely he would not abandon them now.

Midway caught the river road winding through woods toward the iced-over river. The road was well pocked from foot and horse traffic, enabling them to stash the snowshoes, which Andri carried. They headed into the trees whenever they heard horses.

Despite Chantala's weariness, it was Mariana who called for rests along the way. Each time she sat down, grateful to draw in a deep breath, she shut her eyes and tried to still her trembling joints. Astonishing, she thought, how expectations changed. She had never wanted to leave Denwy—had wanted to finish her days in the palace where the duchas had lived. Now, all she wished for was soft ground, the whisper of trees, and Chantala safe.

Ought she to tell Andri? Just a little farther.

It wasn't even noon and they had already stopped five times when Andri studied Mariana's blanched face, listened to her labored breathing, and said, "I'm going back for horses. I smelled them on the wind a little while ago."

Mariana opened her mouth to protest that it wasn't safe, but it was so much easier to sink down, and get a little rest.

Andri loped back, and there they were, horses in rope halter, gathered along an old stone fence that gave them some shelter from the wind. A row of horse faces stared curiously. Horses were so nosy.

He hopped the fence and ran downhill to where he spotted

a winter storage barn. As he'd hoped, it was full of winter mix, salt, and a bucket for de-icing water.

Suspecting that Chantala would not be able to ride on her own, he chose two hardy, shaggy mounts and retraced his steps, ready to be congratulated. But his triumph vanished when he saw Mariana lying in the snow, Chantala crouched at her side.

Over a branch he flung the leads he'd attached to the halters, and knelt down beside Mariana, who gazed up, no longer feeling her fingers. Her tongue had thickened, and her lips numbed. "Andri—"

Andri bent swiftly. "I'm here."

"Promise me—take her to safety—"

"I will."

But that wasn't enough. Mariana struggled to speak. "She is ... yours ... to ... Sles Adran..." The pain was gone, darkness closing in gently. Her work was done. She could rest. Her breathing slowed, and stopped.

Andri sighed as he looked at Chantala. She lay in the snow, her face buried on Mariana's shoulder as she wept silently. "Come on, Orf—what was your real name? Chantala."

Chantala didn't react. Andri sighed again, slid his hands under her armpits and pulled her to her feet. She didn't resist. The moonlight shone on the ribbons of tears flowing, her expression so distraught he did not know what to say, he who had lost so many people in his life.

But he had to say something. Mariana was beyond danger now. They weren't. "We can Disappear her."

"But we did not do the proper forms of respect."

"She'd understand. Her spirit is gone, and some say they watch us, at least for a time. She wanted you safe, more than anything. Wouldn't you agree?"

"At least we shall lay her out properly."

Andri forced himself to wait while Chantala tugged Mariana into dignified repose, her gestures tender. When at last she straightened up, tears splashing on Mariana's still face, Andri whispered the words, and when the snow was empty, "Chantala, can you ride?"

"I can," she murmured, looking sadly down at the imprint in the snow, while Andri brought the horses.

"Let's go," he urged. "It's not safe for us here."

She mounted up with an ease that meant long practice,

Andri was relieved to see.

They couldn't gallop because the snow was so deep, but slow and steady was much improvement over snowshoes. They rode until dawn, the horses never going any faster than a walk.

It began to snow. The clouds cleared away as the sun appeared over the northern hills, leaving a smooth, glistening blanket of snow stretching before them, so bright Andri had to squint. Chantala looked down at the bony ridge of her horse's neck, and never raised her gaze.

In the bright daylight her brown-streaked hair and mottled brown skin was startling. She scratched at her scalp, and rubbed her arms and neck and face. Otherwise she remained silent in her grief. She mounted when Andri asked, dismounted, ate and drank when he suggested it, never complaining. Her quiet disturbed him. No, it was the implicit trust.

Night fell, but they kept going, Andri trying to find any semblance of shelter in the broad expanse of plains. Mariana had said early on that staying as far north as possible would be their best defense — all the southern roads were so much easier.

But now they were nearing the river that marked the border with Enaeran, which meant they would be easily seen.

Occasionally he nodded in the saddle, bobbing almost as if he slept.. Then, quite suddenly, he jerked and threw his head back: he had indeed fallen asleep, and without a mind-shield, Bartal was able to launch a vicious attack.

Chantala stiffened with fear, then urged her horse to his, and reached to slow Andri's horse when she observed the horrible way his eyes gazed sightlessly at the cloudy dark sky.

She remembered his strange behavior during some nights. Chantala squeezed her eyes shut, then reached out a timid hand and touched his sleeve, letting her mind slide into thoughts of sunsets, quiet walks with friends, poetry and song…

She wasn't prepared for the blast of cruel laughter ringing through her head. She snatched her hand away and stared at Andri in stunned surprise.

She began to look around for shelter. She'd made the connection between Mariana's midnight stops and Andri's attacks, and wanted to do the same — but here was only flat plains stretching out. What could she do? Oh! The flask! She grabbed the bag. When her hand closed on the familiar shape she yanked it out and turned to Andri.

"Doing a little midnight tippling?" he said softly.

She shook the flask. "There is little left. It seemed to help you before. I thought it would now, too. Please, have what is left."

He didn't want to point out that most of it had been drunk by Mariana, probably to mask the pain of her failing heart. "Thanks for shaking me free."

"I did?"

"Sorry. I can't talk and raise my mind-shield ..." He brought his hands up and buried his face in them.

Chantala waited, and when Andri hadn't moved, set her mind firmly on the image of the valley they'd seen a couple days before, and touched him again. That terrible blackness swept through her, only this time it was stronger and laughing and thinking her name. Andri jerked away, freeing her, and leaving her bewildered and frightened.

"Don't do it again, Chantala," Andri said hoarsely. "I appreciate your efforts, but you're likely to find yourself in trouble neither of us can handle — there's someone else listening. And he might raid your location from your mind. Ah. He's gone. For another day...heh. Too bad for Bartal that bloodknife connections can go two ways, if you don't have Dena Yeresbeth."

"What does that mean?"

"It means he was relieved of command."

"Has Royal Uncle abdicated?" she said wonderingly.

"Nah. He's still king in Sles Adran. He no longer runs the army...Kinarde. That was it. Do you remember someone in his court called Kinarde?"

"Yes. Arandos Kinarde, from Sarendan. Though I think he moved to Sartor?"

"More like Norsunder Base, is the impression I got. Anyway, I'm pretty sure that was Imry Llyenthur who turned up, told Bartal that bloodknife magic is traceable, and who was he using it on? Out came the truth — including my name. I shut them out before Llyenthur could try to sniff me out."

He tapped his head instead of his nose, which puzzled Chantala. She hugged her arms close to her body as a cold breeze started up.

"Come, let's ride while we can."

The wind soon brought a snowstorm, slowing the tired horses to a stumbling walk. Chantala bent over her horse's neck, trying to make herself as small a target as possible. Andri scanned all sides of the road; if they didn't find even partial shelter soon they'd never make it. How far was this supposed village?

He was thinking this furiously when he realize they were passing a dimple in the road. "Whup!" He turned back, to discover that the snow had nearly obliterated a narrow lane, that led down into a little hamlet beside a small lake of frozen blue-white, cloudy ice. Lake—hamlet—just as the old widow had described.

As they rode up, a small boy pelted out, followed by a woman whose hands were green. Ah. Paint.

Andri realized he was more tired than he thought, as he slipped down from the horse and leaned against its shoulder.

"Welcome," the woman said, her eyes concerned. "Where is my Great-Aunt Mariana?"

Andri was startled. He'd understood that this route was for people escaping Bartal, paralleling that strange plot centering around him. The old widow had not mentioned Andri's name, nor had she paid him much heed, which had made him think that maybe the "Andri Elsarion to the rescue" plot was a Nente aberration. But these kindly folk, so very isolated, mentioned Mariana by name. Because getting Chantala away was a long-laid plan, it seemed. But how much were the two plans related? He got that unsettling feeling he was missing something crucial.

"She died along the road," he said, keeping his voice low as they passed inside and began shedding winter wraps. The house smelled of beeswax and paint; a tall, kindly man returned, saying that the animals had been watered and fed.

"I am sorry to hear that," the woman said. "May she find peace. This will be the duchas's daughter, yes?"

"Yes. I promised to see her to safety."

The woman gave him a smile of approval—and did not ask for his name. Did she see him as a courier, then?

As Chantala thawed, her grief thawed, too, until she lay silently weeping with an arm curled about her turned-away face, the woman sitting beside her until she slept.

In the conversation that followed, Andri also thawed out, body and mind. He saw Mariana's plot now. It even made sense—if you put play-acting figures in place of real people: Andri rescues the missing princess, feels responsible for her, gets rid of Mandracar, and Bartal, unites the kingdoms, and everyone lives happily ever after, the way they do in plays and ballads.

But this was not a ballad. He did not want Sles Adran. Or Chantala, poor soul. Her face was barely discernible, the soft glow smoothing the mottle enough so he could see the shape of her features. Despite Mariana's desperate last wishes, he felt nothing but pity for her.

As soon as they had eaten, he explained about his wound and said that he needed to seek a mage-healer, and would they be able to either take Chantala, or see her to safety?

"She must definitely remain with us," the woman said, her partner nodding. "I promised Duchas Chantal years ago, that were it necessary, we would hide her daughter until — well, until matters were arranged."

What matters? Instinct insisted quite sharply that he was better off getting out of there before Chantala roused enough to mention his name.

The woman went on, "We are an artist's colony here, so far out of the way that no one ever much comes this way. It takes us a week to get our art down to the river, for the spring art market."

"Then I will leave her with you."

Tired and aching as he was — he felt another cold coming on — he thought it better to get while the getting was possible. He thanked the Haries family, and mounted a horse Honor Haries offered. "Just let Prancer go when you can. She'll find her way home. I'll see to it those two you stole are rested and fed before I turn them loose."

Andri thanked him once more, and rode out. They might or might not be part of the duchas's mad plan, but he was very certain that all of Sles Adran was not part of it. Those people in Nente had wanted rescue from Norsunder, not a new king. What Mariana and her beloved duchas had set him up for was the kindling for more civil war, Chantala the completely innocent spark.

He rode on, alone with his own thoughts — and when he spotted traffic on the road, he eased in among them, hiding in company.

Mid-afternoon he crossed the Mesham, following close behind a long train of dour wagoneers. He'd reached Four Corners — the section of the Malamaer range where the borders of Sles Adran, Enaeran, Martan, and Djedan intersected. He was now technically in Enaeran, a surprisingly cheering thought. In fact, he had an urge to embrace the first signpost he saw, pointing the way to a city he knew, Ovaish.

The more he considered it, the more it seemed strange. But it no longer mattered — he was free, he'd cross the border soon, and best of all, poor Chantala had not looked at him with any more interest than he had looked at her.

What was it that made friendship turn to desire? Or what made desire strike like lightning? No telling. He'd leave those questions to the poets; right now, he needed to get over the border and find Liere ...

Five

On the western border of Enaeran

LIERE FER EIDER LAY wrapped in her cloak, eyes closed, breathing even. Ever since she was small she had been able to send what she called a tendril to brush others' thoughts; in recent years she had mastered enough control to both increase her inner warmth when she was unable to get to a fire, and to also walk into the dreams of those she knew well, as long as they were not shielded.

She was supposed to have met Andri Elsarion at this first rendezvous, but unaccountably he had not shown up. They had agreed she was to wait only a night outside Shiovhan, Enaeran's capital—but this was her third day. She kept post-poning her departure, the first day certain that just one more hour would produce Andri. The second day, a fast blizzard had swept through, which she decided to shelter against. And the third day, she convinced herself that the cold Andri had felt coming on had forced him to rest a little longer.

But she was running out of food, and using that much inner control for warmth in particular made her ravenously hungry. While she could also force herself to go without meals, doing the two together would wear her out, and she had a long journey ahead of her.

Tomorrow she would move on, with or without him.

She had been sending out a tendril before sleeping each night to check on her daughter. It had been enough to know that Lyren-Sartora was still very much alive; Liere wanted to try a real contact before she set out again, though it was especially dangerous in the mental realm these days, since Norsunder had invaded the world. Evil minds prowled constantly, like enormous leviathans with rows and rows of teeth, scouring constantly for unwary minds.

She used the sea metaphor to help shape her contact. She was a tiny crab on the sea bottom with antennae narrower than silken thread. She imagined herself near her beautiful, mettlesome daughter, who at age thirteen tended toward the emotions of summer thunder—warm and bright until the lightning struck, then all would clear away.

Lyren-Sartora had flounced off with another of their group of travelers without saying goodbye, and though Liere had sensed her going, she had let her go, partly out of residual guilt and partly because holding on too tight often got her pushed away.

She imagined a quick, tiny fish. She knew Lyren-Sartora's mental signature. A touch of antenna to the sleeping fish— wherever Lyren-Sartora was, it was clearly night for her, too, and she was asleep—and then she was inside her daughter's dream.

The dreamscape was a jumble of familiar figures and spaces, distorted as dreams always are. Liere seized a passing image, ah, a favorite horse, and wrapped its form around her before reaching for Lyren-Sartora's image: *I'm so glad you're safe.*

Lyren-Sartora, thirteen going on thirty, scoffed: *Of course I'm safe. All that training Siamis forced on us while you were gone to the other world. I should be!*

As always, Liere apologized, sending her sincere regret to imbue the image: *I'm sorry I left.*

And there was Lyren-Sartora's immediate response: *Well, I know you had to get away from us. I know I was being a brat.*

Summer thunder.

Lyren Sartora continued: *Where are you now?*

Liere replied: *I'm still in Enaeran. On the run. We split up for a time.*

Lyren-Sartora's response was a little too bright with glee: *You left Banana Brain finally?*

Liere did not like this snide reference to Andri's yellow hair. Nor did she like that glee: *Split for a time. We're going to meet up when things are safer. Lyren, try to understand, Enaeran is to be my home.*

Fast as thought came the correction: *Lyren-SARTORA.*

Once again: *I'm sorry. Habit only. I'll remember.*

Hard on that, Lyren-Sartora added: *It's not your home! Bereth Ferian is your home!*

Liere controlled her own emotional response: *Lyren-Sartora, it's never been my home. Ever. I never fit in there. Andri and I are a match. I don't expect you to understand. Yet. But I do hope one day you will.* And then, recklessly: *I wanted you to be the first to know that as soon as we reach Mearsies Heili and safety, we plan to marry.*

And just like that, Lyren-Sartor's mind-shield shut Liere out.

Liere breathed deeply as her awareness settled back into her body, and for a time she stared upward at the ruined cottage walls, fighting a sense of defeat. Thirteen, she reminded herself. Summer thunder.

She left the next day, severely rationing her food, and a week later, there was still no Andri on the road.

This morning — ever cautious — she had reached Arbanion, and went to the barns first to surveille, hoping to find Andri had somehow reached the place ahead of her. He hadn't. Instead, she recognized Yanji Arbanion, the young nobleman who had returned to his inheritance thanks to Andri. He was mucking out his own stables,. She slipped in and quietly greeted him.

"I remember you," he said. "You were with Andri when he came to free us from the mines. Where is he?"

She studied Yanji Arbanion, and all summer's memories rushed back: the aromatic scent of lemon verbena growing wild around the mines that did not mask the nose-clogging stink of mold and unwashed bodies of the miners: the fatigue and giddy exhilaration of Andri's triumph over Adon Marsael, Andri's distant relation who had thrown in with Norsunder in order to keep a throne that was not his; the intensity of Andri's focus on straightening out the wreckage of the kingdom after years of civil war.

"Andri is in Shiovhan," Liere said to the young man, who had lost his entire family to greed and venality. The only reason he was still alive was because he had been thrown into the mines as a boy of fourteen and forgotten. "He was to meet me here."

"He knows the Norsundrians are here, right?" the young noble flipped up the back of his hand toward the castle on the hill behind them.

"He knows. What happened here?"

Yanji leaned on his pitchfork. "We were bedding down the fields for winter—it was right after harvest—when a company of Adranis rode up, their captain demanding to know where Yanji Arbanion was."

"I take it you did not enlighten them?" Liere asked.

"It was Jaydi who answered before I could get myself killed. Piped up, 'He's run for the mountains. Left all the work to us,' pointing up at the Pass. Then this captain says, 'You just keep on working, but it'll be for us.' Then he ordered a line of his company to find and kill me." He offered a lopsided smile, but his eyes shifted away. "I've been working for my dead self ever since, you might say. At least I can look out for my own land, until we get rid of these ..." He turned to the side and spat into his manure pile.

"Jaydi is quick on his feet," Liere said.

"Living on the streets of Shiovhan, dodging Marsael's bullies, I guess hones the smart ones," Yanji acknowledged. "Come in? We fixed things up for us at the back of the barn here."

He explained as they moved down the clean-swept passage. The Adranis didn't bother them as long as the horses were well cared for. They had their own cooks and supplies, "But we take what we can siphon off," Yanji said. "The locals say life was lean before. They expect it to be now. Hoard and hide what they can."

Liere listened, sympathized, and when scruffy young Jaydi turned up, greeted him and patiently answered the stream of questions he asked about Andri.

Liere answered those without mentioning the Adrani underground, and she also spoke generally about Andri's plans: until Andri said otherwise, she trusted his people, but she didn't trust what might be dragged out of them. Better they didn't know.

Yanji had formed a relationship with a local artisan over the harvest festival, a relationship that had become deeper when the invaders came. She had moved in with Yanji's collection of people, now the staff of Arbanion. Liere stayed with her, and everyone got along well, getting secret pleasure out of their dual identities.

That was the problem. It was so comfortable there, with friendly people, plenty to eat, and easy work. She also liked having a warm bed at night, and not having to scrounge for meals. Well rested, she could check on Lyren-Sartora's well-being each night, before sleeping, even though Lyren-Sartora kept her mind-shield firmly shut against her. But Liere was content simply to know she was there, which meant at least relative safety.

Each day that Andri did not show up, she always had an excuse: why travel in a blizzard if she didn't have to; she couldn't leave before finishing the quilts she had taken over repairing to free up the elderly woman whose eyesight in dim winter was failing; she oversaw the morning school that had lapsed, as everyone was too busy. But Andri had insisted.

Liere knew Andri wasn't dead; she could sense him on the mental plane, though she did not dare reach for him. She just did not know where he was. Andri, with his powerful but untrained Dena Yeresbeth, was more difficult to get images from. Leaked emotions, yes. He was sick again. But alive.

Finally she decided that it was time to leave Arbanion, but before she did, she would try to find Andri in his dreams. When she was satisfied that the predators were focused otherwhere, she reached for Andri—and then recoiled from the hot, distorted, painful smear of his mental landscape. It was a little like Senrid's that one terrible evening, and yet unlike, for instead of the toxins of fermented drink wrenching emotion, memory, and sensation into distortion, this was fever.

No, there was more than that. He was not only sick again, his body taxed by ... another bloodknife?

Bartal. Fury seethed through her. The image was barely a heartbeat, but severe. And nothing she could do. Even if she were with him, performing the spell to remove it would bring every dark magic mage straight to them, because of course it would have tracers attached.

She smothered her reaction and drifted again. Andri was asleep. Restless. Dreams bordering on nightmare, a horrible mixture of his past, still largely unknown, and memories she shared, though distorted almost unrecognizable ...

Ah. There. A flicker of herself in the dream. She slipped into that figure, and without attempting to change the dream at all, her avatar whispered, *Selenseh Redian, Andri. The cure for the bloodknife is there —*

The subtle sense of an awareness floated overhead, not quite quiescent. Listening, not acting.

ANDRI, MIND-SHIELD!

Her antenna snapped back inside her shell and her crab winked out. She jolted back into her body, breathing fast. She had encountered that awareness once before, in Senrid's drunken memory: Imry Llyenthur.

In Larkadhe's tower, Llyenthur reached farther, then farther still. Gone. Both of them — if that image of Liere Fer Eider was even real, and not part of Andri Elsarion's dream.

His chair creaked as he rocked back. Some people, like Detlev's brat, were only interesting as bait, others not even worth that. Liere Fer Eider was definitely bait for Senrid. About Andri Elsarion he'd heard nothing interesting: deposed prince from the ignorant backwater Enaeran; a street rowdy, one of Yeres's targets, though he'd apparently scarpered out of that. But if he could be used to bait Senrid, then it might be worth adding yet another target to the ever-lengthening list.

Andri jolted awake, awash in sour-smelling fever sweat. He gritted his teeth and rebuilt his mind-shield. No use in questioning if that dream was real or not. Whatever "real" meant in the weird world of the mind. Much as he wanted to head south toward Arbanion, he'd forgo that for the northwest road.

Heh. There was something else he might as well try on the way ...

The sky lowered with dark gray clouds as the freezing wind drove down off the mountains and numbed Andri's left side.

He tied the muffler up over his head, but his ear was aching by midmorning, and he wished he hadn't lost his hat.

Prancer was young and strong and seemed glad enough of the chance to exercise and keep warm: when they came across spots where the snow was shallow, her pace sometimes lengthened into a canter. Andri knew he ought to let her go, but this damned cold had gotten into his lungs as well as his joints, and he knew he would never make it on foot.

He had to figure out a place to stay. Actually, he knew where he'd like to stay, but there were two problems. One was finding the place; the second was the unknown attitude of its owner.

Not far off the great east-west road leading to the pass was Elsarion, Andri's ancestral home. He had always wished to see it, but hadn't — the breach that had been made in the family by his father Alored's becoming king had in no way been healed by the civil war. This branch of the family (they called themselves the "senior" branch) had remained aloof. Those left alive.

The road was mushy from being travelled on, and riders were infrequent enough for him to think it better not to be seen. He'd veered off the path to hide behind hedgerows, and in a stand of fir, before he found the signpost he was looking for. It was a four-way one, with a battered "Elsarion" pointing out a lane winding its way into the mountains.

Six

Elsarion – Northwest Corner of Enaeran

IT WAS NEARLY DARK when Andri reached the village of Elsarion. It lay in a valley, the weak yellow glow of lit windows marking slant-roofed houses in the fast-fading light. Above, on a hill across the terraced valley, he could just make out a towered shape that crowned what was once, when the climate had been different, a vineyard on the north-facing hills.

The temptation was irresistible. But then risk and safety were merely states of mind.

He patted Prancer's neck. "A roof, soon, for you, at least. For me, who knows? Let's go."

They skirted the village, no more noticed than another shadow in the deepening gloom. He saw no Adranis: no doubt Bigmouth Marsael had blabbed gleefully about the family conflict, and no one would expect him to show up here.

His idea was to fade back into the surrounding forest and watch for a time, before figuring the best way to break in. But he was tired, the horse was tired, and the open and unattended gates were like an invitation. Which Prancer accepted, walking unbidden across the courtyard, toward the horse-enticing aromas of the stable.

The castle was old—really old, at this end; he'd once read that the original castle had had eight sides, which would explain the blurred outline. The stones on the lee side were black with age, and on the valley side where the wind swept down from the mountains, the stones and corners were smoothing out. But some ancestor had broken the martial ardor by adding spires and corbels and some statuary, now mostly covered with flowering vines. The castle wasn't very large – the whole thing could probably fit in one wing of Brydon – but the way it was set, looking down on the valley and the rising sun from among tall and ancient trees, was far more harmonious than the huge, war-worn royal palace back in Shiovhan.

He dismounted just as a stout girl of about thirteen dashed out of the stable, holding a torch high. She looked at him curiously and not a little suspiciously, but her voice was civil enough: "May I help you?"

"D'you think they'd put up a relative?" He glanced up at the towers. Light glowed in a window.

"D'pends," she said cautiously.

"I'm a cousin. Running from the Adranis," he said.

A man exited a side door and crossed the courtyard to bow to Andri, who wondered how many pairs of ears in this silent castle had been listening to the short exchange.

" – welcome, and his grace invites you to join him inside," the man was saying. And, to the stable-hand, "See to his horse, Linsa."

The man led Andri down a narrow hallway only slightly less cold than outside, then up a short flight of stairs. The man opened a door at the top of the stairs and bowed Andri in. As Andri passed the fellow, he noticed his slightly startled look as he beheld Andri in the light.

Andri found himself alone in a small study with an elaborate carved and gilded wooden ceiling. Two walls bore old, embroidered hangings – on the left a historical scene, on the right a pattern of flowers and animals – and the other two walls were taken up by a bookcase and a fireplace respectively. In the fireplace a large fire crackling merrily.

Hanging in the place of honor above the fire was a head-and-shoulders portrait of a man wearing black velvet. Long black hair framed a bony face with jutting nose, chin and cheekbones. The painted eyes gazing over Andri's head revealed a hint of green, and the mouth curved with humor.

"Uncle Thunder. It's gotta be," Andri murmured aloud, and sank into the large-backed chair facing the fireplace, next to a small table with a fine decanter and a glass set on a silver tray. Andri poured himself a glass of good bluewine, saluted his ancestor, and began sipping. He sat back and regarded his most famous (infamous) recent ancestor as his body began to thaw, and the wine blurred the ache in his chest from his coughing, and the pain of his raw throat.

"I wonder," he remarked presently to the picture, "if this is going to turn out to be one of the stupidest things I've ever done."

He laughed to himself—which turned into a coughing fit. It was weird how everything seemed slightly unreal. Maybe it was the cold, getting to him at last. It was idiocy to permit accident of birth to bring him to the front door instead of sneaking in and spying around as he ought to have done. But every single joint in his body ached as if he'd been racked for a month by Bartal's finest.

He saluted the portrait with a second glass of wine. The door opened. The new arrival and Andri regarded one another in silence as the fire leaped and crackled.

The newcomer was as tall as Andri, long-waisted as well, but powerful in build, contrasting to Andri's feline leanness. Like the portrait hanging over the fire, he had long wavy black hair and a high forehead. The resemblance to Andri was strongest in the shape of his large blue eyes, prominent chin and cheekbones, but unlike in that those blue eyes did not tilt at the corners, and his mouth was a well-shaped line unlike Andri's curving lips bracketed by deep dimples. They were much of an age, though perhaps this cousin was a couple of years the older.

Andri raised his glass in salute. As if this movement freed his host he shut the door, saying, "You must be my cousin." His voice was low, but not raspy like Andri's and his father's. Maybe this side of the family got the music the ancestors were famed for.

Andri remembered that this cousin—if he was who Andri suspected—could make the claim to be *the* Elsarion— n'Elsarion—head of the clan. Should have been, but for Andri's father's treachery against his own cousin.

Andri swallowed off the wine.

"In fact—you are Andri Malcolin?"

"Right again."

"Welcome." His smile was pensive, questioning, as he said, "I am Trevor Macael."

"No Malcolin, eh?" Andri chuckled, and coughed.

"My father decided that it belonged to—er—your side of

the family."

"But your father's name was Malcolin, wasn't it?" Andri croaked.

Trevor Macael laughed. "Amusing, is it not? And I'm sure your father never noticed, and wouldn't've caught the insult if he had. But then there is a lack of Trevors on your side?"

Andri shrugged. "Only because my parents—I suspect in the only fit of family feeling they ever sustained—wanted my sister and me to share their initials. My father said little in praise of anyone, but Uncle Thunder was the exception."

"So we keep his name. And yet—"

"And yet if it hadn't been for him you would be on the throne." Andri's grin turned sardonic. "A year ago it was very much up for grabs. You are even of age."

"It seemed more prudent to wait."

Andri's brows shot up, then the obvious struck him. "Ah. Adon Marsael had you surrounded by spies? Of course he did."

Trevor Macael's glossy head dipped in assent. His manner and voice were quiet, devoid of (justifiable) bitterness as he said, "We tried to make their tenure comfortable, but I fear life here is sadly boring." When Andri's laugh turned into a fit of coughing, Trevor Macael Elsarion's face lengthened into concern. "You're ill! Forgive me. Can I get you some willow steep? A hot meal? I can also promise a warm bed."

Andri waved a hand and tried to speak over the coughing. "Leave it—I'm fine—have to be on my way—only stopped because of curiosity—"

"You're safe here. Adon Marsael recalled his watchers last summer."

"Maybe so, but you're not safe. Adranis are after me," Andri said bluntly, exhausted from the coughing. "If Adon hears, he might be back."

Trevor Macael looked unmoved. "Adon Marsael gave up trying to recruit me. Do at least have some hot food and drink."

"You knew he was a Norsundrian?" Andri sat up suddenly.

"I had a pretty good idea. He dropped hints about aid from a very powerful source—more powerful than Bartal—and how I'd benefit therefrom. I talked about music and my library until he gave up and left."

Andri sank back in his chair, wishing his mind would work better. "I'll take that dinner," he said suddenly, "then I'll be on my way, Trevor Macael."

"Excellent. And—Macael will do. I don't really use the first. Excuse me." He went out of the room, and returned shortly. "The food will be along. I also ordered brandy and coffee for us both."

"Thanks. Tell me. Has Adon been back since he retook the kingdom?"

"A month or two ago. I met him book in hand, and offered to play a melody I'd recently composed. He didn't stay the night."

"Are you still waiting?"

Macael smiled. "Did that seem a threat? I didn't intend it to be. I had hoped you would prevail, but whoever did, it seemed to me to meet the winner over the remains of Enaeran would benefit no one. Certainly not the kingdom." He laughed, a quiet sound. "If you do manage to get rid of Adon Marsael permanently, I have no intention of taking the field against you."

"Perhaps we can heal the break, then."

"A good idea—ah. Thank you, Ranth." Macael got up as the steward came in, bearing a loaded tray.

Macael dismissed the servant, saying that he would serve their guest. This he did gracefully, fending off with light comments Andri's insistence that he not trouble himself. Andri shrugged, and did justice to the heroic quantities brought, while Macael drank coffee.

Presently Andri sat back with his fingers wrapped around a mug of brandy and coffee.

"Tell me about Adon-Marsael," Macael said. "What made him do something so stupid as to give himself to Norsunder?"

"I think he'd ally with anyone who promised to make him king."

"You've had experience with them?"

"Yes."

And since Andri didn't seem disposed to go on, Macael asked, "Have you met Bartal?"

Andri launched into a funny account of his capture, and experiences in Sles Adran's capital—giving a brief mention of the strange business about his being a figurehead. Macael shook with silent laughter as Andri described spraying wine all over the first time he heard it, and how he had to hide his horror afterward.

His voice began giving out, but he added brandy to his coffee and continued, "Bartal knows about it, too. In our interview, he looked me over with his nose in the air, then said, in his oily way, 'You'll have to forgive me, but I can't help wondering what they see in you, I really can't...'" Andri's attempt to copy Bartal's affected tones in his hoarse croak made them both laugh. "And I said, 'But you've got your answer right in front of you. They haven't seen me!'"

"How did he take that?'

"Disappointingly. Probably because Navor Mandracar was there."

"How did you escape?"

"Now that," Andri said, "is the strangest part of all." Andri considered how to describe Mariana, who, despite her plans for his life, had worked hard and selflessly. He did not want to denigrate her, or Chantala, poor soul.

So he said, "The escape was arranged by a servant devoted to a duchas, and to that duchas's daughter, who is also Bartal's niece..."

His mind slipped from memories to wandering, and his eyelids started to drift down. He caught himself in time. "Hmm! Drowsy." He swigged down the rest of his brandy-laced coffee, then set the empty cup down. "Best be on my way. The night air will revive me." He began to rise, then sat back, his limbs heavy.

"Don't go yet, Andri. I have a couple more questions for you."

Andri shook his head. "Time to move along. Safer for us both." He sat up on the edge of his chair. He tried to force himself to his feet, but his vision swam weirdly. But by then his mind seemed even more detached, his thoughts coming from a long way off. He flung his head up. "You drugged me!"

"Sorry. It was that last gulp. Otherwise you never would have known."

Andri gasped and tried to get up, but his body failed him, and he fell back in his chair.

"Don't worry," his cousin's voice floated somewhere overhead. "It's just that you're sick, need rest, and I wish to talk to you further."

Andri's head strained up, and his lips twisted slightly even as his head closed. "I'm a fool," he muttered, and his head dropped back with a clunk.

They sat there for a while, Andri out cold, Macael sipping at his drink and smiling as he stared at Andri while the fire leaped and crackled.

At last he put his empty cup down and got up. He pulled the bell cord, and when the steward entered he said, "Have someone take him upstairs to the tower bedroom, and — carefully, Ranth. He's very ill."

Seven

ANDRI WOKE UP LATE the next morning.

It took him a moment to remember where he was and what had happened to him. When he did, he winced and sat up experimentally. At least he wasn't in a dungeon, wearing clanking chains. His knife lay next to his neatly folded clothes on an elegant fine table whose carvings were blurred with age, but he could make out the stylized lilies of Colend around the edges. Someone had spent the night laundering his things.

The heavy sogginess in his chest had not abated a whit, leaving his mouth dry. Otherwise he almost felt rested.

Nothing terrible had happened to him. He'd needed the sleep. But he wished he'd resisted temptation, even though he knew his distrust was based right now on nothing more than his cousin having blindsided him. He didn't blame Macael — he'd all but begged for it by showing up in the first place.

He dressed, slid the knife into his boot, then went to the door. Locked? No.

He started on down the stairs, pulling the clean collar of his coat around his chin. It was cold. If this stairwell was anything to go by, a deep freeze must've settled in overnight.

A servant was waiting in the hall below. He bowed low, and said quietly, "Would you step this way, sire?"

Sire. Andri resisted the impulse to say, "Nope. Have my horse saddled," and followed, figuring he may's well face the worst, if worst there was to be. Maybe he'd get a breakfast out of it.

He was left in a small, circular breakfast room with large-paned bow windows facing east. The windows overlooked the snowy valley, the village rooftops, and the forest crowding all about its rim. Northward the mountains rose, gleaming white in the pure, peach-tinged golden light of a new day.

Andri took off his coat and sat as a quiet servant came in, bearing a heavy silver tray with a pot and cups, spoons and a cream pitcher on it. "Coffee, sire."

Andri regarded the coffee, then shrugged. Somehow it didn't seem likely that Macael would drug him twice. He poured. It was delicious, and felt good on his raw throat.

His cousin walked in, mouth smiling, eyes curious. "Good morning, Andri; how are you feeling?"

"Fine," Andri said in a voiceless croak, "except for the leftovers of that potion."

Macael lifted his chin slightly, a gesture of the negation he was too polite to speak. "I take it myself when I can't sleep, and I assure you it has no aftereffects. You are very ill, and should be in bed."

Andri dismissed that with an impatient wave of his hand. "Sounds worse than it is. If I can risk breakfast, I'll eat and be off."

Macael laughed soundlessly. "I won't do it twice. But I really wish you would at least stay the day. You are perfectly safe here, you know, and — if you feel half as bad as you look, you'll fall out of your saddle by midday." As Andri glanced out the window at the icy mountains rising in the north, "If not before. A freeze set in during the night, and the accompanying wind is most unpleasant."

Andri was annoyed with himself for being so tempted.

Breakfast was brought in, on two trays. Andri hadn't much appetite and couldn't taste what he was eating, but the food was warm and felt good going down. The conversation was light, mostly about the weather.

After his third cup of coffee, Andri said abruptly, "It's no use. You're right. When coffee fails to get me going, something's wrong. If Norsunder's Host of Lords come calling I'll be up in that tower room."

Andri woke up and went back to sleep three times before he finally felt like rising. Two of those times were at night, when his dreams turned nasty. Both times he got out of bed, wrapped his blankets around him and went to the windows, where he stood looking out over the hidden valley and worked on the sustaining mind-shield that Liere had taught him. Then he drank down the water on the side table and collapsed back in the bed.

Surprisingly, he felt at ease in this castle. If it hadn't been for Uncle Thunder's wanderlust, he would have grown up here. Uncle Thunder's wanderlust and Andri's father's ambition, Andri corrected himself. Andri's father had taken the throne in the teeth of his cousin Malcolin...who had a reputation for being a scribe at heart, Andri remembered.

Andri turned his thoughts to Macael. Seemed a nice enough sort. But then, so had Adon. Andri recognized his longing for Macael's friendship and trustworthiness for what it was — this cousin was his last relative, besides his sister, but she had given her heart to Martan when she married its king.

He wanted his last relative to prove to be an ally, particularly because he was an Elsarion, even though he knew it was sentimental mawk, this foolery about blood and connection.

Time to get moving.

He dressed and found his way down to the breakfast room. After a substantial meal Andri began to feel more himself. He was finishing up when Macael entered. "Good morning, Cousin. How are you feeling?"

"Well enough to push on, thanks."

"I'm glad. I figured you might wish to go. We can have your horse saddled."

"That's not my horse," Andri said. "I borrowed it."

"Oh? I can arrange to have it returned, and loan you one. I have several good cross-country animals."

Andri had planned to turn Prancer loose and steal a new one, leaving Prancer to find the way home again, but this was far better. He described the artist colony, which — no surprise — Macael had never heard of. That led to a recounting of his mission to get Chantala to safety, which he had skipped over in his brief summary of his escape the other night. Less exhaustion and fog-minded than he had been, Andri explained about Chantala, but left out Mariana's unspoken plot. It was immaterial, as it would never happen. Poor Mariana was dead, and Andri did not expect to see Chantala ever again; she was an Adrani affair.

At the end, Macael said, "I'll send someone with the horse today. Take one of mine. I'll also send you with travel fare. Ah, where are you headed? I ask so that the kitchen can better calculate how much to send with you."

""I can forage. Best not to say more. The less you know, the less Adon and his gang can pry out of you, should they trace me here."

"Very well." Macael looked out the window, his smile that pensive one again. The expression Andri had seen before Macael slipped something into his drink. "I can assure you, no one 'gets out of me' what I don't wish to tell, but — you know your own business best. While the horse is being saddled, may I offer you a tour of the ancestral home?"

Andri had been restless to leave, but with Macael readily offering to accommodate him, the prospect of riding into the bitter cold again was not so pressing. And he was curious. "Sure."

The castle was sizable, built to accommodate not only several generations of Elsarions, but their servants and their guards, too, a leftover, Macael said, from the days when organized armies of horse thieves and the like would try to storm the southern pass in order to steal the immensely valuable Marlovan horses.

Marlo*van*, not Marlo*ven* — he gave the word the ancient pronunciation, underlining his awareness of the family history that they shared. As Andri walked, looking at this fading wall painting, or that rebuilt archway, he laughed inwardly: previously he'd thought his awareness of two generations of family history was knowledgeable.

The castle was too well protected to be a palace, but otherwise it could have been called one, designed as it was to please the eye, and to let in as much light as possible in winter. Quite a contrast to oversized Brydon in Shiovhan, showy but shabby, its center a palace thrown up in haste by the first Elsarion king, to house all the exquisite Colendi furnishings he had looted from the palace of a Colendi duchas he'd defeated in a duel.

"And this tower is reputed to be where perhaps our most famous, or infamous, relation, Taumad Dei, stayed — though it is a stretch to call him an ancestor. He never lived here. Or established a permanent home anywhere, though his main line settled across the strait in Imar."

Andri had no interest in Taumad Dei. What he noticed in Macael's explanation was not only his appreciation for, and knowledge of, art, but how he seemed to glide right past all those Marloven marriages back and forth, in favor of connections to the Dei family, who'd never ruled anywhere (so Julian had told him on their journey together, a thousand years ago), but who managed to marry into most of the kingdoms on the continent. Macael might not have ambition, but he did have pride.

As the two of them rounded down the worn tower stairs at the end of the tour, Andri realized that Macael's interests appeared to lie east, past Sles Adran to Colend and Sartor, and not west toward the martial Marlovens. Was that true? Though he'd been talking steadily, Andri found it difficult to see past his polite façade to the man behind.

"And that is all," Macael said. "I shall walk with you to the stables."

Andri thought, I'm a fool. Liere spent days teaching me, why? So I could forget it all? He braced himself and sent his mind out—to encounter a shield as impervious as steel. So much for his Dena Yeresbeth skill! He laughed at himself as they arrived at the stable.

Here, Andri clasped Macael's hands briefly. "Thanks for putting me up. Be well." He checked his gear, then mounted up.

"Travel safely, Cousin," Macael said.

Andri clucked to the horse, who was restless and ready to move. He rode along the walls of the castle, then around the lip of the valley, till he reached the north road.

The freeze had lifted during his long sleep. Wisps of mist from the low gray expanse of the sky obscured the tops of the tallest firs. He let his mind drift, like the distant birds wheeling on the currents far away, and he got an idea. But it would have to wait for when he camped.

The castle people had given him two saddlebags, one full of the very expensive baked and compressed fodder called horse-cakes, of the sort military and governmental messengers carried for long rides. Ordinary folk had to be wealthy to afford them.

Before it turned dark, Andri found a fairly protected crevasse some twenty strides above the road. He cared for the horse, then found a couple thin twigs in the mud below an old, gnarled tree, and a small pebble.

He recollected David's hands flicking up to pinch the air. His own fingers seemed slightly unreal: as if they moved under water, or in a dream. He nipped a streamer of glowing color from the air—he'd always assumed those were part of fire, maybe caused by warmth—and pulled it down the way David had, shaping it into flame with his mind.

Puff! A vagabond fire leaped up from the twigs. A small one—but definitely a vagabond fire. He wrapped up and lay as close to the fire as possible.

He woke up at the first rays of the sun, to find the horse standing over him. "Cold, eh?" he rasped as he sat up, shook his cloak out, and killed the fire with a motion of his hand. This, then, was what the firestick magic emulated? The twigs only showed a discolored spot. He packed them, and was soon on his way.

These mountains seemed too vertical and rocky for anyone to live in—anyway, he'd never seen anyone in them, and he was just settling into what he hoped would be a day-blurring stupor, when he heard horse hooves from behind.

The rider was too close for hiding. He'd completely let his guard down. "Serves me right," he muttered as he pulled his sword from his saddle-sheath, and laid the blade across his knees under his cloak. He turned his mount and waited—

"Good morning, cousin." Macael's voice floated pleasantly on the air. "Thought I'd never catch up with you."

"Macael!" Andri almost dropped his sword in surprise. "What're you doing here?"

"Adon Marsael turned up. I thought it expedient to leave."

"They couldn't have followed me. It was snowing. I was falling out of the saddle, but I know I didn't leave tracks ..." He remembered that dream, in which Liere seemed to be talking to him. All the rest of that dream had vanished like smoke, the ways dreams did, but Liere's words about the Selenseh Redian had remained, and now that he was not feverish, he suspected that she had done her trick of talking to him through his dream.

He also remembered how the dream had ended with that sense of being listened to, and Liere's abrupt departure. Bartal? No, he couldn't listen. Maybe Llyenthur himself. If so, the Norsundrian might have found out where Andri was. Somehow.

"Did you get your people out?" Andri cut in.

"My people are safe." Macael's voice was so even and

polite Andri wondered if he'd offended his cousin with his question.

But Macael said immediately, and in so mild a voice Andri decided he was mistaken, "My messenger with your friends' mare saw your tracks going north. I thought if I could catch up with you, you might help put me on the road northwest. I have some relations up that way. Or if not, company, and a few hints on the art of running. Being inexperienced, I'm sure I'm quite inept."

Andri gave a croak of laughter that dissolved into coughing. Over it he said, "Inept!" soundlessly, a couple times, then he bent over, struggling to catch his breath.

He rolled his eyes over Macael, sitting elegantly on a highbred white charger. Macael looked as though he'd just stepped from the hands of his valet: long ribbon-tied black locks ordered, pale gray mantle spread over the back of his horse and caught at his shoulder by a silver brooch—as clean and unrumpled as his black velvet tunic, black riding trousers and riding boots, and white shirt—eyes clear and face smiling. The white horse had a glistening of sweat down its sides. It had run hard to catch up.

Macael waited patiently under Andri's musing scrutiny.

Andri grinned.

"I am unwelcome?" Macael asked. He tapped the side of his saddle. "I thought to bring an extra sword for you. I ought to have considered that before."

"You and the sword are both welcome," Andri said, not wishing to point out which was the more welcome. "Let's go!" Andri answered, slinging the sword by a very fine shoulder halter over his back.

They started off down the road side by side, keeping the animals at a slow pace. Presently Andri said, "I seem to have done you an ill turn after all. I'm sorry."

"I'm not so certain that you are to blame, cousin. I was hiding when they arrived, judging it the better part of prudence, so I did not speak to them personally. But my valet did: they questioned him concerning my whereabouts. It may not have concerned you. I ordered my people to bide peacefully, and if necessary to depart—I believe the military term it 'fall back'—to a place we had designated when Adon Marsael first brought the Adranis among us."

"I still feel responsible. I'm sorry."

"It won't be forever. And I would cheerfully do it again for the chance to meet you. So we will travel, you and I. Unused to excitement, I shall probably enjoy this." He smiled serenely down into a valley.

Andri turned to hide a grimace so his cousin wouldn't see it.

———⟨⟨⟨⚬⟩⟩⟩———

Liere was very good at going to ground.

She had been trained by exacting teachers on Geth, but also, she was adept at scanning for surrounding life forms, so that whenever danger drew near, she was well hidden. While she would much rather not have had to flounder through mountains in the dead of winter, at least the enemy had the same problems she did, and with a little care, she was safely out of sight whenever any toiled by on patrol.

She also sensed occasional aid.

That was the strangest thing, these interactions.

She knew that human and animal relations had slowly been altering over the centuries, just as had human and indigenous relations. Very slowly—more like millennia. But Dena Yeresbeth, in coming back, seemed to have accelerated it some.

The aid was no more than the occasional creature poised ahead, and looking back intently. If she turned her steps toward the sentinel, it invariably raced off with a flick of tail; she soon understood that she was to follow, for when she did, she found more passable trails. She reached fewer dead ends that forced her to retrace her steps.

Sometimes she heard howling echoing through the woods, a harrowing sound that sent her hiding. Each time she did it, and scanned, she encountered minds intent on killing moving through the woods. Once, as silently as she moved herself.

Her most frequent helpers were gray-coated wild dogs. But there were occasionally deer, and once, wolves.

Finally Liere struggled over the lip of an outcropping onto flatter terrain, densely covered with fir. Dark was closing in rapidly. She crouched down on the lee side of two thick old trees joined together at the base, and ate just enough bread and cheese to ward hunger pangs. When this food was gone, there was no foraging this high.

Over the next stretch of days, Liere severely rationed her food. She traveled by night, mostly unseeing, as there were seldom clear skies. Her path always led upward, sometimes steep climbs and sometimes flounders deep in snow toward the cloud-hidden peaks. Twice, when she crawled, exhausted, into a rocky nook barely affording shelter, she slept deeply — and woke to find herself at the bottom of a pack of dogs.

When she set out, the dogs ran with her, plumed tails wagging. She was glad of the company.

One morning, before she fell asleep, she gazed drowsily over a spectacular valley, rank on rank of mountains below, stretching into the smooth plains beyond, their contours etched by frozen rivers. It would be a horrid irony, she thought, if Andri was floundering somewhere along her trail, but she didn't think he was. Surely she would know, wouldn't she? She did not dare farsense; twice she tried her little crab, to sense Imry Llyenthur drifting overhead. Listening for her, or for who? She dared not probe further, but shut her mind away tight.

She was sure, she thought she was sure, she'd know if Andri were near. She'd always known when Senrid was near. Or far. Though when she was on Geth, she suspected that was just old memories mixing with dreams.

Senrid. He might be in these mountains, too. What an odd thought. The urge to reach for him had to be snapped off, like slamming a door. Weird, how a really old habit, unused for several years, suddenly feels like trespass, as there was no getting around the thought that if he'd wanted to travel with her, he would have waited.

She composed herself to sleep.

Eight

Sles Adran to the Valian Peninsula

WE HAVE SEEN WHAT happened to Andri and Liere after the general breakup of Senrid's group in Nente. While she slipped east, and Andri was forced to return to Nente, Julian and June — two brown-haired, brown-skinned girls of about sixteen, one from Sartor and one from another world — traveled south.

Julian taught June smatterings of languages to pass the time. June learned swiftly, which was as well because Julian was the most impatient of teachers. As it was, June learned the best insults first, which was her favorite way to learn a language.

Julian had always been drawn to people on the margins. It didn't matter where they came from, or how they got here. Nor did she mind prickles. Julian was prickly herself. She'd once overheard her cousin Atan, queen of Sartor, saying sadly to some courtier, *I know Julian is rude. Please don't mind it. She was so small when our families were killed. Her earliest years were difficult, and when the war came, she spent her childhood a pet of other children in a forest glade.*

Once Atan had promised Julian she would not have to be a princess, bound to court and rules and endless classes in statecraft, Julian had tried to be more polite when she was in Eidervaen and around Atan's court life. But she suspected she would have been rude and prickly if she'd grown up in that palace. Her few memories of her mother were vivid with prickles and spikes and glittery things. Especially glittery things: her mother had loved diamonds more than people, and from Julian's perspective had been a diamond herself.

June, who had been thrust through a Worldgate as a sacrifice in another's long conflict, had run, and then kept running. She had hated the version of Earth she came from, which was now consumed in fire.

Her prickles had, at first, all been about being prickly *because I'm crazy* was the most frequent way June had ended sentences, when they were all cooped up in that attic at Rel's house in Lisdan. Sometimes June varied that by elliptical remarks about what a rotten person she was, in a tone that seemed to be meant to shock.

But June also had a sense of humor, including about herself. There was an evening in Rel's attic when people were reminiscing about past adventures, and Julian came upstairs in time to hear Joey saying, *Well, we figured a fire would be faster. Julian did that once, set a pirate's storehouse ablaze. You shoulda seen them pirates run! You'd think they paid for that stuff!*

June had said, *Julian burned down a pirate warehouse?*

To which Julian, in joining them, said, *Hey, just call me crazy.*

June laughed. And since then there had been less about her being crazy.

The two teens had gone south out of Nente, with the goal of reaching Igkai, the hermit-mage, who Julian had met while sailing with Dtheldevor. "Ordinarily," Julian explained to June, "he avoids humans as much as possible. He looks kind of like a frog himself. But we had Sharly and Sidres with us. They knew the way to his place, which is inside the trunk of an ancient hollow tree."

"I have to see that," June exclaimed. "He sounds awesome."

That was another thing Julian enjoyed about June, she appreciated weird people. And she liked animals.

However it took a long time. There were so many patrols, especially in the early days when half were search parties, the two seemed to spend more time hiding than traveling. They also had to scrounge for meals, mostly stealing from Adrani outposts, which were very well supplied. June had noticed that Julian's cloths were worn, almost ragged, yet under her tunic, she wore a chain belt of linked golden coins. A very cool way to have money when needed, June would have thought, except Julian never so much as touched the coins. Even when they went an entire day without getting any food at all.

Julian talked about people and places, coming back most often to Dtheldevor's gang and how much she had loved staying with them. June didn't ask any questions, because that would invite questions, but she became aware that though Julian talked on about Dtheldevor, she did not talk about herself.

"I don't know where they are, of course," Julian said one night as a blizzard howled outside the barn they'd crept into, and time seemed to pass slower than the melt of an icicle. "I keep hoping they might still be in the Sartoran Sea. If so, maybe we could talk them into taking us to Mearsies Heili before they get back to fighting Norsunder."

"Why didn't you go with them?" June asked.

"Because they're fighting on the seas," Julian said. "I can defend myself if some footpad tries to knock me over to get at my coin pouch, but I'm no good against trained fighters. My skill is listening. No one looks twice at me."

June accepted that. "I'm lousy at fighting, too."

"Lousy?"

"English word. It just came out. Bad, rotten, terrible — though it comes from 'lice.'"

"Lice?"

"You don't want to know."

"I do want to know," Julian said, and then added, "Maybe not about lice, whatever that is. I've been talking and talking, and hinting that it might be your turn."

June's arms crossed, her body suddenly sharp angles. "And I've been not hearing those hints."

Julian immediately looked remorseful. "I'm sorry if I'm reminding you of terrible things. This last couple of months ought to have taught me that much. Anyway, I loved living at Dthel Rendm. That's Dtheldevor's island, clear on the other side of the continent. It's got secret entrances and tunnels and everything. I loved it there. I was happiest there, but Dtheldevor never can stay on land long." Julian shrugged.

June decided to sidestep the fact that she had no interest in going on Dtheldevor's privateer unless it was actually offered, and Julian smoothed past the uncomfortable moment by filling the time with language practice.

Another two slow, tense weeks later, they reached the peninsula called Valian, a journey that ought to have taken a week at most. Valian, which Julian had described as quiet and out of the way, swarmed with purple-coated Adranis and gray-coated Norsundrians.

The two girls avoided Al Caba harbor, which had the highest concentration of enemies, and used bad weather to sneak unseen around the point and up the east side, then inland to a tangled wood that the Norsundrians seemed to be avoiding.

As Julian had promised, Igkai did live in a huge hollow tree, with a loft reachable by a staircase cut into wood hardened almost to stone. The loft above that was entirely occupied by birds wintering over.

That was a very promising beginning to what even pessimistic June expected to be an interesting stay—until Julian asked for news.

Igkai stroked his skimpy gray beard, turned his goggle eye away toward the sea, and said, "You probably ought to know that your seafaring friends..." He halted here, shook his wild, leaf-strewn head, whereupon a chipmunk nesting in his snarled hair ran down his arm and he abandoned words to stroke the little creature with one gnarled finger. It crouched on his wrist, eyes half shut.

"No," Julian said, and louder, "No! Dtheldevor can't be dead! It's impossible!"

But there was silence, except for frightened chipmunk vanishing behind a basket of gourds, and the winter wind rustling through the bare branches up above the treehouse. Even the birds had stilled at her shout.

Julian stumbled back through the flimsy door, and crashed through the thick woods and away, leaving June with the mage, who sighed, and went about his affairs.

What to do now? June felt badly for Julian. Dtheldevor had been entertaining—in small doses. She'd also been loud, drank far too much, and June had not appreciated being rousted for swordplay whether she liked it or not, when Dtheldevor decided she was in the mood.

But dead? No one except villains deserved that.

Julian had warned June that Igkai did not like humans around; the ones he tolerated visiting knew to stay a short while, and kept themselves in the loft, unless he spoke to them.

Unsure what else to do, June climbed up to the loft, which she examined. Old, worn quilts lay neatly folded at one side — probably put there by the last visitor, as nothing below was tidy and squared away. She peered over the edge of the loft. Igkai's domicile wasn't filthy, but its order clearly only existed in his head, as piles of books, scrolls, papers, and suchlike lay on every surface, and had been stuffed into shelves along what passed for walls in that oddly shaped space. At one end hung vegetables, and baskets of nuts and tough-rinded fruits of an amazing variety had been stacked.

The sun was already setting, and an enticing smell, of which browned onion and garlic formed the main component, filled the air. June became aware of the weight of tiredness in her joints, and wondered if she ought to go to sleep, which at least ought to help her ignore the yawning hunger inside her.

But then Igkai called, "Supper!"

Julian had said he didn't bother with niceties. That might mean he wouldn't ask twice.

June went down the stairs, hoping that Julian had turned up. Igkai pointed to wooden bowls and spoons, all different sizes, and to a pot in which something that looked like a cross between glue and the dog's breakfast bubbled and popped.

June's appetite, maddened by the delicious aroma of caramelized onions, roared to life and she helped herself. The food was delicious — not unlike garlic mashed potatoes in texture, with bits of carrot amid the onions, garlic, and mashed nuts.

She had devoured half her bowl when Julian moped back in, her tight shoulders shedding snow at every step. She got food, sat down next to June, then said to the mage, "Do you know what happened?"

"One of my high flying friends saw the burning ship. The scent of the evil ones was everywhere, and as they have been capturing birds and doing evil things to them, she did not fly closer."

Julian's eyes closed in pain. She ate silently, then ran to the loft.

June began to follow, and hesitated. "Uh, should I help clean the dishes?"

"I've an ensorcelled bucket," Igkai said. "Go. Be listening ears. Julian has a task, but her heart must be ready."

June nodded awkwardly, and ran to the loft, where she

found Julian wrapped in one of the quilts. June was ready to listen, but it was clear that there would be no talking that night. Only the howl and moan of the wind.

June woke to a sense of warmth, almost to the point of overheating. How many blankets did she have on her? She took in a deep breath, sneezing at an unfamiliar, musky scent. At that loud sound, the quilt moved.

She started, then peered down at herself; a round, ruddy-furred shape lay across her legs. A vixen! Under the blanket, on both sides of her, a litter of kits had crawled in to get the best of the free heat generated by June.

She grinned, and moved a hand to pet one, but the kit bared its teeth and scrambled away, waking the others. They leaped into action, yipping in high-pitched voices as they gamboled and scrambled around the loft.

Their mother's white-tipped tail flickered and she gathered them with a look. Tiny feet pattered. The foxes zipped through a knothole in the bole of the ancient tree, and away.

Julian sat up, dislodging a pair of badgers, who trundled off. She looked around, then at June, her eyes red and puffy. "There won't be any ship ride west, obviously."

From below, Igkai said, "I've a meal waiting. A turtle swims in the sea. An unfinished task awaits."

June mouthed the word, *turtle?*

But from Julian's shrug, Igkai's gnomic utterance was as much a puzzle to her as it was to June.

They went down, to find what June thought of as this world's version of a PB&J—nut-butter smeared on thin pan-fried nut-cakes, with a dollop of jam.

Before they finished, Igkai said to Julian, "She died fighting, as she always said she would."

Julian did not find that the least bit comforting. "But she didn't win." Then understood that he had not meant to be comforting.

Igkai said, not ungently, "When you die fighting, you seldom win."

Julian turned away.

Igkai said to her back, "You made a promise once."

"Not now!" Julian snapped, and threw a scowling look

June's way. "I'm leaving. If you're coming…"

June said to Igkai, "Thanks."

The mage had already wandered off to his scrolls.

The girls tramped back down a narrow trail toward the shoreline. Presently Julian spoke. "We'll have to slog all the way to Mardgar to find a ship. If there are any afloat except Norsunder's."

June shrugged. "Igkai was interesting. But I still don't get that about turtles."

"Not turtles. *A* turtle," Julian muttered. "I don't either. Unless it's part of his nagging."

"That was nagging?" June bit down hard on the wish to add, *You don't even know what nagging means.*

"I know what he wants. But I'm not ready for that. One group of friends dead, and another gang of once-friends should be dead."

June turned, startled, and nearly tripped over a tree root. "What ex-friends should be dead?"

"No one you've met." Julian hissed a sigh. "It was years ago. And yes, he somehow knows I promised to listen after a year. But why go back, just to hear the same lies?"

"There's a story here, I'm guessing," June said.

"And I'm not telling it. I hate depressing stories, and this one is depressing. If you find fake friendship, and lies, in the name of grabbing power, depressing. I do." Julian stalked ahead, and muttered, "I really wish we didn't have to go through Barban. I hope he's not sending one of his furry or flying scouts ahead to be 'helpful.'" Her sarcasm was withering on the last word.

The subject dropped and they kept walking.

Nine

Enaeren northward

ANDRI AND MACAEL RODE on.

The weather worsened. Before darkness completely descended they found a ledge to camp on. While Macael took care of the animals (Andri was relieved he knew how to) Andri started a vagabond fire and laid hunks of bread and cheese near it to warm up. By the time he was done the aroma of melting cheese and toasted bread wafted through the cold air. He turned round and saw Macael with one black glove stripped off, gently stirring the contents of a small pewter wine cup propped over the fire. The delicious scent that rose was scalded beans, ground to powder.

"Coffee!" Andri said exclaimed.

Macael smiled. "Half my contribution." He carefully refolded a small packet and put it in his saddlebag, extracting a beautifully made wineskin as he did. He uncorked it and squeezed a small dollop of its contents into the pewter cup. The liquid sparked amber in the firelight.

"Brandy?"

"This will clear your throat, Cousin." Macael stirred the mixture with his knife handle, then took a tentative sip. "Drinkable...hot, at least," he finally pronounced, passing the cup to Andri. Andri took a huge swig, which scalded his mouth and brought tears to his eyes, but it sure felt good on his raw throat.

"Tastes like horse piss smells, but it sure feels good when it's down," he gasped, passing it back.

They shared the cup till it was empty, then wrapped themselves in their cloaks and spread out, Andri on a fairly large and flat rock and Macael on a folded in half waterproofed cloak, with saddlebag as pillow.

Andri sighed as he relaxed his aching body, preparatory to withdrawing behind his mind-shield if the expected attack came.

It did. Far more insidious than Bartal's generic battering. Andri had to rebuilt his defense, brick by imaginary brick. Until the sense of deadly ice pressure released and he slept.

He woke at dawn, when falling snow began hissing in the vagabond fire he'd made. Macael sat up and stared at it bemusedly. "What time is it? Midnight? Can't be. And yet— that fire, it's not a firestick, but twigs." He shook his head.

Andri rolled over and sat as a coughing fit came. When it was over he got up. "Vagabond magic—" he began to say, but his voice was gone.

He half-dozed on his horse's back over the next stretch of days. Macael found the campsites. Andri roused himself enough to start the vagabond fire, for though Macael copied his movements exactly, Andri could not explain the mental impetus to grab and hold magic, an impetus he scarcely understood himself.

Otherwise, Macael quietly and effectively took charge of the animals, the food, and the route. Andri had begun wondering if his fastidious cousin had ever spent a night in the rough. Whether he had or not, Macael did not flinch at dirt, or cold, or the wearying drip of near-frozen water off branches overhead as they slowly made their way up and up, and finally, one day, Andri roused enough to realize they were descending at last.

They were in Liath. Late that day they reached the east-west road. Andri figured they'd chance this road till they got into trouble—or at least, as long as it wasn't more prohibitive than traveling through the fields and farms north.

When darkness closed in they sought a barn to sneak into for the night. By then Andri's cough racked his body fairly often. He usually muffled his coughs in the crook of his elbow.

It was dark when Andri located a barn suitably distant

from its owners' house. Macael watched with interest as Andri made friends with the animals inside, insinuated their horses in, and found food for them. They each rubbed down their mounts, then climbed their way up into the loft.

Bags of feed sat in the loft, with a stack of empty feed sacks. "We'll sleep warm tonight," Andri whispered hoarsely. "If you put four or five of those sacks one inside of another, keeps you warm and it's easier to sleep on these boards."

They made sack-beds, warmed some food over a candle, then rolled up to sleep.

Andri woke up groggily when his shoulder went from numb to cold, except over the cut. He slid his hand into his pocket till his finger closed around the flask. As he pulled it out Macael stirred. Andri froze.

Macael whispered, "What's wrong?"

"Nothing. Get some rest."

But Andri sensed Macael's alertness, worry, question. He knew that a bloodknife attack was coming, but—he reflected wryly—there was a world of difference between the last time he'd been so marked, when he had no idea what these were or how to effectively fight them, and now, when he not only knew what was coming, he had Liere's calm, sweet voice in memory, reminding him how to effectively shield.

The worst of it was, he had to consciously stay awake and maintain that shield when he would so rather be sleeping.

He waited through the rustle of Macael's feed sacks as he tried to find a comfortable position, then slowed his breathing.

Andri took another tiny sip of the brandy, gasping as the fire spread down his aching throat and lungs. He was beginning to loathe brandy, but it was the only way to kill the cough and pain so he could concentrate on his mind-shield. By midnight he sensed no attack, and so he slept.

They woke before dawn. They restacked the feed sacks and tended their horses; by now Andri was skilled at melting ice and snow for the horses, and themselves, to drink. Macael was his usual pleasant self as they slipped silently from the barn and led their horses out into the cold wind. Andri buried his face in his collar—his throat hurt bad enough without having to breathe that freezing air.

After a time they took out some cold journeybread and gnawed at it.

"Feeling better?" Macael asked presently.

"Yep. If you're done, let's go." Andri whispered.

Macael said, "What is it you wait for, late at night?"

Figures, Andri thought. I was right. He doesn't miss much. His voice was just above a whisper, and sounded as raw as his throat indeed was. He jerked a thumb at his left shoulder. "Norsunder attacks my mind occasionally. They must really be desperate for entertainment, wherever they are."

Macael shook his head. "I am sure the last thing you desire is an over-solicitous relative, but I wish there was something I could do for you. You sound worse than you did when first you showed up at Elsarion."

Andri shrugged. "I catch colds every winter, and I always get over 'em."

Macael gave him a look, as if he wished to say more, but he refrained.

"I'll be fine. Let's go."

The wind was from the north. They rode west with their coat collars turned up over their ears. Snow clouds piled high, and Macael began casting appraising looks at the sky. When they saw a village ahead, they rode toward it instead of away.

The snow started to fall in slow, heavy flakes. Andri honked suddenly, "There's an inn. We haven't seen any Adranis this side of the mountains. I think it will be safe."

"Then let us hasten," Macael said, as the snow started to increase.

Andri led them to a three-story building with welcoming yellow light shining from every window on the bottom floor. They rode into a tiny courtyard and started to dismount as a figure in a heavy, shapeless coat came banging out of the stable. The stable boy took their horses with a lot of cheerful complaining about the weather, and they went inside.

As Macael opened the door, Andri glanced inside the low main room, where some fifteen people made enough noise for fifty. The air was heavy with the aromas of wood, braised fish, and spices; Andri employed his clumsy Dena Yeresbeth, finding himself bombarded by a cacophony of indistinct voices and images driven by emotions: greed, wariness, distrust, but none of the lethal intent he expected of Norsundrians. These people looked more like smugglers or thieves.

As soon as he and Macael walked in, silence fell, and everyone looked at them.

Andri stamped the snow off his boots. "We're illegal but

we're hungry," he whispered in the northern dialect, which was not that different from that common to Elsarion's region of Enaeran — a dialect Andri had learned when very small.

The closest man to the door laughed. "You got money, you're not illegal, far's old Donal is concerned."

Andri waved with supreme confidence at Macael, who tapped his belt, from which a fine, embroidered coin purse hung. "I have plenty of money, and we will not stay long," he said, smiling.

"Come in, come in." An old man with a long innkeeper's apron covering most of his lean frame beckoned. "There's a rule against travelers, but the invaders come around rare. And are about as welcome as cabbage mold. Bad for business."

Andri and Macael entered. Andri threw the right side of his cloak over his shoulder, and worked his sword around so that it lay across his lap, hidden by the cloak on the left. He smiled around — see, we're no threat — then sneezed a few times.

The innkeeper bowed to them. "What would you like, travelers?"

"Hot food, please, Innkeeper," Macael said. "Anything will be sufficient, so long as it's hot. Also a bed — my companion is very ill, and —"

"Nah," Andri croaked, speaking in Sartoran, which he was certain the educated Macael would understand. "No time. We'll eat and ride. And — we may's well get more of this damn drink." He brandished their nearly empty flask. By now he was thoroughly sick of the taste, especially on an empty stomach, but nothing else numbed his raw throat.

Macael suppressed the urge to protest. To him, there was a chasm of difference between the refined brandy fermented from the grapes left from their ancient vineyard, and the rotgut sure to be found here. Andri seemed unable to discern the difference; he might as well be swilling uncouth rye bristic from Marloven Hess.

The innkeeper moved away with the flask. The other patrons resumed their conversations. Under cover of the noise, Macael nodded after the innkeeper, now pouring from a ceramic jug into the flask. Macael averted his eyes. "Should we try to find a healer?"

"Better not. I hate the thought of someone like that being squeezed for word of us. I only need to stay on my feet another week or so," Andri said finally.

"Why a week?"

"Going to a Selenseh Redian, to cure myself. Border of Idego and Visegn. To the west."

Macael had seen the word before, but had skimmed past it as one of those impossible-to-understand ancient things. Andri intending to go to one made him want to ask what exactly a Selenseh Redian was, and how it cured people, but he decided to save that when the food and drink arrived.

Eating was rough on Andri's throat, but he felt better when he was done. Macael ordered and sipped at some coffee, and Andri put his head back on the rim of his chair and shut his eyes. Since to all appearances he was asleep, further conversation was suspended.

Macael stared down into the nearest fire, considering what he had learned so far: Andri was a strange mixture of ignorant and knowledgeable about surprising things. He'd admitted that he was ignorant, his princely education coming to a halt at around age ten, and yet he spoke of this Selenseh Redian with such confidence, and he knew that form of magic that made fire that consumed the twigs very, very slowly. Unnoticed, loud conversations, laughter, and drinking went on around them, until the door slammed open.

Snow and cold air swirled in, hissing in the fires. Black-uniformed Chwahir stamped in, shedding snow in all directions as they spread efficiently along the room's perimeter. A Norsundrian in gray headed them. People started for the exits, then froze into stillness as the Chwahir raised drawn swords.

"Come in if you must, just let me shut the door. You'll put out my fires," the innkeeper said, in a voice totally devoid of friendliness.

"You will do well not to hinder us," the Norsundrian said. His angry brown gaze nicked from person to person, resting longest on Macael as he added, "Meals for nine, at once. And we will ..." His gaze left Macael, then lit on Andri and widened. "That's Andri Elsarion!" He stopped, staring. "Arrest him!"

Instinctively Macael flicked a look Andri's way—to discover Andri standing up, a boot propped on the seat of his chair and his sword resting across his knee.

"Come and take me," he croaked, and sneezed.

"Where is the Adrani princess?" the Norsundrian

demanded.

"I ditched her in Nente," Andri honked. And waited.

But the man in gray did not point out that he was lying, that he'd been tracked with her to the Adrani border. Instead, he looked skeptical, so Andri added, "She couldn't tell right shoe from left! Of course I ditched her!"

The Norsundrian drew his sword, and motioned his team to close in.

"Andri Elsarion of Enaeran?" an old geezer asked.

"Brother to the queen of Martan?" the tough-looking white-haired woman next to the geezer put in. Her forearms were the brawniest in the room.

"Yep," Andri wheezed, and threw his cloak in one swirling motion at the closest two Chwahir.

It caught on their blades and ripped as they tried to disentangle their sword points. He shoved his chair at another with his fist, and pulled his dagger.

"For the queen," the old man said, swinging a chair straight into a Chwahir.

With a whoop the rest of the room erupted into attack and defense, as the Norsundrian cursed the Chwahir, demanding they get Andri alive.

Andri threw a quick glance Macael's way. His cousin had managed to back up to the fireplace, as he dueled against the patrol chief with perfect form. But only the one.

Macael found himself quite busy in the first actual fight of his life. His assailant was soon breathing hard, having not troubled to exercise since the first snows; as the man backed off to survey the scene, Macael spared a glance Andri's way, to discover him using feet, hands, and the furniture as well as his sword against three, no, four assailants.

Crash! Two fell into a table, which splintered. One lay still, groaning; the other picked himself up slowly.

Macael counted. That was seven. Two were missing: unless they had left to chase some of the patrons, they'd gone for help. "Andri!"

"I know. C'mon, let's end it." Andri hefted his sword. He was breathing hard, and occasional coughs racked his body.

The chief attacked Macael again, but kept looking between him and Andri. Macael paused in his fight. His free hand closed around an overturned ceramic candleholder, and when the chief turned toward Andri, Macael lunged and brought the heavy piece down on his head with a crack. The man dropped with a satisfying thud.

Macael leaned against mantle, his sword hanging loosely from his fingers, as his lungs labored. He slung his hair out of his eyes, then studied Andri's situation.

Andri had switched hands: his sword was now in his left and the dagger in his right. Three Chwahir rushed him at once, a heartbeat before the geezer pair brought an entire table down on them. Smash!

"Out," Andri croaked.

Macael sheathed his sword, still breathing fast. "Shouldn't we pay for damages?"

Andri waved a hand tiredly as though pushing the subject aside, then dropped it back on his leg. "You could. But he's gonna be starting over." He sheathed his knife, cleaned his blade and sheathed it.

"I'm afraid your cloak suffered in the fray," Macael said, holding up the sorry-looking garment

"I've worn worse." Andri poked a hand through the biggest hole, wiggled his fingers, and eyed the hem. "I don't suppose you have a sewing kit? No? I wish I'd thought to ask you for one, or even those Adranis. And damnation, am I glad I don't have to go back to rescue those people," he muttered, mostly to himself.

"The Adranis who helped you? You would feel obliged to return to their aid?"

"Yes," Andri croaked, and at Macael's intent expression, "If I didn't drop dead first." An exaggeration, but he did not want to explain how very close he'd come to finding himself mired in Mariana's mad plot. If those kindly, art-minded Harieses had been caught, he knew he'd be again obliged to take responsibility for Chantala, who was perfectly innocent. While being heir to the Adrani throne.

He still felt as if he'd escaped from more than Bartal's bejeweled clutches. He actually shuddered, which Macael took to be a shiver. But before Macael could express concern, Andri said, "Let's go. Everyone hates Norsunder, but right now we're as welcome as a fart in a locked room. Best we can do for 'em is get away fast as we can. Draw the stink after us."

Macael tossed a pair of golden coins behind him as they left.

Ten

Valian peninsula to Barban

JUNE AND JULIAN KEPT going, hiding whenever they heard hoof beats.

The food Igkai gave them ran out one night.

Late the next morning, June's stomach was complaining loudly, but all they'd seen was forest. "How big is Barban?" she asked eventually. "I'm hoping we might be able to score some eats."

"Not far."

Julian's memory was correct; at midday they tramped into a tiny village. The cold, clear air was so dry the light hurt the eyes. The wind blew the snow into smooth expanses across fields and into rounded mounds over obstacles.

Julian's mood had changed from restlessness to dread. As they entered the little village, Julian hunched up, warily surveying their surroundings. Not that there was anything amiss on the surface. Just a village build along a river, like most, with tall-roofed houses of light stone, shuttered against the cold. Sharp and clear rose huge, rocky mountains making a purple-gray line across half the sky. The village center was a widened part of the main road, pocked with foot and hoof prints. No one was around—not unusual in the icy cold.

"If only we could fly," Julian muttered, then looked around. "I hate being in Barban. But we can't go back. Sles Adran is much too hot."

June agreed. At least so far, they had not seen a single patrol—and their road had taken them out of the woods, the road running along the strand.

"Barban," June repeated, hoping to dislodge *something*. "I thought I heard Rel say this place is friendly to teens on the Wander."

"He did say it. The *people* are friendly to those on the Wander. And up in the mountains, they're friendly to morvende, and so on."

June pursed her lips. "But?"

"But. I don't have Dena Yeresbeth, but I'll swear *they* know I'm here."

"They? They who?" June asked. "You don't mean Norsundrians."

"Let's call them rats on two legs. Except that's an insult to rats, who don't pretend to be your friend while destroying everything." And at a side-eye from June, she stopped talking around a subject that was not going to go away. "A few years ago I thought I had friends here. Stupid me, believing their lies."

"Ugh," June said.

"Why don't we find—" Julian cut off when June raised a hand, and they heard the rumble and jingle of horses on the way. "Must be a patrol. And there's no cover at all. We better chance someone's porch."

"And fast."

All the houses on the main road had porches built all the way around. They spotted one stacked with baskets and other supplies, and began a coat-flapping, slipping-and-gooshing dash through the slush, throwing themselves flat on the porch a handful of heartbeats before half a dozen mounted Adranis galloped around the corner ahead. They halted in the square, dismounted, and divided between the three houses across the way.

"Can you see?" June whispered, her face pressed against the support of the bench they'd crammed themselves under. She couldn't move unless Julian got out first.

"Yeah," Julian breathed. "Search. Across the way."

June tried to make sense of the confusion of noises—harnesses jingling, swords clanking, occasional shouted commands in Adrani.

Julian tightened herself into an even smaller ball. "If you bring your knees around now you should be able to—"

With a mighty squirm June rolled over to her hands and knees. She pressed her face to the crack in the railing, and Julian peered over her head at the house across the street as a young woman stumbled onto the porch giving a long, anguished scream.

The Adranis emerged, holding onto two small children, who kicked and struggled vigorously. As they passed the woman, she suddenly turned and attacked the nearest purple coated warrior, nails hooked. He staggered back a couple steps. His prisoner wrenched free and ran. The boy was no more than five; when he saw his mother knocked down, he veered and started for her.

The Adrani nabbed him, and tucked him under his arm.

From surrounding houses, children were dragged out as they and parents or older family members resisted.

"Wonder what happened. The children must've organized into some sort of resistance group and got caught," Julian muttered. "Course some of those look pretty young."

"Maybe some sort of hostage plan."

"Oh, yeah...they seem to be moving on. What're they going to do with the k—ack!" Just as they saw the wagon approaching, two heavy hands landed on the girls' shoulders from behind.

They twisted away, scrambled out and landed on their feet just to face two grinning gray-coated Norsundrians in stockinged feet. Behind the Norsundrians, the front door was open, and inside was a stack of weapons, and several more Norsundrians watching, a couple of them laughing.

Their deserted building was the local headquarters.

They were completely surrounded.

"Come on," one said in wretched Basric, "this way. And no trouble." Then, to the Adranis, in their own language, "I told you, always do a third surprise sweep."

They were led to a long wagon. Julian and June climbed in after a not-so-gentle prod from a sword flat. They crammed in beside youngsters ranging from five to the girls' age. Some of the smaller children were shivering and crying as they tried to struggle into coats and boots. A couple of teens attempted to help. The rest glared at the Norsundrians. There was no roof over the wagon, but the sides were high and solid so no one could see out.

The wagon bumped and jolted on, stopped, and a new

load of children was pushed in, prefaced by screams, shouts, and clanks. Nearly thirty children were squashed in by the last stop. One more teen, then the wagon rolled along without stopping.

The cries and whimpers of the youngest children slowly died away as most of them fell asleep or lay staring up at the sky, puppy-piled in a tangle of bodies and limbs. June found her lap and one shoulder serving as pillows for a pair of little boys, and Julian found herself with a lapful of soundly sleeping little body. Some of the older captives held whispered conversations, but the guards riding to either side discouraged attempts to jump.

The sky clouded just as the trip ended. They were herded out of the wagon and shouted at to line up according to age. Laggards were given shoves and yanks to get them moving faster.

They had to stand still in the snow when they were done, till the local commander came out. He was tall and gray-grizzled, his face sour as he told them in accented Basric that they were in a work camp; they were going to be trained to be productive, and any escape attempts or trouble or chronic sickness would result in death. While they were productive their needs would be seen to, but as soon as they became a burden they would be disposed of and easily replaced.

June pretended to listen, not understanding a word. Julian hadn't said a word to her the entire time since their capture. That they must keep their being foreigners from the Norsundrians—and it was all gray-coats here, no Adranis—was obvious to June, but for some reason Julian didn't want the other kids to know. She was sure of that as soon as the long, meaningless speech from the head gorilla was over.

As the kids broke into groups, muttering and sending angry looks around the fenced-in, snow covered field and the slat-plain barracks along the far end, Julian turned to June and said something in Basric, with a wide gesture around them and a disgusted look on her face.

June scowled as she copied Julian's gesture, which Julian took to mean she was right.

The other kids seemed ordinary enough, the smallest tired and cranky as they were herded in one direction. There seemed to be a rough division by age, into three groups, all motioned toward the barracks.

Julian and June were put with the oldest, about twenty-five teenage girls. The teenage boys were separated off, opposite the girls, and the little kids jumbled together in another building. The dorm was a long room. Slat bunk beds with narrow straw-stuffed mattresses, rough woolen blankets, and hooks for coats, made up the furnishings. At the far end was a cleaning frame.

The rest of that day and the next morning June rarely saw Julian, and the few times anyone talked in her direction it was, of course, in Basric. No one seemed to think it unusual that she didn't answer; there were a whole lot of other kids who weren't talking to anyone either. She followed the line of girls, and stood in silence supposedly listening to harsh-voiced harangues by the Norsundrians because Julian was doing the same. She had pulled her hair into two tight braids and wore a vacant expression. Something was going on; June went along and kept her peace.

The meals were at the other end of the camp, in a big mess hall. The food was utterly bland: oatmeal with nothing to flavor it in mornings, bread-and-cheese (bland cheese, too) at noon.

Right after lunch ended, things changed. As June was rounding a corner to join the line for the next harangue, a pleasant-faced girl rounded from the other direction. She was moving fast, and bumped directly into June. The girl shot out a hand and steadied June, saying "Sorry," in Mearsiean. June' eyes lifted involuntarily to the girl's eyes. They were sky blue. June made a questioning expression, smiled blankly and walked on past.

Shortly after Julian came up next to June, smiling grimly. "No use. Well—prepare yourself for a rescue. There's no way out."

"Oh?"

Julian raised her hand. "I've had it anyway, and you've been picked out, too. They're going to get me now for sure; it's just a matter of timing it around the Norsundrians."

"That was one of your mystery people?"

Julian jerked her chin in a reluctant nod. "Quite sure of it. I'm sorry. I tried to stay away from you so you wouldn't get dragged into it, in case they'd marked me."

June sighed, muttering in English, "That's my life. Wrong place, wrong time. Wrong existence." She thrust an elbow toward the field where they were headed. During each harangue they stood there in lines. "What's going on?"

"Yapping. Rules. What they want you to think and to believe. Near as I can figure Norsunder has some sort of plan to break up families, stick the children in these camps, and train them to be 'useful.' Serves two purposes. We serve as hostages for adults and parents, and we'll be trained as unpaid labor for Norsunder, by the time we grow up." Julian frowned up at the sun for a moment. "They bragged that Llyenthur doesn't expect much success at first. He expects more than half of us to be dead by next year, but the rest would be trained to make up for us in productivity ('us' being the last ones), while at the same time the lesson would not be lost on the adult community." Julian shook her head.

June's brief sneer expressed her contempt for Llyenthur.

"Stupid creep," Julian muttered.

"Stupid is right," June said.

Julian's agreement was rather half-hearted. "If only I was sure he wasn't related to — oh well. It was so long ago, and if some people've said nothing…" Julian's mutter died away till it was almost inaudible. By then they were in line, and since June wasn't interested enough in Llyenthur to pry even if she'd been inclined to, the subject dropped.

There was another boring harangue to go through. It was slightly more bearable this time because they stood side by side and June was aware of Julian's quiet ughs, muffled snorts, snickers, groans and disgusted sharp sighs.

June amused herself by making up an imaginary villain speech, like translations in movies, when voice-actors dubbed lines over the spoken words in badly written English. It cheered her considerably to imagine this guy saying stuff like *And I'm the biggest boss how you imperialist donkey-pigs stupid ambulate no fast, yes? Fear! Bust your corset!*

After that, they were issued spades and made to dig a foundation in the frozen ground. This went on until the next meal bell rang. By then their hands were raw and stiff under their mittens, and their arms and backs ached. Together, the group had accomplished only one-third of their day's task, the Norsundrians informed them before they left for the barracks for sleep. Tomorrow they would be expected to make it up.

The only comment that passed between June and Julian before they flopped onto the hard beds and tried to get comfortable under the scratchy blankets was: "More than half was a cheerful estimate."

The first thing either was aware of was the scent of honey-blossom. It drifted in, sweet but too fleeting to be heavy. Julian's dreams took on a summery turn before she woke abruptly. June, above her, woke at the sudden movement of the rickety wooden bunk bed. She leaned out.

The blue-eyed girl from that afternoon held a candle. In the wavering golden light she laughed softly. She wore a floating silver garment, and the honey-blossom breathed from the garland in her hair.

"You came back to us, Julian," she said in Sartoran. "Welcome, welcome to Barban. But we must free you from this place. You, too." She smiled up at June.

June didn't answer. She rolled the other way and took a scan. Half a dozen teens waited in a semi-circle, their faces lit by candles.

June sighed, and swung her legs out of bed — they all slept fully clothed, including their coats. Julian hunched on the edge of her bunk, looking up at the girl's face. Her narrowed eyes glinted as the girl's candle flickered. She was running a piece of string through her fingers slowly, ruminatively. There was a pause; everything was still save the yellow flames. Then Julian looked around the room, still pulling the string through her fingers.

"It's a ring before the midnight bell."

"Eleventh hour," Julian said with a glare. "Fitting."

In the candlelight, the girl flushed. But her voice was not angry as she said, "There is much magic about. Everyone is under a sleep spell." Then, more quietly, "Have you learned more vagabond magic than your teachers?"

Julian dropped the string, stood up, and shoved her feet into her shoes.

"What happens to the others if we leave?"

"You don't leave. That's why there are so many of us. That is, you will leave behind shadows. And those will be joined by more shadows, each week, until all the children are gone, we hope before the Norsundrians notice. You are building garrisons for the occupation forces, once Norsunder breaks through the barrier round the world."

Julian did not answer. She walked toward the door. The children with the candles closed around her and June, the lights lengthening into a golden glow that seemed to whirl slowly around them in a gleaming fog.

When it cleared, they stood in a throne room of a castle. Moonlight from the open roof shone on the dais with its great chair of stone. Gathered shadows hid the walls.

The only teen who'd made the transfer with June and Julian was the one with the candle. She held her candle high, and its yellow light pushed the moonlight and shadows back only on a small circle, revealing a cracked marble floor and a carved dark-wood table next to Julian.

"Come this way. You must still be tired from all that digging. We can talk tomorrow."

Her circle of light moved over the marble inlay, which Julian saw was in great intersecting patterns that reminded her a little of Sartoran braid-knots in threes. The girl led them up some warm-hued marble steps. The girls noticed gaps in the carved marble balustrade here and there. It was a long climb; at the top, she opened the door to an alcove. "You can sleep here," she said, setting the candle down on the floor.

She withdrew, her long skirts wisping gently on the stone ground, and shut the door behind her. June turned at once to the door, but Julian waved a tired hand at her.

"Don't bother. They don't need to lock it. We'd only get as far as they let us. We may's well explore in the morning."

June shrugged and joined Julian as she spread out on a giant pile of cushions. They pulled large swaths of rich velvet over themselves, and fell asleep at once.

Eleven

North Ghildraith Mountains

LIERE'S LONELY JOURNEY CONTINUED, ever upward.

Abruptly it became more difficult.

It was morning, and the dogs roused not long after settling down. Ruffs fluffed. Breath keening in throats, they ran about, sniffing, restless, ears flattening and rising again, pointing alertly. Not that Liere needed these signs to feel something was very wrong.

The chief female led the way from their crevasse, out along a narrow trail. She seemed to want to hurry along this ancient path cut into the side of a sheer slab of granite.

Liere tried not to look down at the thundering waterfall far below as she edged out on the narrow cliff, her back along it. Danger made her neck tighten.

She shuffled in an awkward crab step as the wind howled along the peaks and tore through the canyons. Big flakes of snow serried down from the heights. Her guide's hackles stiffened. Liere pressed hard against the stone as the female lifted her muzzle and howled.

At once the other dogs set up a frantic barking and howling; their thoughts crashed through Liere's head, splinters of scent and sound that she could make no sense of, but the cumulative effect was fear.

The wind strengthened inexorably, but she forgot that when she sensed intent. Furious, rage-filled intent. She twisted

her head, fighting the stomach-dropping instinct to lean out.
Her ear scraped with painful reassurance against rock as she
peered back where she had been, at a cliff barely in view, to
where a silhouette stood poised, head turning slowly: a wolf.
But wolves didn't peer like that.

She stayed flat against the wall, hands spread like starfish
at her sides, and dared a tendril. What she found sickened her
to the soul, and she shut it out hard.

At first it had seemed like a blurred image but then it
separated into two minds, the wolf's mind utterly without
language, fighting desperately and angrily against the internal
invader. The invader was a human mind, looking through the
wolf's eyes and trying to force human perception onto eyes that
did not function the way human eyes did. Further, it ignored
the world of aromata — including her own scent.

She understood then that the wolf smelled her, along with
all the other thousands and thousands of odors for which
humans had no name, but that invading mind disregarded the
wolf's nature in its quest to see…her? It sought someone.

She breathed slowly, her stomach settling after that
wretched contact. She had to get away. Surely this ledge led
somewhere? She couldn't remain there, nor could she go back,
as that would lead straight toward the wolf.

She began to scrape along in tiny shuffles, heels pressed
against rock.

Abruptly the wind increased to a spine-searing shriek. The
snow buffeted her face, nearly smothering her as the gusts pried
with icy stings to separate her from the wall. Instinct prompted
her to shrink down to as small a target as possible. She began
sliding down the wall, but just as she had nearly hunkered
down a vicious gust whipped against her coat and riding
trousers, causing them to flare just enough to knock her off-
balance.

Her hands scrabbled against the trail —

--and found only rubble. With a wailing cry she pitched
over the edge, smashed painfully against the rock, as the wind
swooped inside her coat, almost lifting her, and out she sailed
into the air.

She tumbled horribly like a cloth doll flung by an angry
child, then twisted about and spread her arms wide. Down she
flew into the depths of the abyss where the rising sun still had
not yet reached. Wind rushed in her ears, nearly smothering an

odd whistling, like birdsong and yet not: there was the cadence of language.

Liere shut that out, trying to relax. She dreaded the smash — could not bear to see it coming, so she closed her eyes against the ferocious buffeting of the icy wind as her mind streamed with images, with remorse and regret as sharp as that wind. She would never again see her daughter's face — and her mind reached along the old path to safety, but she caught herself with a conscious mental cry, *Andri!*

And days of hard travel both west and north, that inward cry hit not just Andri but Senrid heard as well. There'd been another idly listening mind, as high in the Larkadhe tower, Imry Llyenthur rocked back and forth in his chair, eyes shut as Duin read the beginnings of dispatches, tossing most into the flame.

"Bostian, fifth requis —"

"Fire."

"Zranf, from Alsaes, marked urgent —"

"Fire."

"Bartal —"

"Fire."

"Alcandamer. Requisition: we need at least three companies —"

"Those companies stay right where they are until I find who's running the resistance. Colleron, send a message to Connanre. As for Alcandamer, we need a couple of his spies to find that queen running loose. Next?"

"Report from Yuen."

Bang! The chair crashed down. "Yuen? Did he find out Efael's latest game?"

Duin squinted down at the report, which was long, the details neatly listed. Practiced by now, he summed it up. "No sign of Detlev's son. Rumor has it he made it down to the Valian peninsula and took ship —"

"And Efael is trying to imply that I lost that boy by letting him escape to the sea. Wrong. We've got control of everything floating on the Sartoran Sea, from three-masters to rowboats …" Llyenthur's voice drifted.

The staff waited, knowing that blank affect.

Llyenthur caught that mental cry long enough to snag the identity. Liere Fer Eider? Useless herself, at last report, but connected to a lot of very useful people indeed. At the top of that list, Senrid Montredaun-An.

Llyenthur shut his eyes, reached — but to no surprise she was closed off. He cursed under his breath, but without any force. This one he'd have to follow himself.

"Fire," he said. "Next?"

All this time Liere fell through the air, until *fwoosh!*

Someone swooped near, and hard arms clamped around Liere's ribs, knocking her breath out.

Then her stomach dropped as she swept up into the wind. The swoop juddered jerkily, as if a winged creature beat upwards against the gusts.

Her mind caught up, dizzily; she twisted her head to catch sight of a profile that seemed carved from stone, lined and craggy as it was. Wisps of a long silver-white beard blew against her cheek. Her legs dangled in the cold and whistling air.

The astonishing flight reached its apex and then a soaring, swooping curve around a mighty precipice, their shadows thrown against the rock wall. Two humans — one pair of wings, riding the air currents like birds. Liere's panic ignited to giddy thrill. She sensed the working of the flyer's musculature as the wind altered and whipped around them.

They angled, then banked between a great fissure in ancient stone. The wind dropped, leaving Liere feeling as if they floated, but on the other side a waiting wind current smashed into them, and they scudded up and up. When she opened her eyes again, they were drifting down into an enormous cave.

And then she was set on her feet; she stumbled forward a step or two as the old winged man back-flapped, then stopped.

She smiled at her rescuer, who was barely her own height. He smiled, creating more lines in that carved face, made a gesture with gnarled hands the color of new wood, and said, "Sartora?"

East and north of Liere's wild flight, Andri and Macael speculated a little about how that Norsundrian had recognized Andri. "I'd have remembered him if I'd seen him," Andri said hoarsely. "My guess? He saw me when the Adranis who first nabbed me brandished me at the various garrisons when we rode from Enaeran to Nente. I was sicker than I am now, but I do remember some whooping and hollering about rewards and promotions. I expect he would have heard that I'd escaped, taking their princess."

Macael said, "Then you do not think it was a specific hunt."

"No." Andri laughed—then caught his breath, hating the way he really shouldn't laugh lest it stir up the mess inside his chest. Laughter had always been his best defense during the bleakest of days. "I suspect they are a border patrol. He recognized me. Saw a bag of gold. If he was on my trail, he'd have known that I'd ditched Chantala, and maybe even where."

That led to speculation about how far stretched Bartal was, with his army summarily spread all over the southeast quadrant of the continent.

Macael wondered what the cost might be, something Andri had not considered. "You know Norsunder is not going to be paying them."

"Hadn't considered that." Andri chortled, gasped after a fit of coughing, then said breathlessly, "I can predict patrol patterns. But not who gets paid when."

"You won't last long as a king if you don't learn it," Macael observed, slanting an amused glance his way.

"I didn't last long." Andri cackled, coughed, then sighed. "I was beginning to learn. My treasury minister sees the world in numbers. She had a plan for wresting the treasury out of poverty, once I'd reclaimed it. We'd just finished all that when Norsunder made its move; I'd actually gone to Sartor to ask for help when Adon turned up again. Which is probably why I'm still alive." Andri shrugged. "But you were talking about treasuries."

Macael hmmmed softly. Then, "One of the benefits of scholarly pursuits is understanding the ephemerals of value, one might say. Sles Adran will very soon be beggared unless they've raided the treasuries of these other kingdoms being patrolled by the Adranis. Which brings the question, if Sles Adran's reward is annexing the treasuries of all these kingdoms, what exactly is Norsunder getting out of this war?"

"What does anyone get out of war?" Andri countered. "Land. People to push around, or force into labor."

"Toward?"

"According to Senrid and Atan—ah, that's the queen of Sartor. She uses her private name when among friends, anyway—they'll have it that the various chiefs of Norsunder's high command all have different goals."

They paused to water the horses beside a low hill with a running stream. No signs of humankind anywhere, just bare trees grouped in gray-toned upward strokes against white landscape. Macael frowned at the silent countryside, then said, "It would seem that denying them those goals—once you find out what they are—would be the most effective way to get rid of them?"

"And that," Andri said, "is why I'm going to Mearsies Heili. I'm not used to thinking that broadly. I'm going to those who are."

Macael's expression lightened at that. "Now I understand. Yes, excellent plan."

At the same time that Liere was climbing with the dogs, Andri and Macael rode on, foraging for food and fodder, using the horse cakes only when they had to. Perforce, Andri was getting somewhat better at scanning on the mental plane, though it left him dizzy.

This was the pattern until they began to climb the mountains marking the border. Conversation between them was desultory. Often Macael's body ached too much for sleep. He never complained, figuring that Andri felt worse, but he lay awake every night for a long time in contemplation.

Some nights, Andri lay as one dead. This puzzled Macael till he figured that Andri was unconscious, voluntarily, sort of, and his physical self was unprotected. He tested it the second night after they left that friendly farm—when he was sure Andri was out he leaned over and touched his arm. There was no response.

Andri had hidden this weakness as long as he could, without trusting Macael enough to explain it. Salutary!

Andri was grimly cheery when he woke Macael the morning of Liere's fall They'd managed to find a tiny rocky gulley somewhat protected from the weather; though Macael forced himself to wash his face in snowmelt every morning, and used his comb to order his hair, Andri ignored such things. Turning his head, so that his filthy straw-colored hanks straggled down his back, he waved an expansive arm at the clear sky. "Easy traveling today. Which is good. Makes us easier to follow. That's the bad. On your feet. Time to get moving."

The hills were low, and by midday they'd passed a stone plinth that let them know they were approaching the border of Lorgi Idego. They stopped behind a huge clump of bushes beside a frozen stream.

"Where's this Selenseh place that will cure you?" Macael asked after they'd chewed silently on their frozen bread. It nagged at him. He was certain he'd heard, or more likely read, the term before.

"Not a place, a thing somewhere in the hills on the western border of Idego. Selenseh Redian."

"That's Sartoran. Ancient Sartoran—I understand some of the root syllables, but not what they mean. Is someone there who'll do magic to counter that of the Norsundrians?"

Andri shrugged. "Didn't get that impression. Guess we'll have to—" Andri jerked slightly in the saddle as though his muscles had tightened, and his face masked over. He looked so strange that Macael reached over and grabbed the bridle of Andri's horse to stop them both.

They sat there in silence for what seemed a long time. Andri's horse twitched his tail and tossed his head nervously every so often. Macael kept scanning the flat white expanse of fields before them, and the white covered dark gray hills behind. Especially behind.

At last Andri startled Macael by letting out a long sigh. He gazed upward, green eyes the color of spring leaves caught in ice. "C'mon, let's get out of here." Andri shot Macael a wry smile. His lips were dry-looking, the whites of his eyes bloodshot. Macael decided to keep his mouth shut about stopping. He suspected Andri knew as well as he that he couldn't keep up this pace for much longer.

Andri found a farmhouse half-hidden in a huge copse of ancient trees in the bend of a frozen stream. Two old people lived there in an atmosphere of remoteness and serenity. They welcomed the shivering travelers on their doorstep without any surprise or hesitation, and bade all four to come in. The man led the horses through the long, low main room to a wide door in back. Beyond was a stable separated from the main part of the house by a cloth door.

Macael wandered after him, and was told not to worry and to go back inside by the fire and shed those wet clothes. He walked back into the main room, his bootheels loud on the bare wooden floor.

He found Andri collapsed in a chair, his eyes shut and his face pale even in the firelight. Macael began to shed his cloak and coat. The aroma of cinnamon and apples filled the room. Astonishing, how comforting such a simple thing could be.

The woman came back in, smiling and carrying two mugs of hot cider. "These belong to my granddaughters, but they will not mind sharing." She indicated the cups.

The couple made a place for the two Elsarions in that living room, on the floor, with a mighty pile of blankets and quilts. The old folk went to bed early, leaving Andri and Macael sitting cross-legged on the clean-swept floor. By the light of the banked fire, they used colored pebbles from a jar, moving them on the floorboards as Andri taught Macael a simple betting game played by the street youths in Shiovhan; Macael watched, listened, tried, then said, "This is a strategy game, is it not?"

"I don't know. Ah, I suppose it is." Andri grinned ruefully. "I have to admit I've lived on the run so long that I've never had the leisure to think about strategy. I see a problem immediately before me, I use what I've got—which has rarely been much— to tackle it."

"Tactician," Macael said, tossing a pebble on his palm. "Strategy—from my limited understanding—is just one step back."

Andri was going to retort that he'd never stepped back, but heard how pompous that would sound. Anyway Macael's context was different than the usual jockeying to determine who was tougher. There was no challenge whatsoever in Macael's words, or in his attitude. He had been honest from the start about his lack of experience, and how everything he knew came from books.

He was also quick. Macael said, apology in his tone, "I misspoke, I believe. What I meant was, one takes a step back to see the entire map. Not in the sense of whose sword is sharper, or whose courage greater, which I regard as singularly useless in this context, but in the sense of, oh, say, the first Alored, our respective ancestor, facing Mathias Lirendi." Macael tipped his head, considering. "Oddly relevant, in that that was the previous cross-continent invasion. But not a drop of blood was shed."

"Mathias was scared of old Alored." Andri fought against a chuckle. "That's what my father told me once, when showing me the crown. Too bad we haven't the likes of that first Alored now. But then Mathias wasn't a Norsundrian."

"Exactly. And it was not Alored I who halted Mathias Lirendi's expansion, at least not solely. It was partly the king of the Marlovens, there for a visit. Nor was it fear, it was the prospect of battle. The entire point of Mathias's expansion being to unite the continent so there would be no more wars."

"That's what he told the scribes to say, I expect," Andri began, though not with any certainty. He was very aware that his reading of history had stopped when he was ten. He knew the ballads, of course, and various stories, but everyone knew not to trust those entirely.

"There was a war game," Macael said. "The Marlovens won, a foregone conclusion. They were quite ready to turn it into a real battle. In a sense they did. According to another of our ancestors, who was there, and wrote it all down—I can show you the record someday—they killed several Faleth, who were equally determined to win at all costs, unlike the Colendi."

"And so Alored got a kingdom out of it." Andri frowned at the fire. "My head is too stuffed to think, but what you're saying is that Mathias the Conqueror stepped back, eh?"

"Yes. He was never going to go beyond the mountains to Halia in any case. Too difficult to get to, much less administer, and anyway they didn't trouble anyone on our side of the Ghildraith. He went home, the eastern half of what used to be Enaeran Adrani became part of the empire, Enaeran became an independent kingdom, and what Mathias tried to prevent happened anyway: generations of fighting over the rich land between the rivers, which both we and the Adranis covet."

Andri knew that the border between Enaeran and Sles Adran had shifted back and forth from one river to the other over the generations, sometimes in very bloody fights, sometimes in march and retreat, threat and concession. But he'd lost the point. And he was desperately tired anyway. "I know what you meant," Andri said, mostly to end the subject, then he was taken by a terrible fit of coughing, which he valiantly tried to suppress so as not to waken their hosts. He ended up lying flat in his welter of blankets, and murmured, "Better sleep."

"Excellent notion. Forgive me for keeping you awake. It's the delight, you could say curse, of the scholar, arguing over history, and speculating on what if."

Andri waved a hand, and closed his eyes, listening to the

secretive whisperings of the trees outside the windows.

Macael slept fitfully. At one point he woke to Andri staring at the fire. His knees were drawn up and his chin rested on them. The firelight flickered on the ridges and knuckles of his fingers as he massaged his left shoulder as close to the shoulder blade as he could get, on the wrinkles of his once-fine white shirt, off his tangled yellow hair, and off his bony face, which bore that same expression he'd seen on it that morning, during the unexplained pause. Macael turned over; his dreams were noisy and unpleasant.

They left the next morning early, after a hot breakfast, and rode on.

Twelve

LIERE'S GUIDE LED HER deep within the cavern, until the last of the light had faded. Torches smelling of linseed oil waited at a turning. He picked one from a sconce and preceded her into a tunnel, which led down and down until it opened onto a huge cavern with arches and pillars of stalactites and stalagmites. The stone glittered redly in the torchlight.

Liere was still angry, but more apprehensive. As she followed the winged man down a long tunnel, she dealt with the truth: she thought she'd come back so much wiser, but the Sartora business always smashed her flat again. If only it didn't come with such expectation!

By rights Siamis should be dealing with this kind of stuff, or Detlev, was her grimly ironic thought. Not Liere Fer Eider, the Girl Who Accidentally Broke A Very Flimsy Enchantment. And how did these folk even know she was here?

From there to another path. The ground trembled enough to cause her arms to rise, but it was a steady, gentle tremble, never enough to challenge her balance. A deep, low rumble resolved out of that tremor, at first felt more than heard. Two turns and the rumble swelled to a roar. The air, which had steadily warmed, smelled of running water.

The tunnel narrowed abruptly, then opened just as abruptly into a round cavern with a stone ledge wet with the spray from a tremendous waterfall sheeting down, down, down, from high above. Shafts slanting from the mid-morning sun lit the rippling patterns of water into liquid flame. The force of sound thundered in her bones; she laughed aloud at the beauty and power, though she could not hear her own voice.

Her guide led her carefully around the ledge. His hand ran lightly along some indentations in the rock, then part of the rock slid away. A narrow tunnel opened, which they entered. The man's torch, smoking from all the moisture of the outer room, lit the tunnel weirdly.

The tunnel widened abruptly into several, and all of those ended in caverns. They entered a cavern where they found a group of the flying people seated around a black underground pool that glittered in the torchlight. The people looked up as Liere and her guide entered: there were two old men, a woman and some youths who, despite their wings, looked human enough that she recognized in upturned faces and still posture their intensity, their hope.

A tall, skinny teenaged boy brought in some ceramic mugs with steaming liquid in them. It smelled like an herb steep with a little cinnamon, and it was scalding hot so Liere set hers down carefully, permitting the flood of mental imagery, and with it a sense of their language — which (like most) had Sartoran at its roots.

"It is not our custom to interfere with the flatlanders, or to allow them to interfere with us. However, we usually follow them through our territories, to see that they leave. The small-one did not tell us who you were till the wind of the death-ones was called."

"Small-one —" Liere, listening on the mental plane, caught a flicker of image: the white female. "Did you save the dogs?"

"Yes."

"Thank you, I am so glad." Relief washed through Liere, leaving her feeling so exhausted she was a little dizzy.

"You are Sartora," the man repeated, and her relief vanished, leaving the old, familiar anxiousness roiling in her stomach. "You are fighting the death-ones," he stated more than asked.

Utterly dismayed, Liere tried to frame a question that would not sound as accusatory as *What idiot told you that?*

But the guide spoke first. "We will help you through our lands." The word *lands* came with a stunning image of peaks whose snowy tops never thawed. "The death-ones are shooting us out of the skies, and forcing us to carry their minds when they find us. Then they discard the shell." A vivid picture of a wolf, ragged, paws ruined, trembling.

Another wolf besides the one she had seen.

"They…"

"Take the self, and impose their self, until the end."

Sickened, Liere understood now: someone among the Norsundrians, probably Yeres, had found a way to subsume the animals' minds and direct their bodies, much as they did with the soulbound. Apparently not just animals, but also these flying people—if they caught one. Only the more adept Norsundrian riders could see and hear through the victim's eyes and ears. Human or animals, they apparently ran the host to death. After all, there were plenty more.

Now she understood why the wild dogs had helped her, though it was unnerving to contemplate their abilities to sniff out her intent through noses that sifted scents far beyond human comprehension.

"They are killing many people," she said, hugging her elbows against her ribs. "Friends and I were fighting them. We were scattered, but now we are regrouping and will work to free our world, when we are stronger."

"We will show you where they nest," he said. "But now—eat with my family, and we are honored. The snows will be very fierce this dark-time."

———

Liere spent the night in the decorated caves of the winged people. Their light, draped clothing—hearkening back several hundred years to fashions that had traveled from Sartor to Colend, where they became style before they spread outward—hid how the wings worked. Liere was wildly curious to discover if they were born with them or not, but she was hesitant to ask lest her question be intrusive. Their origin might be another world altogether.

They slept on cushioned alcoves carved into the walls of their caverns. Liere slept profoundly and deeply, the noise of the waterfall at this location diminished to a soothing rush. She had no idea that she was given a place of honor—and that afterward it would be known as Sartora's alcove. She was just so grateful to be warm again, and comfortable.

But when she woke, the little details of life must accumulate and demand their due: she was so grimy she itched in every crease of her skin, and though she still thought fondly and gratefully of her canine companions over the high ridges, she smelled strongly of dog.

She was intensely embarrassed to lift the curtain (embroidered over with soaring bird figures) to find the family gathered around a meal laid out on another rich, embroidered cloth set on a stone ledge.

"Do you have a cleaning frame?" she asked, and blushed, her gaze finding the girl nearest her age. "I will help put the bedding through. I shouldn't like to make work for anyone."

"We have not," the girl said. "We fly through the spray, but you must not think about that. We do not. Come! Eat. Then En-mek will take you to where you can see the nest of the evil ones, that you may gather your forces and smite them."

The older folk faded back, letting the girl, Ti-mek, talk to Sartora as they listened to every word she let fall, that they might discuss each for hidden import afterward.

When she finished the odd pudding made (as far as she could tell) of pounded nuts, and wild mountain spices, a young man, maybe five years older than Rel, with a mane of pale hair bound close to his head by a headband, came into the cave and introduced himself as En-mek.

The family vanished before she realized they had, so she could not thank them.

En-mek led her by another route, silent until the air began to get cold again very rapidly.

"You are Sartora?" En-mek asked when they reached an outside ledge, under a windy, leaden sky.

Liere tried not to sigh. "Yes, but I really do prefer Liere."

"It is agreed, I shall show you the stronghold of the death-ones?"

"It is agreed, but I really need to go the Selenseh Redian. Ah, I don't know what you would call it? A cave full of — "

En-mek laughed. "The cave of the singing jewels?"

Singing? Liere thought. But she assented, thinking surely that had to be it.

He raised a hand, his wings lifting and whooshing softly, the great pinion feathers near the ends as long as her leg from knee to ankle. Intense curiosity had to be squashed as he said, "They are near enough, one to the other. We can do both."

He motioned for her to face forward, he gripped his arms firmly around her ribs, leaving her arms free, then edged over the cliff.

Once again she fell. She closed her eyes, stiffening all over — which she sensed made it easier for him as the powerful wings beat once, twice, their bodies jerking up and down. She kept herself rigid, the jerking eased, and then they sailed out, and up, out and up, occasional beats aiding the currents of air.

And so began an experience that almost reconciled her to the horrible Sartora, The Girl Who Saved the World legend rearing up again.

Strong as he was, he could not fly great distances carrying the weight of two. Liere was handed off to a different person at each stop, but they all seemed to think it an honor to lug her.

The first night she was taken to what seemed to be a mighty, hollowed-out tree. The "ceiling" was conical, and a strange greenish light filtered in from tiny windows. The tree was still alive, too — there was no smell of decay from the rough walls. Boards had been fitted into the natural spaces between the bole of the tree and where it ramified into great roots. Below that was hollowed-out ground. And on the other side of the room, an arch-shaped wooden door.

The next night she found herself housed in a cave smoothed to the high ceiling. Possibly a dragon cave incalculable millennia ago? They were certainly high enough in the mountains. Paintings of intricate patterns like woven knots decorated the walls around her. Little was said, though the people she saw treated her with great respect. Too much respect. It worried her, to be served first; she sensed such intense expectation, almost obligation, in the honor.

Then onward.

She gained a view of mountains from above, seeing the many sky-reflecting lakes, the falls, the occasional meadows crossed by animals, and the peaks and crags in their snow-blanketed loneliness. The vegetation had withered or retreated within bark and roots for the winter, so most of the mountain world was a thousand shades of white, pale blue, gray, and silver, dramatically contrasted by the dark green of fir, the spectacular striations of rock, often glittering in the cold, pale winter sun. Wind-polished spires and juts of frozen rock acted as sentinels against the constant, driving-cold wind.

The flying people did not all speak Sartoran, and those few who did were so laconic that even when she ventured quest-ions, she got short answers that left her with more questions. They had different names for pretty much everything, and demonstrated very little interest in the doings of flatlanders. What they wished for was to live in peace, and not be shot out of the skies.

So, though she flew in someone's arms during those amazing days, it was mostly in silence, and as she could not see the person, the journey felt curiously solitary.

Liere's last guide, an older man with a long beard but arms like tree branches, set her down on a cliff overlooking a frozen river gleaming like a silver chain curving back and forth through the mountains. The air, extraordinarily clear at this great height, revealed two branches of the winding river. Between these, built on a long, gradual slope, was a small city of the old fortress type: it looked like a tiny toy from this great distance.

Liere peered intently. Was that the sea, that pale line painted in the farthest distance? Then this must be Idego? Or maybe Visegn — she did not recollect the details of the map. She only knew she had come far, far north of Senrid's country. That toy city was completely enclosed in gray walls, and some of the houses were built right into the walls. In the middle of the city was a castle, constructed around a white tower that appeared to be made from that same strange glistening material that the strange white-stone palace in Mearsies Heili.

"Here is as close as I come. That flatlander city, now it is a place of the death-ones." His voice rumbled with disgust on the last five words. "The jewel cave is down this path, but too many flatlanders go there, so I must not."

Close? Perhaps it seemed that way from the sky. It would take her days just to get down this mountain, and at least a week to reach yon city, were she to want to go there. Which she most certainly did not.

"Thank you," Liere said. "I am so grateful."

"You are Sartora," he said, and his tone carried that same inflection that they all had. "Bring us peace."

"I am doing what I can," she said, knowing that what she could do and what they expected were as separated as these mountains from the sea.

He made a gesture, opening his hands, that she took as a farewell. She mirrored it, and he leaped into the air. His great wings flapped; his long hair and his draped clothes streamed as he sailed around a spire, and vanished into a cloud.

Time to descend, locate the caves, and — she hoped — find

Andri awaiting her.

The trail soon proved to be barely wide enough for a goat. Below the Selenseh Redian it might be a path humans could follow—she was imagining morvende coming this way for millennia—but above the caves, humans rarely came, judging by the steepness and the tumbles of old boulders.

She began picking her way among the rocks. After a long toil in the sinking sun, she could still look back and see where she'd been set down.

She then peered downward, and made out a broader path some distance below, as the flyer had said. She froze; the sound of horse hooves, so faint, must have registered somehow before she saw gray-coated figures riding in twos.

She jerked back, and began to slip-slide down the treacherous path to what she hoped was the Selenseh Redian. Weren't Norsundrians supposed to not be able to enter those caves?

She scrambled, falling twice, before she landed with a splat in the snow of a ledge pocked with footprints. Where was the cave—where was the cave—

Andri? Her thoughts flashed outward in a cry, a lightning bolt in the realm of the mind, but reaching from long habit for Senrid. She cut that off abruptly, returning her awareness to the physical world so fast she swayed, vertigo jolting her unpleasantly.

But she had not gone unheard.

She ran hard, looking desperately for any fissure or crack—

Footsteps, three, four—and a pair of hands clasped her waist, wrenched her off-balance, and let go. She tumbled face down in a drift.

Half-blinded with snow, she eeled out of a second grasp, but her assailant was faster, and caught hold of her arm in a painful grip as he pinned her legs down with a knee. She glared up into a face that seemed familiar for a heartbeat.

She knew two things: that this was Imry Llyenthur, and that she had never seen him face-to-face before. Was it in someone's memory? His eyes were the same spring green as Leander Tlennen-Hess's, and his grin was so smug that she wanted to smack him.

"Gotcha," he said, slanting his brows up under flyaway hair the light brown of ditch water, and waited.

There was no use in fighting. He was tall, his grip strong, and he had several weapons in easy reach. She'd have to dig under the snow, and her coat, to reach that forgotten knife.

Liere cast one glance past his shoulder at the cave. No Andri. He would never have let her get grabbed by the enemy, no matter how many of them there were. She slammed her reaction behind a mental door, and locked it.

Llyenthur pulled Liere to her feet as he said, "Isn't it amazing we haven't met before this?"

So he knew she knew who he was.

The watching Norsundrians, who had spread in a half-circle, closed in, blocking off the cave entrance, as Llyenthur tugged her down the broader path toward where they had left their horses.

The patrol remained behind, Liere noticed with a sinking sensation, before the cave slid out of view entirely. And then she understood what she had missed: the flyers, who did not have mind-shields, had said exactly what they believed, that they brought her here, expecting her to smite the "death-ones." Not necessarily the ones in the city, or maybe those too, but these ones right here. Because she was the Girl Who Saved the World in one dramatic spell. And Llyenthur had sensed them coming.

Meanwhile there was still his question; she caught the end of an inquiring glance. He actually seemed to be waiting for an answer.

"Considering the care I've taken to prevent us ever meeting, no," she said.

"Excellent care. Really, I had not expected it to take so long," he said in a congratulatory tone.

His voice was as timbreless as Kessler's, but unlike too, in that it was not husky or low, but tenor. She shrugged that off and considered possible escape as they reached the waiting horse.

Imry Llyenthur paused, peering around at the rocky spires, the blue sky, the snowy peaks. The world seemed to have gone still, not even a wind.

Llyenthur gave Liere an amused look, though the humor was in no way kind. "Liere, you have before you a choice. As you see, there is one horse per rider. Reputations precede even long-awaited guests, and my people are suspicious of your mighty powers. Ride with one of them, bound like a birthday package, or with me, free."

"I'd prefer the free, without you."

The amusement deepened around his eyes—still not kind—then he indicated she should mount. He climbed up behind her, and they rejoined the others.

Then they rode down the trail, no one speaking. She began to understand that this was a search. She was not the target. She had blundered into the target zone.

She was aware of breathing behind her, then Llyenthur said, "Whew, you stink like wet dog."

For answer, Liere lifted one arm, and waved the other hand at her armpit to fan the reek back in his direction; he uttered a short laugh, but distracted. He was listening, but not to her. She knew he had Dena Yeresbeth.

I am bait, she realized, hating herself for her stupidity and slowness. They're waiting for me to contact someone...or someone to contact me.

She had been so close to extending her awareness, but now she shut down hard on memory and emotion, raising her life-long polished mental shield.

And Llyenthur let go his breath. He slapped something against her arm. Transfer seized her violently, and thrust her into a round tower room.

Thirteen

Barban

THE SCENT OF SPRING flowers woke them.

June turned over and buried her face in the folds of velvet to block out light and smell, nice as it was. Her body ached all over from the digging.

Julian opened her eyes to walls covered by vines. Pale blue morning-blooms, the ones that are usually only seen in late spring, covered the wall, giving off their strong, heady scent.

Julian sighed and stretched. She folded her arms behind her head and stared at the glassless window, not really surprised at how warm the room was, despite the freeze outside. "Argh," she said softly.

June rolled over.

"Sore too?" Julian grinned.

June shrugged. "Imagine how the others must feel."

"I wonder if they're really being rescued." She sat up. "Well, now we're in for a different kind of trouble."

"Maybe it's time to tell me what's going on."

"I don't know what's going on."

"What can you tell me?"

"That girl. Name's Mar—no wait. Changed it. Honey-blossom. She was always nice enough, but—"

There was a knock at the door. "Yeah?" Julian yelled.

"Awake yet? The morning's half gone," came a voice.

"Yeah, yeah. We're getting up," Julian called.

June got up slowly and wandered to the windows. "Think the place is protected?"

"I know it is. By vagabond magic, which is especially powerful when groups do it. They obviously found new recruits, as the old gang got stripped of their magic, except for making illusions, which fall apart if you look hard at them." Julian patted her waist, where the coin belt rode beneath her clothes. "Any other type of magic you try, if it doesn't tip the Norsundrians off, will strengthen the vagabond spells, which feed on magic. We can't leave unless they let us. But if we work it right, they might send us anywhere we want to go."

"I thought they were 'the enemy.' Allies of Norsunder."

Julian shook her head. "It's...not quite that. Some are friends. *Were* friends." She paused, and ran her hands over her face. "The ones I've seen so far are the ones I liked most. I lived with them for two years. Most of them are orphans or from bad situations. I wanted to learn vagabond magic with them, but I hadn't gotten far when I discovered that there was a conspiracy within the group. They pretended to be so friendly. This is why I stay out of politics. Run if there's any sign of... You know how Liere got to Enaeran, and met Andri? It was because of me."

She stopped, scowling down at her hands.

"Is Norsunder in there somewhere?" June commented. She stretched out on silken pillows, figuring, might as be comfortable. Maybe a dungeon would be next.

Julian sighed. "A girl named Feliseh was chief of the group. She was the smartest, and knew a whole lot of magic. She was a great person besides. She started to work toward making the country a refuge for everyone. There was another girl, name of Harana, who led the conspiracy. Harana talked big about unity and freedom, but she wanted to be on top. That's where Norsunder comes in. At least, if she wasn't one, she should have been. She was as power-mad as any of these other chum-brains in gray coats. Told all kinds of lies so we thought she was devoted to Feliseh, then attacked her when they were alone."

"Who retaliated?"

Julian hunched up, her arms wrapped around her knees. "Feliseh was hurt bad. We hid and she made all these spells. When the others found us, they kept banging on the door, promising that they were misunderstood, they discovered too late that Harana as lying, that everything would be fine, just come out and talk. Feliseh handed me this coin belt, each coin binding the magic of Harana and her followers—so of course they'd be promising anything." She yanked up her tunic, showing the coin belt, then hiding it again.

"Ugh!"

"Before she collapsed, Feliseh opened the door, and told them that if the belt is taken from me by force, their magic would be destroyed." She sighed again. "They started polishing my heels, and promising anything. So I left, saying I'd check back in a year. And I meant to. But when a year passed I couldn't bear hearing the fake praise and promises again, from people I'd really liked. But now I couldn't believe a thing they said. Haven't been back until now. It was too much to hope they wouldn't have something worked out to let them know I was around." She stood up, and rubbed her temples. "Now I'm sure I'll have to face a repentant Harana. I never liked her in the first place. She was too much like my mother. Whatever she'll say, fake or genuine, it'll be just as nasty, because I will never believe it's real."

"No wonder you never take that belt off."

Julian started toward the door. "C'mon, let's get it over with. Leave your coat. Won't need it. Whole place'll be warm."

June shrugged and followed Julian out.

They were met with the petals-in-the-wind whirl of flute music. June had heard that winsome, sad melody before, and wondered what it was about. But music could be adapted for any purpose, including evil; she liked it, but didn't trust it. She didn't trust anything that reached right into your emotions, like it or not.

All along the balustrade flowers bloomed on vines. The ancient castle appeared to be alive with flowers, despite great gaping cracks. The marble stairs had been worn down in the center by centuries of feet.

In the huge hall, several people sat around the central table. At one end, a small girl had jury-rigged an easel, and was busy painting. The others looked up as Julian and June approached, but the girl went on painting, obviously completely absorbed.

"Hi Julian," said Honey-blossom, the girl with the light blue eyes. She looked questioningly at June.

Julian said almost brusquely, "June."

Julian took in the others. Her gaze swept round the table

for a second or two. She recognized everyone except the paint-er.

There was the tall, slim half-morvende Yovres. She remembered him being shorter than she was. Now he was the size of Adam of the poopsies. Why did Adam come to mind? Because their expressions were similar, the way their smiles reflected in their eyes. Not big grins, but kind. Forbearing. Her shoulders tightened; she didn't know if it was bad or good to be reminded of a poopsie.

Yovres's smile deepened at Julian's curt nod.

There was Honey-blossom, pale of face, black of hair, probably (they had guessed) all the way from the Land of the Chwahir. Not that she'd ever said. But everyone knew magic was forbidden to the people there, and she had a gift for magic.

Next to her, Dara, whose skinny thirteen-year-old body and bright orange-red hair hadn't changed at all. No surprise, as she had done the Child Spell. Dara and Yovres had been Julian's favorites—until they obeyed Harana.

Julian's expression soured as she took in the last one, the gorgeous Leela. She stood up, swung a long dark braid behind her back, and greeted Julian, all in one fluid motion. She'd grown too.

"Hi, Julian. Welcome back," Leela said, taking Julian's hands before Julian knew what she was about, and could put them behind her back.

Julian shook off her touch, not ungently. But firmly. She faced the group. "Where is she? Let's get it over with so we can leave."

"Who?" Dara said.

Honey-blossom tipped her head, her forehead puckered.

Leela's smile turned wistful.

Yovres thumped his elbows on the table, and his chin in his hands. "She means Harana."

The painter looked up. "Ugh." She went back to her painting.

"Harana is gone, Julian. Has been for…two years, I guess, huh?" Honey-blossom turned to the others. "More like three. We don't know where she is."

Julian made a face as though she obviously expected to see Harana's waving dark hair and round laughing face pop up. She swung a leg over a corner of the table and perched there, arms crossed hard over the coin belt. "Thanks for the rescue, anyway."

"We do what we can." Honey-blossom grinned.

"Then let us out of here. We're fighting the Norsundrians, and we have to get somewhere as soon as possible," Julian said baldly.

"We want to fight them, too," Dara said.

Julian gave her a disbelieving glare.

"We brought you here so you'd give us another chance," Yovres said. "As you can see, we've new people, who handle the magic. Nothing of Harana's plans has been carried out. Dara and I and the old group would like to be able to join them doing something besides stage illusions."

At the stony look on Julian's face, Dara burst out impatiently, "That's not fair! Judging us by old mistakes. We were lied to, too! And you left us before we could explain! Everything's diff—"

Yovres raised a hand, seeing Dara was about to embark on a tirade. From a distant corner of the castle, the echoes of another wind instrument—harmonizing with the flute—started up. "Julian, I'm sure you can understand our wanting to see you again. We will keep you here, but only for a couple days. Whether you change your mind or don't, I promise those of us who can, will send you as far as possible. So you can regain at least some of the traveling time you lost."

Julian turned a sullen look of inquiry at June, who shrugged. Julian laughed shortly. "What's it matter what I say? We're still stuck here, eh?"

Yovres lifted his chin so he could turn out his hands. "You're still stuck here. You did promise to return in a year."

Julian crossed her arms. "I decided that more lies wouldn't be any sweeter after rotting in your mouths for a year. Go ahead. Do your worst."

Dara laughed. "Want something to eat?"

"Wouldn't hurt."

June flicked a considering glance at Julian, whose face wore that tight expression that made her jaw scar writhe, and she was talking in that same half-sullen, half-indifferent voice she'd used after they found out about the Dthel Rendm gang's deaths.

Honey-blossom had been watching the painter, until she looked up and smiled. "By the way, how's Dtheldevor? We haven't seen her since you left last."

"She's dead. Norsundrians got her." Julian's voice flatten-ed.

Yovres's head turned sharply. He got up and disappeared soundlessly down a dark hallway.

Leela said, "By the way, Julian, this is Alian. She's the newest of us," drawing Julian's angry, aching gaze from Honey-blossom's stunned face, just before Honey-blossom's expression gave way to grief. She slipped from her place and stumbled blindly in the direction Yovres had gone, followed by two or three others.

Alian looked up. She had a round face and dark eyes. "Hi," she said rather mechanically.

She went back to work.

Julian's first, distrusting thought was that at least she was *honest*. But she knew that was unfair. That is, Alian didn't know Dtheldevor, and Yovres had been good friends with Joey Warren. Honey-blossom had been pals with Sarmonwilda, Dtheldevor's dawnsinger partner. Maybe their grief was real. Just because Julian didn't want to trust them didn't mean their emotions were fake.

But Harana's had been fake.

To get away from the subject, she leaned out and caught a glimpse of the picture, from which Honey-blossom's face laughed. The gown had already been painted in, red silk over a white under-dress. There were slits in the red around the shoulders, where the sleeve was joined to the bodice, and tiny puffs of white had been pulled through. Her blue-black hair lay in waves over her shoulders and disappeared down her back.

Julian looked away just as Dara entered, carrying an ornate silver tray that she set on the table.

"Egg-cakes. With lots of cheese. *And* summer-steep," Dara said in a subdued voice, as she set two plates out, some heavy silverware, and two bone-white porcelain cups and saucers.

June and Julian sat down and dug in. June sensed Julian's closed off mood, so she waited, enjoying the hot food as she'd enjoyed the soft bed. Alian deftly painted the red and gold embroidery around the neck of the white under-dress.

Julian broke the silence. "What happened to Harana?"

"We voted her out, what, three years ago? She kept insisting she'd changed, but we caught her in lies, and she did sneaky things. Always had a reason, even if her reasons would make your head spin, but you remember, at the center of every utterance she was always the hero."

"And we believed it." That was Yovres, in the background, still upset.

"She sounded so reasonable," Dara muttered. "And she was always asking Feliseh if she could help her, and telling her how wonderful she was. That was the scariest part."

"*So* true." Leela sighed. "As far as we know, she disappeared. Wherever she is, it's not in Barban. We'd know."

Dara turned to June. "Do you like our castle?"

"Pretty old, isn't it?"

"Yep. Ancient. The old stories say that it was built almost six thousand years ago, long before the Fall, but that's probably just the exaggeration of handed-down tales."

Julian glanced at the uneven stone in corners mossy with age. She didn't know much about history. Didn't care. But you couldn't visit Eidervaen and not see that single tower at the west end of the royal palace, which looked like it had been made of a combination of ice and moonlight. That thing was definitely six thousand years old.

"Everybody has different ideas. But you have to try the tall tower. Maybe you'll see what I mean." Dora's eyes reflected the sunlight from the gaps in the ceiling. "Why don't you look around? Feel free to go anywhere in the castle. Not too many of us are around. We do an awful lot of spying on the Norsundrians. We want to ensure that plan of theirs fails." She gathered all the dishes together, flapped a braid back over her shoulder, and bounded away.

Leela said, "The tower stairs are that way," and went back to watching Alian.

June wandered toward the carved arch Leela had pointed out, an arch rounded by time, or something, at the top, so that it was more like those moon doors you saw in some gardens on Earth. Beyond it lay a stairway, the stone steps old and worn, the light slanting down a diffuse shimmer, as if someone had hung the thinnest gauze, then lit it on fire. No, not on fire, it was more like the light reflected in water, both pure and liquid.

Either side of the stairway the narrow, arched windows — June suspected they were from a different century than that round doorway — had long been overgrown by ivy, filtering pinpricks of greenish light.

June started toward the stair, her hands outstretched, as if she could catch that light, as if it might pool in her fingers, warm and soft. That was such a weird thought. She usually didn't have thoughts like that. In fact, when other people yammered on about the beauty of light, she wondered who was impressed. Not her. She'd always claimed the dark was her home. Where she belonged.

Well, that life was...not here. She'd made herself a promise that she wouldn't think about Earth, or the stupid things she'd done just to prove how rotten life there was — and that she could be rottener.

Her footsteps hissed on the stones. The silence closed around her, deep, deeper. The light intensified as she wound slowly up the stairs, then entered a round room with windows at all four cardinal points. The stone was just stone, gray, old, grungy in the grouting. The weird thing was, all four windows streamed with golden light, warm as milk. June's head buzzed faintly, as if she were in an elevator going down very fast, so she moved to one of the windows, and laid her hands on the sill.

It was carved in a stylized pattern; as she ran her fingers over the knotwork, she gazed out. The light — golden, intense, but not quite a glare — shimmered. The ruined walls, gapped and empty, blurred with finished walls pale as mable, with statuary at corbels, and below in the courtyard, people strolled along, the folds of their clothes reminding her kind of like drawings of Persian silks, but kind of not. Bits of jewelry at wrists and on heads glinted in the sun.

She peered down below. A gusty breeze whipped the headdress of a woman giving orders to a man with a cart of vegetables; she beat impatiently at her billowing apron. A small child of about three ran past them, chubby arms spread wide and face turned up as if he expected to take off any moment. June thought it was a boy, though that curly hair cut close to the child's head could have belonged to a girl. The child wore only a loose tunic, below which bare feet twinkled.

A woman two windows away leaned out, sunlight glowing on loose strands of dark hair with reddish highlights as she laughed at the child in the courtyard. She wore an elaborate gown full of folds and drapes, the outer draperies edged with tiny gems that gathered light and glowed. The little boy reached the end of the courtyard and hustled around the perimeter to try again. This time he ran on his toes and arched his back, moving with a grace that suggested some practice.

Bare feet. No snow. How could it possibly be summer? June whirled around. The four windows still streamed with light, but the smooth pale stone hid behind tall bookcases between each window, with a row of tapestries above. Covering the floor, a carpet woven in patterns of golden hares chasing around green.

At the other end of the round carpet, a pair of shoes. Belonging to a girl June's age.

This girl stared, her hands still as if she'd been told to freeze. The girl had a round, brown face and dark almond-shaped eyes, her hair dark also, parted in the middle and pulled smoothly back to a gold clasp at the nape of her neck. She wore a scoop-necked white underdress with an overdress of deep blue, almost black silk of a lustrous kind June had rarely seen. All the edges were embroidered in gold, including the edges of the knee-length sleeves.

She spoke, but June heard nothing. The deep silence had obscured the snapping of banners on the walls, the little boy's laughter, the woman with the headdress talking, and this girl, but June had not been aware until now: she could hear nothing but her own heartbeat.

The girl smiled slightly at June and, with a tiny shrug, sat down at the table and pulled a heavy, open book toward her. The lettering was vertical, right to left, instead of horizontal, left to right. The girl started reading, her finger moving rapidly down the columns.

June became aware of flute music again, coming from far away.

When she turned toward the stair to identify the source, there was the dark, empty tower room again, somehow closer, but that could be the effect of the uneven, moss-dulled stone.

June knew what was happening: once again, she had fumbled smack into a Worldgate.

The light began to fade, as if the sun had gone behind a cloud.

Cold — chilled to shivering — June ran down the stairs.

A burst of laughter surrounded her as she reached the main room. Dara and some other teens crowded around the table, on which posed a boy with white hair. He wore a ragged purple silk pirate-shirt embroidered with swooping birds with long, trailing wings and tail feathers. His face flushed with laughter as he arched his back in a "heroic" pose. Alian seemed to be sketching him.

"I don't want to be remembered like this," he was protesting. "Even for a joke."

Everyone laughed again.

"All you have to say now is 'But I'm not like this,' and you'll finish us off," Leela said, mock-solemn.

"Well, I'm not," the white-haired boy protested.

"Do the shirt justice," Alian said. It was the second time June'd heard her speak.

"What's wrong with my shirt? It's just a plain old work shirt."

The hoots, cackles, and howls that arose reverberated around the stone walls. June crossed the room when she saw Julian standing in another doorway. Julian smiled thinly as June approached. "Hi. Go up into the tower?"

June nodded.

"See the ghosts?"

"Yep," June said, thinking, ghosts? Actual ghosts, or a local idiom for Worldgates?

"That's Gislian, Yovres' brother. A big show off, but nice enough," Julian said in a low voice. June noticed Julian's eyelids were rimmed red.

There was a step behind them, and Yovres said, "I see my brother is posing again. They just return?" His eyelids were red, too.

Julian did not turn his way. "Yep. And Alian asked him to do the pose. For her 'portrait of the group.'"

Yovres said, "We'll celebrate tonight. A memorial for Dtheldevor, a celebration for you. After the sun goes down."

Julian shrugged, a tight movement. "Nothing to celebrate."

"You came back," Yovres said. "You came back."

The celebration happened after supper.

There was one boy with a clear, beautiful voice who seemed to be leading things. All the songs had complicated melodies reminiscent of the flute music Julian and June had heard earlier. Ruddy light glowed from the huge fireplace on the far side of the room, and from the eight or nine tall candles on the table opposite, so as to minimize shadows. When a couple of the girls finally got up and danced together, the candlelight glistened on their worn dresses, flattering them into court gowns, and painted warmly over their hair and skin and in their eyes.

Presently several children brought out instruments, and everyone danced.

That is, everyone but June, who always felt too self-conscious to rubber around a room waving her arms and legs, and Julian who just stood, hands cupping her elbows, shoulders up under her ears.

At the end an older girl danced with a long scarf that kept floating in swirling circles around her as she turned and leaped.

That seemed to inspire the rest, or maybe they had been gathering their strength. The memorial celebration was over, and Julian stalked up the stairs toward the room they'd been given, June trailing after. She looked back once. The others had gathered in a great circle; the glow of magic scintillated in the air as three of the bigger children vanished — to go rescue someone from one of those horrible work camps, June hoped.

The steps carried her around another turn and the great hall disappeared from view. She thought about the words of some of the songs. Most had been adventure ballads, but several were about ideas — peace, longing for freedom, friendship, joy in harmony. Things she had always believed didn't exist.

Fourteen

Ghildraith Mountains (northern)

TWO DAYS BEFORE LIERE'S capture, Andri and Macael reached a promontory that overlooked the long river valley of Lorgi Idego.

They paused to gnaw cold, hard bread and cheese before picking their way across the frozen river, and as their horses crunched and crackled up the other side of the ancient banks, Andri asked, "You mentioned a relation in these parts. I see a fork up ahead. My guess is, if this isn't the border, it leads in the right direction. This might be where you head for safety in Idego." Andri pointed off toward the right. "As you saw back there, any chase is after me."

"I'll stay for now. For one thing, I am easily lost. For another, I want to understand what this Selenseh Redian is. I know I've heard the term. I've been picturing some sort of magical monument. But did you, or someone, say cave?"

"I don't know either, except that it's high in the mountains. Guess I'll find out."

Andri clucked to his horse and they rode toward the rocky hills beyond the river. They came to the fork, each half leading to a different notch between treacherous hills.

Andri scanned as their horses picked their way up the narrow path on the left. No sunlight penetrated into the steep and uneven gorges. There was very little snow here, but the air seemed oppressively heavy with the cold—almost frozen solid—no sound outside of the thud and crunch of horse hooves, the snorting breathing of the horses and the creaks and muted chings of their saddles and trappings.

For a time, Andri rode with his eyes closed as he struggled to maintain his mind-shield and listen beyond it, the way Liere had explained. He was used to using his hands, but there was no using hands in this situation.

*Some*thing was wrong. He was absolutely certain he'd sensed Liere, a quick, startled thought and then nothing. Nothing. Nothing.

He fought the vertigo that worsened the longer the horse jolted and jogged and his mind jolted in another direction, until he was taken by a terrible fit of coughing. When it finally subsided he struggled for breath. His eyes widened in a startled look, then he fell slowly backwards, right off his horse. He landed on his back in the snow, arms outflung and one toe caught in the stirrup. As an afterthought his dagger slid out of his boot and landed with a quiet "chuff!" in the snow.

Macael flung himself off his horse and knelt in the snow beside Andri, wondering what he should do.

Andri's coat had fallen open, and the brandy flask fell out of the inner pocket. Macael pulled it out, uncorked it, and held the thing near Andri's nose. A few drops splashed out and ran down Andri's cheek into his ear. At that his face twitched and his eyes opened. He stared at Macael. Then his eyes crinkled and a flush of embarrassment brought some color into his cheeks—the first Macael had seen since the fight at the inn.

"Ho, that's the stupidest stunt I've pulled in a while." He sat up and wiped his cheek against his shoulder. "Damn."

Macael sat back on his heels. "Perhaps we should abate our pace a little."

Andri shook his head and took a mighty swig. "I wasn't unconscious. I was dizzy." He retrieved his knife, and pulled his foot free. "Let's ride. Can't go on much longer like this."

"Obviously. Your illness has long been past—"

"Nah. Isn't that by itself. Told you, I've had colds before. It's the cold and the bloodknife games and being on the run. I'll make it if I lose at least one. But it's going to have to be soon," he added this last under his breath.

It was late afternoon when they rounded a cliff and got a sudden and breathtaking view of a mountain lake, surrounded by a dark forest stretching downwards and away west, and in the distance a ribbon of frozen river, shining golden in the hazy late-afternoon sunlight. Here and there lay clusters of buildings, tiny villages: from this distance everything looked whole and lovely. The evidence of human wars would not be obvious till they were down amongst the wounds. It was as if the land were asleep, or waiting, and under its snow, the healing going on slowly and unnoticed.

Healing of the land, that is. The people of Idego on one side of the spine of mountains, and of Visegn on the other, had resisted the Norsundrians with all their strength. But it hadn't been enough. The towns were occupied and the reddish haze in the sky warned of a dark magic ward.

Andri's brief search in the realm of the mind reached only angry, frightened people who were suspicious of newcomers; from the glimpses of memory he gained the impression that the treatment of the Idegans' resistance had been exceptionally heavy-handed. He and Macael had to camp in a cave, but he made a large vagabond fire to ward off the bitter cold. As soon as they ate, Andri curled up under his tattered cloak and fell asleep. His breathing was harsh and loud, and Macael, not inclined to sleep in the middle of the afternoon, watched the fire.

Next morning, Andri only spoke once, a wheezy croak. "Keep your sword in reach. Place should be crawling. We're leaving the most obvious of trails."

They rode steadily. There were tracks going in all directions through the forest, which worried Macael. They could be days old, depending on when it snowed last — or they could be fresh. The way Andri squinted around made it obvious he had a crashing headache. Macael kept one hand on his sword hilt.

They stopped at noon to feed the horses. Macael eyed Andri's torpor, reluctant to speak. But Andri was quite alert, focused on thuds and crackling ice somewhere off to the right. "Let's make a run for it." He urged his horse into a gallop.

The animals were too tired for much of a race. Their pursuers gained easily on them. The run seemed pointless, but Macael obeyed.

Just as their horses hit the mushy snow in a clearing Andri yelled, "Now!" He yanked his sword and knife free, dropped his reins in his lap, and wheeled his horse with his knee.

Macael had never trained for fighting on horseback. He was disarmed within two strokes and yanked off his horse. He fell headfirst into the snow with his sword hilt digging into his stomach. Hands grabbed roughly at his arms, wrenched them behind him, and wound tight ropes around his wrists. Then he was pulled to his feet and yanked staggering backwards.

Andri still fought. His horse pranced round and round in a circle, then plunged flat-eared here and there between the Norsundrians' horses. Andri's sword and knife flashed with amazing speed, and Macael could see one badly wounded gray-coat drop away.

In a flurry of fast action someone got behind him long enough to strike from one side, and when Andri back-handed a parry, someone else attacked from the other side, low and hard, unseating him from the horse.

He fell, a pile of bodies flinging themselves on top of him.

When he was bound up, someone gave him a cursory pat down, exclaiming, "Whew! Piss-Hair here reeks even worse than Black-Hair there. Oh, what's this?" The rough hand yanked out the brandy flask.

Andri croaked, "Leave that!" He coughed. "I need it! Even Llyenthur'd grant that, once he sees this cold!"

One of the enemy snorted. "Think you're somebody, if y' think he'll waste his time on the likes o' you."

Another gray-coat barked a couple short words in Norsundrian, and the two Elsarions were forced to mount again, riding without hands as enemies held the reins

They trotted north for a time, till they reached a small town serving as a local outpost. Though it was midafternoon, the place looked deserted—all the doors closed, first story windows shuttered. They rode to a large, dilapidated building in the center of the town. Guards standing around it and boards over the ground-floor windows proclaimed it as the local lockup. The Elsarions and their entourage dismounted at the entrance and tramped up the ancient, weather-warped stairs and in, while a couple of the guards led the horses away.

The two were locked in a room. There was a narrow wood-slat bed against one wall, with a worn and dirty-looking straw mattress on it. As this was the only furnishing, they both sat down, Macael warily.

Andri dropped in his usual careless manner and leaned his shoulders against the wall, so he was half sitting and half lying. He thumped his bootheels on the floor to get the snow off, then smiled at Macael. "Could be worse. They don't know who we are."

"You deduced this from that ruffian's remark?"

"Yep. It's why I said that about Llyenthur and the flask. They were acting on a general order against all travelers. In which case, we should be able to get out when we're ready."

"I wondered why you fought against obviously over-whelming odds."

Andri shrugged. "Always fight. Can't just tamely let 'em take me — besides, they're usually hampered by orders to take me alive." He shrugged and smiled, making the next statement obvious. "If someday they don't have such orders, rather go down fighting."

Macael shook his head. "I have no taste for battle."

"For a pacifist, you do pretty well for yourself."

"Not today, I did not."

"Neither did I." Andri winced and grinned ruefully as he flexed his left hand behind him.

"I was impressed today by the way you handled Bayleaf. He responded as though he'd been trained, but I know he wasn't."

"I've been training him to my signals all along. Best friend Gared taught me to ride. His father was my father's Master of Horse. Wasn't anything either of them couldn't ride. Mind if I try to catch a little sleep? Suspect it'll be a long night —"

"And you have a severe headache; that's obvious. Please, go ahead. Shall I remove myself to the floor?"

"Nah. Gonna stay like this. Easier on the arms. Breathe easier with my head up." He leaned his head into the corner in a way Macael found uncomfortable just to look at, and shut his eyes. Before long he was slumped in sleep, mouth hanging open and breath rasping.

Macael finally got up and tiptoed to the window. Andri stirred but didn't wake. There was not much to be seen: half a street of weather-beaten and empty-looking buildings, and an occasional guard on horseback or on foot, but he preferred that view to staring at the rough wooden walls of their room. He also felt better standing than sitting.

The door was suddenly unlatched and pushed open.

The gray-coat in the doorway jerked his head towards the hall. "Out."

They were escorted by three armed guards in front, three behind, and motioned into a long room with a couple tables and some unmatched furniture scattered around. Seated behind one of the tables was a gray-coated Norsundrian. His head was bent as he wrote steadily.

Andri hooked his toe round the leg of a nearby padded chair, yanked it over, and sat.

The Norsundrian looked up. He was around their age. "You were not told to sit," he said in the local dialect, which was close enough to their tongue.

Andri shrugged. "I'm sick. Will it impress you if I pass out amongst your papers?"

"What are your names?"

"Antivad and Goat," Andri said—giving the names a Sartoran pronunciation.

The man blinked, then wrote them down phonetically. "Why are you traveling?"

"Looking for warm weather, to cure this cold!" Andri said, with a fatuous smile.

"There is a law against traveling without permission or identity papers, and another against bearing weapons. You have broken it, and will be executed at dawn in the local public square."

"No doubt a common occurrence." Andri leaned his head back. "Goat, we have risen from miscreants to martyrs, and we didn't have to do any work."

The Norsundrian waved a disgusted hand and returned to his writing. The attendant guards—one wearing a once-fine green coat (made for someone taller and with shorter arms), and blue riding trousers embroidered in yellow down the outer seam, the other wearing dull brown except for a rose-pink knit scarf—pulled Andri out of his chair and motioned Macael out of the room.

Once they were locked up again, Andri sank down onto the bed and stretched out full length on his stomach.

"How very pointless," Macael said. "It was so obvious we'd lie."

"Wasn't listening. One look at my filthy clothes and my bumpkin conduct, and he assumed we couldn't possibly be on a capital list. I feel like horseshit, Macael. Wake me after the sun goes down. Come midnight, I want to have a plan ready for escape."

"A plan?" Macael repeated; the reality of their situation had begun to catch up with him.

"We could kick our way out of this flimsy room now, but

I've no mind to travel without weapons and mounts. That means a plan. Don't look at me like that. It's just that I've been getting out of worse scrapes than this for years." He studied Macael's face. "You still look angry."

"No, I'm more disappointed with myself for being so useless."

"Look, there's no mystery here. It's a matter of, of habit. There's only about six guards, mostly local hirelings, I suspect, on the inner perimeter. We saw all six walking us because they were bored. No sentries on the roofs, or guarding Witless back there."

"I see. Go on."

"We wait till late, when the night shift is tiredest, before the next shift comes on duty. Two at the most we'll have to deal with, if we're quiet. We can take their weapons. How: in the inside shoulder of this coat I have a small knife. You can get it out, we can cut these ropes, and we can lift the bolt with the knife. There's no one outside this room—they aren't that worried about us. Executions are unfortunately a common occurrence here, or I woulda got a rise of some sort out of Witless. Experience. If we keep on like this much longer you'll know as much as I do. All y'need is a memory."

Andri's voice kept getting hoarser and hoarser as he talked, but his speech had its effect. Some of the tension left Macael's body as he stood looking down at Andri.

"What about our horses? I don't want to leave Firefly or Bayleaf to these mercenaries, or Norsundrians, or whoever they are."

"If we can't get to your horses, they won't be badly treated here. Didn't you see that coming in? Could be orders have gone down about that, especially now that they can't bring reinforcements over from Norsunder's mysterious otherwhere. Not saying that makes it right. Only that the decent treatment might make losing them bearable."

Nothing would make losing his horses bearable, but Macael saw the futility of arguing with someone who had lost everything as a child, and who clearly shrugged off the matter of possessions. "Who told you that about Selenseh Redian curing you? I mean, is it a believable source?"

"Her name is Liere." Andri smiled and shut his gritty-looking eyes.

"Not *the* Sartora, by any chance?"

Andri's eyes opened again at the surprise in Macael's voice. "Adon Marsael threw that in your face, huh? I'm amazed."

"I hadn't believed it. Even if I'd been inclined to lend credibility to his words, reports of you, from sources that I did trust, would have convinced me he was lying."

"What did he tell you? She stepped in and, with one wave of her hand, wrested Enaeran from Adon's well-meaning clutches, no help from me?"

"I believe that was the gist of it. Not that I lend any credence to Adon Marsael's view of events. It's more that I find it difficult to equate someone who consorts with kings, who did rescue the world from Norsunder in one stroke, with…" Too late Macael saw that he had talked himself into a corner.

"…with the likes of me, eh?"

"On the contrary," Macael retorted in the same tone. "I am given to understand, judging by songs and plays, that banditry is at least as sure an attraction as a pleasing countenance. The air of danger being irresistible."

Andri smiled reminiscently in the darkness. "I'd rather believe my success due to my astoundingly handsome face and my fine taste in hats. One of which I wish I had now. In any case, Liere's far more likely to point out helpfully I can't be dangerously irresistible because my nose is too red."

Macael laughed at that, a soft, breathy sound. Then said, "It's more that I don't understand how she would even end up in Enaeran at all, And then, though I don't believe Marsael's denigrations, it does seem you were living on the streets. How would you even meet someone like her? Or is all that about riding a horse of lightning and so forth the hyperbole of tales fostered by balladeers?"

"Oh, the horse made of lightning is true enough, according to her. They went back to their world. Remember the night of the new star?"

"Yes. Erhal's fifth world. It was said that it had been there all along, but masked by Norsunder magic."

"Right. Too bad those horses couldn't have waited around a few years. We could sure use them now." Andri shut his eyes again. He swallowed a couple times, which was visibly painful, then said abruptly, "Time to cut the ropes. Too dark for 'em to see, should they step in. Which is unlikely — wasting food on the doomed." Andri sighed, and sat up with a grunt of effort.

"Left sleeve, just inside the seam. Chest side."

After a long and tense period of awkward fumbling past limbs getting in the way—reminding Andri of adolescent attempts at sex with more than one other person, with absolutely none of the fun—Macael finally got his fingers on the knife. Andri took it from him, being more practiced at unseen-rope-sawing, and as soon as he was free he uncorked his flask and took such a long swig his eyes started to water.

"Whew! More like it!" he gasped, and cut Macael free. "If they come in, hands behind you, so keep that rope wrapped round one wrist. Now I'm going to catch a little badly needed sleep. I'll wake you up at midnight, after Llyenthur—at least, I hope it'll be he—leaves."

"Why do you want to be harassed by him? I thought he was the worst of their sort."

"Nah. Near enough, I s'pose. Anyway, s'morning I was able to read a little of his emotion behind the magical attack. Triumphant about something. Want to see if I can catch a hint about what."

Silence fell. Macael sat against the bed on which Andri lay. He rubbed his abraded wrists, suppressing complaint, as Andri said nothing about what had to be added discomfort. He crooked his arm, laying it over the corner of the rough bed and rested his head on his arm. Andri's snoring sawed away...

He sat up with a jerk and lifted his head. Andri was still lying flat, but no longer snoring. Andri's eyes were open, catching a glint of reflected torchlight from the window.

"Sorry," Andri whispered.

"Quite all right." Macael realized Andri had said something abruptly. "Norsundrians?"

"Something's going on."

"You heard it? How? I don't hear anything."

"Dena Yeresbeth," Andri said, to which Macael looked blank.

Which answered that question; Liere had said that some people had natural mind-shields. She'd had one herself, as a child. Marten as well. As Dena Yeresbeth began to spread in the world again, mind-shields would become habit for all.

Footsteps thudded beyond the door, which was so thin and warped it did not muffle sound. Then voices. "I'm telling you, word is there are a couple of princes in disguise running in the hills. If these are them, we stand to be promoted out of night patrol altogether. Why let Fart Face take all the credit, as usual? Wouldn't you like to sit at a nice warm desk, and send everybody else fetching and carrying?"

"Let's see about that."

Some fumbling noises, then the door banged open. Torchlight flared in the background, rendering the interlopers as silhouettes. The foremost one made an imperious gesture with a sword, and said as menacingly as possible, "We had word two foreign princes might be running in the region. Those fool Chwahir did not see through your disguises—"

"Maybe because we're not disguised," Andri said, and launched to the attack, using a slat he'd pulled up from the bed. The speaker went down, alive or dead, Macael did not know. He stood, doing his best to follow the action, which was a confusion of limbs and grunts and curses, the torchlight throwing wild shadows over everything before dropping altogether.

Andri kicked the torch into the room, where two of the prospective desk jockeys lay groaning, and gestured for Macael to follow.

"Get the horses," he said in Sartoran. "I think those four were on the sneak. So tay quiet. I'm going to find us some weapons."

Macael was going to ask where the stable was, then remembered the direction their horses had been taken. He ran along the side of the building, his heart beating rapidly against his ribs. But he encountered no one. Andri's guess had been right, so far.

No one was in the stable, which was lit by one small hanging lamp. In its dim light he looked everywhere for his fine saddles, then realize the obvious. Of course the conquerors would swap out shabby gear for the finer belongings of prisoners, especially those condemned.

He chose the best of the remaining saddles, and had gotten Firefly ready when Andri showed up again, with swords and knives, and a sack slung over his shoulder.

"I just need to saddle—"

"No time," Andri said. "I'll ride bareback." He grabbed the halter rope and vaulted to Bayleaf's back. The young stallion knew Andri's ways by now. Andri guided Bayleaf out, Macael on Firefly close behind; he'd gained enough experience to spot, and grab, a pair of feedbags and a stack of horse cakes. Banditry, he decided, is easier than one might assume.

Fifteen

Norsunder HQ - Larkadhe

LIERE TESTED FOR WARDS: no transfers.

Llyenthur left her alone for two days, locked in a high tower room with a sentry posted outside the door, and nothing but a jug of water.

After inspecting every stone minutely for some method of escape, Liere settled down to a routine of sleep, exercise, and when she got hungry, meditation from behind a mental shield as solid as cast iron. Disgusted, Llyenthur observed this from a distance while he got on with his endless tasks. Whatever was said about her whining and clinging years ago, it was patently no longer true.

On the third day, he transferred back from a shakedown of his organization in Alcandamer, and a futile attempt to discover who the commander was of the organized and trained forces harassing the Fhlerians occupying Ralanor Veleth. He'd let that one solve itself; the Fhlerians, despite their gaudy uniforms, were just as vicious on the field as the Velethi.

He asked for a report, and discovered that no one had turned up attempting to rescue Liere fer Eider. He ran down to the cell where she'd been locked up. He slammed in, a squad of sentries at his heels.

Liere had been working through a Geth knife form very slowly, as she had not eaten in two days, and that last meal had been scant enough. She looked frail, but looks, Llyenthur knew quite well, could be deceptive.

He sighed. "Let's skip the interview," he said, and fast as a striking snake took hold of her wrist. She blocked half a heartbeat too late and twisted to wrench free, but he leaned into the move and used her own velocity to yank her arm up behind her. Then, with smiling expertise, he jerked until two cracks sent pain like lightning bolts through her.

He let go. She staggered, her knees jellying as she struggled not to puke.

At the look on her face he said, "Cheer up. It could have been a knee."

He walked out. The door shut.

Dizzy, nauseated with pain, she crouched down, exerting all her control as her arm throbbed like iron-work thrust into the heart of a fire.

She was not there long. The door opened again, and an old man wearing a dark tunic entered. His face was set, his mouth thin as he extended a hand. "I'm a healer," he said tightly.

Efficiently, with gentle fingers, he set and bound her arm.

After that, someone brought in a bowl of pickled cabbage over fried fish and rice, which she suspected was what the garrison got. They also replenished her water.

After eating and drinking, she gratefully lay down. But sleep eluded her at first. Had she kept her mind-shield tight when he broke her arm? She was very uncertain about that; had she uttered the mental equivalent of a yelp?

The day wore on, back to the previous routine.

Ghildraith Mountains (north)

Andri and Macael got out of town just as the alarm bell clanged. The outpost chief sent the searchers south, having gotten it stuck in his mind that southern princes were of course running for home, and as a storm blasted through, pelting hail and sleet against fugitives and searchers alike, Andri and Macael escaped.

They worked their way around in a circle before resuming their trail. But not long after that, Andri called a halt. A very old plinth, mostly covered with ivy, caught his eye. Or more correctly, not the plinth itself, but a softly glowing character inscribed? — painted? — somehow imposed on it. This character was reminiscent of the Sartoran word for gem, but different.

And it glowed.

"Do you see that?" Andri asked, tipping his head toward the plinth.

Macael glanced back down the trail, apprehensive of pursuit. Then he peered at the stone glistening in the early morning light. "Rock. Ivy."

"You don't see the character?"

"I see nothing carved, though there is a crack near the top, but it's still so dark…"

"You don't see it glowing?"

"No."

Andri was about to point out that the glow was a lot like the streamers in the air that seemed to tangle with his fire-making, but then remembered that Macael was not able to perceive those, either. "I must be seeing things," Andri muttered. "Maybe another fever coming on. I almost hope it is. Then I wouldn't feel so damn cold. Let's —"

That's when a returning night patrol rode down the trail from above.

Andri had a heartbeat's warning, then the patrol and the two escapees eyed one another, the tired Norsundrians — local mercenaries with a gray-coated Norsundrian at their head — startled. Then the leader said, "Arrest them."

"All right, you road apples, come get me," Andri honked, raising his sword.

He remembered then that he was riding bareback. Which meant he had no stirrups to jam his heels into. One good blow and they'd knock him right off the horse's back.

About five dark figures rode towards him. Andri swung his blade, and got an idea. If the twigs didn't burn…he pulled the glowing currents out of the air, and set them ablaze along the blade he'd stolen. He swung it, and crowed as fire streamed off the steel.

The Norsundrians scrambled back, but not fast enough. Andri's horse plunged among them as he swung right and left, slinging flame in a circle. When he brought his hands up, shouting in his mind, *Rise!*, the flames leaped to tree-height, forcing the enemy to flee back to their camp, where they gabbled about mages prowling around. Their leader, veering between fear of enemy mages and fear of what might happen if he reported the failed arrest, decided that the prudent course was to keep his mouth shut. To the patrol, he said, "Unless you want to be turned into tree stumps, or something worse, we don't know anything."

They agreed, their general feeling summed up by one who muttered, "I signed on for loot, not chasing up in the ice after mages flinging fire around."

Their prudence became Andri's and Macael's protection as they fled up the thickly forested trail.

Once again Andri spotted a glowing character, this time carved into the bole of a huge cedar. He followed the ancient, overgrown path marked out by these characters, as Macael toiled grimly behind him, both unaware that this path was completely unknown to the invaders busily prowling the known paths.

They traveled all day, camped out of the wind for the night, then set out with first light.

Finally the mysterious signs led them up a windy trail along the side of a sheer cliff face. The trail began to wind upwards again as they reached a mountain whose summit was lost in the clouds. The way was rockier and steeper, but they made much better speed; any snow had been scoured off the ledge by the icy winds. The trail was narrow, with dizzying drops beyond the edge.

At noon wisps of cloud drifted down, obscuring the trail here and there. This slowed but did not stop them till they reached a sort of plateau. The shadows had lengthened into elongated shapes that had begun to meld. The trail widened beyond a short tunnel of rock, into a flat place a hundred paces wide or so.

Ahead, suspended a long bridge of planks and rope.

"Oh, no," Macael said, halting. His horse laid her ears back. She did not like it either.

Andri eyed that bridge. "It's here. It has to be stable, or why make it?"

Macael leaned out. He couldn't even see the ground below.

"Tell you what," Andri suggested, squinting skyward, because he didn't like the looks of the bridge either. But it seemed to be the only way to get him where he was going. "Let's camp here. Deal with it come morning. We'll feel better after a meal."

"I suspect I'll only feel better if I waken and discover that that thing was a bad dream," Macael observed.

"We'll risk a fire," Andri said. "We haven't seen an enemy all day, so I'm going to assume there's no one to see the firelight."

Andri brandished the bag he'd taken from the outpost, which he'd been rationing. He rooted inside it, and pulled out one of two loaves of bread, which had squashed dismally flat during the ride. A crumbling pepper-fish pie was also there, mostly chunks by now.

To the two of them, after a judicious toasting of the bread and pie pieces, it looked like the finest meal in the world. The horses even got warmed horse cakes.

"That magic," Macael said at length.

Andri shook his head. "I really don't know how to explain it better than I have."

Macael had to accept that. But he promised himself, if he lived through this adventure, he was going to find somewhere to learn magic.

Sixteen

MORNING BROUGHT DIM LIGHT. The bridge was still there. They hadn't dreamed it.

They ate the crumbs in the bag. By then the eastern horizon had begun to blue, revealing a solid bank of clouds that appeared to be directly overhead. "I'll go first," Andri said.

He slung the sword over his back, dismounted, and walked carefully out along the bridge. It actually didn't sway. Magic? Probably.

He ran back. "I'm going to cover Bayleaf's eyes. He'll be better not seeing it," he said. "Ah, except I don't seem to have anything to use…"

The winter sun had crested the northeast peaks as the two started out, Macael's fine scarf ripped in half and tied over the animals' eyes. Firefly and Bayleaf stepped carefully, trusting steady hands on halter and bridle.

The bridge was perhaps thirty long paces, but surprisingly steady. When they were about halfway across, a patch of spiderweb fog drifted down, and up beyond it the clouds parted. A sudden shaft of sunlight shot down across the left side of the chasm, spilling dazzlingly into the depths below, and reflecting off a frozen stream so far down it looked like a silver bracelet lying at someone's feet. Then, just as suddenly, it was gone as the clouds merged again, and the brilliant light was swallowed up in the gloom.

But they were across. The path narrowed to a goat trail, zigzagging down. The horses stepped carefully, as did Andri and Macael. If it got any worse, Andri thought grimly, he'd have to admit he'd gotten them lost.

But then the goat path dumped them onto a wider path. After following that for a time, they came across an ancient fissure from which steam emerged, bringing the rotten-egg smell of a hot spring.

Andri got an idea. "Let's leave the horses here. I've an uneasy feeling: this path widening suggests to me that it's been used a lot over the years. And that means we're close, and if we're close, others could be around. Including the enemy. I want to scout ahead. The horses need water anyway."

Macael had no argument to make to that; deeper in the cave, the hot spring mixed with a trickle of runoff, affording somewhat bitter-tasting water, but it wasn't bad. Horses and humans alike drank their fill, then Macael tied up the horses while Andri drug out horse cakes. Leaving the animals to munch, the two cousins set out to scout.

More chill wisps of fog drifted along the rock face, obscuring its contours. Andri paused to attempt his scanning. Oh yes. Pairs of minds pacing steadily. Someone was guarding that cave entrance.

He reported that to Macael. They squatted down on the path to wait. Andri picked up the pattern. More wisps of fog trailed along the wall like ghostly fingers.

Andri looked up—into soft, undefined gray fog. The clouds slowly descended, enveloping the mountains in moist, chill embrace.

Andri and Macael had to hide up when one of the patrols tramped right past them and then down along this wider path. When that patrol had been swallowed in the thickening fog, Andri tapped Macael, and beckoned.

One more glowing sign, and they reached a broad ledge. And there, in a stunning anticlimax, was the Selenseh Redian. They ran inside, and pressed against the rock as horse hooves thudded by, then away, the riders hampered by visibility of about five paces.

The two fugitives walked deeper into the cave, the cold lessening at every step. Presently a soft, pearlescent light glowed in the tunnel ahead, brightening at every turn. The air smelled fresher. Sweeter, somehow. But what drew Andri on was a harmonic whisper, not quite chanting, but very close. Compelling.

Then the tunnel widened into a cavern of such brilliance they blinked against the scintillation of color. Instead of rock, every surface coruscated with geometric patterns, refracting light in every hue. Macael squinted, breathing fast. It was almost, not quite, too much to bear.

Andri halted and massaged his left shoulder as far as he could reach. "I guess I have to go on. This thing isn't healed," he said. "And I feel something ahead. In my mind. I wonder if it's true, that the jewels are alive? And read minds?"

"Read minds." Macael repeated the words, his thoughts arrowing back.

He had it now. Long ago, he'd first begun to understand irony when he realized that all the adults never seemed to stop speaking about the Unspeakable Siamis. Years later, Siamis's name once more was on everyone's lips: Selenseh Redian was the name of the caves that the Unspeakable Siamis had been forced to enter, according to the local scribe. Siamis returned alive months later, his mind rearranged by some mysterious magic so that he was no longer a Norsundrian.

That Siamis had come out changed for the better in itself was excellent, of course. It was the method that Macael found disturbing. No *thing*, much less no person, was rearranging his mind for him. He found the prospect of such intimate invasion a breach of privacy of the most repellent.

He gazed into the brilliant shimmer and wiped a strand of damp hair off his brow. It took all his strength to keep his mind-shield shut despite the heat that was not fire, and the brightness that owed nothing to the sun.

With a great effort, he turned to Andri with his customary calm. "I believe I'm more comfortable resting here," he said. "I've no wounds to heal — so. I'll wait."

Andri walked on. His body began to tingle; his mind expanded with each step, exhilarating and dizzying. He let his senses cut free to soar and tumble out into the sky, and beyond the sky. He retained only peripheral awareness of his body, as his shoulder tingled and the dark magic spell dissolved. With every breath the tingle spread through him. He began to breathe deeper, clearer as his mind used the magic surrounding him to shed the infection.

Then, restored, he sent his awareness out. It had never been easier, and beneath the giddiness he was aware that it would not be as easy again: the caves' magic somehow not only

made perception on the mental plane effortless, it effectively
hid him. A huge, malevolent mind loomed somewhere to the
east and north of his physical position (though on the mental
plane everything was proximate) yet it could not perceive him.
And he could not perceive its identity.

He comprehended then that identity would be opaque
unless he was familiar with the mind behind the amorphous
shape. He could hear the whispers of thousands of minds
without mind-shields, a sea of whispers. Those with mind-
shields were like great pearls

There, straight to the west, was Imry Llyenthur. Andri
recognized that one instantly, though there was no getting past
his mind-shield. Much farther away was Bartal, no mind-shield.
He was muttering fretfully about some courtier he hated, but
beneath that was impotent anger at Kinarde commanding his
army.

Andri shut him out, and reached for... Alarm rippled
through him. There was Liere, barely discernable. Located very
close by Imry Llyenthur. A prisoner?

Oh. Here was a surprise: Senrid Montredaun-An not far
from either of them.

He opened his eyes, aware that time had passed, but unsure how much. The world and its problems closed in again,
Liere's situation at the forefront. And here was Macael, a few
steps away, another mind barely discernable, he was so thoroughly shielded.

But Andri, with this new clarity, understood what he
hadn't had time, or focus, to perceive: the little signs of lack of
worry about Elsarion and its people, the deflected questions.
Macael, he guessed, had not *quite* lied. Adon no doubt did come
to threaten him, but Andri was willing to wager it had happened weeks ago, not right after Andri's departure. Macael had
joined him because he wanted to. Why? Curiosity, of course.
Andri would have done the same. And to test himself. He
would have done that, too.

He reached farther out, to see if he could. There was
Gared—no mind-shield. His thoughts galloped along
immediate urgencies as he navigated one of Brydon's many
tunnels. Good. He had recovered that much, then.

Marten—mind-shield. One by one Andri touched others
he knew, each busy with concerns relating to themselves, some
worried, some angry, some tired or hungry or thirsty. Some

amorous, some longing. The intimacy of those emotions people were unaware of sharing clapped him metaphorically upside the head. He was trespassing. Now he understood a little of Liere's reluctance to discuss Dena Yeresbeth, and the strength of her mental wall: not just to keep others from invading her mind, but to keep her own mind from inadvertent trespass. Someday, he thought, learning a shield would be part of early training, along with learning to walk and to talk. But it would take a generation or so.

Right now it was so easy! The sheer reach so exhilarating. There was Julian — oh, and Rel —

And there, suddenly, was Detlev's son. Andri had scarcely exchanged ten words with that quiet, strange youngster. Few had, from what he'd seen.

And yet here came Sveneric's thought, as clear as if they stood next to one another: *Andri Elsarion? You are in a Selenseh Redian.*

: How did you know that?

: I have visited them. And it is the only place where such a contact is safe. This must never happen outside of the caves.

: I wouldn't be able to, Andri admitted with a laugh. And at a wordless invitation from Sveneric, he tried to summarize everything that had happened to him.

His thoughts were a jumble, of course, but Sveneric seemed to understand — both he and another mind that joined, unfamiliar but no threat, one welcomed by Sveneric. Andri sensed the trust between them, and thought that passed between them too quick to catch.

Then it was gone, and Sveneric sent words again: *Detlev will help you.*

: That was the mighty, brain-smiting Detlev? How come I didn't get smited?

Sveneric's inward laughter hit Andri like a sudden shaft of sunlight breaking through clouds: *It's not smiting time, of course.* Then he was serious again: *He must remain where he is. But he will lure Imry Llyenthur from that citadel when the time comes.*

: What time is that?

: You will know. Adam will help you.

Andri sensed another presence: *I am Adam.*

Andri knew a little of who Adam was, one of Detlev's followers. One apparently well liked, at least as well as the one who had been killed protecting the king of Colend.

: I will come in your dreams, Adam said, as clearly as if he spoke from around the next rocky corner. *Don't close me out.*

Feeling as if he'd stumbled through one of Brydon's secret doors and landed not in a dank tunnel but into an altogether different world, Andri agreed, and their minds were gone in a wink.

Time to go.

Macael had drifted into vaguely uncomfortable dreams when Andri's step roused him. "How was it? Ah, I can see the answer. Your eyes are quite clear."

A brief but real smile changed Andri's face. "The blood-knife curse is gone, as promised. Which means it's bleeding again, but at least it wasn't deep." Andri worked his arm carefully as he studied the doubt and question in Macael's face, then said, "Thing you'll really want to hear is that this place is powerful magic of the sort that the Norsundrians can't get near. Which is why they are out there freezing their nuts off, and we're in here. It's a kind of magic that scours your mind inside and out as it repairs your body. I feel like I've had a week's rest, yet I did not sleep at all."

"It sounds like delusion," Macael said.

Andri laughed. "Maybe I am deluded. In there I knew everything—everything! Now I'm locked back inside my skull again, and I know just how small it is." He tapped his head. "Sure you don't want to try it? At least you'll feel rested."

"I'd rather get real rest," Macael said. "What next?"

"What next indeed," Andri said, turning to look down the tunnel toward the entrance. "Another benefit of the caves inside was my ability to, ah, see the situation." Already that extraordinary clarity was beginning to fade, causing him to question his own assumptions. "One thing I do know, they have a prisoner who I intend to spring. And yes, it's probably a trap. But as yet I don't think they know that I know." Andri added, under his breath, "And the trap isn't really set for me."

Macael studied him, uncertain as he had ever been in his life.

Andri said, "Macael, I'm going to be moving fast. I don't want to draw anyone into a rescue that probably won't work. I have to try."

"And if you do?"

"Go to Mearsies Heili, as I said I would. Get help from

anyone who'll give it. Find out the strategy from strategists."

Macael made an impatient gesture. The red stole into his cheeks, but he looked at Andri steadily. "If and when you return triumphant to Shiovhan, and I have no doubt of that, what then?"

"Clean Norsunder out of Enaeran. Keep my promises." He held out his hands, and clapped Macael on the shoulders. "I didn't like your drugging me without consent, but I recognize what was meant as good will. And you've been a good companion. I hope to heal the breach between our branches of the family." He glanced toward the entrance. "Didn't you say you have relations up hereabouts?"

"The Renselaeus cousins, in Lorgi Idego. Distant, but I expect they'll take me in. We met when I was young, and got along well. As for traveling on my own, I believe I've learnt enough to do that, even if I have no mysterious magical skills."

"You will be faster taking Bayleaf. You'll need a remount."

Andri saw the ambivalence in Macael's face; he wanted to be generous, but he also was worried about Bayleaf. Andri liked him better for his obvious concern over his horses. "Really. I can move faster now without a horse. I've got to be stealthy. And if I need one I'll steal one, which I can then let go without guilt."

Macael jerked his chin down in assent.

Andri said, "The fog is still thick, and I know where the patrols are. Let's get back to the horses. Then we'll take our separate ways."

Which is what happened.

Andri saw Macael back across the bridge, leading both horses. They parted there, Andri quickly, as he loathed partings.

He used the cover of the fog and the lingering sensitivity to the presence of other minds to dodge the Norsundrian patrols until he located a narrow goat trail that a horse would not be able to follow, which put him between the patrols.

As he walked, he considered the new set of circumstances. And how to get around Llyenthur using Liere to see who turned up to the rescue; it was great that Detlev's gang seemed to want to help, but they weren't here. Ah, when in doubt, push on. It had gotten him this far.

Seventeen

Norsunder HQ - Larkadhe

SENTRIES STOOD BY EVERY time the healer visited Liere, or a servant came up with food. She was permitted every morning to walk down two landings to where a cleaning frame had been established off a hallway with a lot of doors. She always sensed people watching, though they remained hidden from view.

No one interfered as she marched down and up again, guards before and after her, alert as people under threat of death will be. She could hear the memory, blurred by repetition, as the guards recalled Llyenthur's orders: *If she gets away, you die.*

She could not yet look for escape routes, not under that moral constraint. But once she got a sense of the place, she would find a way around that. Preferably that pointed straight back to their wretch of a commander.

Until then, she moved through her stretches carefully, and she thought back through everything. The mad dash since Zranf was more like a dream, the only sure thing Andri. His smile, his touch. His kisses, fire hot, when everything else was disintegrating around them.

Their plan to meet might have been better worked out — it should have been — except neither of them had expected him to miss the meeting place outside Shiovhan; from there, the chances of finding one another, she could see now, were ever more unlikely.

Whenever her thoughts reached this point, invariably she got up and paced restlessly, around and around the cell. Walking was good, she told herself. But really, walking was a way to distract her mind from the urgency ... the determination to hold to what she wanted most. To make a new home, and a purpose.

What would the others say? She shied away from defining "the others." She knew one thing: she wanted to be married to Andri before they rejoined the rest of the alliance. Then, whatever else happened, she would have this one sure thing, this beginning to a new life that had nothing whatever to do with Sartora. She had found her place in Enaeran, with Andri, without any of that detritus dragging at her. And once they were married, no one would be able to say anything about it.

She had to find Andri, but how? She still could not dare a break in her mind-shield. Around and around she walked, her thoughts whirling in endless circles.

Her cell was kept warm by a firestick, and meals were brought once a day by silent people whose expressions ranged from suppressed anger to resigned sadness. None of them were Norsundrians, and none of them had the mind-feel of willing collaborators.

One day early on a dark-haired woman came in, and Liere said, "Could you possibly get me some pillows? My arm hurts all the time. I'd like to try propping it up."

The woman flicked Liere a wary glance. Her smile was a little thin, but she had such a purposeful air about her Liere wondered if she was a resistance worker. Liere lifted her mind-shield partially and extended a tendril, but there was no contact, nothing but fear and a very wary empathy.

Liere did get the pillows, which surprised her. She'd said it mainly to get a conversation going, and it'd been the most harmless subject she could think of. But the woman apparently was under orders not to fraternize.

The dark-haired woman came back a few days later. She was still silent, but she shot Liere a look so full of sympathy and anger that once again Liere got the feeling the woman was an underground worker — an active one.

The day after that, Liere was summoned for an interview. She stuck her arm in the sling the healer had given her and followed the sentry down a landing. Corridors led off in three directions. She looked around furtively, cataloguing every detail of the hallway, the plastered walls covered by old and faded tapestries. Into a large room with maps on two of the walls, and old books piled at one end of a huge table. Message trays at the other end. A waiting stack of blank paper, ink, and pens.

Norsundrians in gray uniforms moved about or sat doing various tasks as two servants finished tidying a side table, and piled dirty dishes on a tray. Perched at one end of the big table, wearing tunic-shirt and trousers, no uniform, sat Imry Llyenthur amid several people Liere took as scribes and messengers.

He picked up a handful of paper, got up, and pitched the papers into the fire, which flared briefly. Then he turned sharply, his hand moving so fast Liere was caught by surprise as he back-handed her across the face hard enough to send her crashing to the floor.

But she'd been expecting something of the sort, and this time, she kept her mind-shield firmly closed, and whirled into a good fall, keeping the broken arm from hitting the ground. The room stilled as Llyenthur reached down, grabbed her by her good arm and yanked her to her feet.

Then he said in disgust, "I give you a week. If no one turns up, let's see if Efael has more success."

She braced for the expected mind attack, and there it came, Llyenthur frowning in a dire way, as if they stood on a stage before an avid audience.

They *were* on a stage before an avid audience.

She controlled any semblance of reaction, and she knew her mind-shield was solid. She did her focused breathing until she sensed the attack withdrawing.

She opened her eyes to discover that the room was nearly empty, except for the Norsundrians at the duty desks, sedulously attending their work. No one else in sight — they were all out, no doubt gossiping about what they'd just witnessed.

Exactly what Llyenthur wanted.

Llyenthur had been watching. He saw the pain-daze fade from her eyes, which narrowed with realization. But she remained silent, her mind-shield locked. "You're almost interesting enough to keep around."

"I wish," she retorted, "I could say the same."

He grinned, and in that moment he looked like —

"You see the resemblance, Liere?"

Liere had never liked any of Detlev's gang except for

Adam and Curtas. She'd disliked David the most, excepting only MV. But much as she despised him, she couldn't blame him for keeping this connection from general knowledge.

Imry Llyenthur's thoughts obviously paralleled hers. "My brother would be annoyed. I suspect public knowledge of our relationship, were it to get around, could create a rather embarrassing setback in his attempt to be accepted by the lighters."

"I take it you don't wish it to get around anymore than he does."

Llyenthur shrugged. "Don't care one way or another. Not that I have anything against David particularly — except his insistence on following that fool Detlev."

In that moment, Liere recovered the memory that had been poking at her: Detlev talking to someone at Norsunder Base, long ago when Liere was a prisoner there. Was it Kessler? No. She hadn't looked at who it was, she was so miserable, but Detlev was saying, *Yes, the most promising of the group are brothers, Imry and David Llyenthur…*

At the time they'd just been names. She had forgotten that until now.

"I think I'll send you on a few days early," Imry Llyenthur said, perching on the end of the table again. "It's not you I wanted in the first place, but those mountain idiots broadcasted your presence to half the world. It's your swain that I need."

"Swain?" Liere repeated. "Andri?"

"Well, I wouldn't mind him, but I meant Senrid Montredaun-An."

"Senrid?"

"You mean you didn't know he was following you?" Llyenthur gave a snort of contempt. "At great —" His brows went up. " — personal risk to himself, I might add. I freely admit he has managed to evade and avoid several search parties and traps I'd carefully planned for him. I really need him in Marloven Hess, which is — I'm certain you will not be surprised to hear — a disaster."

I really need him. The killer of Senrid's daughter? Fury boiled through Liere.

"But first I'll have to find him." Imry Llyenthur lifted his voice. "Guard!"

Liere was taken out as Llyenthur threw himself into his chair, hoping that this time she'd have the sense to reach for Senrid. All he needed was a heartbeat's time, and the tiniest sliver of an opening —

"Detlev sign," Duin said from his desk.

"What?" Llyenthur lunged for the report in the dispatch tray. "Give me that."

Two wards broken in Bereth Ferian. Three different eye-witness accounts of brief sightings sounded suspiciously like Detlev.

He looked up. "Seems the damned snake is finally poking his head out of whatever hole he's been hiding in. I'd better — no. Better not." He needed to stay right where he was, until his trap was sprung. Especially as this more than likely would turn out to be the hundred sixtieth Detlev sighting that was actually a carter, or a fish-monger, or an owl hooting at the moon.

Liere spent the rest of the day searching her cell yet again, minutely, for any hint of escape possibilities. And when she found nothing, she lay down to rest against the next attempt to get her to reach mentally for help.

And was startled out of sleep by the door swinging open.

"Sartora?" The merest breath of a whisper. It was the dark-haired servant.

Liere rolled out of bed and to her feet.

"Can you see? I'll lead you," the woman said.

Liere shrugged one arm into her coat, and buttoned the other half around her sling. "Please."

The woman walked behind Liere, guiding her by her shoulder.

Down two levels, then along a quiet corridor, then down another stairwell, and back again — avoiding a patrol route.

When they reached the courtyard, Liere whispered, "I don't want to endanger you farther. I can make it from here, if you'll tell me where I am, and which direction is which."

"Larkadhe. North...that way."

"Thanks for the rescue."

The woman took Liere's mittened hand in both of hers, and kissed it. "You saved my parents' lives once. You do not deserve Efael," she whispered. "No one does. Run."

"Fare well, and be careful." Liere was intensely embarrass-ed, and in agony lest Llyenthur spring out and laugh, "Gotcha!" again. From what little she'd seen of him, he seemed the sort of game player who would enjoy that.

There were a few patrollers out, but she used her farsense

to find them, and kept hidden until they passed.

And while she ghosted away, Imry Llyenthur stood in the doorway to the balcony and peered down into the darkness beyond. He was rewarded with a glimpse of movement as a slender shadow ran across the courtyard and stopped near the gate. He could imagine Liere, stiff and afraid, checking thoroughly in all directions, then proceeding. She was very soon out of sight.

He went back inside and stood next to the fire rubbing his hands. A Norsundrian uncovered a lamp so once again the room was lit, and waited quietly. Presently Llyenthur said, "We shouldn't have long to wait."

"Shall I slit the traitor's throat?"

Llyenthur waved a lazy hand. "Let her finish her day's work first. We don't have enough hands as it is."

He ran upstairs, giving orders for a chamber to be readied for Senrid; he would oversee the wards himself, but when he reached his desk, there was Duin with that look on his flat Chwahir face that meant he wasn't going to like the news.

"Let me guess. Efael invited us to celebrate his Name Day?"

Duin said, "Another Detlev sighting."

"Where this time?"

"Bereth Ferian again."

Once was almost always a mirage. Twice in one day? "Tell Elzhier and Yuen to investigate." He named his two best spies, who incidentally loathed each other. That meant they would strive to outdo the other.

"Now, those wards…"

Eighteen

Enaeran to Larkadhe

WHERE WAS SENRID?

While Andri was carted to Nente by the Adranis who had captured him, and Liere had lingered in Arbanion before starting her journey northward, Senrid and Leander crossed Enaeran, avoiding towns and villages except when foraging.

Senrid made a point of stealing from the Adrani outposts when Leander wasn't able to glean from the woodlands they passed through. Senrid lifted not just food, but before they reached the southern pass, he lured a couple of horses from a herd in winter pasture.

They were halfway over the southern pass when Senrid stopped in the middle of the narrow canyon between snowbanks as snow fell all around them; every couple of weeks, the Norsundrians had had to replace the no-longer functioning Road Guild in sending mages to burn a passage through, or else accept that the passes would be closed over winter as in past centuries.

Senrid contemplated the featureless gray clouds overhead in the absent way that meant Dena Yeresbeth scanning. Leader waited.

Presently Senrid stirred. "Liere's in trouble."

"Where?" Leander asked.

Senrid turned slowly, then pointed at the mountain range on the north side of the pass. "Somewhere there."

Leander said, "You're not going to try scaling those mountains?"

"No. Let's get down the pass while we're still between patrols." Senrid started moving again, more briskly than before. "I'll go up through Stalgoreth."

They traveled in silence for a time, then Leander said, "Do you need to? It's not like the old days. Liere has proved she's effective at taking care of herself."

"I'll always look out for her." Senrid's steady, bleak gaze threw Leander back to those last terrible days in Marloven Hess. His manner was different—not restless or nervy, but unyielding. "It's just the way it is."

"All right," Leander said; it would never occur to him to question people caring for one another. "Want my aid?"

Senrid flattened his palm. "You got the two of us through the forests. I'll be heading into other territory, moving fast. More than likely into trouble I may not get out of. Why don't you continue west? I'll try to meet up with you."

"Where?"

"Nowhere near Marloven Hess. Yet. Somewhere north. Not as far as Lindeth Harbor. It'll be as infested with enemies as Choreid Dhelerei. Say, south of there, between Lindeth and the Tirbit River. We surely can find a tough old Iascan fisher who will take us across the sea just to spite the enemy."

They continued on down the pass, and then parted.

When Senrid encountered some locals hiding from the Norsundrians, he asked if anyone had seen Sartora, and then gave her description, his thought being that "Sartora" might ring outward among those resisting, and win her aid, whereas describing a random young woman with blond hair, here in Halia, where blonds were common, would as likely net him a shrug and a shake of the head.

He never got an assent from any of those he asked, but he was right about how word whispered outward. In fact, if anything, he underestimated how frightened people would cling to the legend of the Girl Who Saved the World, hoping for a miracle rescue. The news that Sartora had come to the Ghildraith range spread to the flying folk, resulting in her being plucked from the air.

Unaware of these events, Senrid had been traveling parallel with her ever since, stealing horses through what in his ancestors' day was the great Yvana jarlate, as she was handed off from flyer to flyer.

He crossed the hilly woodlands into Visegn about the time she was captured. He sensed that one brief mental outcry, but she closed it too quickly for direction.

A few days later, Llyenthur broke her arm, and Senrid felt that across the distance. He knew two things, then: where she was, and that she was being brandished.

He bolted for Larkadhe.

Imry Llyenthur had seriously underestimated Liere, he discovered to his disgust. The reports had to be years out of date; though he'd had two good trackers following her, she managed to vanish before leaving the city of Larkadhe, which was not large. With a broken arm, yet.

Alas, the same skill that enabled her to elude Llyenthur's trackers kept Senrid from finding her. They passed within three streets of one another, both thoroughly shielded.

A few hours after her escape, the sun just barely rimmed the mountain peaks, glowing garishly along the edges of the piling snow clouds. The snow was tapering off; Senrid, having woken from a brief and inadvertent sleep, crawled onto a roof protected from the tower windows by the reach of an overhanging eave, and gazed downward as the light strengthened.

He'd spent a couple of days prowling around, mostly regretting the fact that his life in recent years had required him to Be Visible — the very opposite of the skills he needed now. He had to constantly check himself and his surroundings. His only defense, and it was flimsy, was illusion. He was very certain that Imry Llyenthur's inner perimeter guards were trained to examine any blurs or vague patches in the environment.

This spot was the best he could find for watching the main gate. He peered down in the weak light. The myriad hoof prints were a bad sign: a massive search had just been sent out during his sleep, brief as it was.

For whom?

He forced himself to wait patiently. He'd learn more by waiting to see the response than by running off without knowing why the search or where the patrols were going. Two more mounted patrols left, the hoof prints in the courtyard slowly filling up. Servants and armed guards came and went as

Senrid sat motionless, as he had the day previous.

A man with a horse and covered cart pulled in. He climbed down, darting furtive glances around before he began unloading his boxes and baskets from under the cover. He stacked them neatly in the snow.

A door opened in the castle wall. A tall woman carrying a bowl walked out into the courtyard, past the man with the cart. She did not break stride, but Senrid saw the shadows shift slightly on her face as though she'd said something. The man turned, and his face was entirely hidden by a stack of baskets as the woman passed on by.

Lightning swift, Senrid listened on the mental plane – and caught the man's triumph: *She's gone?*

With the "she's" came Liere's image, and the woman who had let her out.

Damn! No, it was good that she was out, but despite his vigilance, he'd missed her.

Senrid slipped and slid down a few feet, scuttled crablike along the roof, jumped down into the shadows of the bridge.

Her escape had been far too easy. So easy, in fact, he sought out the servant who had helped Liere, and confronted her as she carried a tray from the kitchen to the stable.

"That was a setup," he said abruptly, watching her eyes widen, and within the orbs, her pupils contract with fear. Wariness. Anger.

He shrugged. "Believe me or not. But if I were you I would run. Now. Don't even stop at your room, because I will lay you a hundred gold pieces Llyenthur has someone waiting to quietly dispose of you."

The woman set the tray down carefully in a window embrasure, her chalky expression and trembling fingers proof she'd listened, at least.

Senrid did not wait. Maybe she'd be the more convinced by how fast he got out of there, he thought wryly as he slunk along under windows, hopped a fence, then mixed into a crowd of snow-shovelers going out to clear the streets. He worked with them until he was out of sight of the tower guards, and hid up until nightfall. He was nearly to the city gates when he picked out movement in the darkness and swirling snow – a swinging lantern, followed by cursing in Norsundrian. A returning patrol – tired, annoyed –

Senrid braced to attempt a fast, surface-skimming mental

scan, to be distracted by a cry, followed by a shout, "He ran that way!"

He glimpsed a figure running, a teenage boy, who slid in the slush, caught himself, and looked around.

Senrid's nerves flashed cold when he recognized the high forehead, the shape of nose and mouth and jawline. That was Dak of Geth's brother Cath. Hadn't he been taken by Norsunder?

And clearly trying to escape. Cath spotted the patrol that had just arrived, skidded, and ran back in the other direction. Senrid took half a heartbeat to slap his wrists—knives still in place there. Boot knives as well.

He rolled over the tiles, slid, jumped to a wall and down. Then he bolted after Cath. Dashed through the archway into a tiny courtyard off the kitchens, judging by the smells of simmering garlic-chicken.

On the other side of the court Cath stood very still, and when Senrid charged into the court, ready to offer help, Cath sharply raised his hand. His empty hand.

And from every door, and the roof above, guards dropped down, weapons at the ready, and closed in.

Cath was wire-thin, skin and hair bleached of color in the beating light. His gaze cold. Empty. They stood face to face and Senrid processed the fact that he'd walked into a trap. One set by Cath. Who, it seemed, had not been escaping. Who was acting on Imry Llyenthur's orders.

"I felt like you do, toward the end," Cath said, without rancor: not empty after all. But weary, even resigned. He raised his hand toward the stairs in silent command.

It took four brawny sentries to force Senrid into a room and tie him to a chair. Then they searched him, took all his weapons, and tromped out again, except for the duty sentries at the door.

A fire leaped in the fireplace. Senrid stared down at it, trying to see if there was any way to burn the ropes off his hands without catching his clothes on fire. The fireplace was a deep-set one, and he would've had to practically crawl in to get near the fire.

During the bad old days with Tdanerend, the best way to stay alert was pain. He ground his wrists against the tight rope until the door opened, and Llyenthur came in.

"Senrid," he said, smiling a big welcome.

Senrid looked past the smile to the Leander-green eyes wide with mockery. "What a long wait I've had for you! But patience is always rewarded. Here you are at last."

Senrid said nothing. Llyenthur's gaze ranged over him: thin, filthy, clothes wrenched awry in the struggle to get him into that chair. A glint at the open neck of his shirt. A golden chain.

"Senrid," Llyenthur said chidingly, reaching for the chain. He clenched his hand, and the chain broke and dangled, leaving a gold locket in his fingers. He thumbed it open and looked at the blonde curl lying there. "You are disappointingly predictable, Senrid. I expected a much better game. But there is some time pressure." Gold flickered as he flung the locket and chain into the fire.

He grinned at the white-lipped rage Senrid could not hide. "Cut him loose," Llyenthur said to the guards flanking Senrid.

A guard undid the rope. Senrid's right arm twitched.

"Come on. Senrid. Attack me. I'll even give you back one of your knives. That's fair, isn't it? You're a lighter now. You will want everything to be *fair*." Llyenthur crooned the word.

Senrid longed to do just that, but he could see in Llyenthur's stance that he was ready for it. He was also rested and not half-starved. Moreover, Senrid knew that Llyenthur had had the same training as the rest of Detlev's boys — David having told Senrid at their first meeting about the one who left.

In other words, Imry Llyenthur was enjoying himself far too much. Of course. He was expecting not only to win a fight, but to get past Senrid's mind-shield while it was going on.

"What I would like," Senrid said, "is a hot meal."

Llyenthur laughed. "Very good, Senrid! That you shall have. And I will join you. We will discuss my plans for Marloven Hess, and what you can do to help me. But first some necessary chores."

He and his guards went out, locking the door behind them.

Nineteen

ANDRI DISCOVERED THAT HE was still sensitive on the mental plane, his awareness heightened — a dangerous state outside of the protection of the caves because of his lack of training or skill. So Adam cautioned when he walked into one of Andri's dreams right before Andri reached Larkadhe, adding: *But Detlev gave you the Universal Language spell through Dena Yeresbeth.*

Andri did not have time to ask how that worked. Adam continued: *There are three rovers at Larkadhe with rudimentary Dena Yeresbeth, which they have used exclusively to scan others' minds. The rovers trade off watches. The greatest danger is from Imry Llyenthur, whose Dena Yeresbeth is formidable, though he is not often present. Also, there is* (Adam's thought imbued the words with regret) *Cath of Geth.*

With the name was a vivid image of a handsome boy of eighteen or nineteen, bronze of skin and light of hair. His eyes were closed as he played a wooden instrument; Andri liked music when he could get it, and he was educated enough to hear that Cath was very good.

Adam continued: *Do not assume he is cloud-minded. Especially now.* He was gone, the dream changing the way dreams changed.

But Andri remembered when he woke. He thought it over, understanding two things: Adam might be relied on for the weird stuff, but Andri was on his own for scouting. Which was no more than he'd expected. What he couldn't do by Dena Yeresbeth listening he could do by gathering gossip, the way he had for years when running the streets of Shiovhan, staying a step ahead of Adon Marsael's grabby goons.

The castle had four gates, but only the south and northern ones were open during the daylight hours, and all were well guarded. The only people allowed through beside the conquerors were servants, and someone had to recognize each one, both coming and going.

Andri arrived the day after Senrid was taken. Gossip whispered through the town of Larkadhe that He (understood to be Imry Llyenthur) had captured the king of Marloven Hess. Andri wasn't at first able to determine if Liere was still there or not.

He studied the situation for a full day, as promised, understanding the local language. According to the gossip at stables and inns, the castle was desperately short of servants. That ought to be easy, right? A suitable disguise, a shuffling, non-threatening walk. Vagabond magic was known for its illusions, which had contributed to its reputation as flimsy magic — for games.

After some consideration, Andri decided against using illusion to disguise himself, and instead bought red, green, and yellow dye, claiming to be a tailor looking for work.

Slipping into a barn late the second night, he mixed the dyes until he got a good brown, then doused his hair and all his visible skin. He'd already swapped out his ruined clothes on his journey to Larkadhe: a shirt from this outpost, pants from the next, and so on. He even managed to annex another knit hat to warm his ears.

When he talked to the loquacious woman at the inn, she spoke to a brown-haired and brown-skinned lad with a comely smile, even if he was a bit slow. "I'm, uh, good with, you know, horses, but, you won't mind my sayin', uh, I don't work anywhere if they're, you know, killing us off right and left."

She waved that off, looked around, then said low-voiced, "They did at first. But my nephew over in the castle kitchen swears it's because people were poisoning food, and the like." She sat back, mouth prim. "Nobody wants them, of course. But they're here. And they pay. And once the larders are empty of harvest stores, what are we going to eat if we have no coin to buy a bit of rice and a cabbage with?"

Andri bobbed his head. "True, true, true."

Her face relaxed somewhat, her gaze sliding away. "I'm

not saying it's right. But a body has to live, is all I'm saying. As long as they don't expect me to go murdering innocent subjects in their beds. If someone comes in and pays for a meal, says I, they get their meal. No matter where they come from. And I'm not the only one. Pleasure house people have to survive, don't they? If someone offers good coin for a tune or a tumble, does it matter if they wear green or gray?"

"That's fair, that's fair," Andri said. "So where does, uh, a person go who, you know, wants work?"

Apparently there was an interview process at the castle that was more like an interrogation, "…with one of those mind-readers along," was the innkeeper's caution. "My nephew said it's nasty, like someone knocking about the inside of your skull with a hammer."

Next best thing? Get a job at a local stable, which was also short-handed, as apparently the castle had summarily annexed the best workers—along with the best horses.

By the third day, Andri had a job with the local stable, having proved that though he was very slow of speech, and scratched his head and blinked a lot before saying the few words he did speak, he was very good with horses. His boss, who thought herself a wit, named him Gabby, though he'd supplied a perfectly good common name that had taken him some trouble to come up with.

As he hoped, by the end of the week, there was enough traffic between the castle stable and his stable that the gate guards recognized Gabby, who had a head full of air, but who knew how to groom and shoe, moreover who didn't complain if stuck with someone else's mucking-out chores.

Meanwhile Andri gleaned from gossip that the pretty golden-haired girl had slipped off, along with one of the maids (making more work for everyone else), but He was too busy with the King of the Marlovens, and whatever else he was doing up in that tower of nights, to mount a door-to-door search. Everyone knew which tower room belonged to the royal prisoner, and which was the commander's. Andri sometimes looked up that way, noticing lights burning in both rooms very late at night.

A few days later he dropped into his hammock as a blizzard roared outside. After a long day of mucking stalls and laying in fresh hay, he was tired, and wondered if he was ever going to hear from Adam again. At least the barn was warm and dry.

He had no sooner dropped off to sleep when Adam was there: *Go*.

Andri hauled himself up, tiredness forgotten.

During the daylight, in clear weather, he never would have trusted an illusion to get him past the gate. As the wind moaned and howled about the barn, driving sideways gusts of snow, he pulled glowing lights around himself, gathered his things, and left, as up in the tower, Imry Llyenthur exclaimed, "What did you say?"

"Missing books," Colleron stated—Duin being asleep after riding the desk from dawn until midnight. "Just now, Bereth Ferian. All the wards down, and an entire shelf of the old scrolls missing from the Venn collection."

"Venn?" Llyenthur repeated, and transferred.

Of the three rovers whose Dena Yeresbeth was used to patrol the locals, one was on his night off, at the local hot house. The second rode with the outer perimeter patrol, who were losing visibility by the moment. The third, known unfondly as Big Ears, was over at the garrison snooping on a whispered conversation between the watch commander and a riding captain, in hopes that reporting on those who complained about Llyenthur would net him a promotion.

When Llyenthur was away, the biggest threat was Cath, but he was asleep. Music drifted into his dreams, haunting and strange. He began to chase the musician, deeper and deeper into dream territory…

Andri bent into the wind, passed through the gate in the whirl of snow, and headed to Senrid's tower. Time to make his run.

There was a sentry at the door to the tower, and at every landing. Andri used illusion and surprise to attack the sentry at the base of the tower, and took his weapons. Then he ran upward as lightly as he could.

The second floor sentry sensed something amiss, and fought back. Fast blows slammed and blocked as they circled, then Andri lunged, blocked and kicked. The sentry fell backwards down the stairs.

The one on the third landing had to have heard the noise, but there was no way down except the stairs, and no use trying to yell for help over the howl of the wind.

Andri restored his illusion, which gave him a heartbeat's

surprise before the armed guard saw the blur and blinked it away. That fight was the most vicious of all; Andri dropped him, though he took two bad cuts in doing so.

He bent to take the keys, which clashed in his shaking hands, then unlocked the door, and leaned there as black spots swam before his eyes.

Inside was a neat bed, a table with paper on it and a freshly-lit candle. Standing at the window with his hands clasped behind his back was Senrid. He didn't move.

"Senrid," Andri said.

Senrid turned sharply. He gazed across the room at Andri with the tightest mask of a face Andri'd ever seen, puzzled at first by the brown dye, but then he recognized that grin. "It seems you've added dark magic to your long list of attainments," Senrid said, his brows lifting slightly.

"Nope. There were spells all over this place."

Senrid opened a tense hand, palm up.

"I strongly suspect their removal was courtesy of your friend Detlev. Llyenthur is out chasing him right now."

The name seemed to stun Senrid. The tightness in his face eased, and confusion furrowed his brow. "Detlev," he murmured, as though trying to remember the name from a very long time ago. "Detlev…" His gaze wandered from object to object in the room as though looking for something.

Andri recognized this seemingly half-witted behavior: forcible perspective realignment following hard on the cold pitch of tension in which the mind can only grapple with the immediate. After particularly long sessions, during which they fired away at your weak points, your perspective slipped no matter how hard you fought. Especially when you began to believe (as they wanted you to) that you fought alone. In fact, that was the first step along their road.

For Andri, sanity equaled purpose: freeing Enaeran. A though best left unexpressed, considering the gossip about Marloven Hess, he reminded himself as Senrid grabbed a pen off the desk, dipped it, and scrawled something across the topmost paper. Then he threw down the pen. "Can we retrace your steps?"

"I'm ready if you are." Andri indicated the door, and that Senrid take the lead.

Senrid scanned the mental plane, then looked down at the dead guard outside his room.

Andri said, "I had to kill them. They'd die anyway. At least my way was fast."

Senrid had already stepped over the body, grabbing sword and knife as he did so, and Andri understood then that Senrid was not condemning the metaphorical (and real) blood on Andri's hands so much as regretting that *he* didn't hadn't had the chance to do the job. And as Senrid passed directly under a torch, Andri saw fresh as well as old bruises on Senrid's visible skin. Ah, so Llyenthur let his brutes get in their entertainment by kicking around prisoners — no doubt after which Llyenthur would come around offering food, drink, and rest if Senrid would just do the *smart* thing...

Andri had been there, too.

They both cast illusion over themselves, Senrid with a whisper, Andri by pulling magic currents from the air. Back out through the gates they slipped, the steady drip of Andri's blood covered by snow. They made it to his stable, where Senrid said, "Which horses?"

Andri leaned against the wall. "Don't think I can ride," he murmured.

Only then did Senrid take in the spreading darkness of blood on Andri's clothes. He put bridle on one horse, and swung to its back. Then extended a hand to Andri. Who pushed away from the wall, and with a grunt, got up behind Senrid.

Senrid scanned, then rode into the storm. The horse trotted out, but slowed, knee-deep in drifts. Senrid headed eastward, into the rocky hills. They rode in silence for an endless stretch of time, surrounded by the ghostly pale snow. Presently the ride became jarring as the tired horse stumbled over unseen rocky hazards. Andri grunted and slumped against Senrid's back.

About the time the snow started tapering enough to allow a couple sword-lengths of visibility, they started up a steep incline. They rode slowly among the rocky hills for a while till Senrid spotted a likely-looking fissure that smelled like a waystation for numerous animals.

Andri roused. He climbed down, and staggered inside. From the quiet rushing sound, and the smell, the fissure had been widened long ago to a cave.

The cave lay beyond a tumble of rocks. He started a low vagabond fire behind the rock, which limited the light from the entrance. Senrid took care of the horse, then dug one-armed through the saddlebags, to see what was in them. No word was spoken till he came up with someone's freshly cleaned laundry. He ripped that up, then said, "Let's see how bad it is."

Andri groaned, but shrugged out of his coat, and then pulled the sodden shirt away from him, wincing and hissing. The least of the wounds was just above his elbow. The worst had cut down to the ribs on his right side.

Senrid mopped the wound as best he could with the remains of Andri's shirt, then used the torn one to bind the wound closed. As he worked, he noticed that Andri's goose-fleshed skin was covered with white, thin scars.

Andri then said, "I'll wrap my arm. Sometimes the pain is easier to take when you're muffing it yourself than when someone is doing it for you," he added ascetically, and Senrid uttered a short laugh.

He helped Andri into the second shirt, whose owner had been short-waisted and short armed. Andri looked in disgust at his bony wrists protruding from the cuffs, and at the waist button hitting the bottom of his ribcage. "At least it's clean. A nice change."

After that much effort and the blood loss, he leaned against a rock that had supported the back of many a traveler, brigand, and adventurous youngster over the centuries, and longer ago than that, Hawkeye Yvana-Vayir had been caught by a similar storm and had taken shelter, the winter before the Venn invasion.

"Are you going to be all right?" Senrid asked.

Andri leaned his head back, one knee drawn up. "I'll be fine. This is nothing new. Was it bad?" He flicked his eyes toward the entrance, in the direction of the tower hidden by the intervening snow.

Senrid lifted a shoulder.

"Let me guess," Andri said. "His version of seduction swapped off with a dance with the bully boys."

"I gave as good as I got."

Andri sighed a laugh. "I sat through the same thing with Yeres."

Senrid turned his head and spat.

"I wonder if Norsunder conducts classes in Carrot & Stick," Andri mused.

"Way too much stick. But at least I got good meals out of Imry's portion of the program," Senrid said, pausing in the fissure's opening. Weak light outlined the sharp bones in his face, and his coat, which the Norsundrians had thoughtfully laundered for him. "Listen. If you're really all right, I'm going to get going. I'll leave the horse here with you. There was nut-bread and cheese in that bag."

"Liere?" Andri asked, and when Senrid turned up his palm, Andri added, "Can you find her?"

"I can."

Andri considered what that might mean, but nothing showed on his face. They both had lost their kingdoms, but Andri had been at a distance when it happened, after only a couple of weeks of ruling. For Senrid it had been so very much worse, even before the matter of his daughter.

Then there was Liere, whom he could find.

Neither Andri nor Senrid harbored the toxins of envy or jealousy: Andri, being by nature polyamorous, sensed that Senrid's relationship with Liere was something complicated past his own ability to parse. He could only empathize in silence, for he had already seen how much Senrid loathed any hint of pity.

Whatever was to happen would happen. "See you in Mearsies Heili."

Senrid raised a hand, and was gone, leaving Andri alone in that cave. He buried his face into his collar against the drifts of icy air.

Twenty

IMRY LLYENTHUR PROPPED FINGERS on his hips as he looked around the quiet archive in Bereth Ferian.

Detlev was not there, of course. But he had been there. Worse, no one actually knew what was in those scrolls he'd taken—that no one had had time to look at. The catalogue, in Roy's neat hand that Imry instantly recognized, said only: *Artifacts of Time*. And the next one, *Artifacts of Binding*. The third was titled *Explication*, which was maddeningly unclear. Therefore disturbing in its possibilities.

Llyenthur forced himself to take the time to lay an especially vicious ward over the room, one that would take effort to break even from Detlev. Then he added some tracers for not only Detlev, but the rest of his sheep, the idea being that the time it took to take down his ward might be enough for him to respond to the tracer and trap them. Though he didn't invest much hope. Then he transferred back to the command center in the tower at Larkadhe.

He knew instantly that something was wrong: again; his wards had been completely dismantled. And that meant...

Everyone waited in tense silence as Llyenthur walked over the entire scene, examining each dead sentry. Whether or not Senrid had killed them in departing was not clear. No one wanted to speak, and risk drawing attention by self-exculpation, because everyone knew what was likely to happen to anyone who let an important prisoner get by.

Llyenthur turned his head. "Rovers?"

Duin said, "Galeriff was off duty. Shrean and the outer perimeter patrol are still not back. Big Ea—ah, Taulic…" He turned his head. "My understanding is, he was over at the garrison the entire time."

Here Taulic pushed forward, tension rolling off him: he ought to have been roaming, if not physically, then mentally. "I marked an important conversation," he said, too loud, too eagerly. "The watch commander and Tzruid talking sedition—I wrote down the exact words, as I knew they would try to weasel out of it."

Here he flourished a piece of grubby paper. Which Llyenthur looked at for an instant or two, then his eyes narrowed. "Where," he said in the cheery manner that everyone dreaded hearing, "is the sedition? All I see here is grousing about what a shit I am. Everybody knows what a shit I am." He smiled; unlike others who used up time in vituperation, which permitted underlings those moments to form a defense, Llyenthur tended to act first.

Taulic's eyes twitched, his fear a sharp smell. Llyenthur gazed back, his thoughts headlong; there was no chance that Detlev's raid on that library in Bereth Ferian, and Senrid Montredaun-An's disappearance, were coincidences. Tauric might even have been lured. At least one person had come to Senrid's aid, for that door could not be opened from the inside.

Llyenthur was going to have to consider what Detlev's move now meant, beyond the obvious metaphorical face slap. What to do about Taulic? Executions were only useful when the breach of orders was clear. Too many merely fostered lies, mutual blaming, and finally conspiracy.

Taulic was wide open. A mental blow dropped him to his knees, his nose bleeding from the sudden frantic slamming of his heart. It wasn't fatal, but it looked bad to the rest. Lesson learned.

Llyenthur walked out, and continued up to Senrid's chamber. Yes, wards ripped through like so many cobwebs. He paused by the desk, looking down at the reports that he'd given Senrid, to help speed along his desire to get back home at any cost. Across the top, in neat lettering, were no words, only a date. What happened in 4093? No world events. Marloven?

Ah, wasn't what they called Night of the Knives that year?

Llyenthur turned away, laughing. Senrid was giving him back of the hand with his little reminder that even the strongest

Marloven king fell before a knife from within. *Which is not news, Senrid. That is the Norsunder game in essence.*

"Shall we search?" the morning watch captain asked.

Llyenthur considered briefly, squashing the impulse to throw his entire force after Senrid, who could not have gone far. But that would leave his HQ unguarded as well as unwarded.

It was disappointing to lose Senrid, who was more interesting than Llyenthur had expected him to be, but that was a low bar. More important, he recollected the experiment he had going in Marloven Hess, that, so far, was proving to be unexpectedly easy. Senrid's presence in Marloven Hess even as a prisoner would be a distraction that might ruin things.

"You can have no more than two patrols," he said, and mentally shelved the matter.

Larkadhe to the Halian coast

Liere had not run far that first night.

She was offered a ride by a middle-aged couple transporting barrels of a shipment of barley wine to the last inn along the strand of Lindeth Harbor. Liere sensed goodwill from both women—and a silent but ferocious hatred of the invaders.

When they got to Lindeth later that night, with snow imminent, the innkeeper saw her sling, and her tired face, and insisted that she stay the night—no charge. Their rooms were empty anyway, with travel choked off.

"We'll become an eatery, I suspect," he said, waving a farewell to the brewers as they trundled their empty cart toward the home of a relation. "Always assuming we can get goods. But that is a worry for spring. Come, come. You're safe enough tonight," he added shrewdly.

Liere did stay the night, and in the morning accepted a suggestion by the innkeeper's son to come along and help him with fishing.

Thus Liere was out on the water in a grubby fishing boat like the other fifty or sixty out on the gray waters, as a patrol worked methodically through Lindeth in a fruitless search, and Senrid poked around trying to find a trace of her.

She fought down her impatience to seek Andri on the mental plane, and kept her mind-shield tightly closed off, as she worked on healing from within. It was still a slow process — bone does not reknit overnight — but she was able to accelerate the process enough to lessen the pain.

A clear day, followed by another, brought no more searches. It was apparent that she was of minor importance, yet she insisted on leaving, as she had no identity papers — and the inn folk had no way of getting false ones. She would not endanger kindly but hapless people.

Once she was on her own again, she hesitated there on the plains of upper Halia, under the broad gray sky, surrounded by fields of snow. North lay the white-crowned mountains, with Larkadhe somewhere in that haze on the lower slopes.

South lay more fields, and rivers, and eventually Marloven Hess. She could not go that far! But if she returned north, there was the likelihood of another trap set by that horrible Llyenthur.

South seemed safer than north. Then south it was.

She began to tramp down the road, hiding at the approach of riders from either direction.

The inn folk sent her off with plenty of food, so she did not have to forage; she drifted southward toward Enneh Rual, the long, thin polity belonging to the Iascans, who were mostly fisher folk. The Iascans had lived along the coast of Halia for centuries. Their manner of dealing with invaders was to ignore them. They continued to live the way they always had, in their round houses built in kinship villages, with doors always on the east. They traded in fish, kelp, and fine quality driftwood scavenged after storms, along with coral and other gifts from the sea.

Liere had learned about the Iascans long ago, when visiting Senrid, but had never gone over the Rualese border. The night of the great blizzard she came to an Iascan village.

She picked up the language swiftly, and found her first round house utterly charming, their weavings bright and wonderful, without being at all aware of how much she stood out, this slender, thoughtful, beautiful girl barely into womanhood among the tough, stubborn, phlegmatic Iascans.

She passed off her broken arm as "an encounter with an enemy," which solidified her status, and from there she was given exact directions to various tiny villages hugging the palisades of the coast. When she finally ventured a question about overseas travel, she was told that deep water ships did not land along this coast, but, "They sometimes trade along the Tirbit estuary."

Two days outside of that river, Senrid caught up with her. She had been tramping along, careful to step in the prints left by travelers and patrols. She invariably hid when she heard travelers — but when she heard a horse halt, and a familiar voice call, "Liere?" she came out from behind a clump of wind-gnarled scrub oak.

"Senrid?" She gazed in astonishment. "Where did you come from? How did you find me?" Her expression changed. "The people who—"

"No pursuit," Senrid said quickly. "Whoever you sheltered with is fine, as far as I know. I figured you'd probably come this way."

He slid off the latest horse he'd stolen, and half-lifted a hand, not quite touching her arm in its sling. "Is this healed?"

"Nearly," she said with a shrug. There was the old Liere, ignoring such discomforts as a broken arm. "Andri — did you see him? We were supposed to meet, but I blundered into a trap."

"Set for me. I blundered into it, too, but Andri sprang me. With Detlev's help. Andri stayed behind to rest up —"

"He's all right? I've got to go back!"

"And start another round of games with Imry Llyenthur?" When she halted mid-step, he said, "Andri took a wound, but it was not bad. If he's not right behind me, then he'll take another route over the water."

She shook her head. "I have to find him."

Senrid said, "He'll be all right. He's been on the run a lot longer than you or I have."

"True, but..." She turned away from Senrid's observant gaze and looked northwards, toward Larkadhe. She squared her shoulders and let out a sharp breath that clouded, froze, and fell. "Our plan was. Before we go west. We're getting married."

"What?"

Her chin lifted. "Married. I asked him and he said yes."

Senrid hesitated, trying to fit together this sudden news with Liere's not-quite-belligerence. For the first time, he really saw mother and daughter in one another: Lyren-Sartora sounded just the same when she was determined on something she wasn't quite as sure about as she sounded.

In one sense it was not his affair. But in another, if

questions were to be asked, who would dare ask them except for him? "Why?" he said.

Her gaze flicked to him. "What do you mean, why?"

He sighed. "I didn't think I'd have this sort of conversation for…" *Another fifteen years.* He bit that off, but they both heard it. And saw a mental image of little Crystal Ingrid, whose first passion was dogs.

He looked away, then back. "Liere, what I mean is, there's no hurry, is there? Seems to me that a sudden decision like that. In the middle of a war. Is…" He abandoned that path, knowing that whatever he said next would make an already awkward conversation that much worse. "Why not take your time?"

"Because the war is a reminder that we might not have time," she stated. "What have you got against Andri? His lack of magic knowledge?"

Senrid's lip curled. "Liere, don't put words in my mouth that I have never spoken about anyone."

She hissed a sigh. "Then why?"

"I don't have anything against Andri. I like him. But I still don't understand why you're rushing to tie yourself down when you haven't had a chance to get some experience."

She lifted her chin, and there was Lyren-Sartora again. "For once in my life I know *exactly* what I am doing. And for that matter, since when did my actions have to meet your approval?"

"Never. I'm just trying to understand why it can't wait, at least until the war is over. Unless for some reason you have to get a crown on your head now."

"I do not want a crown on my head!"

"Then why —"

"We're in love! We might die! Too many have died, you know that much. We have to grab love where we can, surely *you* can understand that?"

"If I thought you two were really in love, I'd be the first to congratulate you," Senrid retorted. "That's not love." As soon as the words were out, he regretted them.

And she took them badly. "Not love — if that's what you think, all I can tell you is that I feel sorry for you, Senrid. Yes, I do. You have my pity, because you don't know anything about love," she snapped.

Blotches of color ridged his cheeks, but otherwise he didn't move for a long moment, then he said, "Maybe I don't.

But from anything I can see, you don't either."

"You know my feelings better than I do?"

He thought he had a tight rein on his temper, but the words slipped out anyway: "I think you're more in love with the idea of being in love than you love him."

"That's where you are dead wrong. My feelings for Andri—"

"You've got saddle wood for a pretty face. Normal. But you can't seem to let it be normal, you're forcing an everyday itch into something eternal."

"That's not true!"

"Oh, that's right, because you are Sartora. You have to convince the world that *your* feelings are special, eternal, all-encompassing. So you've taken over his life to make certain of it."

"I'm sorry you lost your daughter. But that doesn't give you the right to be a judgmental *hypocrite*," she said through shut teeth.

His face blanched, his lips parted, then he turned to walk away, drawing a long, ragged breath. She'd hurt him—the knowledge hit her like a punch to the stomach. Nausea surged in her, compelled by remorse strong enough for her to perceive how much her righteous anger sounded, well, a bit self-righteous.

The anger vanished like smoke, leaving her afraid that if she let him go she would never see him again. Or she would only see the polite version of Senrid that he showed a world he largely didn't trust.

"I'm sorry, Senrid," she cried, running toward him. "I'm sorry, I'm sorry, I'm sorry. You're *not* a hypocrite. You *never* were. A drunk, maybe—"

He was still facing away, but he let out a short sound that might have been a laugh. "Yep. I'm a drunk. I'm going to have to stop that."

Her voice trembled. "I threw the worst words I could think of at you because it seems, seemed, you're belittling my love, which is all I've got right now. I mean, I know it's not a perfect love—whatever *that* is—the idea of loving someone forever is only true in poems. But I love him *now*. It's real *now*. And now is all I've got."

Senrid halted, listening to this rush of words, his gaze at the ground. He sensed the sincerity, and beneath that the perplexity, and though she had not lost a daughter, or a king-dom, he accepted her words, because he would always accept her words.

He faced her again. "Then grab him with both hands. Andri's an excellent man. You could have done much worse, eh?"

She gave an unsteady laugh, wiping her eyes on her sleeves. He could feel her relief, a flood of sunlight on the mental plane.

He gazed out to sea so he wouldn't have to see the ardency in her eyes—which was not for him. "Listen, there are often deepwater ships off the river not far from here. And if anyone is resisting Norsunder, it would be the Iascans, who honed their skills centuries ago in resisting us evil, invading Marlovens. Shall we try to find a ship that will carry a couple of fugitives?"

She eyed him. He almost could be the old Senrid. There was the old smile, even the tension in his forehead, except he was no longer a boy, he was a man taller than she by half a hand.

Moreover—like those very early days—she could no longer read his face, or feel the tiniest feather-touch of mind. His thoughts, his feelings, were shut behind a smooth steel door that left her looking into a mirror in the mental realm, and standing on the churned-up path shivering in the real world, with sea birds cawing overhead, and the distant thump of breakers on the shore.

"Andri knows about Mearsies Heili. If he doesn't catch up with us in the next day or so, he'll find his way there, and you'll do whatever you believe should be done. But there is also a world to win back," he said. "Sartora needs to ride again. Even if this time, you don't get to flit around on a White Horse."

It was the mildest of jokes, but she laughed, because they were friends again. Not the easy, unthinking friendship of before. She might have ruined that with her petulant words. But she could rebuild it, one careful twig at a time.

And as he said, there was a war on.

"Right," she said. "Let's get to it."

Twenty-one

Barban

FOR JULIAN AND JUNE, the "few days" turned into a month of howling storms. The days slid by, Julian at first avoiding everybody by holing up in the library reading, or watching Alian paint as long as no one talked to her.

The days were indistinguishable, except for the occasional addition of rescues. These were invariably woefully thin, two very sickly. The other looked dead-eyed as Leela hovered, making sure they ate well, then led them off for more sleep.

June found her way up to the tower to look through the Worldgate window and watch the people going about their lives. It was restful and soothing, as nothing much ever happened besides everyday things in that amazing liquid light. Mostly people went about their business, though they seemed to see June. She wondered what she looked like to them. Did they think *she* was a ghost? They didn't seem to be unduly frightened by the sight of a pear-shaped girl with a thick mat of plank-brown hair, brown eyes, and olive skin.

Then one day, June looked out at two women who stood in the court talking earnestly, every so often looking at her in the tower window. One woman wore a long, complicated garment of folds that kind of looked like an Indian sari, except it was folded right over left in the way of clothes depicted in books about East Asia.

The two walked swiftly somewhere below.

They appeared in the tower door, and entered the room. The second one was younger. It was the college-age girl from the day before, now dressed in bright green. She walked over to June with such an energetic stride June could almost hear the rustle and swish of her skirts, except that again there was no sound.

The woman raised a hand with three rings on it, and carefully enunciated a few words.

June's skin prickled with a sense of electric current buzzing, but it wasn't harsh. The woman held her hand out to June, palm toward her, fingers pointing to the sky. She stared straight at June and jerked her head as though to say, "Come on!"

June slowly raised her hand.

The woman extended hers toward June's. June reached slowly, fully expecting the scene to vanish—the hands to pass through one another like illusions—anything but the earthquake jolt that sent shock through her.

Her vision sparkled around the edges. The warmth of another hand brushed against her fingers for a second—

She snatched her hand back and recoiled. The vision blurred.

No, no danger. Go with it. Impatiently she forced herself to recover, to reach again, and this time brace for that weird shock.

The woman began talking quickly and earnestly, her dark-eyed gaze wide and intent.

June shrugged, tapped her ear, and turned out her hands to show them empty.

The woman grabbed a book off the table and opened it in front of June, who looked down at the meaningless vertical handwritten lines, and again shrugged.

The woman pressed her lips together, then sat down abruptly on the rug. The girl in green said something, which the woman answered without taking shifting her gaze from June's face.

The woman gestured to June, raised her hand again, palm toward her. Obviously she wanted to try the touch again. June knew something important was going on. The woman's face wouldn't have that look of urgency if this was just a game of curiosity about people from another land, or even from another world, if magic was everyday here.

But the decorations were so different, the walls so much

newer-looking. What if it was a different time?

She knelt beside the chair so her hand would be on a level with the woman's, and brought it to the other hand. The woman muttered again, and this time the vertigo lasted a couple seconds and the electric shock zapped right through June's mind. She jerked back, glimpsed the woman sinking back exhausted, and the vision ended abruptly.

June rose to her feet. Her head throbbed, and her knees wobbled.

The woman had used Dena Yeresbeth, June realized. The words were in English. Which meant June's being an off-worlder was important to whatever was going on.

"You can get the Safeguard." (Here an image of an ornate silver cup had flashed through June' mind.) "If you say this word ETHE when you see it —" And an image of a hiding place above a door with tapestries on either side of it.

That was it.

This much seemed clear: the cup was some sort of super important magic protection, and June seemed to be the one who had to get it.

For once, she, June Kaifin, was important. She was usually the person who stood in the crowd looking on while someone else was the hero of the hour, the star of the show, blah blah blah. Something was going on, but this woman was turning to her to be a part of it.

Where this cup was, what she was to do with it, and whether it would turn out to be poisonous or something, were not clear.

She had come to distrust adults from an early age. Adults lied, the ones closest to you lying the most. They said it was for your own good, they said it wouldn't hurt, they said a lot of things that you knew were not true, and they used guilt and gratitude as well as authority as weapons. It was the realization that time was inexorable, and the enemy would one day be her, that had driven her through that weird door into total darkness, which turned out to be a Worldgate, briefly aligned with Earth.

All that simmered in her mind, and yet, she had to admit that there had been no sense of lying from this woman. Nothing bad had happened. There was no coercion or compulsion, or June would have run right back down those stairs and never ventured near again.

Therefore. If all these things were true, and that cup was

in this palace (what was left of it—after all these years) she'd find it, or at least look pretty carefully. Why not? If she didn't like the feel of it, she could throw it in the ocean, which she remembered was nearby.

She went downstairs and began to search. She didn't expect the wall decorations to be the same ones from the woman's…time? Environment? She mentally dismissed those and concentrated on door shapes. Most of the doors were arches, but of varying size. This one had been huge—an even bigger round circle. She walked through the entire castle, staring at the tops of all likely-sized archways. None of the ancient black stone matched with the pale carving of the woman's Dena Yeresbeth image.

After an hour of intense looking June was forced to conclude that the needed archway had been in the parts of the castle that had been destroyed. Which was pretty likely, if she really had gotten a glimpse into the past, and not some dream image.

She finally sat down at the top of a flight of stairs, disappointed and a little tired from hustling up and down all those staircases--there weren't more than three rooms on a level with one another--for nothing.

Julian's floated up the stairwell, "Maybe she went up here somewhere. June?"

"I'm here."

Leela and Julian were waiting at the bottom, Julian looking puzzled. "Went up to the tower to look for you. Something happened there."

"Yep."

"You made contact with those people?"

"Sort of." June explained what had happened, and include-ed her fruitless search. She wound it up with a question—"What's going on?"

"Yovres wanted to know if we wanted to go have a look at the local work camp. See if there was any effect from last night's removal."

June' brows went up slightly in a look that clearly meant *They're going to let us out of our cage?*

Julian shrugged one shoulder, an affect of carelessness that fooled no one. "If you wanna go, grab your coat."

They took horses (stabled on the other side of the castle, in a roomy, warm kitchen-converted-to a stable) along a winding back trail. It was bitterly cold out. The snow crackled and crunched under their horses' hooves, and the bare trees seemed almost lifeless, or focused inward against the freeze.

After a long ride, they emerged abruptly on a bluff, overlooking a city. Immediately below great square gouges in the soil indicated the ongoing labors. Small figures moved slowly about, most gathered around an unfinished dig.

"There they rot," said Yovres, with a sweeping gesture of his purple-mittened hand. "So needlessly cruel to force them to dig foundations when the ground is either mushy ice or frozen hard."

"How many?" June asked, since Julian was silent.

"You mean, how many are fake?" Yovres asked. Can't you tell from here? The fake ones don't cast shadows. We couldn't figure out how to manage that."

Once you saw it, it was obvious. It was equally obvious that the bored guards didn't care enough about their charges to see individuals, or else this swap would never have worked. The illusory children worked industriously, though June recognized repeated patterns, kind of like in cheapo cartoons, when the characters run, and the background that whizzes by shows repeats of the same buildings and trees over and over.

Watchers of cartoons don't notice unless looking for it, and it was clear that the Norsundrians didn't look for shadows. It was also clear that this rescue plan had been going on as long as the work camps: there must have been twenty shadowless children below, remarkable considering that one to three were removed at a time. But the Norsundrians noticed nothing.

Yovres said, "Looks like we're safe enough here. Want to go check the next one with us? It's not too long of a ride."

Julian shrugged sharply. "What's the point? I've seen Norsundrians before. Lived among 'em. Right now I'm freezing."

Leela and Dara turned away, their profiles somber. Everyone knew Julian was thinking of her coin belt, and looking for another conspiracy.

She turned her horse and started back up the trail. June heard Dara mutter under her breath, "Glad I'm not wearing it."

———————

Over the next couple of days, June searched the outside of the castle, despite a fairly heavy storm.

More kids appeared, and were taken to rooms to recover. Those who'd recovered were sent various places.

One afternoon, a teen showed up who Julian recognized. Her mood changed again as this boy talked about the good old days when Siamis and Kessler were squabbling down at Norsunder Base, where he'd been a prisoner. He'd tagged along when Siamis blew through, freeing prisoners in a mass escape in what they had thought was his feud with Detlev. He told it in such a way that the entire group, even Alian (who was still working on her painting) laughed.

The subject of the Good Old Days was next, as more kids appeared from out of the gloom and joined them. This soon palled for June. She took a wander around the great hall, this time looking for windows that might have been changed, and left traces in the stone.

When the gloom deepened to darkness, laughing voices echoed down the halls, giving way to the melodic cheer of music.

June returned from her latest fruitless search to find the big table loaded for dinner, and a line of kids holding plates bent around it. That skinny dark-haired boy was singing again, softly, on the other side of the fireplace.

After dinner, instruments appeared out of rooms. The improvisational orchestra got together, and began to find their way into harmony and rhythm. Older teens gravitated toward one another, dark glances laughing, interested, beckoning. Kids danced to be dancing; those who didn't dance sat on the periphery of the circle, talking in quiet voices.

Fire and candlelight glowed on faces and hair and eyes and hands, and in clothing both rich and poor, styles from all over. The far walls disappeared in the darkness, and the warmth and the scent of fresh blossoms created a sense of being outside on a summer's night — augmented by the stars visible through the hole in the roof.

When Julian finally made her decision, June almost missed it. It was so abrupt, so unstated it was almost an anticlimax.

After finishing a dance, Yovres sat down next to Dara, and leaned over her to ask, "Want to dance, Julian?"

She shrugged jerkily and, with a sudden movement, unhitched the belt and handed it to him. "I believe you won't do that plan. That's all I promised." And in a lower voice still,

"The first coin to the left of the clasp if Harana's. Though, come to think of it, if I'm right, she seems to have become a sea turtle."

Yovres laid the belt carefully on the table. "We'll wait until just before midnight, when Norsunder magic is the most intense, and use it against them. Come on!" He held out his hand, and this time Julian jumped up and abandoned herself to the music.

The word must have gone around in a quiet way because slowly the room filled with young people, and the songs played swifter and happier, the faces smiled brighter, with joy and anticipation.

"We're agreed?" asked Dara. "Harana's powers stay bound?"

A shout of agreement rose toward the sky. With deliberate ceremony, that coin was separated from the belt, and Yovres flung it into the fire. "It can stay bound that way," he said. "A turtle is a good end for her. They cannot lie. Form a ring."

The vagabonds sat in a tight circle, holding hands. June remained on the hearth just outside of it; Julian and Yovres stood in the center, holding the belt as the fire leaped and crackled. A faint glow of color began to tinge the air—first making a halo around the fire, then around the circle. Finally Yovres said, "We're ready."

Julian flashed a grin over her shoulder at Leela, then touched each link and murmured her name.

The air filled with the soft golden glow that Julian had seen upstairs, intensifying each time Julian released a bit of magic.

When she had gone around the belt, touching each coin, the room glowed nearly as bright as day.

One of the flutists leaped to her feet and started a song, but three or four notes her flute dropped from her fingers as someone else yelled, "Look!" and pointed above the fireplace.

About thirty feet up in what had previously always been inky gloom, a strange silver glow beat like cool flame. As kids danced unheeding below, June gazed upward at an enormous arched indentation in a solid stone wall, that had obviously been filled in long ago, reflecting. The stone shimmered, as if it had become insubstantial: she could see through it to the pale wall behind. And on a shelf sat a single object, a silver cup, limned in ethereal glow.

June said, "Ethe," under her breath.

The cup appeared suddenly in her hands. The glow died till the cup was left, tarnished and beat-up, with an edge of red-gold glimmering round the rim the fire.

"What's that old thing?" Julian asked, and didn't even wait for an answer. "Well, the gang has their magic back."

"What does that mean?" June asked.

"It means," she said, "that they can shift us all the way to Mearsies Heili."

"Which had probably better happen now," Leela spoke up. "I don't know how far that blast of magic was felt — might not be far at all, but I've got an uneasy feeling about it."

Julian and June exchanged looks, and June thought, at least no one was asking her to get seasick on a ship. "Let's do it."

Twenty-two

Toaran Sea to Mearsies Heili

LIERE FER EIDER AND Senrid Montredaun-An had hoped to find an Iascan deep-waters trader willing to carry them across the western sea, though Norsunder was increasingly tightening maritime control. As Senrid had expected, once the Iascans off the Tirbit estuary understood that he and Liere were fugitives, the only problem was deciding who to choose from the many offers to carry them.

The sea journey took longer than it might have in a fast trysail or raffee; the Iascans avoided any sail sighted hull down on the horizon, counting on their sea-colored sails on masts that never reached to topgallant height to keep them from being seen first. And instead of heading west with the prevailing winds, they sailed north to the Delfin Islands to trade. "There's always someone going west," the fugitives were assured.

What was there to do but agree? Halfway being better than nothing.

During this journey, Liere and Senrid, who once had been the best of friends, maintained an outwardly genial demeanor, each trying a little too hard to replicate what once had been effortless. Though each day's sailing put distance between them and the coast of Visegn, emotionally they still lingered on the shore where eight centuries before, Senrid's forebears had fought an especially bloody battle against the invading Venn. Here Senrid and Liere had fallen into the first conflict they had ever had in all the years they had known one another.

Neither brought it up again. Senrid blamed himself for having lost his temper enough to use sarcasm as a weapon, especially against her.

As for Liere, though she was much tougher now than days of yore, she brooded while standing at the prow, watching the bow cut the waves. She herself had said some pretty unforgiveable things, none of which were true, whereas some (not all! No, not all!) of Senrid's points were ... accurate.

Such as, why *was* she really in such a hurry to marry Andri Elsarion? It certainly was *not* to gain a throne. She'd been around Senrid, and other young rulers, for too long to see ruling as anything but harder work than anyone else did.

As she reflected back over the recent, desperate weeks on the run, she began to consider the notion that rushing into marriage might not be to either of their benefits. Why *not* wait, at least until the war was over? If she was right, and her love was forever, then a wait of however long it would take to gain peace made sense.

Once or twice she almost said something to Senrid, but he looked so exhausted; he had been a prisoner for all that time, and he had not only lost his kingdom, but his daughter. There were a few times, always late at night, when he thought he was alone, sitting on deck and gazing out to sea, that she caught sight of such bitter grief in his profile that she bit back her words, deciding not to add to his burden by bringing up the vexed subject. Once she and Andri reunited, she could take him aside, and if he agreed (and why wouldn't he – he'd once admitted that he'd never thought to marry), they could quietly postpone, and no one but Senrid would be the wiser.

Oh, and Lyren-Sartora. But that would not be a problem, what with Lyren-Sartora's thirteen-year-old resentment of Andri and her disgust toward romance. If Liere postponed the wedding, she was confident that Lyren-Sartora would remain even more silent than Senrid on the subject.

When they reached the Delfin Islands, they discovered Leander Tlennen-Hess there, working as a cook for room and board at one of the main inns; he, too, had been brought by a deep-sea trader. He'd been there almost two weeks. Liere and Senrid had begun to look for jobs when a familiar ship sailed elegantly into the harbor: the Mearsiean privateer *Tzasilia*, sent by Clair of Mearsies Heili.

After they set sail again, with Leander joining them, there was no chance (so Liere told herself) for private conversation. Senrid and Leander spent most of their time together, Leander having been taken in by some morvende just ahead of a Norsundrian patrol. When it was discovered that he was a scholar, they kept him for a week of conversation over ancient texts, and sent him along loaded with copies of valuable manuscripts.

"Artifacts," Leander said, his dark-lashed green eyes wide with enthusiasm. "They think the way to save the world is to find old artifacts salted away four thousand years ago, when it became clear that the Old Sartorans were losing."

Senrid listened, and smiled, and talked history, never sharing his skepticism about lighter magical objects that hadn't done much good the first time around. Liere listened and looked away, finding Leander's spring green gaze a reminder of Imry Llyenthur's eyes of the same hue, though it would be difficult to find two young men more different, outside of the shared eye color.

Liere's old zeal for study had begun to reawaken when they entered the burgundy-blue waters of what the Mearsieans called the Pink Sea, and others the Sea of Rose as the color of the water was altered by great forests of red coral not far below the surface.

Finally they spotted the spires of the white palace gleaming atop a mountain near the east coast of Mearsies Heili.

The three disembarked, unaware that Captain Heraford had already communicated with Clair, reporting their arrival via scribe desk that Norsunder couldn't corrupt because it was a closed circle of two. Liere and Leander headed up toward the white palace to discover who among their friends had arrived before them.

Leander hitched his precious bag of books over his shoulder, chatting with Senrid about the roots of the word *ven*, ("I was right, Senrid. The Venn pinched it from the earliest Sartorans—it simply meant *people* back then. It was the Venn who mucked it up by adding 'the' to it, making 'the ven' an elite separate from other peoples!") Liere strictly controlled her impatience. She silently rehearsed what she would say and do if Andri had preceded her.

They topped the last switchback of the little city, and approached the palace ...

And Lyren-Sartor came dancing out, wearing a gorgeous

gown of white lace over green silk, with long green silk ribbons streaming from her gold-touched dark curls as she cried, "Surprise! Everything is ready!"

Summer thunder.

"Everything?" Liere repeated, rejoicing to see Lyren-Sartora beaming with good will.

With her wafted the scents of a hundred flowers, the fragrance of queensblossom foremost as Lyren-Sartora threw herself into Liere's arms, hugged her fiercely, then whispered so only Liere could hear, "I'm sorry I was so horrible to you in that dream. You can never say I am a judgmental brat again, ever, ever, *ever*."

Utterly puzzled, Liere hugged her daughter back, looking past her shoulder to discover Andri there, a rueful smile curving his lips. Unlike the last time they had seen one another, he was no longer sick or filthy from days of hard riding. Her eyes lingered over his long pale hair clean and neatly combed, his long, lean body flattered by a boot-top length velvet court tunic of green worked with gold edging, and embroidered riding trousers stuffed into a new pair of blackweave boots.

The significance of green — the customary color of wedding clothes — struck Liere then, as Lyren-Sartora added, louder, "Everybody is ready. Atan said she would preside. We even have lemon-almond wedding cakes for everybody. Carl and Jesse Delieth are excited over those. And, I picked out your outfit myself, so you can't wear your usual old rag and say it's perfectly adequate. It turns out there are trunks and trunks of wonderful clothes up in those rooms in the spires, and Clair said everybody can help themselves. So go get dressed. Let's have a wedding!"

"Lyren-Sartora," Liere said helplessly. "We just arrived ..."

"I remember what you said," her daughter proclaimed for all to hear, for in her mind she and not Liere was the center of attention, everyone praising Lyren-Sartora for her generosity in letting her mother practically abandon her *once again*. "You said, the first thing, on your arrival, you and Andri are getting married. I arranged it *all*. You just have to stand there, say your vows, and there you are!"

Other friends had appeared, and crowded around. "So glad you are here," exclaimed Atan, Queen of Sartor; she led the pack, expecting to see delight and surprise. Liere looked more gob-smacked than anything —

Then Atan glanced past her at Senrid, and her nerves flashed to ice. "We could use a celebration," she said, faltering badly, and sneaked another glance at Senrid. To find his usual bland smile. She must have imagined what she had seen. The winter light was so dim.

"There have been far too many memorials," Erai-Yanya said as she joined them at the head of a crowd. As usual, she wore a shapeless shroud of a robe, her gray-streaked brown hair knotted messily on her head with a quill pen. She liked weddings — as long as no one expected her to trouble herself with romance. Weddings were cheerful occasions, and they needed cheering, oh yes they did.

Everyone burst out talking as Liere reached Andri, who closed his arms around her tightly. "I hope this is what you wanted," he murmured into the top of her head. "Your girl is tough to say no to."

Unsure of her answer, Liere put her face up for a kiss, and then another one, as heat kindled deep in her core. So much had happened she had almost forgotten how the fire between the two of them together obliterated war and uncertainty.

"I'd better change." Her fingers laced with his, and she took a step, then another, firmly turning her face toward her new life.

Leander found himself attacked by his step-sister, who could not exist without drama. "I never slept a wink, worrying whether you were safe!" And a great deal more like that.

Under cover of everyone else speaking, Atan said in an undervoice to Senrid, "Are you all right?" Then she remembered that his little daughter was dead, and could have kicked herself for her stupidity.

"Listen, Atan," Senrid said softly. "Did you know I was Imry Llyenthur's prisoner for a time?" His glance strayed to the back of Andri Elsarion's head.

"No," Atan said. "You were? How terrible!"

"The point is, one of his favorite forms of torment was to force me to share meals as he gloated, in the guise of giving me daily sitreps. I think a lot of it was true; he's that kind of game player. And one of the things he told me was that he, personally, took out Dtheldevor's privateers."

Shock flashed through Atan's nerves. She had not liked those mannerless, loud people; she'd thought of them as pirates. But the rest of the young allies had liked them, moreover

Dtheldevor was—had been—an indefatigable foe of Norsunder.

And her young cousin had adored Dtheldevor and her gang, regarding their lair off Wnelder Vee as her home far more than she thought of Sartor.

She drew an unsteady breath. "Thank you for telling me. Julian is not here. This will give me time to think how to tell her." She looked around. "But Darian Selenna from Sarendan is here, he and his friends. One of whom had sailed with Dtheldevor…I'll handle it."

"Thanks," Senrid said. "I don't know any of them well enough to know how best to tell them."

While they followed the rest in, Andri and Liere led the way, arms tight around each other. Andri's head buzzed from all the unspoken emotions he sensed around them. He was still sensitized from his experience in the Selenseh Redian several weeks back; he had found it difficult to know what to do or say to Liere's volatile daughter, whose dislike of him she could not entirely hide. This dislike was nothing so simple as snobbery about Enaeran being poor and ignorant. It wasn't even disappointment in him as a person, as they had scarcely exchanged a hundred words all the summer before. It seemed to be more of a disappointment that Liere was not striving for the world-renown that Lyren-Sartora believed her mother deserved, though Liere herself shied away from such things. There was also the element of a daughter feeling left behind yet again by her mother.

But when Lyren-Sartora was determined upon a course of action, she was like the sun on a summer's day—you could not escape it. Somehow masses of flowers were found, and nearly everyone discovered pretty clothes for dress-up, and the kitchens not only in the palace, but the three inns of the capital, produced quantities of delicious wedding food. All leading to the moment when the two of them stood side by side, repeating vows that changed their state before the community.

"Your prosperity is my prosperity," Liere repeated after Atan, determined with her whole being to cross the invisible threshold into assured adulthood, leaving Sartora and her anxiety-gnawing old self behind.

"Your hardship is my hardship," Andri repeated, enjoying the festival feel, and Liere's warm hand in his.

Atan finished, "…and we call upon all who are gathered

here to celebrate the joining of this family."

A cheer rose, then Atan said, smiling, "Whose custom shall we follow now? It's up to the two of you."

Andri flashed a grin at Liere. "Why, any is fine. Once we're rid of Adon Marsael and can go back home, we'll surely have to do it again. The Enaeraneth won't believe I'm married unless they see it happen."

"A fine reason for another party," Liere said. "In Imar, I remember, it was boring speeches after weddings, before the food came out. But Bereth Ferian had toasts, much shorter."

"In some lands the bride and her sisters and cousins and friends dance, then the groom and his," Atan said. "But in Sartor, the married couple leads the dancing."

"The food is ready," Lyren-Sartora stated, drawing attention back her way. "Why not have the toasts now, and food for those who want, and dancing for those who want?" She opened her hand toward the tables, which she was proud of, each decorated with sprays of aromatic pine and a few hothouse flowers.

Liere sensed that her daughter was fretting, and took Andri's hand, tugging him toward the tables. The guests followed, dispersing to the perimeter, talking and laughing; Lyren-Sartora saw focus splintering, and understood then that her dream vision of everyone marveling over how generous she was, how gracefully she planned the whole, was not going to happen unless she threw a fuss.

She had to laugh at herself, thinking that she understood Kyale Marlonen a lot better now: when that princess wanted attention, she got out there and demanded it.

Liere looked about, unsure what was supposed to be next.

Then quieted when Senrid stood up. "I'll claim the honor of first toast." He held up his goblet. "To happiness and long life!" He saluted the bridal couple, sipped, and all cheered and sipped. Liere smiled across the room, relieved and elated both at his gesture. Everything was the way it should be.

Andri saw the direction of her gaze, and sat back, smiling. He loved a lot of people in a variety of different ways. Life had taught him to live in the moment. The future would take care of itself.

Atan stood next, casting an expert eye around. Veteran of hundreds of court affairs, she offered a quick toast, after which Lyren-Sartora, sensing that it was time, signaled the musicians.

"I actually know your court dances," Liere said to Andri.

"But I don't," he admitted with a laugh, the long dimples at either side of his mouth deepening. "I only went to balls to rob Adon Marsael and his cronies."

"Then let Lyren-Sartora lead," Liere said, eyeing her daughter. "I think she wants to. This is very much her affair."

Lyren-Sartora led the way, executing a very pretty dance that she had learned somewhere, but people were not sitting at the tables to watch her dance. They wandered about to sit with friends, carrying plates and cups as they went, or getting up to adapt their own dances to the music.

And some had vanished altogether, like Tahra Delieth, who disliked the very notion of marriage, and had only attended the vow exchange because she admired Liere and respected Atan. Then there was Caris-Merian Rhoderan, sitting alone and feeling very isolated.

Liere scarcely noticed her—though they had traveled together for weeks, they had not exchanged many words beyond simple practicalities of camping on the road. Liere's gaze slid past her. Who else was missing? Most of the underage guests. Someone was missing. Liere was going to count, then was distracted as two newcomers appeared in the doorway— Julian Landis and June the off-worlder.

They took one look, and before Lyren-Sartora could call a welcome, Julian poked June and they backed hastily out, their obvious dismay causing a ripple of laughter in those who noticed. Liere gave up, and turned back to Andri, holding out her hands. "I'll teach you one of your own dances," she said.

At the other end of the room, just outside the door, Julian and June stood uncertainly. Julian's instinct had been to seek her cousin, for Atan would know what to do. But Atan was surrounded by people as they talked and laughed.

"The flowers and all that. It looked like a wedding," Julian said, appalled. "Didn't it look like a wedding to you?"

"Sure did," June stated.

"Wait, that wasn't my cousin doing it, was it?" Julian asked, even more appalled as she looked for Rel. Who was not there at all. Julian pushed the door shut again.

June smothered laughter at Julian's open horror.

"I don't think—wow. Who's *that?*" June stopped dead as an unfamiliar young man rushed down the gleaming hall toward them.

Julian looked up, then sighed. "That's just Siamis." She scowled. "Is Norsunder attacking?"

"They cannot enter," Siamis said, his gazing raking over them. "It was you who just arrived, yes? What caused that magic?"

Julian and June exchanged glances, then June hauled the battered old cup out of her pack. "You mean this?" She tossed it to him.

Siamis caught it, then stared down at it in perplexity. "This can't be it," he said, mostly to himself.

"What's wrong?" June exclaimed. "Is it, like, radioactive or something? Is my hand going to fall off?"

Siamis breathed what might almost have been a laugh. Except he was too astonished. "It's entirely inert. Are you sure that's all that happened? Where did you get it? No, let's not stand in this hall," he muttered as a door opened to a servant carrying a tray of empty cups, music and the noise of conversation spilling out in his wake.

Siamis led the two girls upstairs to a row of salons, and stopped at a library. "There was a flash of magic that I suspect was felt the world around. By both sides," he added grimly. "But then it snuffed out like a candle. Tell me what happened."

June turned to Julian. "Who's he? Can he order us around?"

"That was a request," Siamis said, striving for patience. "That burst of magic is going to have repercussions. But at least it was too sudden to provide any kind of vector."

"Then how did you know it was us?" Julian asked.

"Because you arrived with a...call it a comet tail, perceivable only in the Selenseh Redian," he said. "Please."

Julian turned to June and shrugged.

June began to give what she meant to be a brief summary, but she started backtracking, and turning to Julian for corroboration. Halfway through this jumble of a recitation, the door opened, and Leander burst in, green eyes wide. "Did anyone else feel that magical starburst?" He grinned. "Erai-Yanya will be coming along behind me. Atan, too."

"Everyone who knows a certain level of magic felt it, I suspect," Siamis said. "As it happens, these two here are in the middle of telling me what it was."

Sure enough, several people showed up, some still in their fancy clothes for the wedding. June waited, only wanting to tell the story once. She took the time to arrange things better in her mind, then once again launched into the tale, doing a better job this time.

As she spoke, the cup passed from hand to hand. And at the end, when she had it again, Leander smacked his palm on a nearby table and exclaimed, "That's exactly what the morvende of Ghildraith geliath advised me to tell you: go forth and find as many old artifacts as possible. It's what they were designed for."

"But he just said this thing is inert." June jerked a thumb at Siamis, then ticked the cup with the edge of her nail. It made a ting sound.

"Maybe the cup is just a cup," Leander said, without believing it for a heartbeat. "But my message still stands. The idea is that there are ancient safeguards all over that were preserved for centuries in case Norsunder returned. They have various strengths, and do various things. Nothing will suddenly restore the world, but if these things can divide Norsunder's attention, or weaken them, then that's useful, right?"

Dirk Sonscarna was one of those who had turned up. He said, "I wonder if there are any dark magic ones, besides that blood mage text that Jilo has. I'll ask my father next time I hear from him, but…where is Jilo? I saw him not two hours ago. Where is Senrid?"

PART TWO

One

JILO AND SENRID WERE still missing a few days later, the mages all noticed; meanwhile, nothing was to be found in Clair's magic library about an old cup named Ethe. No surprise, thought several of the mages who had come for refuge to Mearsies Heili. This was deemed a very small library, suitable for a tiny rural kingdom of minimal importance on the world stage. For research purposes into ancient history, all visitors looked at the modest number of shelves and mentally adjudged this library as sadly insufficient.

Erai-Yanya transferred to the hermitage of her friend Murial, Clair's reclusive aunt, who was a powerful mage, and who had amassed her own library over the decades since she was a mage student along with Erai-Yanya and Gwasan Sonscarna, Princess of Chwahirsland—now deceased. The two women went tearing through the oldest scrolls and books stuffed into Murial's shelves.

Back in the white palace, Atan took a few days to make a book-by-book scan of Clair's library. There were some surprises to be found—several extremely rare texts, which raised some interesting, possibly disturbing questions—but nothing relating to June's discovery.

After a scrutiny of the last shelf, Atan turned to the other mages working in that chamber. "I wish we could consult Tsauderei," she said; she had been queen of Sartor so long that

her expectation that people would listen whenever she spoke
was not conscious.

All eyes turned her way. Her voice had been trained into
clear, mellow articulation, its clarity carrying without strain to
all corners of a large room, and commanding in a small one. As
tall as most tall men, and built upon generous lines, she was an
imposing figure in a gown of silk and lace that she had found
in one of the upper rooms—a rarity, a gown constructed for
someone her size.

She looked around the library, from Leander—formidable
mage as well as a scholar—to CJ, Clair's friend, whose magic
was what the trained mages silently thought of as first year. But
this was CJ's home, whereas all the other mages were guests, so
no one would think of excluding her if she wanted to be there.
They simply paid scant attention to anything she said.

Atan glanced toward Siamis, who checked in briefly each
day. It never occurred to her to ask where he was staying; she
had disliked him as well as Detlev too long for casual speech.
She assumed he had turned up to hide from his former
Norsundrian allies.

The dislike, Siamis thought, had become more habit than
conviction. There was little of the heat of ready anger in her
unsmiling demeanor or her tone as she said, "I don't suppose
you and your...people are hoarding some useful objects?"

Siamis sidestepped this question, getting to what was
important at this moment: "I trust no one is going to go running
off outside the Mearsiean border. This is not the time for magic
student quests for artifacts."

Erai-Yanya looked up from a corner table, where she was
copying one of those rare texts that Atan had uncovered.
"Magic students," she said with the conviction of long experience, "nearly always go through a stage of artifact hunting. I
doubt you'll be able to stop the more venturesome of the young
mage students gathered here."

Atan said, "Going outside into one good blizzard might
send the more prudent right back inside." It was a mild joke—
though the truth underlying her words distracted her momen-
tarily, causing her to glance around, then upward. "This really
is the *warmest* castle I've ever been in. Even with centuries of
overlaying spells to help seal against drafts, Rive Dien is still
cold without a lot of hard work. And every other castle I've
visited in the world is much the same. Except here. We have one

firestick in here, none downstairs, and yet I haven't felt a chill since my arrival. It's difficult to remember it's winter out there, unless one looks out the window. Can it be a property of whatever this stone is they used to build it? Is it something local?"'"

She glanced toward the stairway, and Siamis held his breath. "Another thing," she said, turning to white-haired Clair, the young Mearsiean queen. "The construction is so odd. Not even remotely the usual square. If anything, I'd say I've been walking spirals ..."

Clair said, "I always assumed the stone is from the hills along our northern border. That's where my ancestors landed seven centuries ago."

"Seven centuries?" Atan repeated with polite incredulity. "It feels so much older."

"Almost eight centuries," Clair added.

Atan was going to point out that she meant millennia, then decided it might sound argumentative. "It's remarkable, anyway. Did the architect leave any writings?"

Siamis slipped out then, and transferred back to the Selenseh Redian, which was not even remotely a place for humans to dwell in. But he had done his best to make it habitable.

He sat on a pile of cushions spread over the uneven, diamond-hard floor, shut his eyes, and reached for Detlev: *They're already dispersing.*

: I am almost finished. I think it's time for your surprise.

And he was gone.

Siamis sighed, then sat back and extended his awareness to sweep Mearsies Heili's border. There was always someone trying to get past the deep, disorienting fog to enter the kingdom. It had fallen to him to scan them on the mental plane: anyone who whiffed of Norsunder magic or ill intent never got past the fog, and found themselves elsewhere in sea to the north and east, desert to the west, and wooded mountains to the south.

While he was busy with that, Clair slipped out of the library. Morning court was over; there had been few actual petitions since the kingdom was sequestered. Most of the morning visitors came for another purpose entirely — to stare at the Queen of Sartor.

Clair drifted along, finding it both sad and ironic that she had no sooner re-inherited her throne after her great-grand-mother had sacrificed her life to create the magical border protecting the kingdom, to find herself largely superseded once again.

The urge to get rid of the Child Spell pressed ever more strongly against her consciousness. She was ready. But CJ, best friend and faithful second, wasn't.

"Looking for me?" CJ pattered up, her bare feet silent on the shining floor.

Clair turned guiltily. She always forgot her mind-shield when at home. CJ's Dena Yeresbeth was wayward, but there; had she heard any of that on the mental plane?

One look at CJ's wide blue eyes and her inquisitive grin, and Clair was reassured. CJ could not mask her expression no matter how hard she tried. What she thought showed on her face, a straightforward honesty that Clair cherished.

"I think we found something," CJ said. "Me and Dirk."

"Found something?" Clair repeated, groping for the subject.

"Well, Dirk found it. Somehow. An artifact! Not very far north, in Alcandamer. There's an important thing called a double crown, and it can't leave that kingdom unless the holder grants it. Alcandamer being away from all the places we've heard about terrible fighting, I thought it would be okay to go there. Dirk says that the queen there only shares it with female descendants. He thinks if I go with him, maybe I can talk her into lending it to us."

Clair said, "It sounds like you're giving me reasons why you ought to go."

"Yes! That is, I know you won't argue. But the adults will. They're sure to, beginning with their belief that kids are stupid. But Dirk is even better at sneaking than I am! Kessler's given him some poopsie training."

Clair brought her chin down on every point, then said, "Exactly. Which is why I can tell you that I want to help, too."

CJ's blue eyes rounded. "But…what would you go after? Is there a thing you found in the library, and you didn't tell me?"

"Not a thing," Clair said slowly.

"Not a thing? A person? A secretly hidden mage?"

"In a sense…"

CJ eyed Clair. Something weird was missing here. "Clair,

you're queen again. I mean, I'm sorry that Mearsieanne died, and all that, though it's sure good that Mearsies Heili is totally safe. Thanks to her. Aren't you needed here as queen? Especially with all these visitors, and more bucketing in every now and then?"

Clair entered her own room, and sat cross-legged on the bed. "That was true. For a month or two. Until Atan showed up."

CJ scowled as she flopped down beside her. "What does that matter? She hasn't taken over the kingdom. Has she?"

"No. Of course not. She is very scrupulous in deferring to me. But as soon as word went out that the Queen of Sartor was here, people started showing up. In crowds. Surely you saw that."

"I did, though I went and hid," CJ admitted. "They were grownups, a lot of them looked like snobs, and they definitely weren't here to see *me*. But they all went away again, right?"

"Not the ones who decided to bring their troubles to the Queen of Sartor," Clair said with an ironic smile that looked odd on her usually calm face. "CJ, wait before you start in with the insults and how stupid they are. See it from their perspective. Sartor is thousands of years old, and here's their queen, a woman taller than a lot of men, and those eyes of hers that seem to penetrate rock—"

"Frog eyes," CJ muttered. She and Atan had not started out well at first acquaintance, which CJ struggled not to resent still.

"Whatever you think of her eyes, you know she has presence. And I don't." Clair waved her hand down her short self. She appeared to be thirteen years old—the age she had been when she did the Child Spell that held off puberty. "I don't blame people for trying to go to her. I wouldn't even mind if she did sit on the throne and do morning court for a while." And seeing CJ about to protest, Clair added, "I have the only safe kingdom. In the world. That makes me determined to help in some way."

"How?" CJ asked, her eyes narrowing. "Who would you find?"

"Where the Host has settled."

"*What?*"

Clair went on as if CJ hadn't shouted. "Everyone wants to know where they are. No one is going—"

"Siamis can go. He was their best friend until a few years ago!"

"He was their prisoner, CJ. Anyway, the Host has all kinds of traps laid for Siamis, and Detlev, and probably against Tsauderei and the senior mages. Maybe even against rulers. Anyone famous. But someone like me, listening from a distance—they'd never know."

CJ fumed, wanting to kick something, but as usual she was barefoot. She waved her arms. "Not the Host! They're so spooky we don't even know anything about them, except that they invented Norsunder four thousand years ago, and to them, killing people by mind is old sport!"

"I'm not going to meet them, but to spy out where they are. Then come straight back," Clair said. "We are going to need to know that before any real plans can be made."

"Why *you*?"

"CJ," Clair said, "do you think I'm clumsy enough to get caught?"

"Not clumsy. Never. But them. They are so nasty that they even got Detsie-poopsie-potsie, a zillion years ago, and you know what he's like!"

CJ had always been a firm believer in making villains sound as foolish as possible, to lessen their power. *Detsie-poopsie-potsie* was CJ's nickname for Detlev. Detlev's highly-trained boys had correspondingly been nicknamed poopsies. As with many of the nicknames she made up for people, she had tried hard to get people to adopt it, but few had.

"CJ, stop worrying, and think. This is a spy mission. Not to fight. Or even to talk." Then, seeing the genuine anguish in CJ's face, she admitted, "I'm just thinking about it. And I'd only go if I had someone with me who is good at stealthy travel."

"Oh-h-h-h," CJ said, sagging with relief. "You could wait till Senrid comes back. Ask him to go with you. Or Rel."

Clair smiled, though inwardly she was convinced that spying on the likes of the Host would not be successful if done by big, strong, formidable-looking people like Rel, or famous people like Senrid. "We can't depend on 'everyone else' to do the job of freeing the world. That's how Norsunder caused the Fall four thousand years ago, if I understand right. We each have to do what we can."

CJ studied Clair, who sat there, her moon-pale hair ghostly in the reflected light from the hallway, and knew that this was one of those times.

She swallowed. Humphed. Kicked an innocent footstool. "Well, as long as you go with someone good at sneakery, and it's just spying…" CJ was certain that if Rel turned up, he would feel the same way that she did. As for Senrid, Dirk had pointed out that it was more than likely he'd gone back to Marloven Hess.

Clair laughed. "I have no wish whatsoever to meet any of the Host of Lords, and don't intent to." She got up. "C'mon, let's go get some dessert."

A couple days later, word spread through the castle, to surprise and disbelief, "Siamis has called a meeting of all those going artifact hunting!"

"Siamis?"

"He isn't switching sides *again*, is he?"

"What's wrong? Did Norsunder get in?"

"I'm not sure I want to hear whatever he's going to go on about."

But the prospective artifact-hunters were all there, some, like Kyale Marlonen of Vasande Leror, hiding private misgivings about leaving Mearsies Heili's safety. If everyone was doing it, maybe it wouldn't be so bad—Norsunder couldn't be everywhere!... One couldn't refuse and look like a rabbit… Maybe Siamis would say something that would scare the rest into just staying put, and let someone else deal with the enemy…

Atan, who was not going out artifact hunting, was there anyway. She had another project taking shape in her mind, and decided that while she had them all together, after whatever Siamis said, she could approach her idea.

They gathered in the library, sitting on the tables and the floor when chairs filled. Siamis looked around, then slapped something down on the table next to Leander. "My suggestion," he said, "is that each of you take one of these papers with you. I've been working on this project for some years. I've tested it in numerous ways, and it works about as well as can be expected."

Kyale, who had insisted on a chair, reached past her brother and picked up the top paper from the pile, which she held between thumb and forefinger with a dubious air.

Everyone stared. The paper was rectangular, about the length of a man's hand from fingertip to wrist, and as wide as one's little finger. The paper was very smooth, beige in color. Kyale's mouth crimped as she stared at it, for she could perceive magic woven right into the paper, something she'd never seen before.

"How does this work?" Leander asked, taking up the next one. His lips parted, his bright green eyes wide with delight. "What did you do to it?"

"I made the paper myself," Siamis said. "Spells at every level. You can write to anyone who has one, but only to those who have them. All you need to do is write their name before the message, while envisioning the person."

"Do we have to write with something special?" Dirk asked.

"Anything will do. But always write the name first, and envision the person. If you leave either of those out, the message will not transfer."

"What happens when it fills up?" CJ asked, scowling at the one in Kyale's hand. "It's so small. That won't take long."

"Smear over the words from right to left—opposite direction you wrote in—and the ink, or chalk, will bead up. Shake the paper and it's ready to use again. Or just wait, and the words will fade within an hour." As he spoke, Siamis took up a third, dipped a quill into the ink by Leander's hand, and scrawled on the paper.

He then held it up so all could see. Then he brushed his finger over the words, which ran together into drops of ink. He snapped the paper, and the ink flew off—but it didn't splatter. Instead, it vanished.

"Waste Spell," Atan murmured. "That is quite clever."

It was far more than clever, Clair was thinking. It had taken a great deal of hard work to make that. She turned her serious gaze to Siamis, who merely nodded his thanks for Atan's neutral praise, as if he'd done a small favor like going out to pluck some fresh herbs from the pots on the kitchen terrace. It occurred to Clair that he had not expected any acknowledgment of that hard work.

Then he lifted his head to address the room. "It's inevitable that the enemy will find out about them. If it's you they catch, draw a line while focusing on 'Norsunder' and…"

He slashed the quill in a line across the top, then the paper disintegrated in his fingers.

"Wow! Uh, can it get wet?" CJ asked, "What if you slop on it?"

"It is paper, so treat it as you do any paper — it can get wet, but you'd best let it dry out before using it again, or it will tear."

Conversation buzzed then, everyone marveling or questioning or eager to test for themselves. Atan waited while Siamis fielded a few more questions — repeating himself patiently — then she stood.

"I was going to ask you all to observe what you can, count enemies you see, and remember it all when you come back. I intend to establish a map for future planning, since no one else seems to be making an effort in that direction. Grateful as we are for any aids brought forward." A gesture toward the beige papers as many side-eyed Siamis, who merely stood by, no change in his polite expression. "I was also going to suggest a possible time. If you can get back by harvest month, just as a suggestion, we might begin considering larger plans. But we have to see what we have to work with."

Nobody argued with that.

Atan then added, "I'd also ask that those of you who know others who might help, take an extra paper for them. For example, some of you seem to think that Senrid went back to Marloven Hess. Which makes sense. If anyone's quest leads to Halia, then take one to him? I'd very much like to get him involved in our plans."

Voices rose, suggesting various names. Siamis left as noiselessly as he had entered. No one paid him any heed except for Leander, who had been contemplating the amount of labor Siamis had gone to — it had to have been at least a two-year project if he did nothing else. "Thank you," he called.

Atan heard that, turned, saw that Siamis was gone, and made a mental note to thank him as well. She, too, had an idea of the work involved. But she found the context troubling. That labor had to have commenced years ago. She even recollected Senrid worrying about the scribe desks being compromised if Norsunder did attack, which everyone at that time attributed to Marloven war-thinking. Impossible to interfere with the scribe desks, much less bring them down!

That troubling sense caused her to catch Liere's eye as she was about to leave.

"I take it you are also going away?" Atan asked.

"If there will not be any planning until after harvest, Andri wants to go home. And on the way, we can both do some scouting for your map," Liere promised.

"Good. I'd also like to request another favor."

Liere looked an inquiry.

"Reluctant as I am, I do begin to believe Tsauderei is right that Detlev truly is working against Norsunder, even if he's not quite on our side. In any case, if so, we ought to at least get one of these papers to Detlev. In case he might consider cooperating with us, whatever else he's doing. Or not doing."

Liere's first thought was, *You don't think Siamis already gave him one?* But she kept quiet.

"Will you take one to him? You're the best with Dena Yeresbeth. You ought to be able to find him."

Liere was as reluctant as Atan, but for different reasons. "I will," she said, because she rated her own inclinations as entirely selfish, wanting to go to Enaeran just to be by Andri's side. It gave her deep pleasure to remind herself that she had a whole lifetime ahead for that, and took a second paper from the now much thinner stack.

"I'll set aside two for Senrid and Jilo," Atan said. "If they don't show up soon, no doubt someone else will find them."

Two

THERE CAME AT LAST a day that dawned to a world of drips, the third day of a thaw. Those going north decided to depart in a group while the sky was so clear. The artifact seekers began to talk of departing from Mearsies Heili.

After a lot of internal debate, Mildred, one of Arthur's mage students from Geth, pried Arthur out of his corner of the library, where he was half-hidden by a pile of books and papers, and asked if he could give her some advice.

"I can try," he said, with a lopsided smile. "But you ought to know, I only feel confident about books, scholarship, and archives. For advice about martial matters, you'd do best consulting pretty much anyone else."

Mildred flashed a smile, her pupils narrowing to vertical slits in the manner of a laughing cat. Do cats laugh, he wondered, as she said, "But you are the only person I know here, as yet. And this is a personal matter. You will be far ahead of me. Anyone would be!"

One of the things he liked about her was her frank admission of her very odd past, delivered without an emotional firestorm.

They walked out onto the terrace, where a strong breeze blew rain clouds away. She perched easily on a rail above an unimaginable drop that made him shudder as she said, "The one who raised me told me that making friends was easy. Making enemies was easier. But he never had a thing to say about friends that really aren't friends anymore, but aren't enemies."

"Oh." Arthur noticed that he'd brought the quill he'd been writing with, and stuck it behind his ear, a gesture learned in infancy from his mother, the mage Erai-Yanya. "Let me guess. Caris-Merian Rhoderan?"

Mildred's pupils rounded as she regarded him in dismay. "I didn't show it?"

"No, no," he hastened to reassure her. "I probably would miss the signs even if you had. My guess was process of elimination, the two of you being the only two from Geth. You were in Roth Drael when she came to Bereth Ferian, and then the attack happened. Between that and having to send students home, I forgot to tell you that we had a second Geth person among us."

To his relief, her expression eased. Though she was as tall as he and lean in her loose black clothes, she was one of the kindest people he'd ever met. Martial arts and kindness was an unusual combination in his experience — but one that had first attracted him to Roy.

"It took me by surprise," she said. "Coming face to face with her here, on this world. But when I saw her, everything I'd managed to forget about Les Rhoderan, and the rest, rushed back on me."

"You were involved with that?" Arthur asked. Roy had never mentioned Mildred. But he talked very little about the days when Detlev's boys were living under cover on Geth-deles.

"Everyone in the wanderers' city was involved," she said. "I liked Les. Most everyone did. And Caris-Merian liked those who liked her wonderful, inspiring brother."

"But?" Arthur prompted.

"She was, you might say, my first crush. Ah, those eyes, so true! And yet, the more I liked her, the less I…eh, I did not dislike Les. I thought it was just my past making my view, eh, skewed, but Les's plans scented, ah, I did not have the words. I do not now. I could not choose whom to tell. So when a convoy taking wood west to the Empire in trade for silk needed an extra marine defender, I hired on. By the time I got back, Les was dead. Stabbed by one of the boys I'd scrapped with. Turned out to be Norsundrian spies, so it was said. But they were gone, and Caris-Merian was still there, only she'd changed, or I'd changed. I don't quite know how to describe it."

She flung back a glossy dark braid, and turned a pained smile toward Arthur. She hesitated, trying to find words that would not be unfair – or misleading. Or hurtful, for she knew without ever using marsh-mad to sniff out emotions that the others meant well when they seated the two Geth girls together, and assigned them rooms next to one another.

And Mildred appreciated it. Ten years ago, she would have liked nothing better, and traces of that intense crush still lingered, for Caris-Merian had grown into Mildred's ideal of beauty. But the Charis-Merian of today was not the young teen Caris-Merian of those days any more than Mildred was the young teen who had escaped life imprisonment for accident of birth, changed her name, and began a life of adventure.

"Me, I still like her. When she talks about the things that used to delight her. Drawing. Singing – she was a very good singer, did you know? Sure silent now, eh. I think she still – somewhat – thinks me a friend. But she does not see *me*. Not anymore. I can see it, she doesn't like it when I duck out when she gets around to how somebody ought to take out David. Somebody good at fighting."

"And that somebody is you," Arthur said, rocking back and forth from heel to toe. "I see. And I actually have a suggestion – learned from years of helpful people trying to drag me out of musty libraries to ride, or swim, or do something besides pore over old, moldy tomes. If you want to hang onto the bits of your old friendship, try steering the talk to other things. Maybe even give her another purpose besides her revenge?"

Mildred had tried already. More than once. But she wouldn't reject advice she had just asked for. Advice that in general sounded good. "Thank you," she said, consciously remembering manners.

There was another thing bothering Mildred, and again she ascribed that to her early life. Even so, later that day, Mildred drew Roy aside and asked him to look out for the more hapless of the travelers.

He gazed at her in mild surprise. "That's why I'm going," he said.

Mildred bobbed her head, an action she had consciously learned from watching others.

Emboldened by her success, she decided to follow Arthur's advice. Mildred sought Caris-Merian Rhoderan, her purpose firm in mind when she met those wideset, earnest eyes, under a high, thoughtful brow, but oh, so cold, so cold. "I don't think the younger ones understand the danger," Mildred said, looking at small, bright-eyed Sherry, about as ready for self-defense as a bunny, and Falinneh of the wiry, fire-bright red braids, who turned everything into a joke. Everything.

Caris-Merian gazed back at Mildred, whom Les had admired so much. "As you ask, I will make it my own quest."

She turned away, and Mildred watched her straight back with its entrancing curve from shoulder inward and then out to her hips, and the long, graceful curve of her legs.

Could that be considered a success? Mildred perceived that Caris-Merian still saw her as a martial artist, a potential weapon to be wielded, and not as herself. But perhaps her request might have given Caris-Merian a worthy task that might even take her mind off her revenge plans?

After breakfast the following day, Dirk Sonscarna grabbed CJ's arm.

When she turned her head to protest, he whispered, "Include Kyale Marlonen in our group and I'm off."

CJ shrugged. "Oh, Kyale's not so bad. If you know her." Though, she thought to herself, Kyale had become less fun since she decided to grow up.

"I don't intend to get to know her. Not while anything is at stake. And I won't travel with her." As he said this, Dirk readied for rejection. He wasn't going to tell CJ, or anyone, that going after the double crown was Kessler's assignment to his son—his first important assignment. And he needed someone not male to make it more possible. But not at the cost of traveling with someone who turned every small thing into a dramatic stage play.

CJ protested, "But then we'll lose Troy, whose music is so good, and there'd be more people to keep night watch, and—"

"Without 'em we'll be faster. You can always have a tour with them when the war is over. If Kyale's big mouth doesn't get 'em killed."

War. There it was again, another reminder. Was it wrong, CJ wondered, to try to make your days fun, or at least bearable, while you were doing the right thing? She sighed. "All right. I'll have to think of an excuse — "

"Tell 'em the truth." His voice was soft, and his light blue eyes direct and steady. He didn't look like a kid of eleven or so at that moment so much as he looked like his father — a person who ranked high in CJ's personal pantheon of villains.

She snorted. "Sometimes you are just like Kessler."

"Thank you." He grinned, knowing very well just how much of a compliment that had been. The grin also hid fear. He knew fear was not a moral failing. His father's fearlessness was a defect, Kessler had said, as usual telling the blunt truth. *I'm not sane. No one could be, who survived Wan-Edhe.* But instinct kept Dirk from explaining; many found CJ annoying, but Dirk knew she was loyal to friends. She would not like hearing that Dirk meant to avoid Kyale Marlonen simply because he couldn't stand to be around her.

CJ sighed again, and went to the dining room, where the others about to depart had gathered for breakfast. She did not notice what she ate. The bright glances, the restless jokes and gusting laughter — much more than the jokes warranted — she recognized as that cranked-up mix of excitement and fear. Pre-adventure jitters. You're scared but you know you're going to do it anyway, so you try to make it normal, or even fun.

Here in Mearsies Heili, it was so good to be safe. All the terrors of winter had faded, but that was going to end as soon as they stepped outside the borders. If she and Dirk were not going to start a big stink about going in the same direction as Roy's group, that meant leaving now, while all the others were finishing breakfast, dunking their dishes into the bucket with the magic on it, and packing. It sounded like packing was going to take a while. Kyale's voice fluted above the others about which dresses to take along.

CJ bolted for the library, where she knew that Clair and Atan often met to study. It was a relief to see Clair sitting with books and papers, one bare foot tucked beneath her. No sign of joining any of the traveling groups. CJ hoped that meant someone smarter than she was had talked Clair into staying in Mearsies Heili, and letting some other id — some other brave person tackle smelling out the Host in whatever lair they were stinking up.

CJ spotted little Aurora, Clair's daughter, playing with some dolls on the floor, and swooped down to give her a bone-cracking hug.

The others looked up from the books they had laid out on the table. "We're off." CJ tried to sound casual, but she heard her own voice come out a little too loud and a little too high.

Clair fought her way through her own whirl of reactions. "Promise to keep in touch by the magic-papers?"

"Promise." CJ managed to sound more normal. She turned away, knowing that lingering would make it harder for Clair, who hated letting her feelings show. And besides, there was Dirk, standing in the doorway expectantly. "I'll get my gear," she said to him.

Clair sat on her balcony with Atan, Mildred of Geth, and some of the guild representatives to discuss the latest refugee arrivals at the hereto sparsely populated Tornasio Islands—specifically the blockade Norsunder had set up. Or were trying to set up, despite the weird fog that could not be penetrated, or interfered with by magic.

While the others talked, Clair mentally followed CJ as she and Dirk transferred to the border. CJ had forgotten her mind-shield again.

As they could use magic within the border of Mearsies Heili, they transferred to a Destination at a back road into Ujban. Clair was vaguely aware of the chatter around her as she mentally followed CJ over the border, and shared her relief when CJ did not see any of the fog that confronted travelers from the other direction. No enemy in sight. So far, it seemed, Norsunder had not put anyone permanently along that border. Nothing was there but grassy hills.

CJ began singing a lively song whose lyrics she had rewritten to slander Norsunder as she and Dirk marched together up into the hills. CJ delighted in the balmy air, the sunlight slightly milky, as it often was in early spring, and the sight of the sunnier mud patches fuzzed with green shoots.

"Refugees." Atan's voice broke Clair's concentration, and she swayed a little on her chair as she re-oriented inside her own head.

"Refugees," Clair repeated, striving to recover the subject while aware of a pulse of guilt over being inadvertently rude. "We're getting a lot, I know. But we have space, and there is all the extra farming that the regional governors are encouraging."

"That is an excellent start, and it parallels the secret harvests that Rel and the Colendi and Sarendan guilds at the east end of Sartor have been planting in abandoned fields and hills away from towns or roads," Atan said. "The secret harvest plan also gives those hiding in the hills something to do. But speaking of refugees here, they aren't here to settle. And many don't want to farm. They'll want something else to do, or they might find something to do."

Clair had learned that Mildred had a strange sort of Dena Yeresbeth that was called "marsh-mad." She spoke in that distinctive, rhythmic Geth accent, her voice husky. Clair had been startled on their first meeting when she saw Mildred's pupils shrink to vertical slits, like cat eyes.

Mildred was also learning magic. There was some mystery about her origin, resulting in her being sent to another world to study magic, though Geth had its own schools. Hadn't Liere been sent to one? Maybe Mildred came here for similar reasons to Liere being sent there.

"Me, I took a ride around your mountain here," Mildred said. "I discovered many, many shells of buildings? Empty, but not so old they could not be fixed, eh?"

"That's the old Chwahir outpost, right, Clair? Rebuilding those sounds like a possible suggestion. What do you think?" Atan turned to Clair.

"I think it's a good idea. But I know little beyond that. We've had no occasion for such projects, not for centuries."

"I have to contend with every aspect of such efforts, including dealing with the guilds," Atan said. "If you wish to delegate the task to me, I would be happy to help."

Clair bowed. "Certainly. Offering refugees work to do, and places to stay at the end of it, the treasury will accommodate that. We have Spring Festival coming before long. Perhaps that can be a date to aim for." From the way Atan's expression shuttered into politeness, Clair saw that she had vastly underrated (or overrated?) the time needed to clear out and make weathertight the old Chwahir domiciles left from the military encampment that had once threatened the capital.

Atan and Mildred delved into the mysteries of wood rescue, joiners, stonemasons, and the like. Apparently Mildred came from an island kingdom that had suffered much damage from pirate attacks. She knew quite a bit about city planning.

Clair listened, squashing the instinct to check on CJ — and

so went the next few days, until a message appeared on the scry desk in her room. Captain Heraford's ship had returned, as usual chased by a squadron of Chwahir trysails, which he was in the process of losing in the fog.

When word came, Atan looked up sharply, her expression vivid with painful hope, then fell when there was no message from Rel. Again. But she said nothing, so Clair, Mildred, and little Aurora, the only ones who had witnessed that revealing moment, pretended that nothing had happened.

Intermittently, when neither duty (such as it was) nor love (Aurora's lessons, or her questions) interfered, Clair permitted herself a quick scan on the mental plane as CJ and Dirk progressed north. Quick checks, as the shadows jumped from left to right, until one day, Clair sensed an awareness scanning in a covert manner. Not CJ's — CJ was properly blocked off.

Clair shut away the mental realm, annoyed with herself for forgetting that though she was physically safe, that was not necessarily true in the realm of the mind. No more reaching that way. She would have to try the strange papers that Siamis had made.

But first: to ready for her own quest.

She looked around her room, dug into her trunk for her old travel bag, then startled when her daughter piped up from the doorway, "You're going away, too, Ma? Can I come?"

Clair turned.

Aurora looked so much like Clair now — white hair, and a square face beginning to emerge from the baby-roundness. Others saw in her Clair's observant greenish-gray eyes; Clair saw only question there, and a cautious hope.

"I'm sorry," she said. "It's too dangerous."

Aurora's brow puckered. "Then you shouldn't go."

"I mean to keep the danger at a distance. But someone has to go. Someone who hasn't a ward against them."

Aurora's brow remained puckered, then she said, "They killed Crystal Ingrid, didn't they?"

"Yes."

"So they would try to kill me, too."

"That's my fear."

Aurora had been clutching a doll to her side. It was a stuffed toy, a dog one of Crystal Ingrid's many friends among the Marloven servants had made. She had had so many such toys she had given this dog to Aurora the last time they saw one another.

"If I learn Dena Yeresbeth lessons," Aurora said. "Can I find Crystal Ingrid?"

Clair hid the pang the question gave her. "I don't know. You could ask Liere when she comes to visit."

Aurora tipped her head. "Siamis said he would give me lessons."

Clair remembered that Siamis was around, though elusive at best. Unlike Atan (and many others) she was neutral about him. While she did not know him well enough for trust, she did not distrust him; she could never forget that on their first encounter, before he'd put her under his enchantment (which had merely been a dream state, during which no one had even aged) he had held a conversation with her unlike any other conversation, one in which he had spoken peer to peer. Until then no other adult had done that; though, looking back, he was barely adult age then. But he hadn't treated her like a stupid kid. Further, every word he'd said had proved to be true. "Siamis would be the best to ask," she said.

Aurora didn't want Clair to leave. It seemed to her terribly dangerous. But Clair was going to go. Aurora knew that when the word "duty" was mentioned, there'd be no gainsaying.

CJ had said once that when Aurora got older the girls would all be her sisters, and not her aunties. Right now the girls were still aunties. They could make decisions and act on them, but Aurora had to do what she was told.

Though she would miss Clair even worse than she was already missing CJ and the other girls who had gone artifact-hunting, there would be long sunny days in which to play with the Delieth kids—and, perhaps, get those lessons and find Crystal Ingrid, wherever people's spirits went.

She pattered off to play, and Clair went to find Julian, who had offered to go with her. "He's back," she said. "We can set sail tomorrow, with anyone who wishes to touch at the Sartoran continent."

Julian slipped out to seek June, who had chosen one of the tower rooms, and lay on a round bed in the round room, a scattering of handwritten books around her.

"If you want to come, we're leaving tomorrow."

June had systematically gone through all the books in the library, then asked Erai-Yanya, pursuing any scrap of information about the cup possibly named Ethe, or from Ethe.

Nothing. Maybe travel would disclose a hint. "Okay," she said.

The next day, the last of the quest seekers left, Clair so quietly that many did not realize she was among their number until they realized they hadn't seen her white hair anywhere about. It was Liere and Andri who drew exclamations of good wishes and exhortations to be careful. Both were popular — Liere a legend, surely about to embark on another world-famous adventure.

There was no outward sign of parting from either Clair or Aurora, only an exchange of smiles, and of loving thoughts from mind to mind. But after the little group was out of sight, Aurora's small hand stole into Atan's, and the Sartoran queen forced her worries away for later contemplation — she utterly hated this quest of Clair's, though she understood why she was making it — and exerted herself to make cheerful conversation about the morning's activities.

She never realized that Aurora's gesture was meant to give as much as it was to take comfort.

Three

From the seafloor to the south coast of Drael

SOME YEARS BEFORE, KYALE Marlonen had been sent through a Worldgate, along with Senrid and some others. There, they had been loaned golden armbands with magic that enabled humans to breathe, and see, underwater. Unlike the rest, Kyale had not surrendered hers before returning to Sartorias-deles. She'd brought it back, and had found it useful once or twice, but after she relinquished the Child Spell it became too tight. Once she took it off, she lost interest in it, which made it easy to graciously donate it when Clair asked to see if she could duplicate the magic as a project.

Clair had needed projects like that in those days, after her great-grandmother reappeared in the world, firmly reclaimed the throne that Clair had inherited from her mother, and proceeded to change everything about governing small Mearsies Heili back to how it had been the century previous.

Clair had, with some help from the northern mages, managed to reproduce the armband, and then made a third, her thought being that one day she, CJ, and Aurora might explore the ocean floor. Which was reputed to be both fascinating and very dangerous. "You can see *them*," Kyale had said about the armband. "But no one will see *you*."

After a swift sea crossing, driven by the spiraling winds out of the east, Clair gave armbands to June and Julian.

The *Tzasilia* drifted like a ghost ship toward the Nob, the extreme end of Halia's peninsula, infamous for being raided over the centuries, especially by pirates. Now Norsunder held it, or tried to hold it — every storm seemed to bring new damage to their quarters, supply buildings, and patrols. Impossible to point to any human agency.

Well-primed about the surliness of the Nob folk, Liere and Andri departed under cover of night, immediately swallowed in shadows, followed by the others venturing across the Sartoran continent.

Captain Heraford and Clair had known one another for as long as she could remember, he having rescued her and her cousin when they were small, paid off by the mage Mondros at the time. Heraford had begun life as pirate's get, claiming to be a privateer when it had suited him. His background might have been dubious, but Clair had trusted him — and trust had caused him to become trustworthy, especially when Clair's cousin Puddlenose showed a passionate interest in sailing ships and the sea.

Years and magical aids later, they understood one another, but still he said, "I really don't like your going ashore. I don't think you know how bad it is."

Clair remained mute. He understood then that she would do what she considered her duty. Nothing more to be said. He nodded eastward. "The winter winds and current is still strong, which means we won't be able to outrun anything coming up the strait."

Clair said, "We prepared for that."

Clair, Julian, and June climbed out of the boat that Heraford himself had rowed. Clair waved at the breakers. "Shall we?"

"Ugh, it's cold," Julian complained as they tromped knee-deep in the foaming waves.

June dove suddenly, cutting the water neatly. Her head bobbed up once and she gasped. Her frizzled mat of hair had flattened to her skull, making her almost unrecognizable. She then ducked underwater. And bubbles rose up — she being the first to try breathing under water.

Clair plunged after her, but Julian waded in a step at a time, making faces at each surge and splash, until only her head was left. Then, taking a last breath, she puffed out her cheeks and ducked under.

Instinct was strong, and taking that first breath was

difficult, particularly for Julian, who mistrusted magic even at the best of times. A couple bubbles escaped her nose and she opened her eyes, which promptly stung from the brine. She vaguely made out swimming shapes.

Her lungs began to burn, so she forced herself to draw water into her nose, bracing for the terrible burn, or choke —

Cold, pure air drew from the water and into her lungs. Magic cleared her sight, the salty sting left her eyes, the cold vanished. Clair and June floated near the bottom a few arm-lengths below her. All three watched the *Tzasilia* begin to move, cutting through the water, which created a slow, purling arrow of a wake, as Captain Heraford began his quest to get into every harbor he could in order to evaluate numbers and defenses.

The three girls swam down into the ocean's depths. Magic made the most of the moonlight, revealing the uneven floor, and undersea life, plant and fish, moving with dreamy slowness. Clair and June swam side by side, and glimpsed fish outlined in silver light.

They dove ever downward. The undersea terrain changed, rocky formations giving way to valleys, and great, ancient sea plants of stunning variety twisting upward, the tops waving gently in the never-ending dance of the tides and currents.

Sea-creatures either ignored or shied away from them. From time to time the bottom sheered away into a sudden drop, an wide and apparently bottomless valley wherein even magic did not permit them to see; certainly no light penetrated there. Whatever lived in those depths depended upon other senses, an eerily disturbing thought: they were aliens here, in an environment both interesting and potentially hostile.

Clair really enjoyed this strange journey. They encountered no mer-people, nor sapient sea-creatures who could communicate, though she strongly had the sense of their progress being marked.

The sun rose, lancing down golden rays that danced, revealing and concealing weird structures that might have been natural or made. They avoided anything that could house mer folk, who were reputed to be hostile to land people.

When the sun faded again, they were very tired, and finally slept, suspended in the water, carried along by the strong currents.

That was the pattern for another day and night, which

ended with flashes of purple light, as far, far above, a thunderstorm smashed its way over the sea. Clair and June watched with great enjoyment as they were rocked gently; Julian slept.

One morning they woke to see almond shapes cutting the surface far above them: ships.

Long distance contact was dangerous for many reasons, not the least of which was that the one trying to find someone over great distances would not know how to anchor the physical self, and could lose the way back, wandering in the mental realm until the body, denied its consciousness, withered away to death. So Roy of the poopsies, Detlev's old group, had taught Clair how to construct a false identity behind which to do mental spying. It was this trick that she was going to use in her quest to discover exactly where the Host of Lords had taken up residence.

She thought staring upward, why not practice now?

Keeping her gaze steadily on one of the almond shapes, she quested mentally—and a confused jumble of images and emotions flooded her mind, one impression clear: they were on the hunt.

The girls dove farther down, and swam steadily to the northeast. They only knew that they were approaching land when the ocean floor began to slope upward again, past rocky hillocks, and deep crevasses, and here and there the splintered wooden remains of sunken ships. Julian often explored these, but Clair never did, though she observed how colorful undersea life slowly transformed the wooden hulls and decking and masts into garden floors for amazingly odd plants as well as living space for sea creatures. Julian found an age-crusted knife in one ship, and took it up, intending to clean it.

At last the seafloor turned to sand, and light danced in mote-filled shafts around them. They spotted a harbor from underneath, and veered away again, swimming east against the current until they found a secluded inlet. Up, up, until they rode the waves in, and then stood, feeling as if they had been made of stone, their clothing soggy, their bodies shivering as the magic spell broke.

"I feel like I'm wearing armor," Julian said, stomping ashore. Her voice came out a croak, after so many days of not using it.

They stood in the rising breeze and stared uphill at a

tumble of shore greenery much like that at home.

"The more I dry, the itchier I'm getting," Clair said. "Since we don't seem to have any cleaning frames, let's find a stream and bathe in that."

Julian pointed at a tree-crowded spot between two hillocks. Sure enough, there was a stream, rushing down seaward.

All three were itchy and hot by the time they reached it, and flopped in gratefully. Once again the magic seized them. Clair lay on her back on the bottom of the stream, watching the hand's-breadth of clear water rush directly overhead, sparkling in the sun. Beyond, trees and shrubs rippled. Was this the way fish saw the world above?

Finally she felt she was as rinsed out as she would ever be. The urge to communicate with those at home was strong now, and so she sat up, wrung out hair and clothes, and picked a nice flat stone to sit on in the clear sunlight, so she could dry as she wrote notes.

Now that the magic had relinquished them, they were all hungry. Julian went off to look for fresh food so they wouldn't have to broach the heavy slabs of traveler's bread that each carried.

Clair sat down and opened her knapsack, which was supposed to be waterproof.

It was—her single change of clothes was dry, and there was her beige paper.

> *CJ—We're up from the ocean, a wonderful journey. I'd like to repeat it with you and the gang when we have peace again. We'll find out where we are when we can. Anything to report? Have you heard from the others? — Clair*

As soon as Clair had penciled her name on the odd beige paper the words vanished. She sat there watching the blank paper for a time, then folded it and put it away. She was hungry, and either CJ wrote back — or she didn't.

But just as she was opening her pack a flicker in her head, a lot like a magic alarm, made her think *Letter.*

She flung her pack down and unfolded her note. CJ's distinctive scrawl now covered the beige paper.

*Clair! It's GREAT to hear from you! I'm with Dirk.
We're crossing eastward just along the Fereledria, and
enjoying the cold weather. Was hot in Al Tradhe. Oh, I
could write more, but Dirk is impatient to get
bucketing. Write ANY TIME if something disgusting
happens. CJ*

Clair smiled, swiped her finger along the words, and
watched the ink blob up. She shook both finger and paper, and
observed the ink blurring almost like ashfall, then vanishing.

Julian looked a question.

Clair said, "CJ. They seem to be in a hurry."

June reappeared at a run. "Horseback riders on a road up
that way."

The isolation that had surrounded them under water vanished.

"Let's get moving," Julian said.

———————

North from Mersies Heili to Alcandamer

The first few days of CJ and Dirk's travel had been uneventful.

Midway through the afternoon of CJ's and Clair's
exchange, they spied a market town nestled in a valley near a
lazily winding river, where the ribbons of two roads crossed.

"We're more than halfway through our nutbread," CJ
said, adding mentally that she was getting to be pretty sick of
it. Each day she let hunger build longer and longer, hoping it
would taste good again. "Want to save our stash of food and
get something there?" CJ asked.

"No," Dirk snapped.

CJ bit back a sarcastic comment. She was experienced
enough as a traveler to know that getting into a fight with your
only company turned travel into a misery.

She glanced at Dirk's taut face, and said, "What's going
on?"

He didn't answer. Oooooo-kay, then. She Would Not Pick
A Fight, but she didn't have to talk to him, either. They walked
in silence until stumbling in weak starlight got harder to
endure, then they settled along the banks of a stream. Last thing
CJ saw was Dirk sitting up, watching the horizon.

Another clear dawn woke them, and they wolfed down a slice apiece of nut-studded traveler's bread, and started out at as energetic a pace as the day before.

CJ sneaked troubled glances at Dirk from time to time. This sudden, unceasing wariness she attributed at first to his training and background, but that did not explain his narrowed gaze, the grim line to his mouth, the sharp reactions at unexpected noises.

Late that day, she forced out the question bothering her most. "Is it me you're worried about? It is, isn't it?"

"No. My doubts are about my abilities, not yours," he admitted.

She gaped. "What? But you're the best of any of us! Best at fighting, and running, and scouting—at everything. Good as a poopsie, not that I would ever tell those rockheads they were good at anything."

Dirk sighed, and tipped his head back. All right, here it was. Though maybe needn't tell everything. "Night before last I got a long-distance contact from Sveneric. He said he got one from Detlev."

"Uh oh." If there was anyone more formidable, unreadable, and unhuman-seeming than Detlev, it was his son Sveneric. "What?"

"Yeres and Efael seem to have given up trying to find them. Someone overheard the Black Knives getting orders to seek for me. As a way of getting back at Kessler."

Kessler. CJ was not the only person who was afraid of Dirk's strange father, whose brilliance in the military arts had, it appeared, also extended to magic. It was Kessler who had closed the world so that no one could leave, which meant Norsunder could not reach their waiting forces in the Beyond.

And then Kessler had effectively vanished.

CJ let out a low whistle. "So that's why you don't want to stop in a village?"

"I don't want anyone to see us. We can't know how many spies they have. Sveneric says, even birds flying overhead, their brains taken over by Norsundrians. And…" He sighed, then forced the words out, "I think I might have been spotted. When we crossed the border. I was watching an eagle drifting round and round. Didn't think anything of it, at first."

CJ's neck tightened. She remembered very well what old Tsauderei had told them about the two youngest members of the Host of Lords — the two who, four thousand years before, had managed to hunt down Detlev's nephew Siamis in order to use him as bait to trap Detlev, when Siamis was her own age. CJ could not suppress a shudder.

Dirk said, "Whatever you heard, it's worse. Especially Efael. Though Yeres is not far behind."

"Okay," CJ said, shivering again. "No other people. At the first sight of anyone, let's hide."

Clair and CJ exchanged letters every night. Letters full of jokes, and light-hearted gossip gleaned from friends, for CJ was indefatigable about writing whenever Dirk permitted them to stop.

At sunset on the third, Dirk watched over CJ's shoulder as her pencil dashed over the rumpled beige paper.

> — *Anyway, I hadn't known that Alcandamer was so*
> *big. We've had no success whatever finding a hint of*
> *this Queen Charlana. I'm going to be mad if it turns*
> *out she skipped the country and took that stupid crown*
> *with her. CJ*

Dirk looked away. He knew why they hadn't found a hint of Charlana, who was reputed to be a mage of some ability: because he would not permit CJ to ask questions. As for the double-crown of Alcandamer, Dirk didn't see how it would be useful for a war of liberation, but Kessler wanted it. So Dirk was going to find it no matter how long it took.

CJ watched the ink blob and dissipate, then sat back tiredly.

Dirk said, "You know you can always leave and go north on your own."

Stark blue eyes turned his way, CJ's thin, expressive dark brows above quirked into a frown. Nobody ever was in doubt about what CJ was thinking.

"You think I'm the sort to abandon a friend just because we get a little tired?" CJ retorted. "Look. If you think I'm slowing you up, say so. Otherwise, let's keep going. I understand why you don't want us to ask questions in these little towns — too easy for the villains to ask if anyone has seen any strangers asking questions. Let's eavesdrop instead."

Dirk looked down at his hands. CJ had been as good as her word. She might not be much with weaponry, but now that they were in one of Alcandamer's river valleys, with its frequent dotting of market towns, she listened well in crowds without anyone paying her more than a heartbeat's attention.

And it was a relief to have someone to talk to.

"All right," he said. "Let's get moving."

South coast of Drael

Clair and her companions traveled eastward along the strait. Each night they camped somewhere well away from civilization. When she could sit and concentrate, Clair constructed her phony persona and went mind-questing, skimming only the surface thoughts of the clusters that meant patrols and the like.

Once a sleeping Norsundrian with Dena Yeresbeth woke when she brushed his mental guard, and he demanded identity, reaching for hers at the same time. Clair withdrew so fast she was dizzy for a considerable time after.

She became far more cautious. After crossing a border from one country to another, she tried again outside of a large city built along a river—and discovered a general tension in anticipation of Llyenthur making one of his flying inspections. The charged atmosphere of fearful expectancy, of suppressed anger, caused her and the girls to go to ground and hide. Clair dared another foray, firmly keeping her false persona as an image—a hulking guard   to discover a gloat amid the tension. She eased closer. Ah. Some commander, gloating over a trap. Then appeared the commander's view of Llyenthur, a tall, thin, and very sarcastic young man, who turned his gaze toward the commander—and Clair winked out fast.

"What happened?" Julian asked, low-voiced, as they crouched under some brambles.

"Don't know," Clair said. "I didn't dare stay."

"Can you take a quick poke? I love it when they do our work for us by taking each other out," Julian said.

Clair settled herself, shut her eyes, made sure her false image was firm, and ventured cautiously into the mental plane.

The other two, watching, nearly jumped into the brambles when Clair violently recoiled, then looked around sightlessly, breathing fast.

Clair shuddered. "I don't think I'll do that again without preparing better." She shivered, eyes closed, then said, "He sensed me right away. I think I would have been caught but he was at that moment transferring the one who made the trap."

"By magic?" Julian repeated. "What, where?"

"It was very distinct," Clair said. "Not the image so much as the sense of overwhelming threat, and a location: in Imar."

"Imar," Julian repeated. "That's at the far end of the strait. What now?"

Clair's head ached, and the dizziness caused not just by prolonged contact but by her reaction to the brush with discovery, made it hard to think.

She looked at the other two. June sat as she always did, her expression closed, the late afternoon sun shining through the brambles sparks along the rim of the cup that she turned about, over and over, in her hands.

"I wonder if Imar is enough for Atan. No, it's not. I know little about war planning, other than what I read in a single book, but one thing was clear: the more specific the information the better."

"That's obvious." Julian grinned. "Why d'you think there are spies?"

Clair swallowed. Her throat seemed dry, but she knew it was residual fear, not illness. Instinct clamored so strongly to abandon this quest and to go home, to safety and beauty and peace.

Which would leave the ugly task to someone else.

Oh, if only she knew that someone more qualified was doing the same task—someone like Detlev! Both her royal visitors thought he'd abandoned them all. In fact, Tahra Delieth, whose hatred of Detlev as the embodiment of evil had become a passion, was convinced he'd switched sides yet again, and now worked for Norsunder.

Atan, more reasonable, thought that he was merely hiding, for surely the Host of Lords would have him as their first target. Atan also thought his abilities were overrated, and that his morals—despite his having come to the lighter side—were probably not worth examining too closely. Someone like that would of course put his own safety first.

Clair was not so sure. She'd only met Detlev a few times, and those were brief, but she had seen the poopsies in action from up close, and knew how very well trained they were. She thought suddenly of David, the leader of the poopsies. She doubted very much that he would be hiding. He wasn't the kind to hide — or hadn't been. He was the type who acted.

As for Detlev, Clair remained convinced that everyone underestimated him — even CJ, who considered him just another adult bully, whether Norsundrian or not.

The thing was, no one *knew* what he was doing. Or where he was. He might even be dead, and they would probably never know. Clair hoped not, if only for the sake of Sveneric, Detlev's son, one of the people Clair liked best in the world.

Who did that leave, if he and his gang were — elsewhere?

Ordinary people — like her.

"Let's go to Imar."

Four

DAVID LAY ON A low hill outside Choreid Dhelerei, over-looking a crossroads. Mindful of a betraying silhouette, he peered through the long spring-green grass. He lay so still that small insects flitted or crawled or bumbled about nearby on their business, heedless of the monstrous two-leg in their midst.

David amused himself by observing them until he saw dust rising above the hill to the north. A couple heartbeats after that, the same pattern repeated alongside the river branch to the south.

The two patrols converged at the crossroads, their timing impeccable. David watched the two patrol captains meet and talk briefly, one pointing back to the north, the other assenting. Orders passed and acknowledged. What? No way to find out — yet.

They rode on.

David watched the last four riders of the northern patrol vanish to the south. Soulbound, all four, looking neither left nor right. There was no longer any purpose to their lives, except as directed by the malign will controlling them: they existed as spare pairs of eyes, and to kill when told to kill.

David's hand tingled. If he had a bow ...

But he had deliberately left behind his bow so he would not be tempted to pick off Norsundrians. Not now, not when the Marlovens writhed under the draconian one-for-ten ruling that they all knew the Norsundrians would love, very much, to continue carrying out. Kill one of us, and ten of your children die. In the local square, and you have to watch, or there will be more.

The ten-to-one rule had at first been a disaster; when Imry arrived to find out why Marloven Hess was roiling with unrest, he discovered that there were volunteers to throw their lives away. Parents of dead warriors. Siblings. Lovers.

He'd said, "Make it children. Younger the better." Though he regretted that—he had plans for the young ones. But word spread, just as Imry Llyenthur knew it would, after his executioners promptly and enthusiastically carried out the new orders, and reprisals halted.

David learned this through listening, sometimes talking. The conclusion was clear: Senrid's kingdom would have to rise at once, or not at all.

When the spring-green hills were quiet again, except for the dreamy buzzing of bees and the melodic fall of birdsong, he rose, dusted himself off, and loped toward the city.

By sunset David stood in the shadows of an alleyway, staring reflectively up at the stone towers of the Montredaun-An royal castle. The streets of Choreid Dhelerei were rapidly emptying. In another half an hour no one would be abroad but Norsundrians and spies, and the occasional individual whose private business required desperate risk.

David himself waited on the cover of darkness. The bridges over the river, and the streets along the massive castle, were under constant guard. He stood motionless for another hour, watching the patrol patterns, and glancing up at the mostly dark castle windows. It had been too easy to sneak in. Much too easy. Yes, a very enticing trap, Imry.

David gave his head a rueful shake and slipped noiselessly into the street.

Late the next morning he was on the other side of the city in the old section, drifting along the maze of narrow, winding streets toward a cabinet-maker's shop. Others were already abroad, moving about their business. He knew himself unremarkable in this land, just another blond youth in plain, rather worn clothes, a basket on his arm and a vacant look on his face. Occasional

Norsundrian guards glanced at him with indifference, saw no weapons, observed his stoop-shouldered, shambling walk, and the basket, then dismissed him from their attention.

When he was completely satisfied that he had not been followed, he stepped down into the shop, which was badly lit by two candles at either end of a handsome counter, and sniffed the strong cut-wood smell on the still air.

Quick assessment. No other customers. The old man behind the counter, who had been working slowly at an intricate piece of paneling, kept working.

David did not address the man, but stepped past him to the curtain that divided off the living quarters.

The old woman who sat knitting beside the fire glanced up at David. She gestured toward the steaming cauldron on her fire, saw David's hand-flick, and set aside her knitting to fill a heavy crockery mug with thick soup. He bent his head to sip it, and the old woman looked, with unexpressed anticipation, on the unmistakable bone structure of the Montredaun-Ans in this young man's face. She perceived a strong look of the old king. Well, some of the old man's bloodlust was needed these days.

She cast a glance at the undisturbed curtain and then swiftly lifted the lid to a large cedar trunk and pulled from it the neatly folded clothing and winter-quilts that filled it. Another glance, then she pressed the lock and the bottom of the trunk swung soundlessly up. David stepped into the narrow passage, and down the steep stairs.

He moved fast, but even so his head had barely cleared the bottom of the false trunk when the planking dropped down again, shutting out the daylight.

He snapped his fingers. A small glowglobe lit the tiny cellar room with pale bluish light. He drank off his soup, then picked up one of the quilts lying on a low table. Three sides of the room were lined with mattresses. He wrapped himself in a quilt, lay down, extinguished the light, and dropped with gratitude into slumber.

The secret room was timeless. When he woke he had no idea how long he had been asleep. He had time to realize he'd subliminally heard a creak, or a step, and then came two sharp raps on the planking above. He snapped on the light, folded the quilt, and moved up the stairs, rapping softly twice.

A voice said, low, "The king is back. At Daltan's."

"Coming out," David said.

He retrieved his soup mug as the planking lifted. He climbed out, and discovered that it was still daytime. He'd have to catch up on his sleep later. Senrid was back, but who knew for how long.

As David made his way into the busy streets, he envisioned the news weaving through secret tunnels and rooms throughout the city. Trust the Marlovens to have managed, in a very few months, to organize a complicated communications network, so far solely from mouth to ear.

Daltan's cobbler's shop was full of customers, for she was one of the most skilled of her guild. Both she and her son waited on people, most dressed in unrelieved mourning. It was not so much an expression of grief for those who had fallen defending the kingdom, for the glory of their memory was celebrated in other, fiercely private, ways; the mourning clothing was a kind of silent protest to the occupation force. A warning. Did Norsunder know? Imry would.

Daltan's demeanor did not change at all when her eyes met David's. In-between giving one woman some coins, and turning to fetch repaired blackweave boots for an old man, she glanced just once upstairs.

David drifted around the shop, looking at the finished shoes and boots and belts and baldrics, the repaired gear, the lengths of waxy leddas waiting to be treated and turned into weave, and the strands already treated hung ready to work into footgear. When he was satisfied that every person's attention was away, he eased noiselessly up the stairs into the family's apartments, and found Senrid perched on a narrow bed in an alcove. He and a young boy wolfed down bread and cheese. The pair looked equally threadbare and starved.

"David!" Senrid flashed a grin. "I thought you'd be halfway across the continent by now."

"Had to find out what happened." David smiled at the boy and dropped onto a mat.

Senrid snapped his fingers then turned up his palm: close call, but success. Then, "This is Retren Ndarga."

The boy was thin as a twig, with a head of loose black curls and a sensitive face dominated by a pair of dark-fringed gray eyes: wary, austere, patient. Covertly David studied that face as Senrid described the difficulties of getting cross-country between Norsundrians and spring rains. Senrid treated Retren Ndarga with a sort of casual camaraderie, but there was no mistaking the hero-adoration in Retren's expressive eyes in spite of that easy attitude.

Senrid said, "You stood the last watch, Ret. Go grab some shut-eye while you've got the chance." He jerked a thumb at the adjoining room.

With a smile and a polite nod at David, Retren obeyed.

Senrid went on with the small talk for a time, and then suddenly collapsed back on the bed and rubbed his eyes. "He's asleep. What brings you here?"

"Still on Detlev's orders."

Senrid opened his hand; he'd first encountered David on the border in Methden. David had been mapping permanent HQs and as many field command posts as he could locate. With corroborative detail. It was David who had contacted Senrid, offering help—with Detlev's encouragement, from somewhere far away.

David grinned. "Decided to stretch a point and nose into Imry's business in your capital. I see you resolved things with the boy. What happened to the sister?"

Senrid grimaced. "Closest run I've had in years." He sat up on his elbows. "Thank you for your help."

"It was fun."

"It was anything but fun. If they'd managed to shoot Retren, Imry could've used Marend to torch the kingdom. Close. Damn close."

David remembered just how close: it was only Senrid's skill with a bow that had wrenched victory from Imry's careless fingers. "Did Marend stay out of Imry's toils?"

"Has so far. She wants to get back at him."

David smiled a little. "Ah, my part was fun, keeping Imry on the hop for nearly a day."

"Who said to Marend that old loyalties die hard. What d'you think he meant by that?"

"Not what it sounds like, or why did he leave us? My guess is he's twitching under even nominal restraint, and the best way to give the back of his hand to the Host would be for him to finger Detlev, when they haven't been able to. Where is Marend now?"

"She's in Darchelde, organizing a resistance underground. That after being severely chastened by the experience, and some very rough handling on my part. Go down and take a look yourself if you want to get her measure."

"She kicked the boy out?"

"No. How much of this do you want to hear?"

David had rarely gotten so close a look at Senrid's inter-actions with his own people. "Tell me. I've never seen you with a devotee before."

"It makes me ill," Senrid stated unequivocally. "Soon's he gets some self-respect I'll sic him on someone who can do him some good. No, Marend didn't want him to go. In fact, except for their father's death during the first days of the war I don't think anything hit her harder than my taking Retren away."

"Why did you take him?"

Senrid's gaze diffused. David sensed how very much the incident had upset Senrid. "He was too close to taking the steel exit." A gesture across the throat with a forefinger. Then a sard-onic look David's way. "What did you find in our erstwhile home?"

"Imry doesn't seem to have told anyone about that, has he? No. Nothing. Just regional reports. He must have the sensitive stuff relayed directly to his HQ—which isn't here, to my surprise. Bringing us to Larkadhe. I'm going to make my way north and poke around there. What can you tell me about the terrain?"

Senrid, who made maps in his spare time, briefed David thoroughly on the kingdom of Visegn, once a part of the Marloven empire.

David listened without interrupting, then said, "When Imry finds out you're back, things might get tight."

"I know." A brief flash of teeth. "I look forward to it."

David said, "Want aid? When I finish Detlev's run I could come around and help fill out your entertainment committee."

"What?" Senrid mimed surprise. "Could it possibly be your Montredaun-An blood asserting itself?"

"Montredaun-An bile, more like. I don't know. When I'm away, I scarcely give Marloven Hess a thought. But when I'm here—last night, for example—looking up at the castle of our forefathers, perhaps generations of sons of exiled sons prodded me to take notice of what I'd missed. Just think, if our respected grandfather had been less of a shit I could be fighting with Imry over that same palace."

"What would that make me, Svir's protégé? Detlev's, any-way." Senrid looked appreciative of this flight of fancy. "Where is he? Do you know?"

"Only that he's had to go to ground for a time. But he's almost done."

"Done," Senrid repeated, wondering what Detlev was hiding. "The last I whiffed him was back in fall, when we all split up. Why does it feel like it was years ago? I wonder if Jilo has gone back to Chwahirsland," Senrid mused.

"Dunno. You have recent business with Jilo?"

"Recent shared experience, more like. Kessler sent us off-world for a memorable week, not long ago."

"Off-world! Did he break the ward binding the world?"

"He did. It was not voluntary on our part." Senrid made a grimace of distaste. "But Kessler played fair, and sent me here. That was not long before you contacted me in Methden. Reminds me. You once showed me one of Detlev's little nerve-paralyzers. I think I have it wrong. I did the mind-contact and pressure-point on the nerve clusters as you said, and they pass out, all right, but don't freeze, they drop. Giveaway during sneakery."

"I can show you again, but the only real training is practice." David pointed out the nerve-clusters on himself, then added, "You want the initial adrenaline spike before you strike, or they do fold up."

Senrid turned up his palm. "Will field test some more. There are plenty of Norsundrians to go round."

David took in the tightness of Senrid's mouth, and the tiredness ringing his eyes, and decided it was time to be on his way. He got to his feet, and only then asked what he'd come to ask: "What are your plans?"

Senrid's expression turned sardonic. "Resistance plans. Don't fret. I know an uprising right now would be madness. Nothing, in fact, Imry's blood-suckers would like better."

David twiddled his fingers. "We'll have to give them something else to do. Elsewhere."

Senrid laughed, and David took his departure, leaving Senrid to much-needed rest, from the look of things. He faded into the traffic making its way toward the gates. He soon found someone who needed extra help with a wagonload of barrels, and once again, he became just another scruffy blond gaping vacantly around as the wagon rolled slowly under the scanning eye of Norsundrian sentries.

David did not trust the mental plane, so his report to Detlev was as yet a catalogue at the back of his mind.

As the wagon bumped slowly over the road, David's thoughts drifted back five years, to that very first week after he and the gang had officially hopped the fence. David had gone, first thing, to visit Senrid and warn him that he had cousins. Senrid had shrugged, saying, "I always figured my Uncle Kendred would turn up again, since no one ever reported him dead. Either he or his progeny. Could be worse."

No shock. No dismay. And it had been David, and not Senrid, who had suggested they keep it to themselves.

He had plenty of time to think about that as he made his way northwards. The farther he got from Marloven Hess, the easier it was to slip between the lines. Norsundrians were increasingly scarce — and so were their command posts.

It was not surprising to glimpse a shadow moving orthogonal to the inner and outer perimeter at Nevree. David stilled lest he catch the shadow's attention, did a fast scan, and then came the surprise: he knew that shadow.

David ghost-footed after him, and at an advantageous spot let himself be seen. Knives flashed out, David stepped out into the weak moonlight, and Andri Malcolin Elsarion of Enaeran laughed soundlessly and lowered his weapon.

David matched pace with Andri. "Anything?"

"Blather."

"What brings you here?"

"Assessment up the coast, heading inland along the Marane River. Reporting in to Atan Landis. Making my way home."

"I thought the rest of you were running for Mearsies Heili."

"Some stayed. Some didn't. We're scouting, gathering again in harvest-season. We have magic papers for instant contact, made by Siamis."

David didn't mention he'd known about that project — had even helped test them. "Except for the papers, sounds like our orders from Detlev. Find anything worth scouting in the area?"

"We only arrived today, and that seemed the best spot to listen. You seem to have come to the same conclusion."

"Who's we?"

"Liere's nosing out the HQ in the city. Her assignment is to find Detlev and apprise him of this plan. Give him a paper. Know where he is?"

They had moved to an abandoned stable. David promised

to pass the word to Detlev.

"Your orders parallel ours?"

"Not quite," David said. "I'll be making my way north. Poke around Larkadhe. See what's what."

Andri nicked his chin northward. "I was there three months ago. I can give you a rundown on the place."

They soon parted.

Five

Sles-Adran

Two days later, Sveneric sat on a riverbank outside of a small town in Sles Adran, watching the other prentices playing in the water while he struggled to contain his impatience.

The weather was warm for spring, breathlessly humid in the hazy sunlight and he tugged at the damp neck of his gown. It seemed cooler to sit in the shade of this tree than to lump about in this damned robe, unable to feel any breeze because of the swaths of fabric. How did girls bear it?

It was obvious how girls bore it. They flung themselves into the stream, laughing as they splashed their way into a water fight with some of the boys. All of them in their clothes, for here the sexes separated to swim nude, and no one had brought any swimming-shorts. Their clothes were made mostly of cotton, which molded, when wet, to their bodies. Those with long hair had braided it.

They were mostly under the age of mutual physical awareness, but Sveneric suspected that the most casual glance would see a bump where no bump would be on a girl, and while there might be any number of reasons for this to happen, it was sure to cause talk, and perhaps helpful offers from the local healer, which would assuredly spread through the gossipy town. To be heard by any vigilant Norsundrian spy listening for any anomalies.

He sat on the riverbank and pretended to be too fastidious

for the churned-up mud in the water.

"C'mon, Serena!" called Lisi, the redhead who'd been app-renticed the same day as Sveneric. Her nut-colored gown clung to her scrawny, gangling limbs. Flat she was in front, and would be probably for years yet—but she was still obviously a girl.

Sveneric suppressed a sigh, and called, "No thanks, Lis. I can't abide mud." He flicked the bottom of his yellow robe, which he'd gotten wet to the knees before he'd pretended to be dismayed by the dirt. Already dry in the fierce sun, the cotton was brown-streaked.

Lisi shrugged, flashed a quick smile, and splashed back full length into the water.

Sveneric forced his attention from his sweaty, sticky skin to the water itself. He observed how the light winked and gleamed on its surface, as if someone had taken a piece of the sun, smashed it, and cast the shards over the water. "A tiny line of red, just a thread, between the blue and the white tones," he muttered, squinting. His latest assignment in Master Orthal's house had been light.

Lisi popped up, sending the light splintering out into shards again. How wonderful it was that she'd decided to come to Master Orthal's instead of the more famous Thescar House in Colend! The two of them had come to be known as the Grace Maidens (after a Sles Adrani legend), but when visitors came to see the promising young prentices, Sveneric had taken care to hang back, shy and dull and stuttery. And warm and dear Lisi, for whom art was the world, did not regard "Serena" as competition except in the most invigorating and playful sense.

Life had been good, Sveneric readily admitted. Unex-pectedly good, in spite of the war. But the war was still there, outside the haven of happy work and art, and Sveneric knew that he would be called sooner than later to take part in it: he had managed to escape Efael's hunters. MV, and Adam, had niffed new intent: they were hunting down Dirk in order to get at Kessler through him.

Knowing these things made each day the more precious, but it was not perfect. It was partly his disguise, but mostly how he had to hold himself back. He must not draw attention.

Artificially confined. Like these clothes. No, to be fair it wasn't the robe, which did permit just as much freedom of movement as trousers, it was having to move differently—dain-tily—to rely always on cleaning frames and never to risk a bath lest one of the other girls walk in. The early mornings of exercise not out in the free air, but alone in his tiny room. The forethought required before one walks, speaks, eats.

"Heyo! Get out of that water!"

That was Lemeth, the journeyman in charge of the prentices.

Amid cries of disappointment the others slogged out of the river, shaking or wringing themselves out as they walked. All started ambling back toward town, no one — including Lemeth — feeling inspired to move with any speed. They were relaxed and content. Sveneric mimicked them, but his gaze constantly moved, assessing the crowded street, noting patterns and gaits, angles of approach and various lines of retreat.

"Oh, look!" Lisi cried, pointing.

Sveneric had already marked the flimsy stalls set up round the perimeter of an intersection. His gaze appraised the expectant crowd before a fruit vendor, moved on — and snapped back.

There. Half-hidden in the crowd. Man, mid-thirties. Long brown hair tied back, brown-and-gold vest, white shirt, loose dark trousers stuffed into boots sea-style: the clothes were uncharacteristic but the stance was as familiar as his own heartbeat.

Joy suffused Sveneric. He said to Lemeth with his shyest smile, "I have a few coppers. May I buy a little basket of those fresh blueberries for our group?"

"It's early." Hikolas wrinkled his nose. "Be tart."

"I like 'em tart," Lisi cried. "Course, I like 'em sweet, too. I'm starving!"

Sveneric waited, careful to appear composed, unconcerned.

Lemeth was not supposed to have any favorites, but Serena reminded him of his sister at home — unremarkable, brown-haired — except for those rare times when he'd caught her looking out a window into the snow with the far-seeing gaze of ancient paintings of angels. "Very well. But the rest of you have clothes to change, and work waiting."

Serena walked off, hem held prissily above the mud, and the others massed for the trudge back, many groaning about work on so nice a day.

Detlev stood far enough in the back of the crowd so that it was never quite his turn to be waited on.

Sveneric minced into the line, baggy yellow sleeves float-

ing, and cast a grateful smile upward when a gallant old bearded fellow gave way. Detlev shifted once, twice, and then, when
Sveneric had carefully counted coins into the vendor's palm
and stood struggling helplessly with four brimming baskets he
said, "Need some help, young prentice?"

"Oh, thank you, sir." Sveneric's eyes above all that yellow
looked more green than hazel, and his smile was pensive. "Just
to Master Orthal's."

No one observing them would find anything curious
enough to remain in memory, for Serena was now a frequent
sight on this street, and Detlev was long practiced at moving
through the world unremarked.

Each carried in either hand a flimsy little basket of dusky
blue fruit. Aloud they made polite, rather stilted conversation,
suitable between strangers. By Dena Yeresbeth they carried on
a rapid contact.

Sveneric's opening thought was gleeful: *What would you
have done if I hadn't noticed you?*

From early childhood Sveneric had accepted with amazing equanimity that the nature of his life required constant vigilance; Detlev was delighted when his son showed these occasional glimpses of normal boy bravado: *I'd've scared your braids
off for being lax.*

Wordless triumph, appreciation, and shared humor zap-
ed between them.

: *News?* Sveneric had noticed subtle lines of tension
around his father's narrowed eyes, which indicated he'd been
going without sleep, and possibly without food as well, for a
protracted time. Danger, shut outside of the art school's bubble
of normalcy all winter, closed round him again.

: *The ward will hold.*

Sveneric was one of the very few people who knew how
profoundly important those simple words were.

Detlev went on: *David and I stung Imry in Marloven Hess not
long ago, and more recently in Chwahirsland. Consequently Svir is
stalking me again.*

Sveneric did not make the mistake of comprehending this
in a geographical sense.

: *Magic transfer warded again? By which one?*

: *Svir, I believe. I snapped both of Imry's earlier traps, but I was
not able to break the ward over transfer.*

: *You've just come from Chwahirsland, then? Need me?*

: Are you ready? Detlev sent the query, though he could both see and sense Sveneric's inner turmoil. Sveneric had accepted the amaranthine burden of Detlev's past as his own, never resenting the eternal circumspection, or asking for anything for himself. The winter here, exercising his artistic talent, which was considerable, had been Detlev's gift.

Given the nature of their lives, it was also a kind of test.

Sveneric sighed, and a flood of images came: the restraints of living in his Serena persona; holding back his development and interests; his ignorance of the movement of world-wide events; his isolation from those he loved. His awareness of the demands of duty, in perilous times.

: You know your friends are out?

: I contacted Dirk, as you requested – ?

: No – at least not last time I scanned – but I sent MV as cover.

: Host?

: Svir has a toy.

: We are going to the rescue? Sveneric did not try to hide his fear.

Reassurance. *: Neither. Someone else on the way who I believe will bring it off, and if so the repercussions will be preferable –*

: To us? A drift of bitterness, and a corresponding tightening of loyalties, both quicker than the glancing sunlight, and almost subconscious.

The burden had been less Detlev's actions than the outer world's reactions.

: Perhaps. If you are ready, you are needed to free another before they find out who it is they've nailed.

They had reached the big house at the end of the artisans' street, and as Detlev made a business of handing over the baskets and helping Sveneric to steady them, the already skip-speed contact accelerated to the rapid-synapse of individual thought, minds blended from long practice.

Detlev's hands left the baskets, dropped to Sveneric's, touched for the briefest moment, and then with a last wordless exchange they turned their separate ways.

Alcandamer

That same day, far to the north and west, two small figures

dashed and splashed through the rain sheeting down over the Alcandamer countryside.

As the storm roiled overhead, CJ and Dirk ran on, stumbling and shivering. Lightning flared nearby, suddenly blinding them, and CJ tripped over an unseen stone and splatted full length in the mud.

"Come on." Dirk's voice barely carried over the blast of the thunder.

"A break." CJ's teeth clattered in her skull. "We've been running ... since dawn...no one can find...us in this. No t-t-t-tracks. No scent—"

"That's what we said three days ago," Dirk shouted, his eyes manic, as he fought for breath. "And I know he was there—"

CJ was struggling in the slimy mud, but she couldn't get purchase enough to rise. Dirk bent, and though he was not much bigger than she, he exhibited a measure of his father's strength by picking her up and setting her on her feet.

She windmilled, forced herself to balance, and they started on again. In the lee of a building, the deafening sound abated enough for CJ to yell, "If that stinking Efael does catch up with us...I'm going to save all this up...and barf on his shoes!"

Dirk was too tired to answer, and too grim to even pretend a laugh. He knew that if Efael caught up with CJ, as a useless peripheral she wouldn't live long enough to react.

They ran on.

Six

BEFORE THE ARTIFACT HUNTERS left Mearsies Heili, Roy had used dark magic to give them all the Universal Language spell again.

His group was the largest, and for various reasons, the slowest. Their path took them across Reyte, round the great bay, over marshy territory so ill-suited for human habitation that they did not see a Norsundrian for the entire time they skirted countless salt and brackish fresh-water ponds and marshes. Once they reached Al Tradhe, Roy began scanning, and from time to time said, "Hide."

No one argued. Though Falinneh's soft snickers were often heard once the patrols had passed. From there they reached the belt of the world, the Fereledria — and then, as often happened, a few hours' journey in the magic-charged snows brought them not only to the other side of the great mountains, but at least a week's journey north. Thence through quiet, farm-stitched Lygiera, to Narieth, through the Three Kingdoms.

During those first weeks, the group was intimidated enough by the prospect of danger to be exceedingly careful. They saw few Norsundrians on their long journey northwards, and hid whenever there was a possibility of being seen. But that kind of travel can become tiring. And big groups almost inevitably form fractures into smaller groups.

One night on a plateau overlooking a portion of Three Kingdoms below, the group decided to split up. Roy got them all to promise to return to Mearsies Heili if it turned out dodging Norsunder got to be too much, then they divided.

Caris-Merian kept her promise to Mildred, whom she admired because her brother had admired her. She stayed with the two Mearsiean girls, Sherry and red-haired Falinneh, who had agreed to count Norsundrians up the main north-south trade road through most of the continent of Goerael.

Caris-Merian never relaxed her vigilance, and consequently the other two began to rely on her to provide warning when danger was imminent. Not that that happened often; Llyenthur's strike troops, spread thin, had conquered this particular portion of Goerael's continent by swiftly taking out government leaders, or driving those few they couldn't catch into hiding somewhere in exile, and using violent threat (and prompt reprisal) against the citizenry.

By the time the girls reached the southern border of Goerael Haer they had discovered that life in these sparsely populated outlying areas had long since settled into a semblance of regular habit, tied to the planting, growing and harvesting season; normalcy had returned enough so that Norsundrians were not everywhere to be seen, but came through occasionally.

"Is there a pattern to these sporadic tours of inspection?" Caris-Merian asked one night.

The girls had found that inns and posting houses, desperate for business, were extraordinarily cheap. And as autumnal rains made the roads soggy and the traveling cold, camping was getting tougher.

They sat in a corner booth near the fire. The common room probably had five other customers in it, all out of earshot.

Falinneh scrunched up her shoulders, peered around, and then grinned. "Who cares?"

Caris-Merian hid a spurt of exasperation. "We should. That's why we're here."

"We're here to see how many Norsundrians are stinking up the countryside," Falinneh said with breezy cheer. "We know there aren't very many. Isn't that enough?"

"There has to be a pattern," Caris-Merian replied. "And if there is going to be any kind of successful counter-attack, we have to know where the Norsundrians are, when. And how many."

Sherry propped her chin on her hands, her round, limpid blue eyes for once serious. "I think she's right."

Falinneh groaned. "So we have to follow 'em around? But we'll get ourselves caught fer sure!"

Caris-Merian shook her head. "The road we're on is the main trade route through this area. That means we can ask locals. We don't have to personally count each patrol."

Falinneh rubbed her hands. "Inns? Good! Then we're done with trying to sleep outside when snow-weather is coming? So unfair — we just finished with that down south!"

"We will have to work our way. We have no coins, and we have no travel papers."

"I don't mind work!"

"Me either!" Sherry piped. "I am very good in the kitchen."

Unfortunately, the locals that they encountered either didn't want to talk, or else complained about the weather, and prices, and the roads, because no one seemed to be maintaining them anymore, and as soon as the girls brought up Norsundrians even obliquely, conversations invariably ended abruptly.

They reached a city that seemed quieter than most. Caris-Merian's instincts jangled. They found an inn desperate for help — the family's teen and young men had been marched off to work for the enemy. During their free time late at night Falinneh and Sherry whiled away a long day by writing letters on their beige papers to all their friends, leaving the listening to Caris-Merian.

The rise and fall of talk between strangers who were all trying to pass the time, yet not get too familiar lest there be danger, caused frequent lapses during which all Caris-Merian heard was the snap of the great fire, and the clangs and bangs of kitchen noise beyond the swinging doors.

Punctuating this occasional silence were giggles from the corner booth, where Sherry and Falinneh crouched over their notes, each trying to outdo the other in writing funny letters. From a distance it looked as if they were drawing, and Caris-Merian overheard a comment about the painters' guild, and hadn't they sent the apprentices home?

Still, Caris-Merian endured a pang of danger at every glance. Her life's experience made it impossible to react any other way. And each pang was followed by one equally fierce: exasperation toward the two silliest Mearsieans. She'd thought very highly of the group when she'd first met them, especially CJ, Clair, Dhana, and Seshe. Diana, too; though she seldom talked, she was good in woodcraft and weaponry.

But Caris-Merian wasn't traveling with any of them. Caris-Merian began to suspect that Atan had assigned Falinneh and Sherry here because the danger was expected to be relatively light—and Caris-Merian was to be, in effect, their keeper.

It was a role she was used to. Her beloved brother Les, brilliant, popular, everyone's friend, champion of magic and freedom, had required reminding of things like eating, sleeping, and appointments made. It had been Caris-Merian's joyful purpose in life to devote her life to watching over Les. On her fourteenth birthday, he had said, laughing, *What? Fourteen already? Next thing I know you'll be grown, and fall in love with some handsome, dashing young fellow, and forget about your old, boring brother.*

Never. I'll always be here to help you, she had vowed, appalled at this never-before considered prospect. And so she had kept that vow, even after the never-to-be-hated-enough David had killed Les. With Les's disappearance from the world had gone all meaning, leaving nothing but a sober sense of duty, and a passionate resolve to get revenge. She feared losing this resolve.

At least, Caris-Merian thought as she slid into her place at the girls' table, the Mearsieans hated Detlev and his murdering gang, judging from the energetic insults with which they prefaced mentions. Caris-Merian treasured each one.

She said, "I think we ought to go to the first of their capital cities we come to, and see if there is a Norsundrian headquarters."

Falinneh said, "Winter City is nearest."

This unexpected fact first impressed Caris-Merian, and then irritated her. If Falinneh knew this much, why hadn't she spoken before?.

Falinneh dropped her pencil and frowned across the old, scored oak table at the girl from Geth. It was weird, how Caris-Merian kind of reminded her a little of Laban of the poopsies — not that she'd ever say anything, of course.

A snicker fluttered in her throat, but when she briefly met

those wide-set gray eyes, and saw their expression, the laugh died, and she felt as though someone had put a snowball down her back. Caris-Merian wasn't glaring, or grimacing, but her mouth was pressed into a bloodless line. She looked so ... so, oh, what was the word? Austere, yeah, that was it, but with a little disgust.

Falinneh couldn't help seeing things in people's faces — but she would not say anything, of course. She seldom did, if the question or comment related to the subject she and the girls referred to as You Know What — the code among the Mearsiean girls for Falinneh's despised shape-changing abilities, for she, like Dhana, was not just human. She was a Xubarec, a dwindling people who had been altered by a long-gone mage, and who had resorted to evil during the past century. They were now outlawed pretty much everywhere. Falinneh had run away from them at an early age, ending up with Clair's group. Her current form was the one that felt most natural to her, but all she had to do was see someone once, and she could mimic that person in face and body. Which was why she was so close an observer of human features.

Falinneh scowled at Sherry, then smacked her freckled hands together. "But I like your idea. if we do find any H.Q.'s, let's do something, even if it's only throw rocks through their windows, or maybe stick slugs in their beds. Something."

Sherry nodded vigorously. "We'll do our job, but we'll also have fun."

To their surprise, Caris-Merian shook her head. "No. We can't do anything to draw attention to ourselves. We're here to spy, not to strike."

Annoyance flashed through Falinneh, rare as it was intense. Caris-Merian was now the chief? When had that happened?

Sherry said in what Falinneh thought was a reasonable voice, "But the idea is that we aren't seen."

"No." Caris-Merian responded, desperately afraid of their being marked. How could these two be so dense? She moved away, and did not speak to them again, even later, when they climbed into their bunks in the cold attic.

No one talked much the next day, or the one after. The weather was cold and miserable. Harvest-time still brought many people on the road into Winter City, for business and for pleasure, and so the girls were at least able to catch rides of the backs of wagons, and once even a coach.

They slipped into a barn to sleep.

Next morning, Sherry volunteered to get breakfast before they split up to spy. She trotted to a bakery she had spotted, an while standing in line at a crossroads bakery, listened to people chatter. She overheard one woman say to another: "...and so the Carmael Players are also leaving. Have you seen so many empty playhouses?"

"Not since '36," was the murmured response.

The two women sent quick looks around them, then moved closer together. Sure of being overlooked because she was just a kid, Sherry stepped nearer. "Well, what happened at the Island is nothing to what happened up in Summer City. I'm amazed you didn't hear."

"We did. Something, anyway. People were talking about a whole company being killed after attacking some Norsundrian commander. I thought, players? Real swords? They wouldn't know one end of a real sword from the other."

"Oh, but it's true. Not the attack. That is, it wasn't this." A wave of a finger like a sword. And both glanced round again. The older one bent closer and said in the sort of whisper that carries just as well as a voice does, "They turned that old bore King Barthan into a satire, and made fun of the local command and their new rules. Next day they were all found dead."

Sherry rushed away, unwilling to listen any more, if it meant hearing things like that. She knew she'd have nightmares for ages, just like she had after Irenne was killed by MV of the poopsies. She ran straight back to the barn without buying anything, and amid gulps and fresh springs of tears, reported what she'd heard.

Caris-Merian said, "Let's find an inn that will hire us, do our listening and counting, and get out."

Subdued, the two Mearsieans agreed.

Three inns turned them down flat when they didn't have identity papers.

A sleet storm threatened. They tried a seedy-looking place they'd passed twice. The owner, a sour woman, hired them, and put them to work not waiting on customers who could be overheard, but in the back doing the dirtiest drudgery.

As the evening progressed Caris-Merian's tension increased because the adults seemed uneasy. She was lugging a tray of dirty dishes toward the kitchen when a gust of wet, icy wind blasted into the room and hissed into the fire.

A number of black-cloaked Norsundrians stamped in. All the patrons stilled, a man in civilian dress entered and pointed at several people in the room — the girls among them.

Caris-Merian recognized the man as someone she had seen that morning. More than once. She'd thought him a local, for he'd carried a basket, but now she recognized his type as the enemy spy she'd always feared, who was much better at it than she.

"Papers," demanded the captain of the patrol.

Under her tunic Caris-Merian wore a knife in a sheath, a habit she'd begun during the days on the run with Les. Pulling the blade free, she tried to get past. The fight was quick and furious on her part, bored and routine on theirs, conducted in silence. She, Sherry, Falinneh, and an older man were surrounded by weapon-wielding enemies; all the girls had time for was to zap their magic-papers away.

The Norsundrians herded the four prisoners out into the rain, slamming the inn-door behind them.

Seven

Sles Adran

DETLEV HAD GIVEN SVENERIC an order. He'd also left it to him how and when to carry it out.

Sveneric not only had to contrive his disappearance so that it caused as little comment as possible, he had to lay a false trail, in case Efael or Yeres, who did not willingly relinquish any prey, sent eyes either human or animal to prowl this way again.

He would have preferred to depart without speaking to anyone, leaving at most a note, but writing anything was risky. And he owed these good people closure. It was not just his own sense of right that required he not slip out of their lives without any sign of quittance, though that was a part, he also owed them a peaceful and unremarkable finish. One that would not become a source of town gossip that the Host's spies could sift for clues—and then descend in force, putting everyone to the question.

After dinner, when the others were all in motion, he touched Master Orthal's arm. "May I request a moment's talk?"

The old man courteously held open the door to his study. Then, as Sveneric sorted again through possible openings, he picked up the candle-holder that sat on its shelf near the door and as he lit the wick with one of the wall-sconces, he said, "You going to leave us, Serena?"

Sveneric hunched his shoulders a little. His hands were already clasped tensely before him; how he despised lying to people he respected, cared about! But the pose of girlish unhappiness was necessary. It was to deceive, yes, but the deception was a protection. Let Master Orthal then provide his own story.

"You have to go home, I take it?"

Sveneric looked at the floor. "My father has now completely vanished, and my sister can't run the store alone. I must return and help."

Master Orthal frowned. "No one wrote to me. But the times are so strange," he observed.

"My sister came herself. She was much too ashamed to face anyone here. And was in a hurry to return."

And that closed the circle. "I hate to see you miss any of your training. And I can see that you regret it as deeply as do I. I suppose there is no other way?"

Sveneric shook his head, writhing his fingers to draw attention down to his hands. That mute symbol of inner turmoil would hasten the interview, for Master Orthal would not like to prolong anything painful. "Not while the war is on," Sveneric responded, and in a whisper, "Please don't tell anyone. Outside the house, I mean."

Master Orthal said, "It is nobody's business but yours. I shall keep your place open half a year, and if that time passes and you wish to return and are unable to, send me word and I will extend that. I will extend it almost forever, for you have the makings of a superlative artist. You and Lisi are the best to come through here in twenty years."

Sveneric ducked his head, then lunged toward the door as though overcome. Following right on the end of his exercise in manipulation was the corresponding sense of moral distaste, and beneath that the very real regret—almost pain—at knowing it was unlikely his life and theirs would intersect again.

Heart aching, he trudged upstairs and packed his three girl outfits—he must leave nothing behind—while downstairs the prentices and journeymen and women were all singing. Did Master Orthal keep them deliberately away? Were the choices of songs deliberate? For as Sveneric stole soundlessly down the steps, he encountered no one, and the last sounds he heard were the sweet words of an old ballad about a wandering beloved, and the faith of those who stayed at home.

One great pang of anguish, then he struggled to widen his perspective the way his father had taught him. Everything becomes memory, Detlev had said. For those memories he would want to cherish, he must find something specific for each of the senses to anchor the immediacy: the twining vine shaping the brass lamp for sight; the smell of beeswax polish along the wooden banister he'd run his fingers along each day; for touch, oh, the silken tassel on the narrow tapestry Master Orthal's mother had embroidered to fit into an awkward space between the doorway and the end of the stair. Taste would be the fresh, hot tartlets he'd shared with the other students, and hearing, those voices from the big room, singing "Antivad the Wanderer, Oh!"

Sveneric unlatched the front door. He stepped out and closed the door without making a sound.

It was a cool, clear night.

On the outskirts of town he found a likely place and buried everything except his old shirt and trousers, which he was relieved to find still fit, and the yellow cotton dress, which he carried rolled in a bundle. He queued his hair again, then set off eastward as fast as he could walk.

Goerael Haer

The three days he traveled were spent by Falinneh, Sherry, and Caris-Merian locked in a cell. A real cell, in a very old castle complete with dungeon. There were no windows, only a tiny airshaft in one corner, and once a day two bowls, one of weak, grainy soup, and the other of brackish water, were slid under the door.

They figured they were to share this fare. Caris-Merian only took a few sips of the water, and none at all of the soup. Then she rolled herself in one of the mildewed wool blankets they'd found on the bare stone floor, and faced the wall.

As soon as they were locked in both Sherry and Falinneh earnestly and sorrowfully made lengthy apologies to Caris-Merian.

They couldn't see her face in the inky darkness. Her voice sounded tired and emotionless when she said, "Never mind. What's done is done."

What's done is done. Who had said that to her after Les was killed?

Shock, grief, desolation silenced her. She turned away,

darkness inside her as well as out.

As the slow days stretched out the Mearsieans forgot her as they wrestled with their own reactions.

Their stay in the cell was only three days due to the zealousness of the new commander for that region. Llyenthur had issued orders to the effect that any unusual prisoners were to be reported directly to him. There was quite a bit of latitude to the word 'unusual', of course – and a very sedulous fellow would interpret young girl prisoners speaking a foreign tongue as unusual. A series of guards posted outside the cell finally produced someone who recognized the language being spoken as Mearsiean.

Mearsiean. Wasn't there something about a place with that name in some report or other? The commander sent off his message, rubbed his hands, and smiled.

Next morning, their fourth, the door was unlocked, and gray light streamed in.

"On your feet," a guard said. "Move."

Guards closed in behind them.

They saw from the window high on the opposite wall that rain was still falling hard, and Falinneh shivered in her still-damp clothes, for her cloak had been left behind at the inn. Sherry gazed out wistfully as they walked past, until a jab between the shoulder blades forced her to catch up. Caris-Merian stalked along, head high and eyes remote, as they were led down a hall to a large room.

Long wooden tables and a lingering smell of food indicated that this was the garrison mess hall. Through another door – and the unmistakable, heart-chilling, skin-crawling sound of a man groaning in agony met their ears.

Falinneh muttered to Sherry, "Figures! Torture room right next to the dining room – "

A clout and a snarled "Shut up" cut her off.

Another door was open farther down. The girls were shoved into a bare room – a closet, really – next to the room with the groaning. Two huge guards took up stances at either side of the open door.

Tears blurred Sherry's eyes, horror and pity both, and Falinneh's head still rang with shock from the smack across the back of her head.

From the room beyond, a tenor, drawling voice spoke in the local language, its tone one of amused boredom. "Send a report if he knows anything, Suvenz. I'm afraid I find the questioning of fools tedious. Wasn't there something else?"

"Ah," replied an obsequious voice. "The Mearsieans. Here's what we found on them."

"Looks like trash. No surprise." He waved off the grubby, blank beige papers. "Let's see who we have."

Caris-Merian found that voice terrifyingly familiar. A quick step and here was a tall young man with green eyes and long light brown hair, who was unmistakably the scrawny, nervy, cruelly sarcastic boy from those Geth days. He lounged just inside the doorway, his shirt rumpled and unlaced, a foot wearing a scuffed moc crossing over the other.

"Caris-Merian Rhoderan?" he said in Geth.

"Imry Llyenthur." Her voice was so dry it husked.

"I wonder what brings you to this particular place? I'd thought you were hiding in Mearsies Heili." He paused, slapping at his pockets. "No more transfer tokens." He sighed, turning from Falinneh to Sherry — both of whom looked utterly uninteresting to him. He could question them later if Caris-Merian knew nothing.

"I think you'd better come with me." He watched her blanch, more in anger than fear. He smiled at the hovering Suvenz, and in the local language said, "Find out what they were doing up here, then dispose of them any way you wish."

He flicked a hand comprehensively at Sherry, Falinneh, and the miserable prisoner in the chair; the sycophantic Suvenz dashed into the hall and began issuing orders. Then, before the Mearsieans' appalled eyes, Llyenthur took hold of Caris-Merian, and they transferred out.

Falinneh saw her chance.

She had lost one, but she wouldn't lose Sherry.

With an apologetic glance toward Sherry, she drew a deep breath — and changed to an exact replica of Imry Llyenthur.

Voices were always hardest. Next was moving exactly like the original whose face and form she borrowed.

She took hold of Sherry, gave her head a tiny shake, and Sherry understood: keep silent.

Falinneh shoved Sherry out the door and stalked away with as much purpose as she could muster, her heart hammering her ribs, but far beneath that a weird bubble of hilarity rose, a reckless sense that only gripped her when she used her powers.

The guards jerked, saw her, and stiffened: without orders they remained where they were, guarding the room with two prisoners — or so they thought.

Falinneh pushed Sherry along as she looked desperately about. Dining room that way — kitchen had to be…ah. Through the kitchen, where all the workers stopped short, staring at what they thought was their Evil in Chief.

That bubble of hilarity swelled but Falinneh held herself together until they got outside, in the freezing rain.

Already Falinneh's body felt the strain of stretching its mass into a shape that needed the support of more mass. She snapped back to her natural size, and gasped, "Let's run."

Larkadhe

Night had fallen in the city of Larkadhe when Imry Llyenthur and Caris-Merian appeared in his inner office.

"Sit down, Caris-Merian," Llyenthur said in Geth.

The room was dark, lit only by weak moonlight She lunged, a coiled spring of desperately wound anger suddenly loosed. Fingers crooked into claws, gaze on his neck.

He heard the intake of breath and the subtle hiss of cloth moving in sudden action. He sidestepped, caught her forearm and twisted. She suppressed a gasp of pain as he thrust her into a chair. Then he snapped a glowglobe to light.

She could not prevent herself from looking up, the force of her hatred making her tremble. Llyenthur's expression was appreciative, his attitude mock-sympathetic. "What a waste! Les Rhoderan had such promise, as I recall. But David has always been enthusiastic in pursuing his targets."

Her reaction was no more than a flick of eyelids and a tightening of an already angry mouth, but he was watching so very closely.

He continued. "Ah, trust." He held out his hand, indicating Norsunder's presence on the world.

Pause. No response. Her gaze had gone to the floor, but she was listening. No doubt about that.

Llyenthur was rapidly evolving a new plan, and continued dangling the bait.

"Won't you talk to me, Caris-Merian? I'd like to know why you were in a region I had considered both remote and negligible. I see you won't answer, and I'll have to be patient.

But you realize I'd get the information sooner or later. I'm very good at it, and find it such fun besides, if the, ah ... I loathe saying 'victim', but 'guest' is a trifle disingenuous, so shall we settle on 'subject'? Yes. Quite. If the subject is worthy of interest. And you are. What could bring you here to this world? I did not think you'd be among the Geth visitors until David told me."

Shock made her eyelids flicker.

Ah, how hard it was not to laugh! Hatred was so predictable. She didn't even consider the possibility that that he might be lying.

She did mutter, "I don't believe you." But her tone, her posture, said *Tell me more*.

"Why should you?" he retorted lightly. "Nevertheless, though I chose not to follow Detlev in his somewhat convenient defection, David and I have remained fond of one another, and we meet on the occasions when we can arrange a neutral rendezvous."

Her gaze was unwavering.

Once again he had to exert himself not to laugh. "What were you doing in Goerael Haer? Have you seen David? Did you know he's here, on Halia? I'm quite sure he's on his way here."

Caris-Merian's face had tightened to stone, but she was still listening.

"Do you really enjoy consorting with squabbling, lazy fools who put favoritism over talent? I suspect they think you're dull and stupid, don't they? Just the little sister who used to clean up Les Rhoderan's — well, we won't say messes, because I respect his memory too much for that."

Pause. Not a flicker of disbelief.

"You must enjoy playing dogsbody or you wouldn't do it, I guess. And I can perceive the compensations. At the back of my mind at times is the notion that I might rejoin David and Detlev and the others, but only after I've enjoyed a long, successful career and can tolerate the boredom. Kind of a pleasant thought, being welcomed with home and hearth if I decided to hang my head and repent my wicked ways."

She wasn't even breathing, now.

"No answer? I can see I'm boring you. You'll forgive me. I promise I will not repeat the offense. But then interrogations are seldom boring — at least, for those who are there to answer questions — are they? Next time we meet we'll have to conduct the more traditional type of…interview, let's call it. Because I really ought to find out what you were looking for in Goerael Haer."

Clenched hands. White mouth.

"Guard! Escort Caris-Merian to the tower room. Make her comfortable. Caris-Merian, I'll make time for you in a day or two."

He walked her out. The hallway outside the study was lamp-lit. This was a beautifully-appointed castle, all inlaid wood and fine carpets and each furnishing a work of art.

The guard ushered her down another flight, and they disappeared from view, but for a few moments Llyenthur leaned there, smiling down, and when his chief aide trod up the stairs, carrying a sheaf of reports, he said, "An unlooked-for piece of gold, Duin."

"Who is she?"

"Caris-Merian Rhoderan. You wouldn't know about Les and Geth history of more than a decade ago, I suppose. Suffice it that I had no idea she was on this world. Hadn't given her a thought since I left Geth. But my knack for remembering faces!"

"Someone important?"

"Not at all. But with my usual finesse I provided the tools, and she'll find David, or rather he'll find her. And we won't have to burden our already overworked ferrets at all."

By now Duin was used to sorting through Llyenthur's blather for what concerned him. Anything else he dismissed. "She's joining us, then?"

"Oh, no, her bitterness toward us is unsurpassed — except by her, hmm, passion for my brother. Really, it is an obsession." He started to turn away, then paused, still looking down. "Contrive an escape for her. Say…tomorrow night. She needs a full day in which to brood. Don't make it too easy, for she's not really stupid. Just — obsessed." He took the papers from Duin and idled down the hall toward the study. At the door he paused and looked back. "Remember her name, Duin! When she returns to snitch on my brother, I want her given a warm welcome. I expect I will find her very useful, just as her own brother once was."

Goerael Haer

Back in the Norsundrian garrison, Falinneh stopped, leaning

forward with her hands on her knees. To Sherry, she seemed diminished—even her braids appeared duller.

"Are you all right?" she asked in a tiny voice. "Shouldn't we keep going?"

Still leaning hands on knees, Falinneh turned her head sideways. "Sherry, I think we should go back and rescue that man."

Sherry's eyes rounded in question, her brow puckered.

Falinneh said, "I know he's only one person, and Norsunder is doing that to people everywhere. But we heard him being tormented. And I can't let that go."

"I agree with everything you say," Sherry declared. "I just wonder how? We can't fight even if we had knives."

"One thing I noticed, those Norsundrians in there were scared witless of that man Llyenthur. Witless. I think I should be him again. But I won't run anymore. I can't. I also can't tow the man the way I did you. You'll have to help."

"Just tell me how." Sherry's voice had gone mouse-high again. But she was willing.

"Hide. Behind that stack of barrels. From the looks of them, no one has touched them for weeks. I'll come back this way. We'll go from there. Does that make sense?"

"Yes?"

Falinneh muttered, "Here goes, then."

At Falinneh's embarrassed glance, Sherry looked away, though she found Falinneh's magic fascinating. It wasn't only her body that changed. As Falinneh had explained to the girls a long time ago, the elements that made up her body and the elements of whatever touched her body, like clothes, changed and stretched, or compressed, together. But it was a false thing, like making whipped cream: it looked like more, but it wasn't more. Which was why a spoonful of whipped cream did not weigh down a spoon the way pure cream did. Just so, the clothes that stretched out might look the same, but became easy to tear, like paper.

"You can look now." Her voice had changed with her body, but it still sounded to Sherry like Falinneh, and not at all like Llyenthur as she added in an attempt at that acidic drawl, "'All of you, here are orders.' Do I sound like him?"

"You sound like you, but mannish. Sort of."

"That's no help." Falinneh groaned.

"Slower. Gloaty. Laughing. At us. Not nice laughing."

"Here are your orders," Falinneh sneered.

"Too gloaty. More laugh."

"Here are your orders." Falinneh's snigger made Sherry wince.

"Uh, try meaner. They expect him to be mean, don't they?"

"Here are your orders!"

"That's almost it," Sherry said—on a note of question. Already she was forgetting what his voice had sounded like.

Falinneh couldn't hold a tall shape long. It was now or never. She swung about and stalked back inside. When the guards saw her, they froze, and some backed away a step.

Maybe this could work—if she kept moving. "I want to interrogate that prisoner myself," she said, drawling the last word. "Get him!" she added when they just stood.

Two ran off. The rest stared at her and she stared back, then remembered how Llyenthur had lounged inside the doorway. Ah, that would actually help. She leaned against the wall, and crossed one foot over the other.

Another Norsundrian came in. It was that unctuous commander. "Sir, you did say—" the man began.

Who was he? Oh yes. "Suvenz!" Falinneh said the name out loud.

The effect was startling—the man jolted, and paled. "Your orders?"

Orders? Didn't she already give one? She had to get rid of him. "The cells," she said. "Clean those out. I'm sending you a load of new prisoners. Now!" She waved a hand at them all.

The rumble of departing footsteps caused her to sag against the wall—and tighten immediately when two guards banged in, muscling that older man between them. He was a mess.

"Leave him. Help Suvenz," she said. Her voice was sounding less and less like Llyenthur—or even like a man, to her ear.

But the guards departed.

"Can you walk?' Falinneh asked anxiously. "We need to get out of here."

The man gazed at her incredulously—and then his eyes widened when Falinneh's outline blurred, and she reformed as a short, sturdy, freckled girl.

"Let's get you out of here," she said breathlessly.

Sherry peered out from behind the barrels when the door opened. The man followed Falinneh, and both girls could see that it took all the strength he had. Both sprang to take an arm, and he leaned on them as the three moved away.

No one was in sight. They made it to the adjacent stable, and Falinneh resumed Llyenthur's shape again—knowing it would only work this once.

The Norsundrian stable hands reacted with the usual fear, and Falinneh sent them to help their fellows, who were industriously cleaning the dungeons. "In two hours you'll be receiving twenty-five important prisoners," she called after.

The girls found horses saddled and bridled for a patrol that wasn't going to be going out any time soon. They assisted the man onto one, and each chose another. They rode across fields in the heavy rain, the man leading, and pulled up finally near a ravine from which came the sound of rushing water. The man was leaning at an awkward angle, and there was only dim curiosity in his pain-hazed eyes.

"Are you going to make it?" Sherry asked him anxiously.

He smiled. "Freedom is a great healer. I thank you."

"Sure," Falinneh said. "You better head for some shelter, though."

"If you ever need aid, leave word for Muldor at the Inn of Two Rivers in Gulven-Town." He wheezed horribly as he got all that out.

"Thanks," Falinneh said, and Sherry echoed her.

The man half-lifted a hand in salute, and rode slowly away.

Falinneh collapsed over her horse's withers, as it unconcernedly cropped at the juicy wet grass. "Oh, Sherry," she gasped. "They were so scared of that man I copied! And they're gonna think he's g-gone off his nut..." Laughter hovered near tears. "Sherry! Poor Caris-Merian. Our magic letters!"

"Our cloaks—I'm so cold—our food!"

"What are we going to do?"

Sherry gazed down at the rushing water, foaming over the rocks. "We daren't go back and see if our packs are still there. No one knows what happened—and they won't know! Do you think we should go home and tell Atan what woodskulls we were?"

Falinneh regained control, and wiped her eyes despite the rain streaming into them. "We've been clods and no mistake, but that doesn't mean we still have to be! Let's do our job. We're just going to have to work harder."

Sherry nodded slowly. "Okay. But first, something to eat, and warm things."

Falinneh groaned feelingly, then she began to snicker again, helplessly, shivering with the swooping emotions inside. Defeat, triumph, remorse, gratitude.

As usual, it found its vent in humor

"Oh, Sherry, those Norsundrians! Back there! Busy s-s-s-s-scrubbing those stinky cells! For prisoners who will never come!"

Sherry was afraid that Norsunder would never run out of prisoners, but she laughed anyway, to banish the darkness.

Eight

Zranf – Norsunder HQ - Halarialgre

SVENERIC SLIPPED INTO THE mountain-shadowed city just after midnight.

He made immediately for the fortress. He was tired, and hungry, but he knew he had to act fast — if he was not already too late.

The one frail advantage he has was the local commander's famous conceit. Alsaes was soul-bound to Norsunder, and so his will had been reduced to a tangle of his lifetime motivations and desires, just enough to enable him to follow orders. The strongest of these had been to figure as a great military leader.

Detlev had assured Sveneric that Alsaes contrived to keep his own prisoners secret from his superiors until he had extracted important information. His idea being that he'd then hand over both prisoner and information to Llyenthur, and perhaps get promotion.

: If Imry does check in, he's almost sure to recognize her on sight. Anyone who has been to the Land of the Venn will recognize their royal family, and though I have never personally seen this particular new sprig on the Venn royal tree I'm told that she carries the family resemblance.

Sveneric crouched in his hiding place, watching the guards. He already knew their patrol pattern, but he was concentrating, gathering his remaining strength.

At the right moment he leaped up, soundless in bare feet,

and shot across the wall and under the bridge. Sucking in a deep breath, he slipped into the river, whose water came directly off the snow pack on the mountains, and swam against the current until he was under the second wall.

From there it was easier. His wet clothes shocked his system into adrenaline-speed. He used that to force his heartbeat up, and his skin to generate warmth, as he clambered up the thickly vined wall. It ought to suffice for a couple of hours.

It will have to suffice, he thought grimly as he eased in through a window opening onto a wide roof.

Ghost-footing inside the building, knife in hand, he began a methodical search. Short mind-touches outside each room finally limited him to two chambers. The sleepers inside both were thoroughly mind-blocked.

The risk was, of course, that they could be anyone — Llyenthur included. So he had to check physically, from the outside, which took another half an hour of risky wall-crossing in the tangle of vines, taking care to never make a rustle lest the sentries below hear and glance up. The first room, as it happened, was the right guess. He saw faint starlight on a silvery-gold braid.

He glanced down. He was horribly exposed, clinging here to the vines below a lit window, but the walking guards were as likely to look up as they were to fly — as long as he made no noise.

He shifted his grip on his ropy vine and leaned forward to tap lightly on the window. He couldn't believe the sound carried much beyond the length of a person, but his ears insisted it was loud, and he glanced down again.

Now watch her be the sleeper of the century, he thought, but as he stretched out his fingers for another try he saw the moonlit figure on the narrow bed tense, and then a face turned toward him. He couldn't see its expression — the starlight was too weak — but he gestured, hoping for the best.

Which happened. Instantly the girl swung to her feet and crossed to the window. Eased it open.

"This is a rescue. Can you climb?" he asked in the language of the Venn.

"I do not know. But I shall try."

"It's wet here, but there are good knots to grab."

With no further words she flung one foot over the windowsill. Sveneric lowered himself down. She got a good, sturdy grip, and without being prompted eased the window closed again. And then both climbed, the girl copying every movement Sveneric made.

At the first wall, she whispered, "Who are you?"

"Sveneric. My father sent me to free you. Ah, you are Princess Erenlara?"

"Queen now," she said, and even in the darkness he could see the grief in her face.

"Follow me. Do what I do," he said, though he knew it wasn't really necessary.

He'd picked the retreat route with a soft, untrained, fright-stiffened ex-prisoner in mind, and what he got was someone exceedingly well trained, well-rested, and able to adapt to any situation.

When dawn broke and he collapsed in a rocky cave in the cliffs north of the city, he had just enough energy to murmur, "Can you keep watch?"

"It will be my pleasure." A smile as bright and beautiful as first sunlight was the last thing he saw before he gratefully slid into sleep.

Hours later, the smell of cooking fish woke Sveneric, and he sat up and shook his head into wakefulness, wishing he could perform the warmups Detlev had taught him and the boys, but he dared not until he knew more of this new person.

"There's a stream nearby," came a high, clear voice. "I caught us a couple trout while I kept watch, and got a fire going. You were sleeping so well, I thought I might as well have a thing to do."

Sveneric glanced out the cave, saw afternoon sunlight. He yawned and rubbed his eyes. "I was on the run for three days. Ate once."

"To free me?"

He nodded, and pointed to one of the fish spitted on a trimmed twig. "Those be ready soon?"

"Go ahead and take that one. It went in first. Why, may I ask? I am certain I have never met you. Did you know my honored brother, or did Rel the Traveler send you? He was my brother's friend."

"No, my father did."

"Oh, yes, so you did say. I do not believe I know your father."

Sveneric did not immediately answer this oblique

question. "How he discovered you were a prisoner here I don't know, but when he asks me to do something, I do it. What happened?" He sat cross-legged near the fire and ate his fish, ignoring burning on fingers and tongue. it was delicious.

Erenlara poked at hers, then put it back to cook longer. Her attitude was absent, as though she had little appetite. She appeared to be about his age and height, built on slim lines. Framed by long silver-touched hair the color of ripe wheat, her face was so perfect in its lineaments his fingers itched for chalks.

Sveneric had caught from his father's memory an image of this girl's brother, who had been extraordinarily handsome in exactly the same way. There had also been an image of an old woman, again handsome, with the same shape of eye-socket, subtle bones, and intelligent mouths with an upward curve in the upper lip, marked by a dimple.

Erenlara's long, almond-shaped eyes were a deep, dark blue that looked violet in some light, with a thick fringe of dark lashes above and below, and fine winged brows. The high forehead and long noses that marked her family had refined over the centuries, lending character to her face. Her coloring was peachy and gold, with a scattering of freckles across her nose.

"My honored and beloved brother, whose death grieves me, would not let me fight." She spoke suddenly, after a protracted pause. "Said one of us ought to be safe. I disagreed, and when I would not promise to stay hidden he had the House Arm lock me up in one of the mountain fortresses."

"Arm?" he asked, aware of how very scanty his knowledge was of the Venn.

"Arm of the Crown," she said, as if that explained.

Sveneric decided to wait with his questions. She was so buried in memory it was better to let her narrative progress as she would have it.

"I thought and I thought, and I tried to examine the dilemma from every perspective, and finally I could just not bear to sit there and not do anything. Not know. The feeling increased strongly one day. I could scarcely wait for nightfall so that I could escape. I had not spoken my thoughts aloud so my leaving was unexpected. And—perhaps—permitting me to escape was their last conscious thought before that man with the green eyes enchanted them. I do not know! But I did get away."

Her steady gaze was distant, and unhappy.

"When I reached the flatlands I discovered that the Arm and the Eyes had been both enchanted through their own blood oaths, and were now my enemies! They had been forced to turn their skills toward serving the Norsundrian soulsuckers, and worse, they were being used against neighboring countries. I learned that there had been some skirmishing, but they had been ready for us, and knew where to attack, whereas we had not been prepared. I was *told* that my brother died in battle, as did almost all the Household Arm, in their attempt to protect him. So I knew there would be no more fighting, and I decided to come south to seek help."

"You were going where?"

"Many years ago there was a traveler named Rel who became friends with my brother, and helped him during a difficult time in our land. My brother would have given him rank in the Arm, or lands, whatever he wanted, to get him to stay, but he said no, and finally he admitted he was a liegeman of sorts to the Queen of Sartor. And I had read that this queen was powerful in magic so I wished to make my way to Sartor to ask her aid."

Sveneric considered the enormous distance Erenlara had tried to cover—from the northernmost kingdom in the world to the most southern—and his admiration increased.

She sighed, and turned over her fish. "As I traveled I discovered that the Norsundrians had conquered most everything. I only felt safe once, when I crossed those mountains belting the world. There it was winter and yet not winter—most strange. But my dreams were good, and I even saw my brother again, smiling as if he watched over me."

Her lip trembled, and she turned away, but only for the length of along, hissing breath.

Her voice hardened slightly. "I kept on, believing powerful Sartor would somehow be free. But when I neared there I discovered that it too had fallen. I started back, and was so sick at heart I was careless one night, and walked into a search party. I had no identity papers, and was taken. There you have my tale."

"My father has suggested you go to Mearsies Heili, which is the one land on the world that the Norsundrians cannot get into."

"Do you think they will aid me?"

Her regard was intense, and Sveneric received a wash of

emotions borne with images. One of these was of armies marching.

He said, "I'm sure they'll do everything they can, but you should know it's a small kingdom, and it's protected by strong magic, not by armies."

"Magic knowledge may be more aid to me than armies. As I said, that cursed one enchanted the Arm and Eyes. I do not want anyone fighting, Venn against Venn, if it can be avoided. Venn against Venn, and one side fighting for the damned because their own blood oaths were twisted against them!" Her voice was raw as she made a gesture of repudiation. "Magic aid is what I need. Perhaps I should go there. The generality of us Venn know nothing of magic. It was forbidden by an ancient treaty for so very long."

"Magic knowledge would be useful," he said. "But you would not be able to learn in weeks what it will take to free your country."

"Enchantments can be broken, can they not? They often are in histories." She turned wide eyes on him, then smiled. "Here. Have my fish. I find I am not hungry. That fool Alsaes oppressed me with huge banquets every evening. He was endeavoring to win my trust, I believe — insofar as one can guess at the motives of one who so obviously serves only himself. He seemed to think I was a…what did he call them? Cousin-race to the morvende?"

"A dawnsinger!" Sveneric laughed.

"That was it!"

"It's your hair. Most of them have that shade of gold. They're forest dwellers, related to the Rowens of Geth."

"Geth is a sister world, is it not?" At his nod she sighed. "How I would have enjoyed traveling. It has been in my mind these last three years. Now duty will bind me to home, once we win free. Anyway, I must make my first goal the breaking of that enchantment."

"It's not quite that simple. That is, strength in magic is not all that's required to do it. Not — " He almost said *Not in the way you think*. "An enchantment is not like a door to be battered down. It's actually two or more spells — sometimes as many as a hundred — bound by what we call a key. This key is not necessarily an object."

"So I must discover what is the key to that enchantment."

"Yes."

"Meanwhile the Norsundrians are searching for the key to this enchantment protecting Mearsies Heili."

Sveneric grinned. "They may or may not have found out, but even if they do, they cannot break it." And he told her.

As she listened her dark blue eyes widened, and then the fine winged brows drew down in an expression of determination. "There is no heir to the Sofar line but me, but I would do that, willingly, to free the Venn."

Sveneric finished the second fish and sat back. "It's not that simple. Light magic is bound by certain laws. Just as you cannot sacrifice another's life to bind an enchantment, so can individuals only take their own lives under certain circumstances. And have the magic work, I should say. It's been observed that the only ones for whom the spells are successful are those whose lives have already been lengthened by magic, which is a dark magic spell. The combination means that this sort of enchantment is extremely rare."

"What is to prevent the Norsunder nightcrawlers from killing someone and binding an enchantment onto them using dark magic?"

"The victims come back! Even when they are killed with knives with an enchantment to send them straight to the Host of Lords, there are enough colossal backfires through history to make Norsunder wary of putting that much power even into the hands of one soulbound."

"Oh, I see." She laughed. "How do I search for this key?"

"There are ways. Magic has certain patterns." He hesitated. He sensed that she was very close to coinherence, but that she also knew nothing about Dena Yeresbeth. "Perhaps if I were to accompany you to Mearsies Heili, I could teach you some theories. We can't really do any magic —"

"You know magic?"

"Yes. I'm learning as much as I can."

She clasped her hands, and gave him that brilliant smile again. "My quest does not seem so hopeless anymore! I accept your offer, most gratefully!"

He got to his feet and dusted himself off. "Then let's start moving. I have to find where I stashed my pack, and we can go from there. We'll have to be careful, of course, because Alsaes will be searching."

"I am at home in mountains." She laughed again, and bent to put out her fire, scattering ashes and stones.

He said, "Let's begin our journey by trading stories. You can begin by telling me something about your land. My knowledge is very sketchy at best, and mostly concerns the Venn and their neighbors' interactions in the ancient days."

"You mean the wars we caused." Her smile quirked sardonically.

He said, "But that was long ago. Talk about now! Llyenthur is the type to make keys of symbols. He has so many enchantments going that he must have bound your people right there in your kingdom, in a way that he'll remember whenever he's there."

"Very well. Where ought I to begin?"

"What exactly are the Eyes and the Arms of the Crown?"

"Arms!" She laughed, and then looked contrite. "I apologize. I suppose it makes no difference to someone not accustomed, but the mental image of arms reaching all about—"

"What about the hundreds of eyeballs?" he retorted, grinning.

"Ah, but I see only two eyes in my mind."

They picked their way down the cliffside, being careful not to press down any greenery. "The Eyes see that the laws are obeyed, acting as the queen's—or king's—justice, and the Arm provides the force when force is necessary."

Sveneric caught from her a mental image of blue-robed individuals, and warriors in dark brown with red and gold trim.

"What do they do, spy on people?"

"No. Not at all. They move among them, but are always marked apart by their garb. The Eyes witness and cannot interfere in people's lives, although they are often called upon to judge in disputes between individuals. But when they see laws broken they send the Arm to right the wrong."

"Sounds good in theory, but in practice?"

She smiled. "There have been problems. My honored brother said that other systems have worse records. Anyway it works well for us, and of course they are carefully chosen, carefully trained, and bound by rigorous rules. For instance, Eyes cannot interfere, as I said, and the Arm cannot take action on their own unless they witness an attack. None of them can own land, or carry money, or even marry or have children, while under oath."

"I take it the populace is expected to feed and clothe them, then?"

"Oh yes."

"That must be disliked."

"On the contrary! It is considered a great honor, especially when they mark a place and come frequently. They can offer to turn their hand to any chores, and often do, to barter for clothing and shoes. The Arm are given only their weapons."

She seemed to like questions, and Sveneric was interested. In fact they both found the other interesting, and so, by the time they had escaped through Alsaes's search perimeter and were preparing to head west, despite the fact that the enemy lurked everywhere, and their journey would take them nearly halfway round the world, both—equally accustomed to rigor in their early training—were looking forward to the trip.

Nine

AS CLAIR, JUNE, AND Julian neared Imar, Clair sensed the rusted-metal reek of some sort of ward. Powerful as well as caustically toxic.

The area was watched by spy-birds, enchanted to serve Norsundrian mages. Clair was able to sense them without their sensing her, for their focus was limited to what they saw below, and the few with the ability to impose their minds over the birds' own instincts and wills were equally focused. She detected the presence of non-human minds, tainted with dark magic bindings, and warned the others when the birds were nigh. The frequent need to scramble among the rocks to find a place to hide awhile the birds soared overhead taxed the girls' strength.

Not that anyone but Julian muttered, and hers took the form of insults meant to amuse. As they neared the miasma of border-magic, June became withdrawn. Never known for her garrulousness, she hardly spoke more than four or five words in three days.

They passed into Imar undetected.

Alcandamer

> *Dear Seshe: I think we're in for it, and Clair must not find out. The only thing the Norsundrians would want*

me for would be to do something nasty to force her to let
them into MH and break Mearsieanne's enchantment.
For the same reason I'm not going to write to her, so I
won't know where she is. In case ...

CJ scowled fiercely at the paper. She would never admit
to anyone how terrified she was. The winter days of safety had
long ago receded into dream. Reality had narrowed to running,
and to the horror of being slowly boxed in. It was either run,
and amuse them, or surrender.

CJ would never surrender.

...Dirk keeps being a bucketbrain. No doubt it's his
Kessler side. But I've been in enough chases to know
that when they're ahead of you as often as they are
behind, they're in control, and not you ...

Noises. Breathing. Fear.

Scribbling in haste, for even now she thought of the other
girls and their welfare:

... I'm worried about Falinneh. Hasn't written in a
week, though it could be she got bored, after letters
every night. You know how much she hates writing!
But why would Sherry not answer? It isn't like her at
all. CJ

Seshe wrote back:

CJ, I hope you're wrong about those chasing you. I
won't tell Clair because I can see that the knowledge
would be a burden, not a comfort, but if you vanish
then I *will* tell the others. I haven't heard from
Falinneh either, or Sherry, and what's more, Caris-
Merian does not answer. I really thought she would
write if not to me, then to Atan, if something
happened – but Atan also has not heard from her. Seshe

CJ crouched on the floor of an attic, reading by the light of
a shaded candle. She heard a step, and there was Dirk, outlined
in the dim light.

He dropped down on his knees, his face so taut that fresh
terror jittered through her mind.

"We're out of time," he said. "We have to run. Now."

CJ shoved her beige paper into her shirt and got to her feet. Aware of the sound of rain on the roof, she groaned as she slung her grubby pack over one shoulder. "Into another storm? Why don't we just swim?"

They slipped out of the abandoned house into the night. Big, cold raindrops splashed into their faces as they began to run.

They were on the outskirts of a town that had been deserted months before, judging by the dark windows, and weeds in kitchen-gardens.

They pounded down the empty street, footsteps splashing. Toward the center of town the houses had been built closer together and the streets narrowed. CJ and Dirk ran on, their breath clouding before their faces, the only sounds their breathing, their feet on the brick road, and the slowing patter of raindrops.

CJ lifted her head in an attempt to see where she was going, and perceived a wisp of fog drifting like a fuzzy gray worm between houses and roofs not far ahead. Danger zapped her, followed by the grip of fear. A fast glance at Dirk revealed nothing but his silhouette.

They sprinted into the fog.

Cold vapor clung to skin, making their clothing chilly; the fog thickened. The taint of magic — evil magic — set CJ's teeth on edge. Memory flickered. Her tired mind retrieved the image too late. Just like this she had run once, after she'd been cut by an enchanted knife.

The fog closed in and her steps slowed. She could no longer see ahead. Or to the side, or behind.

Dirk had vanished into the fog. She was alone. Her steps faltered then halted, her knees like jelly. She panted open-mouthed, straining to hear his steps. Her mind groped, tried to clear itself of images, expectations —

And the fog abruptly disappeared, revealing an empty street lit by moonlight between breaking clouds.

She gasped and yanked out her knife as voices echoed, too faint for direction. Girlish tittering, smugly triumphant, and then silence.

She began to run again, with no plan except to get away from that place.

Not five steps into her headlong flight, a shadow slightly darker than the night moved beyond the porch of a house. A hand shot out and caught her arm. The grip was strong as steel. She swung clear off her feet, and just barely bit back a squawk of pain and shock as she was pulled into the inky darkness of the porch.

She drew in a breath to yell when someone hissed in her ear, "They'll be here for you in two heartbeats. Come on."

All she could see was a vaguely familiar shape of a head: tall, male, strong cheek and jawline. She started to bring her knife up, and discovered that a long hand had clamped around that wrist as well. Was this a Norsundrian, or was it some kind of trick?

Was it Efael?

"Let me go," she muttered fiercely.

"They've got him. And now they're after you." The unknown assailant shifted his grip and tugged her away from the street.

She fought. The struggle lasted about the space of a single heartbeat, then one of her arms was bent up behind her to the point of agony, and a hand clamped over her mouth.

Close to her ear came the whisper, "If you bite me I'll break your arm." But there was a breath of a husky laugh, familiar. She hated that laugh. But he was not a Norsundrian.

She relaxed — and at once the hand pulled away from her mouth. The other hand shifted grip from constraining to supportive. "Run."

She ran. Abruptly the rain struck again, a drenching, drumming flood.

She ran beyond her limits, pulled inexorably by the unrelenting grip on her arm, until her head rocked and her knees jarred and her breath hurt at every gasp. She did not stop or make a sound, even when the hand increased its pressure and they sped up, but inside she piled up some choice words for delivery at the first appropriate moment.

He stopped suddenly, and she perforce had to, scrambling to keep her balance. Peering around, she made out of the outline of a horse's head and neck.

She braced herself. Next moment hands gripped her round the waist and tossed her up onto the animal's back. She felt the other person vault up behind her. The horse shifted under his weight; there was no saddle or bridle, she realized, and had just enough time to scramble her soggy skirt from clinging to her legs so her could grip with her knees, and then the horse plunged forward a few steps. She grabbed a handful of wiry wet mane, and rain and cold air and rhythm indicated a gallop, though she still couldn't see.

And so they rode into eternity, for time has little meaning when one is both blinded and frightened and very cold. The horse raced into the rain, and her mind, blocked from testing identity of whoever sat behind her, drifted into the night: he was one of the poopsies. She knew that much. Only which?

Let it not be MV, Irenne's killer…

She was too uncomfortable to sleep, but sank into a kind of shivering stupor, until she gradually became aware that the horse had slowed, and that it was going upward, breathing as hard as she'd been forever ago, when she ran with Dirk.

The horse stopped, trembling. A hand prompted her to slide off. She did, her numb legs nearly buckling under her, but once again a strong hand gripped her arm.

The horse then walked away; she heard it.

"Horse." Was that her voice?

"Be all right," was the murmured response, barely audible over the rain.

The hand now propelled her up a rocky path. CJ stumbled painfully over unseen rocks, wishing she had thought to fetch her mocs from her pack—her pack! It had vanished, and she hadn't even noticed. She let fly with a heartfelt insult, and as her mysterious companion made no demur, she kept it up steadily, gasping only when she encountered more sharp rocks. Uphill. West-facing, she thought hazily, if the storm still came out of the west—unless it had changed direction just to smite them some more.

Then, as abruptly as everything else had happened on this weird journey, they turned, and a roar much louder than the rain thundered around her, too steady to be the storm. A waterfall? A cold stream splashed one arm—and then nothing.

A cave.

She drew in a shuddering breath. Walked forward on damp, smooth stone, then stopped as the guiding hand lifted. She heard the sound of tinder being struck and light flared, shone red-orange, unnaturally bright for a moment. The flame touched the wick of a candle, flinging back the shadows, and revealing the bony features and strange fiery eyes of —

"MV," she whispered, appalled.

MV! The only one she'd hated worse was Laban—but her

mind shied away from dealing with that memory.

She glared at MV. "Is this a rescue, or what?"

He grinned. A long, strong hand lifted to wipe back the wet black hair fanging his forehead.

"You're safe," he said.

She swallowed. Gathered her wits. Realized if he had been intending to croak her, he wouldn't have ridden with her all night in order to do it. "How did you find this place in the dark?"

"Homing stone. One of Detlev's tricks. That's why I was too late. Had to hunt down you two, find a hidey-hole, then get back. My timing was a little off." Irony in that last—she that it was about the closest MV came to expressing regret.

She shook her head, trying to identify and deal with one of the myriad emotions washing through her mind, but it was too much like trying to shape water with your fingers.

"Detlev sent me to give you a hand soon as he learned what direction you'd gone in, and that Yeres and Efael were on your heels."

"Detsie," she murmured, unconscious as usual of the nickname, which had become habit. In addition to her emotional reaction she was still fighting against cold, and exhaustion, and the result was mental fog. "Did you see what happened to Dirk?"

"Yes. He got careless with his farsense, and didn't niff their trap. I didn't actually see them make the grab, but I heard it. Decided the best I could do was to veer and yank you out."

"I suppose you know what they will do with him?"

"He'll be all right. They'll be forced to keep him alive and in good shape because Svir and Ilerian want him for their games with Kessler. But you would just be collateral damage."

"That's what *he* thought." CJ groaned, and shivered even harder.

MV had set the candle down on a stone. CJ knelt, stretching out her numb hands over the flame. "I suppose your rotten dark magic won't extend to dry duds?"

"My rotten dark magic is best unused until I know the turd twins are out of the country. But feel free to use these until then." He pulled a pack from behind a huge boulder, rummaged in it, and pitched some cloth at her. Then he walked to the front of the cave, calling over his shoulder, "I'll check on the storm."

CJ gladly and hastily divested herself of her soggy, muddy clothes. The outfit she was soon nearly lost in was a shirt and long pants. As it happened she'd been wearing a belt (to hold up her knife) so she was able to put it on in order to hold up the trousers. Not that MV's shirt couldn't have served as a dress, there being head, neck, and half a chest in difference between their heights. But the tails of the shirt hit her calves, and she was tired of cold, clammy legs.

She had rolled the sleeves back to her wrists and was working on folding the trousers up to her ankles when he returned.

"Hungry?" he asked, bending over his pack again.

"What d'ya got? Oh." She conscientiously struggled to suppress the yawning chasm that seemed to have taken place of her stomach as she said, "If you wanna change, I'll get out of the way. Fair's fair." She eyed his sodden black shirt and mud-splashed trousers.

A brief smile, the old sardonic one that she'd loathed with such enthusiasm. "A salute to your forbearance, but no need to wait. Here. Take this to start on, and fill this little pot from the fall, and I'll make some coffee —" He considered her. "No. Maybe some steep."

She caught the chunk of bread and crammed it into her mouth. She had no interest in either coffee or steep, but she was willing to get the water so he could have some. Maybe she could hold the cup first, and enjoy its warmth.

She stumbled back to the darkness, feeling her way the last portion, until she heard the fall nearby, and felt the water-laden air. It took some effort to fill the metal camping pot and not get wet all over again. When she returned he was in dry clothes, bent over a tiny fire, toasting cheese-covered bread.

The aroma of melting cheese and crisped bread made the chasm inside her bloom to the size of a sun. She was unable to remove her gaze from that splendor until MV handed it over with a grin that she didn't even see.

She nibbled it, trying to make it last, while he fixed one for himself, and then watched as he pulled from his pack a funny little bunch of rods that turned out to make a kind of tripod, which he fit over the flame, and on its top he set the pot of water.

"What were you two doing in Alcandamer?" he asked finally.

CJ sighed. Her reluctance, she knew, was old grudge. But

Liere Fer Eider's job was to take one of those beige papers to Detlev, so keeping their goals from MV — who was obviously still obeying his old commander — didn't make much sense.

"We all got assignments. The idea is to get as complete a report as possible on the Norsundrians' places of command, and strengths, and status, and all that stuff. Then some are to contact mages and see if they'll help in some kind of big plan, to be organized after we get back around harvest time. Mages, and magic objects that have powers that might help."

MV nicked his sharp-cut chin down in a brief nod. "Go on."

"Dirk's thing was to find someone called Charlana, and also a double-crown, whatever that is. Mine was to measle clear up to Vandary to try to find some mage who's supposed to be brilliant. His name is Randon something — I've forgotten it again. I'll have to write to Atan and get it."

"Amdrelya?"

"That was it! Sounds a little like Erai-Yanya's name. You know him?"

"Yep. You'll like him." MV grinned.

CJ looked extremely doubtful, but after just having been saved by MV she didn't want to say that his recommendation didn't exactly inspire her with any zeal to meet this Randon clod. What was he, some kind of super-poopsie? She sighed, then said, "I guess if they magic-transferred Dirk I won't be able to rescue him, but I ought to take on his task as well as do mine."

"Don't chase after Yeres and Efael," he said with all his old sardonic grimness. "They'll be looking around for you tonight," he added. "It annoys them when they miss someone."

"Because it happens so rarely, I s'pose?" She grimaced, and when he nodded, she produced an enthusiastic and comprehensive snort of disgust. Then she studied him speculatively. "You seem to have evaded them easily enough."

Her voice trailed off, but her expression and tone made the *if what you say is true* clear enough.

His lips quirked at the corners. "Not so easy. In any case, they didn't know I was around. I made sure of that. I'm familiar enough with the Black Knives' methods of the hunt."

"Of course! When you were p — uh, on their side."

"Poopsies. You called us poopsies and they called us babies. Detlev's babies," he said reminiscently, eyes narrowed with ironic amusement.

As her physical discomforts faded, CJ's mental fatigue lifted, or maybe it was just relief not to be running, because she looked up at that bony face with those weird-colored eyes — so light a brown, with these goldy, almost orange flecks, that really did make them look fiery — and curiosity ballooned inside her.

The only poopsies she knew were Adam back when they first appeared, and more recently Roy, but he mostly came to visit Clair, and in any case he'd always been so quiet and discreet he'd made only rare references to the past. And never about his own experiences.

She would never have picked MV, Irenne's murderer, as the one to question. But here they were, stuck in a cave with nowhere to go, and he'd saved her. He also seemed willing enough to talk.

She crouched down, her knees under her chin. "What happened? I take it they didn't just gather you in a circle and explain all their rotten secrets."

"Nope." A brief laugh.

He noticed how her forearms were tucked between her thighs and stomach. His heating water was now sending up little curls of steam. "Steep'll warm you up."

She grimaced. "You drink it. I don't really like most steep, unless there's lots of milk and honey in it. The only kind I like is that rare stuff that Rosey — uh, Mondros —"

"I know who he is."

"Oh." *Did you know he's Rel's father?* No. That was not her tale to tell.

"This steep was a gift from Tsauderei. Give it a try."

"Tsauderei," CJ repeated. The old mage lived high in the Delfina Valley, right on the border of Sartor, and he was close friends with Atan — in fact, hadn't he raised her, or something? "It's got to be the good stuff," she said, with more enthusiasm.

MV grunted, reaching into his pack for a slim heavy-weave packet, which he laid aside. It didn't take farsense to perceive her wary curiosity. He considered what to tell her — and how much. Then he sat back. "So you want to hear more, eh?"

"Well, not anything nasty. How did you learn their tricks? And more important, can you teach them to me?"

"As for how, Efael got bored, and petty, and…" He eyed her again, then finessed. "And he wanted us as targets for various reasons, about the time that —" The faintest pause, and he continued, " —Siamis turned the Arrow over to the Venn. Efael likes to take his targets off world. Says to run. They chase."

"Sounds like fun." She knew as soon as the words were out that this was the wrong response.

MV looked grim and wicked, very much like the old days. Then shrugged. "Let me say this much. It's not fun when you're tired, hungry, and when the Black Knives catch you they either beat the shit out of you or if Yeres was there, and she often was for part of it, she'd experiment with mind tortures on you. Efael would watch, or act, whatever he was in the mood for. Then as soon as you'd recovered enough to stand up, he'd tell you to run. And again. And again." He eyed her, then said, "Then he'd get personal."

Personal. She sensed anger below the drawl, and was afraid to ask what he wasn't telling. "Ick."

"Anyway. Your real question was, training in the hunt. Detlev refined our knowledge."

"Before or after you came over to our side?"

"After."

"Why?"

"Ask him." MV shrugged one shoulder, and flashed that brief grin again. "Should've figured he could outrun those two. They never did bring him down, in the past."

"They snaffled Siamis instead, and tricked Detsie that way, we know that much." CJ nodded. "But it doesn't make sense!" She thought back, remembering how lethal the poopsies had been while they'd been on Norsunder's side — and that hadn't been their best? And why hadn't Detlev given them that training first, before Yeres and Efael had come along?

She said, "What was Detsie doing while all this 'personal' stuff was going on?"

"You mean, for us? Nothing. Efael always made sure to play his games when Detlev wasn't around." MV glanced at the pot, and saw bubbles rising. "Good enough."

He carefully unwrapped the packet, extracted three dark leaves, and cast them into the water. Within moments the cold, moisture-laden air filled with a fresh, greeny scent, like a summer's day in a meadow, or springtime in a forest glade at home.

Euphoria and homesickness both smote CJ. She fought back the homesickness, and watched MV set aside the pot to steep, then dismantle and stow his tripod thing in his pack.

He said, "When you get all this information, how are you going to get your people coordinated? Or are you going to herd 'em all into Mearsies Heili?"

"No, we'll write—oh!" Her hand dove into her clothing, and came out with her beige paper, still damp. "Oh, no! Oh, I do hope Dirk managed to ditch his before the slimes searched him."

MV narrowed his gaze as he wondered if he was seeing Siamis's latest project. "I'd be real surprised if the magic doesn't include wards against Norsundrians."

"You think, or you can tell?"

Another one-shoulder shrug. "Going to let Detlev in on these plans?"

"Yup. The group stuck—that is, Liere was chosen to find him and give him one."

"Mmm." He touched the sides of the pot and fished the leaves out, leaving a fine green liquid. "Here."

They shared the steep back and forth. CJ knew at the first sip that this was the delicious Sartoran kind. It tasted just as it smelled, both warming her and making her think of spring and summer, fresh green growth, balmy air and birdsong. It eased her cold, and even lessened the ache in her arm from MV's initial grab.

Even her scalp somehow felt less itchy and dirty (for she and Dirk had encountered few cleaning frames on their run) and she was tempted to unbraid her hair and get rid of the worst of the accumulated tangles. But as wellbeing spread through her, lassitude followed, and she didn't really want to move.

MV pulled out a tightly rolled black cloth and tossed it into her lap. "Now that you're warm inside, you'll stay warm outside."

"What's this? Oh, a cloak. You have two?"

"Nope."

She looked in doubt at the heavy, fine-woven wool, knowing it would be polite to offer to share. But the truth was, she would rather have shared a blanket with an alligator.

She had not forgotten that he was Irenne's killer, though it was Clair herself who had said that Irenne had twisted into MV's blade. Even harder to accept, they had shared equally in fault—everyone on both sides talking tough, and acting tough, but except for Senrid, no one had really known just what "tough" meant. That kind of knife play, Clair had said later, was what the poopsies did among themselves all the time.

Maybe it really was an accident. But MV hadn't said he was sorry. And that still made CJ feel... She refused to think about it.

"Give me those wet clothes," he said. "I'm going to put 'em under the fall. See if the water will pound some of the mud out of 'em. Then I'm going to do some checking around, so I suggest you get some shut-eye."

She nodded, her shoulders hunching up.

"Tomorrow I'll give you some tips on ditching the hounds, and I won't use Efael's teaching methods. How's that?"

"Great," she said, and swallowed, and said as politely as she could, "There's room for two under this thing."

"Nah. I don't get cold unless it snows."

Her face was a study in valiantly suppressed relief. He gave no sign of noticing, but as he picked up the candle and started out with her filthy duds, he laughed soundlessly to himself.

CJ rolled up and watched the flickering light move farther away, the life-like shadows growing and then melding.

She thought over the long, strange day, and sighed. I know I ought not to keep grudges, but if these creeps had switched sides a few years earlier, then Irenne — and a lot of others — would still be alive. Or if they hadn't been born at all, but of course they didn't choose Norsunder when they were born, they were chosen. By Detlev. Then he switched 'em back. Why?

A horrible thought seized her, now that it was totally dark: what if he chose to switch yet again?

Stop it. Stop it. Get through tomorrow, and the next day, and worry about Mearsies Heili, and let others who actually know what to do worry about Detsie and the Host and all that.

She was soon asleep.

Ten

Western Imar

JULIAN COULD NOT SHAKE the deep unhappiness that haunted her days and her dreams.

She tried, at first, to attribute it to the powerful magic that the Host had woven over the countryside, but finally had to admit, as the girls toiled drearily northwards, that it was her proximity to Dthel Rendm, Dtheldevor's old home. Two kingdoms away, but still her thoughts stubbornly wanted to arrow home to the island on the border of Wnelder Vee and Everon where she had spent the happiest days of her life.

There was no relief when at last she admitted to herself that magic was not at fault, but grief. How she missed Dtheldevor and those crazy pirates!

Her eyelids burned. She leaned her head against the old wood, her nostrils filled with the sharp scent of broken vines, and closed her eyes. Sap! Whiner! Dtheldevor's gang would be the first to laugh at you if they heard such mawkishness.

It was her own excellent woodcraft that had found them this odd little space inside a gigantic dead tree, hollowed over the years by various animals sheltering from weather. The front of the hollow bole was completely covered by growing vines.

Clair had hung her black cloak up inside the vines in order to completely block any pinpoint of light from the outside, and then Julian had made a vagabond fire before retreating into the shadows.

The warm golden light flickered cozily over the wood and curling vines around them. Clair sat nearby, the flames striking gilt highlights in her white hair as she gazed into the fire. June and her cup were gone.

Satisfied that her weakness had not been witnessed, Julian eased back on the soft moss that grew all over the floor of the hollow tree. She thought tiredly that she ought to be grateful to have a chance to enjoy the warmth of a fire, and to be sleeping in relative comfort, safe from those rotten spy birds.

The vines rustled. Clair and Julian stilled. The cloak lifted, and June eased in, followed by a swirl of cold night air. She sat down, and Julian handed her a share of crumbled traveler's cake, which June took in silence.

Clair closed her eyes, her hands on her knees, and Julian realized belatedly that she hadn't been daydreaming. Her pose was the one that the Dena Yeresbeth-types who could do farsense settled into.

Clair blinked, then looked up, and for once they saw, oh, not humor — this journey had been too taxing for that — but a slight smoothing of the tension across her forehead. "Expect some company soon."

Presently the curtain moved once again, and a silhouette stepped into the circle of light, resolving into refined features, with cornsilk hair mostly hiding the winking diamonds in each ear: Zairna Raadi, who had come through a Worldgate. He spoke a quiet, courteous word of greeting.

Clair said, "You were faster than I thought. Either that or I lost my awareness of time. As usual."

Julian frowned. "Why are you here? Weren't you going to Eleyad, to contact the morvende geliath there? Or did you get lost?"

"I did not get lost," Zairna said, his diction precise, but the rise and fall of his words betrayed his off-world origin. "I found the geliath. Or they found me. It was too well hidden. I left signs in the manner Rel indicated."

As he spoke he shrugged off his knapsack and sat down, his movements neat, even elegant. Refined, like his bones. Zairna had been born a prince in a highly cultured land. Bred up from babyhood to his role, not just his features, but his training, movements, tastes, all bespoke the prince. And yet there was no arrogance in his manner, no haughtiness or even that innate sense of superiority that often marked the royally born.

Julian and Clair both liked him. Erai-Yanya had been warned by a mage from his world that Zairna Raadi wasn't quite sane; as a boy he'd survived a charmingly power-mad mother who had intended to make her son an emperor. Someday, after she had a good, long rule herself. She didn't fight on the battlefield, oh no, but in the pleasing chambers of a palace world-renowned for its exquisite treasures. And yet people had ended up just as dead.

Atan had said privately, *There's something especially vicious about the use of the arts as weapons. How can you recover from the wounds?*

Julian leaned forward. "That means Tarael is gone, right?"

"Yes," Zairna said, and hesitated. His eyes were a light shade midway between gray and blue. Their expression was opaque, but his lowered gaze conveyed regret. "He is a friend of yours, is he not?"

Julian crossed her arms, scowling. "A friend indeed. First morvende leader outside of Sartor to make me welcome in their geliaths."

Zairna said, "I am very much afraid that the Host have him in their stronghold."

Julian let out her breath. "Oh, no. Oh, that's —"

Clair looked worried. "You were not thinking of going in to rescue him?"

Zairna spoke, his voice so well-modulated it was pleasing to listen to but difficult to define the tone. "I thought I might try."

The others exchanged appalled glances, then Clair broke the silence. "Are you hungry? We have plenty of travelers' cakes. We stocked up in Djedan."

"No, but I thank you."

Julian turned away, sick with horror, and futile anger. "We don't know where the Host is, exactly," she said. "We've been traveling along, and the land is dying under the blight of their magic — it even changes the sunlight, somehow. People are leaving, if they can."

"I believe I have located their stronghold," he said. "It's north of here, a country estate."

Clair looked down at her hands. "I've been trying to scout by farsense, behind a fake identity, but I've had no success. There's a very weird directionlessness, almost timelessness, on the mental realm here. I have not ranged far, and yet a couple times I nearly got lost."

"I discovered much of what I know by traveling on foot."

"Shall we join together, then?" Clair suggested. "Your sneakery and Julian's, and what little I can do by Dena Yeresbeth. At least we can find out if it's possible to get in to rescue anyone."

Julian hunched forward. "We might also find out who else they have there."

Clair flinched. "That's something I hadn't thought of." She drew in a breath that the others all heard. "I guess that settles it, then. I can't see abandoning anyone without our even trying." She frowned slightly, then said to Julian, "What is it? Bad idea?"

"Do you have any morvende in your family?"

Clair flicked her white hair. "It would seem so, wouldn't it? But there have been few white-hairs in my family over the last hundred years. And before that, no one kept records." She grinned. "Let's plan, shall we?"

Alcandamer

CJ opened her eyes. MV sat on the other side of the cave. Eyes shut, chin on breast, right hand loosely closed around the handle of a long knife.

She sat up, intending to move quietly and not disturb him, but at the first shift of cloth his eyes opened and his head lifted, the knife flashing up — and then he dropped it again.

"They're gone," he said. "Left at dawn."

"Ugh." She grimaced, and stretched. "Yow," she said in a different voice, massaging her right shoulder as best she could. "I'm really glad you came along and all, but did you have to nearly yank my arm off?"

He gave her his brief grin and swung to his feet. "I'll make more of that steep. It'll take the damp out of your bones."

She knew that that was as much of an apology as she was going to get. After all, he had saved her life. She said, "Got any of that bread left?"

"Nope. We downed the last of it last night."

She sighed. "Then I may's well come with you. Where are my duds?"

He'd spread their clothing in the intersection between two caves, where a continuous breeze flowed, but it was a damp breeze, as one would expect so near a vast waterfall, and so the cloth was still unpleasantly clammy.

"Be wearable by afternoon," MV said, fingering a shirtsleeve. "Give us a morning for a little tutoring."

They walked on farther. CJ heard the waterfall's roar, and then felt the stirred air coming off it, smelling of water. The fall sheeted from above, an enthralling translucent wall, and pounded down far below. It was a wintry gray-blue wall under the rain-gray sky. The sun was at mid-morning.

They retreated inside, and as soon as they had drunk their steep, which once again imparted a sense of wellbeing, CJ bent her attention to absorbing everything MV told her.

He spent only a little time on trailcraft. She already knew enough that any further refinement was not going to be possible while they both sat in a cave. What he talked about was how to chase—and how to run from a chase. What signs to watch for—and how not to leave them. How a steady jog would keep one moving far longer than a hard run quickly bringing on exhaustion and carelessness.

"There's more I could show you," he said finally, "but we'd have to be in the field. What you need more than anything is to practice blurring yourself in the perceptions of passersby. It's going to take more concentration than running through a forest does. Not only people from whom you get food and directions, but those who might catch a glimpse of you and wonder who you are ..."

He went on and on, making her practice imaging and blocking until her head ached, and then he had her run at top speed up and back in the cave while holding her focus, until finally she flopped down, panting, dizzy from exertion and hunger.

MV frowned down at her, hands propped on skinny hips. "I wish we had time to make a run with some obstacles—" he began.

"Yow!"

"—but I believe we'd both best hit the road." Detlev's orders had been both abrupt and specific, right down to the place to leave her.

"It's too late. Just tell Clair you disappeared my remains."

"One last thing," he said, looking amused. "Only use—

accept the help of—animals with Dena Yeresbeth. Others can't block mind-probe, and the Norsundrians always kill all but horses."

She sat up. "That horse last night. Did it have horse-Dena Yeresbeth?"

"Yep."

"Wondered. Animals minds are so weird. It's so hard to find 'em because they think so differently from us."

"Dena Yeresbeth ones will usually find you if they want to offer help against the common enemy. All right, that's it. Let's get those clothes and move."

By late afternoon they reached the valley Detlev had required MV to find. He half lifted a hand and said, "I'm off."

She wanted to ask *where to,* but couldn't think of any reason to be so nosy.

He said, "I think your best plan would be to head into the hills rather than back along the populated areas. Might put you on your quarry's trail."

"Okay." She flapped a hand awkwardly, her wide blue gaze intense.

And because she was no coward, she spoke her mind. "Look, I know you poopsies have helped our side. And I know that I'm the worst grudge-holder in the world. And Clair said that Irenne moved. You didn't. And, yeah, you shouldn't have had a knife at her neck, but our side was toting knives, too. But … were you sorry?"

He gazed back, aware that there was a time when he would have despised anyone who thought "being sorry" changed anything, and he would have found her question risible. "Most every day," he said.

She flushed. What had Clair said once? *They're more like a mirror to us girls than you think. A family they made themselves.* She couldn't read his expression, but the simple words, even his flat tone carried more resonance than if he had said the conventional "I'm sorry." And she was just able to perceive it. "All right."

As clemency it wasn't much—and if anyone had dared to say he sought it, he would have hotly denied it—but he was aware of a sense of … call it very incremental ease as he loped off, and was soon swallowed in the leafy gloom of the heavily forested hillside.

CJ's clothes were still damp at the seams, but she'd be wet

by rain soon anyway. At least the grit was gone, and the air wasn't so bitter. She'd walk while there was still light, and practice her trail craft as well as look for something to eat.

Walking in a forest always put her in a good mood. This one was more leafy and mossy than the woodland at home, and the ground much more uneven, but the soft greeny-gold light, the smells, the beauty were so familiar. She found some late berries before too long, and ate some. It was too late in autumn for larger fruit, but there were still gleanings of nuts here and there, shaken down by the recent violent rain.

Nuts, berries, and cold, clear spring water eased the ache in her middle. "Wish I hadn't lost my pack," she thought for the millionth time — and like the previous reminders, it brought on the chilly thought of Dirk captured.

At least she had her beige paper, now safely tucked into her pocket. Even if she got another knapsack, she was never again going to trust it; it had been accident, impatience, really, that had caused her to shove the paper into her shirt instead of her pack.

She dismissed regrets and stared up through the interlaced leaves at the sky. Leaves so many colors, all of them beautiful, and together glorious, more than any jewel box. High above the trees, outlined against the mild blue sky, a bird drifted along on the currents and her spirits soared as well.

Presently the western clouds she'd seen were overhead, and a brief rain misted down, and then departed eastward.

Just before sunset she realized she was being paced.

She looked around, at first covertly, then more openly. Saw nothing.

After more walking she heard slight sounds, and once she just glimpsed the shift of a shadow. She concentrated. If these were Norsundrians, they were experts at masking their evil intent.

When she saw a flock of skylarks hover and dive, not in fear but going about their business with complete indifference to human passers-by, she knew she was not being stalked by Norsundrians, and she began to sing.

Her voice rang high and clear, accompanied by the pleasing random echoes that come in woodlands. She sang in Mearsiean and Alcanda alternately, all the verses of her latest anti-Norsunder song. She got so involved in forming a new verse that it wasn't until she'd decided on the last line that she noticed she had a silent audience walking with her.

She looked from one golden-haired kid to the other, and saw them watching her with expressions of pleasure and merriment.

"Dawnsingers," she exclaimed happily. "What were you doing, following me so long? Trying to figure out if I was a disgusting Norsundrian spy?"

"In part," the girl said. They were a girl and boy, both her size, although their faces were a little older. She spoke Alcanda with a singsong accent that made CJ's nerves tingle the way a new and beautiful song did. "Also we tried to guess what is your purpose here."

"Well." CJ grinned. "I was walking along."

"And after you saw us did not try to hide, or to pursue, or yet to call for aid."

CJ remembered the poopsies in the bad old days, and was about to say *A spy could have acted just as I did* but then she realized that they were walking along an old animal trail, at least a day's ride from any human habitation. They could take off and leave her at any time, and if she got back to report, all she would be able to say would be, *I met two dawnsinger kids. Dawnsingers in the woods.* That stenchiferous wight Llyenthur would certainly pay lots of gold to find out that vital piece of information.

"I'm CJ of Mearsies Heili, a princess if you like to pull rank, and I mention it only because I'm trying to find this queen called Charlana. Uh, and her crown — or someone's crown — a double one, anyway. And I have a message for her from Queen Atan Landis of Sartor." She added this last as ballast, because the other two had been listening without any reaction at all.

They looked at one another. Back at her. "Will you consent to a blindfold?"

"Sure." CJ nodded vigorously, hoping that the blindfold meant that her long search had brought her — accidentally, as usual — blundering onto the right trail.

The blindfold was soft, and tied with care to block all light but not hurt. Then the dawnsingers each took one of her hands and they began to walk.

CJ tried using Dena Yeresbeth to sense around her, but all she got was a confusing sense of color.

The walk was long, but her guides took care to warn her of stones, or vines, or roots, and when the path was about to go downward or up.

When they stopped and pulled off the blindfold she discovered that dark had fallen. They had made a small fire, and one of them produced those dense nut cakes that dawnsingers were famed for, and broke it into three. Delicious, but oh, gone so fast.

"I think you need another portion."

CJ saw the girl smiling and snickered, buoyantly happy. "Oh, you don't know how long it's been since I ate!"

They laughed, and introduced themselves as Alassa and Alander, brother and sister. She was perhaps the older; at least she did most of the talking and the decision-making.

"We have no more now, but tomorrow I promise you plenty," Alassa finally said.

After a night's rest near the campfire, they continued on, the blindfold blocking out the pure morning light. Alassa and Alander did their best to overcome the implied distrust of the blindfold by trading off telling stories and singing songs, and asking for CJ's songs, as they walked on and on.

At last they stopped, and asked her to sit, and she had just enough time to feel a ropy kind of thing at the back of her knees when she discovered that she was being pulled into the air.

She kicked her feet—and then felt herself set down on something wooden.

"Stand, please," a voice murmured, and as she did, the blindfold was slid from her head.

She gazed around at a group of people gathered in what appeared to be a platform built in a mighty tree. Most of the faces were pale, framed by various shades of light hair. A couple of the people were different, most notably a tall, thin young woman with merry blue eyes and a million freckles on a face framed by a wreath of bright red hair.

"Welcome," said the woman. "Who are you?"

CJ spoke her piece again, faltering at the end when she saw the woman shut her eyes, and then smile. "Is something wrong?" she finished.

"Not in the immediate sense." The woman gestured. "This thing always makes me a little dizzy. I'm Charlana, I guess I ought to mention, and this—" She pulled a gold circlet from atop her head, where it had been completely hidden by her curls—"is the crown you seek."

"Um, wasn't it supposed to be double?" CJ gazed askance

at the golden object. Had disaster struck again?

"Only the image the wearer sees if the person viewed is under false guise, spoken or worn."

CJ whistled. "That would be handy! But I suppose you don't exactly pass it around?"

Charlana laughed. "Come. Eat, rest, and we will talk long, come morning, for you have walked far today."

"Okay by me!" CJ nodded, sighing with bliss. "Oh, to be clean and have dry hair again!"

Eleven

LLYENTHUR APPEARED SUDDENLY IN the map room.

His eyes were wide, the pupils small, giving him a manic look that struck terror into his aides' guts. The unpleasant little smile curling his lips only made it worse.

Duin spoke up, hoping that good news would divert the shitstorm about to land on them. "We just got in word—" He pointed at the dispatch relay desk. "—Svirle has Dirk Sonscarna."

"I know." Llyenthur moved to stand before the huge map on the wall, hands behind his back.

The aides hesitated, and when he neither moved nor spoke, they got back to work, finding something to do if there was no immediate task. Look busy, that's right, and maybe he won't ream your skull out. But they all took care to keep him in their field of vision.

The only person in the room who appeared to be unmoved by Llyenthur's presence or absence was a slight blond youth on the verge of manhood, cold of face, with a steady gaze that was so non-reactive the aides had decided that this latest whim of Llyenthur's—giving this damn Geth pretty-boy full run of HQ—was because someone felt bad about accidentally removing his brains.

The youth put his book down, after carefully marking his place. He walked over and joined Llyenthur before the map, and when Llyenthur glanced down into his face, Cath said, "Caris-Merian is gone."

"You were supposed to follow her, were you not?" The gentleness of Llyenthur's tone made the aides watch furtively for the lightning to strike.

Cath of Geth replied dispassionately, "I thought of a better plan." And when Llyenthur looked a question, Cath said, "I planted one of the enchanted knives. She found it and took it."

"A knife? Enchanted against whom?"

"David."

"Why did you think that a better plan?" Llyenthur's drawl lengthened. "Cath, you had specific orders, just to follow her. If I wanted him dead I would see to it myself."

Here it comes, Duin thought, hoping he'd get to watch. That damned Cath, weird as he was, also had a tendency to dole out high-handed orders as if he actually had any kind of command, but so far Llyenthur (for some insane reason) had endorsed them.

Cath ignored the flunkeys, staring back at Imry Llyenthur. In the twisted corridors of Cath's mind, Caris-Merian's old grudge still existed as a mandate: *kill David*. He'd show them all how capable he was. If he was capable, would the torments cease? But to be capable he had to think.

"I don't think she can actually do it," Cath observed. "She'll want to. And all the knife has to do is nick him."

"You," Llyenthur said, "had better be right. My orders still stand. Go track her down."

Llyenthur moved two markers on the map, issued a few more purely logistical orders, and then departed.

Cath, and his book, were already gone.

Twelve

Mearsies Heili

PAUSING TO WIPE TIRED eyes, Atan laid her pen down with her free hand. Then she bent to place a colored pin in the map that she had affixed to a table in Clair's library in Mearsies Heili's white palace.

A knock at the door preceded the entry of Tahra Delieth, queen of Everon. Atan glanced at Tahra's narrow, tense face and her puckered brow. "Can't sleep either?"

"Another almost-mutiny," Tahra said. Her voice was tight.

Atan said nothing. She sympathized with Tahra's children, who fought bitterly against being forced to stay locked in their suite for days, if a visitor came whom Tahra did not like. Which had happened when Roy, one of Detlev's boys, turned up. The elder children had only been released after Roy departed. Atan could not imagine how the mild, quiet Roy could contaminate the Delieth children, but it was not her affair.

"Janil is making hot chocolate in the kitchen," Atan murmured. "Aurora was awake again."

"She's been having bad dreams ever since Clair entered Imar, hasn't she?" Tahra asked, which surprised Atan. She'd thought Tahra was ignoring the progress of the spy missions. She had gotten very angry indeed when Liere Fer Eider had agreed to carry a beige paper to Detlev, and had withdrawn from the planning.

Tahra gave Atan a sour little smile. "I glance at your map from time to time. Especially to follow Clair's progress, now that they are so close to my kingdom. And I watched the progress of Arthur and Mildred when they went through Everon."

"Watched? You mean you wrote to them?"

"No," Tahra said, irony barely masking her anger. "I know what Everon is like when Norsundrians are there. I watched your pins."

Atan lowered her gaze to the map. She knew how Tahra felt — that sickening helplessness, knowing that one's kingdom, one's life responsibility, was in the hands of the enemy, and there was little one could do.

But one did exert oneself to do that little.

At least Atan did.

"Most of them try not to write during night hours here, but sometimes they can't help it, and since I think it better to keep the paper with me at all times, it wakes me up. Darian Selenna, dear boy, was cheered at the welcome he received from the old king of Al Mardeth. Which is good. I didn't like how deeply those children grieved over Dtheldevor's demise."

"I thought it was their friend Deon they grieved."

"Yes." Atan rubbed her forehead, then looked back at the map. "Anyway, apparently this king has taken to the notion that he ought to join his kingdom to mine."

Tahra's straight dark brows went up. "You don't sound pleased. This king is a simpleton, or a villain?"

Atan sighed as she got to her feet. "Let's go get that chocolate...although I'd a thousand times rather drink some steep! I long ago lost a taste for milk, and sugar, and chocolate, but since I did not speak up at the beginning when Clair asked, it seems to do so now would be an unfair reproach."

They descended the stairs, the hems of their fine robes whispering over the steps in a way that had been last heard in the white palace a hundred years ago, in Mearsieanne's day.

"No, he's neither simpleton nor villain," Atan said. "Or at least as far as one can tell from formal correspondence and the silver words of the diplomats. But he's tired as well as old, and the notion of Sartor being an umbrella of safety — and repair, let's not forget the clink of gold here — is so inbred that even in the face of its untruth it still seems to persist."

Tahra murmured, "One can understand seeking safety,

even if in symbol."

"But Sartor fell. In a morning. And everyone knows it."

"Trust the Norsundrians to trumpet that about."

"But it doesn't seem to matter. According to what I'm hearing over the distances, everyone seems to say something to the effect of *When Sartor is free, then we'll see some right action.*

"And they believe Sartor might be stronger than ever," Tahra said. She added in a dry voice, "Have you considered that all this might stem from there being a king in the offing?"

Atan heard the dryness with an inner shrug. The only thing that Tahra hated more than Norsundrians was men. Or more correctly, the idea of romance. Though Tahra had reached adulthood several years ago, she seemed unchanged from the unsmiling survivor of her family's murder in the last Norsundrian conflagration—unchanged except that her prejudices ran deeper, harder, and much, much angrier.

"If so, it would be due to what Rel is doing, not to who he is."

Atan longed for Rel to get one of the beige papers. They had agreed that he would be the right person to give Norsunder a target if it seemed the enemy might discover the underground passage of former prisoners through Remalna, into the mysterious forest along that little kingdom's border. Odd, that, she thought, distracted as she glanced at her map. How two rural inkblot kingdoms had come to be so very important: first Mearsies Heili, then Remalna.

Janil, Clair's pleasant-faced steward, who apparently had been about all the parental figure Clair had had, was carrying a tray. "May I bring this up for you? I'd like to close the kitchen for the night."

"Certainly. Thank you!"

They retraced their steps, Janil carrying the chocolate, which she set down on a little side table in the Magic Chamber. As soon as she was gone, Atan said, "You can have my share."

"Thank you." Tahra smiled, a rarity that brought back, briefly, the happy Hatahra Delieth that Atan first met not long after both their kingdoms had been released from enchantment. So long ago!

"I confess a liking for whipped cream and chocolate," Tahra said, reaching for the pot. "Is Rel spreading these rumors? It doesn't seem like him. But people do change."

"Not at all," Atan said, keeping her voice even. "I suspect

that Rel might be slipping down to Sartor when he's not leading Norsundrian pursuits all over. He is very likely organizing resistance, he is certainly helping to spread the word about the secret harvests up in the mountains and elsewhere, but he is far more likely to neglect to tell anyone his name than he is to trumpet his connection to me."

Tahra gave a short nod. "That does sound like Rel."

"I know rumor's got around about Rel and me, and he's been increasingly popular in Sartor ever since he reorganized the city guard. Everyone who was alive before then remembers the defeat that killed my parents. And the fact that my father, though he'd had plenty of personal courage, was a terrible war leader. Sartorans do appreciate competence. Then there is the old longing for a powerful Sartor, because the old stories persist that Sartor's long existence means peace."

"If you do accept this king's offer, will you become empress, then?" Tahra asked.

"I refuse. It will not happen in my lifetime. Protectorates I guess I will agree to, but only that."

"What does Rel think of it all?" Tahra asked.

"He just shrugs. And when it's time to don all the trappings of state he'll put on those, and the title with 'em, in pretty much the same way he's worn various disguises all these years. Playing king will be the same to him as playing guide over the Redmond Mountains to a party of wealthy Lamancan merchants."

"Half of his friends are rulers."

"And half are not."

"Isn't it strange," Tahra mused, her gaze pensive instead of angry, for once. "My mother was just the same. Those who make no effort to become heroes seem to get the reputation." Her gaze dropped to the map pins. "Is there any kind of picture emerging about the Norsundrian organization?"

Atan once again had to hide her surprise at this evidence of Tahra's interest in the group's plans. "I could have predicted the response I'm getting: steady reports from Seshe, Leander, Darian Selenna, Liere Fer Eider, and a few others. Nothing whatever from Andri Elsarion, Roy, Dirk. Sporadic from the rest. I don't think we'll have a true picture until they all return. If they return: I do not fault Dirk, as he was taken prisoner."

Tahra's gaze wandered over the map for a time, her expression difficult to interpret. When she spoke, her words were a shock of ice water to the heart. "Look," she said, "at how many of us come from broken homes. Even Rel, in a manner."

Atan made a motion of agreement.

Tahra lifted her eyes, and Atan saw that the anger was back, old, cold, and deliberate. "It all seems to come back to Detlev, doesn't it?"

Atan set down a marker, and regarded Tahra steadily. "Except — as you know quite well — Rel's broken family is due entirely to Wan-Edhe of the Chwahir. I don't see Detlev's fault in that horrible man wanting to live forever, a scourge of the worst kind in history. Then there is your broken family — which, I recollect quite clearly, happened at the command of a Norsundrian named Henerek. Who was, if I am not mistaken, once one of your Everoneth Knights of Dei, cashiered for crimes. I still don't see Detlev's hand in any of that."

"He enchanted Carlael Lirendi of Colend into madness on a mere whim," Tahra retorted.

"Very true," Atan said. "Detlev is to blame for many of the ills of the world, but not all. Laying every crime at his feet out of hatred, however satisfying, merely lifts culpability from other villains. What use is that?" She rose. "Good night."

The next morning neither of them referred to the conversation of the night before. When Tahra came down, her children, released from her governance, raced down the stairs and vanished into the garden, where their voices mingled with Aurora's, and with those of other child refugees who were now staying at the white palace.

She found Atan finishing a hasty meal.

"Something happening?"

"Hunger. Liere almost always writes on this day and time once a week, my time, and I hoped to finish my breakfast before I get the call and must begin the day's transcribing." Atan patted a pocket in her skirt, gave a half-wince at the fresh hot chocolate by her plate, and then took her dishes in to put them through the cleaning bucket.

She then left, and Tahra sat down and glanced out the window of the dining room to the flowering pots on one of the terraces. Spring was at its height. Summer stretched ahead, a hovering question.

She shook her head, and pulled from under her arm the book she'd selected the evening before.

Janil came in presently, and found Tahra buried in the old, battered history written early in the history of Mearsies Heili. There was no bowing, no titles, in Mearsies Heili. You either got used to it, or didn't, but the Mearsieans didn't change.

"Would you like anything for breakfast, Tahra?"

"Yes, thank you. Oh, may I give you a piece of information I discovered last night?"

"Please."

"Atan does not like hot chocolate, but is too embarrassed to tell you. She misses steep, specifically that from Sartor, though I don't know if you even get it on this continent."

"Of course we do," Janil said, laughing comfortably. "I keep some against CJ wanting it, usually in winter. Thank you for telling me. I'll take care of that right away." And she kept talking in an agreeable voice about cheery things—the children's good appetites, their learning games from children over the world—all meant to soothe.

Tahra recognized what she was doing, but still felt cheered.

Atan had just settled down and was resting her chin on her hands as she studied the map that Senrid had made, wondering where he was and what he was doing, when the signal bloomed behind her eyes and the beige paper before her suddenly filled with writing.

Liere's handwriting. Atan scanned past the graceful opening, the excuses offered for so late a letter so Atan would not think it inconvenient that Liere stayed up half the night in order to write at the time most convenient in Mearsies Heili.

> *...we reached Andri's friends here in Idego. It appears that the flying folk in the mountains have a friendship with the ruler through one of their children, and thus we were brought directly here...*

Atan scanned through the details about the Renselaeus rulers, to be read and thought over later. Right now she wanted the urgent news, and from the length of the letter, she knew there would be some.

> *...I will give you the report on the local Norsundrians and their present patterns, but first I must detail an incident that disturbs me the more I think on it.*

> *The mountain folk are in contact with one another. The*

ones in the mountains above Shingara had heard about my visit to those above Visegn last year. We were carried over terrain that would have taken us weeks to cross on foot. At first I thought it was mere friendliness, but on my arrival I was told of one of our kind who was also running from the Norsundrians, only they'd found her considerably ill and distraught...

Here it was, then.
Atan began to scan rapidly.

...and they brought me to a cave wherein I found lying on a bed of pillows Caris-Merian Rhoderan. Was she not supposed to be north, on the continent of Goerael? Well, we both entered, but she looked ill, and was not dressed under her blankets, and so Andri left again.

She never even noticed him, that I do swear. She said to me, "They get you, too?"

"Who?" I said. "No one is chasing us. What happened to you?"

"Him. Imry." Her hands plucked at the blankets, but she spoke with a tremulous sort of loathing that I took for granted then, and wonder at now. "Sherry and Falinneh were left, and he gave orders to kill them. He brought me to someplace north. But I escaped."

"And here you can rest safely," I said, and I really believe I was stupid to miss what I think was a cue, for she kept her mind blocked, but there was no expression of relief, at all. If anything, more tension. At the time I thought it was reaction. I do not know her at all!

She said, "Do you know where the others are?"

I thought she meant those she knew from Geth. And so I said, "I haven't heard from the Geth people, but I understand they are fine."

"David?"

"I don't think of poopsies as Geth people! As it happens,

*I do know about him. He and Andri found one another
while spying along the borders of Tiv Evair and Nov
Rual, just a week and a half ago. He was doing the same
thing we are, only on Detlev's orders. He was planning
to work his way north to Larkadhe – why, is something
wrong?"*

"No," she whispered, and closed her eyes, and I left.

*When I told Andri about this conversation he said,
"She's in some kind of trouble. You better find out
what."*

*But when I went back she was gone. Yes, gone, sick as
she had been. I think I might have made a very great
mistake.*

Now for the report

Ghildraith Mountains (north)

Liere finished writing her latest observations on the enemy's
numbers and movements, rubbed her eyes, and laid down her
pen.

The longer time passed, the more certain she was that she
had seen all the right clues, but had put them together wrong.

Tired, dispirited, she returned to the curtained cave that
had been set up as a sleeping chamber, the stone worn smooth
by unknown hands centuries before.

Andri lay in a welter of quilts, a candle set on a tiny table
nearby. Liere let the curtain drop behind her and the candle
flickered wildly, making the shadows jump and leap. The
golden light shimmered on his long pale hair and the diamond
earring in his ear as he turned his head.

Tired as she was, Liere enjoyed the flare of proximity.
Strange, how the mind can be tangled in its own skeins of duty,
expectation, tiredness, obligation, plans, but the body always
lives in the moment.

For the moment.

She dropped down next to him and laid her head on his
shoulder, her senses acute: his scent, his skin warm beneath her

cheek. The sound of his breathing.

"You're troubled," he said.

The sound of his voice, low and husky, reverberating through muscle and bone.

Focus, she commanded herself. "It's Caris-Merian. I am convinced that I ought to have known something was wrong."

"I was wondering how long it would be before you managed to blame yourself." He grinned, and pulled her tighter against him.

"How could I have been so dense? We traveled with her all last winter, from what, Zranf all the way to Nente, and yet I realize I do not know her, not at all."

"She took great care to make certain nobodt did," Andri said.

Liere flinched, and Andri knew — didn't take any insight to guess — that Liere was now thinking of her own preoccupation with Senrid Montredaun-An's inexplicable bitterness. Her oldest friend!

Inexplicable to her, but not to anyone over the age of, say, sixteen. But Andri would not interfere. Senrid and Liere would resolve things, or not, without him elbowing in.

He ran his fingers up her back to the nape of her neck, felt a responsive quiver, and said, "I noticed her grudge against David only because I realized one day that she never spoke to him. Others, else, yes. Not often. But not once did she acknowledge his presence. Though she watched him."

Liere sighed. "How awful. David didn't react, though, or I would have seen that."

"Nope. He kept out of her way, and in retrospect he made sure she never caught him alone. He also took the same watches that she did, so he was never asleep when she was awake."

Liere snuggled her face into the curve between his collarbone and his shoulder. "That's it. I must get to Detlev, not just for this paper thing, but to tell him. He'll know what to do. I don't."

"Good plan," Andri said, and ran his fingers lightly along her temples, and down to her jaw, and then through her long golden hair. She shivered, then smiled, her wide eyes that exact same golden shade. "Meantime, we actually have some privacy. Rare commodity so far in this damn mess, and I for one want to take advantage of it."

"And I for two." She laughed.

Thirteen

Alcandemer

CJ WAS WRITING TO Clair.

> *...but Dirk I guess ran straight into their trap. And I ran straight into — you'd never guess, not in a zillion years — MV the poopsie! (I discover-ed that they think the name 'poopsies' is funny, too. I bet it never was an insult to them, and wouldn't we have hated to find that out, back in the bad old days). We hid in a cave behind a waterfall until the skunk twins were gone, and next day he taught me some poopsie tricks for ditching Norsundrian chasers. Then we split up, him to piddle off on mysterioso Detsie stuff, and me to finish looking for Charlana and the double-crown.*

> *Which I did. With the help of some great dawn-singer kids who live in tree houses, like the ones in Everon! What's more, the way the trees grow, and the way the platforms are made, you can't see 'em from below.*

> *Anyway, it's great. I'd love to spend more time here. Everything is wonderful — the people, the animals, how they live, the music. Oh, the music! But writing about it is boring — it's like writing about great food. The*

person reading gets to feel hungry, and not taste anything.

So anyway, Charlana is hiding out with them. She said she would be glad to help us by coordinating an uprising or whatever, on a signal. She'll stay here and communicate with Atan via her paper.

As for the crown, it would be a waste to bring it to MH. What it does is show the wearer if the speaker is lying or disguised. Since no Norsundrians can get into MH, we don't need it there. So. That finishes Dirk's job. Oh, how I hate to think of him imprisoned by the Host!

Enough of that. One night I was describing my job, once we got everything settled about Dirk's, and I was groaning about the long toil ahead of me, having to go AL-L-L-L the way to Vandary to find this Randon Amdrelya mage. What's so special about his magic, I asked? A mage is a mage. And if he's a kid, then how fantastic can he be? They seem to like my jokes, so I piled it on, until I realized they were not just laughing, they snuck looks over at this kid who was there.

I'd thought he was a dawnsinger. He's short, round face, pale blond curls, big grin. I was really going at how he might look when the kid comes up, bows, and says, "Allow me to intro-duce myself! I am that stenchiferous groanboil Randon Amdrelya. In the flesh, or is that in the groanboil? What is a groanboil, by the way?"

"You could've stopped me," I squelched, feeling like six big stinky feet had been stuffed into my yap.

"You were going too good!" He laughed so hard he almost fell off the rope bridge. Then, when I named people who are on the quests, it turns out he knows Troy, and Rel (who doesn't?) and a couple others — including Julian Landis!

I said, "But she didn't know you when your name came

up in the big meeting."

"That's because she knew me by another name — " He said it just like that, with a break, and a look, kind of like a puppy who knows it made a terrible mistake.

"You must be good at disguises," I said, and he looked away. Aha. No, can't be. Maybe he just had bad memories. So I just said, "I think the only thing left is to go try to rescue Dirk."

"In Imar?"

My natural chickenhood didn't kill me at the very idea only because I knew that you are there.

"If that's where he is." I tried not to bucka-buck and flutter my chicken feathers.

"I'll help, if you like." He shrugged, as if he was suggesting we climb down to the river for a swim. "I've had lots of experience keeping out of the Norsundrians' mitts."

He told me a little, then, when I asked, and indeed that's how he met MV. The fact that he could outrun poopsies, this short, round kid, made me wonder who had trained him! Either that or he had some kind of other really, REALLY clever way around them.

I said, "I'd love it. But unless I can get a friend to come, how do we cross the ocean."

He looked down at his knees in a way that was very familiar indeed and he measled, "Oh, I didn't think about how you'd — "

And this time I knew it. In fact, wasn't that where Falinneh's people had ended up, way north that way? Anyway, I snapped my fingers and said, "You're a Xubarec, aren't you?"

He looked just like Falinneh whenever You Know What unexpectedly gets mentioned — kind of like someone had smacked him with a very old fish. He looked up and down and sideways, just like she used to, and said edgily, "They disappeared years ago – "

I cut in, told him about Falinneh, and how she gets that very same expression. He looked both relieved and unhappy, and I realized he doesn't have any kind of group of friends. Was it because of this secret?

I didn't nose, though. He told me he left them about the same time that Falinneh did, and for the same reasons. He said that copying people and faking being them even if you don't kill them turns you weird after a while, if you do it long enough. He said that here and there are a few more like him and Falinneh, but the rest got caught, "disenchanted," (that means their powers warded) and are living normal lives, or are dead.

Anyway, after he left them he went up north farther and learned magic, and has been causing trouble for all kinds of villains for years. He said, when I asked, that he seldom comes this far south of the Fereledria because he'd thought it was too boring – the proportion of ordinary humans to other kinds of people and to animals is too high.

Interesting! Here everyone in the southern hemisphere thinks we're better because Sartor is in the south, and it's got older history. Everyone who thinks about such things, that is. Boring because of too many humans! We gotta go north more – that is, once we get rid of the villains polluting the world.

He also said that he liked being a kid, and that he avoided grownups.

Of course I pounced on this and asked why.

He shrugged. "They always want me to do things for them – usually against someone else. Things like land grabbing. They always have all these reasons, but that's what it always means, and of course because I'm underage they think I'm too stupid to see their reasons.

People our age don't tend to make land grabs. They're usually the ones who need help, if they come from land-grabbing sorts of families, if you get what I mean."

"Oh, I do," I measled. "All of us do, back in Clair's group."

He looked at me kind of funny and said, "She's a ruler, right?"

"Yep. But don't think we, her friends, got any power, or own one rock of land, because we don't."

He laughed. "I don't care if you do or don't, but if you wanted to – especially to take it away from someone else – then I'd say you are as big a skunk as the adults."

"No chance," I said. "Not even. It sounds like what you've been doing in the north by your-self is what we – Clair's group, I mean – have been trying to do in the south."

"That's it." He smacked his hands on his knees. "I'm going with you, because I have to meet them."

"So we'll cross the ocean and go to Imar," I said, hoping that you can reach Puddlenose...

CJ hesitated, then swiped out those words and shook the ink off her fingers, remembering that Clair's cousin Puddle-nose, who was now captain of the Chwahir ship *Lheit*, its former captain, Fradrisi, having retired to be a full time grandfather. CJ remembered that Puddlenose was using the Chwahir ship to look like one of their transports so he could nose into harbors and report on them to Atan. She scowled, not wanting to appear selfish to Atan.

She sent a look at Randon—who was at that moment asking about anyone who could slip them across to Drael.

CJ let out a sigh of relief, and picked up her pen again. If only she could get Clair to go safely home!

That's it. We can either join you, or better yet, why don't you go home, because there might be some queening stuff that Atan can't do, and we'll tackle the rest, okay? CJ

CJ sat back and sighed. It was done. Maybe eventually the feeling of terror would be replaced by the comfort of doing The Right Thing. Maybe.

She looked up through the crimson maple leaves. It was so peaceful here! Hard to believe that evil existed on the same world. Then recent memory whacked her.

She looked at her paper. Wouldn't Clair have read it all by now? Or was she even there? Or —

"Maybe she's not going to answer," Randon said. He had crouched down nearby, not within reading distance, only watching, because he found the papers fascinating.

CJ shrugged, a sharp up-and-down of the shoulders that would have warned her friends, but Randon was too impatient. Once he'd made a plan he liked to act, and he'd been hiding there too long. It was time to get into action, and do something.

"Let's just go," he said. "Charlana says there are privateers and even pirates still sailing. They get hidden by the big storms, especially this time of year, before the winds and currents change from east to west up the strait — "

"No." She glared.

Randon's impatience turned to irritation. He shifted his gaze from the sun-flooded forest valley below, bisected by the fast-moving river over the rocks. He had been alone most of his life, and though it had been fun, he had to admit that this feeling somewhere in his middle, when CJ talked about her group was — well, envy.

Envy. Huh. He'd made a good life for himself. Did one really need friends, and all their expectations? What if they really only wanted to demand you do things for them?

He turned to CJ, ready to snap right back about the silliness of obligations, but then he saw the sick expression on CJ's face, the worry puckering her brows, and his mood changed again.

Face the truth. The truth was that he had no friends, not like she obviously had, and he wondered if he might have missed anything. Oh, he had plenty of friends who seemed glad enough when he appeared, but would one of them worry if he didn't? No, because they didn't know him.

He considered the surprising fact that CJ and her friends worried about Falinneh. And they knew her secret.

Sighing, he sat down again, and now he was merely curious as he said, "How long do you want to wait?"

"Few more minutes." She did not look up, but watched the paper in front of her bare toes, as she rocked back and forth, her chin on her knees. "And if there's no answer, then I'll write to the others until I find out—oh!"

Suddenly the paper filled with Clair's messy, barely legible script.

> CJ: Just after your letter came I got one from Atan. Multiple rotten news. Falinneh, Sherry, and Caris-Merian seem to have gotten them-selves in trouble. The girls were left in Goerael Haer for the creeps to finish off, but I trust them to find a way free, or for Falinneh to find them a way. Caris-Merian was taken to Visegn, from which she escaped, and some-how she met up with Liere.

> The girls don't answer on their beige papers. I just got done writing to Seshe and Bren and Innon. All three are going to go north and west to see what they can find out.

> In the meantime Liere got the feeling that Caris-Merian had decided to dump our plans and go after David. I just tried a moment ago to get Liere, but she didn't answer immediately, so I decided to go ahead and write to you.

> Will you go check this out? Atan doesn't think Liere is going to, and you know, I'm afraid that maybe something might have happened with Falinneh and Sherry, so in a sense it would be our responsibility to solve the problem.

> Liere says that Llyenthur still uses the city of Larkadhe as his HQ. (It's also supposed to be one of the most beautiful cities in the world. So much for Norsundrians being tough and against beauty, eh? What phonies!) David was supposedly sent by Detlev to spy on Llyenthur.

> I wish you would find and warn him. I won't demand that you don't mess with Llyenthur or Caris-Merian (if

*she's turned Norsundrian somehow) because I'd be a
hypocrite because Zairna and Julian and June and I are
going to try to rescue Dirk and Tarael the morvende
leader, if we can. But I will say please be careful.*

And now I had better go. Clair.

CJ sighed in defeat. Clair was going to do what she
thought was right.

She held out the note to Randon. After he'd skimmed it,
she said, "Do you mind a change in plans?"

He grinned. "I'm just as happy not to have to go to Imar.
This one sounds much easier."

CJ made a horrible face. "I wish Clair wasn't going in
there, but at least there are four of them. That Zairna is supposed to be pretty good with the sword and sneakery stuff, and
I know Julian is good at sneakery. But I'm worried about Sherry
and Falinneh. How far is Goerael Haer from here? Is it farther
than Dielzh and Ytand and those places?"

Randon wrinkled his upper lip and gazed skyward, thinking. "Ytand is southwest, but Goerael is northwest. Dielzh is
south of that."

"So if Seshe and the gang aren't in Ytand, it's a waste of
time for us to go up there as well. I have an idea. Let me write
to Boneribs."

She wrote quickly, while the bridge swayed in the wind.
Birds sang, leaves rustled. For once CJ did not notice.

No answer, no answer.

CJ wrote:

*Jilo: Senrid is not answering letters. Are you in
Marloven Hess with him, or what? He's the closest to
Larkadhe, if he's free, but if he isn't, if you still have
that book that bypasses transfer wards, let me know AT
ONCE, or I promise you'll wake up to a rutabaga-
prune-lima bean pie when we get back to MH! CJ*

Randon laughed. "Who's Jilo?"

"Old enemy, now a friend. He's from Chwahirsland, if
you've ever heard of that disaster. Though he was making it almost livable when Norsunder slimed in and ruined everything
for everybody."

No answer from Jilo, either. Maybe the two didn't have

papers yet.

CJ looked up. "Looks like it's got to be us, then. What do you say?"

Randon shrugged. "A rescue is a rescue and Norsundrians are Norsundrians. I don't know anything about this Llyenthur fool, though."

CJ grinned. "Me neither. Hey, that's one thing we can talk about as we travel — villains we've known. All right. One more letter, to find out if Liere is going after Caris-Merian, which would make the most sense — she's the closest!" After a short spurt of writing and waiting, CJ scanned her last note and sighed. "Isn't that Sartora all over," she exclaimed in exasperation. "She's both in a tearing hurry on an hour of sleep and overcautious. She's not going after Caris-Merian — she's gonna find a way to contact Detlev and stick him with the problem. As if he could do anything but further mess things up! He'll scare Caris-Merian for sure, and clod all over like a typical adult."

"Then it's up to you," Randon said. "And me, because I'm going along. I have to meet this gang of yours."

"Awright!" She cackled.

Fourteen

Western Imar

JULIAN'S HATRED OF THE situation in which she found herself was eased by her having a new oddball to question, watch, and con-sider.

She'd traveled with Zairna, of course, during the run from Zranf to Sles Adran, but the size of the group had made it difficult to observe one who was so skilled at remaining unobtrusive when he wished.

Now he was like a timely gift. She had wondered about him before, having heard interesting stories. Like the time she was visiting on Dthel Rendm, and they were holed up by a thunderstorm, so they'd fallen to taking over old times. Dtheldevor had started talking about her off-world visit. Of Zairna she'd said: *Looks like his pitcher oughter be lookin down its nose at ya from some damn-blasted palace wall, but he ain't no prissy risto. Far from it! Almost as good as me w' a sword. Better with a knife, like assassin better,* she'd finished cheerily.

Julian asked him questions about his own land, which he readily answered, as the four trudged through blighted wood-land, breathing cold, dead, fog-wreathed air. The countryside was so still, as if it had been just killed, and did not yet know it was dead.

June walked warily, sniffing, listening not to her com-panions but outside them, often carrying the cup in both hands. She felt powerful magic tingling in her hands — the sensation increased with each day—but as yet she could not descry what the power signified. And the cup remained inert.

"I think this thing is ready for some kind of action," she said to Clair one morning. "It's like it's charged to the max, but I don't know how to turn on the switch."

Though the metaphor escaped Clair, the meaning was clear.

Clair listened, her pale, tense brow puckered, her eyes so serious June said rather snappishly, "I know I owe it to you people to figure it out."

"No," said Clair, serious and solemn. "You found it. It's yours."

"I don't want the stupid thing," June retorted. "But seeing as I got stuck, I might as well figure out why. Nothing else to do," she added sarcastically, looking around the dreary landscape, on which nothing living moved.

They made very slow progress.

Once they emerged from the woodland they had to travel only at night, when spy birds could not see them. Once they came near a trade route crossroads, and a village. Only the innkeepers had apparently chosen not to leave, for whatever reason. Zairna went to spy them out, and to get supplies if he could find them.

He returned with the supplies, saying that the people moved like sleepwalkers, with vacant eyes. He'd felt it better to steal what they needed than to risk exposure; these people were not capable of keeping any secret. They probably could not even keep any thought.

Clair's skin began to feel as if sandpaper had scraped over it, and there was always a faint, dull headache behind her eyes, which intensified with every physical or mental effort she made. But that only determined her to strengthen her mind-shield the more.

Not long before dawn one day they found a rotting corn bin on an abandoned farm and decided to spend the day there, rather than push on and risk being exposed by daylight before they found another hidey-hole.

June usually stopped to fill the cup at every stream, just in case they started hitting only polluted water. She looked around now, sipped, frowned, and then she blurred, fading from view.

Clair, closing her eyes, could sense her proximity on the

other side of her mind-shield, but making an effort hurt. She dropped heavily down, wondering wearily when she would ever get enough rest not to feel that gritty-eyed tiredness.

Zairna seemed undisturbed as he dug into his pack and brought out a hunk of bread that he'd taken from the inn. He divided it up — pulling with a force that made Clair's mouth go dry — and then silently started on his share. Julian did as well, sighing and grimacing at every bite.

Zairna's lack of complaint, even in expression, made Clair feel obliged to sit up and make a try at eating, but her shoulders were so sore from her pack that it was easier to lean back and let the stale bread lie on her lap. She could always eat it later.

Zairna's head turned, a quick movement, and Clair's heartbeat drummed. "Animal?"

He nodded. Clair wondered if he felt the constant pull at his will, so strength-sapping. He had some kind of odd gift that made Dena Yeresbeth contacts possible, though he said it was not quite the same as what he understood Dena Yeresbeth to be. Ought she to ask more?

He got to his feet. "I will do a quick perimeter check before the sun comes up." A duck, a quiet step, and he was gone.

Clair looked up at Julian. "Do you feel something pulling at your will from inside?"

Julian made a warding gesture with both hands. "No. Maybe that's Dena Yeresbeth, and glad I am I don't have it. I feel more like we're under a thunderstorm about to break. Or maybe in it. Walking through the outer thunder part, if that makes sense, and toward the lightning."

Clair agreed, her thoughts drifting. She was on the edge of sleep when Zairna returned. Dawn began to pale the east; weak light gleamed, blue and unwelcome, along cracks in the old wood, outlining in Zairna's fine skin the shadows of eye socket and cheekbone. He had put back his hood, the fabric briefly brushing his long pale hair back, revealing the spiky inked dragonflower that curved elegantly from the back of his neck up over one ear.

She put back her own hood, wishing that would ease the constant headache. Julian had fallen asleep, her breathing deep and even.

"Zairna?" she whispered. "Is the magic getting stronger as we get closer?"

"Yes."

She rearranged herself, despite the dry, scratchy crackle of old corn husks under her. She was too tired to remove them, and comfort was a long-ago dream. With another glance at Julian, who did not stir, she murmured, "It seems strange…" Her thoughts drifted, and with difficulty she pulled them back, and remembered that she had spoken. What she had said. Saw Zairna waiting patiently. Swallowed. "Seems to be a lot of magic protection for a small group of villains who are here on the offensive…" Did that make sense? She couldn't tell what made sense any more.

Zairna said, "Magic traps, many, I believe."

"Aimed at Detlev, obviously. Kessler. Tsauderei, maybe, and other mages of their ability. But…" She faded, then roused herself, for it seemed that this thought might actually be important. Forced her eyes to focus. "But it seems odd. For them to create this mess, and sit in the middle. Defensive, not offensive. Yes?"

"It's a defense," Zairna agreed.

"What are they defending?" She half-sat, glad to be talking, to be making sense! "They can't be afraid of us attacking. From all we've heard about the Host, that does not sound characteristic." She forced herself to speak slowly and clearly, in complete sentences. It seemed important, somehow.

"Guarding important prisoners?" he countered. "Or protecting something of importance? Perhaps something keyed to the wards elsewhere?"

"Then there is something. Good. But we just don't know yet. So we're here to find out, then, are we not? Rescue people, and discover, if we can, what they might be hiding. Because we are so very close."

"That would seem to be our mission."

Clair sighed, and stretched out. Purpose. She had purpose.

Worry. Had they already had this conversation, or had she dreamed it, during the long walk, maybe, or…?

Oh, it didn't matter. Sleep. Sleep, and purpose. Including staying safe. She had to do that too, for she promised. Why, if she died, CJ would be mad as a wet baggie!

She smiled, her dry lips cracked. She dropped into sleep.

In Clair's capital, in her audience room, Atan held morning

court.

"And during the night they painted it," the old lady exclaimed, trembling with outrage. "When I said no one was to step on my property! And what's more, they made a frightful mess of it—all mottled—looks like a disease!"

Atan impatiently fingered the beige paper in her pocket while maintaining an impassive outward demeanor. Who had just written to her? Was it something important, or just a cheery message? Her thoughts turned to the map upstairs, but she forced her attention back.

It seemed disastrously unfair to be tied to a squabble over a house-painting, but she couldn't throw them all out. This was not her kingdom, and she had promised to keep the peace. And this problem, infinitesimal compared to world-wide events, was very real to the people ranged before her. Her position of guardianship meant that they had a right to her time.

She shifted position on Clair's throne, and then deliberately withdrew her hand from her pocket. "Is this true, you trespassed after you were asked not to step on her property?" She turned her gaze to the man who seemed to act as leader of the group of neighbors.

His bald head gleamed with sweat and his round face was brick-colored. He said, so angry he was nearly in tears, "But it's us have to look at it, and it's so ugly! Forest green I could see, or what they call sea green, but that—that's chartreuse!"

"It's a pretty color. Nice and bright, and it cheers me up," the old woman pronounced as emphatically as her shaky voice permitted.

Atan was secretly drawn to her. Though not to the idea of a bright chartreuse house.

"Everyone on the street thinks it's hideous. We've always asked one another, haven't we?" The man turned to the others, palms up. "Consulted one another first?"

Self-righteous nods of affirmation. A young woman said, "It's true. I asked everyone before I painted my shutters yellow. Even those't can't see 'em from their windows!"

"And if there's a question, you lean toward the ones as will see it most," the man spoke up. "That's being considerate. That's how we've always done it on our street."

"It's not their house, it's my house."

"Chartreuse! My wife says her food tastes bad, it upsets her so. She wants to block up all our windows."

There it was again, another beige-paper signal.

The old woman's chins went up. "Forty-five years, my husband insisted on whitewash, because it's cheap. Now he's gone, and I got my pretty green. I love it."

And again! Three letters waiting. An emergency?

Atan shifted again, fighting impatience, as the man embarked on a long account of the street's history of cooperation, his hands waving as he detailed everyone's house painting over the decades.

The old woman crossed her little bird-arms across her front, and shook her head slowly.

What would Clair do? And how could Atan dispense justice quickly?

She caught a flicker of blue on the periphery of her vision. Tahra stood in the doorway. Atan sent her a pleading glance so eloquent that all the neighbors' heads snapped to face the door.

Tahra walked in.

"Perhaps," Atan said with false-sounding geniality, "we can ask Queen Hatahra of Everon her opinion. Has anyone an objection?"

Rounded eyes. Sartor was foremost in world fame, then Colend, but Everon was right behind it. Atan began to give a brief, objective description of both sides of the argument, but when she paused for breath, both sides burst out with better statements of their positions.

All their attention was now on Tahra. Atan quickly pulled out her beige paper and a pencil-stub and tapped it on the paper.

Then she suppressed a sharp sigh of disappointment.

She was about to pocket the paper when another letter arrived.

This one shot alarm through her nerves:

Atan, this is Gwen. I can't reach Clair, after a day and night of trying —

Atan looked up. Tahra glanced round at her, then back again; the petitioners' voices faltered, then resumed.

Atan walked swiftly out.

A short time later, Tahra found her in the magic chambers, bent over her map, a frown creasing her brows.

Atan looked up. "Resolved?"

"Compromise," Tahra said. "The woman will consider

other colors, the man is to pay. Are you noting all these things down for Clair to see?"

"Yes." Atan pressed fingertips into her temples. "Speaking of whom, she seems to be missing. She's not the only one. Kyale vanished as well."

"Kyale. One of my first friends," Tahra said, thinking of the silver-haired girl from Vasande Leror. "What happened?"

Atan said, as evenly as she could, "It seems she has a birthday coming, and she went to great lengths to warn people not to celebrate it. On account of the war."

Tahra shrugged. "Nobody is celebrating birthdays, at least that I heard."

"Kyale seems to have expected something different, for when the day came and went without a big party, she went off into a tantrum, and Troy — the mildest boy in the world! — was on the receiving end. Winda says he won't say what happened, but she vanished right after." And when Tahra frowned, unable or unwilling to voice a response, Atan added, "No one seems to be able to raise Clair on these letter papers."

Tahra's mouth twisted. "If Norsunder got her, they'd brandish her fast enough. They must be hiding."

Atan rubbed her eyes. "It's only the 20th. Two months, they've been gone. Feels like two years — "

Both looked up as Siamis entered. "Clair is missing?" he asked, with no polite preamble.

"How — where — "

"Aurora overheard you," Siamis interrupted — another thing he had never done. "Where is Clair? That is, where was she when last you heard?"

"She went to Imar."

"*Imar?*"

Both women drew back, startled and affronted at the sharpness of his voice.

"How could you possibly let her go to Imar?"

"She decided to go herself," Atan retorted. "Last I heard, she was not a prisoner in her own kingdom. Nobody else seemed to be finding out exactly where the enemy is lurking — " She laid her hand on her map.

But Siamis did not glance at it. He passed his hand over his eyes, then dropped the hand, and made a visible effort. "It never occurred to you that any one of the Host would easily get the key to the enchantment from her, once they perceive her proximity, in which case this country can be invaded?"

"Your Dena Yeresbeth is a mystery to me," Atan stated stiffly. "But it seems to me that Clair is well versed in it, and can—"

"She would never survive being mind-ripped by Ilerian," Siamis cut in softly. "He would entertain himself for an hour or so by making it as painful as possible and then discard her corpse, bleeding from eyes and ears, without a second thought."

A sickened silence followed. Atan said uncertainly, "You don't seem to understand that Clair felt it was her duty—"

Siamis did not have time for her excuses. He blamed himself as much as he blamed them; he had assumed Clair's lack of presence around the palace was due to her self-effacing habits. He knew she spent a lot of time in that underground hideout she had made for her girl gang, and also visiting her aunt in her hermitage in the western woodland. He'd let her drop to the back of his attention. As he ought not to have done, knowing that she was the most Important person with respect to the ward protecting Mearsies Heili.

It's just that he'd thought that of all those still with the Child Spell, she had the most sense.

He frowned. She *did* have the most sense.

He uttered an oath under his breath and rushed out before Tahra and Atan could get on with their protests.

Atan stopped, then Aurora pattered in, her eyes huge. "Nobody told me...nobody told me..." She burst into tears. "You let her go to *them*." She howled with betrayal.

Clair swallowed thickly.

Was something wrong with the water? No. Aside from tasting dank and metallic it was free enough of magical taint. The wrongness lay in her; the effort of will, day and night, required to resist the unceasing sucking at mental barriers had pushed her beyond exhaustion into illness. Sleep was never refreshing, it was merely a time to lie unmoving. She was cold all the time.

How did the others bear it? She would have abandoned the mission days ago—her brain no longer worked well enough for her to observe or analyze anything—but for the others pushing on. If they could, especially the two who were not even of this world, then so could she. So must she.

And besides, more compelling, there were those who needed rescue, Tarael and Dirk. If she abandoned them to this nightmare existence, the nightmare would haunt her for the rest of her days.

It was a relief when they decided to bury their gear in the floor of a rocky cave. Zairna had vanished one night, reappearing at morning to report that the palace lay just beyond the next rise.

Though the distance was short, they progressed little that day. Three times heavily armed patrols thundered by, and once sleet punished the countryside. Spy creatures drifted over land and in the sky watching without pause.

When they stopped, June murmured, "The cup is cold. Like it's refrigerated. Clair looked up, trying to frame a question about what "refrigerated" meant, but gave up. It took too much strength to form the words.

Julian said, "Does it do anything?"

June shook her head. "Still inert. Just cold." Yawned. "Who has first watch?"

Clair knew she would have to take a turn. How did the others manage? Why was she so weak? She struggled against surrender, bleakly acknowledging that she was going to fight this battle again and again, for eternity—it was either that or just stop. *Stop and lie down and give up.*

And then you will have peace.

The insidious tendril of thought was voiceless, faceless— and even after she shut it out, a stale breath of weariness, pointlessness, lingered in her thoughts.

Not yet eleven at night. The misery would only get worse.

Her hand moved to her knife. Pain cleared my head—and then her fingers zapped back as if burned. Wouldn't Norsunder just love her hacking herself up in order to keep her mind off their magic!

Her burning eyelids lifted to June sitting straight and motionless, on watch.

The insidious whisper continued, *Go to sleep. Ease your mind. You'll only be more and more tired, and it will hurt more in the end.*

She tried to move, to physically shake free of the intruder, but her joints ached so much. I'm lost, she thought. I'm—

A touch on her shoulder. She gazed up into Zairna's face for a long time before she recognized his features, side-lit by the smokeless vagabond fire Julian had made.

"Their magic is getting stronger, which enables me in some wise to descry its structure," he whispered. "Do you know you are in the middle of the spectrum?"

"Spectrum." For a moment comprehension flickered, then went out, a snuffed light. Her tongue moved dryly. "I see nothing but darkness."

"I have experience of dark magic." Zairna's dark gray gaze held hers. His long, fine-shaped hands mimed a rainbow-shape. "Here is Julian, with none of your Dena Yeresbeth. Here at the other end is myself, dark magic background, mental sensitivity that differs from the patterns on this world. And here," he arced his fingers at the highpoint of the rainbow, "you are. This magic is aimed at people like you. Only one step stronger would be magic warded directly against you."

Relief trickled through her mind, followed by regret. "You get it, too?"

"But not like you."

June cut across their whispers. "I think I figured something out here. This cup is kind of like a black hole, in this atmosphere. If I'm not touching it, it's like it vanishes."

"I want to try something." Clair leaned forward and touched June's arm. June tensed—it was clear she did not like being touched without permission—but she did not move away. Then the dark magic beating at the borders of Clair's mind leaped back, like a sea suddenly walled behind glass.

"You both disappeared," Zairna said.

"And it cleared my head for a moment," Clair said doubtfully.

"This might be our way in," Zairna said.

Fifteen

Baragrene, northwest tip of Halia

THE PRIVATEERS MADE CJ and Randon swim the last distance to shore, then rowed back under cover of one of the storms frequent in the area this time of year.

The pair had to tread water for what felt like hours as a patrol boat worked its way along the shore, then at last they climbed out, soggy and salty, onto the coast of Baragrene.

CJ blinked gritty lids, smeared her hair back, then said, "Wow. After floating in water all that time I feel like I turned into a rock, because I'm as heavy as a boulder."

"Yup." Randon shook himself all over, like a dog. "We need a stream to get rid of the salt."

"I see some shrubs over that way." CJ said pointed up the sandy coastline past a jumble of rocks. Thick, waxy, wind-bent shrubs grew, and beyond them, some promising treetops hinted at the existence of running water.

They trudged across the sand toward the bushes, their clothing sticking nastily to limbs and itching at the creases. They pushed their way past and kept walking from the sandy soil into grassy ground filled with wildflowers, until they found a stream winding among some fruit trees, growing in a more or less straight pattern that indicated long-dead hands had planted an orchard many, many years before.

Soon they were settled on grass, munching fruit while they dried in the sun. "I ought to let Atan know where we are." CJ sighed. The sun felt so good, and she was so content, she first wanted to just stretch out—

And woke in the darkness, to the sound and smell of a fire. "Is that safe?" she asked, sitting up.

Randon grinned at her, the mellow light making him look even younger than he did already. "No Norsundrians around. I checked while you were snoring away." He spoke in a cheery voice, poking at some shapes stuck on a makeshift stick grid.

"What are those? Oh!" The sweet scent of baking applies wafted her way.

"I thought we should save those dawnsinger cakes until we haven't any other food, because they do keep," he said.

"Yes," she said, her mouth watering.

After they ate, she said, "Get out my paper, will you? I'd better report in, and then I can write to the rest of the gang!"

"I want to watch," Randon said, starting to hand across her beige paper. "Huh!" He snatched it back and squinted closely at it. "I wish I could figure out the magic behind these things!"

CJ started to comment, but her words turned into a squawk of alarm as figures loomed out of the sheltering shrubs.

Snip! Snap! Meaning to keep the magical paper from the hands of enemies, Randon tossed it onto the fire, where it withered at once into ash.

"Who are you?" a voice demanded in the local language.

"Who are you?" CJ snapped back in the same language, and then she moaned. "Oh, no! You better be Norsundrians, or I'm going to KILL you!"

"What?"

"My paper! Rats, blast, rats, blast, RATS blast you snilch-faced fonebones SNEAKing up on a person like—"

Randon knew enough of CJ by now to suspect that she was just warming up, and as four tallish silhouettes ringed them menacingly, standing at the edge of the circle of firelight with their spears and knives upraised, he jumped to his feet. "CJ! Quiet!"

"YOU be quiet, you popeared, prunebald pickled pill of a—ulp!"

A spear suddenly pointed in her face, and a voice demanded, "Why are you here?"

"Because we're on a picnic!" CJ snapped belligerently, as the ramifications of her having destroyed the paper set in. Now, no one would know where they were. "You-u-u-u-u! Argh."

She sagged suddenly, for the spear had jerked closer, and she'd instinctively brushed the mind of the holder with her small abilities at contact.

She drew in a slow breath, and carefully made contact with them all. None of the people had Dena Yeresbeth — nor did they shield their thoughts. They were not Norsundrians, but they were afraid that CJ and Randon might be Norsundrian spies because they'd been speaking in a foreign tongue, yet knew their own. Obviously they did not know much about magic — specifically the rare and difficult Universal Language Spell.

"Groanboils, what a mess," she said in a more subdued voice. "We're not Norsundrians. We're going to Visegn to help rescue someone."

The spear lifted. "Can you prove it?"

"No," Randon said, his hands out wide. "Unless you turn us in. Norsundrians'd love to get their sticky mitts on both of us."

After a little more cautious give-and-take, the silhouettes stepped into the firelight and joined them, laying down their weapons. They turned out to be two boys and two girls, all in their late teens. The biggest boy had done the talking and spear-poking; once the Baragreners relaxed he was content to sit and munch one of Randon's baked apples, and one of the girls took over the talking.

"We have some animal friends who spot newcomers," she explained. "And you appeared out of nowhere."

"No." Randon grinned. "From a boat hidden by illusion. We swam the rest of the way."

"Oh." She flung back a lock of fire-edged dark, curly hair. "Ay! You'll need magic if you're going to Visegn."

"We know that the Norsundrian commander of the entire invasion is currently stinking up the place — "

"Yes, and last week he smashed the underground they had organized there. Word's been spreading to stay away."

"It was bad," one of the boys said.

CJ and Randon exchanged looks. "What are you doing? Spying on the Norsundrians?"

"Yes. Living off the land while we still can. There's nothing else to do," the girl said bitterly. "They make you get permits to carry on with business — your names, and your family's name, in case you do anything. We ran."

"Sounds horrid." CJ leaned forward sympathetically. "Been nasty here, then, as well as Visegn?"

The newcomers gave them a heartfelt, invective-laced account of the takeover. CJ and Randon responded with stories from other countries, and then the newcomers left.

After a time, CJ said, "What'll we do now?"

"I say we go on."

"Me too. Drat the rotten luck! I wonder who was in that mess they mentioned. None of our people, I hope. But we better find out."

"And I think you better start keeping your weird-ears open so we don't get any more surprises."

"You bet." CJ sighed again. "Toss me my cloak. Let's sleep, and be off'n bucketing soon's there's light."

Larkadhe

Cath of Isolde on Geth sat in one of the Larkadhe towers, watching the westering sun on the distant hills.

The door opened behind him.

"It seems," Llyenthur said, "that Senrid might have turned up in Marloven Hess. I don't have time to go myself. Until we regain egress I have the maximum number there, and yet they seem unable to produce anything but rumors. I want you to go there, and find out the truth."

Cath's gaze drifted back toward the window, his hand tapping soundlessly on the sill. "Caris-Merian is somewhere near. And David," he said. Tap, tap.

"Are they, now."

Cath turned around. "I want to see it through to the end."

"I think we can safely let them bring their little drama to a close on their own. Go find Senrid, Cath."

"You want me to leave this moment?" Cath stood up slowly.

"You might."

Cath walked out, and started swiftly down the stairs.

Much later that night, while CJ and Randon lay sleeping beside their campfire a little to the northwest, and while Cath galloped southward, muffled in a dark cloak, David slid into the city of Larkadhe.

The entire kingdom was paralyzed and watchful. David had discovered that his brother had recently scoured out a newly formed resistance network. A strike the night before they were going to try its first coordinated action, to spring one of their pals locked up in Imry's castle.

Without any forewarning, his agents silently broke into the leaders' houses and dragged them out, and they vanished. No trace. Followed by—nothing. No further hits, no warnings, even. No increased patrols. The silence following the country-wide strike was more effective than the most threatening proclamations nailed up could ever have been.

David thought that over as he noiselessly drifted past quiet, shuttered houses. He wondered, rather grimly, if his brother had had the fellow locked up as a lure all along.

He walked for a while longer, moving through the silent streets, listening on the mental realm to the people hidden in the houses, before he turned toward the towered palace etched against the night sky. He sensed danger, but saw nothing, and finally attributed it to the preternatural stillness.

It took David some time to slip within the outer guard perimeter and circle the palace, observing exits (obvious and the two secret ones that Andri had described), and inner perimeter sentry patrol patterns.

Then, with care, he went mind-questing. Moth-light touches in a room with a lot of people — Imry would not be with 'em. He'd always liked his privacy. Ah. One of them some poor sod who'd just returned from being reamed for inadvertently killing a suspect nailed for questioning. Imry was up there, all right—David got a clear picture of the location of the pleasant room he'd chosen for a study.

What now?

His gaze wandered up a winding street to an intersection bordered by a pleasing array of shops and houses. The city was appealing, but the most striking aspect was the great white tower, made of the same mysterious material as was the palace on the mountain in Mearsies Heili. Larkadhe—enchantment. Now, why had Imry picked this place to hole up?

David shook his head in rueful amusement, heard the rap

of bootheels on stone, then slid soundlessly between two buildings. Two Norsundrians walked by, scanning closely to the side and ahead, and then passed.

They too, it seemed, had taken warning from the other night's events.

Interesting. Again, what now?

Detlev had ordered him to assess Imry's chain of command on this subcontinent, orders which David had obeyed. He'd also said, *Leave Imry to me.* This order David was finding increasingly difficult to heed. David was certain that Detlev was less interested in Imry than in fencing with the Host, and with trying to track Kessler down.

David had said to MV the last time they saw one another, "Whatever Imry can do I can counter—if I find out who he's become."

MV had shrugged. "I'd wait on Detlev. He never holds us back but for a reason." And then he'd added, typically, "If you need backup, tip me the word."

David now settled down behind some bales of rotting hay in an empty stable yard. His intention was to get a few hours of rest, for he'd been on the move too long, but his mind refused to cease its speculations, not with Imry so close.

Twelve years! He hadn't set eyes on Imry in twelve years. Almost thirteen, now. He recalled the last he'd seen of his brother, all bony knuckles and elbows and stork legs, with the fervid green eyes that came from the long ago Tlennen-Hess connection. Ever since he could remember, Imry had been the vortex of simmering energy and tension, as if he walked in the center of a swarm of angry bees.

David could even remember the day, the incident, Imry had at last learned to master and focus that vortex. Anger and restlessness and competition had propelled him into constant fights with the others, in spite of his spindly body and light weight, and he'd never been that successful, especially against MV, who had always been the biggest, strongest, and fastest. In spite of—or maybe because of—a series of thorough drubbings he'd picked fights with MV more than anyone.

That day David sensed a change come over Imry, and he went after and nearly killed MV until Detlev appeared from somewhere and hauled him off. The rest of the boys had been simply too stunned to move at Imry's terrifyingly sudden and savage intensity.

MV and Imry were what, eleven? David thought back, trying to find a comfortable position. He himself had been almost eight.

He meant to sleep, but didn't, for memory, once engaged, refused to relinquish its hold on his thoughts, and so he passed the time in reverie until just before dawn, at which time he shifted to a position on a roof from which he could spend the day watching the routine of the castle without being seen himself.

Sixteen

SUNSET FOUND CJ AND Randon lying side by side on their stomachs atop a precipitous rock. They were waiting for dark to fall so they could slip across the border. Larkadhe was a day's walk—if all went well.

"I wish I could contact the girls," CJ muttered.

There was silence, then Randon said, "You do?"

CJ looked over, startled, then she flinched, red-faced. "Sorry. I guess I've said it a few times today."

"Only a few hundred." He relented with a smile. "I don't mind, really, it's just that there's not much I can say in answer."

"I've been on adventures where I didn't see them for what seemed ages, and it was okay because there was nothing I could do about it. But having those papers was so wonderful, and I miss it like a boot in the trouser-seat."

A boot in the heart, she meant, but CJ loathed the thought of saying anything that might sound even remotely sentiment-al.

"Well, if those four had been Norsundrians, it'd be pretty bad if they'd nipped the paper and used it against your friends."

"I know. I'm not blaming you. I guess I didn't make it clear that Siamis had put a kind of protection on them in case an enemy grabbed one. I'm just mostly worried about Clair. In Imar. What if they get her?"

"From what you say, she's pretty tough."

"I'm not worried about her breaking, I'm more worried

about what they'd do to her to try—oh, it's no use moaning on and on. What shall we do when we get to that city, split and search for David and Caris-Merian? It's great that you know what he looks like, so maybe you can look for him, and I'll look for her. But what if—argh!"

"What now?"

"Oh, I wondered about that stinkbomb Llyenthur, in case he's nosing around. We don't know what he even looks like— and we can't write to anybody and find out! What if he's one of those villains who hangs around pretending to be a normal person, nosing into people's business, then splatting you before you know it? All I know is what Kyale said, that he's tall and skinny, but lots of villains are tall and skinny."

"Eh, we just won't talk to any tall, skinny men. Won't your weird-ears work as warning?"

"My little smidge of Dena Yeresbeth won't work against stinkers like that, who are supposed to have lots."

Randon shrugged. "I've done fine my whole life without it, so we'll just do the best we can. Now, back to the good stuff. Your turn for past adventures."

"Oh yeah!" CJ grinned. "What kind do you want? A creepy one or a funny one?"

"How 'bout a creepy one. Get us ready for yon town."

"Oh, I hope not," CJ said. "Well, this adventure was a double-skunk-reject, where I got sent clear off-world, but it was no nice trip—"

"Let me guess. By Wan-Edhe of the Chwahir?"

"Who else? I guess Kwenz was poking around off-world once, and he met this really rotten villain, and squelch at first sight, they became 'friends'..."

———————

Caris-Merian waited patiently.

Since the silversmith had been hauled out and executed, the shaken remnants of the resistance had begun to check in furtively at the Three Acorn Inn, which had been their favorite meeting place before it became their headquarters. Caris-Merian, long used to observing the patterns of people, watched how the people came for comfort and companionship, and to exchange shocked whispers of what they'd seen, what they'd heard. No one seemed inclined to lay plans. It was as if the

Norsundrian violence had extinguished all purpose. But at least those who knew of her own purpose — of having been sent to find and deal with a Norsundrian spy — left her alone.

It had been a local guild accountant who'd brought her here, days ago, a man who was so trusted, and trustworthy, that she'd decided not to lie to him.

Ah, not that it was the entire truth.

She was not chosen, but her appointment as executioner transcended mere human motivation. Justice is what she sought, and what she would give Leskander at last.

She'd found that talking to her brother in her mind eased her isolation on this world where no one had ever heard of Les Rhoderan. The prospect of triumphing over his murderer helped to keep the rage at bay that had corroded her spirit ever since that terrible day.

How they would laugh, eh, Les? She smiled down at the worn wooden corner table, and in her mind Les smiled back encouragingly, and said, *I trained you well, little sister. Strike fast, and strike true.*

He was so clear! And he would still be here, fighting the enemy, if it had not been for that soul-rotted Norsundrian.

Her fingers slid off the table to her side, caressing the handle of the black-hilted knife she'd found on her way out of that damned palace just visible through the north window. Black. So very like that black steel sword of David's, it was so right that she should find this blade to use for the greater cause of justice.

The only sound David heard as he passed along alleys and side streets toward the south end of town was music. Voices, once a single silverflute, more steel-stringed tiranthes, all gave form to grief.

Why is it, he thought as he drifted downhill, a child's clear voice lingering on the silent air, that the most effective music comes from places where the history has been most violent?

Passion fueled the arts, he knew that. Now he experienced the truth of it. His instinct was to find a way to let these people know that though — through no fault of their own — they'd been cursed with Imry's proximity, they did have allies.

As it happened, he knew just where to carry his message, and at the same time perhaps get something to eat. He'd gone far too long without food, and sleep. One or the other was bearable. Together they constituted a danger.

The messenger undergrounder he'd met at the border two days before, the one who'd told him about the attack on the resistance, had mentioned their headquarters. *My sister works at the Three Acorns Inn. She'd be glad to know that I reached the Ianavair border safely*, he'd said.

A fair trade for news, David had said, promising to let her know.

So David would keep that promise, and see what he could do about bolstering their spirits.

"Ugh," CJ breathed.

It was just after sunset, but at least they were in the city, having mixed successfully into the market-traffic. No one paid attention to a pair of apprentice-age youths. Because Randon had plenty of the sorts of coins often traded in towns in or near harbors, CJ now had a new pack, a cloak that would do as a blanket when sleeping outside, and a change of clothes, each bit bought at a different vendor, along with a different story for each.

CJ stopped and stared at the towers of the royal palace dominating the north end of Larkadhe. She stuck her fists on her hips. "Why is it," she complained in a fierce whisper, "whenever you come to a new city and have to search it, it seems as big as a kingdom? But when you're on the run and want to get lost in a city, all you can find are two-street villages?"

Randon snickered. "Yep, I've noticed. Well, how about we split up and each take a half. We can meet, say…noon tomorrow. I'll take this side, you take that, from the palace west. Then if we have no success, we switch."

"West. Okay. Where do we meet?"

They turned around, orienting themselves with reference to the great palace with its fine towers.

"How about that market, over there?"

"Sounds good. Whether we find them or not, we'll meet, and compare notes."

"Yep. Farewell."

"Same to you!"

They parted and ran off, each on the watch for expected night patrols. CJ had progressed up and down ten or fifteen streets when she began to wonder if this sort of search was a waste of time. "Stench-weasels!" she muttered under her breath. "How am I going to find either of those two? Both with perfect shields, both great at fog-footing."

CJ wondered if the only way to find them was to do something that would draw their attention, but of course the Norsundrians would be nosing around first. Then, as she stepped aside to let two hurrying, basket-laden women pass, one looking furtively behind her shoulder, CJ realized that though Dena Yeresbeth would be useless in locating the likes of David or Caris-Merian, she might be able to contact local minds and at least find out if there was some sort of place where anti-Norsundrian people gathered.

Or used to gather. She could find out from them if some strangers had come to help, or whatever.

She slowed her pace and kept to the gathering shadows, her bare feet soundless on the cobbled streets. Concentrating with Dena Yeresbeth and moving at the same time tended to make her dizzy, so she did each in alternating spurts, resting after the contacts. It still tired her out. The walking spurts got longer and the Dena Yeresbeth ones shorter as she worked southward along the edges of the city, away from the greater concentrations of people. Her plan was to grab a little sleep when she reached the southern end, then come back to town center in the morning, when she could use the market traffic as cover.

A little noise, a moving shadow, up ahead forced her to duck into a recessed doorway, pressing against the brick. Fear and excitement sharpened her focus.

The person did not have any mental shield: an undergrounder! Delivering a message, and the meeting place was...ah, the Three Acorns Inn at dawn.

Okay, so where is it? She shut her eyes. Her farsense was not strong, and the person moved away fast, but she got just the briefest sense of location.

Not distant. And because she was already focused, she tried to find the place on the mental realm —

And glimpsed a fierce mental spear: intent. Murderous intent.

"Caris-Merian," she gasped, and began to run.

David entered the inn, aware of the quick turns of heads, the fear in faces, and he smiled straight at the sister, who looked exactly like her brother: thick shock of black hair, long nose, tilted blue eyes.

His intent was focused on allaying the sudden fear that he felt all around him, and was just formulating the right words when he heard a slight noise behind him, and he realized he had not thoroughly scanned the room.

Exhaustion was no excuse, nor hunger, nor kindly resolve. Detlev had hammered into the boys that eternal vigilance meant just that: days, months, years, decades of care when care was not needed, so one would be ready at that one moment when it was.

Violence hereto had always been when he chose to engage. Now it came to him.

He turned, looked straight into the hate-narrowed eyes of Caris-Merian Rhoderan. Instinct began to torque his body to defend against the upraised arm. He was fast, but she had already brought her arm round, steel flashing in the firelight and the steel jammed between his ribs. She tried to turn the knife, but it scraped off bone...bright blood on his shirt...blood on his lips...he fell, that questioning brown gaze lingering on hers, until at last it let go, and stared past her into the distance.

Pain flared, followed by darkness.

Caris-Merian stood knife in hand as her mind forced her to see over and over the stab, the blood, his loose hands—and the face. Not the David of then, there was no smirking sneer, just a thin, tired face, and brown eyes that held only question.

He vanished.

It shocked her into movement.

For a moment all she could see were the bright splashes of blood on the floor, and then she was surrounded by people yammering at her, but she couldn't hear anything beyond the drum of blood in her head.

"Les?" she whispered.

No answer.

A woman grabbed her by the shoulders. "Was that your Norsundrian spy?"

Caris-Merian wrenched free of her grip, and ran to the door, away from the blood, and the nightmare, and the falling brown gaze, faster, faster.

CJ stampeded round the corner, head down, bare feet

slapping the beautiful stonework streets, as Caris-Merian dashed out, and past her.

CJ sidled to the front door, trying to control her bellows breathing, as she took in the circle of frightened adults staring down at bloodstains on a wooden floor.

"Oh no," CJ gasped, not even aware she'd spoken. Her body chilled to ice. "Caris-Merian?" she croaked.

A couple pale faces turned her way.

Halfway down the torchlit street a girl-shaped silhouette ran blindly.

CJ took off after her. She halved, then quartered the distance, tried to do a mind-cast for Norsundrians, and stumbled as vertigo plucked at her balance.

She tried the direct method. "Caris-Merian! Char—is—mer—yan!"

Caris-Merian was long-legged and fast, but CJ, kept in shape by years of energetic forest games, was an excellent runner. She couldn't close the gap, she was just too short, but at least it didn't lengthen.

The streets widened and the houses were spaced between lengthening bits of garden, grass and hill. They had reached the outskirts of the city. CJ was wondering who would run into a Norsundrian patrol first—with her luck, they'd come from behind—when she heard horse hooves. Of course it had to be a villain.

"I hope the creep stops her first," CJ muttered, plugging on. There was no way to hide, and anyway she refused to hide, and lose Caris-Merian.

The rider changed direction, for the pattern of hoofbeats changed. Now coming straight at them. At least only one rider. CJ thought fumbled in her clothing for her knife.

From the darkness emerged a black horse, visible only against a whitewashed wall, on its back a man's silhouette. The horse and rider angled across Caris-Merian's path. She jerked, stumbled, started up again, but didn't get two steps before the rider had leaped off and taken her arm.

As CJ pounded up, her feet aching from all that running on stone, she saw Caris-Merian look up into the man's face—then make a whimper of terror before she sagged in his hands.

He eased her onto the ground, straightening up just as CJ reached them, waving her knife. "Hey! Leave her alone!" she yelled.

Moonlight pooled in the folds of a dark cape, and glimmered in shoulder-length hair. The man's face turned slightly, so that the weak blue light was strongest, and CJ made out a mustache, and familiar planes. No, it couldn't be—

"She's safe, Cherenneh," murmured a voice that used to give her nightmares.

"Detsie!"

A soft laugh escaped him.

"Whadidya do to her?"

"Nothing drastic. She'll waken in a moment."

CJ thought, well, if she fainted, the sight of your mug, even in that hairy disguise, would certainly do the trick. But just before she demanded to know what he was doing there she remembered her own purpose, and the blood on the floor, and she winced. "Oh, I wasn't in time."

"It was close."

"Cl—does that mean he's alive? Where? He wasn't in the inn, there was only—oh, ish. The Norsundrians got him?"

"Yes. He's in the castle with Imry Llyenthur right now."

"Ugh! Ick!" She didn't bother asking how he knew these things. Detsie always seemed to know things. He could do anything. "D'you think we can get him out?"

"I intend to." Detlev smiled, and bent to pick up Caris-Merian. "But first he has to live, and I am going to have to do something with her so they don't get her as well."

"Can't you—like—help David with your Dena Yeresbeth?"

"No, because that's what Imry is waiting for."

CJ shuddered. All the way across the ocean and down the peninsula she'd thought this would be an easy rescue. Suddenly it had changed, becoming a flash flood where once there'd been a little stream. Her mind worked furiously. "But that Llyenthur creep won't be waiting for a rescue?"

"Yes." Detlev set Caris-Merian across the saddle bow, mounted, and then settled her unconscious form more comfortably.

"Want some help?" CJ spoke with the defiance of one who expected a humiliating squelch from the Grate Ancient Sartoran.

"Shall I enumerate the dangers? There are a number of them, perhaps more than you are aware."

"I don't care. That is, I do, but that's what I'm here for.

And I hate to be too late! Oh, and I'll be Randon will be in on it as well."

"Randon Amdrelya?" The quiet voice was amused. "You Mearsieans have met him at last?"

"Um, I have. So, want us?"

He extended a hand. She hesitated, wary of villain cooties. But he wasn't one any more, right?

She stuck out her small, grubby hand, felt hers grasped, and with a smooth motion he pulled her up behind him.

Up in the White Tower of Larkadhe, a very nervous pair of warriors drafted as orderlies laid David in a bed, stripped off his shirt, and wrapped his chest with bandages, under the merciless gaze of their commander.

Left alone, they would have finished him off, for they knew who he was. It had taken them by surprise when the blood-covered body landed full-length just outside Llyenthur's study where they'd been standing guard. They'd had just enough time to identify the source of blood as a knife-wound, probably through the lung, and were debating who ought to do the honors when the door flung open and Llyenthur stood there, looking seriously irritated.

"Cath of Isolde, it seems, has quite a sense of humor," he said, looking down at the David's bleeding, unconscious body.

The guards exchanged long-suffering glances. They were used to him making no sense whatsoever.

"I fear I was remiss; there appear to be more ironies here than I was aware." Then he issued a stream of orders.

David was taken up to one of the towers, bandaged, and put in a waiting bed by hands better accustomed to assault than care and comfort. They finished, and looked up for clues.

Llyenthur waved them out, and they decamped with evident relief. He shut the door, sat down at the bedside, stretched out a hand—then pulled it back. Intent never justified ignorance. It was better not to try, now, what instinct urged him to try. Instead he thought out what kind of spells would best bind his brother to life.

Seventeen

DAVID SLEPT.

His mind wandered in anguish-driven dreams as he sought escape. He even tried calling mind to mind across continents, and between the temporal world and that of the spirit, to find himself walled. Finally he relinquished the delirious quest to hang onto life, and sank into restless slumber.

Not for long. Inexorably the physical discomforts intensified until he regained awareness, but it was a slow, arduous process, like swimming up with a load of bricks from the bottom of a murky pool.

His immediate awareness was of agony. It sharpened with every indrawn breath, and ached with exhalation. Then there was thirst, and with it the blinding headache that comes with fever. He was still tied to his body, and it was yammering for succor.

He opened his eyes, and a hand withdrew its light pressure from his wrist.

The headache prevented thought — even surprise — as he contemplated Imry sitting on a chair next to the bed on which David found himself stretched. Imry's eyes were that same lambent green but the skin around them was dark and dull. His long, unkempt hair framed an exhaustion-tight face that was (despite the uncompromising bones of adulthood) so very much the same. That expression, watchful and smiling, it had been just like that when they were small.

Imry turned, reached for something beyond the bed, and

David observed his rumpled, unlaced tunic. Dry lips twitched. "Drunk?" he breathed.

"No." Imry poured something.

David could hear the liquid splash, and his dry, sticky tongue moved, making him swallow in a papery throat.

"I've been sitting here with you for three days and as many nights." Imry smiled again. "First time I ever had to put someone back together to get what I want."

David recognized that the implied threat was not mere bravado, it was a reaction-provocation.

"Entertaining?" The word made his chest protest and he shut his eyes until the pang passed, and then he tried to breathe more lightly.

"Once," Imry said. "Here. I woke you up to get some liquid into you. A necessity, according to the fool I keep around here to patch up my victims." One hand lifted David's head, and a cup pressed against his lips.

David tasted watery soup, lukewarm. He swallowed half of it.

"Slowly."

Pain had already taught him not to forget to breathe; he coughed, tasted iron, and the backlash from his tightly bound chest stabbed with each heartbeat.

He closed his eyes to work on catching his breath. His mind was full of questions, but he wasn't ready for speech yet, not yet...

He slept.

When he woke, Imry was still there. That had not been a dream.

"Want some more?" Imry invited.

David's gazed drifted to the window. Dark before, now light slanted in around the curtain edges.

He had better success with the soup this time, then he focused on Imry's face. "Caris-Merian?" he wheezed. The name took three separate breaths.

"What is it you want to know? You don't have to talk, I feel obliged to remind you. I believe my abilities will lend themselves to contact."

"No." David frowned, gathering his strength. Every word felt like someone wearing iron-reinforced ice-cracker boots was stomping on one side of his chest.

Imry's upper lip quirked. "Don't talk. I'll try to guess. Yes, it was Caris-Merian who did the honors. She seems to have forgotten where to strike, if not how, though that jab is vicious enough. Cath set this one up, and I didn't really believe it would actually come to pass. I thought my little demonstration the other day would be sufficient to enable me to flush the both of you out when I had the time, but Caris-Merian appears to have been in a bit of a hurry to cleanse the world of at least one of us."

He paused. David parsed that: so the attack on the resistance was indeed timed, but not simply to thwart efforts of the locals. It was because he'd known — somehow — that David was nearby, and Caris-Merian was coming for him. And the locals were to fear suspicious strangers enough for their fears to show up in a questioning by someone with Dena Yeresbeth.

Imry poured more liquid. David drank it, then sank back.

Imry looked amused, and went on. "No, we don't have her. This surprises me as well. I was convinced she would — supposing she could actually accomplish the dirty deed — come straight to us in a sacrifice of self-loathing, and I could put her to work as an assassin. But she's gone. As well. I have three days of urgent tasks awaiting my attention, and therefore no time for the dramatics of readjusting ethics."

A pause for reaction. David smiled. Or tried to, no more than a twitch of his lips.

Imry sat back, hands on his knees. "The damage is a punctured lung. You'd have drowned in your own blood had Cath not enchanted that knife, which, if you remember, carries a rough-and-ready wound-binding spell until we can get the intended volunteer into our governance. I strengthened it as best I could, but I fear you will be tied to that bed for some time to come before I dare release it."

Pause.

"And?" David said.

"And so we will begin by getting reacquainted, shall we?"

————⟨⟨⟨⟩⟩⟩————

Outskirts of Larkadhe, near the Andahi Pass

Caris-Merian woke up with a sickening headache.

Late afternoon sunlight slanted in through a wall of shrubbery in a dappled glare that made her close her eyes again.

Her hand lifted to shade her eyes, but her fingers trembled, and her arm dropped like a stone.

She was about to try again when an intense pair of blue eyes, framed by long, straight black hair, popped into her line of sight. It took several breaths to put a name to that grubby and unsmiling face: CJ of the Mearsieans.

Where had *she* come from? Where were they, anyway?

"Want some water?" CJ offered. Her voice was high, pleasant—she was the one who sang so well, wasn't she?

Caris-Merian sat up a little, her mind a jumble of disconnected thoughts, until she drank down the water CJ gave her.

Then memory punched through, slamming her down with the weight of years' long hatred. Her head dropped so fast that red lights lanced across her vision, leaving her staring up at leaves, two different types, so closely interwoven she could only see patches of sky beyond.

Memory again. The knife hilt scraping past bone into flesh, the questioning brown eyes, the red smear on the floor…

"David is still alive," CJ said. She sat cross-legged in the grass next to where Caris-Merian lay. "At least, Detsie said so yesterday. We've been here three days, and he made you sleep the whole time, on account of the search, and then the rain that pinned us down, and then we had to find this hiding place. He said to tell you you'll feel rotten only until you eat and drink, then you'll be fine. Here. Drink some more. You look so parched it makes *me* thirsty!"

Caris-Merian drained the cup CJ held out, then she sat all the way up and winced. In truth she already felt vastly improved, just hungry, and—

"Maybe you ought to flake out a little bit longer," CJ said doubtfully.

"No. I have to leave," Caris-Merian said.

"Where?" CJ asked bluntly, as one who had the right.

Caris-Merian frowned at the younger girl. Then she remembered what had happened—what had nearly happened—and looked down at her hands.

CJ said, "Detsie said if you woke up first you might try to do something dumb, and you were to stay here instead, until he gets back."

Caris-Merian's mouth tightened. "I will not obey any command of *his*."

CJ grinned. "You know, he's on our side now."

"So. He. Says." Caris-Merian's voice was so angry it shook.

CJ's mouth rounded.

Caris-Merian pressed her lips together against any more words, and looked around. They were in a sheltered grove of trees with thick hanging clumps of leaves and ferny shrubs. Through the natural curtain of leaves she glimpsed the contours of hills at either side; this grove was set alongside a stream, in a little valley.

A dark cloak lay next to her on the grass. Caris-Merian reached to pick it up, realized it was not hers, and sat back on her heels.

"Well," CJ said, watching. "I suppose old Detsie isn't so bad—now. At any rate he did say to keep you from doing anything fatheaded. So I will."

Caris-Merian stood up, and CJ did as well. Caris-Merian looked down at the much shorter girl, who crossed her skinny arms before her and planted her dusty bare feet foursquare. "Please do not get in my way," she warned.

"Then I'm going with you," CJ declared.

"I don't want company."

"Too bad—"

The rustle of leaves made both girls look up.

A man's hand parted the foliage, and Detlev stepped in. At his elbow was a cheerful boy with a round face and pale blond curls.

"He found me," Randon stated, then he brandished his pack and a covered basket. "And I brought some real grub!"

"Oh," CJ said feelingly. "A welcome sight."

She thrust a hand into the basket, and closed it around a warm roll that was stuffed with smoked chicken and well-aged cheese. She also found an apple, and a chocolate brownie.

"Ahhh!" She turned to display her booty to the others, took one look at Caris-Merian's rigid stance and bloodless face, and gave Randon a significant grimace and a jerk of the chin back the way he'd come.

Randon rolled his eyes, and led the way out again, leaving the hanging clumps of leaves swinging. The two wandered the bright slope of wildflowers, stopping alongside the stream.

"He tell ya what happened?" CJ asked, around bites.

"In about two sentences," Randon said. "He's not exactly gabby with details. But yow! I've never tangled with the really big snakes in Norsunder before. If we try to spring David, we'll have that Llyenthur right on us, hotter'n a volcano."

"Well, I have tangled with 'em—not the Host, but, well, others." She'd been about to name Detlev, and decided to skip it. "There are two things to remember, from my experience. I'll give them to you before I tell you what happened—and I am not, as you well know, about to stint on the details. One. Norsundrians are rockheads, or they wouldn't be Norsundrians. Two, don't worry about sticking to any plan, because they always flub out."

Randon's laugh floated back across the breeze-ruffled grasses to the grove. Hearing it seemed to release Caris-Merian from some sort of paralysis.

She had turned her back on Detlev as soon as she saw him; behind her, she'd heard the little sounds of him unpacking the basket that the boy had set down.

He said, "I think we had better talk, Caris-Merian."

"No. I won't talk to you. I am going to leave—" she began in a strangled voice, but then she stopped, her breathing ragged.

For a short time she struggled for control. The only sounds were leaves rustling, the running chuckle of the stream, and in the distant the two kid voices, almost indistinguishable from the trilling of birds.

Caris-Merian lost her battle. Her chest heaved in a huge sob, and she snarled, hot tears blinding her, "It's all your fault. All of it. None of this would have happened except for you. None of it, so don't tell me you're a lighter now, or that I'm as bad as a Norsundrian because of what I did, just leave me alone!" She dared one glare at him, but her stinging eyes only comprehended a blur. She gritted her teeth, wanting desperately to find strong enough words to blast him with even the tiniest bit of her pain, sending it where it belonged. But she could not see his face, and angrily dashed her knuckles across her eyes.

She could see his face now, but his expression was impossible to interpret. He said, "Nothing I do, for good or ill, will bring Leskander back to life. Likewise nothing that you do will restore him to life."

"He's dead because of you! You and your gang of damnsouled rot-hearted murderers!"

"Did you think that committing more murder in your

brother's name would resurrect him?"

"More? It was not I who—"

"Murder is murder. Is a person less dead if the knife-wielding hand belongs to a Norsundrian, or a lighter? Did you think that killing David would somehow cancel out Leskander's death?"

"Don't you dare to speak his name!"

"If you believe that vengeance rights wrongs I suggest you converse with Imry Llyenthur. He certainly seems to be waiting for you."

Her eyes shifted at that, but she said nothing, only wept silently.

"At least, " Detlev added, "he hasn't left that castle, and he sent out a number of search parties with your name heading the search list."

She countered stiffly, "He's a blathering idiot."

"Perhaps. But the fact remains that he set you up, just as surely as if you had been given written instructions on how to achieve his ends for him without his having to bestir himself."

She choked on a sob of anger.

Detlev went on. "What convenient lies did he tell you, that he and David—possibly the three of us—get together to discuss old times between missions? Laugh over old victims, perhaps? And then you just happened to find an unused knife on your way out, conveniently enchanted against David?"

"Was he lying about their being brothers?" she cut in.

"No. You don't see the resemblance? They are indeed brothers, sons of a man who called himself Kedran Llyenthur—after a kingdom north of here, on which he had designs after he was exiled from his old home. And both boys were in my group, though they never saw one another after Imry joined the regulars thirteen years ago, as we measure time on this world."

"Thirteen—" She scrubbed her knuckles across her eyes again, then said in a low voice that had lost none of its earlier venom, "Fifty, or a thousand years, so what? One of them is as rotten as the other. And what makes it right for him to change his mind about being a Norsundrian and expect to be welcomed by old victims, and walk freely among those whose families were broken by him? That Llyenthur said he might do the same when he got tired of being a Norsundrian!" She raised her hands, then, her flexed fingers expressive of horror. "And I, why should I fare any differently—"

"You are not a murderer yet, Caris-Merian," Detlev said. "David is alive. A prisoner somewhere in that castle. You, those two youngsters, and I are the only people who have a chance of springing him"

It was the right moment to give her unstable emotions a direction. A purpose. The need for action had saved her again and again during the long years since Les's death, and it did now. "There's a city full of people," she began, but she knew that few of them would have the skill to breach that castle, much less the inclination, after Llyenthur's recent strike against them. She drew in a shaky breath and said hatefully, "None of your pet killers near?"

"None," he replied. "And the need to act fast makes it risky to wait for allies."

She rubbed her palms down her sides, and he knew that she had accepted this purpose. Her motivation was self-punishment. His own was not unaligned, in that he was aware that because of time pressures and myriad other conflicting demands he had mishandled the Les Rhoderan situation. He would amend as much of the consequences as he could.

CJ leaned back in the sunlight, feeling replete from her feast. The late spring afternoon was warm and lovely. One would never know that a Norsundrian-infested city lay a few miles to the southeast.

Randon was telling a story of one of his early adventures. CJ enjoyed it thoroughly as images chases vividly through her mind.

But then, suddenly, Detlev was a presence on the surface of her thoughts: *It's time to plan.*

"Yak!" She sat up, which startled Randon into scrambling for his knife. "Oh, sorry," she said. "It was Detsie. I forgot my mind-shield. Again! Anyway he says it's time to plan. He must've got Caris-Merian unmessed, in some way. Could he have somehow zapped her with his Dena Yeresbeth?"

"Zapped?" Randon repeated, shaking his head. "It's hard to believe that mind stuff really works. Oh well, I guess some folk feel that way about magic!"

He got up and whacked dirt and leaf-bits from his tunic. CJ did as well, then they meandered back toward the grove, where they found the other two waiting. Caris-Merian's tear-and-dirt-smeared face was averted, but of course Detlev looked exactly like usual.

Randon shot a glance at CJ, expressing: *What did he do to her?*

CJ responded with a prune-mouth and a tiny shrug: *Dunno, but I'm glad I wasn't in her place!*

"Here, Caris-Merian," Randon said, picking up the basket. "How about some chow?"

Eighteen

Western Imar, near the Dei Manor

THE ONLY HIDING PLACE that Clair's group was able to find that morning lay under an abandoned house. The dirt was damp and the floorboards less than an arm's length overhead were unpleasantly mossy, but at least they had been able to spend an entire day unmolested. Occasional bird spies drifted overhead, unheeding, and the inner perimeter patrol rode by without so much as a glance.

Zairna was watching. He would not admit to Clair how painful the knife-edge sawed between his eyes while scanning mentally in this foreign land. The fact that this type of capability had evolved very differently on his world made the psychic distortion taxing, but it was also his protection; he could discern without much effort that enduring the onslaught of defensive magic on the mental realm was exponentially worse for her.

And she had very little knowledge of defensive strategy, either magic or military. He made it his business to identify the patrol perimeters, and to guide the others through them. Now, at last, they had made it within the inner patrol circle, and they bordered the estate where the Host lived. Tired, dirty, but satisfied that he had done a good day's work, he crawled on hands and knees under the house.

The girls were awake, waiting. "They were all there," he reported in a soft voice. "Something must be going on."

"Rot," Julian muttered, scowling. "We'll starve to death

before we even get a chance to get caught."

"We can get caught right here if you'd rather." Clair tried to smile but it came out a grimace, and her lips cracked. She licked the metallic taste of blood, shuddered, and wiped absently at her eternally gritty eyes. "Zaima, you've been out all day. You ought to rest, and not take a watch."

He looked at her strained face and shook his head. He'd catnapped in his hidey-hole earlier, something he'd learned to do during his own training, and he knew he'd be able to make it.

And he watched her lie back in relief, pulling her cloak about her in an ineffective attempt to lessen the bone-chilling cold. She gave a sigh that she felt through her entire body, without even being aware that she had done so, then with an effort all the others felt, she raised her head. "You'll speak up if you feel yourself bombing out?"

"Yes." Zaima smiled.

Clair nodded, closed her eyes, and slid instantly into sleep.

Her dreams were a jumble. Less frightening than they'd been before the cup had somehow gained so much power. The landscape of her dream changed to vaguely resemble Narad, the capital of Chwahirsland, and though it had gradually began easing into a semblance of what others took as normal life, under Jilo, old memory made her anxious.

She hurried along contorted streets, searching for the girls, because she had to —

An old woman suddenly reached out a hand. It was an incongruous hand. Clair saw that it was long and strong and well-made, the hand of an adult not old — a man's hand.

Alarm chilled Clair's nerves. The old woman said urgently, "Do not waken, do not shut me out."

"Siamis?" Clair-in-dream exclaimed.

Shock almost dissolved the dream, but by focusing on the woman she held it. Then she bent, saw an old face, and the hands now were old as well.

The woman said, "Yes, I am near. Wait until I contact you again. I have found Kessler, and we have a plan. If we are not able to free the prisoners by magic trickery, we will draw the Host off so that you and your friends can slip in, using the cup-magic as cover, and find them."

Surprise and question crowded Clair's mind with such insistence the dream dissolved and she woke. She listened on the mental realm, just the tiniest tendril — and the blackness was waiting.

No Siamis.

She opened her eyes, and found that June and Julian had fallen asleep. Zairna sat, watching the opening into their shelter.

She beckoned, and in a low whisper told him about the dream. And when the dreary sunset smeared into darkness, and the others woke, willing to push on if that was the plan, Clair and Zairna told them what had happened.

Julian rubbed her hands. "Action — at last. But why don't those two do the slipping in, at least with us? Either of them could take on half a dozen warriors, and eat a piece of pie at the same time."

Clair murmured, "Wards. Against them, with their names. No wards against any of us."

"Oh yeah," Julian said, with a slight, dismissive gesture. "Magic."

June fingered her cup. "Then if we have to wait, let's all get some rest," she suggested, and they did.

Imry Llyenthur's HQ - Larkadhe

When David woke a day and a half later, it was to find a middle-aged man hovering about. Guessing that this was the medic to whom Imry had referred so scathingly, David wheezed, "Wouldn't mind another blanket. Cold all the time."

The man gave a curt nod, his face set into lines of disapproval. "You'll get one, now that the fever's down some." He shot a look up behind David's bed, and then straight-ened up.

David's left hand drifted up his chest, and felt a fresh bandage. "Still bleeding?"

"No. It's closed, but not by nature. I didn't dare change the first bandage until today. You need to drink and eat something."

David was ready, willing, but not quite able. The medic assisted him, first in drinking water, then listerblossom steep, and finally in sipping at a nourishing soup that was much better cooked than one would expect of barracks fare.

As the man helped David to lie flat again, he gave David a covertly curious look. "Thank you. And yes, I am his brother.

But I'd take…anything else he says about me…with a sizeable reservation."

The man's mouth opened. He glanced up behind David again, then pressed his lips into a thin line.

"A spy? A guard?" David's whisper was a breath of sound. He almost laughed, but fought the impulse, suspecting that it would hurt.

The medic gave him a doubtful look.

"Fear for my reason?'

The man did not respond, but walked out. Presently a silent servant entered, shook out a quilt and draped it over David, then he too decamped.

David slept. Woke up for food much later. He'd lost track of time; the room was lit day and night, and it would take too much effort to rise and twist around to glance at the curtained windows for signs of daylight or darkness.

Each time he woke, it was to find the medic with food and steep.

Twice he woke up naturally. The second time, Imry appeared. David felt his presence before he entered the room. This amused him, and thus Imry looked down into eyes narrowed with humor.

"And I thought I would either find you asleep, bored, or plotting," he commented, pulling a chair around and dropping onto it. He crossed his arms across the back, put his chin on his wrist, and studied David with interest, watching David study him with the same interest. "You look less like a corpse."

"You too. And I am. Bored."

"Then let us entertain one another with questions. Would you like to begin? This might be easier by contact, you know."

"I'll talk," David whispered, "until I run. Out of breath."

"Twit. What are you afraid of?"

"Noise."

Imry laughed. "No questions? Then permit me to begin by asking you what could have possessed Detlev to hop the fence? Has he some masterly double-cross in mind?"

"Ask him."

"I intend to," Imry said cordially. "If I can get to him before Svir and the rest. More to the point, why did you trot obediently behind him?"

"Because the prospect of spending…an eternity…playing bully-boy in others' games made…just about. Anything else.

Seem attractive."

Imry grinned. "Ah, I'm going to enjoy this interlude. Did you know I had Senrid here a few months ago? Alas, he has no sense of humor."

Senrid? David put together the last of the clues: Andri had been here on an unnamed mission before showing up in Mearsies Heili. Not much later Andri and Liere had married in Mearsies Heili, an act that—David suspected—had been precipitated by reaction, by desperation. Following which Senrid did not stay in Mearsies Heili with the rest of his friends, but went home.

David sorted mentally through the persons, places, and times, and came to the conclusion that Imry's and Senrid's interlude had to have been a masterpiece of humiliation for the latter.

Out loud, he said, "Senrid probably. Found you. Boring."

"Where is he?"

David shrugged with his brows. "Mearsies Heili."

"What were you doing in Marloven Hess a month and a half ago?"

"Nosing into your business...of course. I'm surprised... you didn't niff me before."

"I niffed you then because you wanted me to, you and our mentor. What surprised me was the time and trouble you took over Marend Ndarga, when I've landed half a dozen better prospects before and since."

"But I was there...and you and I...both know...she would have made it...too easy for you...in Marloven Hess."

"Ah, you saw that, did you? Have designs on the place yourself?"

"Haven't decided. Yet."

Imry studied David silently, then said, "I don't know you at all any more. I can't tell if you're lying or not. Never mind! Did you ever meet our father?"

David gave a slight nod. "Couple years. After you left."

"Is he alive or dead?"

"Dead."

Imry's brows rose, but he betrayed no interest beyond that. Irritation made him restless when he saw how the effort of speaking was exhausting David. "That lung might still collapse." He tapped his fingers on the chair-back. "I daren't transfer you out lest I lose you."

"New transfer spell?...Bad one, eh?" David murmured.

"Thanks to Kessler's meddling."

"Heal faster. No wards."

"There are none, beyond the knife-enchantment and the binding on the wound. The only thing I could think of was a spell waiting if you do somehow manage to get outside this room without my leave. The idea is to slow you down."

David's brow twitched.

Imry said, "We will be better allies than we were as boys. You'll see."

"Allies." David curled his lip. "Sure. So long...as I obey orders?"

"Ready to take me on?"

"Name your weapon..."

"I shiver in fear. No — don't talk any more. You're trying my patience enough without inviting setbacks." Imry moved to the door. "Ah. I nearly forgot. I've got the black sword. I'll return it presently."

By then David was too tired to care. He was asleep within moments after Imry closed the door behind him.

Outskirts of Larkadhe, near the Andahi Pass

The sound of footsteps crunching dirt below the tree where CJ sat caused her to stop swinging her legs. She'd been sitting there, struggling to get control of her boiling emotions.

"You look aggrieved." Detlev looked inquisitively up at her.

"First." She raised a forefinger. "I need some chocolate! That brownie the other day, whenever it was — what is the date, anyhow?"

"Today is the 35th of Fifth-month."

"Well, that brownie just reminded me I haven't had a taste of chocolate for weeks. And second, I really hate waiting, especially when I don't know exactly what it is I'm waiting for." She glared down at him. "I don't suppose you really know, and are keeping it to yourself for some typically stupid adult reason? I could see Kessler not telling anyone anything, especially if it's going to help anyone, but I would have thought ol' Siamis would spill the beans a little."

"I don't think they know what form their ruse will take. Long distance contact is risky enough for us to limit our exchanges to what is absolutely necessary."

CJ frowned. "So the Host could, like, catch you traveling around by mind?" She tapped her forehead.

Detlev replied, "Some of them. Quite easily, in fact. Imry as well."

She envisioned her mind being somehow imprisoned far from her body, and shuddered. "Yech. But we have to wait on them?"

"Remember we must get David to the Selenseh Redian near here. We could probably get him out of the castle successfully, but Imry's going to know almost immediately, and he has magic and hunters. We have ourselves until we get to the cave. We'll have allies once we get high enough in the mountains, but still no magic. Unless Siamis and Kessler have some measure of success."

"Oh, I hope Clair's safe, at least." CJ frowned down at Detlev, who still looked piratical to her, with that long loose hair and the mustache. His lack of answer must mean he didn't know where Clair was — CJ tried to reason — and that had to mean she'd gotten herself out of that disaster area. Yes. She was going to believe that, as hard as she could.

CJ swung her feet more vigorously as she stared down at Detlev, who was watching something out of her view. "Hey," she said, making a discovery. "You've got some gray hairs!" She peered down, and yup, a shaft of sunlight touched on strands of silver among the brown strands.

Detlev laughed.

"Those years of villainy catching up with ya, eh?" she asked, snickering at the idea of getting away with this kind of talk in front of the infamous Detsie-poopsie-potsie.

"I've had gray hairs at least since my mother pointed them out on one of my visits home from the dyranarya academy," he retorted equably.

"Before the big splat?"

"Before the big splat."

CJ gave a whoop of laughter, more from relief than actual entertainment.

Randon arrived then, puffing mightily. He plumped his basket on the ground and wiped a sleeve across his sweaty face.

"Here's our grub. Now, what're you laughing about? Tell me the joke!"

CJ began to explain. Randon grinned, but he didn't laugh. He hadn't had any experience of Detlev previous to this so the combination of the unlikelihood of Detlev becoming a pirate, much less looking like one, plus the if-we'd-known-this-would-happen-back-then realization, was not nearly as entertaining for him as it was for her.

She didn't want to admit to anyone that, as the days went by, her feelings about Caris-Merian were changing. In fact — she hated even thinking this about a fellow lighter — the older girl was giving her the creeps.

She eyed Detlev as they began their meal. He looked so ordinary, eating his sandwich and listening to Randon describe his trip into Larkadhe. She thought, he looks like someone's dad who owns a farm down the road. Then she frowned and corrected that, thinking that the farmer down the road wouldn't sit that straight. Then she decided that wasn't right either. There were probably as many farmers who sat up straight as ones who didn't.

It's his stillness, she thought. Nobody I know is quite like that, and I didn't even notice it in him before, because I wasn't around him long. Could he have possibly been like that before he switched?

Except — well —

He glanced up then, caught her frowning gaze, and she burst out, "What does it feel like to be so old?"

"Good question," Randon said thickly, then swallowed his huge bite of sandwich so fast that his eyes watered. "Is time the same in Norsunder? Are — " He coughed.

"Pig!" CJ whacked him on the back.

" — you really and truly four thousand years old? How come you don't have any wrinkles?"

"More than four thousand years have passed on Sartorias-deles since I was born, but I have not experienced them as such because I was seldom here."

"Norsunder is timeless, then? They always said the time is different, but I never really believed it."

"It's not, but the tie is tenuous."

Randon frowned. "So is there a ratio? A day there equals, say, a hundred here?"

"There are no days."

"Oh, you know what I mean! Any sort of ratio."

"No—"

Randon didn't wait for him to finish. Any discussion that related to magic always got him excited. He rushed on. "Then it *is* timeless! It has to be one or the other!"

"It's both, actually, for those who have the knowledge to manipulate it."

Randon looked dubious. CJ said slowly, "It's true."

And then to Randon's impatience she began to compare it to some of her off-world adventures, to places where time had been bent. And Detlev nodded, recognizing her references. Randon fought to contain his impatience; he wished, more than ever, he'd been able to adventure off-world.

"How old are you, then?" CJ finally asked.

Randon turned his attention back to Detlev.

"It would be impossible to calculate."

"How old do you feel?"

"As old as I am." He smiled.

CJ waved her arms. "Are you being a groanboil on purpose?" She went on without waiting for an answer, "But Lilith is really 4000 years old. She *looks* like an old lady."

"She was much older than I when Norsunder attacked, but she too has had access to refuge from time's demands."

CJ frowned, then said, "I think if I ever gave up wanting to celebrate my birthday—I love having birthdays and not having to be a grownup—it would be horrible."

Randon shrugged. "Being an adult would be horrible. Who cares about birthdays?"

Detlev glanced up, then said, "I'll be back in a while. There are some refinements to our plan I'd like to discuss with all of you present."

He walked away, and moments later CJ saw Caris-Merian approaching. She looked tired, strained, and as always she glanced around quickly to make certain Detlev was not around before she accepted her share of the food.

She greeted the two kids with quiet, unsmiling courtesy, then sat down to eat. After a protracted silence, CJ said, "Detlev wants to plan some more, in a little while."

Caris-Merian's shoulders tightened. She said in a flat voice, "Very well." And was immediately lost in abstraction.

CJ hid a shiver by jumping up to run around in the sunshine.

Nineteen

DUIN, LLYENTHUR'S SENIOR AIDE-DE-CAMP, was working in the map room at the command center dispatch desk when a messenger transferred in by magic.

Duin took the sealed letter. "If it needs an answer, we'll send it." He then read out the return-transfer spell. When the runner was gone he sat down and with sharpened anticipation ripped the seal.

The other two in the room paused in their tasks and watched expectantly, for personal transfers were rare, and usually presaged action.

Duin started cursing, habitual Chwahir invective that inevitably caused laughter among the others, as he mentally calculated the time-difference.

"Fourth hour here." He smacked the map, reaching the reluctant conclusion that Llyenthur had probably had less than an hour of sleep. He cursed again.

Bergan gloated, "Won't like being yanked."

Duin muttered, "Why did this come now?"

Ah. A command decision—whether or not to summon Llyenthur. No one wanted that duty. Mistakes were always painful.

Duin repeated the code words, which were part of some spell Llyenthur had set up. He appeared, red-eyed and very annoyed. Even though Duin knew that unblinking stare was transfer-reaction, for Hier Alverian was a quarter of a world away, alarm still burned through him.

Finally, "What is it, Duin?"

"Detlev sighting. Near a geliath we'd thought abandoned, in northern Halarialgre. Arandos Kinarde says Alsaes has commandeered hunting parties from him and from Tiell in the south to go search," Duin reported rapidly.

Llyenthur turned to the map. "It was abandoned half a year ago. I was there." He half-raised a hand, then dropped it again. "It's possible that the lighters are gathering there for some obscure purpose, but it's equally possible that numbers we can ill afford to spare will spend days fruitlessly wandering empty tunnels. David?"

Duin blinked at the fast subject-switch. "Been sleeping. Someone checks on him every hour, as you ordered. Hasn't tried to get up today, hasn't talked to anyone beyond asking about the weather outside once, and asking for something hot to drink once."

Llyenthur showed no reaction, but sometimes no reaction was good. "I want you to go to Halarialgre and see it through. If you find signs that Detlev is indeed there, summon me. If not, I fear it will be necessary to do something about Alsaes. He has no military authority for a reason. Remind him of it, any way you choose. I believe I had better remain here, at least for now."

Duin turned away, favoring his fellows with a covert grin.

Everybody loathed Alsaes.

Tense as it was, this position close to command did have its compensations.

Outside Larkadhe, near the Andahi Pass

Randon and CJ collapsed onto the grass after a long game of tag. A shadow darkened the glow perceivable through her eyelids. She opened her eyes to find Detlev's upside down face.

"We're leaving for the city."

"What? Someone contact you?" CJ leaped to her feet.

"Imry was gone for short time. I used the opportunity to do a little checking before yanking him from sleep." Detlev smiled grimly. Then he was serious again. "Siamis and Kessler intend to make their move tonight, which will be in a couple of hours here. I'm afraid I also tricked an old acquaintance of yours, which will no doubt get him into trouble."

"Who? Who?" She hopped around.

"Do you remember Alsaes?"

"Alsaes!" CJ gave a mighty horselaugh, which sent a number of birds in the trees nearby into a twittering panic. "Horrible villain. How did you trick him?"

"Do you really want the details?" he asked as they walked back uphill toward their campsite in the sheltered grove.

"Yes," she said, more to see if he would answer than because she wanted to hear the answer.

"I required a certain type of mind, and Alsaes is ideal in a number of ways. Easily convinced a vision of my face projected by farsense is me in person, he will supply all the belief necessary to make reality of an image, driven by his overmastering desire to head a mighty force. He is in the process of making a mess of Imry's organization for a considerable distance."

"Giving the local resistance a mysterious break, and leaving them wondering how it happened," Randon muttered.

"And I loooooove the idea of that rat Llyenthur chasing around after phantoms," CJ put in. "Imagine putting that stuffed-shirt Alsaes in charge of anything except a mirror!"

Detlev was considerably amused. "Actually he's a capable enough administrator, sitting behind a big desk and directing flows of paperwork, and he's capable of making show-of-force appearances when necessary."

CJ's mind filled with images of Alsaes at the head of an army of clods just like him, all rushing to defeat.

Randon rubbed his hands. "Well, if Llyenthur is gone then I can fool 'em as long as I want, huh?"

Detlev's smile faded. "He may not have gone. We will know, I suspect, when we get closer. Remember. However good you are at copying faces and outer forms, Imry will know the instant he sets eyes on you that you are not David. You cannot let him see you, Randon, at least not in that form."

Randon and CJ exchanged worried glances.

Caris-Merian turned away and picked up their food-basket.

Imry Llyenthur's HQ - Larkadhe

The sun touched the horizon, a ruddy ball of fire, as Imry ran up the long stairway to visit his brother. When he walked in the guard was there, having just set a tray on a nightstand ranged directly against the bed. Imry waved him out and turned to David, who lay propped up on pillows, sipping at steep.

"And so?" David's voice was hoarse, but had gained a little strength.

His coloring was uneven. Imry touched David's forehead before David irritably flung off his hand. But not before Llyenthur found David's clammy skin still flushed with fever. To be expected because of the magic bindings, but couldn't be helped. To loosen them now would be to risk losing him.

David put the cup down, an exercise which took both hands.

"You have that fever all the time?"

"At night. Tired of running a house party?"

"On the contrary. I have lots more rooms. Tell me where to send the invitations."

David pressed his hand against his middle to ease the sharp pain consequent to a mild spurt of derisive laughter.

Imry said, "I've found what I think is a suitable place. As soon as I am certain you can endure the transfer I'll shift you. No dark magic wards, and I will be able to lift some of that over you."

"Host know I'm here?"

"I haven't told them. If they do know they have given no sign; they have a couple of toys presently occupying their attention."

"So you don't know," David croaked. "Figures."

Imry leaned forward, eyes wide. "Let me in, David. We could have a lot of fun on this world before moving on to better plans."

"No."

"I promise there will be no magic, no suborning of will. I only want to show you my plans."

"Yeah. Sure. And…my name is…Lilith."

Imry smiled a little. "It would have be so much quicker. But I admit that taking our time will be more enjoyable."

David looked sardonic.

"You don't believe me? Why would I waste all this effort

getting you on your feet only to make a hash of you again?"

"I don't think you're stupid. Never did." David ran out of breath, sucked one in, then forced out the rest, "But you used. To have the attention span. Of a gnat. What happens…when you lose interest?"

Imry clasped his hands together and propped them on one knee. "You want to begin with freedom of choice? An excellent topic." And, at David's sudden, soundless laugh, "Now what?"

"You sound…just like him."

Imry smiled. "And he told me—meaning an insult, you understand—that I reminded him of our grandfather. Inspiring, no?"

David smiled in return, but he let the subject of their father drop. He knew he had little strength left. "When you were small…you despised the Host…as much as any of us…Why do you…labor under their command? "

"I should think it would be obvious that I'm doing what I want."

"Are you?" David rolled his eyes in disbelief. "Next…you'll say you can break free…whenever you want… If I had a brick for every fool…who's said that…I could build a stairway…from yon window…to the ground."

"Detlev did it," Imry said gently. "Though he seems to have lost his mind at the last."

The impulse to laugh was sudden, and nearly paralyzed David with pain. He opened his fever-bright eyes. "You can't do it, Imry… Don't you see it?" He paused for a shallow breath. "They'll take you apart in fibers… All the power you're building up…Ilerian will absorb it…right along with you…if you stray once."

"There is a way." Imry murmured, eyes on the window, which had been opened at David's request.

David drew in a slow breath. "You don't think…they don't know that?"

"Of course they do. The issue has not been 'what' for some years." He looked over to see if David comprehended, and met a blank face. He said, with care, "No longer what. But how. And when."

David still had not reacted, except for the increasingly shallow breathing.

Annoyed, Imry said, "I had better leave you to rest. My interest has not abated, but I will admit that my patience is enduring a sore trial."

"Gunna take it out…on Cath?" David retorted.

"Only in a sense. He can practice his method by finding Caris-Merian, if he returns from his present mission empty-handed."

David shifted, his own impatience apparent. "You can play those games…for how long…before you see…you will never. Get beyond reach. Of the leash. What a waste." He drew a breath, closing his eyes. "And what an alternative."

He was barely audible.

Imry's eyes narrowed, and he stilled. Then got to his feet. Ah, you have been summoned, David thought, as Imry said, "I always maintained that Detlev was no smarter or stronger than I, he's merely been around longer. To prove it what better stake than myself?"

Despite everything David sensed the ligature of kinship.

Imry saw it, and smiled. "As for winning, and its relative value, let us save it until you can appreciate the discourse. Drink your steep. Be back later."

David lay back, too tired to reach for the steep. Skirmishing, he thought. Each of us trying to convince the other. The surprise is that he even wants to try.

He closed his eyes, and was dropping swiftly into slumber when he was woken by someone shaking his shoulder.

He opened his eyes. Stared uncomprehending at the half-familiar face of a young boy with a round face and a head of straw-colored curls.

"We're here to get you out," the boy said.

David whispered apologetically, "They took my clothes."

"We thought of that," was the answer. "CJ bagged you some duds on our way in. She said she picked a big hulk to steal from partly because she thought you might have a lot of bandages, and partly because his bunk was the closest to the door in the barracks."

"A hulk?" David murmured. "Not the trousers, I hope."

The boy's face changed. "Uh oh. I didn't think of that. I don't know! Here."

David first had to sit up, an operation requiring intense concentration. This was only the third time he'd done it, but at least he knew what to expect. Controlling his breathing, one forearm pressed against his chest to brace against, he swung his feet to the floor.

"You'll have to help me." He smiled at the boy. "I can't lift my arm very far." He touched his chest.

"That's why I'm here! The other two are outside, waiting until we're done. Case you need help on the stairs. I'm Randon Amdrelya, by the way. You guys chased me a buncha years ago."

"I thought you looked familiar… Randon, Imry said when he saw me last…that he'd be back soon, and I don't know when that was."

"Oh, he's gone, somewhere over the strait." Randon grinned. "Oh! Good ole CJ," he added as he pulled the tunic gently over David's head, then bent down to guide David's feet into the trouser legs. The gray trousers were much too large, but at least the belt could tighten them to settle round his hips; the black tunic-shirt completely engulfed David. "Well," Randon finished doubtfully, tugging the laces with quick fingers. "At least it can't possibly be too tight."

"It's fine," David whispered as he slowly rolled the sleeves back to his wrists. "I assure you…this will draw less attention…than if I tour the fortress…in my drawers."

"CJ didn't think of shoes," Randon added in a self-conscious voice, as his edges shimmered.

Abruptly, David found himself staring into his own face, complete to surprised brown eyes.

"Yep." The real David's voice was slightly deeper than the fake David's. "Got it. I can see it in yer mug."

"You are going to take my place?"

"Fake 'em out long's I can so's you and the others can get as far as possible."

"If Imry sees you, he'll know."

"That's what Detlev said—"

"Detlev is here?"

"Yep. He's the one who told us when Llyenthur went. And where. But he can't come into the castle because there are wards directly laid against him. He's right outside, close as he can be, and he did something weird to the three guards on our way up here. 'Holding,' he called it. But." Randon cleared his throat. "He said we better hurry 'cause anyone with Dena Yeresbeth who pokes around will know it."

David hesitated, reluctant to leave this boy in his place. "You have Dena Yeresbeth?"

"Nope. But Detlev said if the worst happens and

Llyenthur appears, to pretend I'm asleep and think about a black wall."

"It'll work only if. He does not try to. Waken you."

"Wake—" David saw his own eyes round with a horror he'd probably never expressed, at least outwardly, as Randon squeaked, "Ya mean he's already started on the torture and junk?"

"No." A laugh shook David, followed by a spasm of pain so sharp he was forced to steady himself on a chair.

Randon yanked off his tunic, which then shimmered and returned to its normal size, and tied it around his waist by the arms. "Now tell me how this is, and get going!" He threw himself on the bed and pulled the blanket up to his chin, shutting his eyes.

"Fine. I guess." David leaned against the wall, fighting for breath. "Never seen myself asleep. Thank you."

"Sure!" Randon looked away, obviously embarrassed. "See you in a little while," he added, in a voice more hopeful than bracing.

David whispered his thanks, then opened the door.

He paused in surprise on the threshold. There was CJ of the Mearsieans, blue eyes wide with excitement as she brandished a knife that David suspected she had no idea how to use.

And next to her was the cold gray gaze of Caris-Merian.

David took a step through, and the words he'd been formulating were driven out of his mind as a lancing pain flashed through his head.

His vision went black. David recoiled as if he'd been slapped, then rubbed a shaking hand across his eyes. Opened them. Nothing.

"What's wrong?" CJ whispered. "We gotta bucket!"

"Imry's spell," David replied. "He did warn me...one waited...were I to...step out."

"What?" CJ frowned. "You can't see?"

"No." He stretched out his hand. "I fear...going to...need help."

After a hesitation, a small, thin hand closed over his wrist. "I'll tell you when and where on the stairs. Here, Caris-Merian, you better take the knife in case Detsie missed any villains."

"Very well." David heard the soft, tense reply.

Was she going to make another try? If so, well, here he was. No defense this time. But he heard the rustle of her clothes as she moved away, and then CJ gave a gentle but insistent tug on his hand. "Come on. Three steps, then the stairs start."

CJ had counted on being fast. Yeah, she knew David had been stabbed, but somehow poopsies never seemed to show any signs of normal stuff like pain, and she'd expected him to bound down the steps four at a time, only pausing for her to catch up and point the way.

Their journey was exactly the opposite. The impatient looks were all hers as they made their way slowly downward. David's breathing came with such a palpable effort that she maintained a whispered flow of directions much interlaced with encouragements and insults directed against Imry and his Norsundrians, and watched David anxiously. Though they were going downstairs, not up, his breathing soon became even more labored and his hair hung in sweat-damp curls

David sent his mind briefly out as soon as they reached the bottom of the stairs. Two near guards were blanked—they would remember nothing beyond staring at a wall—and other minds were elsewhere in the castle, a number of them gathered in the map room, excited about a Detlev sighting somewhere else in the world. David did not have the strength to pursue farther; it had to be a ploy, for he niffed Detlev's touch in the guards' blanking.

He came back to his body, to find his knees buckling, his head dizzy. He wouldn't last much longer on his feet. A short burst of adrenaline helped. He breathed in and held it as he boosted his effort to walk. He was guided into a place that smelled damp and cold. A secret passage?

Twist, turn, shuffle, step, and then a rush of cool, sweet night air. A step, then a man's hand gripped his upper arm, warmth and strength radiating out from it.

: *Detlev?*

: *Here.*

"That stinkard blinded him by magic," CJ muttered.

"I will ride with him," Detlev answered.

"Poor horse," David commented, and the hand squeezed a warning.

"Save it." Amusement in Detlev's whisper. "You're drunk."

Drunk? David was beyond questioning. It was his job to stay on his feet, which now took all his concentration.

More walking, then the smell of horses, the sound of their

breathing. Detlev helped David to mount, a harrowing process that left his joints as stable as water. David fought for breath, working to control the panic: *Can't breathe! No air!*

A hood slid over his head, and next came the pungent aroma of distilled corn liquor, apparently being splashed about. A sloshing jug was added to the sounds.

The horse began to walk. Movement, slow, and Detlev's supporting arm took his weight as the pace increased. David was vaguely aware of Detlev's voice from time to time, sounding slurry, and distorted, but Detlev was not talking to him, so that, too, didn't matter.

All his concentration went to taking one breath at a time.

At last they stopped. He tried to pull his leg over, but then Detlev lifted him down, long as he was. And then, welcome release, he was permitted to lie flat on a cool dirt floor. He drew a slow, careful breath. Another — and he dropped into oblivion.

"Yech," CJ said to Detlev, staring down at David as Caris-Merian lit a lamp in the storeroom basement they had selected as their first stop. "He looks really bad. Did he pass out?"

Detlev did not answer at first. His gaze diffused as he ran light fingers over David's brow and down his chest. Then he looked up at CJ, his grim expression bringing back the evil Detsie of the old days. "He's worse than I had thought. This wound would have been mortal but for the magic. We're going to abandon the safer route. It's too long. If Imry's forces don't get him, the journey will."

CJ sneaked a peek at Caris-Merian, who was busy spreading out her cloak. Her face gave no clue she had heard. Straightening up, she said to CJ, "Here is your knife back."

"Thanks," CJ muttered in a subdued voice, and to avoid any further conversation with her she busied herself helping Detlev tuck a cloak around David's limbs.

Then she moved away out of the light of the shaded lamp, and crouched in the doorway. Her toes dug into the cool, soft dirt as she stared moodily out at the dark jumble of partially burned buildings. Yuck. She, she rubbed her chin against her knees. Weird, how everything was fun until now. Usually she liked action. But never if someone was in pain.

She paused to savor the memory of Detlev, with his hair clawed into his eyes, offering swings of corn liquor to revolted passers-by. CJ herself had cast an illusion over David, giving him a potato nose and a pot belly, as Detlev did not dare do even such slight magic. Detlev had said that afternoon, *When the inevitable search occurs, what Imry's mind-weasels must burrow out of local people's minds is a disgusting pair of frowsy drunks, and no one who looks even vaguely like David or me.*

Randon would be so mad to miss the spectacle of Detlev acting like a sozzled slob! CJ and Caris-Merian had followed behind, each carrying a basket, as though they had nothing to do with the bleary-eyed pair on the old horse. CJ smiled. The girls at home would love this one — after the mess was over. After they were all together again. Except for Irenne, who would have loved it most…how it still hurt to think about her!

CJ put her head down on her knees, which were hugged up tight against her. She became aware of voices: deep man-tones, soft girl-tones, anger sharpening the girl-words. CJ tried to shut them out, and ground her chin against her knee. Caris-Merian. She'd done her part, and Detlev treated her as if she didn't glare at him hatefully all the time, but she did glare, and CJ's spirit felt the impact of all that anger.

There was something else that bothered her. Even though Detlev readily explained his reasoning for their orders, she had this odd feeling that the real action was taking place somewhere just beyond her range of vision.

She wasn't asking the right questions. It all had something to do with poopsie past, and Caris-Merian. She stared morosely out at the peaceful evening sky. Truth was, she hated the memory of how she'd cracked a mug over Laban's head while he was tied up and helpless, during the early poopsie days, when she and her other friends had taken him prisoner. She sure couldn't shake a finger at Caris-Merian.

All right, then, as soon as this mess was over, she'd ask Detlev to send her to Laban, and then she'd apologize, and if he wanted to boot her straight back home, it was no more than fair.

Her spirits brightened a little. Action, that was the cure. Come on, Randon, she thought, wanting him to get safely out of that nasty castle so she could get some sleep. And if she slept she wouldn't worry about Clair anywhere near Kessler and Siamis going up against the Host.

Though the stars were out, and the weather was neither cold nor creepy, CJ continued to feel uneasy. The night seemed endless, the quiet ominous. Aware after a time of silence behind her, she got up, and went back inside. By the light of the one shaded lamp she saw Caris-Merian wrapped in her cloak, lying still with her back to David and Detlev.

David lay motionless, obviously asleep. Detlev sat next to him, his head a little bent, his profile somber.

When CJ took a step backward in order to retreat, Detlev looked up. CJ frowned, gathering her concentration for a contact, but Detlev's thought was quicker.

: Randon is on his way.

CJ's shoulders dropped as relief washed through her, then faded, leaving the weight of tiredness. She bundled into her cloak, then framed a contact: *You know how it's going with Siamis and Kessler? Can you nose in from here?*

: I've tried. They are still engaging with wards.

David stirred, and Detlev's head turned sharply. David's eyes opened, moved from side to side without focusing on anything, then closed. Detlev uncorked the water, and lifted David's head so he could drink. David smiled when he was done and appeared to sink immediately back into sleep.

CJ looked away, wondering where to settle for the night. She caught a glimpse of Caris-Merian, still lying there unmoving, but her eyes were open, her gaze wide and unblinking as she glared with undisguised hatred at Detlev and David. CJ shivered, seeing the steady glow of the lamp twinned in those eyes, then she turned her back on them all, and curled up on the ground.

Silence. She was dozing in and out of dreams when she heard a soft, steady plop, plop, plop, and Randon loped in, huffing and puffing. He opened his mouth, glanced at David, shut it again, and gave CJ a thumbs-up sign before picking up his cloak.

He was safe—and Imry Llyenthur obviously hadn't returned yet.

Soon he, CJ, and Caris-Merian were asleep, leaving Detlev to watch beside David through the night.

Twenty

The Dei Manor - Imar

CLAIR JOLTED OUT OF a heavy, fractured slumber. It was Siamis's mental voice: *Clair. Come now.* And an image of the Ethe cup.

She sat up, coughing thickly, and blinking sore eyes. She could not see the others. The vagabond fire was out.

"Clair?" A soft whisper from Zairna.

"Siamis. In my dream. Said to come, and stay with the cup." She rubbed her eyes, which made them feel worse.

Soft sounds of movement made Clair look around. She lost her balance. A hand closed over her wrist. Breath and thought came easier. She crawled out after the others, June still holding on, and following beside her.

They stood up, and looked around at the weird cold, dark fog. Clair felt it trying to seep into her skull, and fought to steady herself.

"Yow," Julian muttered. "I can't see one blasted thing. How are we gonna find that castle?"

"Zairna. Is it not...there?" Clair pointed in a direction that seemed to exude more coldness and darkness then the air around them.

A hand briefly collided with hers.

"Yes. Though I do not know how successful we will be in finding it in this terrain."

As if to prove his point Julian took a few steps, then

stumbled over a pile of wood.

"Here," June said. She held the cup out, though it was now so cold it made her hands ache. Even holding it, the cup was difficult to see; perhaps because they strained to see it anyway, the shadows faded back, leaving the swirling vapors around them, moving in languid, hypnotizing patterns. "Hold hands. We really need to remain invisible."

No one spoke as they progressed slowly but steadily into the shallow valley. Then, abruptly, as if a wave had formed and crashed over them, the shadows rolled toward them, an impenetrable miasma.

They heard nothing, but the quiet was eerie, and the air felt like it was filled with icy cobwebs that brushed and clung. The sense of threat sharpened. June was the leader; at the other end of the line, Zairna kept his free hand near the hilt of his knife. Julian dropped hands to yank her own weapon out with a defiant jerk, but then she hastily put her knife in her waistband, and took hands again.

The edges of Clair's vision smeared sickeningly.

June's mouth tightened, and the glow increased.

No noise existed beyond their footsteps. Nothing live moved, cried, or even seemed to breathe. Before them was what appeared to be an impenetrable wall of shadow. They approached it steadily.

After an interminable journey, light flickered ahead. Weird greenish lightning writhed fretfully about a silhouetted tower, then vanished. They tightened their grips on one another; Clair felt June's hand on her shoulder, and her own hand bumped against Julian's damp sleeve as she convulsively altered her hold.

Their progress was agonizingly slow. The shadowed wall seemed endless. But it was no worse than the intensifying shadows that she perceived on the mental realm. If she relaxed her grip, or her concentration on her mind-shield, she would be crushed into oblivion.

When the wall cleared very suddenly, they found themselves standing at the edge of a marble terrace, looking toward tall, candlelit arched windows. The castle was utterly quiet, the atmosphere unremittingly malevolent with threat. They glanced at one another, too disturbed to be reassured at restored vision.

Clair tried farsense—and instantly withdrew as a

terrifying roar of consuming rage rushed at her. She clung to her mind-shield as she focused desperately on the ice-rimmed cup. A soulless wind smashed past, not just in the mental realm but in the physical too, for her clothes and hair fluttered, leaving her numb with horror.

A door ahead stood open, yellow light spilling out.

Clair and her companions gazed into a beautiful vestibule with a vaulted ceiling. Two grand staircases curved their way up to a high balcony. A splendid chandelier glittered in the light of faceted glowglobes that floated in the air.

"There is no one here to see us. Maybe we'd best separate and search," Clair suggested in an under-voice, and dropped her companions' clammy hands. Sounded carried oddly here.

"Are we not to stay together?" Zairna murmured.

Clair whispered, "Do you really think four of us would be any more effective than one against the Host? If we split to search we will at least be faster."

"We've seen no signs of an army," he retorted, too mildly for it to sting. "One thing about armies is, you really can't hide them."

"There could be an army hiding here. This place is huge." Julian cut insect-fast glances around, wary and taut. "But I agree, four or one, it's probably the same."

Then June said, "What does Tarael look like?"

"White hair," Julian began.

"Free any prisoner." Clair was shivering uncontrollably. "But if we see any of *them*, we leave at once."

"What do they look like?" June asked, looking slightly exasperated.

Julian was no mage, but she had spent time around Tsauderei, Erai-Yanya, and Atan, listening. She said grimly, "You'll know them for what they are."

They each went in separate directions. Clair walked slowly up the stairs. How weird the air was. Reminded her of the slowly shifting currents under the sea. There was an odd pull one way, then a shift to the other direction. The air seemed to sparkle darkly, but always at the edges of her vision. When she tried to focus directly, she saw only marble stairs, carved statuary, tapestries depicting a lot of people in old-fashioned clothes, most of them fair-haired. A portrait, larger than most, gazed down from the landing of the stairs. The woman had Liere's eyes.

Clair reached the second floor. Turned slowly. A group of dark-clad phantoms drifted across the hall to her right. They faded, and Zairna emerged through the dissipating shadows. Candlelight gleamed on his tousled hair, on his clothing. He was real.

"Nothing on this half of the floor." His eyes expressed question.

"I'll search the rest," she stated.

"Then I will go up that stairway." He pointed off into the sparkle-shadows to her left.

"Um."

He vanished up to the next level. Clair forced herself to move down the hall, and one at a time open the three doors she encountered. One revealed a splendid library, like the others candle-lit by magic. One a music room, one a kind of parlor. All exquisitely decorated, all empty of life.

As she closed the last door and turned to the stairway leading upward, shadows seemed to flow down toward her. Yet when she jerked her chin up and faced the stairway squarely it was brightly lit by candles in sconces up the walls.

: *Please come.*

The call tugged at the outside of her mind, but evaporated when she concentrated on finding identity. Could it be Tarael? She was terrified to attempt mental contact, but she could, and did, make herself mount the stairs at a quicker pace.

At the top the inner pull was stronger.

: *Come. Come. Please —*

Gently the darkness buffered the edges of her vision, until the stairway was a golden-lit tunnel ahead.

"Tarael?" she called, her voice high and squeaky and flat. As if it didn't reach much farther than a few steps. "Tarael," she tried again, but the result was even softer. A cold weight pressed on her chest when she tried to draw a breath.

She paused, rubbed her eyes, tried to concentrate. But the call persisted. And when she turned, two cloaked figures moved sedately through a wall, and disappeared. Ghostly hands reached for her, but no, that was drifting smoke from an unseen fire. Once again her feet shuffled onward, mounting narrow steps. A cold wind soughed behind her, muffling a vaguely familiar voice.

"Who was that?" she asked, hoping that the effort of speech, the sounds, would help her hold on reality. "Who calls me? Not Puddlenose. Someone – up there."

Up yet again, though the darkness was closing in. She jerked to a stop, as if the angry hand had let go the strings. Ahead yawned a fog-wreathed chasm. Darkness leading down, down. She stared across it to where a female form lifted her hands. She wavered grayly as if seen through water. "Come."

"Tarael? Is he there?" Clair tried to breathe, but felt suffocated. "Do you need help?"

"I need *you*. Come."

Clair lifted a heavy hand, and pointed at the chasm.

"I will help you." And her breathing eased, just a little.

Clair made an immense effort and took a step. See what is real, her inner voice cried, but the sense of what it meant dissolved like the fog. She frowned, trying to recapture the urgent thought, then said, "Tarael?"

"We will get him together."

"Get? Get?" Clair repeated stupidly. Warning sharpened her vision for a heartbeat. She stopped moving toward the chasm, and braced herself against the wall. "I am here to rescue him."

The girl laughed, a soft sigh of sound. "Come. I will explain. We will find him. Free him. Whatever you want."

The warning voice peeped more insistently. Clair leaned against the wall to steady herself, and tried to bring the words into focus. "Wait."

The girl made a sharp movement with her half-visible arms.

Clair jolted, the abyss now reaching up to suck at her disintegrating mind. A last despairing cry from her inner mind flared into just enough of a warning that she did the only thing left: she abandoned her stone-heavy body altogether, diving inward into unconsciousness, while directly below, two floors down, June found a spacious kitchen full of fresh food.

She decided to steal some, grabbing only light things that would still afford some of the nutrition that they all so badly needed. She kept the two doorways always in view, and thus saw Zairna appear framed in one.

"It's Clair," he said.

She laid her bundle down and came at once.

"Something lured her upstairs, and she didn't hear me when I called her."

June grimaced. "Should we go invisible?"

Zairna assented as they dashed round a balustrade and up another flight. "Might be a good idea. And we'd better not separate anymore."

June concentrated. The cup was crusted with ice, and she sensed that the others were enclosed in a bubble of air conditioning, only how that had happened, she had no idea. But it seemed to keep them separate from the castle's toxic atmosphere. They ran upward, arrived at the top of a stairway to find Clair lying very still on a landing with two narrow halls leading off. There was no sign of anyone around. No sign of wounds or violence, but Clair's blanched face was an unpleasant match for the white of her long hair, and the marble flooring beneath it.

June touched Clair with the icy cup. She recoiled, then sat up. Her gaze turned at once toward the flat, half-shadowed wall of the alcove between the two doorways. She stared intently at the wall in a way that creeped both the other kids out, then she gave a faint sigh "Gone," she said.

"Who?" June asked.

Clair's eyelids flickered in surprise. "There." She pointed to the wall, then her brow furrowed. "Don't you see that chasm?"

"I see a wall." June took a step, gave a light rap with her knuckles. The sound, the light of the cup illuminating the cream-colored plaster, caused Clair's eyes to focus, then she got to her feet, shaking her head.

"I guess you don't see the phantoms, then? They're all going that way." She waved eastward, then looked at Zairna. "You know what they are?"

"No, but I have a couple of ideas. Let's get away from here."

They started down one of the corridors, Clair's steps lagging, her face a mask of concentration. Zairna was going to leave her to June and find Julian, so they could stay together, but Clair gave a soft exclamation and started forward. June reached—Clair was beyond her grasp.

"Sheris?" Clair called. She stumbled down to the last door, then turned. "June, it's Sheris. How did she get here? She lives in Teldenor, south of Mearsies Heili."

At least Clair no longer sounded weird, but June didn't trust anything in this dump. "Sure this isn't another of your phantoms?"

Clair paused outside the door, grimacing in effort. "I don't know," she finally said. "I can't tell any more. But if it really is Sheris, and she is a prisoner, I must try."

The other two made no move to stop her, but stood like sentinels, ready for anything, as Clair unlatched the door. They looked in on a small room, bright-lit with the same steady golden glare. On a bed a brown-haired girl in a rumpled yellow gown lay face into a pillow.

"Sheris?" Clair called. And when the girl did not answer, "I'm real, but I can't come in. There's some kind of barrier across the threshold."

The girl sat up, turning a blotchy, tear-smeared face toward them. Her brown eyes were wide with a kind of hope that was painful to see.

"Here." June took an experimental step, then another, and another, walking across the threshold. Zairna and Clair felt the wards tear away like old webs.

Sheris sobbed as she leaped off the bed. "They got you anyway? They wanted me to go into Mearsies Heili to…" She shivered. "How did you come here? And where are those horrible Norsundrians?"

"Gone, but we don't know where, or for how long." The rescue of a real person seemed to infuse Clair with purpose. "Let's finish looking in those rooms over there, and then get out of here."

While they did, Julian progressed slowly from one magnificent room to another. She was used to magnificence, greater and older than this, and did not pause. She trusted nothing: the silence, the light, the apparent emptiness of the rooms. Consequently she lurked in doorways, scanning thoroughly before she passed through.

It was in a tall-windowed library that she found the morvende mage Tarael. She edged in, busy searching over the shelves of books, the beautiful gray and blue and gold carpet on the floor, penetrating every shadow. She almost missed him, and was startled when she saw the white-haired man sitting motionless in the tall-backed, blue-upholstered wingchair before the fireplace.

He stared into the empty hearth, no emotion in his face. Not even recognition when she crouched in his line of sight. Was it really Tarael? His face was a morvende mask. For a sickening moment she thought he might be dead, and propped up here to scare people — it did seem like something the Host would do — but she observed the rise and fall of his breast beneath his tunic.

She touched his arm. "Tarael? Is that you?"

She was ready for — anything. Still, it frightened her when he turned his head and incurious amber eyes lifted to her face. She had spoken in the Sartoran variant used in Eleyad's geliaths, yet his gaze returned to the fireplace, as though he had not comprehended.

"We are here to rescue you," she said distinctly, glancing over a hunched shoulder toward the doorway. "Please. Get up. Come!"

She tried pleading for a few moments longer, but when he remained impassive, she fled back in search of the others.

They were just coming down the stairs. She looked at Sheris, then said, "No Dirk?"

Clair opened her mouth to answer, but then a faint but unmistakable tremor shook the floor, and the chandeliers tinkled faintly, a sweet yet sinister sound, the crystals turning and flaring.

"What was that?" Julian gasped.

"Something horrible has been going on," Sheris said, for they all spoke in Mearsiean. "This night has been the worst one yet."

"Let's get out of here." June frowned, the silver light expanding slightly. The darkness outside seemed to intensify to the same degree.

"Tarael, I found him. But he won't come," Julian said. "I pleaded — tried his language — "

Zairna motioned for her to lead on. They ran to the library, with many looks back over shoulders. In the library the chandelier turned and swayed. Only the figure seated in the wing chair was still.

Zairna stepped up and in a voice of quiet authority said, "Tarael, come with us."

The morvende rose to his feet and followed obediently.

"I hate this," Julian muttered.

They retraced their steps, until they reached the front vestibule. The darkness outside appeared to have coalesced into a solid wall. June pressed her lips together, and raised the cup; she had wrapped her hands in her shirt, but the ache reached to her bones. And yet the bubble of safety widened, including all five of them. Clair reached, tentatively, toward the door. Was that shadow real, or just more of the nightmare?

"Don't go into it," Zairna warned.

Another tremor shook the building, and then another. Walls creaked, chandelier crystal tinkled and clashed. No one reacted, not any more. Time had stopped, and night abided forever.

Sheris began talking in a quick, nervous whisper to Clair, all about how Llyenthur had trapped her group himself when they were leading a party of Rhenish nobles to the border to be sneaked into Mearsies Heili and to safety. "He had them shot because no one would tell him where our secret ways are," Sheris murmured, tears running down her face and dripping onto the marble floor.

They were all sitting by then, in a half-circle facing that black door. June stayed in the middle, the cup in both hands.

"So he stuck me in a tower somewhere, against the time I'd show him our routes, and I'd been wondering how long I could hold out when some other Norsundrian sent me here. And so I've been ever since."

"Has it been bad?"

Tears still flowed, a bright, clear ribbon. Clair realized with heartrending clarity that Sheris had wept so long and so hopelessly she wasn't even aware of it any more.

"Yes," she whispered. "I said I wouldn't do it. Go ask for your help, and bring you out. But sometimes they made me see myself doing it anyway, over and over again."

Clair heard her as if her voice came down a tunnel. She knew that she was only kept from disintegrating by June's will. The silver cup granted enough surcease from the unending bombardment of the will for her to feel shame, and sorrow, at how close she had come to destroying all those lives at home. How could she have forgotten? But the truth was, she had.

She rocked back and forth, arms pressed against her middle. Julian sat with her face covered by her hands. Zairna studied the impenetrable shadow of the door, his eyes narrowed either in effort or in pain—or both. Tarael knelt behind, graceful, utterly isolated. He could have been one of the statues for all the life he exhibited.

She shifted her glance, and then sucked in a terrified breath when she saw the golden light alter outside the bell of June's magic. It was as if motes of darkness grew between motes of light. If it could be called light, for it was more of a glare, a distortion of the glow of candle flame and fire. No shadows fell, and light bleached, distorting objects in subtle ways. The vestibule and its decorations and furnishings looked flat and unreal.

Zairna moved suddenly, turning his head toward the stairs. Did the others not hear those quick footsteps up there? Had to be someone running from room to room, searching. He remembered the weird incident on the upper level, where Clair had seen phantoms, and he knew that whoever it was up there had been summoned to search for Clair. "June?"

June looked up.

Clair watched incuriously as Zairna made a rapid comment in a language outside of Sartorias-deles's Universal Language Spell.

June gave a one-shoulder shrug, and turned to Julian, as Zairna said to Clair, "Can you move?"

She stared at him, rocking back and forth on her heels. He wasted no more time with speech. He got up, went to each person in turn, and put her hands together with the person next. When June touched Julian, she jumped as if shocked. Sheris drew in a long, shuddering breath. Only Zairna and Tarael remained out of the circle. Zairna moved to the morvende, and spoke in a low, urgent voice. Though they were scarcely five paces away, their voices flattened to a mutter. Tarael shook his head once. Zairna bowed, retreated a step, and waited.

And the light vanished.

Disoriented, beyond terror, Clair once again withdrew utterly from the physical realm and knew nothing more.

Zairna had positioned himself deliberately, and he moved fast: left hand touched Tarael's shoulder, right collided with the side of June's head. Neither of the others jerked away, or reacted. He felt the protective magic drop around them just — *just*—in time.

Two breaths, three. The footsteps continued, and a faint flicker of light reflected from somewhere up and to the right. Zairna listened: riding boots, someone with a long stride, searching from room to room. The sounds had descended to the second level. He did not lift his grip, but he mentally checked his knife at his side.

The searcher was coming.

Another sound, from the door.

Zairna turned his head.

Two men stood side by side in the doorway, both looking strained. Zairna recognized Siamis.

Zairna and June both tugged the rest, and they shambled out the door as if they had been chained with stones. The moment they were beyond the reach of the inner wards, a transfer spell seized them all.

Twenty-one

Forest northwest of Imar Noraera

JULIAN WOKE UP LATE, gloriously clean, lazy, and content. Their shelter gave onto a spectacular view over a deep blue lake, surrounded by deep green forest. The blossom-scented cool air drifting over the placid lake felt as good as yet another night's sleep. Tarael sat on a stone nearby, gazing out over the lake, his fine white hair ruffling in the wind.

"Are you all right now?" she asked. "I mean, can you hear us?"

"I can," he said, polite. Reserved. "Thank you." He had the ear-pleasing morvende voice, but it carried no expression. Nor did he look at her, only out over the lake.

She didn't want to say, *Have you forgotten me, Julian Landis?* It was too sickening to have to ask that. She tried again, on a neutral subject. "Do you know where we are?"

"That is Noraera, as we call it. The southern leg of it. We are in the mountains that border Imar, Everon, and Eleyad."

Julian drew in a breath of pleasure. "Then we have to be near your territory, aren't we? Isn't there a geliath somewhere around here?"

"There is."

"Are you going to take us there?"

"If you wish it."

Julian's brow furrowed in perplexity. "What's wrong?" She asked in the morvende language.

"Nothing," he replied.

Zairna appeared then. "We have a meal all laid out here," he said. "Is anyone hungry?"

"Yes!" Julian scrambled past, waking Clair as she did so.

Clair's head and body ached with a deep chill. She gradually became aware of warmth. A pure-smelling breeze soothed her chapped face. Pine, water, blossoms. She breathed slowly, feeling life return to her limbs with each new breath. Presently she became aware of the weight of blankets on her. She opened her eyes to a rough cave-wall above her. Soft bluish light from beyond, and framed in it Zairna sitting with a light-haired man, tall, slender, pleasant of demeanor. Familiar.

Siamis, she realized with mild wonder. She thought about joining them, but couldn't move. Not that she worried, not now. The problem was weakness, not magic, nor threat.

She had forgotten about Siamis. How had he arrived so fast? He had not forgotten about them. She lay back, content to be still and warm and watch the pure pale blue-gray light reflecting off the rugged wind-and-water carved stone. Where were they? Oh, it didn't really matter. They were safe. *Safe.*

She sat up and rubbed her eyes. Sheris, looking concerned, said, "May I bring you something to eat?"

"What I really need," Clair said, "is pure water. Unpoisoned water. And maybe I shall get it myself, because if I move to yon stream, I can get the toxic magical grit out of me as well as off of me." She pointed at her filthy clothes.

She made her way slowly down to the stream that splashed its way downhill toward the lake. The air was warm, the water shockingly cold, but clean and clear. She forced herself into it, gasping, but the cold gave way to a delicious sense of coolness, and so she splashed about, ducking her head again and again, until she felt that she had rinsed the last of the Host palace's residue from her body, if not from her spirit.

When she climbed out she was shivering, and so she lay on a rock in the warm sunshine, and had almost fallen asleep again when a shadow moved across her eyelids. She opened her eyes to see Zairna there, holding out some bread and cheese and fruit. Siamis was not there. "Did anyone say anything about Dirk?" she began around bites.

"Siamis said that Kessler managed to get him out because

of some very complicated ward he'd put over his son when he was born, against just what happened. They were nearly trapped in the process of extricating him. Yet he is safe, and the two of them are hidden somewhere."

Clair gusted a sigh of relief, then stiffened her resolve. "I need to know what happened."

"Kessler and Siamis were endeavoring to break the magic wards over the palace and the adjacent lands. They used a combination of—"

"I don't want to know how," Clair broke in. "Just what."

"Very well. They did not expect to succeed, but to learn something of the Host's magic structure by the process."

His voice was exactly as patient and polite as ever, but Clair sighed, and put her hands over her face. "I'm sorry I was crabby. I want—I want so badly to be home. Tell me whatever you like. I won't interrupt."

Zairna smiled. "Please do, if I am unclear. They used a bluff that Detlev was with them, hoping to deflect some of the counterattack onto a phantom. It worked, at least until they became aware of our presence."

"You mean my presence."

Zairna made a polite, apologetic arc with his hands. "The Host, in their counterattack, were trying to gain access to Kessler and to break through the temporal barrier and retrieve egress to Norsunder. What we saw was the distortion of time and place."

"So that's what the phantoms were! Norsundrians fighting to get through from Norsunder Beyond."

"Yes."

"But you and June didn't see them."

"The seal was very thin, and you were sensitive to it. When they discovered you, they attempted to thrust you through the seal to see what happened. That was before they figured out your identity. They set one of their number to lure you."

"They very nearly had me, too," Clair said, and sighed.

"We were invisible to them until we separated, and then, once they tried to suborn your will, you vanished on them again. But they had shifted themselves in time and place, and so could not shift back without their spells disintegrating."

"That's why we never saw them."

"Yes. They summoned Imry Llyenthur to transfer there

and get hold of you, and as many of us as he could. He must have been the searcher we heard going from room to room. But once we crossed outside the perimeter ward—which we could only do because the cup made us non-existent to the magic—Siamis and Kessler transferred us out."

Clair remembered Tarael's strange demeanor. "Was there magic on Sheris and Tarael?"

"Not much. Siamis said that they prefer to fetter their prisoners by other means."

"That is disturbing."

"Siamis cautioned me to see that you drank as much as you could."

"I shall do so," Clair said, and walked up the little flower-bordered trail, back to the stream.

By mutual consent it was to be an easy day, a day of eating, and sleeping, and resting.

Laughter, conversations, daydreaming, all this Zairna saw in the others, except for Tarael. At night, safe, far from Norsundrians, they made a fire and sat around it. The girls talked, or sang songs. Only Tarael sat, still, silent, his face empty of expression.

Zairna was watching, for Siamis had warned him about this, too.

And so, when Tarael got up and left, Zairna followed. He paced steadily behind Tarael, who walked down into the still forest, the sounds of trickling water heard, even if the source was unseen. Occasionally Tarael paused, and then moved on.

Zairna tracked the morvende deep into the woods, sometimes only seeing the white head in the impenetrable shadows, until at last, Tarael entered a peaceful little moonlit clearing and sat down in the center with ritualistic grace and care.

As Zairna watched from the shade of a great tree Tarael pulled from his clothing something that no one had known he had, a long knife.

The knife now lay across his palm, point toward his breast. Moonlight shafted down from above onto his white head, illuminating his profile, which could have been carved from stone.

Zairna stood behind his ancient tree, as still as the man in the clearing, and waited.

For a long time, nothing moved in the forest clearing.

Then a faint blue glow teased at Zairna's eyes. He was not

certain he was actually seeing anything — that his exhaustion was not tricking his eyes — until the blue glow intensified, then split into two glows. The blue was not quite flowers, though it appeared to bloom. It was not light in the bright sense that "light" usually denotes.

As Tarael sat so still in the center of the clearing, the blue glows split, then split again. Now Zairna could see it more clearly, as if light did bloom, then fall in a thousand tiny strands about the length of one's palm. They faded within a heartbeat or two; he could not tell if they died or rebloomed, or whence the impetus came, but the entire clearing erupted in a startling range of colors, from palest yellow to the violet so dark it was almost black. He could hear a faint, soft zing! A little like the ring of a blade, or the tap of crystal, but so faint the sound blurred as fast as the light.

For a breathless time the entire clearing bloomed with manifold light, and then the blooms diminished in number, diminished, until the last faint green irruptions of color.

Then the clearing was peaceful.

Zairna had no idea what he had seen, but he sensed a sort of benediction. Without knowing if that was a human emotion imposed on something beyond human ken, he drew in a deep breath at last.

Then, slowly, Tarael raised his head to look at the sky, and Zairna stepped out and walked toward him.

"You do not have to carry the evil ones with you," he said, stopping directly before Tarael. The words were simple but the quiet voice carried the conviction of experience.

Tarael indicated the clearing. "So I have seen." Zairna was wondering if he ought to risk asking a question when Tarael said in a low, tired voice, "But there is no going back."

Zairna replied, "I have learned that one's life can never be the same. But it doesn't have to be worse."

Tarael's gaze moved around the clearing, then again up to the moonlit sky. "I am no longer certain what was real." He spoke softly and very slowly. "Two people looking at something see it differently. Which sees the lie? Or are *they* correct, and one makes one's own reality, as nothing else really exists? They permitted me to hope, made me see my desires come to pass, and then exposed them all as illusion. And the things they forced me to do — " He fell silent, staring down at his hands.

Zairna nodded. He'd been the first to see, back in the

palace, that Tarael had not at first responded because he had not believed that it was a true rescue, or that any of them actually were real.

"They found the evil in me, and tried to kindle it. I can take no pride in keeping the geliath keys secret because they made it clear they did not want to know, that I was to be reshaped and sent back among my kindred."

More entertaining, of course, if you have hundreds of years to watch.

Zairna waited in compassionate silence.

"But the tsinge bloomed for me. It never does for them." Tarael lifted the knife in a grip of purpose. "Yet I expect I will never know what during that time I did, and what I dreamed."

He plunged the knife into the ground. "Will you tell my sister I have gone north for a time, and that I am not yet whole, but I seek to be?"

"I will."

Tarael bent his head, a bow that expressed both courtesy and gratitude, then he walked away and his tall, white-haired form was quickly lost among the trees.

Zairna retraced his steps, where he found everyone but June asleep.

"Where is Tarael? He okay?" June asked.

"Yes," Zairna said, and repeated the message to Siamis, who said, "Ah. I know how to get that to his sister."

Zairna bowed his thanks, rolled up in his blanket and lay down to get some long overdue rest.

On the other side of camp, Clair was alone.

Siamis approached. "May I sit down? I think we need to talk a little." He observed Clair who was, despite her calm demeanor, too thin, too pale, her eyes bruised-looking. He hated having to break the illusion of peace.

She looked up. "I have so many questions." She hesitated as well, her grave brow faintly puckered, and then said, "Or is this your inquisition, and not mine?"

Siamis smiled faintly. "I have to leave soon, for there is much that needs my attention. The others are busy elsewhere, and Zairna will be able to answer the rest of your questions. What I have to say is for you alone."

Clair sighed inwardly. Of course she knew what troubled Siamis, for with the pure air and natural warmth came a return of clear thought. She felt guilt, remorse, shame—and with all those came amazement that she, who had always prided herself on careful consideration and decisions made as objectively as possible, could have persisted in a quest that had nearly destroyed her.

She knew it. She also knew that she would think long and hard about the chain of little decisions that had led her into that terrible palace, risking not just herself, but an entire kingdom of people who had come to her for safety. But it was one thing to scold oneself, and another to have an adult chastise her.

She said, "Will I escape the worst of your reproaches if I promise never again to leave Mearsies Heili, no matter what duty seems to beckon, until the war is ended?"

She should have known that Siamis, like Detlev, was never obvious, or belaboring. "Why," he asked, "do you still bind yourself with the Child Spell?"

"Bind," she repeated. The question, so unexpected, struck heat into her face. Anger, defensiveness. Embarrassment: somehow, though she still maintained her mind-shield, he seemed to intuit that the Child Spell had ceased to represent freedom to her, and had become a restraint, like once-comfortable clothes that were now confining at every seam.

Her failure, and the rescue, made her feel she owed him an answer. "All my memories of my mother are bad," she said. "I know from records that she was a happy child, close to her sisters, though my uncle was sour and morose from the start, I think like his father. But then they all grew up, and Mother hated my aunt because Puddlenose's father chose her instead of Mother. Love — lust — whatever you want to call it. I didn't want any part of it, though I understand now that I took the exception for the rule." She paused, her mouth long, and Siamis sensed that she was thinking of her morose, frequently drunken mother.

She was going to add that she worked hard to learn, to study those who showed good judgment, to do a good job despite staying this side of puberty, but then she closed her mouth again. Either her life so far stood to prove it — or it didn't. Self-justification was just so much wasted air.

While she thought this, Siamis considered the little he knew of Clair and her friends. The girls had all come from unenviable environments, found by Clair, and adopted. Like cleaving to like. Had they all been raised affection-starved? Probably.

Siamis said, "You have been around long enough to see

that all adults don't let their passions direct their lives."

"But too many do," she said. "And they all have excuses. Or misery." She thought of Senrid, but did not speak his name.

"It is learning to master that, and the insight that mastery affords, that permits long vision," he said. "And clear vision."

Clair looked down at her hands in her lap. Her eyes stung. "I'll learn it," she vowed.

"At what cost? Or whose?"

She flinched.

He went on. "Do you understand that the highest motives do not justify stupid behavior?"

She whispered, "I know."

Siamis said, his eyes kind, his voice grave, "You girls talked yourselves into this journey of yours because you really believed that you're just as smart as any adult, and at each juncture, when you should have evaluated the signs and made the decision to return, you—not the others, but you—kept going because surely someone who went to rescue the tormented would escape the pitfalls that awaited adults and their passion-clouded minds, their foolish desires, and their tarnished intentions."

Clair was silent.

"You really believed that you, and only you, could rescue the prisoners from the Host, because only you had truly selfless motives?"

"No," she said, heartsick. "I know better than that. I know that high-minded excuses don't keep a person miraculously free. At first we just meant to spy, a group of easily overlooked teens. Then we found out about the prisoners, and, well, it didn't seem that you adults were going to do anything."

"A faulty assumption that would have been easily corrected, had you asked."

Clair frowned, about to deny, then she brought her chin down in agreement. "Yes. And from then on, as we got closer, I couldn't think that clearly because of that magic. The thought of the rescue gave me purpose, and purpose kept me going." She crossed her arms. "You are saying an adult would have seen the mind-clouding magic sooner, and turned back?"

"Not 'an' adult," Siamis said. "You know as well as I do that each individual, of whatever age, is different. But you as an adult would have, that I do believe." He got to his feet. "I think I've said enough on that subject."

"I'll go home," she said again. "And I intend to stay there."

"Yes, I know that," Siamis said, and smiled, but it was a sad smile, almost a tender smile. "But we're having this conversation because you still do not really comprehend the cost, and I fear that you will be the one to pay it."

She stared up at him, and then remembered that he was the one who, at age twelve, had been taken by the Host. For centuries. Until everyone he knew — every place he knew — had died, or been changed forever.

Everyone except Detlev, who had surrendered as a last-ditch effort to save him. And very nearly hadn't.

"Cost," she repeated, and the terror was back.

Siamis said, "Ilerian of Norsunder now knows who you are."

Twenty-two

Mountains outside of Larkadhe

THE NEW DAY BEGAN innocuously enough for CJ.

She woke as dawn blued the entrance, where Detlev made a silhouette, his head bent. He didn't look as if he had moved since nightfall.

"Oh," she whispered, remorseful. "Why didn't you wake me? I woulda been glad to take a watch."

Caris-Merian sat up abruptly, dug fingers into her eyes, and shook her head so hard her braid whipped back and forth. Randon's head popped out of his cloak, his pale hair messy. He gave a gigantic yawn as he looked around.

Detlev said to CJ, "I wanted to monitor David for a night. He will waken soon, and I believe we will have to start at once. Why don't you fill the water bags?"

"Sure." She caught them as he tossed them, and Randon followed CJ out.

They kept a wary eye for local life; so far, none. Residual effect of Llyenthur's violence.

CJ tried not to look at the burned buildings, and instead let her eyes rest on the new light washing over trees, grass, and flowers. "Well, how was it?" she asked Randon, breathing deeply.

"Boring. Just lying there. Coupla guards stuck their noses in from time to time, but I kept my eyes shut. Then, some time at night, I got these bad feelings. Maybe it was just being in a tall body for so long, but I didn't want to take any chances."

"I don't get it. Tall body?"

"When you do a size so different from your own, you feel sorta stretched out and weird, if you do it too long."

"Oh, that's right. Falinneh said something about that, a long time ago. She said it was much easier to copy kids."

"I thought the weird feeling was that, but I wasn't sure. The next guard who peeked in, I peeked at her, copied her, and stuffed the pillow down into a person shape under the blanket, not that I suppose it would fool anyone long. Then I picked the lock and left, using everyone's face I saw along the way, one after the next, just as Detlev told me to do. But whew, that many copies all at once kinda takes the stuffing out of you. How's David?"

"Just sleeping. Detsie said he's in rotten shape."

They found the stream, filled the bags, and made their way back through a cackling wake of loose chickens, who scolded them for feed that no one was going to bring.

"Go on," Randon said, shooing at them. "There are seeds all over the place, you lazy birds!"

The chickens squawked and fluttered, then went right back to clacking and scolding.

CJ and Randon found David on his feet, Caris-Merian nearby and silent. She handed them their packs, and Detlev said, "Let's go."

"Thanks for the bailout, Randon," David said in Randon's direction, though his brown eyes gazed unseeing at the wall.

CJ shuddered, her insides cramping with horror and pity.

"Oh, sure," Randon said with fake cheer. "No problem. That Llyenthur twit never came around at all."

"He was kept away on other errands, I believe," Detlev murmured. "And he has not yet returned. Let's get as far into the hills as we can before he does. The palace probably knows by now that David has escaped, but my guess is that Imry's guards will first search the entire building, and then the immediate surroundings, before they dare to let him know. We have that much time before Imry himself commands the search. We must get as up into the mountains as fast as we can."

Nobody argued.

Detlev turned his head. "Caris-Merian, will you find us a trail, and run point? I'll stay in the rear and obscure our path."

Randon and CJ stationed themselves on either side of

David, who seemed to walk all right, except he kept his fore-arms braced across his middle. The two were good guides, conscientiously warning David where and how to step.

Detlev stayed in the back, as he'd said. At first CJ tried to divide her time between her job and watching Detlev, but he never seemed to be doing anything more arcane than looking about him — though he did drop out of sight briefly from time to time.

At first the day promised to be a warm one, but when Randon complained about heat, CJ said, "Didn't you notice all the dew on the ground this morning? Clouds coming. I hope not rainclouds."

"I was too tired." Randon gaped a big yawn. "Ooop! Watch where you put your right foot."

David obediently altered his step, though he no longer murmured a word of thanks after each warning.

Then Detlev said, "Take cover from the sky, coming from your right."

Caris-Merian sidestepped into a thick shrub. CJ and Randon each grabbed one of David's arms and edged him into a big leafy bush that grew along the trail. They all crouched down, David wincing, but silent.

Detlev had faded from sight.

CJ and Randon peered out as well as they were able, and saw nothing. After a while (during which CJ tried not to sneeze — this bush grew a lot of yellow fuzzy things that put out sharp-smelling pollen) Detlev stepped up. "All clear."

He moved back down the trail.

CJ and Randon flung their way past the leaves and turned, each holding out a hand for David — but he didn't appear. After two, three long breaths, they exchanged a look, then Randon lifted his voice. "Need a hand?"

Behind the lattice-work of leaves David knelt still, head bowed. He didn't answer. A breath or two later, Detlev appear-ed again, moving fast. He bent and lifted David to his feet.

CJ eyed David's greyish complexion and compressed lips, sick inside. Randon pursed his lips and rolled his eyes at her in question: if David was like this now, what was it going to be like, hiking at night? Or tomorrow, when they reached the steeper trails?

They knew that even with the shortest route they had a two or three day walk ahead of them before they reached the high country. And then there was no guarantee that the flyer folk would come to help them.

David shuffled forward. CJ and Randon reassumed their guardianship, but the easy hilarity of earlier had gone.

The ground began sloping upward, the shrubs thicker, and overshadowed by wide-branching trees with glossy dark green leaves. Caris-Merian was barely visible ahead, the dappled light flickering over her messy dark braid and her rumpled clothes as she scanned continually. She picked out a trail that afforded them as much cover from the sky as possible, which meant a lot of zigzags.

The shadows had shifted when Detlev called a halt for food and rest. CJ knew that the rest was for David; the walk hadn't even made her breathe hard.

They sat down on a mossy spot, surrounded by little sprigs of sweet-smelling herbs. CJ found the air bracing, and knew why Detlev had picked the spot, but David did not react, just knelt, one of his long hands pressed against his side, his head slightly bent, eyes closed, expression utterly closed. Randon looked worried; Caris-Merian kept her back to them all.

David didn't eat anything, though he drank some water when Detlev brought it to him and fitted the cup to his hand. And he didn't speak when they started walking again. His face stayed closed, inward. CJ knew that look, it was one of endurance. It unsettled her, to see him looking so, well, so helpless, if it made sense to call him helpless when he was still the tall, strong David of the bad old days, unbeatable in action. But the shadows of ribs around the bandage in the open neck of the huge black shirt, the sightless brown gaze, even the bare toes moving so tentatively forward, all made him look pretty unthreatening. Now she — who loathed shoes — wished she had taken the time to find him some.

Halfway up a pine-dotted slope, David suddenly recoiled as though he'd walked into a wall. CJ's guts cramped as though an invisible, icy hand had squeezed her from the inside. Detlev was there instantly, his hand closing around David's upper arm.

"Imry," he said, in answer to her horrified stare.

"Discovered David's gone? And, what, attacked?" She tapped her head.

"Yes. Will you monitor our tracks?"

"Sure." Her face burned. "Um, MV showed me some stuff

when I was in Alcandamer last—whenever it was," she said, trying to sound reassuring, though she was very aware of her limitations. But I'll do the best I ever have, she promised herself inwardly.

David's steps lagged even with Detlev's help, making their progress slow through the afternoon. Llyenthur's mental attack seemed unending. Once David muttered something in Norsundrian, and up front Caris-Merian stiffened, sending back a troubled glance.

Clouds sailed through the sky, thickening steadily. Though it was a perfectly ordinary spring storm, CJ felt her spirits glooming along with the sunlight.

They walked in silence for a long time more, as the day began to wane toward dusk. Finally Detlev stopped, facing slowly in several directions, and then he pointed off across a rocky hillside.

They picked their way along the base of a cliff as the sun touched the horizon behind them, and then disappeared. At last they reached a hidden glade. Deep in a mossy crevasse behind a thin fall of cold water from a high mountain stream, there was a narrow cave of sorts. CJ now knew how Detlev found places like this—reading the minds of local animals—and was grateful, for she still couldn't do it herself.

David dropped down onto the cool stone floor. At some point Detlev had put his own cloak round him. David clutched it close, though CJ found the air balmy enough. She remembered how sensitive she had felt with her own arm wound—carrying that same terrible enchantment—years ago, and so she dug into her pack and pulled out her own cloak, draping it around David, who didn't react.

Detlev looked up; CJ could barely see the shape of his face. He said in a low voice, "Are you certain you will not need that?"

She shrugged. "He will more than me. It's almost summer. If I get cold, I'll just put on my other duds over these." She shook her head, wanting to get the subject away from herself. "I guess he's getting it pretty bad from Llyenthur?"

"He is indeed."

It occurred to CJ then that concentrating on two people at once must be hard even for ol' Detsie, and so she turned away and helped Randon start a little fire. Caris-Merian had pulled out a share of bread and cheese and was dividing it up. She did not speak at all, and Detlev and David were like a couple of statues, so CJ and Randon had a pretty desultory meal. They ate as fast as they could, then decided to try to get some sleep.

Outside the cave the rain began to patter on leaves. It soon strengthened to a steady shower, adding to CJ's gloom. She pulled on her tunic and her skirt and curled up as comfortably as possible.

There was no use in talking to Detlev now, but if he wanted to rest she meant to be ready to stand a watch. She set herself mentally to waken at the slightest sound. Thus a shifting of gravel and a rustle of clothing brought her awake.

She sat up. The fire had been put out. She could barely make out Randon's pale head near her, and David's not far away. Both were asleep. Farther away Caris-Merian also sat up, her pale face barely visible.

Lightning flared distantly. In the afterimage, CJ saw Caris-Merian's wide gaze, and closer by, two untouched portions of bread-and-cheese. Though as lightning flared again, too distant for much beyond a low rumble of thunder, she saw Detlev pick up his.

"Llyenthur gone?" CJ whispered.

"Yes. I'm going to use this opportunity to scout a little."

"I was going to say, I'll stand a watch if you wanna rest."

"Not necessary," he replied. "But thanks."

"You're not gonna keep going and going until you suddenly splat, like ol' Sartora used to, are ya?"

"I won't splat. I promise." She could hear his smile in his voice. "I'll be back as soon as I can. Keep alert for noise, and don't make any yourselves. The hunt has begun."

"Okay. Uh, that means yes."

Detlev disappeared, as usual without making a sound.

CJ sat up, hugging her knees close and tucking the ragged hem of her skirt under her bare toes. She tried telling herself that feeling chilled was a matter of attitude. Well, or control. Change it — manage it. Of course, it was one thing to issue yourself orders, and another to get your body to pay any attention. She went right on feeling cold.

"CJ?" David's voice was almost inaudible, but it startled her so much she jumped. "Water? Please."

"Sure." She scrabbled for a cup.

Randon woke with a snort.

"Fresh water right outside. I'll get some. Want your share of the grub?"

"No. Thanks. Just water."

She eased out through the crevasse, mostly by feel, and hoped that she would see the water before it landed on her. As she crawled along, patting the rock before moving forward, she paused when she heard the murmur of voices — then wished she hadn't listened.

She scooted farther out, just to get out of range. But then there was the crunch of a footstep beside her, and Randon whispered, "Did you understand 'em?"

"Was in Geth," she whispered back, reaching out — and getting a cold splash on her arm, which totally missed the cup. "Argh!"

"You did, then. She said something nasty, and he was laughing, and it gave me the grips. Tell me, please, I hate not knowing." His whisper was plaintive.

She could sympathize with that: better you saw the monster stalking you than felt it lurking there in the dark. "She said *Why were you ever born?* And he said *You'd have to ask my father that.* Then she said, *I wish you were dead.* And he said, *You can finish what you started — I won't even see you coming.*"

Randon was silent as he considered this, as CJ crouched on a wet, flat rock and once again reached out. This time the cup filled, the fall almost knocking it first from her fingers. When it was full she began to ease her way back, trying not to spill.

Randon muttered, "I don't know what is worse, her, or not knowing what made her that way."

"Exactly," CJ muttered back, then both fell silent as they reentered the tiny cave. "Here I am. Need some help?" She knelt down next to David.

"I'll manage. Thanks."

She couldn't see him, but she felt the effort it took for him to rise on one elbow and take the cup. He sucked up the water as though he'd been parched for weeks; she found out the reason for the thirst when her hand collided with his to take the cup back. He was burning with fever.

"Want some more?"

"No. Thanks." It was barely a sigh.

"I'll get you some just in case," she muttered as he lay back down again.

She made certain he had the cloaks tucked well around him before she scooted away with the cup, which she refilled and brought back, and set it near him for when he woke next.

Randon elbowed her in the side, then thrust a wad of cloth at her — a part of his cloak. "C'mon, we can share. *I* do not have villain cooties!"

She snickered, gratified that he remembered her long explanation of what cooties were — and that only villains had them. She gratefully scrunched down against his solid, warm body. Randon's breathing deepened into sleep almost immediately.

CJ's mind wandered. She thought about Norsunder, and Kessler, and other terrible subjects, all without reaching any insight, or even conclusion. Thinking faded into memories, which in turn metamorphosed into images and dreams.

She was nearly asleep when David gasped.

Llyenthur attack — had to be, she thought in horror.

What was it that Detlev had done for him during the previous attack? She had to try something! Hesitantly she reached toward David — then Detlev's thought flashed into her mind: *Do not use mind-touch. I will be there as soon as I can.*

She snapped her hand back and sat there anxiously by David, hating the thought that there was nothing she could do. He took long, laboring breaths, the kind someone would take if he was holding up a house of bricks and he had very tired arms.

Detlev finally appeared, soundless. Somehow the atmosphere eased. As he settled down, she whispered, "Please tell me what you do? Can I do it?"

"Channel the magic attack."

"Like, you share it?"

"No. It's more like a siphoning off. But you must be able to close off your own identity and your physical location while you do it. It takes training. I'm afraid I will have to wait until later to tell you more."

CJ winced. "Sorry. Go ahead."

Detlev must have touched David, for his breathing eased almost immediately.

Long after what had to be midnight they were still at it, and CJ crept back under her share of Randon's cloak. She slid into sleep without meaning to, and did not waken until Randon poked her in the morning.

"C'mon," he grumped. "We gotta get swimming."

She got up, annoyed with herself for falling asleep. She pulled off her outer layer of clothes and put them back into her pack so she'd have something to wear later, grubby as it all was.

She jammed her share of the stale bread into her mouth as Detlev helped David to his feet, then packed away the cloaks so they'd be dry later. CJ saw that he'd drunk the extra water she'd brought, and she was glad to have helped, even if only that little bit.

They set out into the steady rain.

"It'll make our trail harder to follow," Detlev pointed out as Randon groaned artistically.

CJ sighed, remembering her run with Dirk. Had he gotten rescued? Now was not the time to bother Detlev.

Caris-Merian ignored them all, her face pale and set. After a long, grim hike up the slippery, soggy trail, CJ wondered why the Geth girl didn't just cut and run. But she said nothing to Caris-Merian — or about her.

The rest of the morning she tried to ignore the rain, and to practice good woodcraft skills as they moved higher into forested land. Three times Detlev had them dive for cover. The last time, they actually saw pursuers — a line of Norsundrians working their way up the slope on a lower hill.

CJ and Randon peered down at them from behind a thick shrub, noting the drawn weapons. They scrambled hastily after Detlev, who was now leading them up a tiny valley with a landslide to the left and thick clusters of oak to the right. An animal trail wandered through the luxuriant greenery. They walked single file, as quickly as David could move.

When they were halfway up the trail Detlev peeled off again to lay another false track. He disappeared rapidly in the rainy gloom, leaving no crack or rustle to mark his passing.

CJ watched in envy, muttering under her breath, "If I coulda learned this stuff, I might've volunteered to join the poopsies."

She swung around to check on David, the loose hair coming out of her soggy braid slapping against her arms and sticking painfully. David walked along with his hand on Randon's shoulder.

There was something weird about David. Not his helplessness, so different from days of old. Nor was it his sightless gaze, or his thin, lean-muscled body in the flapping black shirt and baggy pants and bare feet. It was his expression, utterly unlike any she'd ever seen in his face before.

She turned back to the climb. The air was getting colder, the rocky mud more soupy on the feet. She squinted ahead in the relentless downpour, bracing herself for the next steep bit just ahead, when once again David reacted abruptly.

This time he threw up a hand to ward something away, then he stumbled forward to splat full-length into the mud. And when she and Randon sprang to help him up, they discovered he was unconscious.

Randon looked up, his eyes as dismayed as CJ felt. "What now?" he asked, smearing his hair back.

Caris-Merian had stopped a little way up the trail, and stared off into a dark clump of trees. If she'd bellowed the words *I don't care what happens to him*, her attitude couldn't be clearer.

CJ's heart squeezed into a tiny ball of misery. Fighting against it, she turned her face up toward a faint sun-glow behind a thinner patch of cloud.

Still a couple hours before noon.

Twenty-three

DETLEV ARRIVED AT A run.

He knelt and touched fingertips to David's forehead. After a few very long, tense heartbeats, David stirred. Detlev looked up. "He's going to need help walking," he said.

CJ's terror ramped up when she recognized the tension in Detlev's usually unreadable face. "Sure," she said, then stopped. How could she possibly help? "Can he lean with his hands? I'm so much shorter—"

Randon winced with embarrassment and said to his toes, "I'll help. But I don't know how long I can maintain myself at a size beyond what is natural."

"I would appreciate whatever you can do," Detlev said.

Avoiding Caris-Merian's cold gray gaze, Randon eased behind a shrub and came out moments later looking more or less the same, just taller and thinner, the fabric of his clothes flimsier. He and Detlev picked David up, who blanched at the effort it took just to stand.

They started off thus, the three together. The rain increased. Before long all the mud had been washed from David's face, though the thought of how his clothes must feel made CJ shudder.

Detlev made them change direction at one point, and walk in a fast-moving but shallow stream of runoff from the storm. Then they had a difficult climb up a rocky cliff-face, during which they had to scrabble for hiding places. No one spoke unless necessary. The only things they heard for those long, terrible hours were rain, their squelching footsteps, and David's increasingly labored breathing.

Finally Randon stumbled once too often and too hard, and his shirt, stretched thin, ripped across. David crumpled soundlessly to the ground.

"Oh, no," Randon cried, near tears. "I'm sorry. I'm sorry. I just can't do it anymore." And, right before them all, he shimmered and shrank to his normal size, looking worn and miserable in his ripped clothing.

Detlev gave Randon an absent smile, and a small nod; he understood that it was the best Randon could do. Randon breathed somewhat easier as he pulled another, dirty shirt from his pack, muttering about how at least the rain would wash it. CJ breathed a silent sigh of relief, for her long years with Falinneh had taught her something about the peculiarities of Xubarec defensiveness.

Only Caris-Merian burned with disgust, anger – and, deep and unacknowledged – disquiet. She'd forced herself along on this farce half-hoping that the Norsundrians would catch up with them, and shoot her first. But she would not aid them.

What kept her there was her desperate wish to see Detlev betray his true self, to savage one or both of those two stupid brats following at his heels like puppies, or to abandon David and run, leaving them all to the enemy. Something. Anything, to prove that he was a liar. To prove her moral superiority, and his lack.

David stirred, murmuring something under his breath.

CJ flipped her hair back with a loud, wet squelch, then said, "It's getting so dark we're almost as bad off as he is." She pointed at David.

Detlev said, "They will search tonight with a diligence impelled by Imry's anger. I have located a place of reasonable safety, yet we have a ways to go before we reach it."

"I can walk," David whispered, and he made an effort to straighten up.

"Then let us go," Caris-Merian stated.

CJ's and Randon's heads twitched from her back to Detlev.

"This way," he said.

David walked slowly, leaning on Detlev, his face not hiding the effort it took for him to move at all.

"Hey, look. Storm's breaking up," Randon said, squinting

up at a black, star-studded patch to the west. And up to the sky, "Go away, rain."

"Not yet," CJ said. "We're already wet. I'd as soon hide our big fat footprints."

Randon responded with a rude noise, which make CJ snicker softly, and then once again silence prevailed.

After another difficult passage they reached the place that Detlev had selected, an outcropping rimmed with rocks, three sides of which dropped away sheer, some fifteen stories. The one accessible side was wooded with thick, dark, gnarly pine, and huge boulders made a natural doorway, next to which Detlev placed himself.

That it was inaccessible from attack was the best that could be said. It was open to the cold, brisk winds that swept the clouds away, and except for a couple of flat rocks there was only muddy ground upon which to sit.

Detlev helped David to one of the flat rocks, and as the others slipped back along the path one by one to change into their dry clothes, he got the black shirt off and his own extra one onto David, then wrapped him in the three cloaks. David lay shivering as the others forced down their stale bread. He shook his head when offered a share, and that was the last heard from him for a long time.

Randon shared his cloak with CJ again; they sat back to back after a few half-hearted insults about lumpetty elbows and knobby spines.

Then Randon said, "Detlev, how long d'we have to do this climb?"

"I'll show you in the morning. We have perhaps four hours of climbing ahead until we reach the lowest point the mountain folk can reach safely."

"Four," CJ breathed. "Great!"

"Let's get some shuteye, then, and maybe we can be on the road before the sun comes up," Randon said with determination, trying to sound enthusiastic.

And he followed his own advice. It seemed to CJ that he had the same remarkable ability to sleep anywhere, anytime, that Clair's cousin Puddlenose displayed. CJ wished she were so lucky. Her wet hair made her clothes clammy, and she couldn't shift position very well without yanking at the cloak she shared with Randon.

But really, it was because of David, who muttered softly

every now in then in what she was sure was Norsundrian. That sound scraped through her nerves, and as for his difficult breathing, she was certain that that would haunt her dreams for the rest of her life.

She finally gave up on trying to sleep, and just lay there, staring at the sky. The full moon was silver-blue, bright enough to outline Caris-Merian sitting against the rocks on the edge of the cliff farthest from Detlev and David. Her head was turned toward the vista spread out below, the hills just barely discernable. Even as little more than a silhouette, her rigid posture was clear.

CJ turned her back. Exhaustion eventually won over anxiety, and her restless sighs turned into the deep breathing of sleep.

As if released from a bond of silence, Caris-Merian jerked a glare of loathing at Detlev, who raised a hand, palm out. "I realize that you want David as dead as your brother, but I believe it is time to remind you of two things. You may choose not to believe them, though that will not make them any less true."

"I don't believe anything you say."

Detlev went on as if she had not spoken. "First, you are not alone in the world. You still have another brother. You have seen him; you know that he so resembles Leskander they could be twins, though there are several years between them. I want you to consider why you did not know of him until he showed up in the wanderers' city — and why that was the moment when Leskander chose to leave, and to launch his plans. Consider who worked the hardest to erase his existence from your awareness?"

"Les was *not* jealous of him. He wanted to get me away because *you* had ruined him."

"That would only be believable," Detlev said mildly, "if Leskander had known that Laban had been raised by me. But at that time he didn't. He knew only the evidence of his eyes, when Laban first approached him, telling him of their shared heritage and expecting to be welcomed. It was after the boys caught up with your brother that he gave you that excuse for rejecting Laban."

Caris-Merian muttered, "Les spoke the truth when he said that we could not trust our father, that he was a liar. And that Laban's face could have been altered."

"By whom, for what purpose?" Detlev asked. "Harold Dei was long dead by the time Laban joined the others in the wanderers' city."

"He could have been changed to resemble us by you," Caris-Merian muttered, but even she knew it was ridiculous. "How did you get him? Steal him? Or was it you who killed our father?"

"No, and no. Harold Dei sold Laban, then an infant, to me. This after he was exiled for the last time from Everon, and he came to Norsunder, hoping to arrange a deal in his favor."

Caris-Merian retorted with some of her old heat, "What do you expect me to do about it now?"

"I expect you to remember that, if blood relations are as important to you as you have professed, you are not alone in the world."

"Tchah," she muttered in disgust.

"Second, though the fight between your brother and David ended badly, David did not actually kill Leskander. You might not believe Roy, who rescued your brother from Norsunder, but you could ask the Mearsiean Dhana, who was there as well. He was alive. He'd been hidden, unfortunately, by Efael of the Host. It was during that imprisonment that Leskander truly became the hero you always believed, denying Efael what he wanted, though he was without aid or hope. It was a selfless act, unlike his desire to conquer the world—"

"He was not going to conquer the world!" Her hissing whisper was as vehement as a shout.

"He was going to conquer the world," Detlev repeated. "His followers were his army. His weapon—as you are aware—was what we will call vagabond magic, instead of swords and arrows. But you and I know the truth about that magic, do we not? And what do you think would have been the result of that revelation? This war, for one thing, which would have begun on Geth-deles, and after that world was ripped apart, Efael would have brought it here. You know that is true. You were his and Yeres's prisoner for that brief time."

Caris-Merian covered her face with her hands.

"Which is why I sent David to put a mark on Leskander, while I decoyed Efael and his sister. That fight got out of control partly through David's inexperience, but Leskander escalated it when David tried to get him to acknowledge Laban."

"Shut up, shut up, shut up. I don't believe any of it." She

cried that, causing David to stir and mutter feverishly.

Randon and CJ also moved restlessly in their sleep, and Caris-Merian rose to her knees, half-ready to run into the rainy night, but Detlev passed by, saying, "I'm going to make a perimeter check."

He left the cave.

Caris-Merian put her head on her knees and sobbed soundlessly.

CJ woke abruptly much later. The moon now hung over the top of the cliff, and Caris-Merian was half-visible lying in a lump near those same rocks.

Another weak cough; she realized it had been a cough that had wakened her. Detlev was back, sitting next to David.

David said, in Sartoran, "Imry has threatened to release the spell. And I believe he will do it."

His voice was only a whisper, but the sound carried in the utter stillness.

There followed a moment or two of silence, but then David whispered, "No, speak! I want to hear. I need sound. And a sense of the world. Ah...I wish...it was light." His breathing was fast and ragged, as though he'd been running. "He thinks...if I'm a deadweight. You'll leave me."

"He hopes," Detlev said, low-voiced. "It would make his own claims so much more convincing."

A scrape, no more, of stone against stone, from Caris-Merian's end of the cliff. But otherwise silence.

David seemed beyond awareness of anything but Detlev's proximity. CJ could hear his smile as he said, "He thinks I fear death. That surrender is the easier choice."

Then Detlev said in the same smiling tone, "Even in dying—"

"—one can still teach."

Had that saying meant something to them in the past? For it carried more than now-meanings, CJ was sure, as Randon slept on unheeding behind her. It carried memory-meanings, and maybe even changed meanings.

Her eyes blurred with tears, though she could not define why. There they were, outlined in the cool blue-silver light of the moon, Detlev bent protectively, intently, over David, who lay flat under a starlit sky he could not see.

"The blindness," David said, "has helped me to focus the

inner eye. I think he knows that now."

"I can imagine his annoyance." Detlev's voice, unlike his posture, was ironic, light with humor.

"Can you get me past?" It was a quick question, and David did not hide his fear.

"Only if we touch. Remember that."

"I will. I wish I could—ah. So much to do." The whisper was now slow, with regret and longing, and CJ turned her face away and fingered away tears of pity and horror. *David thinks he is dying.* She felt like an eavesdropper, though she suspected that David was beyond caring who heard, and what they thought. Still, she was afraid to move, to call attention to herself. She hoped he thought they were all asleep, if the thought would give him one speck of comfort.

I hate this. She gritted her teeth fiercely against her own emotions. Did Caris-Merian hear him? What could she be thinking?

"When you see Senrid, be sure to tell him—" David gasped, then subsided with a grunt of pain.

CJ forgot her resolve and threw aside Randon's cloak. She scrambled over the rubble to Detlev's side and whispered in agony, "What is it? What happened?"

Detlev slid a hand inside David's shirt beneath the cloaks, and pulled it out covered with a black smear.

"Imry has released the binding spell, and I believe David's lung has collapsed."

"Why? That doesn't make sense! He can't get at him by mind any more, can he? Why would he *do* that? Won't it kill David?"

"Maybe. Imry doesn't need the magic to reach David's mind any more. For a number of reasons. And he doesn't want David to die, but he's taking the risk to slow us down; at this point he has had less sleep than we have, and impulse as well as temper is driving his actions."

CJ stared at David, who was again unconscious, his face thin and eerily pale in the moonlight, his lips black. She wrenched her gaze away.

"Our only chance is to make for the caves as fast as we can."

"Then let's go now." CJ groaned. "How I hate this mess!"

"I'm afraid we cannot leave quite yet. The moon will shortly drop behind the mountain, leaving us only starlight.

The paths we must use are treacherous enough in the light of day, and without pursuers. And David will have to be carried. I do not think he will waken again."

CJ bit back a protest against this calm, logical list. She'd been about to demand if he didn't care, but of course he cared. She could see it, hear it, feel it. So she satisfied herself with a muttered, "Stinking, rotten, fart-brain Norsundrians. If I was alone, I'd go now."

"And die trying," came the inexorable reply. "We have too few resources. Imry has magic, hunters, and now time. We must use everything available to us."

CJ sighed sharply. "I hate it, I hate it, I hate it."

"Try to get some rest. We'll need to be alert come morning."

"Yeah, sure. Sleep." Her voice wavered, and she turned away, hating herself for betraying her feelings, because she knew it did no one any good. She curled up under her half of Randon's cloak, frowning fiercely at nothing —

Twenty-four

AND NEXT MOMENT SHE was being shaken.

"CJ! CJ," Randon whispered. "C'mon, we gotta go!"

"Wha—? Urk."

"Something happened." Randon slid a peek over his shoulder in Caris-Merian's direction, then he leaned closer. "David's not waking up. Detlev said he won't."

"I know. I'll tell you about it when we get going," she muttered, also sidling a glance Caris-Merian's way. Not that she cared if the girl heard, not any more, except it would be horrible if she saw Caris-Merian gloating.

"Here's your stale crust. Got some dirt bits for added crunch."

"Ugh." She prune-faced as she took the hard bread from Randon's grubby fingers, and tore out a bite.

They started off with the dawn light graying the sky above them. Detlev had wrapped David's cloaks tightly around him before he picked him up. CJ turned away when David's head rolled loosely back, his filthy blond hair sliding off his forehead to reveal the taut skin of tension, even in unconsciousness.

Stress kept them moving, as neither had much appetite for the four-day old bread. Detlev led the way, moving steadily along craggy, rock-strewn inclines. They zigzagged their way from the cover of rocky overhands to clumps of greenery, having to pause and hide with nerve-wracking frequency.

Once little stone skittered down from overhead, betraying chasers above. They pressed together under a huge broken slate jutting out from the hillside, and Detlev said, "It is time to call on allies."

"Animals?" CJ asked, trying not to let herself hope.

"And birds. Hawks, most specifically."

They saw, and heard, nothing, merely kept going. Presently CJ and Randon heard a far off hunting cry from a big raptor, followed by angry human shouts echoing down through the valleys. A blow from an eagle's clawed foot was enough to knock one of those hunters clean off the trail. They exchanged looks of triumph: *one for us.*

There were few enough of those. They were still walking, and CJ had begun to permit herself to think that they might just make it, when Detlev ducked under the branches of a huge old evergreen. He put David down carefully on the mat of brown needles, softened by the recent rain, their scent astringent, and straightened up, wiping back his sweaty, tangled hair. "Stay here," he said, and left.

There followed a long, nasty interval which was highlighted by David giving a couple of delirious moans. At first CJ tried to tell Randon about what had happened the night before, but she was too upset, and he didn't press her to finish.

Caris-Merian sat with her back to them and never spoke.

It was late in the afternoon when Detlev returned. The shadow of the mountain west of them had stretched down the slope they were on. Strain still showed in Detlev's face. His eyes went immediately to David, then he said, "Only a little farther. But we'll have to wait for cover of darkness for the fliers."

He picked David up again—no easy task, as David had to be half a palm-width the taller—and led the way out. Up a narrow rocky trail, beneath wind-twisted trees and striated outcroppings. Up, stepping with care, lest one dislodge stones and set them rattling below to alert whoever might be watching.

This time the walk was not as long as the last before. He stopped them again on the side of a cliff, partially sheltered between two great slabs of stone. He set David down, then said, "Here we wait."

"Why?" Randon asked. "They afraid of being seen by Norsundrians?"

"Yes. With reason."

It didn't take any imagination to picture hunting parties of Norsundrians out with their crossbows for some target practice.

CJ and Randon crouched near the edges of their shelter like a pair of gargoyles, gazing fearfully out. No one made any move to fetch any food; Detlev sat with David leaning against him, rather than leave him on the hard, mossy stone. There were no sounds out of David, except for slow, painful breathing, and from the looseness of his hands and head he appeared to be deeply unconscious. CJ looked away fast when she saw the blood on his bluish lips.

The shadows below lengthened and then gathered as above the sky darkened through all the shades of blue. Sunset came — and went, but still Detlev did not move, and CJ realized at last that he was waiting for something. His gaze stayed on the far horizon to the north. What he saw she could not imagine; it had been dark for some time when his head dropped back, his pain unhidden.

CJ pressed her fists against her heart. "What is it? He can't be—"

Detlev's voice was so low she almost did not hear it. "David will not last another hour."

Caris-Merian shifted a little, one foot scraping against gravel.

CJ crouched with her arms locked tightly over her churning middle. "Will they get him? Soulbound? Or can his spirit get free?"

"I cannot say. He is too far withdrawn." Detlev paused, and sighed. "I can't reach him."

CJ frowned fiercely, and was going to give in at last and mutter a really choice string of insults, when a rushing sound brought her head around fast.

Detlev looked up, alert and still again.

Four wiry, slight figures stepped into view, followed by five others.

Not Norsundrians — winged people.

"We must make speed," Detlev said to the leader.

"We were slow to come because we discovered that the evil ones had blocked up the entrance to the jewel cave with rocks," the leader said. "No one can get past."

"But the caves always make a new entrance if creeps block one up," CJ cried. "Sometimes, if there's lots of dark magic wards around, there can be two entrances. I've *seen* it!" Her voice rose to a wail.

The leader of the pale-haired flyer folk glanced her way.

"This we know. I sent two brethren to find the new one, but we dared wait no longer for them. I must say to you that the evil ones know it also, and though I grieve for your friend and his hurts, if the evil ones have found it before we, we cannot land. The peril is too great. Too many of us have fallen in less than four seasons."

CJ opened her mouth to deny, to argue, to plead, but Detlev said, "Very well."

"Less than an hour," CJ whimpered. She hopped from foot to foot. "Let's go, let's go!"

The shadowy figures behind the leader swiftly spread a black cloth on the ground, and a kind of woven litter on top of it. Detlev laid David on the litter and straightened his limbs. David didn't stir at all as he was bound to the litter by the black cloth. Then two more flyers brought a woven kind of chair thing, which was for Detlev; the youngsters were each taken by a single flyer. David's pallet was picked up at the corners by four of them.

Thump, thump, thump, CJ's flyer ran forward a few steps and then flung himself over the cliff edge, dropping far enough that she squinched her eyes closed and felt as if her insides had remained on the cliff. Then whop, whop, whop, up and up they went. She could feel the effort the person made. His arms felt like regular human arms, and he smelled of normal sweat. How had they come to be made, these blends of human and bird? They were shorter than landbound humans, and maybe lighter, though wiry in build and very strong.

And safe enough. She opened her eyes and looked down. She was too upset to enjoy the flight—and too tired, hungry, and dirty—but she looked, because it was better than fearing that the long run would be pointless, that Caris-Merian would win and go away laughing in triumph.

CJ tried not to think, only to watch the night landscape below, which looked strange from this unfamiliar view. The moon hanging low over the edges of the mountains added its own cast of strangeness to the mountain shapes as they flew high and fast over vast peaks. The air was cold at these heights; some of the crests below were dusted with snow, glittering with cold blue light.

Still they flew higher, then finally banked and curved downward toward a line of lower mountains. She wondered where they were. They had to be well out of Visegn, land of nightmares.

Two flyers manifested out of the shadows. There was a short exchange, still at the fast speed, and the two joined the group. The speed increased, until wind numbed CJ's ears and fingers and streamed with stinging strength in her eyes. She ignored the cold, exulting in every evidence of their going faster.

How long had it been? At least half an hour! Where was the Selenseh Redian? She tried to look without moving or twisting—

"There." She heard the leader's voice.

They spiraled down toward a narrow cliff-edge, bare but for a clump of thick trees that had spread from the nearby forested slope. One by one the flyers landed lightly, cautiously. Some of them held knives. CJ pulled her own.

Randon yanked his out as well.

CJ was scarcely aware of flyers taking off one by one, the whoosh and clap of mighty wings on the air. Instead she watched Detlev kneel at David's littler and with rapid movements threw aside the black cloth. Then he lifted David's limp body.

The four of them, flanked by the four biggest flyers, started toward the black mouth of the cave—just as a figure emerged from behind a narrow outthrust of rock, stood directly before the cave entrance, and faced them.

"Imry," Detlev said, unsurprised. The flying folk knew nothing of mind-shields.

Imry Llyenthur sauntered toward them. He raised his hand. At once a sizable number of Norsundrians appeared from behind trees and rocks and flanked CJ and her allies.

The flyers' leader and three companions attacked the Norsundrians. CJ looked around wildly, wondering what to do. Randon! She turned his way; he jerked his chin toward the other side of the ledge, then at Llyenthur. Their duty was clear: deflect the enemy so Detlev could get David past.

Yelling a wild insult in a northern language, Randon ran at Llyenthur at the same time as CJ. Caris-Merian was close behind, silent and grim.

Then several things happened at once.

Detlev dropped to one knee, still supporting David with one arm.

He muttered, pointed, and the Norsundrian soldiers closing in vanished one by one — a reversal of the transfer spell that had brought them up in the first place.

CJ had forgotten that Detlev could do magic, so long had it been. So too had Imry Llyenthur, it seemed, from his reaction: of course the tracers against his use of magic no longer mattered, since he was already face to face with his enemy.

She yelled and swung her knife at Llyenthur, hoping to distract him, and Randon attacked from the other side.

Llyenthur sidestepped Randon's blade. Feinting with one hand toward the boy, who scrambled awkwardly to one side, he followed up with an openhanded slap that struck Randon hard enough to send him crashing against the rocks in a heap.

Caris-Merian leaped over him, knife out, and he looked up, the moonlight full on his face.

CJ stumbled, and gasped. "David?" she exclaimed. Caris-Merian also faltered, shocked.

Llyenthur laughed — and in that moment Detlev threw up an illusion, behind which he took David into the cave.

Caris-Merian and CJ charged, the one toward the cave and the other to Randon's rescue.

Llyenthur assessed in a heartbeat. The flyers had gone, taking their wounded, leaving three of his guards lying motionless. He was alone. He snapped away the illusion of rock, seeing David and Detlev were inside the cave. He ignored Caris-Merian, who slipped inside the cave, and intercepted CJ two steps away from Randon.

Though she was an experienced enough scrapper against another her age, or even a teen, she had never faced a foe like this one. His movements gave no clues to what he would do; his hands seemed to move slightly, slowly, but somehow her knife was wrenched from her fist and she ended up held in an unbreakable grip, her own hair twisted excruciatingly round her throat.

Shoulders, ribs, head ached, but if she moved (what little movement she could manage) the grasp on her hair tightened and she choked.

Impotent rage seized her brain as somewhere over her head a voice she would never forget drawled pleasantly, "Detlev, I never dreamed I would say this to you, but — you know what comes next."

"Yes," Detlev replied from inside. He was walking father in.

"I want David as well."

"You will have to make do with me," Detlev replied.

"Now." And CJ made a gagging noise as her own hair cut off her breath.

Detlev did not appear to notice Caris-Merian, who stood a few steps away, her back pressed against the faintly glowing rock. His eyes searched the inward passage of the tunnel as though measuring the distance and then he silently, carefully, laid David on the ground, pausing only to flick a lock of filthy blond hair from David's closed eyelids.

He straightened up and this time his eyes met Caris-Merian's, for less than a heartbeat. Then he turned away, and walked back down the tunnel toward the entrance.

Caris-Merian flung her knife down with such violence that the steel blade struck bright blue sparks from the rock. She watched as Detlev stepped to the entrance, hesitated, then moved out, hands empty. He stopped a few paces from Llyenthur, just out of reach. For a moment the two studied one another, face to face at last after years of mutual silence, and then Llyenthur moved.

He thrust CJ away, loosed a knife from his sleeve —

And Caris-Merian lifted her hands. Bright color scintillated in the air, off the rock, off all the faces as intense vagabond magic, driven by the limitless power of the Selenseh Redian, shifted not just Detlev, but CJ and Randon into the cave.

Imry Llyenthur sighed, gave them a derisive salute, and vanished.

"Thank you for the rescue," Detlev said.

Caris-Merian made a noise of grief, of anger, of self-loathing, and ran past him, out of the cave, and into the quiet night.

Detlev glanced at the others. CJ wavered weakly to her feet. "I'm okay," she croaked.

Detlev bent, picked David up, and started up toward the glowing colored light at a swift walk.

CJ eased over next to the unconscious Randon, heard breath and heartbeat, and so, safe, unobserved, she put her hands over her face and bawled like a baby.

Twenty-five

Ama-Hazanth

ARTHUR STOOD ON THE city-wall of the capital Torquenda as the sun sank beyond the sea. His expression was thoughtful as he gazed out over the island kingdom from its highest point, his eyes focused beyond the danger so close by him; he appeared to be unaware, or at least unconcerned, with the sheer drop of some five stories a hand's width from his shoes.

Someone eased quietly into the archway at the south end of the wall juncture and stood silently, gazing at Arthur.

Who did not stir. Time passed, punctuated by the boom and crash of waves far below. The last rim of the sun dropped into the distant dark haze, and shadows merged in Arthur's wind-blown brown hair and the wind-ripples in his dark green tunic.

The cold off-shore breeze slowly strengthened. Far below, sea birds circled and landed on the jagged rocks thrusting up from the foaming breakers, their voices spiraling up on rags of salty air.

The watcher observed the rising wind buffeting Arthur, who looked a little like a bird himself, his eyes and chin leading the eye forward to his beak of a nose. Arthur's short, thick dark blonde hair resembled a wind-ruffled crest of feathers, but there the conceit ended: his lanky scholar's body was straight-limbed. Easy.

You shouldn't hate people for being straight-limbed and

easy.

When the fading light had merged the shadows, the watcher stepped out to join Arthur on the wall.

Arthur looked up sharply, and took in the twisted, limping figure. His gaze lifted to the two nearly hidden watchers with their dully gleaming drawn swords, then he cut his attention to the black-clad shadow figure who'd stopped two paces away, and though Arthur was sedentary by nature, and utterly unwarlike, he was glad that Roy had been forcing him to do some rudimentary self-defense over the past year or two.

This shadow figure was bone thin, maybe a bit taller than Arthur, though that was difficult to discern from his stoop. Two narrowed eyes were black slits in a thin, bony face with pain-lines grooved into the broad forehead and from sharp-cut cheeks to narrow jaw. No expression to be read in that face beyond wariness. He wore unrelieved black, with at least three knife-hilts visible about him. Despite the twisted legs, and the cant to the tense body, he moved with a wiry strength that testified to a ferocious will.

When he spoke at last, his voice was so hoarse it was hardly a voice — more like a rasping whisper.

"You could've escaped at least twice," the newcomer croaked. "After you were taken. Why didn't you, unless you wanted to be dragged before the king?"

Arthur betrayed no surprise at this abrupt address — this much Roy had predicted when they had talked over this quest. He returned the intense gaze with his own mild one, then said, "Why do you ask?"

A wide grin from the newcomer, which took many years off. He couldn't be much over eighteen. "I knew it," this surprising figure rasped. "You did get yourself nailed!" He laughed, a sound like a cough from a person with a horrific chest cold. "What's more, you were waiting for me, eh?"

"Let's say I hoped someone might come forward."

"You saw us watching you?"

"I did."

"But you never responded to our signals." The newcomer paused, and Arthur sensed a clumsy contact. He shielded easily against it — in that, too, Roy had trained him well — and the whisper carried a timbre of cautious respect, "Who are you? Not a sailor. A scribe? There's ink under your thumbnail."

"And I thought I had the perfect guise," Arthur said,

knowing how funny they'd find it, for he was in no wise experienced with ships, and nearly everyone on this island had something to do with the sea.

And, yep, there came the wheezy laugh. "Good enough to fool the king's guard. Why did you want to be hailed into The Presence?"

The question was important. Even in the swiftly deepening darkness Arthur could see the intent stances of all within earshot. He said, "It seemed the only way to speak to him without having to divulge my real reasons."

"Which is why you poked around the island? We've known about you since you first came. We watch all strangers. What are you after?"

"Information."

"From the king?"

"I'd thought he would be the one to give it to me."

"But you asked him nothing, and when you escaped from the holding cells this morning, you did not go back for a private interview."

Arthur said, "I learned enough to decide that further conversation with your king would be a waste of time. I came here to think about what to do next."

"And?"

"And if the people who'd been shadowing me ever since my arrival did not come forward, I'd go back empty handed." Arthur grinned, his beaky face slanting in appealing lines.

His raspy-voiced inquisitor smiled back, then said, "You are not a Norsundrian."

"No."

Arthur heard a stirring from the darkness in the archway, and a whisper: "A six-patrol moving north."

"It's enough," Arthur's companion said over his shoulder. And to Arthur, "We're not either. We're not with any of 'em. Come with us? I can't promise to help you unless it'll help us, but I will promise you safe-conduct."

"Lead on," Arthur said.

And so, within a very short time later, when the king's patrol appeared from what they thought was the only access, they found merely a windswept stone parapet and the sound of nightbirds from far below.

The broken, uneven stairs seemed to be moving, Arthur thought grimly as they descended a narrow passage in the thick stone wall, lit only by a wildly flickering torch held high by one of the silent dark clad figures, most but not all, young. They were fast, used to the mossy, worn steps, and Arthur had to watch his feet. The others never seemed to glance down; long habit made them hop, jump, or veer over ancient obstacles.

The stairs ended abruptly at a solid granite wall which then slid with a muted grating sound into the perpendicular wall, leaving a narrow, inky passage.

One by one the others slipped inside, Arthur following in his turn. The rock rumbled into place behind them. This passage was totally dark, and at least it was flat, but so narrow that a slight sway crashed one's shoulders into rock. The torchbearer stepped through last, and light flared headlong down the passage. Arthur saw that most of the figures walked slightly sideways, except for their leader, who was too bent; he walked with one hand out, bracing against each step on that side.

They stopped in a stone chamber. At one end a tapestry hung down. Most of the youths kept right on going through the tapestry. The young teen carrying the torch jammed it into a crack between two stones that obviously served as a sconce, and then left as well.

Arthur and the hoarse-voiced leader were alone. Directly below the sconce-crack was a little table, and around it rugs and pillows.

"Have a seat." The leader dropped onto pillows himself.

Arthur sat down across from him.

Before either could speak a rustling noise came from the ceiling, and a black shape emerged from an equally black slit, wriggled free, and dropped down, sailing: a crow. The bird flapped to the table and perched on the edge.

Arthur watched the bird and the boy regard one another intently, and knew they were communicating. Absently the boy raised his thin hand and stroked the bird's breast, then the crow took off with a racketing of wings and a moment later it had crawled back through the stone-slit and vanished.

"They are why the others call me Crow," the boy said to Arthur. "And not because of my minstrel voice." He laughed, a rusty, coughing sound. "What are you after?"

Arthur had a fair idea who this boy was, now, and replied without any further hedging, "A long time ago, I came across a very old list in the archive at Bereth Ferian." Seeing a puzzled frown, he said quickly, "An archive. At the northernmost end of this continent. Anyway, it was a list of the world's protections, and it included the Fire Ruby of Ama Hazanth. I came to ask for it to be loaned, or used, in the fight against Norsunder."

Prince Marseth Ghandorjien, otherwise known as the Crow, wheezed and rocked with laughter, then finally said, "Go back home, scribe. That thing isn't going anywhere." He limped away, still wheezing.

Later on, it became clear that that was to be his last interview with the Crow or any of his followers.

Arthur gave up, and wrote to Roy:

I failed with the Fire Ruby. If Captain Heraford is still out there at sea, I'll start the long journey back. Arthur

Twenty-six

IN THE SELENSEH REDIAN high in the Ghildraith Mountains, Randon yawned, snorted, then sat up and assessed the passage he'd settled in. So far, it pretty much looked like any other cave. "Ow," he muttered, wincing. "I've got bruises on top of bruises." He gently fingered the side of his face that had met Llyenthur's hand.

A few paces inward, CJ sat up as well, grubby, her face smeared with dust.

Randon was relieved to see her there. Then he blinked his one good eye in surprise. "Hey! We're not dead! What happened? Are we really safe?"

"Yup," CJ said. "You and I are. And ol' Detsie, too. I don't know if David was still alive when they went inside, and I'm too chicken to find out. I've been waiting out here for you to stop sawing logs."

"My head aches like ten anvils fell on it, and I think I bit my tongue when that puke-face smacked me. It hurts. Want to see?" He stuck out his tongue, and after CJ grimaced and made a gratifying noise of disgust, he went on, "Speaking of a big pain, where's Caris-Merian?"

CJ snickered. "She ran away."

"To the Norsundrians?"

"I dunno. That rat-gizzard Llyenthur tried to strangle me, so even after he let go I was a little out of it for a while. Weird.

He looks just like David. Not expressions, not at all, but the rest." She touched her own skull. "Oh, this has been a rotten adventure." She shivered, hugging her arms close.

Randon gave a decisive nod. "I've had better, even when I lost."

CJ said, "Your headache will go away if we go farther in. We should feel better, I think."

"Then why aren't you there?"

"Because I won't feel better if David croaked, you fungus brain! Just hot, and weird, and creepy. Because the caves can do that, too. If you go, I'll have the guts to try."

Randon eyed her. "Could you really leave without finding out one way or the other?" As he spoke he was still feeling the side of his face. "Wow, I really need practice in knife work. That snake wasn't even armed."

CJ sighed. "I don't know. While you've been snoring I've changed my mind ten times. Eleven times."

"Aw, let's go." Randon got up slowly and winced. "If this place gets rid of the headache, at least I can help plan what to do next. Which way?"

"Toward the colored light. And don't mind the heat. You won't burn up."

They walked slowly inside, Randon sucking in his breath in surprise and pleasure when they came upon the glowing jewels.

"Wow," CJ exclaimed, aware of how sound resonated here. "I'd forgotten how beautiful it is. It's been so long since I was in one, all I remember is the weirdness."

Her face began to relax as she looked around at the rainbow array of colors, some gemstones large, some small, most crystalline in shape and facet, and all with fiery color glowing deep within. Measureless numbers of gleaming stones furnished a glareless spread-spectrum light full of magic.

Randon was so transfixed with wonder he never even noticed when his headache faded and the other hurts eased. As they walked, she talked about past experiences in the Selenseh Redian that was located in Mearsies Heili.

"How many are there?" he asked, tipping his head back in wonder. "Why didn't I know about them before this?"

"Somebody said there are seven. All in weird places, a million miles from where humans live. Except ours."

"Wow. Wow. Wow."

CJ had meant to suggest they go on only until they felt better, but somehow the time to stop never seemed to come. They were drawn on, always wanting to see the next cavern, which was surely even more beautiful, the almost inaudible ting from the crystals. Even that sensation of heat was good, for it manifested itself as warmth to tired, chilled, bruised and half-starved bodies.

It was a pleasant surprise when they rounded a last corner filled with healing light and pure, sweet-tanging air, and found Detlev and David both asleep.

Asleep, not dead, both breathing quite naturally, David with healthy color in his face.

CJ let out a sigh that seemed to ease all the way down to the insides of her toes, then she elbowed Randon and jerked her thumb back the way they had come, but then Detlev opened his eyes and lifted his head. He'd been sitting next to David, who lay stretched out on his three cloaks.

"He's really okay?" CJ whispered.

"He has passed the crisis."

She sighed again, the sound reverberating just enough to sound like a whispered musical note, and sagged down. Randon wandered the perimeter of the space, smiling and looking closely at the gemstones. He turned to say, "This is great! You made it sound like being cooped in a jeweled fireplace with a cranky ghost."

CJ shrugged. "That's the way I remembered it. But Detsie, what happened to Caris-Merian? Did she get nailed by the skunks?"

"No. She left after they did," he replied.

"And that was vagabond magic that she made, wasn't it? That saved us? Was that really her?"

"It was."

"Then she could have done that at any time?" Randon demanded, hands on hips.

"Yes."

"Well!" CJ snorted, though her annoyance faded almost immediately. "How did she learn it, and why didn't she use it?"

"It was her brother who discovered it, and so she knows it as well as any. He taught her. But as for using it, that was not so simple."

"Her brother... Oh, I see. Les Rhoderan, wasn't it? I remember some things the others said. When we were on Geth that time, he was this big hero, but a few things others have said since—" CJ frowned, reflecting on how difficult it must have been for Caris-Merian to slog up a mountain in pouring rain with them, and not use it to get away. Why wouldn't she, when she hated them so much? And then to use it to save them...

Detlev said, "The worst of her hatred has been reserved for herself, ever since she stabbed David."

"Okay," CJ said, but she was remembering bits of Caris-Merian's scowling thoughts that she'd accidentally descried, and wondered if the Geth girl had set some kind of silent test for everybody else, and when they did not fail, she had to act.

Weird. Horrible. What would Caris-Merian do now?

But it was hard to hold onto painful emotions here. "At least we're okay now. Will *she* be okay?"

"I think it is possible." Detlev smiled, then added, "Especially if all of us stay out of her life for a time."

"With pleasure!" CJ responded. "But—poor thing, to be out there still cold and hungry in those mountains, all alone, and we're cozy in here." She glanced down at her filthy skirt, and sighed in pleasure. "And we can even do magic in here!"

"We can indeed," Detlev said.

He and David were already clean. Clair had taught CJ the series of spells that were akin to setting up a little one-time cleaning frame. A little proudly, showing off her magical knowledge, she muttered them, and her clothes and skin and hair zapped into cleanliness.

Randon was faster. He grinned at her, his pale curls ruffling over his head once again.

CJ sighed, her attention on Detlev. "You did magic, there, at the end. I know Llyenthur had wards against you, but what about the Host?"

"My gamble was that Imry wanted me himself enough to have fouled their wards. It turned out I was right."

"Ah," CJ said, and her gaze rested on David's face, which once again seemed...peaceful. She realized she was seeing him without that habitual ready-for-action challenge, the anger below the slouching demeanor he'd presented to the world. The not-quite-hidden anger had made his lazy smile creepy. That had vanished on the mountain.

"They really are brothers," CJ observed, turning over that uncomfortable idea. "Somehow I always thought villains didn't have families—that they hatched."

"Just like a snake," Randon said in a dramatic hiss.

"Some snakes are nice," CJ protested. "What have you got against snakes?"

Detlev ended the potential snake argument by reverting to the subject: "David hadn't seen him since Imry left the group."

CJ thought back to something MV had said, a thousand lifetimes ago. "Would that have been before Siamis's second attack, the time we went to Geth?"

"He left us just after that episode."

"Mmm," she said, aware that now she was just being nosy. "Why?"

"His plans for his future did not coincide with mine."

CJ grinned, accepting this.

"Well," Randon said, rubbing his hands. "One thing for sure, and that is, he's on my sna-skunk roster, whether he's got lighter relatives or not."

"Mine, too." CJ frowned. "Trying to strangle me with my own hair." She stood up and whirled around. "Wow, I feel great. If only I knew —" She turned to Detlev, whose eyes were narrowed with considerable amusement.

"Clair is well and on her way home. I believe right now they are sleeping in the mountains of Eleyad, her companions safely with her."

"Dirk?" CJ asked.

"Kessler has him. I do not know where."

Relief! "You've been doing a lot of checking around," CJ observed. "Could you — would you — of course if you're too tired..."

"Who?" He smiled, irony pronounced, but not in any bad way.

Encouraged, CJ said, "Falinneh and Sherry. They were with Caris-Merian when they got bagged, and nobody's heard from them since. Or hadn't, at least, since I had a magic-paper."

Detlev's eyes took on an inner focus as CJ watched anxiously. Finally he looked up and said, "Siamis assures me that they are making their way back toward Mearsies Heili."

"Oh, well, great." CJ laughed in buoyant relief. "Clair on her way home — girls too. With any luck Puddlenose will be back —"

"Luck?" Randon asked, as he had once or twice before.

"Oh, I'll explain later," she said impatiently — again. She was tired of explaining the concept to the people of Sartorias-deles, who never seemed to get it. Especially her version, which was that good luck was like a mirage, but bad luck was always out to get you. "If Puddlenose comes back, then everyone will be safe. Though he might still be nosing around with the *Lheit*. Captain of his own ship! We'll have to do something to celebrate that—our way. Like a good pie in the phizz. How does that sound?"

"I did say I wanted to meet him."

CJ turned to Detlev. "Can magic include transfers? I have my medallion, but what about Randon? What are you going to do?"

"You may use transfer magic within the cave, and you can go safely to Mearsies Heili, but I'm afraid anywhere else is likely to trip tracers or wards."

That's it, CJ thought. He answers, yet doesn't answer. If she asked for details he gave them—or some of them—but she knew she still wouldn't follow everything he said, because she still didn't really know the right questions. Or, there were layers to his answers.

So why worry? The cave was having its usual effect on her. She felt exuberantly rested, healthy, and full of energy, which meant eager for fun among people she understood, far away from the intoxicating intensity of the caves. She turned to Randon. "And if Puddlenose is there, it will be time for the Pie of Doom."

Randon rubbed his hands. "Pie of Doom?"

"I have the spell memorized. How about a real nasty butterscotch-and-cherry-and-lima-bean deluxe? Or, no. A sauerkraut and peach-pumpkin supremo. You sneak up on him, before he knows what's coming, and wham!"

"You wanna get me killed?" Randon gasped.

CJ chuckled evilly, noticing that Randon didn't say no.

They turned to Detlev.

"Thank you for your help," Detlev said. "Both of you."

CJ met his gaze, and her embarrassment at the words whisked away like old dust scoured by a clean wind.

She knew that eyes were just eyes, that they looked out and didn't let anyone look in, and yet her own little bit of sensitivity to the unity-of-three defined itself easiest with the metaphor of sight. When people looked at you, sometimes you could feel their emotions right behind their gaze, and it stopped you, for so many times the emotion was different from what smiling faces or kind words expressed. And it wasn't as if he didn't have feelings. She recollected the anguish in his face when he admitted that David would not last another hour. It was the way he looked back at a person, as if they mattered. As if when he looked CJ of the Mearsieans, he saw a gallant girl whose loyalty and readiness to risk herself for what she saw was right made her a valuable ally.

And it wasn't put in words, which could be so mortifying because words were so public. It was a private message, just for her, so when she turned away she was smiling.

She explained the Destination to Randon, grabbed her medallion, and both transferred out.

———

Meanwhile, in Larkadhe, Imry Llyenthur—who'd still had no rest—tried to sit down and think through his defeat. But there were too many urgent matters besides sleep that he'd postponed far too long, and then couriers kept hovering about outside the door with this or that piece of annoying news. Annoying because Imry knew he should have seen to them all himself, instead of running a damned futile chase.

Futile. Finally he got up and stood at the window, considering the fact that he'd had all the advantages, yet Detlev had snapped his metaphorical fingers under his nose once again.

Without warning, Svir's thought speared into his mind.

: *You lost them.*

: *Yes.*

And Svir had lost those brats blundering about the Host's citadel. They were even, one would think. But with Svir, nothing was ever "even." His contact was urbane, and carried enough firepower in threat to goose rocks: *Your pose as neophyte is entertaining only so long as it keeps you circumspect.*

And he was gone.

Llyenthur dropped back into his chair and contemplated the various warnings he'd perceived, then he transferred down to the map room. There he found Duin with three or four of the other senior aides.

Duin was smirking as he finished recounting his recent trip to Halarialgre. "…and so I decided Alsaes could sit in a dungeon for a while—" He was about to launch enthusiastically into a description of Alsaes' dispatch when he saw Llyenthur.

"Oh! I just got back—"

"You had a good time?"

Duin blinked. "Yes. My report—"

"Later. Bergan." Llyenthur looked up, and that aide stepped forward. The others quickly made themselves scarce.

"Detlev and David," Bergan stated. "You transferred us back—"

"I didn't. Detlev did the honors. I'd had him pegged by tracer-wards for so long I forgot he still had access to our magic. I also spent far too much time on David," he said, and the two aides braced themselves, knowing from experience that Llyenthur's recounting of his own blunders invariably presaged a crackdown.

Bergan interrupted with obsequious bluster, "Do you want us to intercept them when they come out? I've already sent a company back up to the cave site."

"Then call them back," Llyenthur said, eyes wide. "Or are you going to cover all their shifts while they sit up there for six months? A year? Do you want to build them a hut up there while they wait?" As the rest of the staff stood wooden-faced, he said, "Apparently you don't remember when Siamis was forced into one of those caves by Tsauderei. It was nine or ten months before he emerged, with his brains permanently addled. Or were you volunteering to go chasing into that cave yourself?"

"No, no, no," Bergan mumbled. "I forgot those caves torque time, the way that forest does in Sartor."

"I assure you, *I* haven't. More to the point, neither has the Host. There is no telling how long they will be in there. It might even be longer, as I savaged David so thoroughly I expected either to break his will or destroy him altogether. I did neither."

"Musta been that Detlev's doing." Bergan said, even more obsequious.

Llyenthur said instructively, "Most of the time, perhaps, but not at the end. But even so, a person is as strong as the mutual bond, wouldn't you say? Shall we see how long the two of you together can hold out against me, tired as I am?"

Duin shot Bergan a look that said *Shut up, idiot*.

"And, it transpires, Svirle was watching at the end."

Bergan gaped in surprise. Duin merely looked resigned.

Llyenthur smiled the smile they trusted least, and said to Bergan, "I expect he was interested to see what I would do with them had I managed to get hold of them. Svir has patience. I do not."

Bergan's face assumed the expression (and the hue) of a stuffed trout.

"If any of the Host show up — and I expect they will — you will cooperate with them completely. Hide nothing from them. Make any orders first priority, even if they appear frivolous. Meanwhile, Mearsies Heili is to be sealed off. No one to get in. No one to get out. If anyone does come out, shoot 'em on sight, unless he or she is on the capital list, in which case send them directly to me."

"The north side? Around the islands?" Duin pointed up at the map.

"Ah, yes. Get Teredean and…Bendrec from Sartor. It's a waste of time trying to get into Delfina, and old Tsauderei is not going to come out — assuming he isn't already dead. See what they can do about those islands. If the problem is what I think it is, we will put it directly into Ilerian's hands. Now. For the regional commanders, two things."

The two were silent.

"First. The time has come to loosen the reins a little on the cooperative populaces, and let it be known they are doing so. Second. Crack down on any travelers without authorization. They won't catch any of the big problems but it ought to serve to lessen local movement."

"Unauthorized travelers to be shot?" Bergan asked, and Duin thought to himself that the head snakes hadn't broken through in Imar. Norsunder was alone there on this damn world, with a tenth of the numbers they were supposed to have.

"No, the idea is to limit movement. If they are not on my list have 'em beaten, but leave 'em mobile enough to crawl home to serve as examples. Third. No more hoarding prisoners for playtime. Question them, shoot them. If they're on a list, send them on."

"What about the security-holds?"

"They have their own orders. Don't interfere. Go now."

Bergan effaced himself. Llyenthur said to Duin, "You might let the word get out the last order is for their own protect-ion. I expect Svir's going to permit Efael to begin gracing the dungeons. After my blunder, anyone hoarding prisoners, for whatever reason, will probably be ripped apart by Efael. Except, of course, he himself, but we can safely leave him to

Svir's rein. In the meantime you're going to have to call in my trackers. We've as much control of land as we're likely to hold until the Host does their part and brings over the occupation forces. It is time," he said, "to get control of the seas." *First, from Efael.*

"What happened in Imar?" Duin ventured the question everyone had been thinking.

"Svir's annoyed because they didn't break Kessler's seal, though they came close. In the process they lost the morvende mage, and apparently the key to the ward protecting Mearsies Heili. The idiots blundered in and out before I could get to them."

"Then we're definitely penned here," Duin said in dissatisfaction.

"And *they* are confined to the mortal realm." Llyenthur smiled. "Speaking of, even magic won't keep me on my feet past another half-day. Have the trackers in here by morning."

"Anyone in particular?"

"Let's begin," Imry Llyenthur said with a very unpleasant smile, "With Rel the Traveler. His name has come up a little too frequently of late for mere posturing."

Duin noted that down.

"I'll begin in Khanerenth with a salutary demonstration or two, since Efael's attempt at naval command has utterly failed to lay Jehan of Khanerenth by the heels. And then I intend to sleep. Through an entire night. Disturb me only if you experience a sudden desire to take a guided tour of your own entrails."

He vanished, leaving behind the usual stirring of air, and the lightning-crackle frisson of his mood.

Duin heaved a sigh, then went out to convey the orders, finish his brag session, and gossip about the movements of their respective commanders.

PART THREE

One

OF THE SEVERAL QUESTS undertaken this season, so far the most successful were those that never began as quests.

Jilo of the Chwahir hadn't the least notion of pursuing a quest. He was too accustomed to regarding himself as a failure — too unlike Rel the Traveler. Jilo had always thought Rel above emotion, so imperturbable he seemed, as well as effortlessly competent. Until now.

The competence remained. It was the sight of Rel quietly devastated that was so disturbing. He sat on a trunk, forearms resting on his knees, big, capable hands empty and dangling, head bowed. Shontande Lirendi was another who seemed to exist in some rarefied atmosphere above the commonality of fumblers such as Jilo, but even he looked distraught, his dark blue gaze narrowed with pained question. Jilo himself was so numb with shock he did not know what to think. None of them did.

"Did he say anything to any of you? He said nothing to me," Shontande admitted, his regret unhidden. "I attributed his wariness to the fact that we had never met."

Rel lifted his head. "He said little during the escape. Did everything I asked. Ran hard. No sign of surrender."

Jilo sighed. "On the journey out of Chwahirsland. He made a, a kind of joke, but it wasn't funny, about how some are masters only at mediocrity." Jilo blushed painfully. "I thought he was talking about me."

Both Rel and Shontande reacted at that. "But you were the

one who got us in and out alive," Shontande said. "While it is
true that Rel ran the actual rescue, it was you who discovered
that the Host was involved somewhere on the other side of the
strait."

"Right," Rel said. "Never would have gotten past the
guard without your work, much less out. And Conrad knew
that. I made sure of it. Maybe I did wrong? I must have
completely misinterpreted the situation."

Silence fell, as all three contemplated the late Prince
Conrad, uncrowned king of Imar since the death of the former
king early in the invasion. Conrad had been imprisoned in
Narad by Efael, who had not had time as yet to play any of his
games. Nor had the increasingly furious Wan-Edhe, forced to
act as a jailor for Efael, just as he was forced to send four of his
treasured five armies out to do Norsunder's work.

Jilo had also learned through low-level Chwahir contacts
in the army, that Efael's Black Knives were sweeping Colend
for Shontande at the same time that Imry Llyenthur's hunters
were scouring roads and towns for anyone who fit Rel's
description. What better place to hide than in Chwahirsland,
where no one in their right mind would go by choice—and
incidentally spring a prisoner at the same time?

They thought back, each in his own way, over the
successful rescue and escape. Conrad Winstanhaeme—a
moody, rather difficult young man—had cooperated, he had
expressed his gratitude. He had muttered to Rel as they slipped
through a noisome, dripping tunnel beneath the dungeon, that
no one ought to die in Narad's fortress, even Chwahir.

And yet the night after they sneaked back into Colend, he
took his own life. No warning; earlier that evening, as they
celebrated the successful run, he had toasted them all. But late
the next day, when they banged past the door locked from the
inside, he was found hanging in his chamber, no signs of a
struggle.

"Could it be because the Host chose Imar to make their
lair?" Jilo asked, his voice full of doubt.

Shontande, who had only had minimal diplomatic
exchange with Imar's royal family during his very brief reign,
turned in question to Rel.

"I first met him and his sister when they were young. One
of Wan-Edhe's plots. Can't say I really knew them." Rel
shrugged. "They had been trained to keep a distance from

anyone below their rank. It was very important to them, that much I recollect."

"Rank," Shontande repeated. "An insistence on that seems peculiar in a kingdom wherein the nobles are reported to live like kings, right down to private armies, over which the actual king had little to no power. And I had heard that Conrad's time was mainly given to horse racing and gambling."

"Yes," Rel said; when he had traveled through Imar, gossip had made that clear. "'Master of mediocrity.'" He shook his head slowly. "I did not hear that. And I probably would have missed the import had I heard it."

Shontande sighed, passing a hand over his eyes. "He apparently did not want anyone else to catch it. I am sorry, more than I can express. One last guess: I know nothing of his family connections. Was where the Host is rumored to have settled one of his houses, or belonging to a family connection? In other words, might he have taken their presence there as a personal blow?"

Rel said, "That I can actually answer, but only because I used to spend so much time with Commander Dei of the Knights of Dei in Everon. There were no ties with Imar's royal family. That manor is well known in Everon because it once belonged to a branch of the Dei family, though their name changed sometime in the past century or so. Before it became a target of contention when one of the Sartoran Deis attempted to claim it, while laying claim to both the thrones of Imar and Everon. Wnelder Vee, too, I think."

"Ah-ye, Sartor too—until they chased him out of the world altogether. Harold Dei," Shontande said, hands raised in the Colendi shadow ward. "I know that name well." And when the other two turned to him, he added, "My late regency council used to use him as an example of the sort of trouble I would never be able to deal with, if I had not their wise council protecting me. Harold Dei, the wicked Harold Dei, the dangerous Harold Dei, and I too ignorant, too inexperienced, too young, too weak, to deal with the likes of him. Mere mention of his name used to infuriate me, but it all seems sad, and trifling, now."

Rel looked up at that. "At least we have done our best. Conrad Winstanhaeme was the last of his family, his sister having adopted out when she married."

Shontande made the open-handed peace. "We saw to it

that he was Disappeared respectfully, which was dully recorded, now that there is no Road Guild or scribes. I will take charge of that, if you like. I promise to see it delivered to whoever follows next in Imar once we are rid of Norsunder."

"A day we need to be working toward," Rel said, making an effort to shake off the depression Conrad's suicide had caused.

Shontande made another of those airy Colendi gestures Jilo could never interpret. Shon's politeness was invincible — and impermeable. And yet there were verbal patterns that give some clues to what his thought might be. One of them was that he would sometimes sound apologetic when he knew there was a wrong somewhere, maybe one he hadn't solved and felt he ought to have. "Then it is time for Varise to return to her instructional duties."

Shontande referred to the disguise that had, so far, kept him from discovery; he was already finger-combing his auburn hair into braids, preparatory to resuming his woman's clothing. When they left the basement they were hiding in, he would leave as Varise, an instructor at a school for teachers of the arts, located in the countryside north of Colend's capital. Being an exceptionally beautiful young man, Shontande made a very striking young woman, though rather on the tall side.

Jilo said, "I'd better begin that trip I promised to make to Marloven Hess."

Shontande uttered a soft whistle, no more than a breath of sound. "Ah-ye! This would relate to that mysterious magical paper you were given?"

Shontande had still been crossing Erdrael Danara the week previous, when the Mearsiean ship *Lheit* drifted along the coast under a spring storm, and Puddlenose rowed to shore to meet Jilo and Rel for the handoff of the beige papers.

Jilo bobbed in agreement. "I was going to ask if you'd guard mine. If Puddlenose is right that messages can only appear for the intended, I figure, if I get captured, the enemy won't be able to force me to use Senrid's. But me, carrying mine, is too much of a risk. I'm sure to lose it somehow."

"Of course," Shontande said, though there was question in his voice. "These papers would be an enormous boon. If they really do work. Though, I hope you will forgive me for observing, it seems rather short-sighted to craft magical papers that can only be addressed to one person."

Rel grunted. "Short-sighted indeed. Enough that I wonder if Puddlenose got the instructions garbled. He is excellent on the water—he's become one of the fastest captains on the strait. I can attest to that. But he's never been very adept with reading and writing."

Jilo knew this to be true, and he also knew that the breezy, usually easygoing Puddlenose regretted being next thing to illiterate—not for lack of trying.

"Atan probably has one waiting for me," Rel said. "She could not have known I'd meet up with you two. I might as well make my way to Mearsies Heili until the chase dies down. Then it will be time to get serious about communications." And return to Sartor, he vowed internally, to oversee the secret harvest.

Jilo handed Shontande the beige paper that Puddlenose had said was his, and carefully tucked the one for Senrid inside his knapsack. "I feel safer already. Ah. Not safe, but less of a potential threat to others."

"Are you so certain of defeat?" Shontande teased gently. "Jilo, you are twice the mage I am. More."

Jilo looked pained, his narrow, pale face blotching red from cheeks to ears. "I doubt that. In any case, when it comes to martial arts, a ten-year-old could dump me on my butt. No one I can think of, except maybe Senrid, would write to me anyway."

Shontande said, "I would. If I had one."

"I'm sure they didn't think they would find you," Jilo mumbled.

Shontande laughed. "Jilo, it's fine. No one's fault that I don't really know the alliance, though I was nominally included as a member. I will guard your magical paper for you."

"Thanks. I'll travel as a journeyman artist so I have an excuse to carry any kind of paper."

"Good thinking," Shon said.

Noises in the torchlit courtyard above silenced them. Jilo sat in an awkward knot of tense limbs, hoping that if there was a fight he wouldn't stab himself before he got near an enemy.

Shon's posture didn't alter overtly. He was still sitting, one knee up, a forearm across it, but he'd gone from lounging aristocrat to poised for action in some subtle way Jilo couldn't define. He stilled, waiting as Rel, who—despite his height and breadth of chest and shoulders—could catfoot with the best, ghosted up the stairs, then almost immediately reappeared.

"Just a delivery," Rel said. "But we ought to be moving along. I sense that our presence is making our hosts nervous. Two kings and whatever it is that I am might be difficult to explain." He flashed a piratical grin.

"One king," Jilo said under his breath as he stooped to pick up his battered knapsack. *One king, one heir to one throne being pushed toward another ... and then there's me.* Aloud, he said, "I'll go first."

Jilo always felt awkward. But there are highs and lows in the clumsiness, one might say. This was low-intensity, until it occurred to him all his turmoils and ineptitudes were there like glass for Shontande to see through.

Jilo fumbled with the door-latch, nearly broke it, and backed away — straight into the door frame. "Argh."

Shontande reached behind the door for the satchel of travel food that a motherly half-Chwahir miner had put into Shontande's hand right before the tragic discovery, saying, "I put this together for our king. Will you make certain he remembers to eat?" Shontande had promised, reflecting on perspective: to that hard-working woman there was only one king who mattered. And Jilo could not see it.

"Here," he said, intuiting that repeating the generous donor's words would only discommode Jilo. "This was prepared against our leaving. You should take it. I'm now on home ground."

"Do," Rel said. "I have contacts in the area."

Jilo took the satchel, blushing: he'd remembered Senrid's beige paper, and drawing things, and a change of clothes, but he'd forgotten completely about packing trail food.

He stuffed the satchel into his knapsack, said his thanks, and hiked off into the night, glad the air was cool enough to hide his burning face.

Two

TO JILO, REL WAS the embodiment of a hero. Though Rel insisted he merely saw a job to do and did it, the jobs he saw could range from rebuilding a wagon to running a rescue under the eyes of half the Chwahir army.

More to the point, he got the job done. *Isn't it competence that makes kings? Unlike me, who dreams up grand plans and fails at them,* Jilo was thinking as he slipped into a narrow alley that sloped toward the river. *Then there's Shon, new king of one of the most renowned kingdoms in the world. He's another kind of king, the established one with a long family line behind him for stability. And here's me, clumsy son of a single-syllable-name sergeant from a very minor outpost. Still a failure.*

Jilo had labored long under the stigma of having been selected for his unprepossessing appearance by Wan-Edhe's long-dead brother, Kwenz. Kwenz had stayed alive because of his incompetence—a very carefully maintained incompetence, Jilo had come to realize. And Wan-Edhe had permitted Jilo to live because of his own apparent incompetence—putting spells on him in the name of protective wards to make certain that it stayed that way.

While he made his way along, as usual lost inside his head, back in the miner's basement, Rel said, "Ought I to go with him? While I know Jilo can get anywhere inside Chwahirsland, I'm afraid he won't last long elsewhere."

Shontande paused with his braids halfway done. "Something I learned, traveling about with him, while you were running between Remalna and Sartor: there are a surprising number of Chwahir occupiers who secretly look out for him."

"Really?"

Shontande resumed twisting his braids up into a style favored by Colendi women. "I saw it. I heard it, after a couple of my own scouts witnessed it."

Rel watched Shontande's long fingers as the light of a single candle caressed his elegant contours, and lit strands of his hair to ruddy gold. Rel enjoyed the mild twitch of attraction as Shontande transformed himself from male to female; Rel had never responded to other men in the ordinary way, but Shontande knew exactly how to soften and blur the masculine line, and to artfully suggest female curves, both rounded and hollow. And Rel's own inclination was toward strong women.

Shontande went on, "Though he is ill-equipped for stealth in, ah-ye, what do you call it? A hard target pursuit, with the willing aid of an increasing number of people, he moves between both sides without causing distrust, enmity, anger."

"I know he is familiar with all the outposts in Chwahirsland," Rel said. "To him, support staff, squadron captains, ordinary flatfoots, they're all of equal importance. I did not realize he's moving about so adeptly here."

"I would not say adept, in the sense of a method or design," Shontande said, placing the last hairpin, and dropping his hands. "At least, not that I perceive, but then I am unable to distinguish between all the tabs and shoulder flashes and armband stripes and the like, even before one gets to the various colors."

Rel gave a snort of disbelief. "Easiest system in the world. You don't want to know it."

Shontande raised both hands, too polite to say the word *no*. "Truly, truly, when it comes to this one with peach markings on a uniform that I believe is meant to be forest green, and another with spring green color tabs on a uniform that appears a shade of purple that perhaps has not been washed properly ..."

Rel shook his head. "Those uniforms began all black. But crimson and green armbands and flashes and tabs, those two armies are the lowest of the five, always left last when supplies are handed out. Chwahir flatfoots and sailors can tell the region and the year a person joined by the fading shades of black. Before Wan-Edhe was forced to split First Army—gold— among the fleets, you can be very sure their uniforms were pure black, and their rank markings are either real gold, or, for company and lower, goldenrod. The rest of the kingdom starves so that the army is well fed and supplied, but those supplies are unevenly distributed; Fifth Army, the greens, are also known as the tatters."

Shontande opened his hands politely.

Rel, like Jilo, loathed the world's thinking of the Chwahir as a faceless mass not worth distinguishing in its component parts. No one saw the immense tragedy of a king out of the worst nightmares forcing them into a war not of their own making; meanwhile, Rel's father Mondros, alone of all the admittedly hard-pressed senior mages, fought singlehandedly to keep Wan-Edhe from creating border wards over Colend.

Somewhat grimly, Rel went on. "Gold. Silver. Purple. Crimson. Green. Five colors, five armies, five divisions in today's navy. Five groups in each category: eight to a squad, five squads in a company. Five companies in a battalion. Five battalions in a brigade. Five brigades in a division, and five divisions per army."

Shontande bowed. Any kind of military thinking was new to him, and his Colendi soul found it dispiriting, but he sensed that he had erred. This lesson was, in a way, a remonstrance; he said hesitantly, "I must confess that our histories seemed to make reference to a great many titles for generals and admirals, and in my ignorance I was unable to comprehend the outer structure."

Rel's tone was a bit less acerb as he said, "Those were centuries ago. Back then, especially before the standing army was organized, generals and admirals were appointed by mission, and the rank only existed for that mission. But some were so successful that the prestige of this or that mission title persisted, handed down to its army or division. For example, the great admiral Thog of the Two Blades, who cleared the strait of the last of the Venn right after the great defeat, had accrued so much prestige that her rank, meant only for the duration, persisted for at least a couple of centuries."

Shontande made the peace. "Thank you for enlightening me."

Rel was not done. "Tabs on collars for command. Shoulder flashes for mid-rank. Armbands for service. Tabs, flashes, and armbands, are broken down further by the number. It's easy."

Shontande bowed again. "I will endeavor to be more

observant." And when Rel finally sat back, he said, "We did watch Jilo during the early days of the invasion — after I escaped captivity." Here Shontande gazed down at his hands, which had held Curtas as he died. Grief and regret still hurt.

He looked up, dark blue eyes almost black in the glow of that one candle. "While I learned to like, and to respect, Jilo last summer, he is a Chwahir, and it was Chwahir that Norsunder sent against us, under the command of Norsundrians. But my scouts discovered that Jilo avoided the Norsundrians. He spoke randomly to those Chwahir warriors with little or no rank — as you say, to cooks and horse tenders and ordinary spear carriers. To them, he spoke similar words to the effect that every gesture that escapes Wan-Edhe's notice, every sign, every object, is its own magic, turning humiliation into dignity. I confess I have contemplated this message, without arriving at any true understanding."

"I believe I can help with that," Rel said, as the rhythmic tramp of a patrol passed in the street outside the high window.

"Please enlighten me."

"In Colend — before the war — the ordinary person chats at the Hour of the Bird," Rel said as Shontande unself-consciously shucked his clothes. Rel looked up at the window. "They go to plays, and express their opinions with shouts, or thrown flowers. Sometimes thrown mud, I've heard, though no one I know has seen that."

"All true," Shontande said, poking his head carefully through the neck of his under gown.

"In Sarendan, the ordinary folk draw slogans and criticisms on walls and fences. Most of it is unmemorable as art, though it expresses sharp emotion. A lot of it is still pictures, crude sometimes — stick figures — rather than words, but the idea is conveyed. In Sartor, in certain areas, that has also happened, though the guilds frown on it. Decorations appear on certain statues, and everyone knows what's meant. And so on."

Shontande bowed courteously, then he dug out his carefully folded gown in shades of rose.

"What the world, which despises and hates the Chwahir, does not understand is that when the Chwahir have been denied the freedom to utter certain words, or to write them, they make gestures. When gestures were denied them, they resorted to signs. Wan-Edhe knows that the more words the

Chwahir were permitted to use, the freer their existence. He does not want them free. He wants them obedient, the entire kingdom to exist entirely as an extension of his will."

"I am familiar with Wan-Edhe's evil intent," Shontande murmured as he deftly folded and tied the gown so that the panels hung straight.

"Familiar, but I wonder if you comprehend what it means," Rel said. "It's the word 'random'. Let me finish, and you shall tell me. Jilo could not save Chwahirsland from Wan-Edhe's return. He regrets that deeply. Profoundly. So profoundly that he sees himself only as a failure, after years of unrelenting effort to undo Wan-Edhe's damage before his return."

"This, I know," Shontande said, gesturing Rue, his long sleeves like butterfly wings.

"Jilo also believes, with equal conviction, that the Chwahir belong only to themselves. Eh. I wonder if that might give us an insight into Conrad of Imar — the fact that he had no consolation of conviction or purpose. No loyalty except to a rank that no longer existed?"

"Worth contemplating," Shontande said, hands touching lightly in the peace. "Please go on."

"I am nearly done. Jilo believes that if words are banned, then the Chwahir must assert themselves through gestures, signs, even objects. They are more difficult to identify, to interpret, and therefore are less likely to arouse suspicion. But they are there, oh yes, they are there. And each carries tremendous meaning among them, all the more for being unspoken."

"Oh?" Shontande said on an interrogative note. "Are you saying that Jilo, in speaking those words I repeated, was giving the Chwahir what he could? He did not succeed with magic, so he encourages them with what he considers mere words?"

"Yes," Rel said. "But, in his grief over what he considers his failure, he, in his turn, does not quite see that to people who have been denied and forbidden everything, his words are not 'mere'."

Shontande accepted this with another open-handed gesture, as if he held a fan. "While we were there in Chwahirsland, I did see him make covert signals, especially as we left Narad. But I never saw that in my own kingdom."

"Oh, the signs are not only made with fingers and hands,

one to one. There are signs left for others to see. And not only in Chwahirsland. There are all over Colend, I expect," Rel said. "Ah, you misunderstand," he added as Shontande raised a hand in the shadow ward. "You won't notice most of them. And if you did, they have no military meaning. If you're right, and he's visiting people in outposts and the like, he's finding those people not randomly, but by these signs. Made for Chwahir resisting Wan-Edhe to recognize one another."

"Ah-ye. I am unobservant after all; I missed that entirely."

"You aren't Chwahir."

Shontande smoothed the gown over his manufactured curves—and once again, Rel appreciated Varise in the way he couldn't warm to Shontande's true physical self, though he knew Varise was all art.

Shontande said, "I believe I comprehend a little better, and I amend my conviction that he goes about randomly. But now I worry that someone will betray those signs."

"It's possible," Rel conceded as he shook out his cloak and repacked his satchel. "But more unlikely than you would think. You have to remember that so much of Chwahir life is centered in one's twi—chosen after much discussion over years by the families. People live in twis. If they marry, it is discussed among the twi. Those intended for the army enter as a twi, a group of eight, never on their own; more frequently than not a twi becomes a squad when they join the army. Twis are only broken up over squads when there are missing numbers, but a good company commander tries to keep all of a twi in the same company. Trust happens between twis, and between connections of twis. And Wan-Edhe, in attempting to outlaw that ancient custom, is hated more by the Chwahir every day."

Rel stood, hefting his pack. He frowned at the clean-swept stones of the basement floor, then sat down again. "One thing I noticed coming north was relatively little evidence of violence between Chwahir and Colendi. Is that Jilo's doing? It can't be — he has no influence in Norsunder."

"I can actually answer that, with some certainty," Shontande said, as he rolled his man's clothing up and fitted it inside a bright yellow stuffed neck-warmer with a hidden pocket. "Jilo explained this to me. Wan-Edhe—quite unintentionally—is an unexpected aid in that he has given his occupying forces the strictest orders not to slaughter the populace, or rob them. Wan-Edhe reserves the pleasure of witnessing mass executions for when he is rid of Norsunder at last, and can take possession of my kingdom, and preserve or dispose of it entirely at his leisure. Instead, the Chwahir scribes are enjoined to list every cup, every plate, every coin, for his future treasury."

"That sounds exactly like Wan-Edhe. I take it that the fighting then has largely been against the Norsundrians?"

"Very little fighting, because of vicious reprisals in the early days. But here is where Jilo gains credit: he elicited a promise from me early on that I would encourage the Colendi to resist killing Chwahir, or even baiting them. Fear, and a lack of training, did contribute, but for the most part, the Colendi and the Chwahir are existing in a semblance of truce. One contributing factor is that the Chwahir appear to have never experienced the foods that are common here, and related commodities ... ah, I will not describe the peculiar barter system of the hidden market, by which Chwahir smuggle such things home, and in they turn overlook small matters such as traders forgetting their identity papers and the like. My worry," Shontande said soberly, "is what will happen if we do defeat Norsunder. And yet the Chwahir are still here." He made an effort to ease his tone as Rel rose, picking up his pack. "Jilo says that he has plans for that, too. Since there is little I can do, I wait."

Rel uttered a short laugh, mostly of admiration. "It seems that once again I've underestimated him, though no more than he underestimates himself." He raised his hand in salute, and ran up the stairs.

After a scan, he faded into the night, a sword strapped to his back, the hilt sticking up above one massive shoulder.

Very soon after, Varise the tall, elegant teacher, passed in the opposite direction, directly east.

Three

JILO MADE HIS WAY to the riverside, and to the flat-bottomed supply boats lined along the quay. He found what he was looking for: a character, worked in three rusty, bent nails, along the warped wood of one of the flat boats. The sign was the first character in a homophone for *hum*.

Jilo stepped aboard, and waited for someone to feel the vibration of his step and come out from the modest houseboat section at the rear of the flatboat. When a silhouette appeared with a lantern swinging, Jilo said diffidently, "I am reporting for work."

The woman peered at the gangling figure in the shapeless Colendi laborer's clothes, his black hair tied back, and she smothered a gasp. Could it possibly be *him*? "Your name?" she croaked.

Jilo dropped his head at what he heard as a sharp tone. He said the homophonic word.

"Your bunk is..." She was going to say at the back, but what if it really was him, Jilo, Chwahirsland's champion, the uncrowned king?

"If you haven't room, I don't mind sleeping among the barrels," Jilo said. "The nights are warming."

She had heard that he was truly humble. "No, no, no, we have a hammock set aside."

He was soon settled, with tender care, and as the army paid no attention to Chwahir civilians, and the Colendi disdained just another platter-faced, black-haired Chwahir, Jilo embarked on an easy journey down the river into the capital, his only labors helping load and unload. He was so spindly that the boat people gave him the lighter chores, the ones the young daughter of the family usually saw to. He was invariably kind, rather absent, and always insisted that the family eat first.

By the time they saw Alsais on the horizon, the family had enfolded him into their hearts—which Jilo managed not to notice. He was adrift inside his head, wondering how he'd find his way to the far west without getting totally lost. Or captured.

When the boat stopped for the last time before reaching the capital, Jilo changed to the worn uniform he'd carried for years, to which he'd added the brown armband of a lower level stable worker. He bowed low to the family, and when he turned away, they bowed even lower, and remained that way until he was out of sight beyond a stack of barrels.

He walked into Alsais, ignored by the Colendi and Chwahir alike. When he reached Headquarters, which occupied the royal palace, he took care to report to the stable, where he picked up a wand and went to work in the stalls, getting rid of waste, then hauling fresh water in for the animals. He found the work soothing, especially when he experimented with what he thought of as his meager version of Dena Yeresbeth to check the emotional states of the horses.

It was while he was doing this that he caught an inward scream of rage, coming from outside the stable. It ripped across his awareness like a burning arrow, a wordless and inhuman wrath.

He kept at his labors, but when he reached a stall with a small window, he glanced out. Across the training court, he spied what had to be an old chicken coop, now full of dark shapes—raptors. One section had been closed off. In it was a big raptor, dark except for what appeared to be a golden collar of feathers and a ring of scarlet under its beak. It flew upward, thumped against the ceiling of the roost, fell then flapped upward again, over and over. Trying to escape.

Seeing any creature in pain sickened him. He turned away, and moved to the next stall.

He worked until the watch bell rang melodiously. Jilo was convinced that Wan-Edhe did not know about the carillons, or he would have ordered them destroyed. The interesting thing was that the army commander apparently hadn't reported carillons instead of obtaining the requisite iron bells. Impossible to guess at motivation. He tried to avoid those who might be called before Wan-Edhe, lest they be put into an impossible situation—if, that is, they didn't betray him outright.

Jilo eased across the HQ until he reached the comms wing. When he spotted a familiar buck-toothed, caterpillar-browed face, he rejoiced inside—an expression that matched the one that flashed in Dassler Anjit's unprepossessing face when he spotted Jilo.

Dassler Anjit still wore company and regimental flashes on his arm; he had managed to avoid promotion to the collar tabs of upper command yet again, though everyone knew he had the fastest pen in at least two of the five armies.

Anjit flicked up his quill, then said, loudly, "Stable Hand Four, take this list to Requisitions."

He handed a stack of papers to Jilo that ought to go to a runner, but anyone could send a lowly stable hand anywhere.

Jilo went to the supply annex—and turned down one of the narrow corridors between stacks of winter gear to await Anjit, whose midday meal time this was.

Anjit was not far behind him, a tall, thin young man of indeterminate age—one of the Sunrise Generation, the covert name for those whose lives Jilo had saved when he lessened Wan-Edhe's wicked pocket Norsunder, which fed on the life forces of those serving in Narad's fortress.

"What news?" Anjit asked.

"I've just come from the capital," Jilo said. He told Anjit nothing that could get him into trouble, even obliquely, such as the fact that he had been a part of the prisoner raid at Narad. Instead, Jilo had used the time while Rel was making his way to Narad fortress's dungeon to meet covertly with low ranking guards, shopkeepers, and wagon drivers, resulting in the most precious commodity to the average flatfoot: family news.

Anjit listened thirstily, gave a short nod, and promised to convey news to those who would want to hear it. Then he said, "No new orders, other than that an important prisoner supposedly escaped, and The Hate is using that to send four regiments into Erdrael Danara to search. The Norsundrian chief in Erdrael Danara is angry as a result. Sees it as encroachment. Word through the relay is that The Hate received a visit from Imry Llyenthur, more threats, more demands, especially having to do with naval matters. They're tripling the patrols off Toar, and the old outpost."

Mearsies Heili, Jilo translated. "Something happened?"

"Giam on the coast desk says there's evidence that..." Anjit glanced upward, meaning the high command—Norsunder's Host. "...*they* lost prisoners."

"Oh?" Jilo wondered if that was garbled news about Conrad, then recollected that Efael had been summoned to Imar, which had enabled Rel and Shontande and him to slip into Narad. He'd managed to forget that, what with all the tensions in Narad, the escape, and then Conrad's shocking end.

It was frustrating, building a picture a piece at a time, often distorted or weeks late—but that was life now.

Anjit went on with the rest of Wan-Edhe's latest spate of orders, all petty, intrusive. Inconsistent. The King of the Chwahir was writhing under the control of his Norsundrian masters, still angry that his prized First Army had been broken up and put to sea as marine warriors, and Second, Third, and Fourth dispersed, leaving him with only Fifth army—fifty thousand, many literally as well as figuratively in tatters—to protect himself.

Jilo listened, and when Anjit had finished venting, said, "Those birds out in the training court. One of them is battering itself trying to escape."

Anjit's face soured. "New spy birds. Orders are to begin using them. Not many can stomach it," he added. "The big one is for the general. He hates it. The bird hates the spells." Anjit cast a quick look to either side, then lowered his voice. "The general says, he knows that the spells on that bird are also spying on him. He's sure that when he forces the bird to look, someone is spying on his own mind. Gives him a headache."

"The bird keeps crashing into the roost ceiling, and screeching," Jilo said.

Anjit looked away again. "The general keeps hoping one of the Norsundrians will get sick of the noise and kill it. The blame will go to the Norsundrians," he added unnecessarily. "It's *she* who is in charge of the birds, I'm told. And the young soulsucker Hyath. Bespelling as many big birds as they can capture. We're supposed to be using them to cover all ground."

"You can't just let them accidentally escape?" Jilo asked. "Surely you can't keep big birds like that in a roost all the time."

"Oh, the Norsundrian who brought them lets them out once a day, but the magic on the birds forces them back, even before those of us chosen to train in using the birds for spying get to them."

A bell rang once on a sweet note. "Got to go," Anjit murmured.

Jilo retreated to the stable, falling unconsciously back into the Chwahir warrior posture, which was head slightly bent, gaze lowered. Looking at a superior straight on could get you killed.

On Wan-Edhe's return to Narad from Norsunder, the Chwahir king had had all five of his top generals shot for not having anticipated Wan-Edhe's wishes and killed Jilo. Though two had tried, balked by Kessler's magic. There had been other purges, mostly of people who dared to speak, to explain. Wan-Edhe did not reward initiative. Such contradictory insanity had been a grim reminder of what life would be like again under Wan-Edhe: his sojourn in Norsunder had not mellowed him.

Jilo did not personally know any of the current generals. But from various signs, he suspected that Crimson General Furo was not a bad person. Just a survivor. As they all had to be, especially burdened with the blood-poison spell Wan-Edhe forced on them, so he could keep control.

Jilo stopped in the courtyard, studying the roost full of angry birds.

He wavered. He needed to start on his journey to Marloven Hess. But he listened to that rage-filled shriek, the desperation under it harrowing his nerves. He had seen blood glistening on feathers. He knew he was going to try.

The first step was taking over the feeding duty — and since these birds were carrion eaters, no one liked toting buckets of dead rats and fish guts and leftover chicken parts out to the roost. Jilo didn't either, but the reward was proximity, which enabled him to test the magic over the birds.

The gold-necked condor screeched hate at him. Jilo blocked against the searing rage, trying to send calm. I'm trying to figure out how to free you, he thought — knowing that his inner voice probably sounded like blah-di-blah-di-blah to the bird. But maybe they were akin enough in emotion for the idea to get across?

The condor turned away from Jilo and continued to fly, scratching at the roost roof with its long middle talon before falling.

Jilo had spent so long testing Wan-Edhe's magic that the cautions and the methods were habitual by now. He reached, then his eyes blinked wide. A simple lattice of two links?

Lattice wards are the most complex in magic. The most difficult to master. But Jilo had been striving against this magic for immeasurable time, and he immediately recognized the type.

Yeres's mage, he exulted, was either lazy or rushed. The spells were basic — once you understood lattice wards — and she hadn't even bothered to put wards over the lattices. He knew the fundamentals of this magic; by the time he had distributed his noisome cargo to those in the roost, he had broken the links on them all. At first cautiously, then faster each time.

The big condor, ignoring him until then, fluttered back to its roost, eyeing him. It was still furious, but curious. Jilo looked about. No one paid them any heed.

He said, hoping that the idea would get across even if the words didn't, "You'll be free soon. Keep screeching."

The bird opened its beak, flapped its wings, and shrieked. Jilo winced, backing away a step as he wondered if that was an answer, or a random noise.

Buoyed in spirit, he returned to Anjit's wing. He passed by the door twice before catching Anjit's attention. By that time he'd rehearsed what to say.

"Does anyone want more water?" Anjit asked. "I'm going to refresh the jug."

"Send a runner," someone else said as he pored over a message.

"I need to stretch my legs," Anjit said.

Likely they all knew that meant a private conversation, but no one reacted, and Anjit and Jilo were soon outside.

"I daren't be gone long," Anjit said.

"You don't have to be. Tell Crimson General Furo to find some way to be late to the birds' training court."

Anjit's eyes widened and his jaw dropped, making him look like a rabbit with those enormous front teeth. "Birds," he repeated.

Jilo said, "I'm going to leave now. And fix as many of them as I see in the skies."

A shout from around the corner caused both to turn away; when Anjit turned back, Jilo was already sloping around a corner, vanishing from sight.

A short time later, Anjit reported to Crimson General Furo. "The bird master is here." As promised, he murmured, "If the general pleases, I can brush your jacket again."

Furo glanced at him in surprise. "But this is not the Court of Rule. The only punishment we're likely to face is bird droppings on us. Doesn't it make more sense to brush down afterward?"

Anjit was already beside him, clothes brush in hand. "*He* was here," Anjit said under his breath. "Visited the birds himself. Said to delay you."

Furo was quite content to delay another vertigo-inducing "training" session, during which, he was convinced, the only thing accomplished was some distant Norsundrian twi-banned no-family laughing heartily as Furo and his scouts got vilely sick, their minds full of misery. He already lived with a slight sense of heat and nausea, induced by Wan-Edhe's loyalty spell. He'd said that the nausea was a reminder.

The general sipped Colendi ginger steep, which did seem to help the nausea, as Anjit fussed over the fresh jacket Furo had put on scarcely half a watch ago, and then summoned the scouts.

When they reached the stable court, they found a hubbub of underlings busy saddling horses, as the Norsundrian who had brought the birds cursed and shouted for them to get on the road — follow the birds — capture them.

Furo was very careful to keep his expression impassive as he approached the Norsundrian. "Send a runner when you have retrieved them." As if they would ever be able to ride those birds down!

He returned to his office, and the never-ending flow of reports, while secretly exulting. Later on, he murmured to a wooden-visaged Anjit, "Next time *he* comes, make sure he has everything he needs."

Four

Such was Jilo's conviction that that beige paper was Senrid's (his own being left behind with Shontande Lirendi) he ignored the infrequent signals he felt during his subsequent travels, believing they were communications meant for Senrid.

There were few enough Norsundrians patrols in quiet Colend, and its even quieter neighbors, that even someone as unpracticed in evasion as Jilo was able to hear them and get out of their way. The area was mostly patrolled by spy birds, though not all of them had human riders. Jilo detected them by the magic on them. He still hid from these, but from behind cover as he broke the lattices binding them, and then watched with quiet glee as the birds invariably squawked and flew rapidly off. Since the most of those birds did not have riders, he was fairly certain no one could map where the magic was broken and find his trail.

Not that the journey didn't have problems, particularly his sort of problems. He was so used to traveling at night that he'd forgotten how hot the sun could get during this season, and he had to get a hat. In a little village alongside the river, he found a nice woven gray one with a wide brim, though buying it used most of his little store of coins.

He crossed the river behind a slow ox-cart full of plain linens, and dared an illusion warding himself at the other side. He was careful to match the plodding pace of the oxen, and the bored Norsundrian posted there never looked twice.

After that, he ventured into pleasant country, avoiding all

villages and sticking to woodlands.

The satchel of food lasted until he'd reached the Sea of Mists midway in the continent. This vast lake was a study in spectacular contrasts: layers of striated rock, deep gorges, and tumbling falls cascading down, down toward the lake. The best vista was the island and its huge castle silhouetted against a fiery summer sunset. He spent an entire day sketching, while he ate the last of his food, then licked the crumbs from the bottom of the satchel.

He tried willing himself to go on despite hunger, but he tired much faster, and lamented having so little endurance. Now he regretted shrugging off Senrid's invitations to waken before dawn just to toil through physical exercise, which Jilo loathed, and Terry's similar invitations when Jilo was living over the Chwahir border in Erdrael Danara, after Wan-Edhe's return. He was a very good walker, after slipping in and out of Chwahirsland over that stretch of time, but that only meant his feet were in shape; the rest of him was as tough as overcooked noodles, he though grimly.

He would have run into trouble had he not been able to sense fearful people, or angry ones, or the willing collaborators. He begged at farmhouses, and once was given a ride by some underground resistance folk. And another of these, an old and very crafty river-woman who plied the Naldwer rescued him when she found him half-drowned on the shore alongside a great river. She took him to relations, told him to always ford a river with a good, stout branch at hand if he didn't have a boat, and cautioned him to head south. She said that the forest folk there would help him. "You don't want north," she said. "Unless you want to get betwixt the brigands and those hunting 'em."

He sketched their faces in his book, which he used to reinforce his tale of being a starving journeyman portrait-painter whose shop had been closed. He knew his talent was untrained—he could see it, but not how to fix it—but the people's appreciation was genuine when he apologized for his lack of mastery. Art, they said, nodding to one another, was, as you might say, art.

This gave him license to observe, and to record differences in people: regional, inherited, age, personality. He wondered how languages contributed to facial characteristics and gestures. And he wished he could meet up with Leander of

Vasande Leror, Senrid's friend, and ask him how languages branched.

One morning he freed six birds in a row as he wandered along the Sha Vira river looking for a place to cross over. He didn't trust bridges, but as he was a rotten swimmer, the fast-rushing water disinclined him against using it as a method of travel. The hot afternoon sun finally made him brave, and selecting a spot from which he could see a reasonable distance over both banks, he waded out.

The water was cool, but footing was exceedingly difficult. Inevitably he slipped, soaking his hat and knapsack, but he made it across, and camped early in a pleasant, secluded grove of trees so he could spread Senrid's paper and the leaves in his sketchbook out to dry in the balmy evening air. Hunger, and no way to escape it, forced him to try escape in sleep.

He was dreaming at midnight when an ancient cowherd he'd observed a couple days before drifted into his dream and suddenly spoke to him with David's voice.

Jilo startled out of the dream, thrown back in memory to when the entire pack of Detlev's boys had chased him across Erdrael Danara. After David had spent weeks aiding him in the struggle against Wan-Edhe's magic.

Jilo had always wondered about that, though he found Detlev's boys far too intimidating to ever ask, even after they and Detlev had left Norsunder. Not that he saw them but rarely — and the one time he initiated a conversation that he'd assumed would be innocuous, it wasn't.

Sharp remorse banished sleep, and for a moment he was in Bereth Ferian's library, late in winter up there. He and Terry had transferred to Arthur's library to ask about something; Jilo didn't even recollect the question. What he did remember was finding Roy there, as usual, talking to Adam, David, and Curtas, while Arthur searched through stacks of papers and scrolls on a long table.

They'd broken off their conversation to greet Jilo and Terry — the latter making a sort-of joke about how much they must miss the fine air and delicious food of Norsunder Base.

It was David who had turned it into a joke, but Jilo remembered feeling uncomfortable, and so he'd said to Adam, who he hadn't seen for a couple of years, "Do you get to study art now?"

Jilo flinched, remembering how the sudden silence had

gripped them all. How David had turned to the door, and Curtas had picked up a book from the table and began leafing through it, as Adam said, "Oh, I'm doing something else how."

Adam's smile had been exactly the same as always, and the subject changed to Curtas's new building project, but on their return to Erdrael Danara, Jilo had said, "What happened back there?"

Terry said, "Did you see his hands?"

"Whose hands?" Jilo asked.

"Adam's. Wearing gloves."

"I didn't notice. You know I never notice what anyone is wearing. It's winter up there, anyway, so gloves would be expected, yes?"

Terry shook his head slowly. "He never took them off, even when Arthur brought out the cakes and pear cider. It's the same thing I did, for a long time after I lost these." He held up the hand with the missing fingers. "I even stuffed my glove, until I realized it looked even weirder. I think something bad happened to his hands, and he can't do art."

"When? What?" Jilo remembered being bewildered. "I recall him having a broken leg, but ..."

Yet another painful blunder, the sort only he seemed to make. Ever since then, Jilo had avoided any encounters with them. Not that there were many.

Too wakeful to sleep, he shook out his cloak and got up. The moonlight was bright enough to see the world in shades of gray and silver, so he decided to walk on.

He made it halfway through the next day when the noon heat drove him to seek shade, water, and then to rest his eyes ...

And here was David once again in his dream, wearing that same shape of a cow herder, though the voice was David's. "Jilo — hold this dream if you can. I'd like to talk to you." The cowman smiled with David's brown eyes.

In other words, this was not one of those surreal twists that dreams take, it was a real contact. Recognizing it almost thrust Jilo into wakefulness again. He hovered on the threshold, more curious than fearful.

"You can see why this only works with Dena Yeresbeth folk," the cowman said. "Talk to this figure."

"An enemy is — listening in — via Dena Yeresbeth?" Jilo asked in astonishment.

"No, but one could be, and this is good practice for us

both." The contact was shot with humor, though the figure of the cowman poked about placidly. "Detlev says you are heading for Marloven Hess."

"How did he know?"

"He will explain when you meet. I too am going to Marloven Hess. Do you want to join forces?"

"Only if you know where you're going. I confess I don't really know the map, and I'm just walking west."

"You've got to head south, not west —" Briefly, a map glowed into his mind, held, and he saw that David meant to go by ocean, and that the mountains would take him months to trudge.

"Meet me in Al Caba. I will get a boat." An image of a harbor flashed into Jilo's mind. "Should take you four days to get there, but cross the Kerga foothills at night. You are heading directly into danger."

The cowman reverted to a dream figure, and Jilo slept.

Five

SUSPECTING THAT FOUR DAYS at what the Mearsieans would call poopsie-pace would be roughly four times that at Jilo-pace, he pushed hard. Probably too hard. A sudden cloudburst caught him on a particularly treacherous hillside as he skulked from shrub to shrub, tracking a low-flying spy bird. When at last the bird was directly overhead, which enabled him to break the lattice link, he made the mistake of watching the bird react and swoop away. He'd thought it a very small recompense, enjoying the sight of the birds discovering their freedom — but forgot that he stood on the side of mountain under a downpour.

When the ground beneath his feet began to slip, he had just enough time to whoop in a surprised breath before he tumbled down, smothered in mud. Down, down he slid, thoroughly buried, until he smashed into an outcropping of rock.

Mud flew in every direction, freeing his face enough for him to gasp for air — inhaling what felt like half the mountain along with it. He gagged, coughed, and spat, then flopped back, letting the rain beat down on his face before he dared open his stinging eyes.

The storm finally began breaking up. He watched the sun sink behind the gold and pink-edged clouds, then at last hauled himself upright, to discover that he'd tumbled to the foot of a woodland. He had no idea where he was, other than an occasional whiff of brine. Had he finally reached the peninsula?

He slogged until he reached a stream that ran clear, where he could drink, then dunk himself again. After which he spread out his things on the grass, and slept until something crawled over his face.

It was not quite dawn. The air was cool, not cold. Trees soughed overhead, a sound he had loved when he was small, sneaking out of the Chwahir outpost whenever he could, and into the Mearsiean woodland.

He drank some water, then sat back against the bole of a tree to watch the new day's light filter into the forest, something he hadn't done since he conceived his "early morning patrol to catch the Mearsieans" dodge, back in the bad old days of the Chwahir outpost below the Mearsiean capital.

First a thousand shades of gray and blue and brown emerged from the darkness, gradually transforming silhouettes into forms of three dimension. Flat brown shot with umber here and there, blue spangled with gold high in the trees. The spangles worked downward as the sun rose, then blended into the greens of foliage. The character and scents of this forest differed from Mearsies Heili in ways he did not have the vocabulary to define.

The enchantment of dawn had ended. It was now day, and he was not getting any closer to Al Caba by sitting there.

He got slowly to his feet, so hungry the light-headedness that came on gradually worsened to dizziness; at first he thought he was hallucinating when a raspy voice broke the quiet: "My friends said there was a human needing help. They are right?"

Peering into the green-brown shadows, he made out the half-visible figure of an old, bearded man.

His experiences with bearded old men had been mixed. Kwenz had largely left him be, outside of sporadic discussions of magic. Tsauderei had been observant, sardonic, but benign. Against them there was the horror of Wan-Edhe. This man was, unlike those three, short and squat, with goggle eyes above that beard.

"Go ahead and laugh," Jilo said. "I'm lost."

The frog-round eyes crinkled. "And yet you still found it worthwhile to free a being from evil bindings."

"And then I managed to fall down a mountain," Jilo mumbled.

The old man laughed, a rusty sound. "Come. You will eat, spend this night in comfort, and we will teach each other some things. You will lose no time from your journey."

He led Jilo into the deep-shadowed grove from which he'd emerged. There was no discernable path; they ventured farther into the forest, and though foliage and branches and vines were thick about them, the old fellow knew how to move so they were not hindered. Even after darkness had fallen, and Jilo could not see where he was putting his feet.

Then they stopped, in a dwelling built within a gigantic husk of a tree. A lit candle sat on a little rock-shelf against their coming, and on entering the man crouched down and snapped a firestick to light. Soon the welcome glow also exuded warmth, and a clean cedary sort of smell.

"What name shall I call you by?"

"Jilo. And you?"

"Call me Igkai."

Igkai spoke Sartoran, with an oddly archaic flavor that Leander could probably have identified. An image entered Jilo's mind and he said, "Turtle?"

Igkai sat back on his heels and grinned rather impishly. Though he was obviously old, small — the top of his messy nest of hair did not go beyond Jilo's nose — and thin, with gnarled, age-spotted hands and a wrinkled face, he moved like a much younger person. His hair and beard were grey-white and very long, tangled but clean, and he wore a shapeless brown robe tied at his waist with a sash. Several bags and implements hung from the sash, but no knife. His feet were bare.

"That I was named many years ago, by someone who tried unsuccessfully to argue me out of abjuring the human world. I kept it because my then-friends liked it." Once again the rusty laugh. "The turtle is slow, and careful, and endures. The turtle lives long without harming others in order to continue life. I thought it a good name for me, for turtles also live alone. I have changed a little since then, but it is still a good name." He carefully unwrapped a cloth-bound mass of brown, broke it in half, then held out part to him. "Now you must eat."

"Must?" Jilo repeated, trying not to grab with overeagerness. He was ravenous.

The piece of what he bit into was a very dense cake, mildly sweet, and touched with a little cinnamon. It had nuts and fruit-bits in it, but unlike the fruit-cake he'd tried — and hated as cloyingly sweet — this was savory. By the time he was halfway through it his body was reacting as warmth and vigor reached his limbs. When he was three-quarters done with his piece, he was full, and he carefully wrapped up the last bit for his next starvation-stretch. Even stale, that cake would be welcome.

"Now, you must tell me what you did to free my winged friends." And, to forestall Jilo's question about how he found out, "You freed a red-tail hawk before you fell down the mountain. She followed you down, then came to tell me. It was she who brought me to you."

"It's a lattice," Jilo said.

"I know *of* this magic, but do not know it. My skills lie in another direction entirely, and it is rumored to be very tricksome. One might say dangerous, especially forced bindings against the will of the bound. But what they are doing to the birds ... can you teach this spell to me?"

"I can," Jilo said. "But I only know how to do it with dark magic."

"Dark, light, it's two paths leading in the same direction," Igkai said with a dismissive wave of his hand.

Jilo ducked his head in a nod; he'd long thought so, but so many of the lighters were adamant in their belief that light magic was exclusive to those who did no harm, and dark magic exclusive to villains ... with the occasional exception. Igkai clearly lived here separate from all social, political, and cultural expectations.

Jilo drank some of the well water, which was cold and tasted slightly of wood, and then — fumbling and backtracking — commenced teaching Igkai. Who listened intently, and then wrote everything down in a script that Jilo did not recognize.

Igkai finally said, "I fear not many will be able to perform this spell, but I will see to it my mage colleagues get it."

Jilo agreed, adding, "And I don't have to be afraid every time I look up."

To his surprise, Igkai made a sharp negating gesture. "That would not be wise."

"Why not? If I see them, I will break the spell."

"Because there are those who have not the spell," Igkai said. "Who spy for one or another of the enemy from choice."

Jilo sat back. "Why?"

"Why does anyone cleave to another? Why does a horse choose a donkey for a lifelong friend, and the donkey choose the horse? Why does a beaver and a duck choose one another? Ah, they *chose*, for whatever reason, they chose, they chose. This spell, it is good for those who are forced into bondage. But you must still watch the sky."

Jilo stirred uncomfortably, but was not going to argue. "Might I trade for some food when I leave?" Jilo asked.

"I will give you what I have." Igkai poked a finger toward Jilo's knapsack. "But forests are bountiful for all creatures. And the rest of your walk will be through forest."

"I don't know much about nuts and berries and so on. I'm just as likely to pick and eat poisonous berries because they have rich color."

"Yes." Igkai bowed his head, rocking back and forward a couple of times, then leaned over and extended his arm toward the floor. Two small ferrets swarmed over each other, leaping to that arm and running up to disappear under Igkai's thick, grizzled hair. "Tomorrow I will walk with you, and you will learn. Now you must sleep, for we will be gone at first light." He pointed to a loft overhead.

Jilo climbed up, found a welter of clean blankets, stretched out — and dropped immediately into a long and refreshing slumber.

Their walk together was pleasant and instructive, and passed with easy speed. Jilo learned about plants and finding food. He learned how to look at forestland differently. He had always observed the fall of the light, and the colors and shapes of forest-growth. Igkai showed him how to watch the ground so he could discover where water might be flowing. And, therefore, where he'd find the plants that grow only along streams. Igkai pointed out the signs in leaf shape and lobe, in berry and fruit and flower, that indicated what could be safely eaten by humans, and which to be left alone. Igkai taught him how and why forests grow thick and why they thin out, and told him many stories about birds, beasts, and people like him, and about enemies who are not.

Igkai shared more of that wonderful bread with Jilo, who asked if he could sketch the mage. Igkai consented, but laughed from time to time as if he thought it funny. He asked to see other sketches, glanced through, and at the end he said, "You have a patient eye. This, I find, is a good sign."

Jilo had no idea what to do with that; his ears burned as he mumbled and shuffled his feet.

The mage handed the rumpled, crackling stack back, and the two parted as suddenly as they had met.

Jilo's walk became much easier as he put to use what Igkai had taught him. He was so absorbed that when he reached a ridge and the trees thinned, he was surprised to discover below him lay the distant bright line of the ocean.

Once he reached the outskirts of Al Caba he found himself enthralled by the bright sun winking and gleaming off glass, metal, and the restless sea. After the cool hush of the forest, the world seemed a panorama that he passed through without quite being a part of it, but he began to have doubts about ever finding one person in that chaotic mass.

He was soon sweating heavily as the day wore on. He was once again wearing his weather-beaten hat, and despite the heat he had the collar and cuffs buttoned on his grimy shirt.

Finally he couldn't bear wearing the tunic. He stopped in the middle of a broad road, hauled it off, and stuffed it into his knapsack. When he began to close the knapsack, Senrid's paper fluttered out, stirred by a breeze off the water. As Jilo bent to retrieve it and shove it back into the knapsack, he heard an angry shout.

The world, so distant until now, closed in abruptly. He wiped his forehead against his sleeve, fighting against a sneeze from air that was dusty and pungent from dark-ale and spiced fish-on-a-stick vendors.

He slung the knapsack over his shoulder, aware that in the short time he'd bent over, silence had fallen in his immediate vicinity. People had moved away, leaving him to be surrounded by a patrol.

A hard buffet slammed his shoulder, and iron fingers dug into his arm. He was barely aware of loud, harsh laughter nearby as he jumped. He looked up into the cruel eyes and curled lip of the sort of bully who used the gray jacket as a way to legitimize slapping and kicking others into gratifying fear and obedience.

"Let's see your papers, shit-for-brains," he snarled in corrosive Aliande.

"I haven't any—"

"Where you from?"

Jilo stared, aware that he hadn't updated his story since he'd left Wardrael. Igkai flashed in his mind and he said, "Sartor."

A voice behind him said, "He doesn't look like any

Sartoran. Looks more like them fish-pale platter-faces up north."

"You a deserter?" The Norsundrian shoved his face close, squinting at Jilo. "Here. Search this." The man yanked Jilo's knapsack free, nearly pulling one of his arms out of its socket, and tossed it to his partner.

Off balance, Jilo stumbled, and the Norsundrian grabbed the front of his shirt to straighten him up again. "What're you doing in Al Caba?"

"Looking for work. I'm a journeyman artist —"

He never saw the fist. Suddenly the world exploded into red and orange and black shards, and when it coalesced again his vision was hazy. "Traveling is forbidden. You know that or you wouldn't have been skulking here. What are you doing in Al Caba?"

The other Norsundrian dropped his knapsack and its contents into the street with a derisive gesture. Senrid's being paper fluttered among the drawings. "Nothing but scribbles and dirty rags."

The one holding Jilo turned his mean gaze back on him. "Take him in."

Pain splintered impressions as he was cursorily searched, bound, and shoved toward a couple other unfortunates the patrol didn't like the looks of: sun glinting on a swirl of dust motes; one of his drawings kiting into the street, propelled by the rising breeze. He coughed against dust and the sharp scent of horse sweat.

After a miserable but short trip, Jilo found himself shoved through a shadowy stone doorway along with the other prisoners. The gloom, his hair in his eyes, and his lack of balance made him stumble.

A Norsundrian barked questions at him, and when he remained silent, the leader of the group who'd brought him said, "Then he's ours."

"Not if he's on a capital list," was the response.

He was taken to a big room, busy with Norsundrians coming and going. A wall-length parade-window looked out onto a torch-lit courtyard, black with blood around a post. More wall-torches lit the room.

A tall Norsundrian strode in, scattering underlings left and right. To him clung the smell of dried blood. He pointed a crusted gouging tool at Jilo. "That one is a Chwahir! Let's begin with an eye—"

Crash!

Everyone in the room—prisoners and Norsundrians—spun around as the big window smashed into shards. Glass flew everywhere, glittering in the light of the flickering torches, as a black figure on a huge black horse leaped through.

Six

JILO GLIMPSED THE WHITES of the horse's eyes, and an outstretched black-gauntleted hand above the animal's head — then
the room erupted in noise, shouts, and fighting, with glass
tinkling everywhere.

Aldon, the tall Norsundrian who liked conducting his
own tortures, was one of Norsunder's top commanders, of late
shifted to the south. He was the first to react, throwing the
gouging tool at the figure on the horse. The gauntleted hand
moved in a tight arc and knocked the spinning torture
implement back at Aldon, edges glittering wickedly. The horse
plunged among the Norsundrians, who scrambled out of the
way, many picking glass from their faces and hands.

The black figure brandished a sword and a long knife as
the Norsundrians ran to the attack. Despite the rider's superlative skill the sheer number of attackers might have brought
him and the dancing, snorting horse down but three or four
dark-clad people leaped over the jagged-edged window sill and
spread out in a circle, throwing the wall torches at papers,
warriors, and the great table full of reports.

Glass crunched underfoot, kicked up by everyone as the
figure on the horse slashed his sword in an arc. Aldon had
picked up a sword from a stack beside the table and lunged, to
be blocked, then driven back by a furious onslaught. The horse
reared, hooves pawing near Aldon's face.

He jumped back — and fell heavily over a chair that a
black-clad figure shoved behind his knees.

A female voice murmured urgently to Jilo and the prisoners behind him, "Come on."

The prisoners scrambled after her, skidding on glass as they ran. Another figure helped at the window. The air in the courtyard was cool with the strong sea-breeze. Norsundrians and Adrani guards lay like lumps here and there, some moving painfully.

"Hold still," a voice said at Jilo's shoulder, smothering a laugh, and someone sawed energetically. A moment later his hands were free.

A mass of Norsundrians waving swords erupted from the door. The poised rescuers bent, did something close to the ground, and Jilo heard an odd, rattling hiss.

The first wave of Norsundrians skidded, and at least half went heels over head into spectacular parabolas, crashing into the rest.

"Dried peas," someone near Jilo gasped. "Come *on*."

Jilo stumbled after the speaker through a narrow door in the wall.

Out in the street two or three others waited, guarding several horses. People flung themselves in the saddles, and pulled others up behind them. Then they rode into a bewildering maze of narrow streets, riders peeling off every so often and vanishing up narrow alleys.

The few left stopped briefly in the back of a sail-maker's house. A hefty woman emerged, holding a lamp high. The black-clad rider wore a hat, under which his hair was covered by a kerchief. His skin was swarthy, his fine-ridged cheeks marked on one side by a writhing purple scar and on the other by three huge, hairy warts. One of his eyes was hidden by a patch, and the other squinted narrowly. He bent down, held a quick and low-voiced exchange with one of the other rescuers, then straightened and beckoned to Jilo.

When Jilo neared his rescuer, Wart Face pulled him up behind him with a remarkable surge of strength. Jilo barely had time to grab hold of the rider's belt when the horse leaped into a gallop as though it hadn't been out of its stall in a month.

The ride was long. Jilo couldn't see much. The rider was taller than he, and dizziness and exhaustion narrowed his focus to staying in that saddle.

Morning light had brightened into day before they slowed. Jilo's head ached badly, making him squint against the summer glare as his rescuer gave a long sigh. The horse ambled into a barnyard adjacent to a weather-beaten farmhouse. A door banged open and two children raced out, followed more slowly by a tall woman on crutches.

The rider threw his leg over and jumped off. The woman dissolved into wheezing, gusting laughter as Wart Face put his hands on his hips and grinned up at Jilo, who gazed down blankly.

"Come, Jilo! Midnight deserves a rubdown and feed, don't you think?" As he spoke, he yanked apart the laces of his black tunic.

Jilo gazed uncomprehendingly at the bulky black tunic now sagging, the narrow V of visible flesh some shades lighter than his face. A disguise?

The woman gave a gasp and a snort. "Three warts? Three?" She leaned heavily on the crutches, her silver-streaked brown head bent. "You just had to put on three?" She wheezed, laughing helplessly.

"Handsome, aren't they? I couldn't choose between 'em, so why not go for full splendor? Besides, I guarantee, the only useful description that will come out of that gang, including from Aldon, will be the three warts. I'm tempted to keep them, except they itch." He yanked his hands free of the heavy, steel-ring reinforced blackweave gauntlets, and wrung his fingers. "Also, hot. I thought I'd melt."

Then, right there in the barnyard, he stripped off all the black gear, the weapons, even the boots, flinging down the hat last. He stood there in swimming shorts as he pulled the kerchief over his face and rubbed vigorously. When he pulled away the brown-streaked kerchief, there stood David of Detlev's gang.

Jilo gaped.

David was either taller or thinner than Jilo had remembered, maybe both, and definitely browner. He looked as if he'd been living in those faded, frayed swimming cut-offs — his hair had sun-bleached in pale blond streaks and it curled unkempt on his neck. His skin was marred by thin scars here and there, an ugly purple one high on his ribs on one side.

"You didn't guess that was me," he asked, laughing up at Jilo.

"No, not for a moment."

"There, y'see?" He turned his head to address the woman,

who was wiping her eyes on her sleeve. "And I didn't disgrace the Black Phantom, did I?" Back to Jilo, who remembered that window exploding into millions of flashing pieces, the horse and rider leaping through.

"Oh, no," he said.

"See? See?" David waved at the pile of clothes and stuff on the ground. "Though I did sweat 'em up something fierce," he added ruefully, leaning against the worn slats of the barn.

He was laughing, but his hand shook as he brought it up to wipe his grimy hair out of his eyes. The woman eyed him narrowly, but said only, "That always happens. Always did, according to my grandparents' book. Never mind! One trip through the cleaning frame, and they're fine."

She turned her attention to Jilo. "You, don't you want to get down? The children want to take care of Midnight."

"Oh. Right."

Jilo slid off the horse, and his knees nearly buckled. He clutched at the saddle, struggling to keep his feet under him.

The woman wiped her eyes again. "Oh dear, if only my grandmother could have seen those warts."

"You hurt, Jilo?" David asked.

He was still leaning against the barn wall. Jilo didn't know him well enough to ask if David was all right — he was looking a little pale — so he just said, "Headache, nothing more."

The horse was led away by two youngsters, who cooed and promised treats and water and a good rubdown as they unbuckled the trappings.

"C'mon in, we'll getcha fixed up," the woman said. "Life! Those warts. I guess it's no worse than my grandmother in a beard ... but I'm not putting warts on my face! They'll just have to disappear, adding to The Phantom's mystery."

"The scar is very fine, I thought," David offered. "You can stick with that."

David moved away from the wall rather stiffly. He vanished into the barn and reappeared, holding out a battered object — the knapsack. With Senrid's paper safely among the drawings.

"Here, Jilo. I hope all the sketches are there. They were too good to lose. Almost forgot 'em in the saddlebag."

Jilo did not know what to say, but his rescuers did not seem to expect anything. David ran down the hall yelling, "I'll get dressed!" as the woman said, "I'll fix my special elixir. Bring the Phantom in, will ya?"

"Right." David disappeared again.

The farmhouse interior was cool, dim, and smelled of strong soap. Jilo sank into an upholstered chair staring uncomprehendingly at the leaf pattern embroidered on the chair-arm cover until David pressed a warm cup into his hands. "Drink this. Should help some."

Jilo smelled herbs, and tasted sharp steep with a hint of vanilla. Strange, but not unpleasant. Warmth spread through his head, easing the ache and leaving lassitude.

David knelt by his chair, wearing shirt and pants now, and peered into his face. "Better?"

"Much, thank you." Jilo drained the cup. "Won't they search?"

"Sure they will." David grinned. "They won't find that stuff, though."

"Horse?"

"He's a bay farm horse, turned into Midnight with dark green cloth dye. Remind me to teach you how to fall." He stood up. "Think you can eat?"

"Oh yes. I'm very hungry."

"Good. Sit and relax. We'll be leaving as soon as we've eaten."

Jilo said awkwardly, recollecting his doubts about meeting David at all, "Thanks for the rescue." Remembering that spectacular arrival, he added, "I can't imagine how you did it without getting cut."

The two children brought in trays. The boy dumped his and ran out, but the girl sat down nearby and picked up some sewing. Her poised manner reminded Jilo of Liere when he first met her. Dena Yeresbeth had given her that same self-possession.

The woman came in and dropped into her chair, easing her leg with a heavy sigh. She waited while David wolfed down a few bites, then said, "Land! Takes forever for a leg-break to heal. Now, tell me, where were the prisoners you rescued, and what did you do?"

"Main garrison."

"Never say! And whom did you take to help?"

"Sail-maker's cell."

"That all?" She raised her hands. "Well, you're alive — and here. How'd you do it?"

"Rode Midnight through the parade window, and while

they picked up their jaws, the cell-members piled in, grabbed the prisoners, we tossed the torches onto the papers, and absconded. Used dried peas to slow 'em down a bit. My guess is," David laughed easily, "some of those Norsundrians will be employed in cementing up that window today. Didn't manage to kill Aldon, and for that I'm sorry."

"Hm!" She grunted. "Never mind, Tobias and the others will keep trying. Well, sounds like you added a little luster to The Phantom's list of crimes, which is all I asked. Good for The Phantom to be seen again, good alibi for me. But I'll be glad to get back on my feet."

She ran a hand through her thick hair, and scratched her head. "What gravels me still, though, is how you knew about me. I know, I know, you hear unspoken things, same's Norfa here, and you knew about me same way she knew you were to be trusted. But makes me wonder all the same! Could be someone like that cursed Aldon will hear as well."

"Not from my source. I promise," David said, piling his dishes together. He started to rise, then fell back again.

This time Jilo saw color flood his face, then ebb.

"I'll get the dishes," the daughter chirped suddenly. "Cubby's here. You're supposed to be ready."

"Fewer people who know you weren't upstairs asleep last night, better," the woman said. "Though Cubby's a good enough young fella."

"Done, Jilo?" David turned to him, and his face changed. "Blast, I forgot about that shirt. Pants'll have to do, but not the shirt."

The woman nodded. "Just thinking that myself. Brown trunk. An old blue one, black leaves and vines around the neck. Should do fine. No one's seen it here for almost two generations. Nora. Hold Cubby off."

David and the girl moved in two directions. Jilo stood up, carefully picking up the dishes.

"You can leave 'em. Youngsters'll take care of 'em," the woman said, smiling at him.

David reappeared. "Here," he said. "Off with that shirt. Hurry."

It sank in then that David had not been talking about his lack of a shirt, but about the one Jilo was wearing. He glanced down. Dirt—rips—blood splatters from his nose and lip the night before. These stains were superimposed over the rest of the grime, and there were also several tears. He eyed the shirt David held out, and saw that it did not have buttons. "Did I stand out, is that why they nabbed me?"

"Yep," he said, and pitched into the fire the one that Jilo had just taken off. "That's it. You've got to learn about protective coloration."

"Aldon knew me for a Chwahir," he said, tying the black sash that David handed him. "I don't mean to sound grabby or ungrateful, but these socks are pretty ripe. I've been wearing 'em for days."

"Hang on! You'll be rid of 'em soon."

Cubby turned out to be Jilo's own age. David said good bye to the woman and her family (and he noticed neither he nor the woman addressed one another by any names); Cubby led them away, talking about local resistance plans. David seemed very knowledgeable. Jilo, listening, twice caught oblique references to parents and a family business in Nardarian. Was that true? He knew nothing of the poopsies' backgrounds.

They reached the shoreline mid-afternoon. Cubby led them out onto a pier, to which a variety of small boats were tied. They climbed into an old dinghy and Cubby rowed them toward a tiny island that lay not far off. Anchored all around it was a variety of sailboats and even some small two masted vessels. Cubby took them to one of the larger sailboats. It was fifteen or twenty paces long, with sleek, rakish lines, and one mast.

"Here you go," Cubby said cheerfully. "And here's the water-barrel I promised. Should easily be enough magic on it left to get ya to Valian."

"Looks good," David said, rolling the barrel out from under his bench. With a grunt of effort he hefted it aboard the sailboat. "Hop on, Jilo!"

This was a tricky process that involved two independently rocking vessels. Somehow he managed, though he nearly fell in a couple of times — finally Cubby shoved him from behind. "Landsman, are ya?" He chuckled, flipped up a hand, and rowed away.

David rolled the water barrel to the hatch and disappeared with it. He reappeared shortly and said, "Go on below. Bunks're there. You can flake out while I get us going. Time enough for questions after we both catch a little rest."

There was the hatch. A short ladder led down; Jilo clung

to it like a spider, moving a sweaty, tense limb at a time. But he finally reached the lower deck, and held on as he looked about him. He was in a sort of small room, with supplies and ship equipment stowed neatly all around him. Two benches had been built into the hull.

In one direction was the galley, and the other the cabin. Entering this last, he saw two bunks built up against the walls, with storage above and below. He kicked off his shoes and lay down on one of the bunks ... and while he tried to decide whether or not he'd need a blanket, he fell asleep.

Seven

JILO WOKE WHEN THE late afternoon light hit his face through an open scuttle, the slanting shafts sending sun-reflections dancing across the curved cabin walls and ceiling. How to paint that?

He climbed onto the deck—after lurching painfully into doorways, ladders, anything that could bruise.

Wearing only swimming shorts again, David lounged lazily on the clean, smooth planked deck, one bare foot propped on the rudder pole. The sail's ropes had been bound in such a way that he didn't have to hold it; the wind thrummed the sail's heavy canvas.

As Jilo made his way cautiously toward him, David's eyes opened. "Feel better?"

"Much." Jilo swallowed. Swallowed again.

"Hungry," David said appreciatively. "Know how to cook?"

"I'm afraid I have no skills beyond what you know from your stay in the royal castle at Narad."

"You'll learn. Here. Take over. I'll fix us something."

"What do I do?"

"Just keep this steady. The wind should stay on this side of you as you face the bow."

Jilo sat down stiffly, his body aching from the Norsundrians' rough handling, and David vanished below. The pull of water against the rudder was rhythmic, and easy enough to counter. Meanwhile the late sun beamed warm on his back, easing his bruises.

When David reappeared he said, "We've plenty of food. I even have clothes – sorry about the socks, but magic is limited in those parts, and the woman's cleaning frame needs renewal. I didn't want to use it for us when I knew we'd be coming to this boat. We'll be able to wash things easily."

"Ah." Jilo looked down, then up. "Though I probably should just stay in long clothing, because I burn easy."

"We'll take care of that." David passed him a bowl – and Chwahir eating sticks. "Eat up."

Jilo said, "I am grateful for the rescue. But why am I here?"

"Because I need your help." David saluted Jilo with his bowl.

Jilo laughed at the incongruity of one of Detlev's hyper-competent boys needing anything from the likes of him. The laugh hurt his throat. "Help you what? Learn to fumble?"

"I fumble enough on my own." David's finger brushed absently over the livid purple scar over his ribs. "Senrid wants you for something, I do know that. And you're going there. So am I. Why not this way?"

Senrid, that was who David reminded him of. Well, both were blond, with square faces. Maybe a little of the old Chwahir prejudice had gotten into Jilo after all, thinking that everyone outside of Chwahirsland looked alike. "Senrid wants me? For what?"

"Dunno. You'll find out soon enough. Meantime, I need someone to watch MV's boat while I do some experimenting. In case I mess up."

Jilo shook his head. "I know absolutely nothing about sailing."

"You'll learn. I don't plan to do anything for a while. If I do. Or if there will be any result. Here. We've time, a rare commodity these days. Let us use it with some awareness and control drills. You're going to learn to avoid sunburn while we work on removing from that Chwahir hide of yours the patina of long dead fishbelly."

"There's some mysterious way to deflect the sun's rays?"

"Not without magic." He wiped his fingers on his shorts and leaned back to prop his foot on the rudder again. "Do you know what Dena Yeresbeth means?"

"The lighters all define it as the unity of the three. Body, mind, and spirit."

"That's the poetic translation. Some say those words are mere poesy, barren of meaning. A tighter translation is cohesion in Chwahir, or in Sartoran, coinherence. Imprecise as 'the unity of three' may seem, the idea is clear enough."

"I think I get it."

"So. However you define it, you cannot integrate the three if you ignore a couple of the components."

You singular: David meant him. Jilo reached past that. "It's a continual process? For everyone?"

"Yes. You like music?"

"Very much."

"Then we'll try a music analogy." David eyed the sail, the water, and the distant feathering of clouds, then said, "Why haven't you discussed any of this matter with anyone who could give you these basic definitions?"

"Too recent. And, well, it always seemed the wrong time—" Jilo struggled to express his incompetence without sounding self-pitying, and found no words.

David said, "All right. You hear a melody all your life. You sing it, you recognize it when sung. You find an orchestra who plays it—that was your unity. Now, you can either call up the memory of it, or you can then go on to learn the instruments and eventually conduct the orchestra. And if you want, change the melody." He sniffed the air.

Jilo wanted to ask where David himself was on this path, but it seemed trespass. He confined himself to practical matters. "Did you steal this boat?"

"Didn't I mention? It belongs to MV."

Jilo thought of the sauntering, fiery-eyed tough he'd glimpsed a few times. "Did *he* steal it?"

David flashed a grin. "Paid. Has the sved to prove it. He saved up his earnings fighting pirates, not long before we hopped the fence. I worked on it one summer, while he was taking paying customers between Jaro and Khanerenth, bypassing Wan-Edhe's cruisers off The Fangs."

Jilo suppressed a grimace at this reminder of Wan-Edhe's toxic presence in Narad. "I take it one person can run it?" Jilo looked doubtfully at the tangle of ropes and blocks.

"Yes. You have to not mind constant work. He doesn't— though he's added some labor-saving systems. In a few days, you'll know all there is to know."

The last of the sun sank beyond the horizon and a cool

breeze sprang up. As the air chilled, David's hand once again rubbed absently at his ribs. He got to his feet. "Let me get a shirt. I'll show you how to anchor down for the night."

He vanished, and Jilo looked around at the deepening blue of the sky overhead and the purple horizon, its glowing embers reflected in west-facing rills of water.

When they'd readied the vessel for the night, David dropped and Jilo laboriously climbed down into the galley, which was invitingly lit by a small lamp affixed to a bulkhead. David explained the little fitted drawers, cabinets, and shelves neatly organized around the tiny stove. He started a vagabond fire in that, firesticks being far too difficult to get hold of on shore, these days.

David set Jilo to grinding beans for coffee while he fixed a simple meal of olive pressings-fried potatoes with carrots, and freshly caught fish. He dashed some wine over the latter, and pinches of herbs. It was difficult for Jilo to equate the hard-riding, hard-fighting MV with those small, tightly stoppered, neatly labeled jars of herbs, but David insisted that was MV's handwriting.

"Tomorrow you'll learn to make biscuits," David said, as he pointed to the clean-water barrel that Cubby had given him. He'd already filled it while Jilo was asleep. Judging from the bluish snap as they dipped their plates, there was plenty of magic still left on it, which meant they didn't need to wait for rain to refill the barrel.

They took the coffee back to the cabin and sat on the bunks, sipping coffee by the light of the single lamp. Life, thought Jilo, had become surreal, and regret washed through him for Conrad, whose life could have taken a better turn in the freedom Rel had won him.

Then David said, "What happened in Chwahirsland?"

"Didn't Detlev tell you?"

"No details, only that you teamed up with Shontande Lirendi in evading Efael's hounds by slipping into Chwahirsland to make a raid on the prison. Bold move. They have to be loaded down with orders to shoot you on sight."

"Actually, to drag me to Wan-Edhe so that he can have the pleasure of killing me, as slowly as possible. Rel was with us, too. We did rescue a couple of prisoners, one of whom was the new king of Imar. But ..."

David then saved Jilo having to figure out what to say by

wincing. "Ah, I heard a little of that. Sounds like Conrad Winstanhaeme gave up, and blamed everyone else for it."

Jilo remembered that painful statement about masters of mediocrity, which he had been so sure was aimed at him. Maybe it even was. But not altogether. "Oh, he blamed himself. I think he didn't see any way out of it."

"Other than the easy exit, leaving everyone else to clean up the mess. Enough of him. Tell me instead about the earlier episode in Chwahirsland, when you slapped Ilerian hard."

"That," Jilo said, "was mostly Detlev."

"He said it was you and Hibern who made it possible, as he had to deal with a few thousand layers of wards against him. Wasn't there something about a book?"

"Prince Kessler gave me one," Jilo said on an exhaled breath.

"About?"

"Lattice wards."

David leaned forward. "Same stuff you and I beat our heads against that time when I joined you in that poisonous fortress?" He shook his head slowly. "How much did you figure out?"

"Some — some." Jilo rubbed his eyes, remembering the headaches he'd endured while studying that book. "I felt stupid. I've studied dark magic for years, but I was a beginner when I saw the complicated knots of spells there. I did see where Wan-Edhe had superimposed some of his own spells in an effort to shortcut some of the purposes. "

"Dangerous — and stupid."

"Typical of Wan-Edhe. Of course he'd use others for his experiments, so the danger was never to him. Anyway, I felt less stupid when I complained to Hibern — this was right before she vanished — about how difficult it was to study. She said she felt the same way when studying Ancient Sartoran taerans. That there is another level entirely to the magic that we don't comprehend — "

David stilled, his eyes widening.

Jilo paused, waiting for him to speak. When he didn't, he went on. "Anyway, Detlev warned me it should be destroyed first if there is any chance Norsunder might get it."

"Here's a piece of information we learned the hard way. Detlev actually gives orders very rarely. But when he does, it's better to do exactly what he says."

"I did heed him. That's why I went to Mearsies Heili, to hide it there, where Norsunder can't get to it. What I don't understand is why Detlev didn't just take it from me, and use it himself."

David shook his head. "If it really was the old magic, he can't use it."

"Wait. I don't get it. I've seen him use dark magic."

"Not dark magic, the old magic. From their day, you understand? Precedes the arbitrary divisions we call 'dark' and 'light', which just has mainly to do with intent, and safety controls."

Just as Igkai had said.

"For thousands of years no one could use it, partly because magic itself was nearly destroyed in this world. Dena Yeresbeth as well. Both are needed, but using it for major magic would act like a beacon to the Host."

"New ... old ... I cannot imagine how and why it differs. But if it's that powerful, it's a shame we cannot master it and use it against the Host."

"Yes," David said, getting up. Jilo could not see his face. "I'll wash the cups. Then we'll get some shut-eye."

Jilo watched him make his way to the galley, and wondered what his experiment was. Something was missing, or misunderstood if not only the leader of Detlev's boys wanted Jilo for something, but Senrid—equally hyper-competent, and acknowledged king of a powerful kingdom. Senrid was everything Jilo wasn't, no doubt at this very moment assembling his resistance army.

No, David had to have misheard.

Eight

SENRID LAY FLAT BEHIND a flowering bush, pounding a fist against the ground and mouthing curses into the tufting summer grass as he stared down into the torchlit Eveneth garrison.

As the execution squad marched out and unslung their bows at a sign from the commander who stood squarely in the center of the parade ground, Senrid's fist moved longingly toward the bow strung across his own back. His feelings found momentary relief in the image of the commander crumpling with an arrow in his chest. It would be a long shot, but not difficult. That wasn't the reason Senrid withdrew his hand from temptation and formed it back into a fist.

The reason — reasons — were the two squads of Norsundrian heavies, armed and waiting, in the hills at either side of Senrid — and the ten youngsters who'd been marched out just before the execution squad, and now stood in a ragged line facing their foes. And those, in turn, were the reasons Senrid's local resistance command sat in a small house in the town, waiting grimly while Senrid forced himself to lie there and watch the execution of one he cared about while he did nothing to stop it.

The commander was taking his time, possible to let any would-be rescuers get into attack position, most probably to stretch the tension and misery out as long as he could.

The row of mostly fair heads turned toward the iron-studded doors.

Senrid had been trying to discover Llyenthur's evolving

orders for Marloven Hess. The most recent general order had been for ten random youngsters to be executed for every one Norsundrian brought down. So far, it had happened three times, the first causing shock, the second an angry upsurge in spitting wherever Norsundrians walked — or sat, or ate — and the third had sparked a riot, led by the mothers and grand-mothers of the victims, that had taken two days to put down. With heavy loss.

Senrid was betting that Llyenthur had changed the orders again, but if he was wrong, not only was the city ready to rise, he would lose them. For he had ordered them to stand down.

A squad of four Norsundrians marched out in square formation. At their center was a gangling blond teenage boy in dark clothes who walked straight and tall, with a jaunty stride, despite his hands being bound behind him.

Senrid gritted his teeth. He was even denied the question-able relief of being with Aldrend at the end. There were two Norsundrians hidden inside the fortress who had enough Dena Yeresbeth to sense a contact.

It didn't help at all that the boy had brought it on himself by flouting Senrid's order to hold off. He hadn't been the same since his twin sister had been shot three months ago in an almost-successful weapons-raid against the garrison, and he had gathered the remains of her group, nine of whom stood there watching him now, practiced for a month or two, then struck against the local command in a swift series of raids, culminating in the shooting of a local commander rumored to have a taste for torture.

Senrid knew that Aldrend had received the message to lie low because the runner carrying Senrid's commands had re-peated them face-to-face.

None of that helped Senrid be anything but agonized at having to lie there impotent. The fact remained, Senrid was doing nothing as the Norsundrians prepared to shoot one of his most promising academy third years.

"Aim." The commander raised his hand.

Arrows were nocked, strings pulled back.

"Victory!" The kid's voice broke, and then the arrows thudded into his chest, the sound only partially masked by the treble voices of the four teenage girls and five-ten-year-olds who shouted, their faces tense and stony, "Victory!"

The commander strolled over to the body, and reached out

a toe to nudge it.

Senrid sat up, careful to make certain he created no sil-houette against the night landscape, then pulled his bow and nocked his own arrow. If that shit down there gave the signal for the rest of the youths to be put against the wall, he was going to give himself the satisfaction of nailing him first, and as many of the others as possible before the two squads raced in. Take them all to damnation with him, because he knew, he *knew*, that that act would torch the tinder-dry, angry kingdom into a fire that would consume them all to the last standing person.

Better than serving Norsunder, they said bitterly. They would throw their lives away because that was the Marloven way.

And the failure for that is mine.

The thick, corrosive sense of blame churned in Senrid's guts. He controlled the nausea by an effort of will, but his eye stung as he gazed down into the court, while the commander took his time studying the row of young faces, their trembling limbs, and then lifted his head to sniff the air.

No sound from his hidden force.

No sound from the youths.

The commander lifted his hand... and pointed to the doors.

The execution squad unslung their bows and marched back inside. The youngsters were herded after, several looking back toward Aldrend's still form sprawled in death, arrows sticking up like an obscene parody of reeds.

The commander stepped over him, and followed the line inside, leaving the body to the medics to Disappear. After that, no one was left but the sentries on the towers. And the watchers on the hills.

You failed them, whispered the inward voice.

The roiling in Senrid's mostly-empty gut won its duel with his mental control. He fought a silent battle there, as bitter as any duel with steel. When his insides settled at last, and his watery limbs could move, he forced himself away, pausing only at a trickling stream to rinse out his mouth. When he sat up again, black spots swam before his eyes, darker than the starlit night. He ignored them. He had to stop the wildfire.

Senrid eeled through the grass to the cover of a standing of trees before fading away down the hillside.

A little while later he entered the low-ceilinged kitchen where seven people sat around an old wooden table, heads bowed, as in the background two gray-haired women and a grandfather with sparse white hair sang the eerie threnody called the Andahi Lament.

At the head of the table the parents sat, the man leaking tears, the woman with a face like stone, her empty arms, which had once cradled the two infants, crossed tightly against her chest: Aldrend was the second of her children to be executed in three months.

Senrid stood until the third repetition, and the old people fell silent. The only sound was the snap of the fire, and the shift of cloth as the father wiped his eyes.

Senrid chose then to enter.

The four men, two boys, and one woman stilled, except for their eyes, which tracked the arc as Senrid threw down his bow. The unspoken question intensified the silence.

"The others?" The older boy clenched his fists.

"Marched 'em back inside —"

A noise from without silenced them, hands moving to weapons.

A short red-haired girl bounded through the door, gasping, "All nine. Alive! Thrashed 'em . . Sent 'em home with ... a warning! I saw 'em."

The older boy sighed, sinking back in his chair, a bony-knuckled hand shading his eyes. The woman closed her own eyes, her compressed lips trembling.

"That's why I waited. To make sure." Senrid's voice came out hoarse. He shut his mouth until he could get better control.

While he tried to get a grip on himself, he watched the others process the news. Only one had died. The Norsundrians had new orders to replace the ten-for-one.

The adults turned Senrid's way, those not locked in grief assimilating the fact that the king had calculated correctly. This was why he had not taken out the commander, which was to be the signal for the retaliatory attack.

The younger boy, Retren Ndarga from Methden on the southwest border, watched everyone with his intense gray gaze as the family began stirring a little, talking a little, releasing their inheld tension very slowly.

Their host, Holned, a solid man with bristly red hair, got to his feet and began ladling stew into bowls and setting them out for anyone who would take one. At a sign from him, his thirteen-year-old son Evred hopped up and poured out ale from a huge stone crock.

Senrid gratefully took a sip, and then he couldn't resist another. The home-brewed ale was better than most, soothing the churning in his guts a little. He now faced two tasks, and he had to get them right. Today. Now, or there might not be a second chance.

First task. The parents were waiting for words of praise from the king. Those at least they could take to a home with two empty places, now.

The old warrior leaned his mangled arm heavily on the table as he swallowed the last of his ale, his gray-streaked yellow horsetail, long out of fashion, sweeping his chair seat behind him. Old cavalry vets would die first before cutting this evidence of old glory. "To young Aldrend, who would have ridden proud for Eveneth."

"Here, yes," Holned said over his shoulder as he stirred his cauldron. "Let's drink to Aldrend. Evred! Pour out ale all around. Did he give the victory cry?" He came back briskly to the table, wiping his hands on his apron.

"Yes he did," Senrid said, leaning back in his chair, as Evred carefully poured from the stone jug. "As did the nine."

"What did the Norsundrians do? Get mad?" Evred demanded with the truculence of barely-held-in tears over the death of his elder cousin.

"I was at the extreme range of bowshot, which makes it hard to see faces clearly," Senrid said. "I can't imagine they were pleased by that, or by the fact that Aldrend died well. He strode out there like he was in command of the place ..."

He went on to describe what he'd seen, emphasizing the boy's courage and heroism. The mother smiled faintly as she stared down at her work-worn hands. She grieved for the loss of two bright stars, but she was being honored by the king, a fact that would spread by gossip throughout the region by sundown the next day.

Even his exact words would be repeated, which was why he had to be so careful.

"... and the young ones were marched back into the prison wing," Senrid finished. He took a sip of his second cup of ale, knowing his drifting ending held their attention. "He died well. As Aldinor had, from what I have been told by everyone in Eveneth."

"Yes," young Evred said fervently, and all the adults agreed either by grunts or palms turned upward.

"A bad loss." Senrid struck his fist lightly on the table. "I had long plans for those two." He paused and studied the faces.

The transition had been made. So far they were with him.

"I can't give either of them enough praise," he said, emphasizing the "enough."

The mother looked up, her lower lids bright with gathering tears. Senrid smiled at her. "Remember when I first put them in the academy?"

Nods from the men, a little smile from the mother.

"They marched out of here so proudly—and their good moods lasted about a week. How they hated the discipline, especially Aldinor! And the pranks she pulled in revenge ..." Senrid tipped his head back as though trying to recall, though in reality he had prepared this speech all during the long day and night, lying there on the hillside.

He recounted a few of the twins' exploits, saving the most outrageous for last. "When I made an inspection that first summer Aldinor told me she might not ever make much of an captain but she was ready for field command with scrub-brush and broom." Another laugh, and then: "But you all knew them, too. I'm sure you remember as well as I do how only their second year they started taking awards as though they'd stolen them, including at the Games."

Fervent mutters of agreement, and one or two thin smiles.

"Shall I tell you the plans I'd made for them? Just this last year I'd had it in mind to season them for a few years in the desk jockey corps. Aldrend had a wanderlust. If city-travel turned out not to be enough range for him I would have used him for training missions to foreign lands. After that it's hard to say, but at the least I expect he would have ended with his own company. And Aldinor ..."

He paused, searching the expectant faces. "One of two candidates I had in mind to take Earl Waldevan's place." He pretended not to hear indrawn breath from one or two of them. "You know he had no heir, and I told him years ago I would give him one, he being the last of the old commanders from my father's time. Aldinor would have been, if she had turned out as I expected, an excellent Jarlan and Commander. And now—" He lifted his hands. "I guess I can say to finish that I shall miss them sorely. It will be hard to find replacements with as much promise."

There. I should have started ten years ago. Fifteen. But I will begin now, if they will hear me. One person at a time.

Underneath the glorious words he had to plant the idea that a live person can take on meaningful work in the future. But a dead hero remains a dead hero.

Yet he could not leave the parents empty-handed. This family was old Marloven; though all the various children were loved, and most were good at their chosen crafts, it was those two eldest who had brought pride to the family by choosing the army life. And so he finished his panegyric.

There were appreciative ducks of chins, and raps of knuckles on the table. Holned's brother and his bereaved wife departed, along with two of the grandparents. Curfew was still rigidly enforced.

Holned was left, as host; his grizzled old father supervised the youngsters into collecting and dunking the dishes. Then he herded them off to bed. As Retren left with dragging footsteps, he looked expectantly at Senrid, but received a smile and a jerk of the thumb: yes, bed for him as well.

The youngsters' settling noises upstairs had diminished when Holned poured out two more cups of ale and sat down opposite Senrid. "Everyone in town will be finding excuses to come by to either my brother or me tomorrow."

"Then you will be the one to decide whom to trust for spreading my communication system."

Holned flushed, rubbing one of his protuberant ears. He said doubtfully, "It's hard to learn something new. You know, without drill."

Senrid leaned forward. "Not this one. You probably know I've been working on this problem off and on for years. I always got too elaborate. "

Holned poured out more ale and sat opposite Senrid, his mug in his hands. "I know. I remember hearing tell of the games you set up in the city."

"And how my great ideas failed." Senrid lifted his hand. "This is how my new idea came about. When I sneaked back into the kingdom, I had nothing, not even a change of clothes. I didn't dare let anyone know I was here, except for Keriam."

Holned opened his hand. Everyone knew Commander Keriam, sometimes nicknamed Kingmaker Keriam (though he didn't know if the king knew about that). Keriam headed the

Marloven academy, he'd had command of the city guard in the old days, and he'd been a father to the king when Indevan-Harvaldar was knifed by his own brother, when Senrid was just five.

"Well, to keep this yak short, I began stealing food. Not from anyone poor. But careful as I was, word got around anyway, and ahead of me. I don't know how. The important thing is, word got ahead—but the Norsundrians didn't hear it. People talk. We all know that. But they were very careful who they talked to. Then I started finding open windows, with a chicken pie cooling. Fruit tarts. Rye biscuits, just baked. Fruit. Too often to be coincidence; and if I nipped something, the hue and cry about theft did not go up."

Holned chuckled; a cook himself, now, he knew that in some villages there was fierce competition to see whose house the king took food from as he passed by in the wind. But, he wondered, what did 'the open window for the king' have to do with a comm system?

Senrid said, "I thought, we need a communication system that's as simple as the open windows. But can travel fast. And what is faster, and yet more simple, than a candle in a window—set to the left or the right on the sill, or maybe upstairs instead of down? Two candles in the upstairs windows to mean one thing, downstairs for another. Only for a short period, say second-bells watch, as people go about their evening inside, so they never draw attention."

Holned chuckled, rubbing his hands.

"I will explain the code to you, and you and whoever you think best divide up watches. Now, simplest is: Norsunder coming in force ..."

Presently, Holned set aside his mug. "Got it. You're right. It's easy enough." Then a shrewd look. "We are going to rise and fight, then."

Now Senrid was on familiar ground. Not easy ground, but familiar.

"Of course we are," he replied. "But not today. Or tomorrow. They are waiting for just that. As I told you before the execution, the entire setup was a steel trap."

Holned rubbed his ear again. "You were right."

"They're backing off a little because they're stretched too thin elsewhere in the world not to. But if they have to shift too many of them here to hold us, well, then they'll lift the gate as we become a battleground in a war we can't win. If we shout out 'Honor!' and go down fighting to the last, then I'm left with a kingdom of empty houses, and Norsunder uses word of the slaughter here to tighten their grip on the world."

"The world," Holned said—like most Marlovens, having not given a thought outside the border.

"Think of the message to the rest of the world: if we are destroyed, no one dares rise. Their bully-boys use us as target practice, and when we're all dead, they noise that to their own benefit elsewhere."

Senrid watched the impact of those words. "What should we do instead, you're about to ask? I'm communicating with other leaders. Mages. The entire world will rise on a signal. We have to be ready. Alone, we can't win. Together? We can."

"Yes. Our defeat made that clear enough. But it's hard."

Senrid turned up his hand. "No matter what we do, we've hard times ahead. Let's make it harder for them, if we can. But we have to choose the right battlefield, and the right time to attack."

Holned smacked his hands on the table in agreement, then rose. "Can I get you something to eat? I noticed you didn't like my stew." He smiled.

"Stew's fine. But watching your nephew get shot, without my having lifted a hand, took away my appetite."

Holned's smile winked out. "Maybe you ought to hit the bedroll, especially if you mean to be on the road again. But before you do ..."

Here it comes, Senrid thought. He gestured assent.

"It's about Jarend Ndarga's boy." Holned paused, and when Senrid opened his hand in invitation, he said, "Talk is going round you've taken him on as ..." Holned hesitated, hating to mention the little princess so newly dead. "Your heir. No one is saying he could *replace* the little princess," he added hastily, blundering even worse, though unknowingly. "But a king's got to have an heir. That's reasonable."

There was nothing reasonable about putting a suicidal eleven-year-old on a throne, Senrid wanted to retort, but he didn't. Senrid detested inquiries into his private life. At the same time he knew that the expectation of a private life was an absurdity in kingship; he had spent years trying to convince his Marlovens that changes in government did not always have to be by violence. Of course they wanted to know what to expect if Senrid died, which could happen any day, and what's more, they had a right to know. A peaceful changeover meant getting used to the heir beforehand, and the heir getting used to them.

Senrid looked down at his empty hands. "I'm still considering this question."

"Ah. Give us a fighter, that's what we'll need, Senrid-Harvaldar, though everyone hopes it will not come to pass for many years."

"Thank you. As for Retren, he's with me for the sake of expedience. He's expressed an interest in learning magic, and I'm waiting for a friend to arrive who would be an excellent teacher. He is likely going to leave the kingdom altogether, at least for a while."

Holned pursed his lips. "He's a good boy," he said. "And Jarl Ndarga had a good rep."

"True, and true," Senrid said. "Come, we're both tired. Time to rack up. In case I don't see you come morning, thank you for housing us. I'll be back again this way before too long."

Holned smiled. "Ah, we'll see you come dawn. I myself would not see you off without a good meal inside you."

The boys were asleep in the loft. Holned could not prevail on Senrid to take his narrow bed in the little room off the kitchen, Senrid saying he preferred the floor by the window. He lay there until Holned's breathing slowed and deepened, then he got up and returned to a chair to sit staring at the kitchen fire as he considered persons and events of the past five years. An idea was evolving in his mind ...

He fell asleep without meaning to, woke suddenly (with a crick in his neck) when he tried to change position, and discovered he was still in a chair. Shaking off drowsiness, he mind-touched with Retren and was joined noiselessly a short time later.

Retren grinned in triumph. One thing he'd learned while traveling with Senrid was quiet arrivals and departures. They picked up their gear—for both were armed like a couple of arsenals—and slipped outside.

Dawn was still an hour or two off. The air was cool, and wisps of fog blurred distant shapes. The city was quiet, and Senrid and Retren passed through and out, easily evading the night patrol.

It was not until they were in the open fields, with gray edging the eastern horizon and morning birds beginning to drift along, calling, that Retren said pensively, "What now?"

"Roam around for a day or two, make sure they are doing what I want, then take my semaphore-system to Toth and Telyerhas and see if they want to join us. Perideth if we have time — and patience."

"South," Retren said speculatively, grinning with anticipation.

Senrid glanced at him. "Glad you know some geography."

Retren's grin winked out like a snuffed candle. "Are we going to stop and see Marend?"

Senrid looked down at the wide, watchful gray eyes, and saw no anticipation there, no joy. Retren had braced himself, the subtle signs of which brought Aldrend unexpectedly to mind, right before the commander gave the order to shoot.

Senrid said, "We shall see what trail proves fastest."

Retren turned away, accepting, and Senrid thought, no Darchelde, then. Not yet.

They kept walking, eventually coming in sight of a small village, sheep dotting the gentle hills. Their stomachs were gnawing with hunger when they spotted an open window, and not just a chicken pie cooling, but a hefty wedge of cheese, and a jug of fresh milk, and another of ale.

Senrid sent Retren to fetch the food, which they ate sitting down by a stream out of sight of any roads.

The king is abroad, that was what the open window meant. And, *The king will free us*.

I'll run until I die, isn't that what my ancestor said? Senrid gave a mental shrug as he washed out their dishes in a stream then put them back in the open window.

Senrid picked up his bow, shouldered his pack, and they left.

Nine

FOR SOME DAYS DAVID and Jilo worked at sailing techniques interspersed with all kinds of games and drills. Jilo knew he was getting remedial poopsie training. Remedial for the likes of him. He was grateful to get it, especially as David never said anything about Jilo stumbling when the boat lurched unexpectedly. He just waited for Jilo to get back up again.

For a time his head as well as his body ached. His body, as muscles long ignored now were exercised, his head as new avenues of thinking, new ways of concentrating, new focus, tested him. Jilo learned to reach deep within and alter his skin's ability to use what it needed from the sun and shed the rest.

He learned to handle the tall, beautifully curved mainsail, and the jib sails that extended from the mast to the bow when the winds were light. He learned how to cook. There was no mention of experiments but, sensitive as he was, he caught a distinct flare of excitement from David when he explained how the Sartoran Sea was a bowl for winds, thus making sailing there as problematic as it was around the islands at the eastern end of the continent.

"Then the weather might turn bad on us?" Jilo asked as he scowled in suspicion at the bright, benign blue sky.

"Oh, yes." David laughed.

Jilo studied the deep blue waves, the sparkle in the wavelets, and shrugged. It obviously wasn't now.

When he wasn't tending sail, or working through complicated

drills of his own, David whittled at a piece of wood. He liked keeping his hands busy.

Between drills one day, as Jilo tried to recover from an especially tough lesson (every night he fell into his bunk, his muscles like unraveled strings) he said, "How do you navigate, out of sight of land like this? I take it you want to be out of sight of land. Is Norsunder patrolling?"

"Yes, though they rely more on spy birds. Shortage of forces, since Kessler closed off the world and left the occupation armies waiting in Norsunder. I have to admit this is my first attempt at navigating on my own, but we passed the Dessre Islands when I thought we would, so we're doing all right."

"Show me?"

He did. He also showed Jilo the log. In turn, Jilo was glad that for once he could teach something: he gave David the spell for breaking the controls on spy birds.

"This," David exclaimed, "is valuable. And too difficult for most of those I know." But he'd see to it that MV would learn it. Sveneric. Detlev likely knew it, but he'd been spending so much time where no spy birds flew ...

The days passed one after another, full of lessons, talk, and more lessons.

They were becalmed toward the latter part of the month. The ocean, which Jilo had discovered had its moods, turned a glassy green. Somehow that color made him aware of the distance between their stick of floating wood and the ocean floor far below. Later in the day a breeze from the north tugged fretfully at the sail and jibs, too uncertain to sail by.

By late afternoon the heat was back. They sat on deck eating the meal that Jilo had prepared, and watched the slow, steady march of tiny puffs of clouds eastward.

"About the old magic," Jilo said, and David flicked a sharp look his way. "Something wrong?"

"No. Go on with your question."

"Why hasn't Detlev taught it to you?"

David dropped his head back and squinted at the sky. A hot puff of breeze fingered his hair, which had turned pale yellow. "He's taught me the theory. Practice is impossible because it's still a secret. Though not for much longer. And most wouldn't be able to use it."

"But the Host knows, right?" Jilo grimaced. "I don't

understand why they haven't blasted us with it, killing us all?"

David looked upward, considering what he could say and what he couldn't. "One aspect to them remaining deep in Norsunder-Beyond is that they lose awareness of time. We have the mainsail set, no reefs, and the jibs. All the canvas we've got, but we're barely moving, because there isn't a breeze."

Jilo's brow puckered, then he said, "Oh yes, you said that magic has been coming back into the world. So the Host didn't know how much had recovered, is that it?"

"Pretty much. Each century more evidence of it. The Host doesn't want to bother hanging out their sails until there's a wind worthy of them."

"But they are out now."

"Yes."

"So they know how much magic is back in the world."

"Not ... quite."

"Does that mean there isn't enough? There's more to come?" Jilo kept at it.

"Yes."

Silence fell as Jilo considered these things. David lay back, his fingers moving over his ribs. Jilo had noticed that gesture from time to time. As their skin armored itself against the summery sun by browning, that livid purple scar slowly began to fade to pink.

Jilo knew plenty about scars from his days in Wan-Edhe's castle. That wound of David's, located where it was, had been serious, and it was newly healed. Maybe because of the wound he got cold easily, sooner than Jilo did, unless he was exerting control. But David rarely did that, telling Jilo (though he found it difficult to believe, for their wrestling matches proved that David was far stronger and faster) that he was recovering his strength. He admitted that after his Phantom ride, he'd nearly fallen off the horse in a faint. Jilo doubted it, but he appreciated the oblique boost. And in truth he was getting stronger.

In the evenings, when the wind often died down, they floated on the water in silence, after a hard day of work. The sight of David there whittling away at a new handle for one of the storage lockers, which had cracked, made Jilo's internal dialogue shift from magic to the nature of friendship.

MV, who had rebuilt most of the boat himself, David had told Jilo, trusted David enough to permit him to take it. And to bring it back.

Jilo thought about his own friends. He did not consider the false twi who had sycophantically followed him back in the days with Kwenz—reporting in secret to Wan-Edhe on everything they heard and saw Jilo doing. Wan-Edhe had scorned the idea of friendship, saying it was merely another name for using others. Jilo had seen the evidence of Wan-Edhe's lies in Clair's group of girls. But in those days it was easy to dismiss them as "just girls"—lighters—sentimental—all Wan-Edhe's ideas. Jilo had envied the camaraderie of Clair's gang, and also their strong bond, so strong it made them as a group far stronger than any of them could have been as an individual.

Jilo had discovered what friendship meant to Clair after Wan-Edhe was tricked by Kessler into Norsunder-Beyond. Clair had offered to share magic books. No demands, no promises, no superiority—no claims. She loaned him her books, trusting that he would not use the knowledge against her.

From there to kingship. He'd told Senrid, Atan, and Rel that he didn't feel like a king, despite all the years that had passed. More of a custodian. Senrid had laughed and told Jilo that all kings were custodians.

How was he to win Chwahirsland back?

That thought drove him to get up restlessly, to get physical space by roaming the length of the boat and back. The air was hot and sultry, and when David sent a considering look his way, he recklessly dove over the side.

The water, so cool after that humid press of heat, was delicious. The mental turmoil receded as he concentrated on using what he'd learned about swimming. Then he turned on his back and floated on the rising swell as he stared at the sky.

Even supposing he did manage to free Chwahirsland, who would rule? The next in line through blood would be one of the two Sonscarnas—Kessler or Rel—but both had made it clear they would never return to Chwahirsland in a permanent way.

Kingship—friends.

Clair, Shon, both rulers. Senrid. Terry. All rulers. They understood how much work lay ahead, reversing Wan-Edhe's damage—

"Jilo?" David's head appeared over the edge of the rail. "I think you'd better come up. Heavy weather on the way."

Jilo saw that he'd been staring not at woolly tuft clouds, but towering gray leviathans. He scrambled back on board and helped David get everything battened down tight except for the reefed sail, angled to the wind. Used as he had gradually become to the rolling of the deck, the sudden sharp angles and pitches nearly dashed him overboard and he began to use the life-rope David had strung along the length of the ship.

David sent Jilo below to batten down everything there, the lockers not just shut but wooden bars shoved between the handles and knotted tight.

Then Jilo leaped back on deck in time to see the last of the daylight smeared in glaring orange across a sky filled with vast, mountainous black clouds. Far to the east the sky was clear, but that would change — the whitecaps tossed all the way out to the horizon.

He gripped the life rope, ready to follow orders as David braced himself at the rudder, forcing the boat round southward against the east-running current.

The sail thrummed. The wooden hull and the mast creaked. Ropes hummed as the wind rose, and the breakers began to smash against the bow, sending foaming jets of water washing down the deck.

Uncertain, Jilo had just decided he needed to see whatever was coming — he wouldn't hide below — when mind-touch from David sent him to the sail to add another rope as brace.

It took far too long to do this otherwise simple job, for he was thrown down once by a sharp pitch of the bow, another time by a massive wash of water over the deck. Jilo understood viscerally now how important it was to know how to fall, for he rolled to his feet again, hand gripping the life rope. Then up for another try. It seemed to take forever, and his hands shook. But at last he got the job done. Lightning flared; thunder crashed and rumbled across the sky.

"Reef!"

Jilo sprang to that job, as the deck slanted dangerously. He had to stand on the rail. The ties were like ice, and his hands bled before he was done, but the straining sail eased, the wind now whistling under it, and the boat lifted higher out of the water, sending the smashing waves down its length faster. It began to move instead of wallow, the mast creaking warningly.

Finally Jilo had everything braced as well as human effort could make it, and toiled back to David, who stood with his face into the wind, his hair blowing straight back; he had braced the rudder pole, the ropes iron-taut. "Forgot about danger to life and limb," he shouted, grinning. "When one plays in storm weather."

"What?" Jilo shouted back, and then remembered David's mysterious experiment.

Surely not *now?*

David said, "You know vagabond magic?"

"I know of it. I'm no traveler —"

"It's a state of mind." A mask, actually, but David was cautious out of long, trained habit, even during the extremity of this storm, as MV's boat rode up kelp-veined waves higher than the mast, then crashed down again. "Let me teach you how to gather it," he yelled.

He showed Jilo how to use Dena Yeresbeth to see and gather magic potential. Jilo grasped it so fast he began to comprehend that he'd always done that, but in a passive way. Jilo saw at once how the supposed limits — traveler, sunrise, sunset, music — were in truth human-imposed limits, to give the shapeless a sense of form; his long, painful labors in Narad made it easy to gather the potential and shape it. "If something happens to me, and the boat begins to break up, use this magic to bind it," David shouted. "Storms are wild with magic potential."

Jilo already sensed that — the charge of it, like lightning gathering, only it was discernable in the mental realm.

"Is what we're doing traceable?"

"Not for such a small purpose." He indicated the mast swinging in a wide parabola. "Your falls on this heaving deck were well done. If we had any swords we could get in some practice with steel. Assuming we live through this one."

"You lost that black sword?"

"Taken from me." David lanced a brief smile Jilo's way. "I'll get it back. Remind me to teach you some sword forms." As lightning flared closer this time, he laughed, not the breathy chuckle Jilo thought characteristic, but a ringing laugh that somehow expressed both tension and joy.

The storm worsened steadily. Whenever Jilo thought it had reached its maximum an even larger wave would loom up, high as a rooftop. The boat slanted up at an angle nearly vertical, and just as the boat seemed to hang in the air — he feared it would fall backwards into the abyss between waves — the bow would crest the foam, water washing all down the length. Then it slid down into the trough, water crashing over the rails as the wind failed. The sails sagged, and they wallowed as the seas poured out of every scuttle. Then began the gradual climb up the next wave, jolting as the screaming wind caught the scrap of sail again, and wrenched the boat taut.

They tied ropes round their waists as rain slashed with stinging cold needles, and lightning glared. The bracing ropes at the rudder trembled violently, sending vibrations through bones and teeth. Lightning flared, followed by a crash of sound so loud Jilo's bones juddered with the boat under him. When he could see, it was only shapes, the rare glitter of rain and water in the reflection of distant lightning. And what he saw was an impossible tall wave forming behind the two or three coming at them. Higher than a castle tower, clots of seaweed veining its greenish-black wall as it swelled closer, and higher.

The intervening waves abruptly diminished, as if the monster drained their strength. David flung one last bracing noose around the rudder.

They hit the trough at the base of the monster. An enormous surge of water struck Jilo in the chest, and he fought for breath, fought to keep his hold on the life rope; a block glanced off his head, but he scarcely felt the pain.

When the water sloughed behind, the boat pitched, riding upward, upward, and in the glare of lightning Jilo saw David laughing, the sound ripped away by the wind.

He lifted his hands, not holding on at all.

What? Had he lost his mind —

Lightning forked to the left.

The boat shot upward, water pouring off. Up straight into the wind, the sail racketing madly. Bewildered, Jilo braced his numb, bleeding hands on the rope, waiting for them to smash down as three, four heartbeats passed and they rode the monstrous wave.

David threw back his head, laughing into the angry sky, his blood-dappled hands raised, the tendons standing out.

Lightning branched and crackled directly overhead, branched, then shot down toward the boat. Glare-blue light coruscated around David's fingers. His laughter vanished in the roar of wind and thunder, the enormous swell and crash of water. Then he threw the lightning back at the sky.

Jilo stared witlessly as light shot skyward, an incandescent bolt joining storm and human in light.

Jilo tried mind-touch. David's head jerked his way, then the mental realm exploded with a force impossible for his tenuous grasp and he fell into oblivion.

Ten

JILO WOKE UP STRETCHED out on his bunk.

His shoulder hurt where he'd smashed against the mast. His forehead throbbed as well. He didn't remember what had struck him. His ribs ached, along with a knee, and one badly stubbed toe.

"Awake?"

Dressed in clean shirt and trousers, David dropped on the edge of his bunk, a steaming cup in his bandaged hands.

Jilo raised his own hands, and discovered they too were bandaged. The ropes burns added their clamor to the other hurts.

"I would have gotten those wet clothes off you, but you tried to sock me," David said. "Drink this."

The listerblossom washed away some of the ache. Jilo's awareness ventured farther, to the boat rocking gently, and the light in the open scuttles clear, bright, and mild.

"I'm all right. I *am* all right," Jilo discovered. "How much of that was a dream?"

"It happened," David said. His expression was pensive, but Jilo sensed mirth, like sunlight on water. That and triumph.

"What's so funny?" Jilo asked, drinking down a gulp.

"It was a pretty rotten evening for you. I apologize."

"Not for you. Not the way you were laughing. I thought you'd gone mad—and I couldn't remember that vagabond magic because my own wits had fled. I thought lightning hit you. Except I distinctly remember—or dreamed—that you tossed it back into the sky?"

David half-raised a hand and stretched the fingers, holding it there tensely, then dropped it to his knee. He said, softly, "I raised the old magic."

"That's what you meant about playing with the weather?"

"It was the only way to try it and not catch the attention of the Host. I planned it very carefully. It's been a long month." He lifted his head, looking sightlessly at the decking above their heads. "A month ago today, in fact. I didn't know if I could hold it. Which is why I taught you that spell."

"Does anyone know what you did?"

"No one but you and me."

"Not even Detlev?"

"No. But I think he knew it would happen. He would probably have wanted to be there to monitor me. And not in the middle of a war, though he knew that was coming."

"If he didn't teach you—"

"He taught me the theory. I figured out the practice." David flexed his hands slowly, as if his rope burns hurt, too. "It began when I was assigned to investigate vagabond magic. Which I'd thought as useless as illusion, a lighter parlor trick. I should have known better. Les Rhoderan wouldn't have bothered with parlor tricks. He wanted to build himself an empire, and he was the first to figure this stuff out. Worked hard to keep it secret."

David's gaze diffused, and he smiled sardonically. "But it took time for me to recognize the clues. There was no one on the lighter side I could ask—and few enough knew of it. Autumn of Bermund is not human, so her understanding of magic wouldn't match ours. No one could find Rel after he learned it."

"He wouldn't have talked to you anyway," Jilo said, remembering those bad days—Terry's wild grief over the killing of his friend Karhin Keperi. Glenn Delieth killed, and by David himself, even if it had been a duel.

Shon hadn't lost a friend to death, but to betrayal. He and Curtas had bonded, something Jilo hadn't even known until Thad said to Jilo at the end of the alliance shambles, *You people probably won't see Shon again, at least for a while. It's not your fault. I want you to understand that. It's just that—until Curtas found him—he never had a friend. Not a real one, or what he thought was a real one. That betrayal, well, if he goes back into isolation, it's because of that. Tell the others, if they ask.*

Not that they had. No one had really known Shon, except Thad.

David gazed down at his hands. "The irony is, Curtas would have willingly stayed friends with him."

"But you, several of you, killed people on our side. You saw us as enemies. Didn't you?"

One side of David's mouth tightened, less anger than a grimace of ... regret? "How to answer that? I don't think any of us saw you as enemies in the same sense as we regarded Efael, Aldon, Henerek, and the rest of them. No, make that most of us. We saw ourselves as isolated. There were individual jobs. I can tell you this: though people died, Detlev never ordered us to kill any of you. He explained, quite reasonably, that he did not want us to be annexed and used as assassins. If it helps, think of the two of us working in that stinking fortress of Wan-Edhe's, for months. I never once tried to take you out, right?"

"That's true. And you could have. With ease."

"Not ease," David admitted. "Not in that poisonous atmosphere. I still don't know how you survived it."

"I almost didn't," Jilo mumbled. "That time. In Erdrael Danara. When the lot of you tried to nab Wan-Edhe's enemies book from me. After Autumn destroyed it, she did some kind of magic on me. Said she was removing poison. I was poisoned, and didn't even know it."

David eyed Jilo. "It was evident. Did she also remove the Child Spell from you, or did you do that?"

"I never had it," Jilo said. "Or maybe I did. If I did, Prince Kwenz put it on me, to keep me from growing tall enough for Wan-Edhe to see me as a threat. But I don't know. You remember how time is distorted in that fortress."

"But you've been growing since," David said.

"I have?"

"I think you've grown since we climbed onto this boat. Not certain, but one thing I do know, you've got a couple of hairs sprouting on your lip there."

Jilo fingered his face. "I do?"

If David had needed any proof of his suspicion that the sun of awareness was still below the horizon for Jilo, there it was. He masked his amusement; he and the boys had spent their years on the houseboat in the secret bay mostly without clothes, as they were constantly in and out of the water, but when they were in Norsunder Base, they slept in clothes designed for action, with weapons in reach.

David had long ago learned that the easiest way to fit into a social situation was to dress in similar fashion to whoever he was with, and so, though the two of them were alone in the middle of the Sartoran Sea, David matched Jilo's comfort level by wearing swimming shorts night and day. Jilo was already uncertain enough, whether that was due to surviving Wan-Edhe, or his going without the support of a twi, or his own natural reticence.

David waited to see what direction Jilo would take, as Jilo stopped fingering his lip; he had already forgotten the superficial changes in his own body, never much of a subject of interest. He was still trying to understand Detlev's boys' place between Norsunder and the lighters. The thought occurred that no one had ever heard their side of anything. He was especially sensitive to such matters, having endured countless reactions of disgust and revulsion at the mere sight of a Chwahir.

Of course, some of that was due to Detlev's gang's collective silence. "So the deaths were truly accidental?"

Jilo could see from the marks under David's eyes that, clean as he was, he hadn't slept, and wondered if he would be hearing as much as he was if David had been rested.

David said, "Glenn's death I didn't regret as long as I probably should have. He was going to be the worst sort of king, and he was better at dividing your allies than we were. But Karhin Keperi—" He shook his head. "Was killed by one of us whose brain never quite healed."

He half raised a hand, then flicked it aside—a gesture Jilo had seen many times from Senrid. "Back to vagabond magic. The Norsundrian understanding of vagabond magic as harmless illusion was a carefully constructed mislead."

"Didn't you say that vagabond magic is the Ancient Sartoran magic?"

"Not quite, but it's the first step, one might say. The magic we grew up learning, with all its signs and spells, those are protections as well as aids to focus. I told you before, artificial walls and stairs and doors made to protect the finite human mind from the raw power of magic potential. There are many more doors and walls in light magic, which is what makes its fundamentals such a grind to memorize. But the result is, a botched spell dissipates. Dark magic builds faster, as you know.

You also know it will consume you if you err. With the old magic, you focus the inner eye, and the raw power is there, to be held, by mind only, and shaped."

"Sounds dangerous."

"It is."

"And yet Detlev assigned you to investigate it? He ought to have known all that."

"He did. Remember what I said about Norsunder's understanding of it."

"Oh. A ruse. Yes?"

"Hiding in plain sight. Though we didn't know it at the time. Part of that assignment was meant for us to be learning."

"And who besides the Host, and Detlev and so forth, knows how to do what you did last night?"

"I ... think Imry has found his way to it. The irony is, we stand in exactly the same danger if Svir or Ilerian find out."

"You sound as if you don't want him to."

David looked out through the scuttle, then back. "Imry is my brother. You'd probably better know that."

Jilo sensed hesitation. There was more. "Who was your father?"

"He called himself Kedran Llyenthur."

"But you don't call yourself David Llyenthur. Or do you?"

"No." David looked up, then down again. "You really want to hear the details?"

"Why not?"

"I don't talk about it generally, not for my own sake, you'll soon see. Kedran Llyenthur was born a prince. When Detlev caught up with him, Imry was four years old. Kedran had made a mess of trying to train him into an assassin. He tried again, wanting a docile child for his plans to get his father's throne. I was born. Then his father died, and the brother he'd liked took over, and he abandoned his plan in favor of assassinating his way to the top of a pirate federation. Before he sold us to Detlev, he gave me a name from his home country."

"Home country. Which is?"

"Marloven Hess. Kedran was born Kendred Montredaun-An. Disinherited and exiled."

"Senrid knows?" Jilo didn't even try to hide his astonishment.

"Oh, yes. First thing I did was go to him after we left Norsunder. Senrid hasn't told anyone. I leave that to him. But I don't think he'd mind your knowing."

Jilo flinched. "Llyenthur killed Senrid's daughter."

"Yes." David drew a slow breath. "In no way does this exonerate him — far from it — and yet his method was a mercy compared to what Efael had intended."

Jilo's mind was already running in another direction entirely. "If you had been born a girl, what then?"

"The same. He didn't pick boys deliberately. That's what he found."

"So when you took Clair to the fifth world, that wasn't an experiment to try girls?"

David finished his coffee, then said, "No. It didn't make sense at the time, except as a distraction as tensions escalated with Norsunder. But Detlev told me later she was there to make Roy's break easier on him."

"Roy?"

"Yes." David's sardonic almost-smile was back briefly. "He made his break early, and I almost killed him for it. Not for being a lighter. For betraying us. Detlev, with the long view, knew, and again permitted it to happen. One of those distractions. Efael and Yeres were watching avidly in those days, veering between wanting to command us, and wanting us as target practice. Eh, I think I've blabbed long enough. And this boat isn't going to repair itself."

Jilo swallowed down his coffee, smothering the questions he wanted to ask.

They went to the deck to deal with the storm damage, and thus began a series of summer days while they repaired the boat in a hundred little ways, and played games the rest of the time — wrestling, drilling, and mental contact games, meant to strengthen Jilo's mind-shield and enable him to be more focused, and more subtle, with contact and farsense.

Gradually the continual ache of unused muscles gave way, and his head no longer felt like his skull would split by the time he fell into his bunk.

As promised, David taught him simple vagabond magic, calling fire.

They had no more personal talk — as Jilo had surmised, after David slept, he retreated behind his easy-going persona. They did discuss the old magic once more, when Jilo asked about the lightning round his hands, and David told him that he'd used his hands as the physical focal point. From what he'd gathered, the Ancient Sartorans often had a focus object when they were learning. After mastery, most did not need such aids.

"The dyra," Jilo said, remembering those long hunts in the early days.

"Actually, those were for another purpose," David said. "Though you're right that they were aids."

Leaving Jilo puzzled: why had Detlev searched so assiduously for them? But he had learned that any question about the dyra invariably got the response, "You'll have to ask Detlev."

Eleven

AT LAST THEY WOKE to a dark jut on the horizon: the mountains surrounding the Bay of Jaire.

The bay was full of patrol boats, so they continued the practice sessions as they sailed by night along the coast, until they found a suitably protected little inlet between high rocky cliffs, with birds wheeling and crying far overhead.

They drifted in on the tide, dropped anchor, and stripped the boat down to bare poles. Then they covered the boat with canvases that had been layered with spells to reflect sea and sky, effectively hiding it unless someone investigated up close. Last, they opened the lockers to fetch out knapsack, shoes, and socks. A smell of dust, a whiff of forest leaves on the knapsack brought Jilo's earlier journey to his mind. So much had happened it seemed years ago instead of a few weeks. Jilo blinked at the handsome shirt the woman had given him, and he wondered who had worn it before, under what circumstances. All that embroidery — it was a festival shirt.

He tucked it into the knapsack and pulled on a volumenous undyed one that MV kept in a locker for guests when he hired the boat out. David had said to help himself.

"Need a blade?" David asked, half in and half out of another locker.

"Sure," Jilo said, not wanting to admit that he was useless with weapons

"Here." David tossed a long double-bladed knife to Jilo, then dove back in. "Ah! Trust MV. Here's a wrist stiletto as well."

He handed Jilo a blade about as long as his hand, fitted into a blackweave sheath with a little square sewn at the top.

"How's it work?" Jilo asked doubtfully, envisioning himself digging desperately in his sleeve and then dropping the knife.

"See this little piece? You loosen it by flexing your wrist like this." David demonstrated. "And then again when you want it to drop into your hand. But you have to practice."

"Won't MV miss it?"

David snorted. "If it's here it's extra. MV is a walking armory, you know that."

Jilo strapped it on, tried—and of course the blade first stuck, and when it dropped it passed right through his fingers and clattered onto the deck.

"Practice," David said. "No mystery to it. When we were eight years old, that kind of practice was fun. Now it'll be dull, but if you need it, the skill will be there."

———◄║═►───

Under moonlight they walked up a steep, rock-scattered promontory, desolate in the darkness. A brisk wind blew off the land, smelling of loam, and grass, and horse, and the lingering traces of baked cabbage.

"There's a place over that hill," David said. "Under another name, Detlev did a signal service here a couple of years ago, so we should find a welcome."

A very small village sat tucked against a semi-circle of striated rock cliffs, the buildings long and low as if hunkered against the wind scouring off the mountains to the north. David said that the rain seldom made it that far past the mountains, and that the locals earned money mainly as yeath herders. Jilo was hoping to see some yeath, the long-legged animals with the long, silken fur that was clipped at the beginning of each spring and sold at fabulous prices below. The animals were rare, that much Jilo knew, living only on mountaintops.

They crunched their way up a stony path, to find that the locals already knew someone was coming. As soon as the sentinels saw David, they relaxed, hidden hands coming out empty of weapons, and weather-worn faces easing into smiles. If David had been part of that "signal service," he did not say.

But they soon had a room with clean bedding and a good fire, after a supper of plain but plentiful food.

Morning brought coffee fresh from Sartor, fried pepper-potatoes, and David paid with some of MV's coins while Jilo ordered trail food to slide into his knapsack, where Senrid's brown paper was carefully folded.

"We ought to have hired horses," Jilo said.

David shook his head. "Not enough money — and no local mounts to spare. No, we need weapons as much as we need horses. We're sure to run into a likely maneuverable arsenal. What say?" David turned his head, smiling.

Jilo did not try to hide his dismay. "You're saying we ought to ambush Norsundrians?"

"Mmmm, if it's scruples you have, I ought to point out that what I'm looking for is the type to ambush us first. Live and let live is my usual policy."

"Ah, that wasn't what I was thinking. It seems to me that if someone volunteers to join Norsunder, they are the type to want to make trouble. But attack Norsundrians, just you and me? With knives?"

David shrugged. "Remember what I told you, break any task into pieces, not just an impossible lattice ward that would defeat anyone but a completely mad Chwahir mage who will go unnamed."

Jilo blushed and shuffled his feet as David went on, "We're not attacking all Norsunder. The elites are in the security-flagged kingdoms. Around here we're likeliest to find some newly-joined thugs who thought fighting for Norsunder would net them easy loot, license to slap people around, and no real work, and who'll soon get a bellyful of constant orders, mind-raids, and sneak attacks. Not all from the locals. Most of those recruits eventually desert."

"Desert?"

"Tough on both sides, actually. They seldom become model citizens."

Jilo took a deep breath. "Won't there be reprisals?"

"Not if we catch a patrol at a distance, and claim we were sent by another garrison. There are a couple of local outpost commanders ripe for trouble of this sort. It's at the outposts you find the worst, as Norsunder is so short-handed."

"All that makes sense, but I also know that a few weeks of drill on the boat won't make me into anything useful. I'll only get in your way."

"Think of it as just more practice. We're not likely to find martial arts experts out here."

Those were likely to be up in Marloven Hess — where they were headed, Jilo thought wryly. But he'd consented to this journey, so he'd see it through.

David led the way into the hills up a trail strewn with rock and shale. He stayed silent, using farsense to scout. Since Jilo couldn't scan with farsense and walk without getting dizzy or tripping, he practiced with the little knife, over and over and over as he watched for wild-growing foods. (And, being Jilo, he failed to notice how much more stamina he had going uphill.)

Before they lost the light they camped, high enough that they could have a fire and not draw attention. They ate well, courtesy of the village they first visited, with the addition of sprays of juicy berries that Jilo had found as they walked.

After a time, David said, "You seem pleased."

Jilo said, "The control. It's actually getting easier."

"Don't forget your limits."

"I'm always aware of my ... You don't mean me. Do you?"

David gazed out into the darkness. "Don't worry. I'm just tired. Beware of impatience, that's all."

"What do you mean?"

David shrugged. "Not long before we met up I had some trouble. Thought I was more recovered than I am. I'll be all right, but I wouldn't mind holing up for a week or so, once we reach Marloven Hess."

They settled down and slept. When Jilo woke, it was to a gray, mysterious world of fog. David was already awake, and said, "We'll warm up by doing some drills."

This they did. And then set out.

The next day they encountered their first patrol, a pair riding along the same road. David flicked a glance at Jilo, who remembered to space himself so he wouldn't foul David's reach, as one of the Norsundrians said, "Papers?"

David pulled a map of the local area from his inner pocket. The Norsundrians didn't even look at it. Seeing them unarmed, they waved them on, continuing their conversation. David bobbed his head and tramped on. Jilo, after a heartbeat's hesitation, followed, suppressing the urge to glance back.

After a time he realized David meant what he said about live and let live, which caused Jilo to wonder what did inspire people to join Norsunder. He could not believe that anyone volunteered for good motives, but might some motives be mixed? Those two they'd first passed might have joined having lost their old work, and so long as they were left to ride the trails, could keep their heads down and eat their three meals a day. Maybe even sneak some back to families. Then there were always those who would try to destroy the enemy from within.

The next day, they encountered a patrol of four. Jilo squinted at them in the summery sun, danger prickling at the back of his neck. The tension in shoulders and arms, the way two of them smirked with anticipation—this was the sort of encounter he'd expected. And dreaded.

"Papers?" the chief roared.

David pulled out the map again.

And again, the Norsundrians didn't bother looking to see if they were genuine or not. The chief grinned at his cronies, a tough-looking woman with red bows in her braids and two hulks who had to be brothers or cousins, saying, "Looks like we've got ourselves some rule-breakers, begging for a lesson, eh?"

"And here we go," David murmured. "Those back two probably fight together. Pick one. Keep them off me."

Before Jilo could react, David leaped between the two in the front, his body twisting as he snap-kicked in both directions, sending the chief and the woman tumbling from their mounts. After that, the fight was confusing. One of the hulking twins came at Jilo, swinging his blade. Jilo bobbed and danced about, dodging his swings long enough for David to take care of the others, then whack him from behind.

Three were out cold and one groaning and twisting from side to side over a broken knee as David gasped, "Catch the horses."

Jilo caught two by the reins. David caught the others. Moving swiftly, David searched through their gear, tossed what he wanted to keep into a pile, then evaluated the animals by some standard Jilo could not perceive. He loosened the saddle buckles on two of the horses, then whacked the animals on the flank, sending them bolting away; the saddles would eventually fall off, but not anywhere nearby where they might be of use to the enemy.

David spoke casually in one of the local languages as he scanned papers then destroyed them. He set aside food and weapons and discarded belongings, except for the chief's sturdy gray Norsundrian coat. He referred to someone in Perideth; Jilo remembered that they were supposed to be from another garrison, but he didn't know how to fake that, so he only grunted in response.

Then the one with the broken knee fainted. Now all four were unconscious. Jilo said, "That jacket. Is it for a plan?"

David looked surprised. "I'm cold."

"Oh." Jilo hated the gray jackets too much to take one, so he scrounged through the clothes that David had discarded, and discovered one of them had been carrying a well-made tunic of undyed wool. If cold weather was coming, why not be prepared?

They mounted the two horses David had kept and rode northward into the mountains, climbing steadily into bands of dark, strong-scented pine.

They slept better that night, despite the cold from the heights. Next morning they practiced with actual swords. Jilo felt the blocks; the shock of blade on blade stung down to his bones, but he discovered that the drills had actually given him the wherewithal to handle it.

David then demonstrated how to use that force to twist aside, turn it down, or up, away. Though Jilo worked far past what he'd always assumed was his limit in the old days, he still didn't match David, mysterious recovery notwithstanding. His arms trembled when David said at last, "Good enough. Let's hit the road."

Twelve

THE NEXT FEW DAYS fell into a pattern—eat, drill, sleep, wake up, drill some more, eat, then ride through hills, sticking to trails that did not expose them to view. Gradually the silences lengthened.

Jilo got used to drill every day, instead of when convenient.

After drill, they'd ride. Gradually, as the days brought them higher, the silences grew longer. Jilo sat on his horse, tried to be observant, and practiced the wrist knife drills, first right hand, and then left. Jilo assumed David was doing long distance scanning of a sort he could not even attempt to comprehend, or to emulate, during those protracted silences. Jilo left him to it, figuring his part was to not interrupt.

But four days along, Jilo sensed searching eyes, by a strange sort of awareness that he could not categorize. David did not move, just rode, his gaze diffuse. But Jilo had formed a habit of watching the skies. He glimpsed a dot high above, coasting in a slow circle. He and David were riding under trees, so the bird vanished and appeared again. Its line was too methodical for a bird: it had to be a spy bird. Jilo muttered the spell to bread the lattice link.

Nothing happened. The bird continued its slow, deliberate circle. Jilo halted his horse. David halted as well, looking up as if startled.

Jilo fixed his gaze on that bird, and slowly performed the spell.

Nothing happened.

"Wait," David murmured softly, as if that bird winging far away could possibly hear him.

Jilo waited, every sense alert.

David tracked the bird as best he could, grateful for the trees that concealed him, Jilo, and the two mounts. The horses nosed at the grass, unconcerned, as the two humans watched until the bird's circles — neatly described as if drawn against the sky — vanished to the north.

David turned his gaze to Jilo, uncertain what to say. He couldn't be sure of the human awareness riding that bird. Too well blocked, except through the bird's eyes. That was definitely a careful scan.

David rubbed his jaw, conscious that he'd pushed much too hard. It was insane to test himself now that they were so close to the border. Marloven Hess was not the place for such blunders.

"That was some other kind of sky bird," he said to Jilo.

Who nodded awkwardly, mumbling, "Igkai said. Some birds. Animals. Pair with humans on their side."

"There is no sides for animals," David observed. "Threat levels, yes. And friends."

They pushed on through the forest, and when that showed signs of clearing, they camped and waited till night. Under a drizzling summer rain, they descended to the plain through which ran the border river.

Jilo knew that subtle, carefully made border wards could have warned someone and they wouldn't know it. Such wards were extremely difficult to make on so large a scale, but Marloven Hess was definitely the sort of kingdom that Norsunder's commanders would deem worth taking the time over.

Despite it being night, with low clouds and rain, they waded out, senses alert to any shift in the wind, a new scent, a sound beyond the slosh of water around them and the plash of warm raindrops. It was unnerving, to feel so exposed in spite of the darkness. The horses were skittish, whether from sensing the humans' moods or some other cause, and would not be ridden. One balked mid-stream, and the other whickered, ears back.

David slid off, gripping the bridle, and tugged gently, steadily. The balking animal began to move.

They'd reached the rocky shore, and the horses surged out

when David gave a bit-off exclamation and landed with a splat in the mud.

"Take them," he gasped when Jilo looked back.

The horses were near panic. Jilo took the reins of both as David hauled himself painfully to his feet, cursing steadily under his breath.

"What happened?" Jilo asked when they reached the upper bank.

"That woke me up," David muttered. "Foot caught in a vine. Twisted."

"Better get the boot off," Jilo said. "Before it swells."

"Have to remain as it is. Listen, Jilo, I think we ought to head directly for Darchelde, which has the least number of patrols, and no garrison, as Norsunder believes it to be uninhabited. Senrid has a kind of outpost there."

"Isn't that a huge forest? How will we find them?"

David hissed a strangled laugh. "I believe they will find us."

———————

They made their way eastward through hills gradually descending into broadleaf and flowering shrub terrain. The storm moved on, but at least David had shed the worst of the mud.

An hour or two before dawn David said, "Jilo, everything will be easier if you have an identity that the Marlovens will understand."

"I've been here before. Stayed with Senrid. In the capital," Jilo said.

"You haven't met any of Senrid's borderland Marlovens. These are youths, and life has been rough. My point is, I'm suggesting you use this opportunity to explore vagabond magic. In the Marlovens' eyes there is a wide difference between an unknown foreigner they have to feed and guard, and a mage who might help them. A vagabond."

"But ... isn't that dangerous?"

"First, there are no wards against you in this kingdom. I'm pretty sure there are wards against me. Second, anything you'd be able to do won't catch attention. I'll stop you if you suddenly begin smashing mountains or throwing lightning around without a storm to cover it."

Jilo agreed, but he was full of questions.

They proceeded into a dark, thick forest adrip from the recent rain. The clean smell of duff, wood, and foliage gave Jilo a pleasant, heady sense that intensified the sense of unreality caused by too little sleep.

It seemed one moment the horses walked in single file along a narrow creek chuckling along, moonlight striking silver gleams in the dripping trees, then the next they were surrounded by slender youths mostly dressed in brown and green, except for a small one wearing black, nearly lost in the shadows.

A boy in his early or middle teens said, "What is your favorite season?"

"Harvest," David replied.

Jilo noted that all these teens bore bare steel. He was certain that even the smallest of them was more adept with steel than he was, in spite of his few weeks of lessons.

"Why?"

"Because it's Van's," David said, with no hint of amusement at this awkward passphrase.

"You can't take the horses," the shadow said.

David replied, "Didn't intend to. It's just that I twisted my ankle rather badly, so we came as far as we could while mounted."

"I'll take the horses where they will be welcome," one of the foresters whispered to the short one.

"Good idea."

Jilo and David dismounted—David painfully—and so began a journey on foot, single file once again.

The east was graying, the dark tree shapes taking on hints of color, when the leader pointed down into a dark, dank-smelling pit dug into the side of a rocky hill. Steep, uneven steps had been worked into a hole slanting down beneath the hillock, into a round cave that was partly natural, but mostly dug out of the clay-soil. It smelled of mud, mold, old food, smoke, and wet wool, the air so dank and stuffy Jilo grimaced.

Lamps barely fought back the gloom. Against the far wall were three rickety, rudimentary triple decker bunk beds, set inward from the mud-weepy wall. On the other side a jumble of gear, a rocky cook pit, and a lot of weapons. Burlap bags and shovels were stacked near the tunnel entrance.

David dropped onto a pile of canvas bags, the lamplight bright on his pale hair.

"I'm Kethadrend," a blond boy said.

Jilo realized they were all staring at him. "I'm ..."

"He's a vagabond mage," David said. "There are wards and warrants against his name in several kingdoms."

"Oh." The Marlovens said on a respectful note.

Kethadrend went round the room introducing his companions. None of them looked any older than he was.

The little shadow, Marend, then said flatly to Jilo, "Does vagabond mage mean you can do magic?"

"When the time is right," Jilo said.

"We've already had two bad rains and we're not so sure we won't lose at least part of that wall," a tall, thin boy said — Jilo had already forgotten his name.

Jilo nodded. Not just one but all of the walls glistened with seepage. "I see. If I can help, I will. Perhaps under cover of the storm, so the Norsundrians won't sense the magic."

A girl came forward, and said with hands propped on hips, "How about letting him sit down first, rock-heads?"

"Yeah. And are you hungry?" a small, round boy asked. He grinned, poured something from the cook rocks into a cup, then said, "I'm Kelsan. Bet you didn't catch a one of our names, with Keth spitting 'em out like that." He handed Jilo the cup. "Sorry. It's kinda cold. We only cook once a day, or the smoke and smell kinda gets to us."

"That I can fix now," Jilo said, relieved his first essay into being "the vagabond" was something easy — he had been making all their campfires. He snapped a vagabond flame. "It won't smoke unless you stick wood into it, and you don't need to do that. It'll continue to draw the magic it needs, until you douse it."

The Marlovens stared, so impressed that Jilo became self-conscious. He forced down some of the tasteless, cold vegetable soup until a practical girl with long braids pointed to one of the beds.

"Sleep," she said, and with a thumb at David. "You two look like you're about to fall over."

Jilo didn't even remember stretching out on the nearest bunk. He woke abruptly to thunder rumbling around him, shaking down glops of mud from overhead. Bare tree roots dripped, splat, splat, splat.

David stood over him. "There's a good storm out there. We'll have to act now."

Jilo rubbed his eyes. "Marlovens?"

"Turfed them out. They're patrolling, or making a supply run."

"How will we do this?"

"I'll draw the magic down. You do the shaping. Remember, be precise or it falls apart — and might be discerned."

Jilo said, "I think I can do that."

Jilo had spent what had felt at the time like an eternity longing for the Mearsieans' underground hideout. He understood later what he wanted was only in part the actual structure. What he'd craved was the laughter, the friendship, the enticing aromas of meals shared with friends. Every Chwahir, no matter how humble, belonged to a twi of peers — except Jilo. And of course that had also been true of the royal family, as Wan-Edhe could not tolerate his own relations' loyalties going to anyone but him.

But as a young teen, all those realizations lay in his future. He had dreamed of the Junky, as the Mearsiean girls termed it. All those old dreams proved to be useful now.

As for vagabond magic, he didn't need David's help for too long. After all the time he had spent wrestling with incredibly dangerous and lethal lattice magic, while enduring the most toxic atmosphere in the world, his concentration for magic (David realized, monitoring him from the mental plane) was almost unparalleled. Not that Jilo was aware of just how skilled he was. He only saw what was to be done, did it, then wistfully reflected on how much he still needed to learn.

The walls hardened, leaving a narrow bench all around, the water sinking to the aquifer he sensed below. He smoothed and hardened ceiling and walls and floor, and scooped out the two caved-in rooms that the Marlovens had been forced to abandon. He lifted the unwanted soil up through the entrance and scattered it through the woods, leaving the round rooms dug deep, so as not to disturb tree roots. He added an air shaft reaching inside a hollow tree, and another that he sheltered by a rock fall to keep out rain. He reinforced the entry tunnel so that it stayed weather proof.

By then his vision started glittering dangerously. His last act was to set up a cleaning frame. When that was done, both he and David collapsed, and slept.

Thirteen

THEY WOKE TO VOICES.

"Hey, it doesn't stink!"

"Look — it's warm!"

"The walls, how did he do that?"

The Marlovens wandered around exclaiming as they fingered the cleaning frame, the smooth walls, the water bucket.

"Could you do that again?" asked Marend. She was very serious, very intense. She spoke the least, invariably spending evenings writing something that she did not show anyone, as the others talked and planned.

"I can," Jilo was pleased to say. He wouldn't even need David; he had learned how to find and draw in ambient magic, shaping it in his mind. "As soon as there is another storm. Preferably with thunder."

No one asked why, which Jilo found interesting. They seemed to distrust magic, though they liked its results just fine. But no one wanted to be around it lest something go wrong and an arm or a leg fell off.

They got their summer storm two days later; the Marlovens led Jilo on a fast journey through the forest to a site they had already begun excavations at. When they reached it, David took Jilo aside. "You can handle this task, yes?"

"I can," Jilo said. "I know what to do now. Even thought up some refinements."

"Then make them a closed comm system. Can you do that?"

"You mean, just between the two undergrounds? Yes, I can do that. Not sure I could go beyond that."

"Just the two," David said. "Anything else increases the risk. I'm off to explore a little. I'll be back soon." And to Jilo's questioning face, "There's an old, abandoned castle not far. I've a mind to poke around it for a few days while this foot of mine heals up." He vanished into the woods.

Jilo created a second hideout, relishing the flow of magic that he shaped with his mind. He had visualized things all his life, deliberately committing to memory sights that pleased him, and that habit served him now. He envisioned the water flow to the aquifer, the smoothing and hardening of dirt, the shifting of mud through the air, to line the stream not far away. He enjoyed the process so much it never felt like work, until his vision began to glitter around the edges. But when he halted, here was a fine cave to match the other one.

The Marlovens marveled all over again, and Jilo was gratified at how they welcomed him, encouraging him to take the first helping of meals, or the first cup of fresh-ground and scalded coffee. This, in Chwahir terms, was honor.

But that also meant that Jilo was invited to join their drills. Used to being the weakest, slowest, and worst trained, he was surprised to discover that David's tutoring on the boat and on the trail subsequently had changed him more than he was aware. In other words, he did not disgrace himself, though they'd clearly pegged him as a mage and not a warrior; for some reason, they had settled it among themselves that David was in secret a captain in the cavalry, though he'd said absolutely nothing to them about his identity.

Jilo noticed that his being able to keep up with their drills included him among them to a higher degree. He adapted to their routine, and was just getting used to it when it was interrupted once again. A tall messenger named Cam turned up to report that someone was coming to conduct Jilo and David to Senrid.

The following morning, the Marlovens woke to discover Marend, the quiet one, vanished. Tdor, the girl with the braids, crossed her skinny arms, and said, "She told me she was going last night."

"Where?" Ramond ran a hand through his brown hair, looking more tousled than ever. And exasperated.

"Methden."

Ramond turned his face skyward in a dramatic eyeroll.

Kelsan looked from one to the other and murmured, "Van said he didn't want anyone going back."

"I know, I know, I told her that. And what did she say? 'What's he going to do? Court martial me? I'm not in the army.'"

"Argh." Ramond flung himself down on the wall seat (which by now had cushions, made by Cam's friends in some village, after the Marlovens had been gathering down from the feathered creatures who had fledged during spring).

"What if that Llyenthur scum gets her again?" Nollard spoke up.

Tdor sighed. "If he does, and if she doesn't get a chance to use her knife, we go out, find her and shoot her." She flung her scrawny, freckled arms out wide. "What's the problem? She'd do the same for us."

"Why'd she go?" Nollard asked. "Not to attack Norsundrians? That'd be unfair!"

"Not without us. She's gone, big-nose, to try to patch things up with the Jarlan. And then to take Lesra to Toth somewhere, so the Norsundrians can't put her in some weird Norsundrian experiment that Marend was stewing about. Using ten-year-olds and the like. And she promised if she saw anything that needed group action she'd come back for us."

Jilo spoke up. "The border is being watched, and there are wards."

Ramond waved a hand. "If anyone can get around that, it's Marend."

After that the atmosphere eased — drills continuing, but with a measurable increase in play and laughter.

While they drilled and learned, Jilo learned more on the mental plane, by tentative degrees, until one night he ventured farther out, aware of forest life. By now he could sustain the vastness of distance only by using mental landmarks. He sensed evil intent on one horizon, and so he warded that direction. In the real world, you do not want to turn your back on danger. But in the mental realm it's the only way to stay unperceived when powerful and inimical minds are prowling.

Once Jilo knew the space around him, he lingered above the forest, conscious of the connection between his mind-self here and his body-self lying in bed in the hideout below the ground. Living things glowed in colors. The trees he perceived as a diffuse, stationary blue. Toward the southeast the hue altered to a purple, gaining more red until there was a place with the disturbing glare of burning embers. Yet as he watched, he sensed an infinitesimal change in shade, the red lessening, the blue gaining strength.

Between the trees darted many lights, golden or sun-shard yellow. Gold strengthened imperceptibly. Westward gleamed a steadily moving cluster made up of various shades of ugly orange and red, the glare of anger, the red of blood-lust: a Norsundrian patrol.

The gold and yellow were animals and people.

Back to the east and now Jilo found, nearly hidden in the center of the changing hues of the forest, only perceptible as a kind of echo where it had been, a single light of steady green: David.

Jilo did not contact him, only observed. David was quiescent in a ring of darkness. Jilo wondered if it was the ruin David had mentioned wanting to explore. Most of the red embers surrounded him.

Exhilaration suffused Jilo and his consciousness expanded until he perceived a beacon lancing an orange glare from horizon to horizon in a slow sweep. Jilo hurled his mind back into a body he discovered was dizzy, sweating, trembling. Time to abandon experimenting.

After that, life returned to drills, and the group talked about what they would do when Van gave the signal at last to turn on the conquerors and fight to regain the kingdom. Jilo found himself enjoying the life. He was not part of this twi, but they had accepted him, much as a twi might accept a cousin of one of its members. He relished every little, unconscious sign of that acceptance.

He became far more circumspect with his experiments on the mental realm. And when Senrid's courier turned up, Jilo said to the Marlovens, "Before we do anything else, I think you people need to be aware of mind-shields."

To his surprise they didn't scoff, they all sat down and faced him expectantly. "You know what those are, right?"

"Sure!" Sindan, Tdor's twin, called out.

"Then engage it now."

Several of them frowned portentously. Kelsan put his fingers in his ears and squeezed his eyes shut. The rest mostly looked uneasy or puzzled.

Jilo went from person to person, using mind-touch on the surface thoughts, and he spoke their thoughts aloud. Consternation and amazement replaced the confidence, puzzlement, and question.

Jilo said, "All it would take is one Norsundrian with Dena Yeresbeth riding by and he'd find the hideout without even having to search. You thought practicing mind-shields boring?"

"Hard," Rom said.

Lemarden put in, "And if we were tough enough —"

"Shut up, Lemarden," Rom muttered.

"It's not hard once you get used to it. But thinking of a wall for the space of ten or twelve breaths is not a mind-shield. You have to make it and keep your thoughts behind it. Make it a habit not just when you're awake, but even when you're asleep."

Kelsan said in horror, "Asleep? They could get us then, and read the signals out of our heads, and —"

"The password!" Sindan jumped up, flapping skinny arms.

They got serious about practicing, so that Jilo felt their surface thoughts winking out like doused snapfires. Satisfied, he went to get some rest before what he was certain would be hard travel once again.

To his surprise Tdor followed him down to the far chamber, its air shaft below a long-blasted tree that not only let in air but a little light.

Jilo flicked open the bedroll, then discovered Tdor standing in the door. She eyed the smooth walls with a few roots dangling, his knapsack, and the trunks and neatly lined up bedrolls. Then she said, "There might be no other chance to get you alone. I'd like to ask you to pass on a message for me. Would you?"

"To — Van?" Jilo almost said *Senrid's name.*

"Nah. To Ret."

"Who?"

"Marend's brother, Retren Ndarga. He's with Van, or at least was when they left during spring. If he's not there anymore, of course forget it."

"No written messages?" Jilo asked.

"Right. Yeah, I hate being a noser. But she left a message for him with me. And I have a feeling he's not hurrying back any time soon. Tell him this: she went to make peace with the

Jarlan."

"Went to make peace with the Jarlan," Jilo repeated obediently.

"Yeah. And tell him—no, that's enough from me in that mess," she said, but her thought was clear, *And she went to help Lesra because you liked her, and she misses you so bad ...*

The grief that suffused these thoughts rocked Jilo back a little. He said, "Mind-shield."

"Oh. Yeah. Right." Tdor hunched a bony shoulder up. "Thanks."

Fourteen

JILO WOKE AT A mind-touch so subtle he almost thought he was waking naturally, but for its familiarity: David.

: Bring your gear. She wants to be on the way before sunrise.

Kelsan, whose long line of antecedents apparently had bred in him innkeeper-habits, had already risen and had a hot breakfast awaiting them.

The courier, who introduced herself simply as Tree, was silent until they reached the road. She was about his age, almost his height, square, capable hands, light brown braids, a keen light blue gaze. She carried a bow and arrows as well as a travel knapsack.

David flicked a grin at Jilo. "Ready?"

"It's raining. Isn't it," Jilo said sourly.

"Only misting," David soothed. Then he buckled across his back the sword he'd taken from the Norsundrian patrol. Despite the rain he wore no jacket or cloak, in fact his sleeves were rolled to his elbows. Whatever he'd been doing on his expedition had apparently been good for him.

"It was you who let Senrid know we're here?" Jilo murmured as they emerged from the tunnel into a cool gray mist.

David slanted a smile his way, and Jilo fell silent.

With two alert, quiet companions, Jilo was free to range in thought, scanning his surroundings from time to time as the forest gradually thinned, revealing rolling hills, some green with grass and smelling of wild herbs and flowers, others dotted with trees in full summer leaf. Tree had refused to take any of Kelsan's stores (and he had not argued with any conviction), saying she was prepared.

At nightfall they camped in a little gully next to a stream, eating the dense, heavy travel rations that Marloven warriors and traders had eaten for centuries. Jilo loathed the blend of rye and honey; he discovered if he chewed it into paste he got it down easier. Early the next day they were skirting a village when he saw Tree studying one of the houses with a long, intense gaze. She murmured, "We'll find food here, I think."

And she led the way back a ways to a hillock, and they sat behind a hedgerow through which they could see the houses below. Presently people emerged and walked out to the fields beyond, scythes in hand in order to get in a very early hay crop. Leander had once told him that the horses got most of the oats, and the people what was left.

They walked down to one of the houses, which had a back window partially ajar. She reached in, brought out a hot chicken pie, half a loaf of fresh bread, a small jug of milk, and two fat apple tarts.

"We'll eat the pie and drink the milk here," she said. "They will need the dishes back."

They retreated to a grove and sat down to eat. Delighted with a much better repast, Jilo asked, "Do you know those people?"

She gave him an enigmatic glance—the same one the teens had given when their signals were mentioned. "We're on the king's business," she said, as if that was an answer.

The way Tree and David devoured their share made Jilo wonder how much they liked the travel rations, then Tree returned the dishes, and they walked on, careful not to be seen.

They crossed a wide, slow river, and entered a little valley sheltered by a grove of very old oak. She reslung her bow, and said, "Wait here. If the Norsundrians come first, go into Ihr and find Solet the wood-joiner." And she left, soon vanishing from sight.

They stretched out on the grass in the sun to dry from the river crossing. The air was balmy, smelling of sage and oak, and in the distance birds chattered.

Now that he and David were alone, Jilo said, "You seem to have benefited from your stay in the abandoned castle."

"There's a lot of blight left from an ancient magic battle, kept there by a, ah, call it a pool of toxic magic. It's been lessening incrementally over the centuries. Now it's going to lessen a little faster, but unless a Norsundrian actually walks right in, they won't notice. Very restful, I found it. I wonder if we're going to have to play spy versus spy for a week or two until we dig Senrid out from wherever he's holed up."

Jilo's eyes were closed. He relished the warmth on his eyelids. "In this kind of weather I am in no hurry." As he said the words, he was aware that the Mearsiean girls would have warned him that such a statement, said out loud, would be an open invitation for Senrid, or better yet one of the Host of Lords, to pop out from a bush, uttering a sinister laugh. He chucked under his breath, memory sliding into the dreams of a light doze before some subliminal signal—maybe only a quick breath—woke him to David sitting very still, his narrowed gaze northwards.

Then he flicked a grin at Jilo. "Senrid begs for the honor of our presence."

They picked up their gear and trudged north, rejoining the river again. Through another close-growing oak grove, up a hill, and when they emerged from the trees, they looked down at a secluded lagoon, blue and enticing in the hot summer sun. Two startled faces stared up.

Jilo had just recognized Senrid with his hair plastered against his skull when he exclaimed, "Damnation, David, do you have to skulk around looking like that?"

"Like what?" David sauntered down the little trail to the lagoon's edge and dropped his sword harness. Then he laughed at the revulsion in Senrid's expression. "But I don't look anything like Imry!"

He did, a little, Retren Ndarga was thinking as he tried to calm his jangling nerves. David saw this at a glance, and laughed ruefully as Senrid surged out of the water and sat down on a rock to dry.

Jilo blinked at Retren Ndarga, who at first he took for Marend, until he noticed Retren wearing swimming shorts, something his sister would never do. Later he'd notice more subtle differences, in particular the bone ridges that promised growth spurts soon, whereas her bone structure was fine, indicative of a girl who would never be taller than she was now.

The biggest difference was in their expressions. If Marend sometimes reminded Jilo of that strange, silent girl from Geth, Caris-Merian, this boy's face called Sveneric to mind.

"Ret, this is ... Jilo? What have you been doing to your-self?"

"Nothing. Unless you mean my tan. Have you ever seen a Chwahir with a tan? I got that sailing with David." He was too embarrassed to say anything about the control lessons.

Not that he had to. Senrid saluted David with a fencer's gesture. "Been turning him into one of Detlev's boys, eh?"

"Prime candidate." David gave his soundless laugh. "We had some fun messing with MV's boat and playing around with this and that."

Senrid was watching him with an odd expression. David met his gaze with unimpaired good humor. Finally Senrid laughed and said nothing more about their appearances, but that night baths, haircuts, and new clothes were all made available. They'd followed the feeder stream back up to a river and walked to the outskirts of a town, then waited until night to enter.

They stayed at a glassmaker's, in a secret room. This room had a mirror, and it was here that David and Jilo saw the changes wrought in their appearances.

David glanced at himself and grimaced; he was thinner than he'd been since he was fifteen — as thin as Imry — and his neglected hair had grown. Though Imry's was brown and flyaway-fine and David's was yellow and thick, he had to acknowledge that at a glance he might have been mistaken for his brother.

He left to find the barber Senrid had provided. Jilo linger-ed, not really seeing the smooth light brown skin stretched over his familiar bones, or the muscle definition in what used to be scrawny limbs. He frowned, leaning so close to the mirror his breath clouded it as he sought the hairs David had insisted had sprouted on his lip. Yes, two fine black hairs, barely discernable. The beard spell was still a long ways off in the hazy future; that led him to reflecting sourly about Wan-Edhe's edict that the only beards permitted were certain ranks and above.

Jilo had learned about the concept of fashion from Shontande Lirendi. There was no such thing as fashion in Chwahirsland, whatever might have existed in the past. There was only Wan-Edhe's will. Why would he force people to get the beard spell? Because it reduced men to boys, of course. If I am king, anyone can have a beard.

If I am king, he repeated as he eyed the long, lank black

locks that to his eye made his jaw look even more receding, his ears bigger, and his forehead more narrow. You don't look like a king, you look like a stable sweep. Laughing inwardly at himself, he left the mirror, and got in line for the same Marloven military haircut that was given David.

Over a hearty supper Senrid and David exchanged local news, to which Ret and Jilo listened in silence. As they'd expected, Senrid explained the mysterious signal system, adding that it was successful enough he'd taken it to the neighboring countries to introduce to the rulers there—suitably adapted. "Jan Senelac took over that duty, as my chief courier. All our comms are in his hands now."

David leaned forward. "I met him in Choreid Dhelerei a year or two ago. Seemed to be quick on his feet. Definitely good with his hands."

Senrid said, "Yes, and yes."

"But surely he, or someone, is watching this whole window scheme of yours. Seems ripe for a spy to mess with. Your candles, too."

Senrid's lip curled. "You are forgetting how angry the Marlovens are. Those open windows are watched, you can be sure. Shepherd on a hill. Carter loading vegetables. Children out weeding the rye. Any stranger touches that food besides Jan Senelac, or Stad, or Marlovair or any of their couriers—and by now people know them all—they won't live long."

"I trust you're going to give Perideth a different system completely?"

"Everyone knows Halmaer Nothalin of Perideth or his son Valta won't be able to resist trying to get me killed. But I can trust Jan not to let that outride us, and if we can get everyone else used to expecting communication, we might be able to raise everyone at once."

"Conditionally promising," David said.

"There's one immediate benefit. One of Van Stad's roaming patrols rescued a pair of traders from Telyerhas from being shot. There's a secret forge being set up in the high mountains. With some funding, which I've sent Senelac to take to them himself, they'll make weapons and stockpile them against the expected uprising."

At length Senrid turned to Jilo. "What news from the northeast?"

Jilo considered what to say, then decided that if the

Marlovens really wanted to know, they'd ask. He pulled out the much-battered beige paper, saying, "Siamis made these. According to Puddlenose, the allies can write to you. And you can write back."

"Do you have one?"

"Yes, but I left it with Shontande Lirendi. In case I got myself in trouble. Uh, which I did."

Senrid said nothing, nor did he niff any thoughts, but as Jilo handed him the paper, he got the strongest, strangest sense that he was handing Senrid a yoke.

Senrid merely took it, and stuck it in his pocket, saying, "Thanks. This should be useful if we do coordinate an uprising against the enemy."

Senrid had to go to a meeting not long after. He invited the two newcomers along, but Jilo declined, preferring to stay behind and catch up on sleep. Knowing Senrid's habits of old, he'd be up before dawn, and stay awake and moving until midnight. Jilo now had to—somehow—get to Mearsies Heili, and he did not want to embark on such a long journey already tired.

Then, as he rolled up in his blanket, he remembered David's comment aboard the boat the very first day, that Senrid might need him for something. Even though Jilo went to sleep early, as he expected, the next morning he emerged into the main room, where Senrid and David were up, dressed, and talking. The air was dry and even though the sun was an hour or two from rising, the day was already warm.

Senrid turned his way. "Jilo, I have to travel fast to Choreid Dhelerei and back. Could I get you to stay with Ret here and wait on two important messengers I'm expecting from the south? One is from that group of forge workers I mentioned last night."

"I can," Jilo said, though he wondered why Senrid didn't hand off such a task to a Marloven.

Senrid stepped closer. "Listen for him here." Senrid tapped his forehead. "Ret will insist he's fine even when he gets tired. Last week he was nearly sick."

And there was the reason—Dena Yeresbeth. "I can try," Jilo said, doubting that even an eleven-year-old Marloven would listen to him.

Senrid then turned abruptly to David, who had been sitting with his eyes half closed. "What have you been doing?"

David grinned. "When you have more than half your attention to give to me, I will tell you. Until then it can wait."

Senrid's palm came down flat on the table. "I knew it. Knew it! A plan. How I knew it, I haven't laid eyes on you in weeks. Months. No contact. Nothing. Must be the bile."

David laughed. "Must be the bile."

Bile? Then Jilo translated that as a joke on their shared blood.

"Want to come with me?"

David only gave a lazy shrug. "Not really. I want to nose around here for a time."

"Then I'm off." And Senrid strode swiftly out.

David turned to Jilo, his expression serious. "Last night I niffed someone stalking Senrid. I'm going to find out who."

"Did you tell Senrid?"

"Yes, last night. He's been stalked for so long and by so many he can't take time or attention for a new one. His way of dealing is just to keep moving fast. But his wanting you to stay with Retren is his way of acknowledging my warning." David finished his coffee, and drifted out.

When Retren emerged he scanned the room once, then twice more slowly. His wide gray gaze lowered, but not before Jilo saw hurt.

"David is off to scout, and Senrid went off to a meeting that he said he could travel to fastest alone. We are to remain here for two important messengers. I hope you'll help me identify them."

Ret flicked out his hand in the Marlovan equivalent of assent, then turned his attention to the food on the table. "Is that for me?"

"Yes. I just ate. I'll be back in a moment."

There was something Jilo wanted to do, but he wasn't sure whether Retren would prefer to be alone or invited along. He took his crumpled, smeared drawings from the knapsack, and smoothed them as best he could.

When Jilo returned, Retren was done eating. He sat very still, obviously waiting for orders. Jilo said, "David and I were in Darchelde." Retren's demeanor sobered. "There was a girl named Tdor." And Jilo repeated her message.

As he spoke, Retren lowered his gaze, his expression

bleak. Jilo said into a silence he did not understand, "Though it's hot out, I want to make some sketches. You know any places that might be good for drawing?"

It was no more than a polite question, but for the first time Jilo saw interest, even a wary enthusiasm in Retren's demeanor. "You're an artist?"

"No. I've had no training at all. But that doesn't stop me from trying to draw."

"I think I know a place. But of course if you think it's bad. Just say!"

And thus began a day that ended up as one of the best days of Jilo's journey.

Retren led him to a knoll with three twisted trees growing round one another, dappled light falling on wild herbs with clusters of tiny white flowers. As Jilo sketched, Retren watched intently, without the usual barrage of questions like *Why are you making it that way? Or How come it's not bigger? Smaller?*

Then he began practicing handstands on the grass, and when he laughed at one of his falls, he clowned. They discovered they shared a similar sense of humor.

After that the questions began, but Retren was so shy, so tentative, that Jilo discovered he did not mind. "Are you really a king? How big is Chwahirsland?" And finally, "He says you know magic."

"You are interested in magic?"

"Oh, *yes!*"

"But Senrid hasn't taught you?"

"He said he's a bad teacher, and hasn't the time. The last I know is true. I mean, I've had fun, traveling with him. And I've learned many things. But we've had less time for questions and answers in the last month than the first days I saw him. I counted," he added, and from that Jilo discovered he really was a kindred spirit.

Jilo said, "Ah, I can teach you some."

Retren's mouth opened, then closed, and his face reddened and then paled as he assimilated the enormity of this gift.

"We can't actually perform anything but the simplest illusion," Jilo hastened to add. "All I can teach you is the basics, and most people hate those —" He stopped there. It was clear that Retren would learn anything.

They kept at it until they lost the light, and then Jilo said, "I'm sorry. You've been sick, and I forgot about lunch. It's past supper time."

Retren shrugged. "I'm used to it. Skipping meals, I mean. I like skipping 'em and knowing I get to eat." And as they returned, Jilo on the watch, Retren began whispering his lessons in an undervoice of acute concentration.

Over dinner Jilo asked why Retren hadn't studied magic, and from Retren's impassioned but jumbled explanation, got some insight into Retren's situation: a father who expected him to become a warrior leader, despite his interests, which could be relegated to private hobbies. Music, art, poetry, those were for idle hands and idle moments, not the future pursuits of the son of a jarl and commander, and everyone in the family had believed that. Or at least his father and Marend had; his mother had been quiet about such things.

So much Jilo learned, but he forbore asking more when Retren's voice trembled on his single mention of his sister.

They practiced magic until Retren was so tired he started confusing obvious things. When Jilo suggested that he get some rest, Retren rolled up and slept only because he was in the habit of obedience, but Jilo could feel his reluctance.

Next morning, just as Jilo was planning the day, he got a sudden contact from David: *Senrid is being ambushed. I need backup fast.*

Fifteen

RET INSISTED ON GOING.

Jilo had only to say that the king might be in trouble, and the owner of the secret room promptly arranged for horses and the dreaded travel bread. They were riding side by side before the shadows had hardly had a chance to shorten as the morning sun began its climb into the sky.

Once again a contact from David, a vivid, sudden blast of image that gave Jilo direction and even glimpses of terrain — a reminder of just how powerful his abilities were, and how well he controlled them.

They skirted some farms, riding along the edge of a woodland on the other side of a local branch off the main river. Abruptly Jilo spotted the rock-crowned hill David had shown him, sticking up above the dark green canopy of trees. A flick of the reins on the halter, and the beautifully trained horse sensed his wish and changed direction, Ret's following.

The horses thundered down the trail. Jilo crouched over his mount's neck, watching the dirt for prints — saw them — ducked low, leafy branches —

And there were the three figures in a long, rock-bordered clearing.

Ret dismounted while his horse was still moving, rolling up and pulling his knife. Jilo labored to follow, fighting the inbred Chwahir instinct to wait for orders.

Ret led the way to a dark-haired young man in night maneuver blacks kneeling over a blood-splashed figure whom

Jilo recognized with a sickening jolt as Senrid. The young man glanced up. He was rail thin, his height, and tense as a blade. In the fasted move Jilo had ever seen — faster even than MV — he pulled an obsidian stiletto from his clothes.

"David said to wait for you." His accent was strong. Jilo was sure he'd heard it before, but could not immediately place it.

Ret lunged, and with no change of expression the young man in black disarmed him in one brief, effective move. He then grasped Ret's wrist with long, thin fingers, and said, "This one lives." He pointed down at Senrid. "It was Cath of Geth who attacked him, not I. I disarmed Cath."

And he indicated with a jerk of his chin another blond figure lying at the other end of the clearing, partially obscured by long grass.

Ret tried to wrench free. The young man let him go.

Ret yelled, his voice cracking, "You've a knife. Van's been knifed. That Cath fellow's got no blood on him!"

"If I wanted, Senrid would be dead," was the calm reply. "David, he went after the two who watched Cath. Asked me to guard here. You will find, his cuts are not serious."

The fellow had Dena Yeresbeth but was not blocked. When Ret turned to Jilo in agonized question, Jilo said, "He's speaking the truth as he sees it."

Ret sighed, picked up his weapon, sheathed it, then sank worriedly down next to Senrid.

"What happened?" Jilo asked. "Who are you?"

"I am Lyal. I followed Cath. I saw him track this one. Senrid? This Senrid. Cath tracked but did nothing. I was trying to discover where his mind was." He touched his temple. "Today he decided to strike."

At that, Ret lifted his head. "Why didn't you stop him?" he accused in a high, angry voice.

"This was no quarrel of mine. I waited, hoping there would be speech, for I needed to understand why Cath was here. What was his purpose. Who was this person he stalked. They confronted here. Cath used a knife-shape I once taught him, to reflect the sun's light off the blade to blind your opponent, cut once, and then finish. The first, it worked, but then it did not work, for this one here — Senrid? I got it right?"

"Yes."

"He's quick with his hands. But the cut, the blood in his

eyes, he could not see, and so Cath cut him across the ribs, and ...." He mimed a crashing blow to the jaw. "And knife hilt at the back of the head. I beg pardon. My tongue is slow. I have spoken very little for very long months. You see I am right?"

Ret stood. "What about that Cath, is he a Norsundrian? Out to kill the king?"

"Yes. Mostly. He was putting Senrid over a horse when I intervened. A quarrel is not my concern, but to make someone prisoner of Norsunder. That I make my concern."

Jilo saw there was much going on here that they were not being told, but all he said was, "If a lot of people have been stalking one another around here, maybe we'd best move along."

Lyal said, "I know a good cave, on the other side of the water."

Ret scowled at Cath's unconscious form. "He's alive. Shall I slit his throat?"

"No," Lyal and Jilo said together.

Lyal added, from Ret to Jilo, "David said to watch over him as well."

"We'll take him along," Jilo said. "If he shows signs of waking, we'll tie him up. But I know him from long ago, when he was younger. He was once friend to my friends. I don't know what happened, how he could come to do Norsundrian's work. Perhaps we ought to wait and find out."

Lyal and Jilo left Ret to clean the blood off Senrid's face and bind his ribs with the fabric of his extra shirt while they carried Cath into the cave. There, Lyal produced some cord from his clothes and securely bound him. When they returned, they found Senrid lying on a bed of moss gathered by Ret. His chest rose and fell with steady breathing.

They shared out some travel rations, and had finished Senrid stirred, and put a hand to his bandaged head. One eye was covered. He sat up, winced, then said, "Did my brains fall out? It's got to all be there, it hurts too much not to be." His uncovered eye took in Lyal. He frowned slightly. Then he saw Jilo, and Ret. His expression eased.

Just then Cath stirred. He was still unconscious, but not for long.

Senrid levered himself to one elbow, then gripped his head. "What happened?" he asked hoarsely.

"Cath attacked you. Lyal there rescued you," Jilo said.

"David. Where's he?"

"Gone after the two Norsundrians Lyal said were on Cath's heels."

"I'm thirsty," Senrid said irritably, and though he had not aimed that at anyone, Retren leaped to his feet, grabbed a cup, and raced down to the river. Senrid sat up, muttering, "I notice it's my shirt that got sacrificed to the cause."

"Actually, that's Ret's extra. Yours was full of mud and blood."

Senrid winced, then lifted his chin. "Cath!"

To his surprise a voice answered from inside the cave, "Yes?"

"What did you have to jump me for?"

"Imry Llyenthur put me under orders to bring you to Larkadhe."

Lyal silently helped Cath to sit up, and lean against the rocky wall, which could not have been even remotely comfortable, with his hands bound behind his back.

Retren reappeared, gave Cath a narrow look, but did not speak as he helped Senrid get the cup to his lips. He drained the water, then let out a long breath. "I was thirsty *before* all this assing about." He sat back, closing his good eye. "I should have stayed and lazed out for the day."

Cath replied, with some humor, "I would have waited."

Senrid opened the eye that had swelled shut. "Maybe. But I wouldn't have left my wits behind." From that it became clear that his anger was with himself. "Damn, how old Keriam will curse if he finds out."

Retren spoke for the first time. "You found proof that Aldren Keriam was behind the trouble?"

"Yep. Fool. I should have thrown him out of the academy when Commander Keriam suggested it. But it was his name — grand-nephew-in-law, adopted in by marriage. And now he's trading on the Keriam name."

"Collaborator problems?" Jilo asked.

Ret and Senrid both turned his way, and even in the weak greenish gray light filtering through the thick leaves outside the cave, Jilo could see their utter revulsion at the idea of collaboration.

But Senrid just said, "No. One accusation that cannot be made. His ambitions are limited to riding in my boots, not Llyenthur's. He's smart enough to figure he has a better chance of challenging me now while we're all equally on the run, but not smart enough to see that for every hothead or trouble-maker he attracts in his wife's great-uncle's name he makes more enemies. When Van Stad catches up with him, or especial-ly Jan Senelac, he'll get a dose of reality, especially for trying to dust things up when we all should be working together." His voice got progressively hoarser, and on that last word he shift-ed, and lay down flat, pulling the edge of Jilo's cloak over his goosebumpy flesh. "I've got to go," he said, muttered his own curses, and then was silent.

No one spoke for a time. The sun had begun its afternoon descent, and more light sifted in. Jilo glanced further inside the cave to discover Cath outlined against the rock, his face square now. Cath was older and bonier than the small, quiet boy Jilo remembered from years ago on Geth.

"I remember you," he said to Jilo. "You came to Isul Demarzal, when it was enchanted. You have changed."

"You too."

"Yes," Lyal agreed, sounding tired and dispirited. "Every-thing Yeres says is a lie. Everything."

"Except there is no freedom," Cath replied flatly.

"You were a Norsundrian?" Retren broke in, addressing Lyal. And, seeing his gesture of assent, "Did they teach you how to fight like that?"

"No. I learnt it at home." The even voice betrayed no pride whatsoever. "My home is what your people here call the fifth world. Efael took me away to make me into an assassin." He spat after the name.

Jilo glanced up. "Cath. Was that blade you used on Senrid enchanted?"

"No."

Cath shifted, looking uncomfortable. Senrid's breathing had deepened. Lyal stared down at his hands, his thoughts impossible to guess. Ret's eyes glittered and glimmered with reflected pinpoints of light as he watched them all.

Jilo glanced at his knapsack. The rations for two were already half gone. What he had left would divide into very little for so many. "I'll scout something to eat."

"I will watch here," Ret said, with a look Lyal's way be-traying his ambivalence.

Jilo crawled out and walked back down the trail, dis-covering one of the mounts at the riverside.

He rode along trails, wary of patrols. As he hoped, he spotted an open window with a loaf of bread, a huge chunk of cheese, and a berry tart waiting. There was also a jug of soup and one of milk. He left the milk, as he could not ride and carry two jugs. The soup was thick, smelling of onion, pepper-and-wine braised trout, and olive-braised potato, an aroma that made his stomach wring as he rode.

When he made his way back (not forgetting his mental markers, as Igkai had taught him) Jilo left the horse to wander over the grass, and carried his armloads up, to be met by David, who took some of the burden from him. "More food — excellent!"

"I thought you were searching for Norsundrians," Jilo said.

"I found 'em," David said with his usual smile. "No problem."

"You mean you saw them, or they got away, or they weren't Norsundrians?"

Senrid's wry voice interrupted. "Means he knifed 'em, Jilo."

"Only one," David said cheerily. "Tried to kill me first. The other merely needed a fresh point of view. Shall we eat?"

They entered the cave, where Senrid was slowly wincing his way into a tunic David had brought out of his pack.

"Here we go. Six portions! Here, Lyal. Should we free Cath? My head hurts too much to watch him."

Retren's breath hissed in.

David glanced sideways as he dug into his pack. "Cath's not going anywhere, on foot or by mind, while I'm here. Are you, Cath?"

Cath made no answer, at least aloud, and his face was difficult to see in the gathering darkness.

"Ah," David said, pulling from his knapsack a long, narrow shape.

Jilo was not the only one who tried to see that object as weapon, but then David pulled out a second one, and scooted closer to the fire. Everyone could see that he held two reed pipes of the sort that anyone could make.

Senrid looked away again, wincing against the throbbing of his head. Retren stared, his eyes huge, pupils so wide they were black. Jilo gazed from one to the next as David said, "Cath, it's time for a little talk."

He laid aside one of the reed flutes and blew softly across the top of the other. His upper lip twisted briefly. He dug out a knife and carefully trimmed one, then another of the holes, wood curling off no wider than a thread.

He blew again, and everyone could hear the notes follow true. He tested the other flute, used the knife to adjust three of the holes, and when he was satisfied, he sat up, crossed his legs, shut his eyes, and began to play.

The sound was breathy, plaintive at first, then rippled into a breezy melody. Twice through he played that, as Ret unconsciously swayed in time, and Jilo surprised himself by finding his fingers tapping the floor on the beat.

Then the song shifted to something slower, mournful. Simple melodies all — the sort of song sung by workers in the rice fields, or sewing, or building, or baking. David was skilled enough not to make errors and to keep a beat, but he was no court-trained musician, astonishing sophisticated listeners with complicated passages. Perhaps that was why the emotions came through so well.

At any rate, Jilo enjoyed the songs, once he'd consciously dismissed the old prejudice against lighters who could have music whenever they wanted, without fear of Wan-Edhe's punitive descent. Between a sorrowful tune and another of the merry ones, he glanced at the others to see the effect. Senrid had lain back, his eyes closed as he listened. Retren had also closed his eyes, his head slightly tilted. Lyal sat in the shadows, his expression difficult to interpret.

Jilo glanced at Cath — then glanced again, his nerves chilling at the way the strange young man leaned out, his face at an angle, his eyes narrowed.

When David came to a pause, he laid aside the flute, then surprised Jilo and Ret by pulling his knife and moving toward Cath. He used the knife tip to loosen the knot binding Cath's wrists, coiled the rope, then sat back in his place before tossing the second flute to Cath.

Who picked it up, blew across the top, then dug a fingernail into one of the middle holes.

David picked up his flute again, and this time began with a fast, skipping melody. He got partway into the refrain when Cath raised his flute to his lips, and brought forth a silvery ripple of notes so pure, so airy that Retren gasped, and Senrid's eyes opened, though he did not move.

Cath began slowly. Painfully. His fingers uncertain, as if he were an old, old man, dredging memory for long-forgotten scraps of song, of skill. He found the key, and followed the skipping tune in an echo, like a round.

David finished out that song and began another, with a more compelling melody, and once again Cath echoed — but when they reached a certain point, he played four notes over and over as David carried on with the melody. The four notes began discordantly, but David shifted key, and what had clashed now harmonized.

That began a duel. No. Not a duel, but a conversation, entirely carried out in music. Cath's skills far outstripped David's, but the passion, the shifts in focus and emotion, were as sharp as if they debated in words, until the listeners realized that the two had changed places: Cath had taken the lead, dashing headlong into the intricacies of regret, grief, discovery, consolation, fury, mercy. David now played in harmony, usually the same four notes in complementing chords.

They didn't stop until Cath launched into an impossibly complicated passage, his hair lying in sweaty curls on his brow, his gaze arrowing straight to another world, until he reached a note so high it hung there in the sky, trembled ... and the reed split with a shriek.

Cath dropped the flute and turned away, stumbling farther back into the smelly interior of the cave, where animals had obviously nested.

Lyal rose, and put one hand flat to his breast. In his quiet, accented voice, he said, "Yeres took everything else away, but she could not take my memories of Jeory, my brother, who heard ..." He gestured upward, then out. "That music, the one that binds all things." He considered his words, then said. "When I could hear it again, I promised him. I would make recompense for what they made me do. I would find all her targets. And try to undo the lies." He turned his face toward the back of the cave. "I know what he is thinking."

"Then we can leave him to you," David said.

Sixteen

SENRID SAID TO RET, "How was your day?"

"Jilo taught me magic!" Retren talked a little about that, and art.

Senrid made interested noises, but Jilo could tell his mind was elsewhere, and presently he said, "Messengers?"

"No," Jilo answered.

Senrid said, "Damn, my head aches. I suppose the only escape is sleep."

Jilo wondered if Senrid had been roughed up more than he'd assumed. He'd never known him to be abrupt, almost rude like that to an obvious dependent like Ret. To his longtime friends, yes.

He turned toward David, who successfully read the question in his face. Contact from David came, with considerable amusement: *Senrid's inept way of dealing with hero treatment. Take pity on the boy. Invite him along to scan the outer perimeter for Norsundrians while we finish up with these two.*

Jilo turned to Retren. "Let's do a scouting run."

Retren rose instantly, and trotted at Jilo's heels.

"Wow, that David," Ret said, when they were away from the cave. "Nailed two Norsundrians and acts like it was nothing. Van told me David's tougher than he is, and that there's another one with a funny name who's ever tougher than him. Who do you think is the toughest?"

"I don't know," Jilo said, trying not to laugh. "One thing I can say for certain is that I wouldn't want any of them coming at me angry."

"Did David run drills in Darchelde?"

"No. He was mostly away."

"Did you know Llyenthur is his brother?"

"Yes."

"Did you know Llyenthur almost turned my sister in a Norsundrian?"

"No." That made Jilo uncomfortable.

"Well, he did. He was going to let her command the warriors in Methden. Her, not even in the academy. Da wouldn't let her go. I was to be the warrior. But she had to prove herself by having me executed. She almost did. But Van saved me." His voice trembled.

"Oh?" Jilo said, his neck prickling.

"Instead of being dead, I will learn magic. When I go back, I'll show them. But first I want to learn magic. And I want to see everything. Everything!"

"Then you have to leave this kingdom."

"I know. But I think I ought to stay and help Van. He saved my life." And his thought came clear: *I want them in Darchelde to see me at his right hand.*

Jilo had been about to offer to take Retren to Mearsies Heili with him, but hesitated.

"Are you disgusted?" Ret asked, after a time.

Jilo realized he'd been silent too long, and he thought he knew what Retren was feeling: that sickening sense that you've spoken too much, and you wish you could take all the words back.

"Norsunder stinks," Jilo said. "And so do their allies. But here's something that probably will make me sound like I'm lecturing. Yet I'll say it. There are better things to strive for than being tougher than anyone else."

"So Van says." And, in a lower voice, "That's what they all seem to feel they have to say after they're already there."

Jilo laughed. "I'm not there. Never will be. Yet I do feel that way."

Retren was quiet for a long moment, then said warily, "When you're tough, no one looks down on you, and they do what you say, and don't expect you to always follow them."

"Sometimes. But other times you just make a bigger target and get killed faster. Wan-Edhe Sonscarna is tougher than me in all ways but physical. He's surrounded by rings of guards enchanted to do nothing but protect him, so it doesn't matter that he can hardly lift a sword much less use one. But I am still going to throw him out of Chwahirsland. Kill him, if I must."

Ret's eye widened. "What you are saying is, the goal is the true measure of strength."

Jilo scratched his head. He hadn't been talking about strength at all, but it let it pass, and they went on to finish the magic lesson.

Later on, in the cave again, David showed up. "They're gone. That was unexpected."

"Cath?" Senrid said, gingerly touching his eye.

"With Lyal."

"Do you really think it was a good idea to let those two go off like that?" Senrid asked skeptically. "Seems to me they're ripe for grabbing again,"

"Not Lyal," David said. "He could teach the Black Knives about stealth. I think they are the best thing for one another. They know what they were forced to do while torqued by Yeres's mind-games."

Senrid opened his hand in acceptance, and then pulled out a map, and began quizzing Retren on it. He was patient but distant, and presently he rolled it back up and said, "Good enough for today. Get some rest."

Retren obeyed instantly, as always, and the talk was desultory until Senrid tipped his head back, then said, "He's out. Jilo, are you going back to Chwahirsland?"

"Not yet," Jilo admitted soberly. "If Wan-Edhe even thinks there is a trace of me, he will burn everyone and everything in his way to get at me. I think…Rel agreed…that I need to work on the army from outside Chwahirsland. Not just the army, the navy, too. They are all outside the homeland, forced to fight for Norsunder, hated by all, and…" He made himself stop. "I thought I'd go to Mearsies Heili first. There is a blood-poison spell Wan-Edhe put on the five armies upper command. I'm going to free them."

There, it was out, his utterly mad plan.

"Go ahead. Laugh. Tell me it's impossible."

"Not doing that," Senrid said. "I'm sure what I'm doing here looks just as mad, and from what I can see, your task is that much harder. As for impossible? Ah, you run till you die."

David said, "Jilo, you'll have some help."

Jilo's head lifted at that. "Oh?"

"Early yet," David said. "There are...things...that need doing. But don't think you're alone. You're not."

Jilo had been alone so long that he couldn't quite believe that this would not continue, but he appreciated the thought.

Senrid waited, and when David said nothing more, he spoke. "Two items. Jilo, since you are not going back into Chwahirsland yet, do you think you could take Ret with you for a time?"

Surprised, Jilo hesitated, then said, "I'm not sure he'd want to go."

"Why?"

He repeated the gist of the conversation he'd had with Retren.

"He owes me nothing," Senrid said. "I can easily convince him of that. The rest is typical Marloven arrogance. I want him to find something better to do with his life than dream it away as a desk jockey job in the military, which his family expects, as it's traditional, but he'd hate it. If you don't like him or don't want to be saddled with him, we'll drop the subject."

"I like him a lot, but he seems to want to see his friends again in Darchelde."

"No he doesn't," Senrid said, with calm conviction. "In fact he dreads it so much I've had to put off going there. He thinks he ought to go back, for all the wrong reasons. Did he tell you anything about Imry's game with his sister?"

"Just that her almost having him shot was the condition for her getting a command." He thought of Marend's blankness, her refusal to participate in decision-making, and knew that he had missed far more than he'd guessed.

"'Almost' doesn't convey it. She gave the signal to the execution squad. He saw it. He'd been her shadow until then, living entirely to please her, to act up to her expectations. I got him away, but even so, for a time afterward he came close to finishing the job on his own, by his own hand. So I let him shadow me for a time, but now it's time for him to define his own goals, and not try to live someone else's. Above all he needs to see new things, try new things, and make mistakes outside of the awareness of his sister and their friends."

"I will ask him in the morning," Jilo said. "If he wants to

come, he's welcome."

"Excellent. And I promise I will strive to find a way to repay what I consider a tremendous favor. As for..." He touched his eye again, then glared in David's direction "Damn! How I wish I could have been on that boat. I always thought studying those ancient taerans a waste of time. Made no sense. So there's a stage between our magic and the old. Can you teach the rest of us? Can we use it against Norsunder—or will they retaliate? And if so, will our efforts be the equivalent of grass blades thrown at arrows?"

David laughed. "I don't know, I don't know, and I don't know. As for your first question, not yet. But that's not to say that some might not figure it out on their own. I'm pretty sure Imry has."

"If so, what's he waiting for?"

"Same reason we are."

Senrid cursed under his breath, then said derisively, "And he's doing their work for them."

"His own as well."

"Any idea what's riding him?"

David tipped back his head. The firelight flickered, ruddy, on his face from below, hiding his eye-sockets. "At the end I was seeing him as clearly as he was seeing me, which was why he released the physical ties. But he had enough of a stake, whatever it was, to keep it up far too long. He used too many to chase me, and he himself invested too much time and effort. It would be a mistake to assume he has any regrets about the past. So, the short answer is, though I see these things, I cannot add them to any satisfactory answer. And I suspect he feels the same about me."

"I'll kill him if I can." Senrid dropped his hand. "As he'll do to me. Forget about him. To what Jilo said. An inside line of communication would put us so far ahead...I thought it was impossible. Yes, Jilo, do find out more about the potential of these papers, from Siamis, if you can. And we should get them to all the mages. Like Hibern, who has completely gone to ground—"

"She is in Norsunder," David said gently. "Did you not know that?"

"What?" Senrid spoke sharply.

"Kessler told Siamis. After the attempt in Chwahirsland failed. Ilerian found her, and sent her to await him. It was then that Kessler commenced the magic to close us off."

Jilo thought back—and he could see from Senrid's expression that he was as well. Those last days or so in Lisdan had been so disorderly no one had noticed her missing.

"But they'll rip her to shreds!"

"No," David predicted. "Because she has Ilerian's mark on her. It will keep his underlings from touching her just as surely as if she wore paint on her brow warning them off. No one, ever, interferes with Ilerian's prey."

Senrid cursed, then said, "And I'll have to be the one to tell her cousin Collet. Who lost her older brother last fall, in the fighting. Speaking of fighting." He drew a hissing breath. "David. I have something to ask. And I need Jilo here as witness, in case I get the answer I want."

David responded with a trace of humor, "If you get reticent, I really worry."

"For my peace of mind," Senrid said.

David cut in with a soft laugh. "Oh, no. Don't do it."

"I am. You can say no, but I'm asking."

David sighed. "Are you sure you want to re-establish the connection?"

"Since when do I care what anyone says? Especially after I'm dead! And you don't have to use the name. Let it die. I don't care. That is, I won't if I'm dead."

"I wouldn't, but the label is not my objection."

"What have you against the name?"

"It's not mine."

Their voices were so quiet, light-toned, they were almost indistinguishable.

"What is," Senrid asked, the irony back. "Llyenthur?"

"No! I've yet to decide, I think. Maybe I won't have a surname. Those really only make sense for families. Which I might never have. But this for certain, nothing to be thrust on me. Who is heir now?"

"Leander, perforce, though he actually agreed to be regent for Ingrid if I died. He would never last as king even if he wanted it. Of those who are most eligible, Van Stad would be the best, but he's the one with the lowest birth. And he doesn't want it. The one with the closest thing to a blood claim is Van Marlovair, but he's far too devoted to Marlovair, and everyone knows it. He'd be constantly defending every decision. Jan Senelac has the vision to be king, but he's got that Senelac temper, and like Stad, he would avoid it if he can. He hates being tied down."

He shrugged one shoulder. "They'd do their duty, but they'd catch it hot for one reason or another. No one could hold it but you."

"And tell them I'm the spawn of the Wicked Prince Kendred? No, no, no. I refuse."

"Suit yourself — though at least half of them would consider that an attribute."

"The wrong ones," David said, crossing his arms.

Senrid opened his hands.

David sighed, and sent a sour curse into the void, aimed in Detlev's direction. No answer.

"No titles, tags, demands about my comings and goings?"

"Nothing you do not agree to first."

"Will you promise not to die for another hundred years?"

"I shall do my best!"

David laughed, then he said, "You know that Detlev's strategy, raising me on Five and then keeping me on Geth, worked, to the extent that I don't have any more interest in Marloven Hess than I do any other kingdom."

Outside the cave, an owl hooted.

David said, "And you know you cannot control what I, or anyone, would do after you're gone? I'll tell you right now, I don't want Marloven Hess any more than Leander does. And I do have plans."

"But you could hold it."

"So you are willing to ease your kingly soul at the expense of my free one."

"Adamantly."

"Ah, damn. Then I shall have to exert myself to see that your existence is continued."

"No argument here." Scraping sounds, and Senrid sighed as he lay down. "Better. Except my eye. Couldn't Lyal have gotten to Cath before he had to jump me?"

The owl hooted, its mate hooted back, and presently everyone slept, for once with peaceful dreams.

About the Author

Sherwood Smith writes fantasy, science fiction, and historical fiction. Her full bibliography can be found on her website at https://www.sherwoodsmith.net.

About Book View Cafe

Book View Café is an author-owned cooperative of professional writers, publishing in a variety of genres including fantasy, science fiction, romance, mystery, and more.

Its authors include New York Times and USA Today best-sellers as well as winners and nominees of many prestigious awards such as the Agatha Award, Hugo Award, Lambda Literary Award, Locus Award, Nebula Award, RITA Award, Philip K. Dick Award, World Fantasy Award, and many others.

Since its debut in 2008, Book View Café has gained a reputation for producing high quality books in both print and electronic form. BVC's e-books are DRM-free and distributed around the world.

Book View Café's monthly newsletter includes new releases, specials, author news, and event announcements. To sign up, visit https://www.bookviewcafe.com/bookstore/newsletter/